Introducing the Short Story

Introducing the Short Story

edited by
Henry I. Christ
Jerome Shostak

Dedicated to serving

AMSCO

our nation's youth

AMSCO SCHOOL PUBLICATIONS, INC.
315 Hudson Street / New York, NY 10013

Illustrations by Bert Dodson

When ordering this book, please specify:
either R 531 S or INTRODUCING THE
SHORT STORY.

ISBN 0-87720-791-7

Printed in the United States of America

CONTENTS

ELEMENTS OF THE SHORT STORY

People have always loved a tale well told. For thousands of years, myths, legends, fables, fairy tales, and anecdotes have helped satisfy the human yearning for a good story. These short prose narratives go far back into history, but many critics think the *modern* short story was born as late as the 19th century. Edgar Allan Poe is often mentioned as the father of the modern short story, especially in the detective story form.

Perhaps Somerset Maugham's definition of a short story is as good as any: "a piece of fiction that has unity of impression, that can be read in a single sitting, and is moving, exciting, or amusing."

Young journalists are taught to answer six important questions in writing the lead, or opening paragraph, of a news story: *Who? What? When? Where? How? Why?* Short stories tend to answer these questions, often by emphasizing one question more than the others.

Let's consider the major elements of the short story: *plot, character, setting,* and *theme.*

Plot

J. A. Cuddon defines plot as "the plan, design, scheme or pattern of events in a play, poem, or work of fiction." Here we are concerned with *What?* and *How?*

A fully developed plot is often divided into six sections: *situation, complication, conflict, development, climax, outcome.* Let's see how it works in a famous story, *Romeo and Juliet.*

Romeo sees Juliet at a ball and falls instantly in love. (Situation) Unfortunately, the two lovers belong to rival families. (Complication) The warring families continue to feud. (Conflict) A duel results in Romeo's killing Juliet's kinsman. (Climax) Romeo and Juliet try to be together but die as the result of a failure in communication. (Outcome)

1

The plot shows us *what* happens and *how* it happens. It is the strongest element in stories for children and young readers. A good plot also causes adult readers to turn pages rapidly!

Short stories may be divided into three plot types. The first, in *Romeo and Juliet*, may be diagramed in this way:

The action rises to a climax and then winds down to the end. The second is sometimes called a *rocket plot*:

Here the climax ends the story. There is no "winding down." You'll meet several examples in this collection.

The third is sometimes called a *slice-of-life story*. This kind of story shows characters in a series of scenes—and stops without coming to a dramatic climax. It may be diagramed in this way:

In this story type, plot is often a minor element.

Character

A short story may be nearly plotless, but it always needs characters. They help answer the questions *Who?* and *Why?* A novel may have dozens of characters; a short story has a limited number, sometimes only two or three. It features real people in recognizable situations.

Setting

"Certain dank gardens cry aloud for a murder; certain old houses demand to be haunted; certain coasts are set apart for shipwreck." (Robert Louis Stevenson)

The setting of a story often plays a major role in the interaction between the characters and their environment. By answering the questions *Where?* and *When?*, setting provides a locale, a stage for the dramatic action. In a well-developed story, plot, character, and setting are interwoven.

Theme

The central idea of *Romeo and Juliet* is the tragic waste of young people's lives because of the stupidity of a feud. Similarly, the central idea, or *theme*, of a short story is an important element in its development. Theme often depends upon human emotions like greed, love, jealousy, hatred, and courage.

Other Elements

Awareness of plot, character, setting, and theme increases enjoyment of the short story, but there are other elements.

The *mood* and *atmosphere* of a story are dependent upon character and setting. The mood of "The Most Dangerous Game" is one of tension, both because of the setting and the character of the hunter.

Motivation is a term associated with character. What makes a person tick? Why does he or she act in a certain way? If a mild-mannered person like Walter Mitty suddenly seems courageous, we should know why.

The short story is usually characterized by *compression* and *economy*. A novel can afford long stretches of description and digression. A short story usually seeks a *simple impression*.

Introducing the Short Story is divided into two major parts. In the first, the emphasis is upon the techniques of the short story. This section explores the elements of the short story as outlined in this introductory presentation.

In the second section, the emphasis is upon content and theme. Stories are grouped by similar central ideas to show how different authors approach the same areas.

The selection of authors and stories in this collection reflects the universal appeal of short stories; they are not the exclusive property of any age group or nationality. Short stories are always popular. You will see why!

1

Plot: What Happens Next?

"What happens next?"

Stories that emphasize plot are always popular. Will the detective solve the crime? Will the space travelers find their way back to planet earth? Will the boy and girl meet again after a long separation?

A great many films emphasize plot. James Bond, for example, gets into a series of hairbreadth adventures, each time barely escaping with his life. In *It's a Wonderful Life,* a favorite on television at Christmastime, Jimmy Stewart gets into an unhappy situation because of a foolish remark made in a moment of despair. Will he be able to regain the happiness he failed to recognize at the beginning?

Like a film director, a novelist has time to develop the plot. The novel may take fifty pages to get into the story. It may jump around from place to place, from character to character. It may retell events that happened in the past. It may devote some pages to the author's commentary on the action. The short story is another form altogether. The short story writer must capture the reader's interest quickly and hold it.

The stories in this unit use a variety of methods to keep the reader interested. "Runaway Rig" starts with a bang and doesn't let up until the very end. "The Most Dangerous Game" suggests a mysterious setting, puts the hero into this strange setting, and then gradually builds a sense of great danger. "The Lady, or the Tiger?" uses a different approach. The leisurely opening gives subtle hints of complications to come. It ends with one of the most famous concluding lines in all of literature. "Archetypes" has two events of heightened interest and excitement. All four are guaranteed to keep you reading to find out what happens next, one of the strongest of all motivations for reading.

Runaway Rig

Carl Henry Rathjen

◆ **Faster, faster, faster they went down through the Corkscrew. The black-and-white police car screaming interference for the rocketing runaway. But Barney felt no elation, no triumph, no hope. What good was this going to do with that final spine-busting S a mile ahead? Neither of them could take it at this speed. And they would take a lot of other guys with them.**

Few stories can match the level of excitement in "Runaway Rig." The opening sentence tells you that something is wrong. The extent of the problem becomes abundantly clear as the story goes on. You find yourself in the cab of a runaway ten-wheel combo truck and trailer with a skilled but apparently doomed driver.

You have undoubtedly ridden in a car down a steep mountain grade at night. Perhaps the thought occurred to you, "What if our brakes failed? How would we keep from riding wildly down the twisting mountain road and crushing other cars or plunging to our deaths?" Barney Conners found himself in such a position in a "runaway rig loaded with tons of machine parts."

You will find the story expertly written, as the excitement builds. As the speed increases, the lives of innocent people are threatened. A frightened driver unknowingly cuts off Barney's access to an escape ramp. A state trooper, once a source of annoyance to Barney, is Barney's only hope for survival. This story, based on a true incident, never lets up.

Hold on! You're in for a terrifying ride!

RUNAWAY RIG

The kid burned out the rig's brakes on the Corkscrew grade at eleven thirty that night. Then, panicking as the ten-wheel combo—tractor and semi-trailer—gained speed, he raced the diesel, double-clutched, and tried to jam into a lower gear ratio. The stripping grind from the transmission jarred up into the bunk behind him. Barney Conners came awake fast.

"Easy, kid!" he yelled, even before he got his eyes open. But he knew he was too late. He also knew, without seeing, but just by feel, that they were rolling unchecked downgrade. And that could only mean the Corkscrew, the truckers' graveyard.

"Lay on the horns!" he shouted, so Joel Nichols and the other highway troopers stationed on the grade would be alerted to the emergency. He swung out of the bunk. Ahead, sharp red clusters of taillights and beady truck markers brokenly traced the dropping twists of the divided highway. It was the Corkscrew, all right. And worse, they were already past the patrol-car spot!

Fingers of fear squeezed his stomach. It was a sickness worse than the indigestion he'd been trying to sleep off—the only reason he'd let the kid drive up the Hill, with a strict order to wake him at the top. But the kid hadn't obeyed. He'd boomed across the ridge's level four miles. Now the Corkscrew had him.

But this was no time for jawing. Not with five miles of murderous downgrade ahead of the runaway rig loaded with tons of machine parts.

Barney shouted. "Let me have it!"

"Barney, I didn't mean to take her down. But you looked so comfortable I thought I'd take her across the top and then—"

Barney jammed his left forearm on the wheel ring. He

7

hoped the blasting air horns would carry back to the patrol-car station. Ahead, the driver of a hay rig heard it and changed his mind about cutting out to pass a tanker.

That's what the kid had probably done. Swung out to pass a box or something big enough to hide the large illuminated sign warning about the downgrade, ordering trucks to use low gear. Then he was into it, burned out his brakes trying to check her, and then stripped her because he was going too fast for the next lower ratio.

"Barney!" the kid shouted above the horns as the rig's headlights plowed faster and faster into the darkness.

"Shut up!" Barney snapped. The kid's hands fluttered as though to help with the wheel. Barney elbowed them away, then shot a glance in the big outside mirror. Not a sign of a police car coming to help them down to the emergency escape ramp for runaway trucks, the one night when he needed some citation-happy trooper like Joel Nichols breathing into his rearview mirror!

"Better get out, kid," Barney yelled through the clamoring horns. The kid stared down at the streaming blur of the divider. Then he turned back, his face like a white mask punched with wide holes for eyes and mouth. Barney didn't give him a chance to protest. "Jump while you've got the chance. I don't want to shove you out, but I need room." He reached over, grabbed the door handle, and crowded the kid's trembling body. "Out! Break it with your feet. Relax. Then double. Knees over stomach. Arms around head. Don't try to stop it. Here you go, kid!"

Barney bumped him out to the step, but the kid hung onto the door. Wind roared into the cab. The rig's heavy treads machine-gunned the pavement. Barney slid solidly behind the big wheel. Inching as close as he dared to the streaking edge, he kicked on the far beams. Weeds waved in the night wind, leaning away from the onrushing rig. Glass and beer cans glinted among them. The kid was in for a cutting-up, but that was better than being mashed to pulp. Willowy bushes swept into view.

"The bushes, kid!" Barney shouted. "Hit 'em!"

He didn't wait for the kid to find his nerve. He hammered his fist on the fingers hooked over the windowsill. From the corner of his eye he saw the kid sail out of the cab. He twitched the wheel, angling away, then gave a sharp but smooth swing back to whip the trailer box away from the rolling body. He played the wheel to get that whipsawing trailer in line again.

His glance darted side to side to the mirrors again. In the left one he vaguely glimpsed the kid staggering to his feet. In the right one he hoped to spot a highway patrol booming around a curve after him. But all he saw was the glare of truck headlights.

Where the devil were the troopers tonight? Joel Nichols, he remembered now, from the grapevine, was probably off duty to stand by his wife, who expected her first baby. But usually there was someone riding Barney's tail in this sector, because years ago, wheeling a rush shipment, he'd gone overboard, telling off Joel Nichols for delaying him with a truck inspection. After that he figured he'd better watch his driving, his gross axle loads, his lights, everything. So maybe, in a way, he could

thank Joel and the others for the way he began winning safety awards.

But he didn't feel like a safety-award driver now, at the wheel of a runaway monster on the Corkscrew. He squinted ahead, the wheel tremoring in his fists. Even if those two gearshifts just under his right hand had anything left beneath them, it was no good to him now. He was going too fast to mesh anything. He flicked his far beams on and off as a warning to other drivers.

Just stay out of my way, boys, he prayed. *Let me look good, like a reckless driver who only gets by because the other guys have sense enough to let him through. Give me a chance to get down to the emergency turnoff ramp.*

Rocketing down the dark grade, horns blasting, lights flashing, he rubber-burned around a curve and spotted the twin bull's-eye taillights of a car. A half mile ahead on the straightaway, and in his lane!

His forearm jostled the ring. His foot beat a frantic tattoo on the light button. Words that might have been a prayer or a curse burst up from deep in his chest. But he never knew what they were. They jammed in panic in his throat. That driver didn't hear or see him coming. That driver was doing a legal fifty-five, but this runaway truck didn't know any of the rules.

Come on, come on, guy! For the luvva Pete! Don't those lights blazing in and out of your rear mirror mean anything?

Barney's eyes searched desperately. To his left was the divider, sort of hollowed like a shallow gully. He couldn't take the rig in there. But he couldn't go to the right either. Not with the serpentine line of hay haulers, pole dollies, tankers, boxes, and stakers creeping down the Corkscrew. But that guy ahead could slip in between them. He would burn rubber, slide onto the shoulder maybe, go into the ditch, but wasn't that better than what could happen?

Hadn't he been reading the papers lately? Hadn't he seen the pictures of what happened to a guy like himself? The big wheeler went right over that other guy, flattened him and his passengers and the new car right down to a fourteen-inch pancake and kept going.

Barney held the wheel steady, locked in position like his teeth as he bore down on the ranch wagon's taillights. Then, at the same instant that the driver must have become aware of him, Barney saw the tousled little head lift just inside the rear window, a pink blanket draped around the tiny shoulders. And ahead of the waking child his blazing headlights caught the woman beside the driver as she jerked around to peer back.

Barney winced. This was like his family traveling at night because it was cooler and the kids could sleep—and because he knew he could count on the nighttime wheelers to give him a break if anything went wrong.

Yeah, he'd have to play along. Looming down on that ranch wagon with his runaway rig crammed with tons of machine parts, he knew he could never wipe out this family and then face Flo and his own kids. He eased the combo toward the sunken divider.

But then the ranch wagon began frantically seeking an escape niche in the wall of trucks to the right. Barney shook his head. There wasn't time or room enough for him to get by. The box would careen the rig over. He'd lose control completely, go gouging on his box sides right across the divider into the on-coming upgrade lanes. A nightmarish shambles. He wasn't too sure he could prevent it by deliberately swinging into the sunken divider. But maybe, at least, he could keep it all for himself right there in the weeds between the strips of pavement.

Then blue smoke burst from the ranch wagon as the driver gunned her. Barney nodded grimly, holding his thundering rig steady. Maybe this was an out. Maybe not. But he wasn't thinking just about himself. It was that guy ahead.

Watch yourself, mister. You ain't geared for this. You've been driving easy back and forth to work every day, Sunday picnics. You can't suddenly come out here and let all those horses run wild with you. I've picked up too many of you guys who thought they could.

Barney sucked breath through his teeth as the light car, matching his own speed, slowed on a turn and threatened to sideswipe a semi, inching down in creeper gear. Barney took his heavy rig around as though he were on tracks. But even so, he was scared, wondering if all the pushing-weight in the trailer would jackknife his unit.

His eye caught a flash of red from the big outside mirror. He waited until he had the rig lined up smoothly on the straightaway, a hundred feet behind that fleeing ranch wagon. Then he whipped a glance toward the mirror. That red light came from a pursuing police car. At last!

Barney smiled tightly. Then he heard the siren undulating in the surging rhythm that was the distinctive style of Joel Nichols. Barney shook his head. He'd been right in telling Joel he took his job too seriously. Out here chasing a truck instead of standing by his wife in the hospital.

The police car closed in behind Barney's trailer, bobbing over a rough dip in the pavement. The siren screamed to give warning ahead. Barney, going downgrade faster than he'd ever driven in gear under control, began overtaking the ranch wagon. But why? That job had more soup than that packed under her hood. And the guy should be able to hold her on this straightaway. Then, looking over and beyond the car, Barney saw that the driver was planning to swing into a long gap in the trucks in the right lane.

"No!" Barney shouted, blasting his horns, flicking his lights. "Keep going!" he yelled, waving his right arm. Behind him the siren shrilled frantically. Ahead, a hay-hauler whipped off onto the shoulder in a cloud of dust. Two hundred feet farther on a flat-bedder with a tarped-load shot a plume of black smoke toward the stars as the wheeler spurted ahead to clear the entrance to the emergency ramp, a strip of pavement that gradually angled away from the highway, and went up a hill that would slow a runaway truck and then bog it in soft sand.

But the ranch wagon swerved into the right lane, blocking Barney's chance to ease into the escape route. The bull's-eye stoplights blazed, the guy's tires smoked to keep from rear-ending the flat-bedder. His arm came out, waving Barney on by.

Barney's locked teeth combed his curse into explosive hisses. Why shouldn't he try to hit that ramp? His life was just as important as that guy's. He would smack across the rear of that ranch wagon. Maybe the guy could keep from rolling over or slamming ahead into the heavy flat-bedder while Barney steadied his rig on that ramp. Barney nodded, and in that split instant of decision, words came from way back in his memory, as clear as though he were speaking them again.

Barney held his runaway rig straight on its way down the Corkscrew. He flicked his markers off and on twice to the white-faced driver of the ranch wagon. That's the way you usually thanked a guy for giving you a chance to keep rolling. But thanks for what now? Just a chance to live a little longer and wonder if he could somehow manage to die alone.

The police car shrieked right after him. Tailgating. A sure citation if Joel Nichols caught somebody else doing it. Not a chance to stay out of it when Barney hit something or piled over. "Cut it out, you fool," Barney muttered.

He fought the swaying combo around into another straightaway, surprised that his rear tractor wheels were still in contact with the pavement. Another curve. This one to his left. Thank God there was nothing on it, because he couldn't hold her in this lane. She screamed rubber across the white line and kept on scorching toward the shoulder. Leaning to his left, bracing into the wheel, fighting to hold her on the last inch, the corner of his eye caught the police car squalling by on the inside of the turn. Its black top tilted toward him like a gleaming ebony table reflecting his markers. She slewed right in front of him.

Faster, faster, faster they went down through the Cork screw. The black-and-white police car screaming interference for the rocketing runaway. But Barney felt no elation, no triumph, no hope. What good was this going to do with that final spine-busting S a mile ahead? Neither of them could take it at this speed. And they would take a lot of other guys with them. Downgraders and upgraders. Because there wasn't any divider in there. Too narrow. Just a little hump of concrete between the opposing lanes of traffic.

Barney wished he had thought of that sooner. Why had he let Joel lead him into this trap? He should have piled her up before he caught other wheelers and people in private cars in a rending, smashing charnel of litter. He desperately sought some way to do it now. But how in this canyon with rigs and cars lining both shoulders? It would be just as horrible as in the S.

Wait a minute. Both shoulders? Yeah. Nothing moving on either side of the highway. Nothing except a police car on the upgrade side. It swung into a turnoff, made a wild U-turn, and began to race down on the wrong side, trying to pace him, like Joel ahead of him.

That could mean only one thing. Joel had been shouting

into his radio way up and back there on the way down, maybe almost from the moment he spotted the runaway. He'd gotten them on the job down here. They'd stopped traffic, got it off the pavement. But what could anybody do about that S?

Barney saw he was creeping up on Joel. Creeping? He was catching up as if Joel had his brakes on. Barney began flicking his lights. An arm reached gingerly out of the police car into the blast of wind. It waved for him to come on. Then the car spat exhaust smoke and barely held its lead.

Bewilderedly, Barney tracked after it. Here came the S. Joel and the others were fools to think he could make that first swing to the right. Never. Not even at half this speed. Then he sensed, rather than saw—because his eyes were on that police car—there were no trucks or cars in here! Both sides, both shoulders were clear! Joel's car didn't even try to take the start of the curve. It went straight over the six-inch hump as though it weren't there, to the far side of he road.

"O.K. Gotcha!" Barney muttered, eyes unblinking. Maybe he could straighten this thing out enough to get through. It was his only chance. He never felt his left tires cross the hump. And he didn't unfreeze the wheel until he was sure the right trailer wheels were over too.

He swerved a bit, then held her straight to streak across the far shoulder, skinning by the canyon wall and the drainage ditch. Back on the pavement. Over the divider hump again. Then the other shoulder.

All he saw was straightaway. He yelled. No words. No meaning. Just a bottled pressure that had to get out of him, and it came as a yell. He would bet they could hear it way ahead. Even beyond Joel's police car shrieking yards in advance of his front bumper.

Far ahead down there, red lights winked on police cars. Minutes later he waved as he flashed by them. On past drive-in eateries, people out of their cars, staring, holding half-eaten 'burgers, bottles of pop.

Seven miles farther down the valley, where it leveled off, he scraped his sidewalls screechingly along a curb. The rig slowed, but still rolled across an intersection against a red light. But Joel was holding back traffic while another police car leapfrogged ahead to the next intersection.

Finally the rig stopped.

Barney sat on the running board. Nothing would hold still in him. His clothes stuck and dragged with sweat. He wanted a cigarette, but his hands were all fingers that wouldn't behave. Joel came back, his boots glistening. His face had a grin that looked as sickish as Barney felt.

"Hi," Barney managed to say. It was silly, crazy, but it was enough. Joel sat down beside him and put both hands around Barney's right one holding the pack of cigarettes.

"Now try it," Joel said shakily. "And get one for me."

Some other trooper struck a match for them. Barney stretched his legs out, then drew them back. Everything shook, no matter what, even his left hand gripping the edge of the running board. Joel blew out a deep puff.

"Nice wheeling, Barney."

"The other guys, you mean. The ones who got out of my way. Except one darn fool."

Joel looked at him. "Why didn't you jump, after you got the kid safely out?"

"Why didn't you stay at the hospital?" Barney retorted. He stood up. "Before you write out a citation, I better set out my flares and reflectors."

Joel, smiling, stood up, too. "I'll help you. It's a boy, Barney."

"Congratulations," said Barney, holding out his hand. "I hope the stork gave him a better ride than we had."

His legs felt wobbly, but the rest of him began to feel good. Real good.

Reading for Understanding _____

Main Idea

1. The story demonstrates the importance of   (a) fun and games   (b) courage and cooperation   (c) curiosity and daring   (d) truck inspections and licensing of drivers.

Details

2. The kid burned out the brakes by (a) making sharp turns (b) using too much gasoline (c) going too fast (d) listening to Barney's advice.

3. Barney forced the kid out of the truck to save the kid's life and to (a) get more room in the driver's seat (b) show how displeased he was with the kid's driving (c) have the kid get in touch with the troopers (d) warn all cars following the runaway.

4. Barney didn't use the safety exit ramp because (a) Joel signaled him away from it (b) at his speed the ramp wouldn't have stopped the rig (c) it was closed for repairs (d) a ranch wagon was in the way.

5. The boy in "It's a boy" belonged to (a) Barney (b) the kid (c) Joel (d) a friend of Joel and Barney's.

Inferences

6. "Now the Corkscrew had him" meant that (a) the rig was threatening to go out of control (b) the kid had correctly estimated the danger (c) Barney would certainly get a citation for reckless driving (d) a quiet part of the downhill was just ahead, with the greatest danger miles beyond.

7. The driver of the ranch wagon unintentionally (a) drove below the speed limit (b) put Barney's life in grave danger (c) prevented Joel from doing his duty (d) nearly hit the kid.

8. Barney was especially sad to see the occupants of the ranch wagon because they (a) were all asleep except the driver (b) waved their fists in anger at him (c) caused their car to go out of control (d) reminded him of his own family.

9. Fortunately for Barney, the police (a) were off duty that night (b) cleared the road of cars (c) were at the hospital (d) did not understand what an experience Barney had gone through.

10. What Joel and Barney had in common was   (a) a love of babies   (b) a bitter hatred of slow drivers   (c) great driving skill   (d) a fondness for driving.

Order of Events

11. Arrange the items in the order in which they occurred. Use letters only.
    A. The ranch wagon shoots into the right lane.
    B. The kid jumps.
    C. Barney gets through the S.
    D. The kid fails to awaken Barney
    E. Barney sees a child's head in the ranch wagon.

Outcomes

12. After the story ended,   (a) Barney and Joel took up their old disagreement again   (b) Barney gave up driving a truck   (c) the kid scolded Barney for making him jump   (d) Joel probably did not give Barney a citation.

Cause and Effect

13. Because the kid wanted to give Barney extra rest, he (a) disobeyed Barney's orders   (b) became expert in driving a huge combo   (c) earned Barney's gratitude (d) managed the Corkscrew like an expert.

Fact or Opinion

Tell whether the following is a fact or an opinion.
14. Barney was a thoughtful, considerate driver.

Author's Role

15. The tone of this story is   (a) quiet and reserved (b) dull and boring   (c) sarcastic and hopeless (d) urgent and swift-paced.

Words in Context _____

1. Not a sign of a police car coming to help them down to the emergency escape ramp for runaway trucks, the one night

when he needed some *citation*-happy trooper like Joel Nichols breathing into his rearview mirror.
Citation (8) means   (a) a summons to court
(b) an award for good driving   (c) an invitation to a police party   (d) a piece of advertising.

2. But usually there was someone riding Barney's tail in this *sector*.
Sector (9) means   (a) road   (b) mountain   (c) rise   (d) area.

3. He squinted ahead, the wheel *tremoring* in his fists.
Tremoring (10) means   (a) remaining steady
(b) coming loose   (c) vibrating   (d) going out of control.

4. Barney saw the *tousled* little head lift just inside the rear window, a pink blanket draped around the tiny shoulders.
Tousled (11) means   (a) skinny   (b) mussed up
(c) strange   (d) determined.

5. Barney *winced*. This was like his family traveling at night because it was cooler and the kids could sleep.
Winced (11) means   (a) flinched   (b) chuckled
(c) wept   (d) screamed.

6. But then the ranch wagon began frantically seeking an escape *niche* in the wall of trucks to the right.
Niche (11) means   (a) open spot   (b) stone wall
(c) small truck   (d) speedy turn.

7. A nightmarish *shambles*. He wasn't too sure he could prevent it by deliberately swinging into the sunken divider.
Shambles (11) means   (a) problem to solve
(b) bloody mess   (c) script of a story   (d) point of view.

8. Then he heard the siren *undulating* in the surging rhythm that was the distinctive style of Joel Nichols.
Undulating (12) means coming in   (a) loud noises
(b) a monotonous beat   (c) long periods of silence
(d) waves.

9. Its black top tilted toward him like a gleaming *ebony* table, reflecting his markers.

Ebony (13) means (a) polished (b) maple
(c) black (d) new.

10. But Barney felt no *elation*, no triumph, no hope.
Elation (13) means (a) curiosity (b) joy
(c) sadness (d) interest.

Thinking Critically About the Story _____

1. What were some of the dangers faced by Barney on his wild downhill ride? How did he meet them?
2. The two principal characters are Joel and Barney. Why do their differences make the final cooperation so meaningful?
3. The author writes, "In the left one he vaguely glimpsed the kid staggering to his feet!" Why is it important for the reader to get this information?
4. Point out realistic touches all through the story to make this story seem as real as today's news reports.

Stories in Words _____

Panicking (7) Pan was a minor Greek god of the forests, usually associated with gaiety and pipe playing. He was also a kind of goblin, who loved to frighten unwary travelers. When hikers are lost in the forest, often unreasoning terror sets in. This scary state is called *panic*, after Pan himself.

Willowy (8) The willow tree gets its name from older words meaning *to turn, twist, bend*. You can see a willow tree turning, twisting, and bending with the wind.

Tattoo (10) There are two *tattoos*. The first refers to designs on the skin, from the Tahitian *tatau*. For the second tattoo Dutch pubs once signaled closing time by drumming with fingers or feet. The Dutch words *tap toe* meant *shut the tap*. Then the word acquired the more general meaning of continuous drumming.

The Most Dangerous Game

Richard Connell

◆ **For a moment the general did not reply; he was smiling his curious red-lipped smile. Then he said slowly: "No. You are wrong, sir. The Cape buffalo is not the most dangerous big game." He sipped his wine. "Here in my preserve on this island," he said in the same slow tone, "I hunt more dangerous game."**

You are marooned on a lonely island in the Caribbean. You are greeted on the island by a smooth, polished, mysterious stranger, with an obscurely menacing manner. You are treated as an honored guest . . . until you realize that your host has some strange plans for you.

Sanger Rainsford finds himself in just such a predicament. After reaching the island that has a "bad reputation," he soon finds himself playing the most dangerous game of all. But at the end of the story, you will realize that the title has a double-barreled meaning.

"The Most Dangerous Game" is an excellent story to demonstrate how a writer can arouse and hold the reader's interest. The opening sentence is a device sometimes called a "grabber." After reading a few lines, you are hooked by the author's cleverness in building atmosphere. He quickly introduces the principal character, Rainsford, who at first seems unsympathetic. For example, in talking of hunting, he coldly says, "Who cares how a jaguar feels?" This remark comes back to haunt him and foreshadows the ordeal to come. Our attitude toward Rainsford changes, and we experience, with him, a different kind of hunt.

In this story, setting (page 3) plays a major role as backdrop for the action of the two main characters. Conflict (1) is at the heart of the story, as suspense builds and builds until the last sentence.

Come. Learn the real meaning of "The Most Dangerous Game."

THE MOST DANGEROUS GAME

"Off there to the right—somewhere—is a large island," said Whitney. "It's rather a mystery—"

"What island is it?" Rainsford asked.

"The old charts call it 'Ship-Trap Island,'" Whitney replied. "A suggestive name, isn't it? Sailors have a curious dread of the place. I don't know why. Some superstition—"

"Can't see it," remarked Rainsford, trying to peer through the dank tropical night that was palpable as it pressed its thick, warm blackness in upon the yacht.

"You've good eyes," said Whitney, with a laugh, "and I've seen you pick off a moose moving in the brown fall bush at four hundred yards, but even you can't see four miles or so through a moonless Caribbean night."

"Not four yards," admitted Rainsford. "Ugh! It's like moist black velvet."

"It will be light enough where we're going," promised Whitney. "We should make it in a few days. I hope the jaguar guns have come. We'll have good hunting up the Amazon. Great sport, hunting."

"The best sport in the world," agreed Rainsford.

"For the hunter," amended Whitney. "Not for the jaguar."

"Don't talk rot, Whitney," said Rainsford. "You're a big-game hunter, not a philosopher. Who cares how a jaguar feels?"

"Perhaps the jaguar does," observed Whitney.

"Bah! They've no understanding."

"Even so, I rather think they understand one thing—fear. The fear of pain and the fear of death."

"Nonsense," laughed Rainsford. "This hot weather is making you soft, Whitney. Be a realist. The world is made up of two classes—the hunters and the hunted. Luckily, you and I are hunters. Do you think we've passed that island, yet?"

"I can't tell in the dark. I hope so."

"Why?" asked Rainsford.

"The place has a reputation—a bad one."

"Cannibals?" suggested Rainsford.

"Hardly. Even cannibals wouldn't live in such a God-forsaken place. But it's got into sailor lore, somehow. Didn't you notice that the crew's nerves seemed a bit jumpy today?"

"They were a bit strange, now that you mention it. Even Captain Nielsen—"

"Yes, even that tough-minded old Swede, who'd go up to the devil himself and ask him for a light. Those fishy blue eyes held a look I never saw there before. All I could get out of him was: 'This place has an evil name among seafaring men, sir.' Then he said to me, very gravely: 'Don't you feel anything?'— as if the air about us was actually poisonous. Now, you mustn't laugh when I tell you this—I did feel something like a sudden chill.

"There was no breeze. The sea was as flat as a plateglass window. We were drawing near the island then. What I felt was a—a mental chill; a sort of sudden dread."

"Pure imagination," said Rainsford. "One superstitious sailor can taint the whole ship's company with his fear."

"Maybe. But sometimes I think sailors have an extra sense that tells them when they are in danger. Sometimes I think evil is a tangible thing—with wavelengths, just as sound and light have. An evil place can, so to speak, broadcast vibrations of evil. Anyhow, I'm glad we're getting out of this zone. Well, I think I'll turn in now, Rainsford."

"I'm not sleepy," said Rainsford. "I'm going to smoke another pipe up on the afterdeck."

"Good night, then, Rainsford. See you at breakfast."

"Right. Good night, Whitney."

There was no sound in the night as Rainsford sat there, but the muffled throb of the engine that drove the yacht swiftly through the darkness, and the swish and ripple of the wash of the propeller.

Rainsford, reclining in a steamer chair, indolently puffed on his favorite briar. The sensuous drowsiness of the night was on him. "It's so dark," he thought, "that I could sleep without closing my eyes; the night would be my eyelids—"

An abrupt sound startled him. Off to the right he heard it, and his ears, expert in such matters, could not be mistaken. Again he heard the sound, and again. Somewhere, off in the blackness, someone had fired a gun three times.

Rainsford sprang up and moved quickly to the rail, mystified. He strained his eyes in the direction from which the reports had come, but it was like trying to see through a blanket. He leaped upon the rail and balanced himself there, to get greater elevation; his pipe, striking a rope, was knocked from his mouth. He lunged for it; a short, hoarse cry came from his lips as he realized he had reached too far and had lost his balance. The cry was pinched off short as the blood-warm waters of the Caribbean Sea closed over his head.

He struggled up to the surface and tried to cry out, but the wash from the speeding yacht slapped him in the face and the salt water in his open mouth made him gag and strangle. Desperately he struck out with strong strokes after the receding lights of the yacht, but he stopped before he had swum fifty feet. A certain cool-headedness had come to him; it was not the first time he had been in a tight place. There was a chance that his cries could be heard by someone aboard the yacht, but that chance was slender, and grew more slender as the yacht raced on. He wrestled himself out of his clothes, and shouted with all his power. The lights of the yacht became faint and ever-vanishing fireflies; then they were blotted out entirely by the night.

Rainsford remembered the shots. They had come from the right, and doggedly he swam in that direction, swimming with slow, deliberate strokes, conserving his strength. For a seemingly endless time he fought the sea. He began to count his strokes; he could do possibly a hundred more and then—

Rainsford heard a sound. It came out of the darkness, a high screaming sound, the sound of an animal in an extremity of anguish and terror.

He did not recognize the animal that made the sound—he did not try to; with fresh vitality he swam toward the sound.

He heard it again; then it was cut short by another noise, crisp, staccato.

"Pistol shot," muttered Rainsford, swimming on.

Ten minutes of determined effort brought another sound to his ears—the most welcome he had ever heard—the muttering and growling of the sea breaking on a rocky shore. He was almost on the rocks before he saw them; on a night less calm he would have been shattered against them. With his remaining strength he dragged himself from the swirling waters. Jagged crags appeared to jut into the opaqueness; he forced himself upward, hand over hand. Gasping, his hands raw, he reached a flat place at the top. Dense jungle came down to the very edge of the cliffs. What perils that tangle of trees and underbrush might hold for him did not concern Rainsford just then. All he knew was that he was safe from his enemy, the sea, and that utter weariness was on him. He flung himself down at the jungle edge and tumbled headlong into the deepest sleep of his life.

When he opened his eyes he knew from the position of the sun that it was late in the afternoon. Sleep had given him new vigor; a sharp hunger was picking at him. He looked about him, almost cheerfully.

"Where there are pistol shots, there are men. Where there are men, there is food," he thought. But what kind of men, he wondered, in so forbidding a place? An unbroken front of snarled and jagged jungle fringed the shore.

He saw no sign of a trail through the closely knit web of weeds and trees; it was easier to go along the shore, and Rainsford floundered along by the water. Not far from where he had landed, he stopped.

Some wounded thing, by the evidence a large animal, had thrashed about in the underbrush; the jungle weeds were crushed down and the moss was lacerated; one patch of weeds was stained crimson. A small, glittering object not far away caught Rainsford's eye and he picked it up. It was an empty cartridge.

"A twenty-two," he remarked. "That's odd. It must have been a fairly large animal too. The hunter had his nerve with him to tackle it with such a light gun. It's clear that the brute put up a good fight. I suppose the first three shots I heard were when the hunter flushed his quarry and wounded it. The last shot was when he trailed it here and finished it."

He examined the ground closely and found what he had hoped to find—the print of hunting boots. They pointed along the cliff in the direction he had been going. Eagerly he hurried along, now slipping on a rotten log or a loose stone, but making headway; night was beginning to settle down on the island.

Bleak darkness was blacking out the sea and jungle when Rainsford sighted the lights. He came upon them as he turned a crook in the coastline, and his first thought was that he had come upon a village, for there were many lights. But as he forged along he saw to his great astonishment that all the lights were in one enormous building—a lofty structure with pointed towers plunging upward into the gloom. His eyes made out the shadowy outlines of a palatial château; it was set on a high bluff, and on three sides of it cliffs dived down to where the sea licked greedy lips in the shadows.

"Mirage," thought Rainsford. But it was no mirage, he found, when he opened the tall spiked iron gate. The stone steps were real enough; the massive door with a leering gargoyle for a knocker was real enough; yet about it all hung an air of unreality.

He lifted the knocker, and it creaked up stiffly, as if it had never before been used. He let it fall, and it startled him with its booming loudness. He thought he heard steps within; the door remained closed. Again Rainsford lifted the heavy knocker, and let it fall. The door opened then, opened as suddenly as if it were on a spring, and Rainsford stood blinking in the river of glaring gold light that poured out. The first thing Rainsford's eyes discerned was the largest man Rainsford had ever seen—a gigantic creature, solidly made and black-bearded to the waist. In his hand the man held a long-barrelled revolver, and he was pointing it straight at Rainsford's heart.

Out of the snarl of beard two small eyes regarded Rainsford.

"Don't be alarmed," said Rainsford, with a smile which he hoped was disarming. "I'm no robber. I fell off a yacht. My name is Sanger Rainsford of New York City."

The menacing look in the eyes did not change. The revolver pointed as rigidly as if the giant were a statue. He gave no sign that he understood Rainsford's words, or that he had even heard them. He was dressed in uniform, a black uniform trimmed with gray astrakhan.

"I'm Sanger Rainsford of New York," Rainsford began again. "I fell off a yacht. I am hungry."

The man's only answer was to raise with his thumb the hammer of his revolver. Then Rainsford saw the man's free hand go to his forehead in a military salute, and he saw him click his heels together and stand at attention. Another man was coming down the broad marble steps, an erect, slender man in evening clothes. He advanced and held out his hand.

In a cultivated voice marked by a slight accent that gave it added precision and deliberateness, he said: "It is a very great pleasure and honor to welcome Mr. Sanger Rainsford, the celebrated hunter, to my home." Automatically Rainsford shook the man's hand.

"I've read your book about hunting snow leopards in Tibet, you see," explained the man. "I am General Zaroff."

Rainsford's first impression was that the man was singularly handsome; his second was that there was an original, almost bizarre quality about the general's face. He was a tall man past middle age, for his hair was a vivid white; but his thick eyebrows and pointed military mustache were as black as the night from which Rainsford had come. His eyes, too, were black and very bright. He had high cheekbones, a sharp-cut nose, a spare, dark face, the face of a man used to giving orders, the face of an aristocrat. Turning to the giant in uniform, the general made a sign. The giant put away his pistol, saluted, withdrew.

"Ivan is an incredibly strong fellow," remarked the general, "but he has the misfortune to be deaf and dumb. A simple fellow, but, I'm afraid, like all his race, a bit of a savage."

"Is he Russian?"

"He is a Cossack," said the general, and his smile showed red lips and pointed teeth. "So am I."

"Come," he said, "we shouldn't be chatting here. We can talk later. Now you want clothes, food, rest. You shall have them. This is a most restful spot."

Ivan had reappeared, and the general spoke to him with lips that moved but gave forth no sound.

"Follow Ivan, if you please, Mr. Rainsford," said the general. "I was about to have my dinner when you came. I'll wait for you. You'll find that my clothes will fit you, I think."

It was to a huge, beam-ceilinged bedroom with a canopied bed big enough for six men that Rainsford followed the silent giant. Ivan laid out an evening suit, and Rainsford, as he put it on, noticed that it came from a London tailor who ordinarily cut and sewed for none below the rank of duke.

The dining room to which Ivan conducted him was in many ways remarkable. There was a medieval magnificence about it; it suggested a baronial hall of feudal times with its oaken panels, its high ceiling, its vast refectory table where twoscore men could sit down to eat. About the hall were the mounted heads of many animals—lions, tigers, elephants, moose, bears; larger or more perfect specimens Rainsford had never seen. At the great table the general was sitting alone.

"You'll have a cocktail, Mr. Rainsford," he suggested. The cocktail was surpassingly good; and, Rainsford noted, the table appointments were of the finest—the linen, the crystal, the silver, the china.

They were eating *borsch*, the rich, red soup with whipped cream so dear to Russian palates. Half apologetically General Zaroff said: "We do our best to preserve the amenities of civilization here. Please forgive any lapses. We are well off the beaten track, you know. Do you think the champagne has suffered from its long ocean trip?"

"Not in the least," declared Rainsford. He was finding the general a most thoughtful and affable host, a true cosmopolite. But there was one trait of the general's that made Rainsford uncomfortable. Whenever he looked up he found the general studying him, appraising him narrowly.

"Perhaps," said General Zaroff, "you were surprised that I recognized your name. You see, I read all books on hunting published in English, French, and Russian. I have but one passion in my life, Mr. Rainsford, and it is the hunt."

"You have some wonderful heads here," said Rainsford as he ate a particularly well-cooked filet mignon. "That Cape buffalo is the largest I ever saw."

"Oh, that fellow. Yes, he was a monster."

"Did he charge you?"

"Hurled me against a tree," said the general. "Fractured my skull. But I got the brute."

"I've always thought," said Rainsford, "that the Cape buffalo is the most dangerous of all big game."

For a moment the general did not reply; he was smiling his curious red-lipped smile. Then he said slowly: "No. You are wrong, sir. The Cape buffalo is not the most dangerous big game." He sipped his wine. "Here in my preserve on this island," he said in the same slow tone, "I hunt more dangerous game."

Rainsford expressed his surprise. "Is there big game on this island?"

The general nodded. "The biggest."

"Really?"

"Oh, it isn't here naturally, of course. I have to stock the island."

"What have you imported, General?" Rainsford asked. "Tigers?"

The general smiled. "No," he said. "Hunting tigers ceased to interest me some years ago. I exhausted their possibilities, you see. No thrill left in tigers, no real danger. I live for danger, Mr. Rainsford."

The general took from his pocket a gold cigarette case and offered his guest a long black cigarette with a silver tip; it was perfumed and gave off a smell like incense.

"We will have some capital hunting, you and I," said the general. "I shall be most glad to have your society."

"But what game—" began Rainsford.

"I'll tell you," said the general. "You will be amused, I know. I think I may say, in all modesty, that I have done a rare thing. I have invented a new sensation. May I pour you another glass of port, Mr. Rainsford?"

"Thank you, General."

The general filled both glasses, and said: "God makes some men poets. Some He makes kings, some beggars. Me He made a hunter. My hand was made for the trigger, my father said. He was a very rich man with a quarter of a million acres in the Crimea, and he was an ardent sportsman. When I was only five years old he gave me a little gun, specially made in Moscow for me, to shoot sparrows with. When I shot some of his prize turkeys with it, he did not punish me; he complimented me on my marksmanship. I killed my first bear in the Caucasus when I was ten. My whole life had been one prolonged hunt. I went into the army—it was expected of noblemen's sons—and for a time commanded a division of Cossack cavalry, but my real interest was always the hunt. I have hunted every kind of game in every land. It would be impossible for me to tell you how many animals I have killed."

The general puffed at his cigarette.

"After the debacle in Russia I left the country, for it was imprudent for an officer of the Czar to stay there. Many noble Russians lost everything. I, luckily, had invested heavily in American securities, so I shall never have to open a tearoom in Monte Carlo or drive a taxi in Paris. Naturally, I continued to hunt—grizzlies in your Rockies, crocodiles in the Ganges, rhinoceroses in East Africa. It was in Africa that the Cape buffalo hit me and laid me up for six months. As soon as I recovered I started for the Amazon to hunt jaguars, for I had heard they were unusually cunning. They weren't." The Cossack sighed. "They were no match at all for a hunter with his wits about him, and a high-powered rifle. I was bitterly disappointed. I was lying in my tent with a splitting headache one night when a terrible thought pushed its way into my mind. Hunting was beginning to bore me! And hunting, remember, had been my life. I have heard that in America businessmen often go to pieces when they give up the business that has been their life."

"Yes, that's so," said Rainsford.

The general smiled. "I had no wish to go to pieces," he said. "I must do something. Now, mine is an analytical mind, Mr. Rainsford. Doubtless that is why I enjoy the problems of the chase."

"No doubt, General Zaroff."

"So," continued the general, "I asked myself why the hunt no longer fascinated me. You are much younger than I am, Mr. Rainsford, and have not hunted as much, but you perhaps can guess the answer."

"What was it?"

"Simply this: hunting had ceased to be what you call 'a sporting proposition.' It had become too easy. I always got my quarry. Always. There is no greater bore than perfection."

The general lit a fresh cigarette.

"No animal had a chance with me anymore. That is no boast; it is a mathematical certainty. The animal had nothing but his legs and his instinct. Instinct is no match for reason. When I thought of this it was a tragic moment for me, I can tell you."

Rainsford leaned across the table, absorbed in what his host was saying.

"It came to me as an inspiration what I must do," the general went on.

"And that was?"

The general smiled the quiet smile of one who has faced an obstacle and surmounted it with success. "I had to invent a new animal to hunt," he said.

"A new animal? You're joking."

"Not at all," said the general. "I never joke about hunting. I needed a new animal. I found one. So I bought this island, built this house, and here I do my hunting. The island is perfect for my purposes—there are jungles with a maze of trails in them, hills, swamps—"

"But the animal, General Zaroff?"

"Oh," said the general, "it supplies me with the most exciting hunting in the world. No other hunting compares with it for an instant. Every day I hunt, and I never grow bored now, for I have a quarry with which I can match my wits."

Rainsford's bewilderment showed in his face.

"I wanted the ideal animal to hunt," explained the general. "So I said: 'What are the attributes of an ideal quarry?' And the answer was, of course: 'It must have courage, cunning, and, above all, it must be able to reason.'"

"But no animal can reason," objected Rainsford.

"My dear fellow," said the general, "there is one that can."

"But you can't mean—" gasped Rainsford.

"And why not?"

"I can't believe you are serious, General Zaroff. This is a grisly joke."

"Why should I not be serious? I am speaking of hunting."

"Hunting? Good God, General Zaroff, what you speak of is murder."

The general laughed with entire good nature. He regarded Rainsford quizzically. "I refuse to believe that so modern and civilized a young man as you harbors romantic ideas about the value of human life. Surely your experiences in the war—"

"Did not make me condone cold-blooded murder," finished Rainsford stiffly.

Laughter shook the general. "How extraordinarily droll you are!" he said. "One does not expect nowadays to find a young man of the educated class, even in America, with such a naïve and, if I may say so, mid-Victorian point of view. It's like finding a snuffbox in a limousine. Ah, well, doubtless you had Puritan ancestors. So many Americans appear to have had. I'll wager you'll forget your notions when you go hunting with me. You've a genuine thrill in store for you, Mr. Rainsford."

"Thank you, I'm a hunter, not a murderer."

"Dear me," said the general, quite unruffled, "again that unpleasant word. But I think I can show you that your scruples are quite unfounded."

"Yes?"

"Life is for the strong, to be lived by the strong, and, if needs be, taken by the strong. The weak of the world were put here to give the strong pleasure. I am strong. Why should I not use my gift? If I wish to hunt, why should I not? I hunt the scum of the earth—sailors from tramp ships—lascars, blacks, Chinese, whites, mongrels—a thoroughbred horse or hound is worth more than a score of them."

"But they are men," said Rainsford hotly.

"Precisely," said the general. "That is why I use them. It gives me pleasure. They can reason, after a fashion. So they are dangerous."

"But where do you get them?"

The general's eyelid fluttered down in a wink. "This island is called Ship-Trap," he answered. "Sometimes an angry god of the high seas sends them to me. Sometimes, when Providence is not so kind, I help Providence a bit. Come to the window with me."

Rainsford went to the window and looked out toward the sea.

"Watch! Out there!" exclaimed the general, pointing into the night. Rainsford's eyes saw only blackness, and then, as the general pressed a button, far out to sea Rainsford saw the flash of lights.

The general chuckled. "They indicate a channel," he said, "where there's none: giant rocks with razor edges crouch like a sea monster with wide-open jaws. They can crush a ship as easily as I crush this nut." He dropped a walnut on the hardwood floor and brought his heel grinding down on it. "Oh, yes," he said, casually, as if in answer to a question, "I have electricity. We try to be civilized here."

"Civilized? And you shoot down men?"

A trace of anger was in the general's black eyes, but it was there for but a second, and he said, in his most pleasant manner: "Dear me, what a righteous young man you are! I assure you I do not do the thing you suggest. That would be barbarous. I treat these visitors with every consideration. They get plenty of good food and exercise. They get into splendid physical condition. You shall see for yourself tomorrow."

"What do you mean?"

"We'll visit my training school," smiled the general. "It's in the cellar. I have about a dozen pupils down there now. They're from the Spanish bark, 'San Lucar,' that had the bad luck to go on the rocks out there. A very inferior lot, I regret to say. Poor specimens and more accustomed to the deck than to the jungle."

He raised his hand, and Ivan, who served as waiter, brought thick Turkish coffee. Rainsford, with an effort, held his tongue in check.

"It's a game, you see," pursued the general blandly. "I suggest to one of them that we go hunting. I give him a supply of food and an excellent hunting knife. I give him three hours' start. I am to follow, armed only with a pistol of the smallest caliber and range. If my quarry eludes me for three whole days, he wins the game. If I find him," the general smiled, "he loses."

"Suppose he refuses to be hunted?"

"Oh," said the general, "I give him his option, of course. He need not play that game if he doesn't wish to. If he does not wish to hunt I turn him over to Ivan. Ivan once had the honor of serving as official knouter to the Great White Czar, and he has his own ideas of sport. Invariably, Mr. Rainsford, invariably they choose the hunt."

"And if they win?"

The smile on the general's face widened. "To date I have not lost," he said.

Then he added hastily: "I don't wish you to think me a braggart, Mr. Rainsford. Many of them afford only the most elementary sort of problem. Occasionally I strike a tartar. One almost did win. I eventually had to use the dogs."

"The dogs?"

"This way, please. I'll show you."

The general steered Rainsford to a window. The lights from the window sent a flickering illumination that made grotesque patterns on the courtyard below, and Rainsford could see moving about there a dozen or so huge black shapes; as they turned toward him, their eyes glittered greenly.

"A rather good lot, I think," observed the general. "They are let out at seven every night. If anyone should try to get into my house—or out of it—something extremely regrettable would occur to him." He hummed a snatch of song from the Folies Bergère.

"And now," said the general, "I want to show you my new collection of heads. Will you come with me to the library?"

"I hope," said Rainsford, "that you will excuse me tonight, General Zaroff. I'm really not feeling at all well."

"Ah, indeed?" the general inquired solicitously. "Well, I suppose that's only natural, after your long swim. You need a good, restful night's sleep. Tomorrow you'll feel like a new man, I'll wager. Then we'll hunt, eh? I've one rather promising prospect—"

Rainsford was hurrying from the room.

"Sorry you can't go with me tonight," called the general. "I expect rather fair sport—a big, strong black. He looks resourceful—Well, good night, Mr. Rainsford; I hope you have a good night's rest."

The bed was good and the pajamas of the softest silk, and he was tired in every fiber of his being, but nevertheless Rainsford could not quiet his brain with the opiate of sleep. He lay, eyes wide open. Once he thought he heard stealthy steps in the corridor outside his room. He sought to throw open the door; it would not open. He went to the window and looked out. His room was high up in one of the towers. The lights of the château were out now, and it was dark and silent, but there was a fragment of sallow moon, and by its wan light he could see, dimly, the courtyard; there, weaving, in and out in the pattern of shadow, were black, noiseless forms; the hounds heard him at the window and looked up, expectantly, with their green eyes. Rainsford went back to the bed and lay down. By many methods he tried to put himself to sleep. He had achieved a doze when, just as morning began to come, he heard, far off in the jungle, the faint report of a pistol.

General Zaroff did not appear until luncheon. He was dressed faultlessly in the tweeds of a country squire. He was solicitous about the state of Rainsford's health.

"As for me," sighed the general, "I do not feel so well. I am worried, Mr. Rainsford. Last night I detected traces of my old complaint."

To Rainsford's questioning glance the general said: "Ennui. Boredom."

Then, taking a second helping of crêpe suzette, the general explained: "The hunting was not good last night. The fellow lost his head. He made a straight trail that offered no problems at all. That's the trouble with these sailors; they have dull brains to begin with, and they do not know how to get about in the woods. They do excessively stupid and obvious things. It's most annoying. Will you have another glass of Chablis, Mr. Rainsford?"

"General," said Rainsford firmly, "I wish to leave this island at once."

The general raised his thickets of eyebrows; he seemed hurt. "But, my dear fellow," the general protested, "you've only just come. You've had no hunting—"

"I wish to go today," said Rainsford. He saw the dead black eyes of the general on him, studying him. General Zaroff's face suddenly brightened.

He filled Rainsford's glass with venerable Chablis from a dusty bottle.

"Tonight," said the general, "we will hunt—you and I."

Rainsford shook his head. "No, General," he said. "I will not hunt."

The general shrugged his shoulders and nibbled delicately at a hothouse grape. "As you wish, my friend," he said. "The choice rests entirely with you. But may I not venture to suggest that you will find my idea of sport more diverting than Ivan's?"

He nodded toward the corner where the giant stood, scowling, his thick arms crossed on his hogshead of a chest.

"You don't mean—" cried Rainsford.

"My dear fellow," said the general, "have I not told you I always mean what I say about hunting? This is really an inspiration. I drink to a foeman worthy of my steel—at last."

The general raised his glass, but Rainsford sat staring at him.

"You'll find this game worth playing," the general said enthusiastically. "Your brain against mine. Your woodcraft against mine. Your strength and stamina against mine. Outdoor chess. And the stake is not without value, eh?"

"And if I win—" began Rainsford huskily.

"I'll cheerfully admit myself defeated if I do not find you by midnight of the third day," said General Zaroff. "My sloop will place you on the mainland near a town."

The general read what Rainsford was thinking.

"Oh, you can trust me," said the Cossack. "I will give you my word as a gentleman and a sportsman. Of course, you, in turn, must agree to say nothing of your visit here."

"I'll agree to nothing of the kind," said Rainsford.

"Oh," said the general, "in that case—but why discuss that now? Three days hence we can discuss it over a bottle of Veuve Cliquot, unless—"

The general sipped his wine.

Then a businesslike air animated him. "Ivan," he said to Rainsford, "will supply you with hunting clothes, food, a knife. I suggest you wear moccasins; they leave a poorer trail. I should suggest too that you avoid the big swamp in the southeast corner of the island. We call it Death Swamp. There's quicksand there. One foolish fellow tried it. The deplorable part of it was that Lazarus followed him. You can imagine my feelings, Mr. Rainsford. I loved Lazarus; he was the finest hound in my pack. Well, I must beg you to excuse me now. I always take a siesta after lunch. You'll hardly have time for a nap, I fear. You'll want to start, no doubt. I shall not follow till dusk. Hunting at night is so much more exciting than by day, don't you think? Au revoir, Mr. Rainsford, au revoir."

General Zaroff, with a deep, courtly bow, strolled from the room.

From another door came Ivan. Under one arm he carried khaki hunting clothes, a haversack of food, a leather sheath containing a long-bladed hunting knife; his right hand rested on a cocked revolver thrust in the crimson sash around his waist. . . .

Rainsford had fought his way through the bush for two hours.

"I must keep my nerve. I must keep my nerve," he said through tight teeth.

He had not been entirely clearheaded when the château gates snapped shut behind him. His whole idea at first was to put distance between himself and General Zaroff, and, to this end, he had plunged along, spurred on by the sharp rowels of something very like panic. Now he had got a grip on himself, had stopped, and was taking stock of himself and the situation.

He saw that straight flight was futile; inevitably it would bring him face to face with the sea. He was in a picture with a frame of water, and his operations, clearly, must take place within that frame.

"I'll give him a trail to follow," muttered Rainsford, and he struck off from the rude path he had been following into the trackless wilderness. He executed a series of intricate loops; he doubled on his trail again and again, recalling all the lore of the fox hunt, and all the dodges of the fox. Night found him leg-weary, with hands and face lashed by the branches, on a thickly wooded ridge. He knew it would be insane to blunder on through the dark, even if he had the strength. His need for rest was imperative and he thought: "I have played the fox, now I must play the cat of the fable." A big tree with a thick trunk and outspread branches was nearby, and, taking care to leave not the slightest mark, he climbed up into the crotch, and stretching out on one of the broad limbs, after a fashion, rested. Rest brought him new confidence and almost a feeling of security. Even so zealous a hunter as General Zaroff could not trace him there, he told himself; only the devil himself could follow that complicated trail through the jungle after dark. But, perhaps, the general was a devil—

An apprehensive night crawled slowly by like a wounded snake, and sleep did not visit Rainsford, although the silence of a dead world was on the jungle. Toward morning when a dingy gray was varnishing the sky, the cry of some startled bird focused Rainsford's attention in that direction. Something was coming through the bush, coming slowly, carefully, coming by the same winding way Rainsford had come. He flattened himself down on the limb, and through a screen of leaves almost as thick as tapestry, he watched. The thing that was approaching was a man.

It was General Zaroff. He made his way along with his eyes fixed in utmost concentration on the ground before him. He paused almost beneath the tree, dropped to his knees, and studied the ground before him. Rainsford's impulse was to hurl himself down like a panther, but he saw that the general's right hand held something small and metallic—an automatic pistol.

The hunter shook his head several times as if he were puzzled. Then he straightened up and took from his case one of his black cigarettes; its pungent incenselike smoke floated up to Rainsford's nostrils.

Rainsford held his breath. The general's eyes had left the ground and were traveling inch by inch up the tree. Rainsford froze there, every muscle tensed for a spring. But the sharp eyes of the hunter stopped before they reached the limb where Rainsford lay; a smile spread over his brown face. Very deliberately he blew a smoke ring into the air; then he turned his back on the tree and walked carelessly away, back along the trail he had come. The swirls of the underbrush against his hunting boots grew fainter and fainter.

The pent-up air burst hotly from Rainsford's lungs. His first thought made him feel sick and numb. The general could follow a trail through the woods at night; he could follow an extremely difficult trail; he must have uncanny powers; only by the merest chance had the Cossack failed to see his quarry.

Rainsford's second thought was even more terrible. It sent a shudder of cold horror through his whole being. Why had the general smiled? Why had he turned back?

Rainsford did not want to believe what his reason told him was true, but the truth was as evident as the sun that had by now pushed through the morning mists. The general was playing with him. The general was saving him for another day's sport! The Cossack was the cat; he was the mouse. Then it was that Rainsford knew the full meaning of terror.

"I will not lose my nerve. I will not."

He slid down from the tree, and struck off again into the woods. His face was set and he forced the machinery of his mind to function. Three hundred yards from his hiding place he stopped where a huge dead tree leaned precariously on a smaller living one. Throwing off his sack of food, Rainsford took his knife from its sheath and began to work with all his energy.

The job was finished at last, and he threw himself down behind a fallen log a hundred feet away. He did not have to wait long. The cat was coming again to play with the mouse.

Following the trail with the sureness of a bloodhound came General Zaroff. Nothing escaped those searching black eyes, no crushed blade of grass, no bent twig, no mark, no matter how faint, in the moss. So intent was the Cossack on his stalking that he was upon the thing Rainsford had made before he saw it. His foot touched the protruding bough that was the trigger. Even as he touched it, the general sensed his danger and leaped back with the agility of an ape. But he was not quite quick enough; the dead tree, delicately adjusted to rest on the cut living one, crashed down and struck the general a glancing blow on the shoulder as it fell; but for his alertness, he must have been smashed beneath it. He staggered, but he did not fall; nor did he drop his revolver. He stood there rubbing his injured shoulder, and Rainsford, with fear again gripping his heart, heard the general's mocking laugh ring through the jungle.

"Rainsford," called the general, "if you are within sound of my voice, as I suppose you are, let me congratulate you. Not many men know how to make a Malay man-catcher. Luckily for me, I too have hunted in Malacca. You are proving interesting, Mr. Rainsford. I am going now to have my wound dressed; it's only a slight one. But I shall be back. I shall be back."

When the general, nursing his bruised shoulder, had gone, Rainsford took up his flight again. It was flight now, a desperate, hopeless flight, that carried him on for some hours. Dusk came, then darkness, and still he pressed on. The ground grew softer under his moccasins; the vegetation grew ranker, denser; insects bit him savagely. Then, as he stepped forward, his foot sank into the ooze. He tried to wrench it back, but the muck sucked viciously at his foot as if it were a giant leech. With a violent effort, he tore his foot loose. He knew where he was now. Death Swamp and its quicksand.

His hands were tight closed as if his nerve were something tangible that someone in the darkness was trying to tear from his grip. The softness of the earth had given him an idea. He stepped back from the quicksand a dozen feet or so and, like some huge prehistoric beaver, he began to dig.

Rainsford had dug himself in in France when a second's delay meant death. That had been a placid pastime compared to his digging now. The pit grew deeper; when it was above his shoulders, he climbed out and from some hard saplings cut stakes and sharpened them to a fine point. These stakes he planted in the bottom of the pit with the points sticking up. With flying fingers he wove a rough carpet of weeds and branches and with it he covered the mouth of the pit. Then, wet with sweat and aching with tiredness, he crouched behind the stump of a lightning-charred tree.

He knew his pursuer was coming; he heard the padding sound of feet on the soft earth, and the night breeze brought him the perfume of the general's cigarette. It seemed to Rainsford that the general was coming with unusual swiftness; he was not feeling his way along, foot by foot. Rainsford, crouching there, could not see the general, nor could he see the pit. He lived a year in a minute. Then he felt an impulse to cry aloud with joy, for he heard the sharp crackle of the breaking branches as the cover of the pit gave way; he heard the sharp scream of pain as the pointed stakes found their mark. He leaped up from his place of concealment. Then he cowered back. Three feet from the pit a man was standing, with an electric torch in his hand.

"You've done well, Rainsford," the voice of the general called. "Your Burmese tiger pit has claimed one of my best dogs. Again you score. I think, Mr. Rainsford, I'll see what you can do against my whole pack. I'm going home for a rest now. Thank you for a most amusing evening."

At daybreak Rainsford, lying near the swamp, was awakened by a sound that made him know that he had new things to learn about fear. It was a distant sound, faint and wavering, but he knew it. It was the baying of a pack of hounds.

Rainsford knew he could do one of two things. He could stay where he was and wait. That was suicide. He could flee. That was postponing the inevitable. For a moment he stood there, thinking. An idea that held a wild chance came to him, and, tightening his belt, he headed away from the swamp. The baying of the hounds drew nearer, then still nearer, nearer, ever nearer. On a ridge Rainsford climbed a tree. Down a watercourse, not a quarter of a mile away, he could see the bush moving. Straining his eyes, he saw the lean figure of General Zaroff; just ahead of him Rainsford made out another figure whose wide shoulders surged through the tall jungle weeds; it was the giant Ivan, and he seemed pulled forward by some unseen force; Rainsford knew that Ivan must be holding the pack in leash.

They would be on him any minute now. His mind worked frantically. He thought of a native trick he had learned in

Uganda. He slid down the tree. He caught hold of a springy young sapling and to it he fastened his hunting knife, with the blade pointing down the trail; with a bit of wild grapevine he tied back the sapling. Then he ran for his life. The hounds raised their voices as they hit the fresh scent. Rainsford knew now how an animal at bay feels.

He had to stop to get his breath. The baying of the hounds stopped abruptly, and Rainsford's heart stopped too. They must have reached the knife.

He shinned excitedly up a tree and looked back. His pursuers had stopped. But the hope that was in Rainsford's brain when he climbed died, for he saw in the shallow valley that General Zaroff was still on his feet. But Ivan was not. The knife, driven by the recoil of the springing tree, had not wholly failed.

Rainsford had hardly tumbled to the ground when the pack resumed the chase.

"Nerve, nerve, nerve!" he panted, as he dashed along. A blue gap showed between the trees dead ahead. Ever nearer drew the hounds. Rainsford forced himself on toward that gap. He reached it. It was the shore of the sea. Across a cove he could see the gloomy gray stone of the château. Twenty feet below him the sea rumbled and hissed. Rainsford hesitated. He heard the hounds. Then he leaped far out into the sea. . . .

When the general and his pack reached the place by the sea, the Cossack stopped. For some minutes he stood regarding the blue-green expanse of water. He shrugged his shoulders. Then he sat down, took a drink of brandy from a silver flask, lit a perfumed cigarette, and hummed a bit from *Madame Butterfly*.

General Zaroff had an exceedingly good dinner in his great paneled dining hall that evening. With it he had a bottle of Pol Roger and a half bottle of Chambertin. Two slight annoyances kept him from perfect enjoyment. One was the thought that it would be difficult to replace Ivan; the other was that his quarry had escaped him; of course, the American hadn't played the game—so thought the general as he tasted his after-dinner liqueur. In his library he read, to soothe himself, from the works of Marcus Aurelius. At ten he went up to his bedroom. He was deliciously tired, he said to himself, as he locked himself in. There was a little moonlight, so, before turning on his light, he went to the window and looked down at the courtyard. To the great hounds he called: "Better luck another time!" Then he switched on the light.

A man, who had been hiding in the curtains of the bed, was standing there.

"Rainsford!" screamed the general. "How in God's name did you get here?"

"Swam," said Rainsford. "I found it quicker than walking through the jungle."

The general sucked in his breath and smiled. "I congratulate you," he said. "You have won the game."

Rainsford did not smile. "I am still a beast at bay," he said, in a low, hoarse voice. "Get ready, General Zaroff."

The general made one of his deepest bows. "I see," he said. "Splendid! One of us is to furnish a repast for the hounds. The other will sleep in this very excellent bed. On guard, Rainsford." . . .

He had never slept in a better bed, Rainsford decided.

Reading for Understanding _____

Main Idea

1. Of all possible hunted animals, the most dangerous game is   (a) the jaguar   (b) the tiger   (c) the bear   (d) man.

Details

2. Sanger Rainsford had a reputation as   (a) a soldier   (b) a hunter   (c) a sailor   (d) an animal trainer.

3. Rainsford considered the most dangerous game to be   (a) the tiger   (b) the jaguar   (c) the Cape buffalo   (d) none of these.

4. Rainsford found himself on the island because of
   (a) a fall   (b) a storm   (c) a shipwreck   (d) an invitation.

5. General Zaroff was slightly injured by   (a) a knife
   (b) a falling tree   (c) Ivan   (d) the hunting dogs.

Inferences

6. The shots that Rainsford heard aboard the yacht had been
   fired by   (a) Ivan   (b) Captain Nielsen   (c) Zaroff
   (d) Whitney.

7. The "animal in an extremity of anguish and terror" (23)
   was really   (a) a jaguar   (b) one of the hunting dogs
   (c) a person   (d) the Cossack.

8. Zaroff sought an animal that   (a) can reason
   (b) was not a source of danger   (c) lived on the island
   (d) was stronger than a Cape buffalo.

9. Zaroff stocked his island with creatures to hunt by
   (a) shipping them in from Africa   (b) breeding them in a
   zoo   (c) buying them in South America   (d) arranging
   shipwrecks.

10. Zaroff enjoyed a hunt only when it was   (a) brief
    (b) difficult   (c) relaxed   (d) friendly.

Order of Events

11. Arrange the items in the order in which they occurred.
    Use letters only.
    A. General Zaroff tells Rainsford what the most dangerous game is.
    B. Rainsford talks to Whitney about hunting.
    C. Zaroff is surprised to find Rainsford in his bedroom.
    D. Ivan dies.
    E. Whitney tells Rainsford about the island.

Outcomes

12. After the story ended,   (a) Zaroff apologized to Rainsford   (b) Whitney appeared on the island   (c) Zaroff
    was arrested   (d) Rainsford left the island.

Cause and Effect

13. Rainsford was able to survive only because of
    (a) his previous skills as a hunter   (b) Zaroff's cowardice
    (c) an unexpected change in weather   (d) Zaroff's change
    of heart toward him.

Fact or Opinion

Tell whether the following is a fact or an opinion.
14. Zaroff could have killed Rainsford the first morning after
    the hunt began.

Author's Role

15. The major purpose of the author is to   (a) discourage
    hunting   (b) emphasize a worthy theme   (c) contrast
    two admirable characters   (d) build suspense.

Words in Context _____

1. The dank tropical night was *palpable* as it pressed its
   thick, warm blackness in upon the yacht.
   Palpable (21) means   (a) felt by the senses   (b) mysterious and strange   (c) moist and uncomfortable
   (d) unnoticed by the crew.

2. "But it's got into sailor *lore* somehow."
   Lore (22) means   (a) songs and dances   (b) traditional
   knowledge   (c) weird superstitions   (d) disagree-
   ments.

3. "Sometimes I think evil is a *tangible* thing—with wavelengths, just as sound and light have."
   Tangible (22) means able to be   (a) understood
   (b) discovered   (c) carried   (d) touched.

4. Rainsford, reclining in a steamer chair, *indolently* puffed
   on his favorite briar.

Indolently (23) means   (a) nervously   (b) quickly
(c) pleasantly   (d) lazily.

5.   Desperately he struck out with strong strokes after the
receding lights of the yacht, but he stopped before he had
swum fifty feet.
Receding (23) means   (a) blinking   (b) going away
(c) hard to see   (d) unchanging.

6.   They had come from the right, and *doggedly* he swam in
that direction, swimming with slow, deliberate strokes,
conserving his strength.
Doggedly (23) means   (a) with a dog paddle
(b) suddenly   (c) cheerily   (d) stubbornly.

7.   It came out of the darkness, a high screaming sound, the
sound of an animal in an extremity of *anguish* and terror.
Anguish (23) means   (a) agony   (b) irritation
(c) noisiness   (d) headache.

8.   The jungle weeds were crushed down and the moss was
lacerated; one patch of weeds was stained crimson.
Lacerated (24) means   (a) mangled   (b) smooth
(c) missing   (d) uncovered.

9.   His eyes made out the shadowy outlines of a *palatial*
château.
Palatial (25) means   (a) modest   (b) dignified
(c) magnificent   (d) mysterious.

10.   But it was no *mirage*, he found, when he opened the tall
spiked iron gate.
Mirage (25) means   (a) disappointment   (b) false
vision   (c) garden   (d) large courtyard.

11, 12.   Rainsford's first impression was that the man was
singularly handsome; his second was that there was an
original, almost *bizarre* quality about the general's face.
Singularly (26) means   (a) remarkably   (b) moderately
(c) darkly   (d) cruelly.
Bizarre (26) means   (a) striking   (b) gentle
(c) ugly   (d) weird.

13.   He was finding the general a most thoughtful and *affable*
host, a true cosmopolite.

Affable (27) means　　(a) intelligent　　(b) sharp
(c) loud　　(d) friendly.

14. "After the *debacle* in Russia I left the country, for it was imprudent for an officer of the Czar to stay there."
Debacle (29) means　　(a) disaster　　(b) experience
(c) amusing incident　　(d) earthquake.

15. "What are the *attributes* of an ideal quarry?"
Attributes (30) means　　(a) finances　　(b) characteristics
(c) weaknesses　　(d) impressions.

16. "I can't believe you are serious, General Zaroff. This is a *grisly* joke."
Grisly (30) means　　(a) humorous　　(b) thoughtful
(c) horrible　　(d) intentional.

17. "Do not make me *condone* cold-blooded murder," finished Rainsford stiffly.
Condone (31) means　　(a) describe　　(b) enjoy
(c) pardon　　(d) attack.

18. "Dear me," said the general, quite *unruffled*, "again that unpleasant word."
Unruffled (31) means　　(a) calm　　(b) irritated
(c) interested　　(d) alert.

19. Then he added, hastily; "I don't wish you to think me a *braggart*, Mr. Rainsford."
Braggart (33) means　　(a) murderer　　(b) weakling
(c) dreamer　　(d) boaster.

20. "Ah, indeed?" the general inquired *solicitously*. "Well, I suppose that's only natural, after your long swim."
Solicitously (33) means showing　　(a) anger
(b) concern　　(c) fear　　(d) curiosity.

21. "One foolish fellow tried it. The *deplorable* part of it was that Lazarus followed him."
Deplorable (35) means　　(a) regrettable
(b) outstanding　　(c) hopeful　　(d) favorable.

22. He saw that straight flight was *futile;* inevitably it would bring him face to face with the sea.
Futile (36) means　　(a) vital　　(b) desirable　　(c) useless
(d) expected.

23. He executed a series of *intricate* loops; he doubled on his trail again and again, recalling all the lore of the fox hunt, and all the dodges of the fox.
Intricate (36) means   (a) similar   (b) simple
(c) circular   (d) complicated.

24. An *apprehensive* night crawled slowly by like a wounded snake, and sleep did not visit Rainsford, although the silence of a dead world was on the jungle.
Apprehensive (36) means   (a) unusually cold
(b) anxious   (c) warm   (d) uncomfortable.

25. Then he straightened up and took from his case one of his black cigarettes; its *pungent* incenselike smoke floated up to Rainsford's nostrils.
Pungent (37) means   (a) sharp   (b) visible
(c) soothing   (d) blinding.

26. Three hundred yards from his hiding place he stopped where a huge dead tree leaned *precariously* on a smaller living one.
Precariously (38) means   (a) insecurely   (b) solidly
(c) well balanced   (d) lightly.

27. His foot touched the *protruding* bough that was the trigger.
Protruding (38) means   (a) irregularly shaped
(b) well concealed   (c) sticking out   (d) rough.

28. Even as he touched it, the general sensed his danger and leaped back with the *agility* of an ape.
Agility (39) means   (a) knowledge   (b) cry
(c) unsteadiness   (d) quickness.

29. That had been a *placid* pastime compared to his digging now.
Placid (39) means   (a) rough-and-ready   (b) unpleasant   (c) common   (d) quiet.

30. It was a distant sound, faint and *wavering*.
Wavering (40) means   (a) pleasant   (b) uncertain
(c) musical   (d) timeless.

Thinking Critically About the Story _____

1. The heart of irony is the clash of opposites. It focuses on the difference between what *is* and what *appears* to be. Someone may say something that has a meaning quite different from what was expected or intended. Early in the story, Rainsford says smugly, "The world is made up of two classes—the hunters and the hunted. Luckily, you and I are hunters." How does this statement seem ironic in light of the events to follow? How does Rainsford change his opinion about the hunters and the hunted?

2. Character and plot are often well intertwined in a story. Character advances plot, and plot shapes character. Is this statement true of "The Most Dangerous Game"? Support your point of view by referring to the story.

3. Apparently, Zaroff originally planned to have Rainsford as a hunting partner, but he changed his mind. At what point did he begin to look upon Rainsford not as a fellow hunter but as a person worth hunting?

4. Despite Zaroff's claims of fairness, how did he demonstrate his unfairness when ordinary methods of hunting failed?

5. What part does Ivan play in the story? How does he add an element of dread?

6. How did Zaroff make sure to get sufficient numbers of persons to hunt?

7. *Immorality* is sometimes defined as "wickedness." *Amorality* is defined as the "inability to distinguish between right and wrong." How would you classify Zaroff? Is he *immoral? Amoral?* Is he just downright evil? Or does he really fail to understand the difference between right and wrong? Explain.

8. Sporting attitudes have changed recently. Many people no longer look upon big-game hunting as a worthy sport. How do you feel? Develop your point of view in a composition of

200–250 words. You might use the following as a topic sentence:

In my opinion, the hunting of big game like tigers, jaguars, and Rocky Mountain sheep is . . .

Stories in Words

Philosopher (21) The two parts of this word are common. *Philo*, which means "loving," appears in *philology*, "a love of learning," and *Philadelphia*, "the city of brotherly love." *Soph*, which means "wise," appears in *sophomore*, "a wise fool" and *sophisticated*, "worldly wise." A philosopher is "one who loves wisdom."

Bizarre (26) The Basque word *bizar* means "beard." Since knights tended to be bearded, Spanish produced the word *bizarro*, meaning "bold, knightly." Then came the Italian *bizarro*, meaning "angry, fierce, strange." The last meaning is at the heart of the English word. *Bizarre* means "strange, odd, unbelievable."

Aristocrat (26) The two parts of *aristocrat* are *aristo*, "the best," and *crat*, "rule." By derivation, an *aristocracy* is a "rule of the best people." But in addition to its good meanings, the word *aristocrat* has also developed some negative ones of snobbishness and unconcern for the welfare of others. The context (words surrounding the word in question) will suggest which meaning is intended.

The Lady, or the Tiger?

Frank R. Stockton

♦ **He turned, and with a firm and rapid step he walked across the empty space. Every heart stopped beating, every breath was held, every eye was fixed immovably upon that man. Without the slightest hesitation, he went to the door on the right, and opened it.**

Game shows sometimes have contestants choosing doors to open. Behind one door may be an expensive product; behind another may be a nearly worthless "gag" object. There is always suspense as the contestant pauses and then points to the chosen door.

"The Lady, or the Tiger?" also involves a choice of doors, but here the wrong choice is not something for a laugh. It is something much more serious, as you will see. The choice of door presents one of the greatest puzzles in literature.

On nearly any list of the ten most famous stories, "The Lady, or the Tiger?" has a place. The central point has become part of our folklore. The phrase is sometimes used for a terrible decision, with one choice a deadly one.

The plot (1) is simple, but characterization (2) is everything. The king's character is interesting, and the author paints it with a certain amount of humor. It is the princess's character, though, that arouses our keenest interest. In her, many conflicting emotions are balanced—almost perfectly for the sake of the story. It isn't her lover who is presented with that terrible decision. It is the princess herself. Does her love prevail over jealousy? Do her finer emotions tip the scales against her almost barbaric nature? What do *you* think? You see, *you* must also make a decision!

THE LADY, OR THE TIGER?

In the very olden times, there lived a semibarbaric king, whose ideas, though somewhat polished and sharpened by the progressiveness of distant Latin neighbors, were still large, florid, and untrammeled, as became the half of him which was barbaric. He was a man of exuberant fancy, and, withal, of an authority so irresistible that, at his will, he turned his varied fancies into facts. He was greatly given to self-communing; and, when he and himself agreed upon anything, the thing was done. When every member of his domestic and political systems moved smoothly in its appointed course, his nature was bland and genial; but whenever there was a little hitch, and some of his orbs got out of their orbits, he was blander and more genial still, for nothing pleased him so much as to make the crooked straight, and crush down uneven places.

Among the borrowed notions by which his barbarism had become semified* was that of the public arena, in which, by exhibitions of manly and beastly valor, the minds of his subjects were refined and cultured.

But even here the exuberant and barbaric fancy asserted itself. The arena of the king was built, not to give the people an opportunity of hearing the rhapsodies of dying gladiators, nor to enable them to view the inevitable conclusion of a conflict between religious opinions and hungry jaws, but for purposes far better adapted to widen and develop the mental energies of the people. This vast amphitheatre, with its encircling galleries, its mysterious vaults, and its unseen passages, was an agent of poetic justice, in which crime was punished or virtue

* *semified*   a humorous word invented by the author to suggest why the king was only *semi*barbaric.

51

rewarded, by the decrees of an impartial and incorruptible chance.

When a subject was accused of a crime of sufficient importance to interest the king, public notice was given that on an appointed day the fate of the accused person would be decided in the king's arena—a structure which well deserved its name; for, although its form and plan were borrowed from afar, its purpose emanated solely from the brain of this man, who, every barleycorn a king, knew no tradition to which he owed more allegiance than pleased his fancy, and who ingrafted on every adopted form of human thought and action the rich growth of his barbaric idealism.

When all the people had assembled in the galleries, and the king, surrounded by his court, sat high up on his throne of royal state on one side of the arena, he gave a signal, a door beneath him opened, and the accused subject stepped out into the amphitheatre. Directly opposite him, on the other side of the enclosed space, were two doors, exactly alike and side by side. It was the duty and the privilege of the person on trial, to walk directly to these doors and open one of them. He could open either door he pleased: he was subject to no guidance or influence but that of the aforementioned impartial and incorruptible chance. If he opened the one, there came out of it a hungry tiger, the fiercest and most cruel that could be procured, which immediately sprang upon him, and tore him to pieces, as a punishment for his guilt. The moment that the case of the criminal was thus decided, doleful iron bells were clanged, great wails went up from the hired mourners posted on the outer rim of the arena, and the vast audience, with bowed heads and downcast hearts, wended slowly their homeward way, mourning greatly that one so young and fair, or so old and respected, should have merited so dire a fate.

But, if the accused person opened the other door, there came forth from it a lady, the most suitable to his years and station that his majesty could select from among his fair subjects; and to this lady he was immediately married, as a reward of his innocence. It mattered not that he might already possess a wife and family, or that his affections might be engaged upon an object of his own selection: the king allowed no such subordinate arrangements to interfere with his great scheme of retribution and reward. The exercises, as in the other instance, took place immediately, and in the arena. Another door opened beneath the king, and a priest, followed by a band of choristers, and dancing maidens blowing joyous airs on golden horns and treading an epithalamic measure, advanced to where the pair stood, side by side, and the wedding was promptly and cheerily solemnized. Then the gay brass bells rang forth their merry peals, the people shouted glad hurrahs, and the innocent man, preceded by children strewing flowers on his path, led his bride to his home.

This was the king's semibarbaric method of administering justice. Its perfect fairness is obvious. The criminal could not know out of which door would come the lady: he opened either he pleased, without having the slightest idea whether, in the next instant, he was to be devoured or married. On some occasions the tiger came out of one door, and on some out of the other. The decisions of this tribunal were not only fair, they were positively determinate: the accused person was instantly punished if he found himself guilty; and, if innocent, he was rewarded on the spot, whether he liked it or not. There was no escape from the judgments of the king's arena.

The institution was a very popular one. When the people gathered together on one of the great trial days, they never knew whether they were to witness a bloody slaughter or a hilarious wedding. This element of uncertainty lent an interest to the occasion which it could not otherwise have attained. Thus, the masses were entertained and pleased, and the thinking part of the community could bring no charge of unfairness against this plan; for did not the accused person have the whole matter in his own hands?

This semibarbaric king had a daughter as blooming as his most florid fancies, and with a soul as fervent and imperious as his own. As is usual in such cases, she was the apple of his eye, and was loved by him above all humanity. Among his courtiers was a young man of that fineness of blood and lowness of station common to the conventional heroes of romance who love royal maidens. This royal maiden was well satisfied with her lover, for he was handsome and brave to a degree unsurpassed in all this kingdom; and she loved him with an ardor that had enough of barbarism in it to make it exceedingly

warm and strong. This love affair moved on happily for many
months, until one day the king happened to discover its
existence. He did not hesitate nor waver in regard to his duty
in the premises. The youth was immediately cast into prison,
and a day was appointed for his trial in the king's arena. This,
of course, was an especially important occasion; and his
majesty, as well as all the people, was greatly interested in the
workings and development of this trial. Never before had such
a case occurred; never before had a subject dared to love the
daughter of a king. In after-years such things became commonplace enough; but then they were, in no slight degree, novel
and startling.

The tiger cages of the kingdom were searched for the most
savage and relentless beasts, from which the fiercest monster
might be selected for the arena; and the ranks of maiden youth
and beauty throughout the land were carefully surveyed by
competent judges, in order that the young man might have a
fitting bride in case fate did not determine for him a different
destiny. Of course, everybody knew that the deed with which
the accused was charged had been done. He had loved the
princess, and neither he, she, nor anyone else thought of
denying the fact; but the king would not think of allowing any
fact of this kind to interfere with the workings of the tribunal,
in which he took such great delight and satisfaction. No matter
how the affair turned out, the youth would be disposed of; and
the king would take an aesthetic pleasure in watching the
course of events, which would determine whether or not the
young man had done wrong in allowing himself to love the
princess.

The appointed day arrived. From far and near the people
gathered, and thronged the great galleries of the arena; and
crowds, unable to gain admittance, massed themselves against
its outside walls. The king and his court were in their places,
opposite the twin doors—those fateful portals, so terrible in
their similarity.

All was ready. The signal was given. A door beneath the
royal party opened, and the lover of the princess walked into
the arena. Tall, beautiful, fair, his appearance was greeted with
a low hum of admiration and anxiety. Half the audience had
not known so grand a youth had lived among them. No wonder

the princess loved him! What a terrible thing for him to be there!

As the youth advanced into the arena, he turned, as the custom was, to bow to the king: but he did not think at all of that royal personage; his eyes were fixed upon the princess, who sat to the right of her father. Had it not been for the moiety of barbarism in her nature, it is probable that lady would not have been there; but her intense and fervid soul would not allow her to be absent on an occasion in which she was so terribly interested. From the moment that the decree had gone forth, that her lover should decide his fate in the king's arena, she had thought of nothing, night or day, but this great event and the various subjects connected with it. Possessed of more power, influence, and force of character than anyone who had ever before been interested in such a case, she had done what no other person had done—she had possessed herself of the secret of the doors. She knew in which of the two rooms, that lay behind those doors, stood the cage of the tiger, with its open front, and in which waited the lady. Through these thick doors, heavily curtained with skins on the inside, it was impossible that any noise or suggestion should come from within to the person who should approach to raise the latch of one of them; but gold, and the power of a woman's will, had brought the secret to the princess.

And not only did she know in which room stood the lady ready to emerge, all blushing and radiant, should her door be opened, but she knew who the lady was. It was one of the fairest and loveliest of the damsels of the court who had been selected as the reward of the accused youth, should he be proved innocent of the crime of aspiring to one so far above him; and the princess hated her. Often had she seen, or imagined that she had seen, this fair creature throwing glances of admiration upon the person of her lover, and sometimes she thought these glances were perceived and even returned. Now and then she had seen them talking together; it was but for a moment or two, but much can be said in a brief space; it may have been on most unimportant topics, but how could she know that? The girl was lovely, but she had dared to raise her eyes to the loved one of the princess; and, with all the intensity of the savage blood transmitted to her through long lines of

wholly barbaric ancestors, she hated the woman who blushed
and trembled behind that silent door.

When her lover turned and looked at her, and his eye met
hers as she sat there paler and whiter than anyone in the vast
ocean of anxious faces about her, he saw, by that power of
quick perception which is given to those whose souls are one,
that she knew behind which door crouched the tiger, and
behind which stood the lady. He had expected her to know it.
He understood her nature, and his soul was assured that she
would never rest until she had made plain to herself this thing,
hidden to all other lookers-on, even to the king. The only hope
for the youth in which there was any element of certainty was
based upon the success of the princess in discovering this
mystery; and the moment he looked upon her, he saw she had
succeeded, as in his soul he knew she would succeed.

Then it was that his quick and anxious glance asked the
question: "Which?" It was as plain to her as if he shouted it
from where he stood. There was not an instant to be lost. The

question was asked in a flash; it must be answered in another.

Her right arm lay on the cushioned parapet before her. She raised her hand, and made a slight, quick movement toward the right. No one but her lover saw her. Every eye but his was fixed on the man in the arena.

He turned, and with a firm rapid step he walked across the empty space. Every heart stopped beating, every breath was held, every eye was fixed immovably upon that man. Without the slightest hesitation, he went to the door on the right, and opened it.

Now, the point of the story is this: Did the tiger come out of that door, or did the lady?

The more we reflect upon this question, the harder it is to answer. It involves a study of the human heart which leads us through devious mazes of passion, out of which it is difficult to find our way. Think of it, fair reader, not as if the decision of the question depended upon yourself, but upon that hot-blooded, semibarbaric princess, her soul at a white heat beneath the combined fires of despair and jealousy. She had lost him, but who should have him?

How often, in her waking hours and in her dreams, had she started in wild horror, and covered her face with her hands, as she thought of her lover opening the door on the other side of which waited the cruel fangs of the tiger!

But how much oftener had she seen him at the other door! How in her grievous reveries had she gnashed her teeth, and torn her hair, when she saw his start of rapturous delight as he opened the door of the lady! How her soul had burned in agony when she had seen him rush to meet that woman, with her flushing cheek and sparkling eye of triumph; when she had seen him lead her forth, his whole frame kindled with the joy of recovered life; when she had heard the glad shouts from the multitude, and the wild ringing of the happy bells; when she had seen the priest, with his joyous followers, advance to the couple, and make them man and wife before her very eyes; and when she had seen them walk away together upon their path of flowers, followed by the tremendous shouts of the hilarious multitude, in which her one despairing shriek was lost and drowned!

Would it not be better for him to die at once, and go to wait for her in the blessed regions of semibarbaric futurity?

And yet, that awful tiger, those shrieks, that blood!

Her decision had been indicated in an instant, but it had been made after days and nights of anguished deliberation. She had known she would be asked, she had decided what she would answer, and, without the slightest hesitation, she had moved her hand to the right.

The question of her decision is one not to be lightly considered, and it is not for me to presume to set myself up as the one person able to answer it. And so I leave it with all of you: Which came out of the opened door—the lady, or the tiger?

Reading for Understanding _____

Main Idea

1. When given a terrible choice, the princess had to
   (a) seek the advice of the king, her father   (b) choose happiness or death for her lover   (c) turn her head when the door was opened   (d) refuse to signal her lover.

Details

2. The choice of doors took place in   (a) the king's palace   (b) the princess's suite   (c) a public arena   (d) an isolated field.

3. The lady behind the correct door was always
   (a) the man's wife or sweetheart   (b) a princess
   (c) a plain-looking peasant   (d) a beautiful lady.

4. When the correct choice was made,   (a) a marriage was performed immediately   (b) the king had the second door opened anyway   (c) the people were unhappy
   (d) the king personally congratulated the happy man.

5. In this story, the lady behind the correct door
   (a) hated the princess   (b) gave a signal to the man in

the arena   (c) was pleasant but plain in appearance
(d) knew the princess's lover.

Inferences

6. The king is labeled semibarbaric ("half barbaric") because he   (a) gave the accused persons a 50-50 chance of
   happiness   (b) encouraged his daughter to find out
   which door concealed the tiger   (c) set up a judicial
   body like our Supreme Court   (d) preferred to see the
   accused person choose the correct door.

7. "When he and himself agreed upon anything, the thing
   was done." This sentence is meant to be   (a) irritating
   (b) serious   (c) misleading   (d) humorous.

8. Until the fateful decision in this story, all previous choices
   of doors had been strictly matters of   (a) corruption
   (b) chance   (c) the public's feelings toward the accused
   (d) unconcern to the public.

9. The young man's love for the princess was really
   (a) untrue   (b) not returned   (c) ill-advised   (d) unimportant to the story.

10. If the wrong door had been chosen, the lady would have
    been   (a) set free   (b) also put to death   (c) quickly
    married to a substitute husband   (d) made a lady-in-
    waiting to the princess.

Order of Events

11. Arrange the items in the order in which they occurred.
    Use letters only.
    A. The princess signals.
    B. The young courtier opens the door on the right.
    C. The king invents his trial by doors.
    D. The young courtier is caught in a love affair with the
       princess.
    E. The princess uncovers the secret of the doors.

Outcome

12. After the story ends,   (a) the young man is happy
     (b) the princess is happy   (c) the king is infuriated
     (d) the outcome is uncertain.

Cause and Effect

13. The outcome of the story depends entirely upon
     (a) hope   (b) the king's prejudices   (c) the princess's
     character   (d) the young man's courage.

Fact or Opinion

     Tell whether the following is a fact or an opinion.
14. The king did not know that his daughter had found out
     the secret of the doors.

Author's Role

15. The author's purpose in this story is to   (a) tell a true
     story of the past   (b) present a perfect riddle
     (c) show how chance operates in our lives   (d) describe
     an ideal love affair.

Words in Context _____

1, 2. In the very olden times, there lived a semibarbaric king,
       whose ideas, though somewhat polished and sharpened
       by the progressiveness of distant Latin neighbors, were
       still large, *florid*, and *untrammeled*.
       Florid (51) means   (a) showy   (b) stupid   (c) civ-
       ilized   (d) dreary.
       Untrammeled (51) means not   (a) understood
       (b) desirable   (d) hindered   (d) sincere.
   3. He was a man of *exuberant* fancy.
       Exuberant (51) means   (a) modest and unassuming
       (b) understated   (c) uncertain   (d) high-spirited.

4, 5.   When every member of his domestic and political
systems moved smoothly in its appointed course, his
nature was *bland* and *genial.*
Bland (51) means   (a) fierce   (b) critical   (c) smooth
(d)   searching.
Genial (51) means   (a) interested   (b) pleasant
(c) curious   (d) nervous.

6.   The arena of the king was built, not to give the people an
opportunity of hearing the *rhapsodies* of dying gladiators.
Rhapsodies (51) means   (a) emotional cries
(b) complaints   (c) silent agonies   (d) challenges.

7.   This vast amphitheatre . . . was an agent of poetic justice,
in which crime was punished, or virtue rewarded, by the
decrees of an impartial and *incorruptible* chance.
Incorruptible (52) means   (a) easily bribed   (b) fair
and honest   (c) thoughtful and considerate
(d)   weak but well-intentioned.

8.   Although its form and plan were borrowed from afar, its
purpose *emanated* solely from the brain of this man.
Emanated (52) means   (a) shuffled   (b) crept
(c) arose   (d) tipped.

9.   A hungry tiger, the fiercest and most cruel that could be
procured, immediately sprang upon him, and tore him to
pieces.
Procured (52) means   (a) borrowed   (b) described
(c) visualized   (d) obtained.

10.   The moment that the case of the criminal was thus
decided, *doleful* iron bells were clanged, great wails went
up from the hired mourners posted on the outer rim of the
arena.
Doleful (52) means   (a) huge   (b) soothing
(c) sad   (d) cast.

11.   The vast audience, with bowed heads and downcast
hearts, wended slowly their homeward way, mourning
greatly that one so young and fair, or so old and respected,
should have merited so *dire* a fate.
Dire (52) means   (a) dreadful   (b) strange
(c) unexpected   (d) dreary.

12. The king allowed no such subordinate arrangements to interfere with his great scheme of *retribution* and reward.
    Retribution (53) means   (a) respect   (b) apportion   (c) fame   (d) punishment.

13, 14. The semibarbaric king had a daughter as blooming as his most florid fancies, and with a soul as *fervent* and *imperious* as his own.
    Fervent (53) means   (a) gentle   (b) hot-blooded   (c) murderous   (d) humorous.
    Imperious (53) means   (a) forgiving   (b) proud   (c) likable   (d) impish.

15. He was handsome and brave to a degree unsurpassed in all this kingdom; and she loved him with an *ardor* that had enough of barbarism in it to make it exceedingly warm and strong.
    Ardor (53) means   (a) emotional warmth   (b) slight indifference   (c) love-hate feeling   (d) mild affection.

16. The tiger cages of the kingdom were searched for the most savage and *relentless* beasts, from which the fiercest monster might be selected for the arena.
    Relentless (54) means without   (a) strength   (b) friendliness   (c) appetite   (d) yielding.

17. The ranks of maiden youth and beauty throughout the land were carefully surveyed by *competent* judges, in order that the young man might have a fitting bride in case fate did not determine for him a different destiny.
    Competent (54) means   (a) able   (b) powerful   (c) interested   (d) elderly.

18. He saw, by that power of quick *perception* which is given to those whose souls are one, that she knew behind which door crouched the tiger, and behind which stood the lady.
    Perception (56) means   (a) signaling   (b) awareness   (c) eagerness   (d) excitement.

19, 20. It involves a study of the human heart which leads us through *devious mazes* of passion, out of which it is difficult to find our way.
    Devious (57) means   (a) roundabout   (b) annoying   (c) obvious   (d) carefully laid out.

Mazes (57) means   (a) cruel traps   (b) veins and arteries   (c) networks of paths   (d) series of circles.

21, 22.   How in her grievous *reveries* had she gnashed her teeth, and torn her hair, when she saw his start of *rapturous* delight as he opened the door of the lady.
Reveries (57) means   (a) rooms   (b) verses of poetry (c) arguments   (d) daydreams.
Rapturous (57) means   (a) surprised   (b) ecstatic (c) well-concealed   (d) nervous.

23, 24.   Her decision had been indicated in an instant, but it had been made after days and nights of *anguished deliberation.*
Anguished (58) means   (a) repeated   (b) shared (c) steady   (d) painful.
Deliberation (58) means   (a) freedom (b) punishment   (c) thought   (d) agony.

25.   It is not for me to *presume* to set myself up as the one person able to answer it.
Presume (58) means   (a) dare   (b) hasten   (c) hesitate   (d) restore.

Thinking Critically About the Story _____

1. How does the character of the princess dominate the story, overshadowing the character of the colorful king? How does the interpretation of her character decide the reader's answer to the question at the end?

2. Why was the choice in the arena the perfect solution to the king's disapproval of his daughter's romance?

3. When the reader answers the question at the end, does the answer tell something about him or her? Explain.

4. The young courtier knew his princess very well. Was that knowledge sufficient to guide him in his choice? Should he have chosen the other door? Explain.

5. Though the situation described is serious, the author generally writes in a light, humorous tone. Point out examples of humor in the story.
   Example: *The accused person was instantly punished if he found himself guilty; and, if innocent, he was rewarded on the spot, whether he liked it or not.* Note the ironic twist in the *whether* clause.

6. In a book called *The Lady, or the Tiger? and Other Logic Puzzles* (Knopf), Raymond Smullyan uses the puzzle as the basis for a number of brainteasers all dealing with the puzzle element in the story. Why has "The Lady, or the Tiger?" retained its popularity for nearly a century, though nearly all other works by Frank R. Stockton are forgotten?

7. Note the author's use of suspense. Halfway through the story, the young man marches into the arena to make his choice. Then we are held in suspense while the author concentrates upon the princess. It takes the rest of the story to reach the end—and then the reader is put off by the puzzle! Is this an effective device? Explain.

8. Who or what do you think came out of the open door? In a sequel of 150–300 words, write what happened after the man made his choice.

Stories in Words _____

Barbarism (51)   To the ancient Greeks, those who did not speak clear Greek were barbarians. To the educated Greek, the foreign words sounded like "bar-bar-bar," not like any intelligible word. Thus someone who spoke those "bar-bar-bar" syllables was a barbarian. Even today, a *barbarism* is defined as an *inappropriate or nonstandard expression in a language.*

Barleycorn (52)   The usual expression is "every inch a king." Why say instead "every barleycorn a king"? A barleycorn was originally a unit of length equal to ⅓ of an inch. The use of *barleycorn* is the author's humorous exaggeration to poke subtle fun at the king.

Deliberation (58)   One of the zodiac signs is Libra, the *scales* or *balance*. What connection does *deliberation* have with scales? To deliberate is to weigh something carefully, to put the matter into the scales to see which alternative should be chosen. Note that the word *weigh* itself is associated with thinking.

Archetypes

Robert Greenwood

♦   **I hadn't recognized him when he entered my shop. His appearance was changed. Not his huge bulk; nothing could disguise that. But his hair was now jet black, long and coarse. And, of course, his eyes weren't pink. They were dark green.**

These words begin a series of suspenseful events that lead the reader on a wild chase. The setting of the story is the narrow limits of a coin dealer's shop. Within this setting two characters play out their destiny: an apparently mild-mannered coin dealer and a brutal criminal. The action doesn't let up, as the suspense builds. It's a rare reader who can put the story down once it has been begun.

"Archetypes" provides a study in how suspense can be built. By using a flashback technique, the author develops a sense of dread that gets the reader in the mood for the events to follow. Will the brutal visitor repeat the events of two years previous? Can the coin dealer overcome an enemy twice his size, a man without anything resembling a conscience?

The major characters are well defined. They influence the plot and are in turn influenced by the events as they develop. Within the short space of the short story, the author develops a complete little world that shuts out everything beyond the doors of the shop.

An archetype is an original model, a pattern from which other things of the same kind are made. In a sense the two principal characters are archetypes, patterns of two persons in the kind of conflict that has appeared and reappeared throughout history. In life, there are conflicts of a person against nature, a person against society, even a person against himself. But one of the most primitive and enduring of all is the conflict between two persons who face each other in a savage, often fatal, encounter.

ARCHETYPES

Through a ten-power glass I was looking upon the face of Alexander the Great. When I saw that distinctive cut on Alexander's cheek, I'd first thought it was an old banker's mark, left there by some harpagon of antiquity. But then I realized I'd seen this particular coin before. The cut on the cheek. That was the clue.

The man who had brought the coin into my shop was sitting opposite my desk. We were alone in my shop. I could feel his eyes upon me as I examined the coin.

"Yes, it's a very rare coin," I said, although he'd not asked for an opinion.

He'd simply handed me the coin in its plastic envelope, seated himself, and asked, "How much for this?"

"You know what it is?" I asked, looking up.

He looked at me indifferently. He didn't answer.

"It's a silver tetradrachm," I said. "Issued during the reign of Ptolemy I, King of Egypt. On the obverse is the head of Alexander the Great. The reverse is Athena, holding a javelin and shield. But the coin isn't in the best condition. There's an old cut on it. That hurts its value. You understand?"

He'd turned his shoulders and was looking around my shop, taking everything in with a rapid glance, his eyes pausing at the entrance, where he did a quick study of the security door and the wall area around the door. His eyes flicked back to me.

"How much?" he repeated. There was authority in his voice. Authority or contempt. I decided it was contempt.

Then I remembered.

I remembered where I'd seen the coin before. It had been almost two years ago, a day in later summer, in the month of September. I could recall the exact hour. I'd closed my shop

early that day to make a few calls on my colleagues, dealers in
the numismatic trade. That morning I'd got a telephone call
from a close friend and competitor, Doc Parker, a specialist in
ancient coins, who told me he'd just bought a small hoard of
Greek and Cretan coins. "Come on over and take a look," he'd
said. "There's some pieces here you won't be able to resist."

Doc's shop was located in a small shopping center at the
other end of town. When I arrived he saw me waiting outside
and reached under the counter to press the button that automatically released the security lock on the door. The buzzer
sounded, and I heard the lock open. I went inside. There were
two customers looking at some Roman bronzes in a display
case. Doc came over and brought out a tray from underneath
the counter and opened it. "Look through these," he said.
"There's some nice coins here. But the best ones are back in my
office. If you want any of these, pick them out and we'll settle
up later back in my office."

He walked back to the two customers and talked about
Roman bronzes. I took out several coins and studied them with
the glass I always carry in my pocket. I was especially interested in an unusual Cretan coin. I guessed it had been struck
in about the fifth century B.C., probably in Knossos. The design
was one I'd not seen before. On the obverse was the head of the
minotaur; on the reverse, a complicated pattern in the form of
a labyrinth. I put it aside, intending to look at it again.

It was then I saw the silver tetradrachm with the head of
Alexander the Great. I had a customer who'd been looking for
this particular coin for years, but one only in a fine state of
preservation. I focused my glass expectantly. When I saw the
cut on Alexander's cheek my hopes faded. My customer for this
coin was a finicky man. Difficult to please, you might say. He
would quibble over the defect to beat down my price. I put the
coin aside.

I walked around to the cash register. Doc nodded at me
and I went through the turnstile and into his private office.
He'd put two trays of coins on his desk for me to look at:
"pieces you won't be able to resist," he'd said. Doc's private
office was closed off from the rest of his shop, except for the
door, and I'd closed that behind me. But there was a small
one-way window that looked out into the shop. When you were

seated at Doc's desk it was at the level of your eyes. From inside the shop, if you happened to look at it, surrounded as it was by a lot of framed coin displays, it looked like an innocent mirror hanging on the wall.

I looked down at the desk at the trays of coins. Doc hadn't exaggerated their quality. They were all excellent pieces. Good enough to consign to the best auction house in the trade. I got out my glass and turned on the high-intensity desk lamp. I vaguely remember hearing the buzzer and the automatic unlocking of the shop door. I was too absorbed in my study to pay any attention. But after a while, perhaps because of a kind of tension I sensed, I glanced up and looked through the one-way window.

Doc was standing in the center of the shop with his hands raised above his head. The two customers were down on the floor, spread-eagle fashion, a gun pointed at them. I looked at the man holding the gun. He was enormous. Almost a giant. I guessed he was well over six feet tall. With a powerful torso, massive shoulders, a neck as thick as a bull's. His head jutted out of that huge neck, arching and thrusting forward. He had a great mane of white hair, thick folds of it. His eyes were as brutal as the rest of him, fiery, the whites considerably inflamed or bloodshot. I guessed he'd weigh close to three hundred pounds. Middle thirties, you couldn't be positive. The white pullover sweater he wore emphasized his albino appearance. I fully expected, were I to see his eyes closely, that they would be pink. He held a .45 automatic in his hand.

I knew that Doc always carried a gun on his person during shop hours. He wore it in a small holster clipped to his belt, at the small of his back, concealed by his coat. He had a license. The first chance he got, Doc would reach for that .38 special of his. And he wouldn't hesitate to use it.

The man with the bull neck had opened one of the display cases and was dumping trays of coins into a canvas bag. With a sweep of his powerful arm, he gathered up the coins I had left on the countertop, including the two I'd removed from the tray. As he moved around the shop, Doc turned slowly, facing him. Doc's back was turned toward me. I noticed he'd dropped his right arm slightly, almost imperceptibly.

My first thought was to help Doc. I opened the desk drawers, looking for a gun. Nothing. I looked in the corner beside the desk. Doc had kept a shotgun there at one time. My own gun I'd left in my shop, in my top desk drawer. I never carried it on my person. Hoping that I was not too late, I reached for the telephone and dialed the police. I spoke softly, keeping my eyes glued on the window. He gave no sign he heard me. He was intent on his looting. When I'd reported the robbery in progress, I gently cradled the telephone and looked again for a gun.

Doc's right hand was now almost down to the level of his waist. He'd turned his body at an angle in an effort to conceal the movement of his right arm. The two customers were still down on the floor.

I racked my mind to think of something I could do. I realized if I were to open that door and enter the shop I might very well be shot down on sight. Perhaps I could create a diversion that might give Doc a chance to get his gun. Maybe, without actually entering the shop, I could stand behind the office door, give it a wild push forward, duck, and hopefully dodge the gunfire.

As I started toward the door I saw Doc reach his hand up underneath his coat. Before I could move, two shots rang out. The roar was deafening, the sound only a .45 makes. Doc was thrown back by the force of the impact, and crashed into one of the display cases. He was probably dead before he hit the floor. A .45 does terrible things to human flesh. A shot from a .45 can blow a man's arm off. Doc wasn't hit in the arm. He had been shot twice, in the chest and abdomen.

The man with the .45 was backing toward the door, carrying his loot. His eyes flashed. He was like a bull enraged, gathering his muscles for a ferocious charge. I knew then he was going through the security door. It could only be unlocked from inside the shop by pressing the button to release the automatic lock. He didn't have time to look for that button. He wheeled suddenly around, facing the door. It was a strong door. Steel frame with reinforced glass. He lifted one leg straight out, balanced himself on the other, then lunged forward, aiming at the frame with the heel of his shoe. The door popped out like a slice of toast from an automatic toaster. Didn't even break the glass. The force of the blow was so great it tore the anchor bolts out of solid concrete.

I ran out and grabbed Doc's gun. He'd at least got it in his hand before he was shot. The two customers were still on the floor, watching me. I leaped over the broken door and out into the mall of the shopping center. The parking lot was crowded with cars. Then I saw him lower his huge bulk into a blue Mustang, glancing back at the shop before he pulled his head inside. The engine started up with a roar. It was a hell of a thing I had to do—to take a shot across a parking lot crowded with cars. But I did. I hit the window on the passenger side as the Mustang swung out of the lot. I saw the glass shatter. But I'd missed him. I hadn't time to get another shot. And I couldn't see the license plate at that distance.

When I got back to the shop a crowd of people had gathered outside. Someone had telephoned for an ambulance. But Doc was beyond that. I went inside and looked at him. But there was nothing I could do for him. He had done a great deal for me. He'd helped me to get started in the business. He was twice my age. But I'd never thought of him as old. In the ten years I'd known him I'd never even noticed him aging. He had been given the name of Doc because there were a lot of us in the trade that respected him. Not only respected him as a man but because we respected his knowledge. He knew as much about ancient coins as anyone I'd ever met. He could read six languages. Knew as much about ancient history as most college professors. Maybe more. He had a memory for coins the way some people remember baseball scores, almost total recall. But he hadn't been one of those mousy antiquarian types. He'd been a big man, over two hundred pounds, robust, and he liked a good time. He'd liked hunting. One morning in the river delta we had watched a flight of geese very high up in the sky. So high you could barely hear their honking. Doc had liked that. Another time we had gone hunting wild boar in the Big Sur. We were in rough country when suddenly an enormous sow charged us. She was as large as a boulder and black as fury. With long white tusks that could disembowel a man. I shot twice from my hip, a tricky thing to do with a rifle. Hit her in the neck and snout. The momentum of her charge carried her right to my feet, where she had collapsed in a heap. Doc had hugged me like a bear, dancing me around. Now he lay dead at my feet.

When the police came, I gave them a full account. Every detail. One thing I hadn't mentioned before; when he'd shot Doc with that .45, the recoil hadn't even jerked his wrist up, the way it does with most people. The recoil of a .45 has quite a kick. It hadn't fazed him. I described him to the police. When I'd finished, they looked at me like maybe I was exaggerating. "That's the honest truth," I'd told them. "He's one of the biggest men I've ever seen. And he's as brutal as he looks. He has the body of a man, a powerful man, with the head of a bull." The last I'd heard, they'd not yet caught him.

I hadn't recognized him when he entered my shop. His appearance was changed. Not his huge bulk; nothing could disguise that. But his hair was now jet black, long and coarse. And, of course, his eyes weren't pink. They were dark green.

Early that morning I'd got a telephone call from a man who told me he had some coins to sell. I'd given him directions how to find my shop. When he appeared at my door I'd pushed the button underneath my desk to release the automatic lock. There was no help for it now. He was sitting opposite my desk in one of the big red-leather chairs I keep there for my customers.

He wore a black sweater over a sport shirt, open at the throat. I noticed the sweater was pulled down over his waist. A good place to conceal that .45, I thought. He reached into his pocket and pulled out another plastic coin envelope, and leaning forward, put it on my desk.

"How about this one?" he asked. His huge head jutted toward me. Then he settled back in the chair. There was an arrogance in his attitude, a kind of contempt. If not for me personally, then for everything in life. It wasn't a pose, you understand. That was simply the way he was.

I looked at the coin with my glass. It would give me time to think. I saw it was the other coin I had seen that day at Doc's, the Cretan coin with the design of the minotaur and the labyrinth. It was as though he'd handed me the final proof, and with a gesture of ultimate defiance and challenge, fantastic in its implications. But I was certain he hadn't seen me that day in Doc's shop. It just hadn't been possible. Not in the natural order of things. Even when he'd glanced back at Doc's shop, before pulling his head inside the blue Mustang, I was sure he hadn't seen me.

He was looking toward the corner behind my desk. To my right. I have a walk-in vault there. I leave it open during shop hours and lock it up every night. I keep most of my inventory in there. From where he was sitting he could see it was a vault and that the door was open, nothing more. I'd been working on a catalog to mail out to my customers and I had my book truck in there, loaded with reference books. The book truck is about four feet high, has a steel frame, and holds a lot of weight. It runs on rubber wheels, and when loaded it's plenty heavy. He kept looking at the vault and I guessed I knew what he was thinking.

I'd bought coins from a lot of people. Usually when people have coins to sell they keep their minds on business. Sometimes they try to exaggerate the value of what they have. Or if they don't know what they have, they try to pick your brains. Maybe get a free appraisal. Then use your own appraisal to go somewhere else and try to get a better price. He hadn't even been interested when I'd told him about the silver tetradrachm. But I was ahead of him. I knew he wasn't here to sell me any coins.

I continued to examine the Cretan coin, or pretended to, turning it over under my glass. I had to have time. Time to think. I knew I was no match for him. I hadn't the weight, not by half. He could break my bones with as little effort as it might take him to crack two walnuts in his fist. If he got his hands on me, I knew I hadn't a chance. When I have to fight, I want every advantage I can get. I'd been held up and robbed before. I've been pistol-whipped in my own shop. I've never stood still for it. But I've never done anything reckless, either. I'd never rush a man holding a gun on me.

"This is a valuable coin," I told him. "I'd like very much to buy it."

He turned his head quickly. He seemed somehow amused.

"I'm not sure I can really pay you what it's worth. But I'll go as high as I can." I put my glass down on the desk.

"Name a figure," he said. His mouth was forming a smile, of insolence.

"You see," I said, "right now I'm getting a catalog ready to mail out to my customers. I'd like a coin like this to feature in my catalog. It would create a minor sensation. My customers like to compete for really valuable coins. It gets their juices flowing, if you know what I mean."

He simply stared at me, cold but not withdrawn. I thought he acted as though he already owned everything I held of value. That I was an intruder in my own shop. He made you feel like that. That intimidation which radiated from him made you feel your dignity was in jeopardy. That your integrity as an individual was about to be destroyed. He said nothing. Just that cold stare.

"Not that I don't have some really valuable pieces in the shop," I said. "I do. I've been saving up some of the best things for my catalog." Then I tossed him the teaser. "I've got them in my vault over there," and I nodded toward it.

"Make me an offer," he said, and he seemed amused again.

"Oh, for the Cretan coin," I said, picking it up. "How about a thousand?"

He shrugged his shoulders. His face seemed to change. He'd got a figure from me, and he took it as a kind of victory. But more. He was looking at me as a victor might look at his victim. Now he was watching my hands, as I'd been watching his. I'd made sure during our conversation that my hands had always been in plain sight. My .38 automatic was in my top desk drawer, only inches away from my fingers. But I knew were I to open that drawer, even casually, he would probably go for his .45. He couldn't risk it. Not knowing what was in the drawer. Watching him, smiling at him, I understood that he'd always forced others to his will. That his lust for power had no restraints. He would make a sacrifice of anyone who opposed him. I knew I was in danger of my life. His or mine, I thought, smiling at him again, I knew that one of us would very probably die. He looked toward the vault again.

"I can go five hundred on the silver tetradrachm." I picked up the coin with the portrait of Alexander the Great and turned it over in my fingers. "Fifteen hundred for the two coins." I didn't want to lay it on too thick. Or be too obvious. "Would you prefer cash or a check? I think I've got that much cash in the vault."

He seemed contemptuous of me in that moment. A fool, he had taken me for. An easy mark. A piece of cake. It was written all over his cruel face. His eyes had an expectant look, like an animal contemplating its prey. Good, he had taken the bait.

I thought: in our age the ways of sacrifice have changed. We no longer slaughter younger boys and maidens to appease the gods or demons. Maybe we do symbolically. But not often literally. Sacrifice usually begins with intimidation. Today the threat of bodily harm is most often a means to an end, not an end in itself. There will always be those who demand sacrifice of others. Either through legislation or raw force. The end might not be the taking of life itself, not in the direct sense, though it had been in Doc's case, but rather the extortion of one's property. If an individual has invested knowledge and time in acquiring values and property, then what is extorted is life in its abstract form. When intimidation fails and the intended victim refuses to yield up what he values, the looter will resort to greater force. Threats, or worse. The victim, if he continues to resist, may find a gun pointed at his head. I wondered where on his person his .45 was concealed. Perhaps in a holster at the small of his back. Maybe strapped to his leg.

"You must have some interest in numismatics," I said, trying to keep a straight face. I stood up from the desk. I did it as casually as I could, keeping my hands in plain sight. He was watching me like a hawk. "Otherwise you wouldn't have these coins. Maybe you'd like to see some of my best pieces. The ones I've been saving for my catalog." I nodded toward the vault. "In any case, I keep my cash in the vault. The fifteen hundred I owe you, you know."

He stood up, drawing himself to his full height. He towered over me. I'd hoped to put an idea in his mind: that in volunteering to show him my most valuable coins it would save him the trouble of guessing which ones to rob me of. I hoped I hadn't overplayed it. He watched me, waiting for me to move.

"I'll go with you," he said. There was nothing in his face to suggest that he considered me a dangerous adversary. Only an amused look. And contempt.

I walked toward the vault. The door stood open. I paused at the threshold. He could now see inside the vault. His eyes flicked, taking everything in. He saw the trays of coins on the shelves. Stacks of silver dollars on the countertop. The book truck loaded with my reference books. I stepped inside.

He seemed to hesitate a moment. Then he looked at me

and walked in. I said, "Over here is my rarest coin." I'd put on my best shopkeeper's manner. Chatty and confiding. "A really rare piece. A French twenty-ducat gold piece. On today's market it's worth at least ten thousand." That was some exaggeration. It wasn't a twenty-ducat in gold. Only a common one-hundred-franc gold piece, worth maybe eight hundred. I picked it up and set it on the counter, beyond his reach. As he moved toward it, I pivoted, got behind him and drove my shoulder into his back with all my weight. I'd taken him by surprise. I'd used the forward motion of his own body, when he was slightly off-balance reaching for the coin, to send him sprawling against the far wall of the vault.

As I leaped outside, grabbing for the steel door of the vault, I saw him struggling to regain his balance. I shoved against the heavy door, and almost had it closed when I felt him hit it from inside. The jolt shook me, but I only pushed harder. The door was about six inches short of locking position. I'd known I would have the advantage with the vault door. You understand: the door was balanced in my favor. Although it weighed over a ton, it was balanced so that it closed much easier than it opened, by at least half the effort. For a minute I gained nothing on him. But I didn't lose anything to him, either. The door seemed frozen there, motionless, as both of us pushed against it, from opposite sides, with all our strength. I felt sweat on my forehead. Neither of us spoke a word. I could feel my heart pounding against my rib cage.

We couldn't see one another. But suddenly I saw him shove his hand through the narrow opening. I saw the .45. He tried to turn his hand to fire the gun where he guessed I would be. But he couldn't turn his hand in that small space, not without dropping the automatic. I summoned up all my strength. I knew that with one hand in the opening of the vault he had lost some of his leverage against the door. With a lunge that made my back and legs ache, I threw myself against the door. I pinned his hand. Or thought I had, when suddenly he jerked it free, the .45 disappearing inside. I lunged again and heard the lock catch. With my left elbow I spun the wheel, and then reached down and turned the combination lock.

I had him.

I turned around and leaned my back against the door. Sweat

was dripping down my face. I took several deep breaths, making my body relax. Then I walked over to my desk, opened the top drawer, and got my .38. I picked up the telephone and called the police. They wanted to know all the details. I must have been on the line with them at least five minutes. I told them it was the same man who had robbed and killed Doc Parker two years ago. He'd tried to rob me today, I said. I had him locked in my vault. They said they would send over a squad car with three men. I told them I would meet the car outside.

I had good reason for telling them I would meet them outside. My shop is located in a large building. It covers an entire city block in the downtown section. Five floors. There are at least eight corridors on each floor, many of which intersect. Three stairwells connect all five floors. The building is rented out to shops and professional offices. Unless you're familiar with the building, or with a particular shop or office,

you can easily lose your way. Some of my customers jokingly call the building "The Maze." But they know where to find me after one or two visits to my shop. One of my customers, a very charming young lady, once told me that I should carry a ball of string with me every day I entered the building. Meaning that if I played out the string on my way in, I would be able to find my way out again by retracing the string.

I locked my shop and started outside to meet the police. I met them in one of the corridors on the first floor. When we got back to my shop, I explained the situation. "He has a .45 automatic. He'll use it. He's a big man, as big as any two of us."

They wanted to know if there were any vents into the vault. They thought they might even up the odds if they could shoot some tear gas in there.

"No vents," I said.

"Can we talk to him in there?" the older cop asked.

"No way," I answered. "It's a walk-in vault."

"Will he know it when we unlock the vault?" the fat cop asked.

"Yes," I said. "He will hear the combination and see the wheel turning when I unlock the door."

"I'd better go down to the squad car and get the tear gun anyway," the young cop said.

"Bring up the shotgun too," the older one said. "Then you wait outside in the squad car. Keep the front entrance covered. And phone in for an ambulance. We might need one before this is over."

The young cop left. The older one decided that I was to open the vault. Just a crack. Not more than an inch. That way the guy inside couldn't get the barrel of the .45 through the opening. The fat cop would help me with the door. I explained to them how the vault door was balanced in our favor.

"When we get it open just a crack," the older cop said, "I'll stand behind the door and tell him to throw out his gun. Or the clip. If he refuses, I'll tell him we're going to shoot tear gas in there. Actually, that might be a tricky thing to do. Especially if he won't give up the gun or the clip. But with two of us holding the vault door I think we can manage it."

The young cop came back with the shotgun and the

tear-gas gun. "I loaded them both and called in for an ambulance," he said.

"If you hear any shooting," the older one said, "call in for another squad car."

I pressed the button for the security door and let him out.

The two cops drew their revolvers and took positions in front of the vault. I put my automatic in my waistband and wiped my hands with a handkerchief. I turned to the older cop. "Ready?" I asked.

"Okay," he said. "Easy does it."

The fat cop stood to my right, his weight against the vault door. I worked the combination and spun the wheel lock. We pulled the door open a crack. At first, for one wild second, I thought we had everything under control. Then I saw the flat end of a crowbar thrust into the opening. I had completely forgotten about the crowbar. I'd left it in the back of the vault two weeks ago when I'd moved some of the storage cabinets I keep in there.

He got terrific leverage with it. The door literally flew open. I hung on, but was lifted off my feet as it swung out. The fat cop was thrown against the older one standing in front of the vault. Then out of the corner of my eye I saw the book truck poised at the entrance of the vault. He was crouched behind it, like a runner, bracing himself, his bull neck arched forward. I cried out, but I was too late. The book truck shot out of the vault like a thunderbolt and hit the two cops. The older one went over backwards. The truck ran right over the fat cop's leg, making a sick crunching sound.

He burst out, .45 in hand. The whites of his eyes were red with rage. I saw his pocket bulging with my coins. In his left hand he had one of my canvas moneybags, heavy with coins.

The older cop had struggled to his feet. He had lost his revolver. The fat cop was still on the floor, his leg broken. The bone had come clean through his flesh and trouser leg. It looked ghastly.

Seeing that the older cop was not armed, he looked around for me. His face was twisted with fury, his teeth clenched. I ducked behind the vault door. The older cop moved to grapple with him but he swung the moneybag at his face and sent him reeling halfway across the shop. He seized the book truck and aimed it straight at the security door.

His back was toward me now. I leaned out and took careful aim at his right leg. He'd already sent the book truck crashing through the security door when I shot him. He didn't go down. He wheeled around and fired two shots at me. I ducked, and heard them ricochet off the vault door. He was limping out, still carrying the moneybag, when I leaned out again and shot him in the other leg. He let out a terrific bellow, like a maddened bull. Then he went down. When he hit the floor in the corridor outside, the .45 fell out of his hand and slid from his reach. I walked out, keeping my gun on him.

Several people had run out of the other shops and were standing in the corridor. One woman raised her hand to her mouth, but she didn't scream. No one said anything. The air was so thick with tension you could have measured it with a barometer. He turned and looked at me. I'd never seen so much hate concentrated in a human face.

In a voice so low I could barely hear him, he said, "You should've killed me when you had the chance." Then he fixed me with his eyes, as if to say, "I'll never let you stop me. Nothing can. Nothing short of death itself." Then he rolled over and dragged himself toward the .45. His arm shot out, grasping for it. He grunted with pain, but I knew it was not for his life he was fighting. It was mine. He got his fingers around the butt of the .45. Someone screamed and I heard people running.

"Give it up," I shouted, my gun aimed at his heart.

He didn't say anything. He rolled over quickly, bringing the gun up with him, getting it into position to fire. He'd left me no choice. I pulled the trigger.

His eyes went blank, staring at some chaos known only to himself. He fell back heavily, firing the .45 twice into the ceiling, harmlessly.

In the distance outside I could hear the sirens of the ambulance and police cars. Several people began looking out of the shops, stepping timidly into the corridor. The dead man lay on the floor. I looked at him. His great mane of jet black hair almost obscured the features of his face.

There are men in this world, I thought, who live by the expected sacrifice of others. The mark of rage is upon them.

You have probably noticed them. They intimidate and bully you. They are quick to fight over a card game. If they are jostled in a crowd they fly into a rage. You get the feeling that people like this expect you to apologize merely because you exist. Or that you owe them an apology simply because reality exists. Everything that happens to them is always somebody else's fault. In the moment of his death, when I'd seen that look of chaos in his eyes, I thought of his victims. I thought of Doc Parker, and of those victims unknown to me whose bones he had scattered in the wake of his lifelong rage.

The older cop staggered out into the corridor. He was dazed. I could tell by the slant of his mouth and chin that his jaw was broken. He pointed at the body on the floor and mumbled something to me that I couldn't quite make out. So I said "Dead?" just to make sure I understood what he was trying to say, and he said it again, nodding, and I answered, "Yes, he's dead." Then I volunteered something of my own. I said, "He had the body of a man, with the head of a bull."

Reading for Understanding _____

Main Idea

1. The major purpose of the coin dealer is to   (a) get a fair price for the Greek coin   (b) prevent a repetition of a previous theft   (c) demonstrate his own skill with a weapon   (d) try to reason with the brutal criminal.

Details

2. Doc was a   (a) physician   (b) college professor   (c) detective   (d) coin dealer.

3. The narrator of the story was protected from the robber because of   (a) a false mirror   (b) a desk   (c) a table   (d) the book truck.

4. The robber was temporarily restrained by   (a) his love of old coins   (b) his friendship for Doc   (c) the vault   (d) his own cowardice.

5. The robber almost succeeded because of   (a) an explosion in the shop next door   (b) a crowbar   (c) the dealer's friendship for him   (d) a mysterious accomplice.

Inferences

6. Doc can be characterized as   (a) uncertain about the value of coins   (b) a false friend   (c) too brave for his own good   (d) someone in the business only for the money.

7. The dealer mentions the recoil of the gun to   (a) show how strong the robber was   (b) demonstrate his own knowledge of guns   (c) comment on the inferiority of modern guns   (d) suggest that all dealers ought to learn about firearms.

8. The dealer tried to   (a) get an excellent price for the Greek coin   (b) interest the robber in coin collecting   (c) show that he understood coin values   (d) trick the robber.

9. In his escape from the trap, the robber showed   (a) a lack of courage   (b) some sympathy for his victims   (c) a complete lack of emotion   (d) incredible strength.

10. In a sense, the robber's downfall came about because of his own   (a) contempt for others   (b) lack of skill with a weapon   (c) knowledge of ancient coins   (d) reluctance to shoot a police officer.

Order of Events

11. Arrange the items in the order in which they occurred. Use letters only.
    A.   The robber is trapped inside the vault.
    B.   Doc calls the narrator to inspect some coins.
    C.   The narrator offers the robber a thousand dollars for the Cretan coin.

D.   The narrator kills the robber.
E.   The narrator sees the robbery from Doc's office.

Outcomes

12.   At the end of the story, the narrator probably
(a)   was sorry for his part in the death of the robber
(b) attended the funeral of the robber   (c) never collected Cretan coins again   (d) continued in his coin business.

Cause and Effect

13.   The narrator was able to trap the robber because
(a) the robber had become a little careless   (b) a policeman happened to walk into the store   (c) Doc returned unexpectedly   (d) of an explosion outside the shop.

Fact or Opinion

Tell whether the following is a fact or an opinion.
14.   The narrator turned out to be braver than the robber.

Author's Role

15.   The author's style can best be characterized as
(a)   leisurely and thoughtful   (b) rapid and direct
(c)   flowery and poetic   (d) dull and uninteresting.

Words in Context _____

1.   "On the *obverse* is the head of Alexander the Great. The reverse is Athena."
Obverse (67) means   (a) main side of a coin
(b) coin of excellent design   (c) explanation
(d) catalog of rare coins.

2. I'd closed my shop early that day to make a few calls on my colleagues, dealers in the *numismatic* trade.
   The *numismatic* (68) trade deals in   (a) stamps
   (b) autographs   (c) documents   (d) coins.

3. He would *quibble* over the defect to beat down my price.
   Quibble (68) means   (a) exclaim noisily   (b) make small objections   (c) argue violently   (d) walk silently away.

4. I guessed he was well over six feet tall. With a powerful *torso,* massive shoulders, a neck as thick as a bull's.
   Torso (69) means   (a) hips   (b) legs   (c) trunk
   (d) head.

5. I noticed he'd dropped his right arm slightly, almost *imperceptibly.*
   Imperceptibly (69) means   (a) not easily seen
   (b) noticeably   (c) in a threatening manner
   (d) intentionally noisily.

6. The *momentum* of her charge carried her right to my feet, where she had collapsed in a heap.
   Momentum (71) means   (a) sight   (b) force
   (c) sound   (d) awareness.

7. There was an *arrogance* in his attitude, a kind of contempt.
   Arrogance (72) means   (a) expression
   (b) thoughtfulness   (c) insulting pride   (d) fearful concern.

8. His mouth was forming a smile of *insolence.*
   Insolence (73) means   (a) interest   (b) goodwill
   (c) generosity   (d) contempt.

9. That *intimidation* which radiated from him made you feel your dignity was in jeopardy.
   Intimidation (74) means   (a) neutral feeling
   (b) terrorizing   (c) easygoing acceptance
   (d) pleasant manner.

10. His eyes had an expectant look, like an animal *contemplating* its prey.
    Contemplating (75) means   (a) devouring
    (b) guarding   (c) studying   (d) upsetting.

11. We no longer slaughter younger boys and maidens to *appease* the gods or demons.
    Appease (75) means   (a) satisfy   (b) annoy
    (c) report to   (d) describe.

12. The end might not be the taking of life itself, not in the direct sense, but rather the *extortion* of one's property.
    Extortion (75) means   (a) destruction
    (b) mortgaging   (c) listing with a realtor   (d) theft.

13. There was nothing in his face to suggest that he considered me a dangerous *adversary*.
    Adversary (75) means   (a) opponent   (b) gunman
    (c) coin dealer   (d) actor.

14. I ducked and heard them *ricochet* off the vault door.
    Ricochet (80) means   (a) make a whining noise
    (b) be blocked   (c) make a large circle   (d) rebound.

15. If they are *jostled* in a crowd, they fly into a rage.
    Jostled (81) means   (a) noticed   (b) bumped
    (c) robbed   (d) discovered.

Thinking Critically About the Story _____

1. "Archetypes" uses the flashback technique at the beginning. We see the brutal criminal in his attack on Doc's coin shop. Many movies and stories use the flashback technique cleverly. By using this method, a writer sacrifices the suspense of "What?" We know what happens. But there is another kind of suspense: "Why? How?" In "Archetypes," Robert Greenwood has the best of both worlds. The flashback tells all about the brutality of the criminal, but it adds additional suspense. How? Why? Explain.

2. In developing his story, a writer may choose one of several viewpoints. "The Lady, or the Tiger?" uses the omniscient (all-knowing) third-person point of view. The writer is

outside the story and can report everything, including a character's innermost thoughts. "The Most Dangerous Game" uses a more limited third-person point of view. Though the story is reported directly from Rainsford's point of view, we cannot look into the heart and mind of Zaroff. "Archetypes" uses the first-person point of view. The principal character reports everything, using the pronoun *I*. We know only what he or she knows. Which method do you prefer? What is lost or gained by each method?

3. Writing is sometimes divided into two principal types: subjective and objective writing. Subjective writing makes judgments and does the work for the reader. "The Lady, or the Tiger?" tends to be subjective. The writer does much of the interpreting for the reader. "Archetypes" is more objective. Events are reported directly. Though the coin dealer does make some judgments about his dangerous opponent, for the most part he reports, in realistic detail, only what is happening, not what he thinks about what is happening. Which type of writing do you generally prefer? Why?

4. One test of suspenseful, economical writing is the tendency not to waste words. Look back over the story. Can you find any sizable block of writing that can be omitted without loss, without harming the impact of the story? If you can, compare your findings with those of your classmates. Discuss the writer's skill in telling his story.

5. Many great short stories can be enjoyed on more than one level. At its simplest level, "Archetypes" is the story of a conflict between two antagonists locked in a life-and-death struggle. At this level alone, the story is a satisfying, suspenseful tale. But there is a deeper level. Discovering the deeper level in any story increases the enjoyment of that story. "Archetypes" is a story that suggests more than appears on the surface. In a subtle way, this is a retelling of an old Greek myth, the story of Theseus and the minotaur. The minotaur was a monster with the body of a bull and the head of a man. It lived in Crete, in the Labyrinth: a maze, a complicated and confusing series of

passages. At intervals, the minotaur required the sacrifice of seven youths and seven maidens. The hero Theseus destroyed the creature and ended the sacrifices. Study the following quotations from the story and tell how these quotations suggest the myth of the minotaur.

a. "I was especially interested in an unusual Cretan coin. The design was one I'd not seen before. On the obverse was the head of the minotaur; on the reverse, a complicated pattern in the form of a labyrinth."

b. "Almost a giant. I guessed he was well over six feet tall. With a powerful torso, massive shoulders, a neck as thick as a bull's."

c. "The man with the bull neck had opened one of the display cases."

d. "I saw it was the other coin I had seen that day at Doc's, the Cretan coin with the design of the minotaur and the labyrinth."

e. "There are men in this world, I thought, who live by the expected sacrifice of others. The mark of rage is upon them."

f. "The building is rented out to shops and professional offices. Unless you're familiar with the building, or with a particular shop or office, you can easily lose your way. Some of my customers jokingly call the building 'The Maze.' "

g. "I said, 'He had the body of a man, with the head of a bull.' "

6. *Archetype* is derived from two Greek words. *Arche* means "original, primitive." *Archaeology*, for example, is the study of the life and cultures of primitive people. *Type* is our common word meaning "class" or "group." The dealer and the robber are archetypes, representatives of the two sides in a primitive conflict of good and evil. Does knowing about the deeper meaning of the story add to your enjoyment? Explain.

7. The central character is a dealer in rare coins. Perhaps you have a hobby. Do you collect coins, stamps, license plates, minerals, or some other? Are you interested in craft work: weaving, sewing, carpentry, painting, or some

other? In a composition of 150–200 words, tell about your favorite hobby. Mention whatever special appeal it has for you.

Stories in Words _____

Labyrinth (68)   In the myth of Theseus and the minotaur, the monster inhabited the Labyrinth, an intricate maze with so many corridors it was almost impossible to escape from it. After killing the minotaur, Theseus escaped with the help of the princess Ariadne. He laid down a golden thread as he entered and found his way out by following the thread. The word *labyrinth* has come to mean
(a) "any actual maze with winding passages" or
(b) "a complicated course of affairs."

Delta (71)   The fourth letter of the Greek alphabet was delta, equivalent to our letter *d*. The shape of the letter was a simple triangle. If you look at a map of the mouth of the Nile river or the Mississippi, you will find a triangle-shaped land created by the flooding of the river at its mouth. This land is appropriately called a *delta*, after the Greek letter.

Jeopardy (74)   Jeopardy comes from two old French words meaning "game divided." It refers to an evenly divided game, with neither side having an advantage. If neither side has an advantage, there is an element of *uncertainty*. If there is uncertainty, there may be danger. From there it was but a step to the meaning *extreme danger*. The first part of *jeopardy* is related to the English *joke*, which is derived from the Latin word for *game*. It is interesting to think that jeopardy is now no joke.

Plot: What Happens Next?

ACTIVITIES

Thinking Critically About the Stories ____

1. All the stories sustain the reader's interest from beginning to end, but you probably have a favorite. Tell which kept you most interested and explain why.

2. In what ways are General Zaroff ("The Most Dangerous Game") and the robber ("Archetypes") similar? In what ways are they different? Which did you find the most repulsive? Tell why.

3. Two of the stories have clear-cut villains. A third story has no villain at all. The fourth has a person who may or may not be considered evil. Identify each.

4. All the story settings are appropriate for the tales you have read. Which story setting did you find *most* exciting, *most* helpful for the development of the story? Explain.

5. Which plot (1) did you find most interesting, most readable?

Writing and Other Activities ____

1. Write a letter to a friend recommending one of the stories in this unit. Tell why you liked it and why you think he or she would enjoy it. Use correct letter form.

2. If you were looking for a story to expand into a full-length movie, which would you choose? In a composition of 200–250 words, tell which story you would choose and explain why.

3. In a book of mythology, look up the story of Theseus. Retell for the class the Theseus story with events both before and after the minotaur.

4. Select an interesting suspense movie you've seen on television and compare it with one of the stories in this unit. How effectively did the movie sustain interest?

5. If you were providing musical background for a television play based on a story in this unit, what kind of music would you choose? First identify the story you've chosen and then describe the kind of music you'd provide.

6. Could any of these stories be made into a television play? Explain.

Stories in Words: A Review _____

A. aristocrat
B. barbarism
C. barleycorn
D. bizarre
E. deliberation
F. delta
G. jeopardy
H. labyrinth
I. panicky
J. philosopher
K. tattoo
L. willowy

Answer the following questions by choosing a word from the list above. Use letters only.

Which of the words above . . .

1. . . . is associated with a Greek god of the woodlands?

2. . . . has to do with scales?

3. . . . is one who "loves wisdom"?

4. . . . has a meaning based on the shape of a Greek letter?

5. . . . is from Dutch words meaning "shut the tap"?

6. . . . comes from a root meaning "turn, twist, bend"?

7. . . . is associated with a famous monster in Greek myth?

8. . . . suggests a dislike of foreigners?

9. . . . has a root that suggests "the best"?

10. . . . comes from old French words meaning "game divided"?

2

The Magic of Imagination

"**A**nd then a giant bird flew into the yard, and I said to it . . ."

The child's world is filled with talking animals, friendly genies, and other creatures of dreams and daydreams. Imagination is not only a childhood quality, however. It is also the source of great invention, important discoveries, and magnificent fiction. Anything that takes you out of the humdrum into another world expands your life.

The four stories in this unit are good examples of imaginative fiction. Each one takes you into a new world, a strange world, a different world. For a moment you will share life in a lonely part of England, a mysterious forest near New Orleans, a strange hospital in Italy, and a French village. These are not tales of the everyday. Rather, they suggest something offbeat, something not quite normal, something imaginative.

What are the common ingredients in all four stories? First of all, they are well written, without padding or dull sections. Second, they challenge you to think differently, to look at life in an unaccustomed way. Third, they hold your attention, keep you glued to your chair, eager to find out what happens next.

Though the endings are not necessarily happy, they do have a kind of logical necessity, given the nature of the stories. These stories were grouped together for a purpose: to show how writers from regions as varied as England, Italy, and America can stimulate your imagination.

The Monkey's Paw

W. W. Jacobs

◆   **The matches fell from his hand. He stood motionless, his breath suspended until the knock was repeated. Then he turned and fled swiftly back to his room, and closed the door behind him. A third knock sounded through the house.**

"What's that?" cried the old woman, starting up.

"A rat," said the old man, in shaking tones—"a rat. It passed me on the stairs."

Suppose you had three wishes to satisfy all your dreams. Would you take them? But suppose there was a strange curse attached to the wishes. Would you still take them? That is the central problem of "The Monkey's Paw." The Whites are offered three wishes and decide to take advantage of them. What happens next may be coincidence . . . or something more deadly.

There is an old saying, "If wishes were horses, beggars would ride." Young people daydream of success on the athletic field or some other activity. "If I only had . . ." is a common expression. In the eternally popular Christmas movie, *It's a Wonderful Life,* the character played by Jimmy Stewart gets his wish, but lives to regret it.

Wishes play a major role in the folklore and daydreams of people around the world. A genie from a bottle may build a mansion in a moment. A leprechaun, one of the Irish "little people," may provide a pot of gold. Often a talisman or charm is the key to wish fulfillment, but usually common sense breaks in and the wish is often shown to be empty.

The plot of "The Monkey's Paw" is a perfect example of effectiveness through economy. There isn't a wasted word. The dialog, the descriptions, and the powerfully limited action make this a classic. Besides, it is a worthy addition to all those stories that ask, "What if . . . ?"

THE MONKEY'S PAW

I

Without, the night was cold and wet, but in the small parlor of Lakesnam Villa the blinds were drawn and the fire burned brightly. Father and son were at chess, the former, who possessed ideas about the game involving radical changes, putting his king into such sharp and unnecessary perils that it even provoked comment from the white-haired old lady knitting placidly by the fire.

"Hark at the wind," said Mr. White, who, having seen a fatal mistake after it was too late, was amiably desirous of preventing his son from seeing it.

"I'm listening," said the latter, grimly surveying the board as he stretched out his hand. "Check."

"I should hardly think that he'd come tonight," said his father, with his hand poised over the board.

"Mate," replied the son.

"That's the worst of living so far out," bawled Mr. White, with sudden and unlooked-for violence; "of all the beastly, slushy, out-of-the-way places to live in, this is the worst. Pathway's a bog, and the road's a torrent. I don't know what people are thinking about. I suppose because only two houses on the road are let, they think it doesn't matter."

"Never mind, dear," said his wife soothingly; "perhaps you'll win the next one."

Mr. White looked up sharply, just in time to intercept a knowing glance between mother and son. The words died away on his lips, and he hid a guilty grin in his thin, gray beard.

"There he is," said Herbert White, as the gate banged to loudly and heavy footsteps came toward the door.

The old man rose with hospitable haste, and opening the door, was heard condoling with the new arrival. The new arrival also condoled with himself, so that Mrs. White said, "Tut, tut!" and coughed gently as her husband entered the room, followed by a tall burly man, beady of eye and rubicund of visage.

"Sergeant-Major Morris," he said, introducing him.

The sergeant-major shook hands, and taking the proffered seat by the fire, watched contentedly while his host got out whisky and tumblers and stood a small copper kettle on the fire.

At the third glass his eyes got brighter, and he began to talk, the little family circle regarding with eager interest this visitor from distant parts, as he squared his broad shoulders in the chair and spoke of strange scenes and doughty deeds, of wars and plagues and strange peoples.

"Twenty-one years of it," said Mr. White, nodding at his wife and son. "When he went away he was a slip of a youth in the warehouse. Now look at him."

"He don't look to have taken much harm," said Mrs. White politely.

"I'd like to go to India myself," said the old man, "just to look round a bit, you know."

"Better where you are," said the sergeant-major, shaking his head. He put down the empty glass and, sighing softly, shook it again.

"I should like to see those old temples and fakirs and jugglers," said the old man. "What was that you started telling me the other day about a monkey's paw or something, Morris?"

"Nothing," said the soldier hastily. "Leastways, nothing worth hearing."

"Monkey's paw?" said Mrs. White curiously.

"Well, it's just a bit of what you might call magic, perhaps," said the sergeant-major offhandedly.

His three listeners leaned forward eagerly. The visitor absent-mindedly put his empty glass to his lips and then set it down again. His host filled it for him.

"To look at," said the sergeant-major, fumbling in his pocket, "it's just an ordinary little paw, dried to a mummy."

He took something out of his pocket and proffered it. Mrs. White drew back with a grimace, but her son, taking it, examined it curiously.

"And what is there special about it?" inquired Mr. White, as he took it from his son and, having examined it, placed it upon the table.

"It had a spell put on it by an old fakir," said the sergeant-major, "a very holy man. He wanted to show that fate ruled people's lives, and that those who interfered with it did so to their sorrow. He put a spell on it so that three separate men could each have three wishes from it."

His manner was so impressive that his hearers were conscious that their light laughter jarred somewhat.

"Well, why don't you have three, sir?" said Herbert White cleverly.

The soldier regarded him in the way that middle age is wont to regard presumptuous youth. "I have," he said quietly, and his blotchy face whitened.

"And did you really have the three wishes granted?" asked Mrs. White.

"I did," said the sergeant-major, and his glass tapped against his strong teeth.

"And has anybody else wished?" inquired the old lady.

"The first man had his three wishes, yes," was the reply. "I don't know what the first two were, but the third was for death. That's how I got the paw."

His tones were so grave that a hush fell upon the group.

"If you've had your three wishes, it's no good to you now, then, Morris," said the old man at last. "What do you keep it for?"

The soldier shook his head. "Fancy, I suppose," he said slowly. "I did have some idea of selling it, but I don't think I will. It has caused enough mischief already. Besides, people won't buy. They think it's a fairy tale, some of them, and those who do think anything of it want to try it first and pay me afterward."

"If you could have another three wishes," said the old man, eyeing him keenly, "would you have them?"

"I don't know," said the other. "I don't know."

He took the paw, and dangling it between his front finger and thumb, suddenly threw it upon the fire. White, with a slight cry, stooped down and snatched it off.

"Better let it burn," said the soldier solemnly.

"If you don't want it, Morris," said the old man, "give it to me."

"I won't," said his friend doggedly. "I threw it on the fire. If you keep it, don't blame me for what happens. Pitch it on the fire again, like a sensible man."

The other shook his head and examined his new possession closely. "How do you do it?" he inquired.

"Hold it up in your right hand and wish aloud," said the sergeant-major, "but I warn you of the consequences."

"Sounds like the *Arabian Nights*," said Mrs. White, as she rose and began to set the supper. "Don't you think you might wish for four pairs of hands for me?"

Her husband drew the talisman from his pocket and then all three burst into laughter as the sergeant-major, with a look of alarm on his face, caught him by the arm.

"If you must wish," he said gruffly, "wish for something sensible."

Mr. White dropped it back into his pocket, and placing chairs, motioned his friend to the table. In the business of supper the talisman was partly forgotten, and afterward the three sat listening in an enthralled fashion to a second installment of the soldier's adventures in India.

"If the tale about the monkey paw is not more truthful than those he has been telling us," said Herbert, as the door closed behind their guest, just in time for him to catch the last train, "we shan't make much out of it."

"Did you give him anything for it, father?" inquired Mrs. White, regarding her husband closely.

"A trifle," said he, coloring slightly. "He didn't want it, but I made him take it. And he pressed me again to throw it away."

"Likely," said Herbert, with pretended horror. "Why, we're going to be rich, and famous, and happy. Wish to be an emperor, father, to begin with; then you can't be henpecked."

He darted round the table, pursued by the maligned Mrs. White armed with an antimacassar.

Mr. White took the paw from his pocket and eyed it dubiously. "I don't know what to wish for, and that's a fact," he said slowly. "It seems to me I've got all I want."

"If you only cleared the house, you'd be quite happy, wouldn't you?" said Herbert, with his hand on his shoulder. "Well, wish for two hundred pounds, then; that'll just do it."

His father, smiling shamefacedly at his own credulity, held up the talisman, as his son, with a solemn face somewhat marred by a wink at his mother, sat down at the piano and struck a few impressive chords.

"I wish for two hundred pounds," said the old man distinctly.

A fine crash from the piano greeted the words, interrupted by a shuddering cry from the old man. His wife and son ran toward him.

"It moved," he cried, with a glance of disgust at the object as it lay on the floor. "As I wished it twisted in my hands like a snake."

"Well, I don't see the money," said his son, as he picked it up and placed it on the table, "and I bet I never shall."

"It must have been your fancy, father," said his wife, regarding him anxiously.

He shook his head. "Never mind, though; there's no harm done, but it gave me a shock all the same."

They sat down by the fire again while the two men finished their pipes. Outside, the wind was higher than ever, and the old man started nervously at the sound of a door banging upstairs. A silence unusual and depressing settled upon all three, which lasted until the old couple rose to retire for the night.

"I expect you'll find the cash tied up in a big bag in the middle of your bed," said Herbert, as he bade them good night, "and something horrible squatting up on top of the wardrobe watching you as you pocket your ill-gotten gains."

II

In the brightness of the wintry sun next morning as it streamed over the breakfast table Herbert laughed at his fears. There was an air of prosaic wholesomeness about the room which it had lacked on the previous night, and the dirty, shriveled little paw was pitched on the sideboard with a carelessness which betokened no great belief in its virtues.

"I suppose all old soldiers are the same," said Mrs. White. "The idea of our listening to such nonsense! How could wishes be granted in these days? And if they could, how could two hundred pounds hurt you, father?"

"Might drop on his head from the sky," said the frivolous Herbert.

"Morris said the things happened so naturally," said his father, "that you might if you so wished attribute it to coincidence."

"Well, don't break into the money before I come back," said Herbert, as he rose from the table. "I'm afraid it'll turn you into a mean, avaricious man, and we shall have to disown you."

His mother laughed, and following him to the door, watched him down the road, and returning to the breakfast table, was very happy at the expense of her husband's credulity. All of which did not prevent her from scurrying to the door at the postman's knock, nor prevent her from referring somewhat shortly to retired sergeant-majors of bibulous habits when she found that the post brought a tailor's bill.

"Herbert will have some more of his funny remarks, I expect, when he comes home," she said, as they sat at dinner.

"I dare say," said Mr. White, pouring himself out some beer; "but for all that, the thing moved in my hand; that I'll swear to."

"You thought it did," said the old lady soothingly.

"I say it did," replied the other. "There was no thought about it; I had just— What's the matter?"

His wife made no reply. She was watching the mysterious movements of a man outside, who, peering in an undecided fashion at the house, appeared to be trying to make up his mind to enter. In mental connection with the two hundred pounds, she noticed that the stranger was well dressed and wore a silk hat of glossy newness. Three times he paused at the gate, and then walked on again. The fourth time he stood with his hand upon it, and then with sudden resolution flung it open and walked up the path. Mrs. White at the same moment placed her hands behind her, and hurriedly unfastening the strings of her apron, put that useful article of apparel beneath the cushion of her chair.

She brought the stranger, who seemed ill at ease, into the room. He gazed furtively at Mrs. White, and listened in a preoccupied fashion as the old lady apologized for the appearance of the room, and her husband's coat, a garment which he usually reserved for the garden. She then waited as patiently as her sex would permit for him to broach his business, but he was at first strangely silent.

"I—was asked to call," he said at last, and stooped and picked a piece of cotton from his trousers. "I come from Maw and Meggins."

The old lady started. "Is anything the matter?" she asked breathlessly. "Has anything happened to Herbert? What is it? What is it?"

Her husband interposed. "There, there, mother," he said hastily. "Sit down, and don't jump to conclusions. You've not brought bad news, I'm sure, sir," and he eyed the other wistfully.

"I'm sorry——" began the visitor.

"Is he hurt?" demanded the mother.

The visitor bowed in assent. "Badly hurt," he said quietly, "but he is not in any pain."

"Oh, thank God!" said the old woman, clasping her hands. "Thank God for that! Thank——"

She broke off suddenly as the sinister meaning of the assurance dawned upon her and she saw the awful confirmation of her fears in the other's averted face. She caught her breath, and turning to her slower-witted husband, laid her trembling old hand upon his. There was a long silence.

"He was caught in the machinery," said the visitor at length, in a low voice.

"Caught in the machinery," repeated Mr. White, in a dazed fashion, "yes."

He sat staring blankly out at the window, and taking his wife's hand between his own, pressed it as he had been wont to do in their old courting days nearly forty years before.

"He was the only one left to us," he said, turning gently to the visitor. "It is hard."

The other coughed, and rising, walked slowly to the window. "The firm wished me to convey their sincere sympathy with you in your great loss," he said, without looking round. "I beg that you will understand I am only their servant and merely obeying orders."

There was no reply; the old woman's face was white, her eyes staring, and her breath inaudible; on the husband's face was a look such as his friend the sergeant might have carried into his first action.

"I was to say that Maw and Meggins disclaim all responsibility," continued the other. "They admit no liability at all, but in consideration of your son's services they wish to present you with a certain sum as compensation."

Mr. White dropped his wife's hand, and rising to his feet, gazed with a look of horror at his visitor. His dry lips shaped the words, "How much?"

"Two hundred pounds," was the answer.

Unconscious of his wife's shriek, the old man smiled faintly, put out his hands like a sightless man, and dropped, a senseless heap, to the floor.

III

In the huge new cemetery, some two miles distant, the old people buried their dead, and came back to a house steeped in shadow and silence. It was all over so quickly that at first they could hardly realize it, and remained in a state of expectation as though of something else to happen—something else which was to lighten this load, too heavy for old hearts to bear. But the days passed, and expectation gave place to resignation—the hopeless resignation of the old, sometimes miscalled apathy. Sometimes they hardly exchanged a word, for now they had nothing to talk about, and their days were long to weariness.

It was about a week after that that the old man, waking suddenly in the night, stretched out his hand and found himself alone. The room was in darkness, and the sound of subdued weeping came from the window. He raised himself in bed and listened.

"Come back," he said tenderly. "You will be cold."

"It is colder for my son," said the old woman, and wept afresh.

The sound of her sobs died away on his ears. The bed was warm, and his eyes heavy with sleep. He dozed fitfully, and then slept until a sudden wild cry from his wife awoke him with a start.

"The monkey's paw!" she cried wildly. "The monkey's paw!"

He started up in alarm. "Where? Where is it? What's the matter?"

She came stumbling across the room toward him. "I want it," she said quietly. "You've not destroyed it?"

"It's in the parlor, on the bracket," he replied, marveling. "Why?"

She cried and laughed together, and bending over, kissed his cheek.

"I only just thought of it," she said hysterically. "Why didn't I think of it before? Why didn't you think of it?"

"Think of what?" he questioned.

"The other two wishes," she replied rapidly. "We've only had one."

"Was not that enough?" he demanded fiercely.

"No," she cried triumphantly; "we'll have one more. Go down and get it quickly, and wish our boy alive again."

The man sat up in bed and flung the bedclothes from his quaking limbs. "Good God, you are mad!" he cried, aghast.

"Get it," she panted; "get it quickly, and wish—Oh, my boy, my boy!"

Her husband struck a match and lit the candle. "Get back to bed," he said unsteadily. "You don't know what you are saying."

"We had the first wish granted," said the old woman feverishly; "why not the second?"

"A coincidence," stammered the old man.

"Go and get it and wish," cried the old woman, and dragged him toward the door.

He went down in the darkness, and felt his way to the parlor, and then to the mantelpiece. The talisman was in its place, and a horrible fear that the unspoken wish might bring his mutilated son before him ere he could escape from the room seized upon him, and he caught his breath as he found that he had lost the direction of the door. His brow cold with sweat, he felt his way round the table, and groped along the wall until he found himself in the small passage with the unwholesome thing in his hand.

Even his wife's face seemed changed as he entered the room. It was white and expectant, and to his fears seemed to have an unnatural look upon it. He was afraid of her.

"Wish!" she cried, in a strong voice.

"It is foolish and wicked," he faltered.

"Wish!" repeated his wife.

He raised his hand. "I wish my son alive again."

The talisman fell to the floor, and he regarded it shudderingly. Then he sank trembling into a chair as the old woman, with burning eyes, walked to the window and raised the blind.

He sat until he was chilled with the cold, glancing occasionally at the figure of the old woman peering through the window. The candle end, which had burnt below the rim of the china candlestick, was throwing pulsating shadows on the ceiling and walls, until, with a flicker larger than the rest, it expired. The old man, with an unspeakable sense of relief at the failure of the talisman, crept back to his bed, and a minute or two afterward the old woman came silently and apathetically beside him.

Neither spoke, but both lay silently listening to the ticking of the clock. A stair creaked, and a squeaky mouse scurried noisily through the wall. The darkness was oppressive, and after lying for some time screwing up his courage, the husband took the box of matches, and striking one, went downstairs for a candle.

At the foot of the stairs the match went out, and he paused to strike another, and at the same moment a knock, so quiet and stealthy as to be scarcely audible, sounded on the front door.

The matches fell from his hand. He stood motionless, his breath suspended until the knock was repeated. Then he turned and fled swiftly back to his room, and closed the door behind him. A third knock sounded through the house.

"*What's that?*" cried the old woman, starting up.

"A rat," said the old man, in shaking tones—"a rat. It passed me on the stairs."

His wife sat up in bed listening. A loud knock resounded through the house.

"It's Herbert!" she screamed. "It's Herbert!"

She ran to the door, but her husband was before her, and catching her by the arm, held her tightly.

"What are you going to do?" he whispered hoarsely.

"It's my boy; it's Herbert!" she cried, struggling mechanically. "I forgot it was two miles away. What are you holding me for? Let go. I must open the door."

"For God's sake don't let it in," cried the old man, trembling.

"You're afraid of your own son," she cried, struggling. "Let me go. I'm coming, Herbert; I'm coming."

There was another knock, and another. The old woman with a sudden wrench broke free and ran from the room. Her husband followed to the landing, and called after her appealingly as she hurried downstairs. He heard the chain rattle back and the bottom bolt drawn slowly and stiffly from the socket. Then the old woman's voice, strained and panting.

"The bolt," she cried loudly. "Come down. I can't reach it."

But her husband was on his hands and knees groping wildly on the floor in search of the paw. If he could only find it before the thing outside got in. A perfect fusillade of knocks reverberated through the house, and he heard the scraping of a chair as his wife put it down in the passage against the door. He heard the creaking of the bolt as it came slowly back, and at the same moment he found the monkey's paw, and frantically breathed his third and last wish.

The knocking ceased suddenly, although the echoes of it were still in the house. He heard the chair drawn back and the door opened. A cold wind rushed up the staircase, and a long loud wail of disappointment and misery from his wife gave him courage to run down to her side, and then to the gate beyond. The street lamp flickering opposite shone on a quiet and deserted road.

Reading for Understanding _____

Main Idea

1. Which of the following best expresses the main idea of the story?
    (a) Trying to interfere with fate may bring sorrow.
    (b) Friends may unintentionally injure those they love.
    (c) Greed is an unpleasant sin to watch.
    (d) Every person is truly master of his or her fate.

Details

2. The sergeant-major had obtained the monkey's paw in
    (a) Arabia   (b) Africa   (c) Australia   (d) India

3. The three wishes on the monkey's paw were available to only   (a) one person   (b) two persons   (c) three persons   (d) four persons.

4. When Mr. White wished on the paw, he said it

(a) felt slimy   (b) twisted in his hand   (c) felt strangely
warm   (d) stung his hand.

5. The amount of money asked for by Mr. White was
    (a) one hundred pounds   (b) two hundred pounds
    (c) three hundred pounds   (d) not mentioned.

Inferences

6. Mr. White complained violently about the weather be-
    cause   (a) it was snowing   (b) the sergeant-major
    couldn't get through   (c) it had turned cold
    (d) he had lost a chess match.

7. When the monkey's paw was first mentioned, the
    sergeant-major   (a) said he had lost it   (b) boasted of
    his success with it   (c) offered to sell it to Mr. White
    (d) didn't want to talk about it.

8. It may be inferred that the sergeant-major   (a) was a
    close friend of the Indian fakir   (b) really disliked Mr.
    White   (c) was not happy with the result of his three
    wishes   (d) didn't tell the truth.

9. The Whites thought that   (a) they were being punished
    for wishing on the paw   (b) Herbert was a careless
    worker   (c) Herbert's death had nothing to do with the
    paw   (d) the sergeant-major was intentionally cruel to
    them.

10. The third wish was to   (a) ask for more money
    (b) send Herbert back to his grave   (c) get a gravestone
    for Herbert   (d) help Mrs. White with her grief.

Order of Events

11. Arrange the items in the order in which they occurred.
    Use letters only.
    A. Mr. White wishes for a sum of money.
    B. The sergeant-major mentions the monkey's paw.
    C. Herbert and Mr. White play chess.
    D. Mrs. White forces Mr. White to make his third wish.
    E. The Whites are visited by a man from Maw and
        Meggins.

Outcome

12. After the end of the story   (a) Mrs. White puts the monkey's paw in a place of honor   (b) Mr. White tells Mrs. White she had made a good decision   (c) Herbert is found injured but alive   (d) Mr. White says not a word about what he had wished for.

Cause and Effect

13. In the minds of the Whites, Herbert's death had been (a) the fault of the company   (b) completely expected (c) a result of their wish   (d) purely an accident.

Fact or Opinion

Tell whether the following is a fact or an opinion.
14. As a family, the Whites were greedier than most families.

Author's Role

15. The tone of the story can be described as   (a) down-to-earth and straightforward   (b) wild and exaggerated, (c) dull and dreary   (d) good-humored and lighthearted.

Words in Context _____

1. It even provoked comment from the white-haired old lady knitting *placidly* by the fire.
   Placidly (95) means   (a) nervously   (b) fearfully (c) calmly   (d) hopefully.

2. Mr. White, who, having seen a fatal mistake after it was too late, was *amiably* desirous of preventing his son from seeing it.
   Amiably (95) means   (a) tactfully   (b) good-humoredly   (c) impatiently   (d) tenderly.

3, 4. Her husband entered the room, followed by a tall *burly* man, beady of eye and rubicund of *visage*.
Burly (96) means   (a) handsome   (b) dark
(c) silent   (d) muscular.
Visage (96) means   (a) face   (b) shoulders
(c) clothing   (d) height.

5. Mrs. White drew back with a *grimace*, but her son, taking it, examined it curiously.
Grimace (96) means   (a) cheerful grin
(b) expression of disgust   (c) cry of great pain
(d) sudden, unexpected movement.

6. The soldier regarded him in the way that middle age is wont to regard *presumptuous* youth.
Presumptuous (97) means   (a) too bold
(b) handsome   (c) somewhat interested   (d) cowardly.

7. Mr. White took the paw from his pocket and eyed it *dubiously*.
Dubiously (99) means   (a) carefully
(b) enthusiastically   (c) rapidly   (d) doubtfully.

8. His father, smiling shamefacedly at his own *credulity*, held up the talisman, as his son, with a solemn face somewhat marred by a wink at his mother, sat down at the piano and struck a few impressive chords.
Credulity (99) means too willing to   (a) challenge
(b) struggle   (c) believe   (d) take the easy way.

9. There was an air of *prosaic* wholesomeness about the room which it had lacked on the previous night.
Prosaic (100) means   (a) unsettled   (b) commonplace
(c) unexpected   (d) imaginary.

10. "Might drop on his head from the sky," said the *frivolous* Herbert.
Frivolous (100) means   (a) serious   (b) bold
(c) playful   (d) courageous.

11. "I'm afraid it'll turn you into a mean, *avaricious* man, and we shall have to disown you."
Avaricious (100) means   (a) bitter   (b) changeable
(c) menacing   (d) greedy.

12, 13. He gazed *furtively* at Mrs. White, and listened in a *preoccupied* fashion as the old lady apologized for the appearance of the room.
Furtively (101) means   (a) secretly   (b) admiringly   (c) obviously   (d) happily.
Preoccupied (101) means   (a) intense   (b) inattentive   (c) angry   (d) alert.

14. "You've not brought bad news, I'm sure, sir," and he eyed the other *wistfully*.
Wistfully (101) means   (a) sadly and longingly   (b) quickly and intently   (c) cheerfully and slyly   (d) humorously and sentimentally.

15. The visitor bowed in *assent*.
Assent (102) means   (a) dismay   (b) hostility   (c) agreement   (d) gladness.

16. There was no reply; the old woman's face was white, her eyes staring, and her breath *inaudible*.
Inaudible (102) means cannot be   (a) felt   (b) seen   (c) tasted   (d) heard.

17. "They admit no liability at all, but in consideration of your son's services they wish to present you with a certain sum as *compensation*."
Compensation (102) means   (a) sympathy   (b) pity   (c) payment   (d) insurance.

18. But the days passed, and expectation gave place to *resignation*—the hopeless resignation of the old.
Resignation (103) means   (a) quitting   (b) faith   (c) outrage   (d) acceptance.

19. The room was in darkness, and the sound of *subdued* weeping came from the window.
Subdued (103) means   (a) repeated   (b) soft   (c) angry   (d) loud.

20. The candle end was throwing *pulsating* shadows on the ceiling and walls.
Pulsating (104) means   (a) brightening   (b) lengthening   (c) sparkling   (d) throbbing.

Thinking Critically About the Story _____

1. Like "The Lady, or the Tiger?" this story is open-ended. The reader must supply his or her own explanation. Is this a story of the supernatural, or merely the story of an unfortunate coincidence? What do *you* think?

2. Is *suggesting* sometimes more effective than *showing?* Which is scarier, a long, dimly lit street with just the sound of footsteps—or a grinning corpse? Movies use both methods, with the trend in recent years toward more and more graphic pictures of horror. Yet some people maintain that a rippling curtain in a lonely bedroom may provide more shivers than a prowler with a gun. Which method do you think brings more chills? Why?

3. Which of the two methods mentioned in 2 does "The Monkey's Paw" use? Suppose the door had opened to show a mangled body in the doorway. Would that have improved the story? Why or why not?

4. There are two short sentences in "The Monkey's Paw" that provide an essential clue to the events described. Why are the following two sentences so important?

    His dry lips shaped the words, "How much?" (page 102)

    "For God's sake don't let it in," cried the old man, trembling. (page 105)

    Don't overlook the importance of the pronoun *it.*

5. The plot of "The Monkey's Paw" is a classic of economy. Let's follow the six steps (page 1). The *situation* at the beginning involves a simple family of mother, father, son, in a peaceful setting. The *complication* is the arrival of the sergeant-major. The *conflict* arises out of the monkey's paw. Should the Whites try it? The *development* follows the Whites through their various wishes. The *climax* comes with the third wish and the mysterious knocking. The *outcome* is an empty doorway and "a quiet, deserted road." How do you feel about this plot? Is it well handled? Point out examples of economy in the telling.

6. *Suspense* comes from the Latin root *pendere*, "to hang." When you are kept in suspense, you are "left hanging." One method of suspense is to get you to a high point of tension and then change the action elsewhere. In "The Monkey's Paw," great suspense is built up by another method. A single paragraph builds the tension. It begins, "Neither spoke, but both lay silently listening to the ticking of the clock. A stair creaked, and a squeaky mouse scurried noisily through the wall." Why is this section especially suspenseful?

7. "If I had three wishes!" Suppose you were given three wishes without strings attached. What would you ask for? In a composition of 150–200 words describe your wishes.

Stories in Words _____

Enthralled (99)   Thrall is another word for "slave" or "bondman." The word itself can be traced through Old Norse, to an Indo-European root meaning "shove, press hard." Thralls were indeed "pressed hard." Indo-European is the common ancestor of most European languages. What connection does *enthralled* have with "slave"? A person who is *enthralled* is a *slave* to a person, an idea, or a suggestion. When the Whites listened "in an enthralled fashion" to the sergeant-major, they were enslaved by his tale.

Apathy (103)   The Greek word *pathos* means "emotion." The Greek prefix *a* means "not, without." It appears in such words as *asocial*, "not social," and *anonymous*, "without a name." *Apathy* thus means "without emotion." *Pathos* also appears in *sympathy*, "together feeling," and *pathetic*, "arousing emotion."

Scurried (105)   This simple word may have two related origins. One suggests that *scurry* is a blend of *scatter* and *hurry*, just as the colloquial *happenstance* is a blend of *happen* and *circumstance.* The other suggests that *scurry* is part of the reduplicated *hurry-scurry.* Reduplication is a common, playful tendency in language. It appears in such expressions as *bric-a-brac, crisscross, dingdong, flimflam, flipflop, riffraff, seesaw, singsong,* and *zigzag.* Sometimes the two parts rhyme, as in *bowwow, harum-scarum, helter-skelter, hobnob, hocus-pocus, hodgepodge, hubbub, hurdy-gurdy,* and *pell-mell.*

Lonesome Boy, Silver Trumpet

Arna Bontemps

♦   **But the morning breeze blew stronger and stronger. The curtains flapped, and a gray light appeared in the windows. By this time Bubber noticed that the people who were dancing had no faces at all, and though they continued to dance wildly as he played his trumpet, they seemed dim and far away. Were they disappearing?**

Every once in a while a story comes along all clothed in mooonlight, mist, and magic. Such a story, simply told, holds a reader's interest and stimulates both curiosity and imagination. "Lonesome Boy, Silver Trumpet" is that kind of story. It has a dreamlike quality that is pleasant to read and difficult to write.

The setting, so important to the story, is New Orleans and the magical countryside nearby. Bubber, the central character, is a natural-born trumpet player, able to entrance listeners with his musical ability. But he is a young man who knows his own mind . . . or thinks he does. The lonesome boy takes his silver trumpet off into a strange land, where nothing is as it seems. Come. Experience with him a strange dance where the music is eerie and the dancers are weird. This is a *haunting* story in several senses of the word.

LONESOME BOY, SILVER TRUMPET

When Bubber first learned to play the trumpet, his old grandpa winked his eye and laughed.

"You better mind how you blow that horn, sonny boy. You better mind."

"I like to blow loud, I like to blow fast, and I like to blow high," Bubber answered. "Listen to this, Grandpa." And he went on blowing with his eyes closed.

When Bubber was a little bigger, he began carrying his trumpet around with him wherever he went, so his old grandpa scratched his whiskers, took the corncob pipe out of his mouth, and laughed again.

"You better mind *where* you blow that horn, boy," he warned. "I used to blow one myself, and I know."

Bubber smiled. "Where did you ever blow music, Grandpa?"

"Down in New Orleans and all up and down the river. I blowed trumpet most everywhere in my young days, and I tell you, you better mind where you go blowing."

"I like to blow my trumpet in the school band when it marches, I like to blow it on the landing when the riverboats come in sight, and I liked to blow it among the trees in the swamp," he said, still smiling. But when he looked at his grandpa again, he saw a worried look on the old man's face, and he asked, "What's the matter, Grandpa, ain't that all right?"

Grandpa shook his head. "I wouldn't do it if I was you."

That sounded funny to Bubber, but he was not in the habit of disputing his grandfather. Instead he said, "I don't believe I ever heard you blow the trumpet, Grandpa. Don't you want to try blowing on mine now?"

Again the old man shook his head. "My blowing days are long gone," he said. "I still got the lip, but I ain't got the teeth. It takes good teeth to blow high notes on a horn, and these I got ain't much good. They're store teeth."

That made Bubber feel sorry for his grandfather, so he whispered softly, "I'll mind where I blow my horn, Grandpa."

He didn't really mean it though. He just said it to make his grandpa feel good. And the very next day he was half a mile out in the country blowing his horn in a cornfield. Two or three evenings later he was blowing it on a shady lane when the sun went down and not paying much attention where he went.

When he came home, his grandpa met him. "I heard you blowing your horn a long ways away," he said. "The air was still. I could hear it easy."

"How did it sound, Grandpa?"

"Oh, it sounded right pretty." He paused a moment, knocking the ashes out of his pipe, before adding, "Sounded like you mighta been lost."

That made Bubber ashamed of himself, because he knew he had not kept his word and that he was not minding where he blowed his trumpet. "I know what you mean, Grandpa," he answered. "But I can't do like you say. When I'm blowing my horn, I don't always look where I'm going."

Grandpa walked to the window and looked out. While he was standing there, he hitched his overalls up a little higher. He took a red handkerchief from his pocket and wiped his forehead. "Sounded to me like you might have been past Barbin's Landing."

"I was lost," Bubber admitted.

"You can end up in some funny places when you're just blowing a horn and not paying attention. I know," Grandpa insisted. "I know."

"Well, what do you want me to do, Grandpa?"

The old man struck a kitchen match on the seat of his pants and lit a kerosene lamp because the room was black dark by now. While the match was still burning, he lit his pipe. Then he sat down and stretched out his feet. Bubber was on a stool on the other side of the room, his trumpet under his arm. "When you go to school and play your horn in the band, that's all right," the old man said. "When you come home, you ought to put it in the case and leave it there. It ain't good to go traipsing around with a horn in your hand. You might get into devilment."

"But I feel lonesome without my trumpet, Grandpa," Bubber pleaded. "I don't like to go around without it anytime. I feel lost."

Grandpa sighed. "Well, there you are—lost with it and lost without it. I don't know what's going to become of you, sonny boy."

"You don't understand, Grandpa. You don't understand."

The old man smoked his pipe quietly for a few minutes and then went off to bed, but Bubber did not move. Later on, however, when he heard his grandpa snoring in the next room, he went outdoors, down the path, and around the smokehouse, and sat on a log. The night was still. He couldn't hear anything louder than a cricket. Soon he began wondering how his trumpet would sound on such a still night, back there behind the old smokehouse, so he put the mouthpiece to his lips very lightly and blew a few silvery notes. Immediately Bubber felt better. Now he knew for sure that Grandpa didn't understand how it was with a boy and a horn—a lonesome boy with a silver trumpet. Bubber lifted his horn toward the stars and let the music pour out.

Presently a big orange moon rose, and everything Bubber could see changed suddenly. The moon was so big it made the smokehouse and the trees and the fences seem small. Bubber blew his trumpet loud, he blew it fast, and he blew it high, and in just a few minutes he forgot all about Grandpa sleeping in the house.

He was afraid to talk to Grandpa after that. He was afraid Grandpa might scold him or warn him or try in some other way to persuade him to leave his trumpet in its case. Bubber was growing fast now. He knew what he liked, and he did not think he needed any advice from Grandpa.

Still he loved his grandfather very much, and he had no intention of saying anything that would hurt him. Instead he decided to leave home. He did not tell Grandpa what he was going to do. He just waited till the old man went to sleep in his bed one night. Then he quietly blew out the lamp, put his trumpet under his arm, and started walking down the road from Marksville to Barbin's Landing.

No boat was there, but Bubber did not mind. He knew one would come by before morning, and he knew that he wouldn't be lonesome so long as he had his trumpet with him. He found a place on the little dock where he could lean back against a post and swing his feet over the edge while playing, and the time passed swiftly. And when he finally went aboard a riverboat, just before morning, he found a place on the deck that suited him just as well and went right on blowing his horn.

Nobody asked him to pay any fare. The riverboat men did not seem to expect it of a boy who blew a trumpet the way

Bubber did. And in New Orleans the cooks in the kitchens where he ate and the people who kept the rooming houses where he slept did not seem to expect him to pay either. In fact, people seemed to think that a boy who played a trumpet where the patrons of a restaurant could hear him or for the guests of a rooming house should receive money for it. They began to throw money around Bubber's feet as he played his horn.

At first he was surprised. Later he decided it only showed how wrong Grandpa had been about horn blowing. So he picked up all the money they threw, bought himself fancy new clothes, and began looking for new places to play. He ran into boys who played guitars or bull fiddles or drums or other instruments, and he played right along with them. He went out with them to play for picnics or barbecues or boat excursions or dances. He played early in the morning and he played late at night, and he bought new clothes and dressed up so fine he scarcely knew himself in a mirror. He scarcely knew day from night.

It was wonderful to play the trumpet like that, Bubber thought, and to make all that money. People telephoned to the rooming house where he lived and asked for him nearly every day. Some sent notes asking if he would play his trumpet at their parties. Occasionally one would send an automobile to bring him to the place, and this was the best of all. Bubber liked riding through the pretty part of the city to the ballrooms in which well-dressed people waited to dance to his music. He enjoyed even more the times when he was taken to big white-columned houses in the country, houses surrounded by old trees with moss on them.

But he went to so many places to play his trumpet, he forgot where he had been and he got into the habit of not paying much attention. That was how it was the day he received a strange call on the telephone. A voice that sounded like a very proper gentleman said, "I would like to speak to the boy from Marksville, the one who plays the trumpet."

"I'm Bubber, sir. I'm the one."

"Well, Bubber, I'm having a very special party tonight— very special," the voice said. "I want you to play for us."

Bubber felt a little drowsy because he had been sleeping when the phone rang, and he still wasn't too wide awake. He yawned as he answered, "Just me, sir? You want me to play by myself?"

"There will be other musicians, Bubber. You'll play in the band. We'll be looking for you?"

"Where do you live, sir?" Bubber asked sleepily.

"Never mind about that, Bubber. I'll send my chauffeur with my car. He'll bring you."

The voice was growing faint by this time, and Bubber was not sure he caught the last words. "Where did you say, sir?" he asked suddenly. "When is it you want me?"

"I'll send my chauffeur," the voice repeated and then faded out completely.

Bubber put the phone down and went back to his bed to sleep some more. He had played his trumpet very late the night before, and now he just couldn't keep his eyes open.

Something was ringing when he woke up again. Was it the telephone? Bubber jumped out of bed and ran to answer, but the phone buzzed when he put it to his ear. There was nobody on the line. Then he knew it must have been the doorbell. A moment later he heard the door open, and footsteps came down the dark hall toward Bubber's room. Before Bubber could turn on the light, the footsteps were just outside his room, and a man's voice said, "I'm the chauffeur. I've brought the car to take you to the dance."

"So soon?" Bubber asked, surprised.

The man laughed. "You must have slept all day. It's night now, and we have a long way to drive."

"I'll put on my clothes," Bubber said.

The street light was shining through the window, so he did not bother to switch on the light in his room. Bubber never liked to open his eyes with a bright light shining, and anyway he knew right where to put his hands on the clothes he needed. As he began slipping into them, the chauffeur turned away. "I'll wait for you at the curb," he said.

"All right," Bubber called. "I'll hurry."

When he finished dressing, Bubber took his trumpet off the shelf, closed the door of his room, and went out to where the tall driver was standing beside a long, shiny automobile. The chauffeur saw him coming and opened the door to the back seat. When Bubber stepped in, he threw a lap robe across his knees and closed the door. Then the chauffeur went around to his place in the front seat, stepped on the starter, switched on his headlights, and sped away.

The car was finer than any Bubber had ridden in before; the motor purred so softly and the chauffeur drove it so smoothly, that Bubber soon began to feel sleepy again. One thing puzzled him, however. He had not yet seen the driver's face, and he wondered what the man looked like. But now the chauffeur's cap was down so far over his eyes and his coat collar was turned up so high Bubber could not see his face at all, no matter how far he leaned forward.

After a while he decided it was no use. He would have to wait till he got out of the car to look at the man's face. In the meantime he would sleep. Bubber pulled the lap robe up over his shoulders, stretched out on the wide back seat of the car and went to sleep again.

The car came to a stop, but Bubber did not wake up till the chauffeur opened the door and touched his shoulder. When he stepped out of the car, he could see nothing but dark, twisted trees with moss hanging from them. It was a dark and lonely place, and Bubber was so surprised he did not remember to look at the chauffeur's face. Instead, he followed the tall figure up a path covered with leaves to a white-columned house with lights shining in the windows.

Bubber felt a little better when he saw the big house with the bright windows. He had played in such houses before, and he was glad for a chance to play in another. He took his trumpet from under his arm, put the mouthpiece to his lips, and blew a few bright, clear notes as he walked. The chauffeur did not turn around. He led Bubber to a side entrance, opened the door, and pointed the boy to the room where the dancing had already started. Without ever showing his face, the chauffeur closed the door and returned to the car.

Nobody had to tell Bubber what to do now. He found a place next to the big fiddle that made the rhythms, waited a moment for the beat, then came in with his trumpet. With the bass fiddle, the drums, and the other stringed instruments backing him up, Bubber began to bear down on his trumpet. This was just what he liked. He played loud, he played fast, he played high, and it was all he could do to keep from laughing when he thought about Grandpa and remembered how the old man had told him to mind how he played his horn. Grandpa should see him now, Bubber thought.

Bubber looked at the dancers swirling on the ballroom floor under the high swinging chandelier, and he wished that Grandpa could somehow be at the window and see how they glided and spun around to the music of his horn. He wished the old man could get at least one glimpse of the handsome dancers, the beautiful women in bright-colored silks, the slender men in black evening clothes.

As the evening went on, more people came and began dancing. The floor became more and more crowded, and Bubber played louder and louder, faster and faster, and by midnight the gay ballroom seemed to be spinning like a pinwheel. The floor looked like glass under the dancers' feet. The drapes on the windows resembled gold, and Bubber was playing his trumpet so hard and so fast his eyes looked like they were ready to pop out of his head.

But he was not tired. He felt as if he could go on playing like this forever. He did not even need a short rest. When the other musicians called for a break and went outside to catch a breath of fresh air, he kept right on blowing his horn, running up the scale and down, hitting high C's, swelling out on the notes and then letting them fade away. He kept the dancers entertained till the full band came back, and he blew the notes that started them to dancing again.

Bubber gave no thought to the time, and when a breeze began blowing through the tall windows, he paid no attention. He played as loud as ever, and the dancers swirled just as fast. But there was one thing that did bother him a little. The faces of the dancers began to look thin and hollow as the breeze brought streaks of morning mist into the room. What was the matter with them? Were they tired from dancing all night? Bubber wondered.

But the morning breeze blew stronger and stronger. The curtains flapped, and a gray light appeared in the windows. By this time Bubber noticed that the people who were dancing had no faces at all, and though they continued to dance wildly as he played his trumpet, they seemed dim and far away. Were they disappearing?

Soon Bubber could scarcely see them at all. Suddenly he wondered where the party had gone. The musicians too grew dim and finally disappeared. Even the room with the big chandelier and the golden drapes on the windows was fading away like a technicolor dream. Bubber was frightened when he realized that nothing was left, and he was alone. Yes, definitely, he was alone—but *where?* Where was he now?

He never stopped blowing his shiny trumpet. In fact, as the party began to break up in this strange way, he blew harder than ever to help himself feel brave again. He also closed his eyes. That was why he happened to notice how uncomfortable the place where he was sitting had become. It was about as unpleasant as sitting on a log. And it was while his eyes were closed that he first became aware of leaves nearby, leaves rustling and blowing in the cool breeze.

But he could not keep his eyes closed for long with so much happening. Bubber just had to peep eventually, and when he did, he saw only leaves around him. Certainly leaves were nothing to be afraid of, he thought, but it was a little hard to understand how the house and room in which he had been playing for the party all night had been replaced by branches and leaves like this. Bubber opened both his eyes wide, stopped blowing his horn for a moment, and took a good, careful look at his surroundings.

Only then did he discover for sure that he was not in a house at all. There were no dancers, no musicians, nobody at all with him, and what had seemed like a rather uncomfortable chair or log was a large branch. Bubber was sitting in a pecan tree, and now he realized that this was where he had been blowing his trumpet so fast and so loud and so high all night. It was very discouraging.

But where was the chauffeur who had brought him here and what had become of the party and the graceful dancers? Bubber climbed down and began looking around. He could see no trace of the things that had seemed so real last night, so he decided he had better go home. Not home to the rooming house where he slept while in New Orleans, but home to the country where Grandpa lived.

He carried his horn under his arm, but he did not play a note on the bus that took him back to Marksville next day. And when he got off the bus and started walking down the road to Grandpa's house in the country, he still didn't feel much like playing anything on his trumpet.

Grandpa was sleeping in a hammock under a chinaberry tree when he arrived, but he slept with one eye open, so Bubber did not have to wake him up. He just stood there, and Grandpa smiled.

"I looked for you to come home before now," the old man said.

"I should have come home sooner," Bubber answered, shamefaced.

"I expected you to be blowing on your horn when you came."

"That's what I want to talk to you about, Grandpa."

The old man sat up in the hammock and put his feet on the ground. He scratched his head and reached for his hat. "Don't tell me anything startling," he said. "I just woke up, and I don't want to be surprised so soon."

Bubber thought maybe he should not mention what had happened. "All right, Grandpa," he whispered, looking rather sad. He leaned against the chinaberry tree, holding the trumpet under his arm, and waited for Grandpa to speak again.

Suddenly the old man blinked his eyes as if remembering something he had almost forgotten. "Did you mind how you blew on that horn down in New Orleans?" he asked.

"Sometimes I did. Sometimes I *didn't*," Bubber confessed.

Grandpa looked hurt. "I hate to hear that, sonny boy," he said. "Have you been playing your horn at barbecues and boat rides and dances and all such as that?"

"Yes, Grandpa," Bubber said, looking at the ground.

"Keep on like that and you're apt to wind up playing for a devil's ball."

Bubber nodded sadly. "Yes, I know."

Suddenly the old man stood up and put his hand on Bubber's shoulder. "Did a educated gentleman call you on the telephone?"

"He talked so proper I could hardly make out what he was saying."

"Did the chauffeur come in a long shiny car?"

Bubber nodded again. "I ended up in a pecan tree," he told Grandpa.

"I tried to tell you, Bubber, but you wouldn't listen to me."

"I'll listen to you from now on, Grandpa."

Grandpa laughed through his whiskers. "Well, take your trumpet in the house and put it on the shelf while I get you something to eat," he said.

Bubber smiled too. He was hungry, and he had not tasted any of Grandpa's cooking for a long time.

Reading for Understanding _____

Main Idea

1. Which of the following best summarizes the main idea of the story?
    (a) Playing a trumpet is a waste of time.
    (b) It's a good idea to stay away from New Orleans.
    (c) Music is a universal language.
    (d) Grandpa knows best.

Details

2. Grandpa said his horn-blowing days were over because of his (a) arthritis (b) lips (c) teeth (d) cheeks.

3. Bubber left home and picked up a boat at (a) Marksville (b) Barbin's Landing (c) New Orleans (d) none of these.

4. Bubber paid his boat fare by   (a) money he had saved
   (b) dancing   (c) playing the trumpet   (d) mention-
   ing his grandpa's name.

5. When the party ended and daylight came, Bubber discovered he was sitting in   (a) a pecan tree   (b) a big car
   (c) a lonely shack   (d) a boat on the Mississippi River.

Inferences

6. After Grandpa gave Bubber advice, Bubber was
   (a) respectful but disobedient   (b) pleased but rude
   (c) willing to give up the trumpet   (d) bitterly angry.

7. Blowing the trumpet   (a) was hard work for Bubber
   (b) made Bubber feel good   (c) did not please most
   listeners   (d) awakened grandpa.

8. Down in New Orleans   (a) most people did not appreciate good music   (b) it was very hard for Bubber to
   make a living   (c) Grandpa finally found Bubber and
   brought him back   (d) Bubber's fame spread.

9. The dance that Bubber played for could be described as
   (a) ghostly   (b) friendly   (c) cheerful   (d) uncontrolled.

10. It could be said that   (a) Grandpa didn't know what
    had happened to Bubber   (b) Bubber learned from his
    experience at last   (c) good trumpet players are com-
    monplace in New Orleans   (d) New Orleans people did
    not appreciate good music.

Order of Events

11. Arrange the items in the order in which they appeared.
    Use letters only.
    A. Bubber is picked up by a chauffeur.
    B. Bubber gets lost while playing his trumpet.
    C. The people of New Orleans approve of Bubber's
        trumpet playing.
    D. Bubber finds himself up a tree.
    E. Grandpa warns Bubber about playing the trumpet.

Outcomes

12. After the story ended,   (a) Bubber ran away again
(b) Bubber sold his trumpet   (c) Bubber listened to
Grandpa   (d) Bubber again played at a wild dance in
the forest.

Cause and Effect

13. Bubber's scary experience came about because
(a) his trumpet playing was not as good as he thought
(b) Grandpa gave him bad advice   (c) Bubber refused
to listen to Grandpa's warnings   (d) Bubber had put an
ad in the paper for his services.

Fact or Opinion

Tell whether the following is a fact or an opinion.
14. Bubber was the best trumpet player in New Orleans.

Author's Role

15. The mood of the story can best be described as
(a) dreamy and mysterious   (b) merry and happy
(c) irritable and angry   (d) sarcastic and aggressive.

Words in Context _____

1. That sounded funny to Bubber, but he was not in the
habit of *disputing* his grandfather.
Disputing (116) means   (a) encouraging
(b) alarming   (c) contradicting   (d) forgetting.
2. It ain't good to be *traipsing* around with a horn in your
hand.
Traipsing (117) means   (a) dancing   (b) singing
(c) walking   (d) sneaking.

3. In fact, people seemed to think that a boy who played a trumpet where the *patrons* of a restaurant could hear him or for the guests of a rooming house should receive money for it.
    Patrons (119) means   (a) employees   (b) owners
    (c) critics   (d) customers.

4. He went out with them to play for picnics or barbecues or boat *excursions* or dances.
    Excursions (119) means   (a) trips   (b) launchings
    (c) shows   (d) departures.

5. Bubber looked at the dancers swirling on the ballroom floor under the high swinging *chandelier,* and he wished that Grandpa could somehow be at the window and see how they glided and spun around to the music of his horn.
    Chandelier (122) means   (a) drape   (b) lighting fixture   (c) flag   (d) banner.

Thinking Critically About the Story _____

1. When Bubber first began to play, Grandpa said, "You better mind *how* you blow that horn, sonny boy." Later Grandpa said, "You better mind *where* you blow that horn." Why does Grandpa change *how* to *where?*

2. At one point (page 117), Grandpa says, "You might get into devilment." Why does the word *devilment* take on greater significance when we read of Bubber's later adventure?

3. Bubber's love for the trumpet seemed innocent enough. Yet it led him into trouble. Is it possible that an excessive love for any hobby or activity can have harmful results? Explain.

4. The composer Modest Mussorgsky created a musical masterpiece, "A Night on Bald Mountain." This piece was featured in Walt Disney's *Fantasia.* In it, demonic spirits have a wild dance under the guidance of the devil himself. The music suggests the increasing speed and tension of the

dance. In folklore, the night before May 1 was associated with Walpurgis Night, or the witches' sabbath. On this night, witches and sorcerers gathered, again under the leadership of the devil. How does the "devil's ball" resemble these two weird get-togethers? Are there differences?

5. Novelists and playwrights often write character studies of the people they're about to create. These character studies help to give consistency and reality to the characters. In a composition of about 150 words, write a character study of Grandpa. Use all the clues presented in the book and add any traits that you consider consistent with this character. Though relatively few lines are devoted to Grandpa, he is a strong and interesting personality.

Stories in Words

Cricket (117) When you hear the word *cricket*, you undoubtedly think of the special chirp that crickets have. The history of the word is tied up with the sound. *Cricket* comes from Old French through Middle English. The root means "to creak." When a cricket gets into the house and starts chirping invisibly, you'll think of the old meaning.

Telephone (119) Classical Greek has added thousands of words to English. Because Greek roots are easily combined, scientists call upon Greek in coining new words. *Telephone* has two roots meaning "distant sound." When *tele* is combined with *scope*, we have *telescope:* "distant seeing." When it is combined with *gram*, we have *telegram:* "distant writing."

Chauffeur (120) This word gives us a glimpse into an older time. It comes from a French root meaning "to heat." The *chauffeur* originally was the stoker, the operator of a steam-driven car. Though steam-driven cars have disappeared, the old name remains to remind us of how things once were.

Seven Floors

Dino Buzzati

◆　The patients were housed on each floor according to the gravity of their state. The seventh, or top, floor was for extremely mild cases. The sixth was still for mild cases, but ones needing a certain amount of attention. On the fifth floor there were quite serious cases and so on, floor by floor. The second floor was for the very seriously ill. On the first floor were the hopeless cases.

Horror movies have a faithful following. Modern movie wizardry makes all kinds of terrible effects possible: severed heads, corpselike faces, monsters that burst from ordinary bodies. After a while, these effects become almost funny. They are mechanical and obviously designed just to shock. Moviegoers become callous.

This story presents another approach to horror: a normal and recognizable setting; apparently sympathetic doctors and nurses; a likeable and understandable patient. There are no bloody gashes, no grinning skulls, no ghostly figures. At the beginning, all is sunshine and bright color. Then the feeling of terror builds slowly, almost without notice. Each step is described in such reasonable and believable detail that readers are carried along with Giovanni Corte.

Dino Buzzati has a reputation in his native Italy for unforgettable short stories. This story may stay with you for some time to come!

SEVEN FLOORS

One morning in March, after a night's train journey, Giovanni Corte arrived in the town where the famous nursing home was. He was a little feverish, but he was still determined to walk from the station to the hospital, carrying his small bag.

Although his was an extremely slight case, in the very earliest stages, Giovanni Corte had been advised to go to the well-known sanatorium, which existed solely for the care of the particular illness from which he was suffering. This meant that the doctors were particularly competent and the equipment particularly pertinent and efficient.

Catching sight of it from a distance—he recognized it from having seen photos in some brochure—Giovanni Corte was most favorably impressed. The building was white, seven stories high; its mass was broken up by a series of recesses which gave it a vague resemblance to a hotel. It was surrounded by tall trees.

After a brief visit from the doctor, prior to a more thorough one later on, Giovanni Corte was taken to a cheerful room on the seventh and top floor. The furniture was light and elegant, as was the wallpaper; there were wooden armchairs and brightly colored cushions. The view was over one of the loveliest parts of the town. Everything was peaceful, welcoming and reassuring.

Giovanni Corte went to bed immediately, turned on the reading lamp at his bedside and began to read a book he had brought with him. After a few moments a nurse came in to see whether he needed anything.

He didn't, but was delighted to chat with the young woman and ask her questions about the nursing home. That was how he came to know its one extremely odd characteristic:

the patients were housed on each floor according to the gravity of their state. The seventh, or top, floor was for extremely mild cases. The sixth was still for mild cases, but ones needing a certain amount of attention. On the fifth floor there were quite serious cases and so on, floor by floor. The second floor was for the very seriously ill. On the first floor were the hopeless cases.

This extraordinary system, apart from facilitating the general services considerably, meant that a patient only mildly affected would not be troubled by a dying cosufferer next door and ensured a uniformity of atmosphere on each floor. Treatment, of course, would thus vary from floor to floor.

This meant that the patients were divided into seven successive castes. Each floor was a world apart, with its own particular rules and traditions. And as each floor was in the charge of a different doctor, slight but definite differences in the methods of treatment had grown up, although initially the director had given the institution a single basic bent.

As soon as the nurse had left the room Giovanni Corte, no longer feeling feverish, went to the window and looked out, not because he wanted to see the view of the town (although he was not familiar with it) but in the hopes of catching a glimpse, through the windows, of the patients on the lower floors. The structure of the building, with its large recesses, made this possible. Giovanni Corte concentrated particularly on the first floor windows, which looked a very long way away, and which he could see only obliquely. But he could see nothing interesting. Most of the windows were completely hidden by grey venetian blinds.

But Corte did see someone, a man, standing at a window right next to his own. The two looked at each other with a growing feeling of sympathy but did not know how to break the silence. At last Giovanni Corte plucked up courage and said: "Have you just arrived too?"

"Oh no," said his neighbor, "I've been here two months." He was silent for a few moments and then, apparently not sure how to continue the conversation, added: "I was watching my brother down there."

"Your brother?"

"Yes. We both came here at the same time, oddly enough, but he got worse—he's on the fourth now."

"Fourth what?"

"Fourth floor," explained the man, pronouncing the two words with such pity and horror that Giovanni Corte was vaguely alarmed.

"But in that case"—Corte proceeded with his questioning with the light-heartedness one might adopt when speaking of tragic matters which don't concern one—"if things are already so serious on the fourth floor, whom do they put on the first?"

"Oh, the dying. There's nothing for the doctors to do down there. Only the priests. And of course . . ."

"But there aren't many people down there," interrupted Giovanni Corte as if seeking confirmation, "almost all the blinds are down."

"There aren't many now, but there were this morning," replied the other with a slight smile. "The rooms with the blinds down are those where someone has died recently. As you

can see, on the other floors the shutters are all open. Will you excuse me," he continued, moving slowly back in, "it seems to be getting rather cold. I'm going back to bed. May I wish you all the best . . ."

The man vanished from the windowsill and shut the window firmly; a light was lit inside the room. Giovanni Corte remained standing at the window, his eyes fixed on the lowered blinds of the first floor. He stared at them with morbid intensity, trying to visualize the ghastly secrets of that terrible first floor where patients were taken to die; he felt relieved that he was so far away. Meanwhile, the shadows of evening crept over the city. One by one the thousand windows of the sanatorium lit up; from the distance it looked like a great house lit up for a ball. Only on the first floor, at the foot of the precipice, did dozens of windows remain blank and empty.

Giovanni Corte was considerably reassured by the doctor's visit. A natural pessimist, he was already secretly prepared for an unfavorable verdict and wouldn't have been surprised if the doctor had sent him down to the next floor.

His temperature however showed no signs of going down, even though his condition was otherwise satisfactory. But the doctor was pleasant and encouraging. Certainly he was affected—the doctor said—but only very slightly; in two or three weeks he would probably be cured. "So I'm to stay on the seventh floor?" inquired Giovanni Corte anxiously at this point.

"Well of course!" replied the doctor, clapping a friendly hand on his shoulder. "Where did you think you were going? Down to the fourth perhaps?" He spoke jokingly, as though it were the most absurd thought in the world.

"I'm glad about that," said Giovanni Corte. "You know how it is, when one's ill one always imagines the worst." In fact he stayed in the room which he had originally been given. On the rare afternoons when he was allowed up he made the acquaintance of some of his fellow-patients. He followed the treatment scrupulously, concentrated his whole attention on making a rapid recovery, yet his condition seemed to remain unchanged.

About ten days later, the head nurse of the seventh floor came to see Giovanni Corte. He wanted to ask an entirely personal favor: the following day a woman with two children was coming to the hospital: there were two free rooms right next to his, but a third was needed; would Signor Corte mind very much moving into another, equally comfortable room?

Naturally, Giovanni Corte made no objection; he didn't mind what room he was in; indeed, he might have a new and prettier nurse.

"Thank you so much," said the head nurse with a slight bow; "though, mark you, such a courteous act doesn't surprise me coming from a person such as yourself. We'll start moving your things in about an hour, if you don't mind. By the way, it's one floor down," he added in a quieter tone, as though it were a negligible detail. "Unfortunately there are no free rooms on this floor. Of course it's a purely temporary arrangement," he hastened to add, seeing that Corte had sat up suddenly and was about to protest, "a purely temporary arrangement. You'll be coming up again as soon as there's a free room, which should be in two or three days."

"I must confess," said Giovanni Corte smiling, to show that he had no childish fears, "I must confess that this particular sort of change of room doesn't appeal to me in the least."

"But it has no medical basis; I quite understand what you mean, but in this case it's simply to do a favor for this woman who doesn't want to be separated from her children. . . . Now please," he added, laughing openly, "please don't get it into your head that there are other reasons!"

"Very well," said Giovanni Corte, "but it seems to me to bode ill."

So Giovanni Corte went down to the sixth floor, and though he was convinced that this move did not correspond to any worsening in his own condition, he felt unhappy at the thought that there was now a definite barrier between himself and the everyday world of healthy people. The seventh floor was an embarkation point, with a certain degree of contact with society; it could be regarded as a sort of annex to the ordinary world. But the sixth was already part of the real hospital; the attitudes of the doctors, nurses, of the patients themselves were just slightly different. It was admitted openly that the patients on that floor were really sick, even if not seriously so. From his initial conversation with his neighbors, staff and doctors, Giovanni Corte gathered that here the seventh floor was regarded as a joke, reserved for amateurs, all affectation and caprice; it was only on the sixth floor that things began in earnest.

One thing Giovanni Corte did realize, however, was that he would certainly have some difficulty in getting back up to the floor where, medically speaking, he really belonged; to get back to the seventh floor he would have to set the whole complex organism of the place in motion, even for such a small move; it was quite plain that, were he not to insist, no one would ever have thought of putting him back on the top floor, with the "almost-well."

So Giovanni Corte decided not to forfeit anything that was his by right and not to yield to the temptations of habit. He was much concerned to impress upon his companions that he was with them only for a few days, that it was he who had agreed to go down a floor simply to oblige a lady, that he'd be going up again as soon as there was a free room. The others listened without interest and nodded, unconvinced.

Giovanni Corte's convictions, however, were confirmed by the judgment of the new doctor. He agreed that Giovanni Corte could most certainly be on the seventh floor; the form the disease had taken was ab-so-lute-ly negligible—he stressed each syllable so as to emphasize the importance of his diagnosis—but after all it might well be that Giovanni Corte would be better taken care of on the sixth floor.

"I don't want all that nonsense all over again," Giovanni Corte interrupted firmly at this point, "you say I should be on the seventh floor, and that's where I want to be."

"No one denies that," retorted the doctor. "I was advising you not as a doc-tor, but as a re-al friend. As I say, you're very slightly affected, it wouldn't even be an exaggeration to say that you're not ill at all, but in my opinion what makes your case different from other similarly mild ones is its greater extension: the intensity of the disease is minimal, but it is fairly widespread; the destructive process of the cells"—it was the first time Giovanni Corte had heard the sinister expression—"the destructive process of the cells is absolutely in the initial stage, it may not even have begun yet, but it is tending, I say tending, to affect large expanses of the organism. This is the only reason, in my opinion, why you might be better off down here on the sixth floor, where the methods of treatment are more highly specialized and more intensive."

One day he was informed that the Director of the nursing home, after lengthy consultation with his colleagues, had decided to make a change in the subdivision of the patients. Each person's grade—so to speak—was to be lowered by half a point. From now on the patients on each floor were to be divided into two categories according to the seriousness of their condition (indeed the respective doctors had already made this subdivision, though exclusively for their own personal use) and the lower of these two halves was to be officially moved one floor down. For example, half the patients on the sixth floor, those who were slightly more seriously affected, were to go down to the fifth; the less slightly affected of the seventh floor would go down to the sixth. Giovanni Corte was pleased to hear this, because his return to the seventh floor would certainly be much easier amid this highly complicated series of removals.

However, when he mentioned this hope to the nurse he was bitterly disappointed. He learned that he was indeed to be moved, not up to the seventh but down to the floor below. For reasons that the nurse was unable to explain, he had been classed among the more "serious" patients on the sixth floor and so had to go down to the fifth.

Once he had recovered from his initial surprise, Giovanni Corte completely lost his temper; he shouted that they were cheating him, that he refused to hear of moving downwards, that he would go back home, that rights were rights and that the hospital administration could not afford to ignore the doctors' diagnosis so brazenly.

He was still shouting when the doctor arrived to explain matters more fully. He advised Corte to calm down unless he wanted his temperature to rise and explained that there had been a misunderstanding, at least in a sense. He agreed once again that Giovanni Corte would have been equally suitably placed on the seventh floor, but added that he had a slightly different, though entirely personal, view of the case. Basically, in a certain sense, his condition could be considered as needing treatment on the sixth floor, because the symptoms were so widespread. But he himself failed to understand why Corte had been listed among the more serious cases of the sixth floor. In all probability the secretary, who had phoned him that very morning to ask about Giovanni Corte's exact medical position, had made a mistake in copying out his report. Or more likely still the administrative staff had purposely depreciated his own judgment, since he was considered an expert doctor but overoptimistic. Finally, the doctor advised Corte not to worry, to accept the move without protest; what counted was the disease, not the floor on which the patient was placed.

As far as the treatment was concerned—added the doctor—Giovanni Corte would certainly not have cause for complaint: the doctor on the floor below was undoubtedly far more experienced; it was almost part of the system that the doctors became more experienced, at least in the eyes of the administration, the further down you went. The rooms were equally comfortable and elegant. The view was equally good; it was only from the third floor that it was cut off by the surrounding trees.

It was evening, and Giovanni Corte's temperature had risen accordingly; he listened to this meticulous ratiocination with an increasing feeling of exhaustion. Finally he realized that he had neither the strength nor the desire to resist this unfair removal any further. Unprotesting, he allowed himself to be taken one floor down.

Giovanni Corte's one meager consolation on the fifth floor was the knowledge that, in the opinion of doctors, nurses, and patients alike, he was the least seriously ill of anyone on the whole floor. In short, he could consider himself much the most fortunate person in that section. On the other hand he was haunted by the thought that there were now two serious barriers between himself and the world of ordinary people.

As spring progressed the weather became milder, but Giovanni Corte no longer liked to stand at the window as he used to do; although it was stupid to feel afraid, he felt a strange movement of terror at the sight of the first floor windows, always mostly closed and now so much nearer.

His own state seemed unchanged; though after three days on the fifth floor a patch of eczema* appeared on his right leg and showed no signs of clearing up during the following days. The doctor assured him that this was something absolutely independent of the main disease, it could have happened to the most healthy person in the world. Intensive treatment with digamma rays would clear it up in a few days.

"And can't one have that here?" asked Giovanni Corte.

"Certainly," replied the doctor delighted; "we have everything here. There's only one slight inconvenience . . ."

"What?" asked Giovanni Corte with vague foreboding.

"Inconvenience in a manner of speaking," the doctor corrected himself. "The fourth floor is the only one with the relevant apparatus and I wouldn't advise you to go up and down three times a day."

"So it's out of the question?"

"It would really be better if you would be good enough to go down to the fourth floor until the eczema has cleared up."

"That's enough," shrieked Giovanni Corte exasperated. "I've had enough of going down! I'd rather die than go down to the fourth floor!"

"As you wish," said the doctor soothingly, so as not to annoy him, "but as the doctor responsible, I must point out that I forbid you to go up and down three times a day."

The unfortunate thing was that the eczema, rather than clearing up, began to spread gradually. Giovanni Corte couldn't rest, he tossed and turned in bed. His anger held out for three days, but finally he gave in. Of his own accord, he asked the doctor to arrange for the ray treatment to be carried out, and to move to the floor below.

Here Corte noticed, with private delight, that he really was an exception. The other patients on the floor were certainly much more seriously affected and unable to move from their beds at all. He, on the other hand, could afford the luxury of walking from his bedroom to the room where the rays were, amid the compliments and amazement of the nurses themselves.

He made a point of stressing the extremely special nature

---

* *eczema*   skin disease

of his position to the new doctor. A patient who, basically, should have been on the seventh floor was in fact on the fourth. As soon as his eczema was better, he would be going up again. This time there could be absolutely no excuse. He, who could still legitimately have been on the seventh floor!

"On the seventh?" exclaimed the doctor who had just finished examining him, with a smile. "You sick people do exaggerate so! I'd be the first to agree that you should be pleased with your condition; from what I see from your medical chart, it hasn't changed much for the worse. But—forgive my rather brutal honesty—there's quite a difference between that and the seventh floor. You're one of the least worrying cases, I quite agree, but you're definitely ill."

"Well then," said Giovanni Corte, scarlet in the face, "what floor would you personally put me on?"

"Well really, it's not easy to say, I've only examined you briefly; for any final judgment I'd have to observe you for at least a week."

"All right," insisted Corte, "but you must have some idea."

To calm him, the doctor pretended to concentrate on the matter for a moment and then, nodding to himself, said slowly: "Oh dear! Look, to please you, I think after all one might say the sixth. Yes," he added as if to persuade himself of the rightness of what he was saying, "the sixth would probably be all right."

The doctor thought that this would please his patient. But an expression of terror spread over Giovanni Corte's face: he realized that the doctors of the upper floors had deceived him; here was this new doctor, plainly more expert and honest, who in his heart of hearts—it was quite obvious—would place him not on the seventh but on the sixth floor, possibly even the lower fifth! The unexpected disappointment prostrated Corte. That evening his temperature rose appreciably.

His stay on the fourth floor was the most peaceful period he had had since coming to the hospital. The doctor was a delightful person, attentive and pleasant; he often stayed for whole hours to talk about all kinds of things. Giovanni Corte too was delighted to have an opportunity to talk, and drew the conversation around to his normal past life as a lawyer and man of the world. He tried to convince himself that he still belonged to the society of healthy men and women, that he was still connected with the world of business, that he was really still interested in matters of public import. He tried, but unsuccessfully. The conversation invariably came round, in the end, to the subject of his illness.

The desire for any sign of improvement had become an obsession. Unfortunately the digamma rays had succeeded in preventing the spread of the eczema but they had not cured it altogether. Giovanni Corte talked about this at length with the doctor every day and tried to appear philosophical, even ironic about it without ever succeeding.

"Tell me, doctor," he said one day, "how is the destructive process of the cells coming along?"

"What a frightful expression," said the doctor reprovingly. "Wherever did you come across that? That's not at all right, particularly for a patient. I never want to hear anything like that again."

"All right," objected Corte, "but you still haven't answered."

"I'll answer right away," replied the doctor pleasantly. "The destructive process of your cells, to use your own horrible expression is, in your very minor case, absolutely negligible. But obstinate, I must say."

"Obstinate, you mean chronic?"

"Now don't credit me with things I haven't said. I only said obstinate. Anyhow that's how it is in minor cases. Even the mildest infections often need long and intensive treatment."

"But tell me, doctor, when can I expect to see some improvement?"

"When? It's difficult to say in these cases. . . . But listen," he added after pausing for thought, "I can see that you're positively obsessed with the idea of recovery . . . if I weren't afraid of angering you, do you know what I'd suggest?"

"Please do say . . ."

"Well, I'll put the situation very clearly. If I had this disease even slightly and were to come to this sanatorium, which is probably the best there is, I would arrange of my own accord, and from the first day—I repeat from the first day—to go down to one of the lower floors. In fact I'd even go to the . . ."

"To the first?" suggested Corte with a forced smile.

"Oh dear no!" replied the doctor with a deprecating smile, "Oh dear no! But to the third or even the second. On the lower floors the treatment is far better, you know, the equipment is more complete, more powerful, the staff are more expert. And then you know who is the real soul of this hospital?"

"Isn't it Professor Dati?"

"Exactly. It was he who invented the treatment carried out here, he really planned the whole place. Well, Dati, the mastermind, operates, so to speak, between the first and second floors. His driving force radiates from there. But I assure you that it never goes beyond the third floor: further up than that the details of his orders are glossed over, interpreted more slackly; the heart of the hospital is on the lowest floors, and that's where you must be to have the best treatment."

"So in short," said Giovanni Corte, his voice shaking, "so you would advise me. . . ."

"And there's something else," continued the doctor unperturbed, "and that is that in your case there's also the eczema to be considered. I agree that it's quite unimportant, but it is rather irritating, and in the long run it might lower your morale; and you know how important peace of mind is for your recovery. The rays have been only half successful. Now why? It might have been pure chance, but it might also have been that they weren't sufficiently intense. Well, on the third floor the apparatus is far more powerful. The chances of curing your eczema would be much greater. And the point is that once the cure is under way, the hardest part is over. Once you really feel better, there's absolutely no reason why you shouldn't come up here again, or indeed higher still, according to your 'deserts,' to the fifth, the sixth, possibly even the seventh . . ."

"But do you think this will hasten my recovery?"

"I've not the slightest doubt it will. I've already said what I'd do if I were in your place."

The doctor talked like this to Giovanni Corte every day. And at last, tired of the inconveniences of the eczema, despite his instinctive reluctance to go down a floor, he decided to take the doctor's advice and move to the floor below.

He noticed immediately that the third floor was possessed of a special gaiety affecting both doctors and nurses, even though the cases treated on that floor were very serious. He noticed too that this gaiety increased daily; consumed with curiosity, as soon as he got to know the nurse, he asked why on earth they were all so cheerful.

"Oh, didn't you know?" she replied, "in three days time we're all going on holiday."

"On holiday?"

"That's right. The whole floor closes for a fortnight, and the staff go off and enjoy themselves. Each floor takes it in turn to have a holiday."

"And what about the patients?"

"There are relatively few of them, so two floors are converted into one."

"You mean you put the patients of the third and fourth floors together?"

"No no," the nurse corrected him, "of the third and second. The patients on this floor will have to go down."

"Down to the second?" asked Giovanni Corte, suddenly pale as death. "You mean I'll have to go down to the second?"

"Well, yes. What's so odd about that? When we come back, in a fortnight, you'll come back here, in this same room. I can't see anything so terrifying about it."

But Giovanni Corte—as if forewarned by some strange instinct—was horribly afraid. However, since he could hardly prevent the staff from going on their holidays, and convinced that the new treatment with the stronger rays would do him good—the eczema had almost cleared up—he didn't dare offer any formal opposition to this new move. But he did insist, despite nurses' banter, that the label on the door of his new room should read "Giovanni Corte, third floor, temporary." Such a thing had never been done before in the whole history of the sanatorium, but the doctors didn't object, fearing that the prohibition of even such a minor matter might cause a serious shock to a patient as highly strung as Giovanni Corte.

After all, it was simply a question of waiting for fourteen days, neither more nor less. Giovanni Corte began to count them with stubborn eagerness, lying motionless on his bed for hours on end, staring at the furniture, which wasn't as pleasant

and modern here as on the higher floors, but more cumbersome, gloomy, and severe. Every now and again he would
listen intently, thinking he heard sounds from the floor below,
the floor of the dying, the "condemned"—vague sounds of
death in action.

Naturally he found all this very dispiriting. His agitation
seemed to nourish the disease, his temperature began to rise,
the state of continued weakness began to affect him vitally.
From the window—which was almost always open, since it
was now midsummer—he could no longer see the roofs nor
even the houses, but only the green wall of the surrounding
trees.

A week later, one afternoon about two o'clock, his room
was suddenly invaded by the head nurse and three nurses, with
a trolley. "All ready for the move then?" asked the head nurse
jovially.

"What move?" asked Giovanni Corte weakly, "what's all
this?" The third floor staff haven't come back after a week have
they?"

"Third floor?" repeated the head nurse uncomprehend-
ingly, "my orders are to take you down to the first floor," and
he produced a printed form for removal to the first floor signed
by none other than Professor Dati himself.

Giovanni Corte gave vent to his terror, his diabolical rage
in long angry shrieks, which resounded throughout the whole
floor. "Less noise, please," begged the nurses, "there are some
patients here who are not at all well." But it would have taken
more than that to calm him.

At last the second floor doctor appeared—a most attentive
person. After being given the relevant information he looked at
the form and listened to Giovanni Corte's side of the story. He
then turned angrily to the head nurse and told him there had
been a mistake, he himself had had no such orders, for some
time now the place had been an impossible muddle, he himself
knew nothing about what was going on . . . at last, when he had
had his say with his inferior, he turned politely to his patient,
highly apologetic.

"Unfortunately, however," he added, "unfortunately Professor Dati left the hospital about an hour ago—he'll be away
for a couple of days. I'm most awfully sorry, but his orders

can't be overlooked. He would be the first to regret it, I assure you . . . an absurd mistake! I fail to understand how it could have happened!"

Giovanni Corte had begun to tremble piteously. He was now completely unable to control himself, overcome with fear like a small child. His slow desperate sobbing echoed throughout the room.

It was as a result of this execrable mistake, then, that he was removed to his last resting place: he who basically, according to the most stringent medical opinion, was fit for the sixth, if not the seventh floor as far as his illness was concerned! The situation was so grotesque that from time to time Giovanni Corte felt inclined simply to roar with laughter.

Stretched out on his bed, while the afternoon warmth flowed calmly over the city, he would stare at the green of the trees through the window and feel that he had come to a completely unreal world, walled in with sterilized tiles, full of deathly arctic passages and soulless white figures. It even occurred to him that the trees he thought he saw through the window were not real; finally, when he noticed that the leaves never moved, he was certain of it.

Corte was so upset by this idea that he called the nurse and asked for his spectacles, which he didn't use in bed, being shortsighted; only then was he a little reassured: the lenses proved that they were real leaves and that they were shaken, though very slightly, by the wind.

When the nurse had gone out, he spent half an hour in complete silence. Six floors, six solid barriers, even if only because of a bureaucratic mistake, weighed implacably above Giovanni Corte. How many years (for obviously it was now a question of years) would it be before he could climb back to the top of that precipice?

But why was the room suddenly going so dark? It was still mid-afternoon. With a supreme effort, for he felt himself paralyzed by a strange lethargy, Giovanni Corte turned to look at his watch on the locker by his bed. Three-thirty. He turned his head the other way and saw that the venetian blinds, in obedience to some mysterious command, were dropping slowly, shutting out the light.

Translated from the Italian by Judith Landry

Reading for Understanding _____

Main Idea

1. The progress of Giovanni Corte's ailment can best be described as   (a) placid   (b) encouraging   (c) upward   (d) downward.

Details

2. Corte's first change of floor was blamed on   (a) a storm   (b) the arrival of a woman and two children   (c) a vacation for the staff   (d) refurnishing.

3. The second change was blamed on   (a) a change of hospital organization   (b) Professor Dati   (c) a request by another patient   (d) the death of a patient.

4. Corte moved to the third floor (the fourth change) to (a) help a really ill patient   (b) meet Professor Dati (c) treat his eczema   (d) get a better view of the outside world.

5. The order to go to the first floor was   (a) forged (b) signed by Professor Dati   (c) a joke   (d) quickly reversed.

Inferences

6. Throughout, the manner of doctors and nurses might be characterized as   (a) cruel   (b) bitter   (c) weary (d) optimistic.

7. The fate of Corte could be described as   (a) inevitable (b) basically humorous   (c) the result of Corte's disobedient nature   (d) deserved.

8. Throughout his stay, Corte was constantly being (a) sent out on errands   (b) drugged   (c) misled (d) moved to higher floors.

9. According to advice received by Corte,   (a) the lower the floor, the better the treatment   (b) higher floors had

the most able doctors   (c) nobody ever got out of the sanatorium   (d) most of the nurses were inefficient.
10. All Corte's moves were   (a) a signal of his improvement (b) thoroughly "explained" by the staff   (c) designed to get more money from him   (d) immediately accepted by him.

Order of Events

11. Arrange the items in the order in which they occurred. Use letters only.
    A. Corte is moved to the first floor.
    B. The staff on one floor goes on vacation.
    C. Corte is given a bright, cheerful, elegant room.
    D. Corte moves to the fourth floor.
    E. Corte arrives at the town where the sanatorium is located.

Outcome

12. After the story ends, Corte   (a) has a special meeting with Professor Dati   (b) starts moving up, floor by floor (c) dies (d) is pleased by the way he has been treated.

Cause and Effect

13. As Corte was moved down, floor by floor,   (a) he made a study of hospital routines for a book he'd write (b) he fell in love with one of the nurses   (c) his spirits got lower and lower with each change   (d) he tried to bribe one of the doctors.

Fact or Opinion

    Tell whether the following is a fact or an opinion.
14. All the doctors and nurses were thoughtful, kindly, honest, and highly professional.

Author's Role

15. The tone of this story is   (a) straightforward and optimistic   (b) rapid and explosive   (c) sweet and gentle (d) quiet but subtly menacing.

Words in Context _____

1. This meant that the doctors were particularly *competent* and the equipment particularly pertinent and efficient.
    Competent (131) means   (a) famous   (b) thoughtful
    (c) talkative   (d) qualified.

2. He recognized it from having seen photos in some *brochure.*
    Brochure (131) means   (a) movie   (b) television
    program   (c) map   (d) pamphlet.

3. This extraordinary system, apart from *facilitating* the general services considerably, meant that a patient only mildly affected would not be troubled by a dying co-sufferer next door.
    Facilitating (132) means   (a) helping   (b) hurting
    (c) broadcasting   (d) studying.

4. This meant that the patients were divided into seven successive *castes.*
    Castes (132) means   (a) rooms   (b) groups
    (c) numbers   (d) floors.

5. He stared at them with *morbid* intensity, trying to visualize the ghastly secrets of that terrible first floor.
    Morbid (134) means   (a) extreme   (b) lax
    (c) gloomy   (d) occasional.

6. Only on the first floor, at the foot of the *precipice,* did dozens of windows remain blank and empty.
    Here *precipice* (134) is used to suggest a   (a) cliff
    (b) tunnel   (c) volcano   (d) field.

7. A natural *pessimist,* he was already secretly prepared for an unfavorable verdict.
    A *pessimist* (134)   (a) enjoys laughter   (b) expects
    the worst   (c) is shrewd and clever   (d) believes
    nobody.

8. He followed the treatment *scrupulously,* concentrated his whole attention on making a rapid recovery, yet his condition seemed to remain unchanged.

Scrupulously (134) means   (a) rapidly   (b) fearfully
(c) carefully   (d) hopelessly.

9. The seventh floor was regarded as a joke, reserved for
    amateurs, all *affectation* and caprice.
    Affectation (136) means   (a) artificial behavior
    (b) emotional attachment   (c) confusion   (d) con-
    sistent failure.

10. "No one denies that," *retorted* the doctor.
    Retorted (136) means   (a) reported   (b) whispered
    (c) wept   (d) replied.

11. "It is fairly widespread; the destructive process of the
    cells"—it was the first time Giovanni Corte had heard the
    sinister expression.
    Sinister (136) means   (a) threatening harm
    (b) opening up favorable possibilities   (c) one-sided
    (d) strange and novel.

12. He shouted that they were cheating him, that rights were
    rights and that the hospital administration could not
    afford to ignore the doctors' diagnosis so *brazenly*.
    Brazenly (137) means   (a) swiftly   (b) boldly
    (c) noisily   (d) cheerlessly.

13. More likely, the administrative staff had purposely
    depreciated his own judgment, since he was considered an
    expert doctor but overoptimistic.
    Depreciated (138) means   (a) deeply appreciated
    (b) carelessly forgotten   (c) reduced in value
    (d) bitterly attacked.

14. He listened to this *meticulous* ratiocination (reasoning)
    with an increasing feeling of exhaustion.
    Meticulous (138) means   (a) obviously false
    (b) carefully detailed   (c) extremely inaccurate
    (d) somewhat incomplete.

15. Giovanni Corte's one *meager* consolation on the fifth floor
    was the knowledge that, in the opinion of doctors, nurses,
    and patients alike, he was the least seriously ill of anyone
    on the whole floor.

Meager (138) means   (a) prominent   (b) generally accepted   (c) cruel   (d) tiny.

16. "That's enough," shrieked Giovanni Corte *exasperated.*
Exasperated (139) means   (a) cheerfully hopeful
(b) extremely annoyed   (c) quickly satisfied
(d) able and willing.

17. The unexpected disappointment *prostrated* Corte.
Prostrated (140) means   (a) encouraged   (b) propped up   (c) laid low   (d) puzzled.

18. The desire for any sign of improvement had become an *obsession.*
Obsession (141) means   (a) overpowering idea
(b) means of entertainment   (c) pleasant hobby
(d) time for thought.

19. "The destructive process of your cells, to use your own horrible expression is, in your very minor case, absolutely negligible. But *obstinate,* I must say."
Obstinate (141) means   (a) surprising   (b) improving
(c) easily cured   (d) stubborn.

20. Further up than that the details of his orders are glossed over, interpreted more *slackly;* the heart of the hospital is on the lowest floors.
Slackly (142) means   (a) intensively   (b) carelessly
(c) strangely   (d) cheerfully.

21. "And there's something else," continued the doctor *unperturbed.*
Unperturbed (142) means   (a) unwilling
(b) uncertain   (c) undisturbed   (d) unimpressed.

22. But he did insist, despite nurses' *banter,* that the label on the door of his new room should read "Giovanni Corte, third floor, temporary."
Banter (143) means   (a) teasing   (b) objections
(c) howls of injustice   (d) lack of sympathy.

23. Giovanni Corte stared at the furniture, which wasn't as pleasant and modern here as on the higher floors, but more *cumbersome,* gloomy, and severe.
Cumbersome (144) means   (a) well made
(b) lightweight   (c) bulky   (d) angular.

24. Naturally he found all this very *dispiriting.*
    Dispiriting (144) means   (a) reassuring
    (b) unexpected   (c) unimportant   (d) discouraging.
25. After being given the *relevant* information he looked at the
    form and listened to Giovanni Corte's side of the story.
    Relevant (144) means   (a) appropriate   (b) unim-
    portant   (c) upsetting   (d) repeated.

Thinking Critically About the Story _____

1. There is a brooding sense of mystery about "Seven Floors."
   There are many questions to consider. Was Corte's disease
   a fatal disease to begin with? If so, why did the staff keep
   putting him off with excuses for moving him? Did the
   lowering of floors lower Corte's morale and his resistance?
   Or did the doctors try to make the inevitable result a little
   less shocking? Were the doctors following a calculated
   plan, or were they just reacting as they went along? Early
   in the story, were there clues to Corte's serious illness?
   Explain.
2. Sometimes a hearty cheerfulness disguises a basic indifference and impersonality. Do you think the staff members
   were sincere in their talks with Corte? Explain.
3. If there were such a hospital, would the organization by
   floors be sound? Explain.
4. On page 136, Corte tells his companions on the sixth floor
   that he'd be with them only a few days. "The others
   listened without interest and nodded, unconvinced." What
   does this sentence suggest about Corte's chances of moving
   back? Why?
5. Supposedly, Corte was given a choice before being moved.
   Suppose he disagreed and refused to go. What do you think
   might have happened?
6. Rationalizing is making up reasons for unreasonable or
   emotional decisions. "I won't study tonight because I'll

learn more by watching TV" is an example of rationalizing. Point out examples of rationalizing in the story.

7. The number *seven* suggests mystery and magic. The seventh son is supposed to be lucky and gifted. There were Seven Wonders of the World. There is a constellation "The Seven Sisters." We talk of the seven seas. *Seven* appears over and over again in literature. Would this story have been equally effective if it had been titled "Five Floors" or "Ten Floors"? Explain.

8. In a composition of 200–250 words, rewrite the ending of "Seven Floors." Decide on a plan for Corte's survival and trace his course upward and out. Provide an excuse for each change of floor. (You may wish to skip a few floors!)

Stories in Words _____

Alarmed (133)   When danger threatened, an old Italian cry, "All'arme," roused the defenses of the place being attacked. It literally meant, "Get your weapons!" Notice how the current word *alarm* has broadened its meaning for any warning of danger. We may now be alarmed without rushing to get our weapons!

Caprice (136)   This word can be traced both to the Latin *caput*, "head," and *caper*, "goat." The most colorful origin is the latter. As Wilfred Funk reports, "When a girl is *capricious* and cuts up *capers*, she is imitating the frisky playful antics of the male cousin of a sheep." *Capricious* does suggest a quick change of mood and actions, often without reason. *Taxicab* comes from *taximeter cabriolet*. A *cabriolet* was a light two-wheeled carriage that bumped about a bit, like a prancing goat!

Jovially (144)   *Jove* was another name for Jupiter, father of the
gods. Supposedly, in astrology, people "born under the
sign of Jupiter" were certain to be "full of hearty good
humor." Other planets have given us descriptive adjec-
tives. *Mercurial*—"quick-witted, changeable, fickle"—is associated with Mercury. *Martial*—"warlike, eager to
fight"—is associated with Mars. *Saturnine*—"sluggish,
gloomy, quiet"—is associated with Saturn.

Roads of Destiny

O. Henry

◆ "I swore there and then, by ten thousand devils, that she should marry the first man we met after leaving the château, be he prince, charcoal burner, or thief."

Somerset Maugham, English writer (page 240), tells a fable about a Baghdad merchant whose servant came home trembling from the market-place.

"Master," cried the servant, "just now when I was in the marketplace I was jostled by a woman in the crowd and when I turned I saw it was Death that jostled me. She looked at me and made a threatening gesture."

Terrified, the servant asked his master for a horse to escape Death. After the servant had ridden off to Samarra, the merchant became annoyed at losing the services of his servant. He went down to the marketplace to confront Death and complain.

Death explained that the gesture was not a threat but rather an expression of surprise. "I was astonished to see him in Baghdad, for I had an appointment with him tonight in Samarra."

Does fate or chance rule our lives? This is a question that can never be settled, but it sparks a lot of interest. "Roads of Destiny" is a fitting follow-up to the Maugham fable about Death and the servant. It further explores our destinies in a creative and imaginative way. In this story, the theme (3) stresses the inevitability of fate and sides with fate in the discussion.

Here, in a plot (1) with three different but parallel threads, your imagination will be captured as you follow David Mignot along three different roads, only to discover that . . . But you must read the story to find out.

ROADS OF DESTINY

I go to seek on many roads
   What is to be.
True heart and strong, with love to light—
Will they not bear me in the fight
To order, shun or wield or mould
   My Destiny?
   UNPUBLISHED POEMS OF DAVID MIGNOT.

The song was over. The words were David's; the air, one of the countryside. The company about the inn table applauded heartily, for the young poet paid for the wine. Only the notary, M. Papineau, shook his head a little at the lines, for he was a man of books, and he had not drunk with the rest.

David went out into the village street, where the night air drove the wine vapor from his head. And then he remembered that he and Yvonne had quarrelled that day, and that he had resolved to leave his home that night to seek fame and honor in the great world outside.

"When my poems are on every man's tongue," he told himself, in a fine exhilaration, "she will, perhaps, think of the hard words she spoke this day."

Except the roysterers in the tavern, the village folk were abed. David crept softly into his room in the shed of his father's cottage and made a bundle of his small store of clothing. With this upon a staff, he set his face outward upon the road that ran from Vernoy.

He passed his father's herd of sheep huddled in their nightly pen—the sheep he herded daily, leaving them to scatter while he wrote verses on scraps of paper. He saw a light yet shining in Yvonne's window, and a weakness shook his purpose

155

of a sudden. Perhaps that light meant that she rued, sleepless, her anger, and that morning might——But, no! His decision was made. Vernoy was no place for him. Not one soul there could share his thoughts. Out along that road lay his fate and his future.

Three leagues across the dim, moonlit champaign ran the road, straight as a plowman's furrow. It was believed in the village that the road ran to Paris, at least; and this name the poet whispered often to himself as he walked. Never so far from Vernoy had David traveled before.

THE LEFT BRANCH

Three leagues, then, the road ran, and turned into a puzzle. It joined with another and a larger road at right angles. David stood, uncertain, for a while, and then took the road to the left.

Upon this more important highway were, imprinted in the dust, wheel tracks left by the recent passage of some vehicle. Some half an hour later these traces were verified by the sight of a ponderous carriage mired in a little brook at the bottom of a steep hill. The driver and postilions were shouting and tugging at the horses' bridles. On the road at one side stood a

huge, black-clothed man and a slender lady wrapped in a long, light cloak.

David saw the lack of skill in the efforts of the servants. He quietly assumed control of the work. He directed the outriders to cease their clamor at the horses and to exercise their strength upon the wheels. The driver alone urged the animals with his familiar voice; David himself heaved a powerful shoulder at the rear of the carriage, and with one harmonious tug the great vehicle rolled up on solid ground. The outriders climbed to their places.

David stood for a moment upon one foot. The huge gentleman waved a hand. "You will enter the carriage," he said, in a voice large, like himself, but smoothed by art and habit. Obedience belonged in the path of such a voice. Brief as was the young poet's hesitation, it was cut shorter still by a renewal of the command. David's foot went to the step. In the darkness he perceived dimly the form of the lady upon the rear seat. He was about to seat himself opposite, when the voice again swayed him to its will. "You will sit at the lady's side."

The gentleman swung his great weight to the forward seat. The carriage proceeded up the hill. The lady was shrunk, silent, into her corner. David could not estimate whether she was old or young, but a delicate, mild perfume from her clothes stirred his poet's fancy to the belief that there was loveliness beneath the mystery. Here was an adventure such as he had often imagined. But as yet he held no key to it, for no word was spoken while he sat with his impenetrable companions.

In an hour's time David perceived through the window that the vehicle traversed the street of some town. Then it stopped in front of a closed and darkened house, and a postilion alighted to hammer impatiently upon the door. A latticed window above flew wide and a night-capped head popped out.

"Who are ye that disturb honest folk at this time of night? My house is closed. 'Tis too late for profitable travelers to be abroad. Cease knocking at my door, and be off."

"Open!" spluttered the postilion, loudly; "open for Monseigneur, the Marquis de Beaupertuys."

"Ah!" cried the voice above. "Ten thousand pardons, my lord. I did not know—the hour is so late—at once shall the door be opened, and the house placed at my lord's disposal."

Inside was heard the clink of chain and bar, and the door was flung open. Shivering with chill and apprehension, the landlord of the Silver Flagon stood, half-clad, candle in hand, upon the threshold.

David followed the marquis out of the carriage. "Assist the lady," he was ordered. The poet obeyed. He felt her small hand tremble as he guided her descent. "Into the house," was the next command.

The room was the long dining hall of the tavern. A great oak table ran down its length. The huge gentleman seated himself in a chair at the nearer end. The lady sank into another against the wall, with an air of great weariness. David stood, considering how best he might now take his leave and continue upon his way.

"My lord," said the landlord, bowing to the floor, "h-had I ex-expected this honor, entertainment would have been ready. T-t-there is wine and cold fowl and m-m-maybe—"

"Candles," said the marquis, spreading the fingers of one plump white hand in a gesture he had.

"Y-yes, my lord." He fetched half a dozen candles, lighted them, and set them upon the table.

"If monsieur would, perhaps deign to taste a certain Burgundy—there is a cask—"

"Candles," said monsieur, spreading his fingers.

"Assuredly—quickly—I fly, my lord."

A dozen more lighted candles shone in the hall. The great bulk of the marquis overflowed his chair. He was dressed in fine black from head to foot save for the snowy ruffles at his wrist and throat. Even the hilt and scabbard of his sword were black. His expression was one of sneering pride. The ends of an upturned moustache reached nearly to his mocking eyes.

The lady sat motionless, and now David perceived that she was young, and possessed a pathetic and appealing beauty. He was startled from the contemplation of her forlorn loveliness by the booming voice of the marquis.

"What is your name and pursuit?"

"David Mignot. I am a poet."

The moustache of the marquis curled nearer to his eyes.
"How do you live?"

"I am also a shepherd; I guarded my father's flock," David
answered, with his head high, but a flush upon his cheek.

"Then listen, master shepherd and poet, to the fortune you
have blundered upon tonight. This lady is my niece, Mademoiselle Lucie de Varennes. She is of noble descent and is possessed
of ten thousand francs a year in her own right. As to her
charms, you have but to observe for yourself. If the inventory
pleases your shepherd's heart, she becomes your wife at a
word. Do not interrupt me. Tonight I conveyed her to the
château of the Comte de Villemaur, to whom her hand had
been promised. Guests were present; the priest was waiting;
her marriage to one eligible in rank and fortune was ready to
be accomplished. At the altar this demoiselle, so meek and
dutiful, turned upon me like a leopardess, charged me with
cruelty and crimes, and broke, before the gaping priest, the
troth I had plighted for her. I swore there and then, by ten
thousand devils, that she should marry the first man we met
after leaving the château, be he prince, charcoal burner, or
thief. You, shepherd, are the first. Mademoiselle must be wed
this night. If not you, then another. You have ten minutes in
which to make your decision. Do not vex me with words or
questions. Ten minutes, shepherd; and they are speeding."

The marquis drummed loudly with his white fingers upon
the table. He sank into a veiled attitude of waiting. It was as if
some great house had shut its doors and windows against
approach. David would have spoken, but the huge man's
bearing stopped his tongue. Instead, he stood by the lady's
chair and bowed.

"Mademoiselle," he said, and he marveled to find his
words flowing easily before so much elegance and beauty.
"You have heard me say I was a shepherd. I have also had the
fancy, at times, that I am a poet. If it be the test of a poet to
adore and cherish the beautiful, that fancy is now strengthened. Can I serve you in any way, mademoiselle?"

The young woman looked up at him with eyes dry and
mournful. His frank, glowing face, made serious by the gravity

of the adventure, his strong, straight figure and the liquid sympathy in his blue eyes, perhaps, also, her imminent need of long-denied help and kindness, thawed her to sudden tears.

"Monsieur," she said, in low tones, "you look to be true and kind. He is my uncle, the brother of my father, and my only relative. He loved my mother, and he hates me because I am like her. He has made my life one long terror. I am afraid of his very looks, and never before dared to disobey him. But tonight he would have married me to a man three times my age. You will forgive me for bringing this vexation upon you, monsieur. You will, of course, decline this mad act he tries to force upon you. But let me thank you for your generous words, at least. I have had none spoken to me in so long."

There was now something more than generosity in the poet's eyes. Poet he must have been, for Yvonne was forgotten; this fine, new loveliness held him with its freshness and grace. The subtle perfume from her filled him with strange emotions. His tender look fell warmly upon her. She leaned to it, thirstily.

"Ten minutes," said David, "is given me in which to do what I would devote years to achieve. I will not say I pity you, mademoiselle; it would not be true—I love you. I cannot ask love from you yet, but let me rescue you from this cruel man, and, in time, love may come. I think I have a future, I will not always be a shepherd. For the present I will cherish you with all my heart and make your life less sad. Will you trust your fate to me, mademoiselle?"

"Ah, you would sacrifice yourself from pity!"

"From love. The time is almost up, mademoiselle."

"You will regret it, and despise me."

"I will live only to make you happy, and myself worthy of you."

Her fine small hand crept into his from beneath her cloak.

"I will trust you," she breathed, "with my life. And—and love—may not be so far off as you think. Tell him. Once away from the power of his eyes I may forget."

David went and stood before the marquis. The black figure stirred, and the mocking eyes glanced at the great hall clock.

"Two minutes to spare. A shepherd requires eight minutes to decide whether he will accept a bride of beauty and income!

Speak up, shepherd, do you consent to become mademoiselle's husband?"

"Mademoiselle," said David, standing proudly, "has done me the honor to yield to my request that she become my wife."

"Well said!" said the marquis. "You have yet the making of a courtier in you, master shepherd. Mademoiselle could have drawn a worse prize, after all. And now to be done with the affair as quick as the Church and the devil will allow!"

He struck the table soundly with his sword hilt. The landlord came, knee-shaking, bringing more candles in the hope of anticipating the great lord's whims. "Fetch a priest," said the marquis, "a priest; do you understand? In ten minutes have a priest here, or—"

The landlord dropped his candles and flew.

The priest came, heavy-eyed and ruffled. He made David Mignot and Lucie de Varennes man and wife, pocketed a gold piece that the marquis tossed him, and shuffled out again into the night.

"Wine," ordered the marquis, spreading his ominous fingers at the host.

"Fill glasses," he said, when it was brought. He stood up at the head of the table in the candlelight, a black mountain of venom and conceit, with something like the memory of an old love turned to poison in his eye, as it fell upon his niece.

"Monsieur Mignot," he said, raising his wineglass, "drink after I say this to you: You have taken to be your wife one who will make your life a foul and wretched thing. The blood in her is an inheritance running black lies and red ruin. She will bring you shame and anxiety. The devil that descended to her is there in her eyes and skin and mouth that stoop even to beguile a peasant. There is your promise, monsieur poet, for a happy life. Drink your wine. At last, mademoiselle, I am rid of you."

The marquis drank. A little grievous cry, as if from a sudden wound, came from the girl's lips. David, with his glass in his hand, stepped forward three paces and faced the marquis. There was little of a shepherd in his bearing.

"Just now," he said calmly, "you did me the honor to call me 'monsieur.' May I hope, therefore, that my marriage to mademoiselle has placed me somewhat nearer to you in—let us say, reflected rank—has given me the right to stand more as an equal to monseigneur in a certain little piece of business I have in my mind?"

"You may hope, shepherd," sneered the marquis.

"Then," said David, dashing his glass of wine into the contemptuous eyes that mocked him, "perhaps you will condescend to fight me."

The fury of the great lord outbroke in one sudden curse like a blast from a horn. He tore his sword from its black sheath; he called to the hovering landlord: "A sword there, for this lout!" He turned to the lady, with a laugh that chilled her heart, and said: "You put much labor upon me, madame. It seems I must find you a husband and make you a widow in the same night."

"I know not swordplay," said David. He flushed to make the confession before his lady.

" 'I know not swordplay,' " mimicked the marquis. "Shall we fight like peasants with oaken cudgels? *Hola!* François, my pistols!"

A postilion brought two shining great pistols ornamented with carven silver from the carriage holsters. The marquis tossed one upon the table near David's hand. "To the other end of the table," he cried; "even a shepherd may pull a trigger. Few of them attain the honor to die by the weapon of a De Beaupertuys."

The shepherd and the marquis faced each other from the ends of the long table. The landlord, in an ague of terror, clutched the air and stammered: "M-M-Monseigneur, for the love of Christ! not in my house!—do not spill blood—it will ruin my custom——" The look of the marquis, threatening him, paralyzed his tongue.

"Coward," cried the lord of Beaupertuys, "cease chattering your teeth long enough to give the word for us, if you can."

Mine host's knees smote the floor. He was without a vocabulary. Even sounds were beyond him. Still, by gestures he seemed to beseech peace in the name of his house and custom.

"I will give the word," said the lady, in a clear voice. She went up to David and kissed him sweetly. Her eyes were sparkling bright, and color had come to her cheek. She stood

against the wall, and the two men leveled their pistols for her
count.

"*Un—deux—trois!*"

The two reports came so nearly together that the candles
flickered but once. The marquis stood, smiling, the fingers of
his left hand resting, outspread, upon the end of the table.
David remained erect, and turned his head very slowly, searching for his wife with his eyes. Then, as a garment falls from
where it is hung, he sank, crumpled, upon the floor.

With a little cry of terror and despair, the widowed maid
ran and stooped above him. She found his wound, and then
looked up with her old look of pale melancholy. "Through his
heart," she whispered. "Oh, his heart!"

"Come," boomed the great voice of the marquis, "out with
you to the carriage! Daybreak shall not find you on my hands.
Wed you shall be again, and to a living husband, this night. The
next we come upon, my lady, highwayman or peasant. If the
road yields no other than the churl that opens my gates. Out
with you to the carriage!"

The marquis, implacable and huge, the lady wrapped
again in the mystery of her cloak, the postilion bearing the
weapons—all moved out to the waiting carriage. The sound of
its ponderous wheels rolling away echoed through the slum-
bering village. In the hall of the Silver Flagon the distracted
landlord wrung his hands above the slain poet's body, while
the flames of the four and twenty candles danced and flickered
on the table.

THE RIGHT BRANCH

*Three leagues, then, the road ran, and turned into a puzzle. It
joined with another and a larger road at right angles. David stood,
uncertain, for a while, and then took the road to the right.*

Whither it led he knew not, but he was resolved to leave
Vernoy far behind that night. He traveled a league and then
passed a large château which showed testimony of recent
entertainment. Lights shone from every window; from the
great stone gateway ran a tracery of wheel tracks drawn in the
dust by the vehicles of the guests.

Three leagues farther and David was weary. He rested and

slept for a while on a bed of pine boughs at the roadside. Then up and on again along the unknown way.

Thus for five days he traveled the great road, sleeping upon Nature's balsamic beds or in peasants' ricks, eating of their black, hospitable bread, drinking from streams or the willing cup of the goatherd.

At length he crossed a great bridge and set his foot within the smiling city that has crushed or crowned more poets than all the rest of the world. His breath came quickly as Paris sang to him in a little undertone her vital chant of greeting—the hum of voice and foot and wheel.

High up under the eaves of an old house in the Rue Conti, David paid for lodging, and set himself, in a wooden chair, to his poems. The street, once sheltering citizens of import and consequence, now was given over to those who ever follow in the wake of decline.

The houses were tall and still possessed of a ruined dignity, but many of them were empty save for dust and the spider. By night there was the clash of steel and the cries of brawlers straying restlessly from inn to inn. Where once gentility abode was now but a rancid and rude incontinence. But here David found housing commensurate to his scant purse. Daylight and candlelight found him at pen and paper.

One afternoon he was returning from a foraging trip to the lower world, with bread and curds and a bottle of thin wine. Halfway up his dark stairway he met—or rather came upon, for she rested on the stair—a young woman of a beauty that should balk even the justice of a poet's imagination. A loose, dark cloak, flung open, showed a rich gown beneath. Her eyes changed swiftly with every little shade of thought. Within one moment they would be round and artless like a child's, and long and cozening like a gypsy's. One hand raised her gown, undraping a little shoe, high-heeled, with its ribbons dangling, untied. So heavenly she was, so unfitted to stoop, so qualified to charm and command! Perhaps she had seen David coming, and had waited for his help there.

Ah, would monsieur pardon that she occupied the stairway, but the shoe!—the naughty shoe! Alas! it would not remain tied. Ah! if monsieur *would* be so gracious!

The poet's fingers trembled as he tied the contrary ribbons.

Then he would have fled from the danger of her presence, but the eyes grew long and cozening, like a gypsy's, and held him. He leaned against the balustrade, clutching his bottle of sour wine.

"You have been so good," she said, smiling. "Does monsieur, perhaps, live in the house?"

"Yes, madame. I—I think so, madame."

"Perhaps in the third story, then?"

"No, madame; higher up."

The lady fluttered her fingers with the least possible gesture of impatience.

"Pardon. Certainly I am not discreet in asking. Monsieur will forgive me? It is surely not becoming that I should inquire where he lodges."

"Madame, do not say so. I live in the——"

"No, no, no; do not tell me. Now I see that I erred. But I cannot lose the interest I feel in this house and all that is in it. Once it was my home. Often I come here but to dream of those happy days again. Will you let that be my excuse?"

"Let me tell you, then, for you need no excuse," stammered the poet. "I live in the top floor—the small room where the stairs turn."

"In the front room?" asked the lady, turning her head sidewise.

"The rear, madame."

The lady sighed, as if with relief.

"I will detain you no longer, then, monsieur," she said, employing the round and artless eye. "Take good care of my house. Alas! only the memories of it are mine now. Adieu, and accept my thanks for your courtesy."

She was gone, leaving but a smile and a trace of sweet perfume. David climbed the stairs as one in slumber. But he awoke from it, and the smile and the perfume lingered with him and never afterward did either seem quite to leave him. This lady of whom he knew nothing drove him to lyrics of eyes, chansons of swiftly conceived love, odes to curling hair, and sonnets to slippers on slender feet.

Poet he must have been, for Yvonne was forgotten; this fine, new loveliness held him with its freshness and grace. The subtle perfume about her filled him with strange emotions.

On a certain night three persons were gathered about a table in a room on the third floor of the same house. Three chairs and the table and a lighted candle upon it was all the furniture. One of the persons was a huge man, dressed in black. His expression was one of sneering pride. The ends of his upturned moustache reached nearly to his mocking eyes. Another was a lady, young and beautiful, with eyes that could be round and artless, like a child's, or long and cozening, like a gypsy's, but were now keen and ambitious, like any other conspirator's. The third was a man of action, a combatant, a bold and impatient executive, breathing fire and steel. He was addressed by the others as Captain Desrolles.

This man struck the table with his fist, and said, with controlled violence:

"Tonight. Tonight as he goes to midnight mass. I am tired of the plotting that gets nowhere. I am sick of signals and ciphers and secret meetings and such *baragouin*.* Let us be honest traitors. If France is to be rid of him, let us kill in the open, and not hunt with snares and traps. Tonight, I say. I back my words. My hand will do the deed. Tonight, as he goes to mass."

The lady turned upon him a cordial look. Woman, however wedded to plots, must ever thus bow to rash courage. The big man stroked his upturned moustache.

"Dear captain," he said, in a great voice, softened by habit, "this time I agree with you. Nothing is to be gained by waiting. Enough of the palace guards belong to us to make the endeavor a safe one."

"Tonight," repeated Captain Desrolles, again striking the table. "You have heard me, marquis; my hand will do the deed."

"But now," said the huge man, softly, "comes a question. Word must be sent to our partisans in the palace, and a signal agreed upon. Our stanchest men must accompany the royal carriage. At this hour what messenger can penetrate so far as the south doorway? Ribout is stationed there; once a message is placed in his hands, all will go well."

* *baragouin*   gibberish

"I will send the message," said the lady.

"You, countess?" said the marquis, raising his eyebrows. "Your devotion is great, we know, but——"

"Listen!" exclaimed the lady, rising and resting her hands upon the table; "in a garret of this house lives a youth from the provinces as guileless and tender as the lambs he tended there. I have met him twice or thrice upon the stairs. I questioned him, fearing that he might dwell too near the room in which we are accustomed to meet. He is mine, if I will. He writes poems in his garret, and I think he dreams of me. He will do what I say. He shall take the message to the palace."

The marquis rose from his chair and bowed. "You did not permit me to finish my sentence, countess," he said. "I would have said: 'Your devotion is great, but your wit and charm are infinitely greater.' "

While the conspirators were thus engaged, David was polishing some lines addressed to his *amorette d'escalier.** He heard a timorous knock at his door, and opened it, with a great throb, to behold her there, panting as one in straits, with eyes wide open and artless, like a child's.

"Monsieur," she breathed, "I come to you in distress. I believe you to be good and true, and I know of no other help. How I flew through the streets among the swaggering men! Monsieur, my mother is dying. My uncle is a captain of guards in the palace of the king. Someone must fly to bring him. May I hope——"

"Mademoiselle," interrupted David, his eyes shining with the desire to do her service, "your hopes shall be my wings. Tell me how I may reach him."

The lady thrust a sealed paper into his hand.

"Go to the south gate—the south gate, mind—and say to the guards there, 'The falcon has left his nest.' They will pass you, and you will go to the south entrance to the palace. Repeat the words, and give this letter to the man who will reply, 'Let him strike when he will.' This is the password, monsieur, entrusted to me by my uncle, for now when the country is disturbed and men plot against the king's life, no one without

---

* *amorette d'escalier*   stairway romance

it can gain entrance to the palace grounds after nightfall. If you will, monsieur, take him this letter so that my mother may see him before she closes her eyes."

"Give it me," said David, eagerly. "But shall I let you return home through the streets alone so late? I——"

"No, no—fly. Each moment is like a precious jewel. Some time," said the lady, with eyes long and cozening, like a gypsy's, "I will try to thank you for your goodness."

The poet thrust the letter into his breast, and bounded down the stairway. The lady, when he was gone, returned to the room below.

The eloquent eyebrows of the marquis interrogated her.

"He is gone," she said, "as fleet and stupid as one of his own sheep, to deliver it."

The table shook again from the batter of Captain Desrolle's fist.

"Sacred name!" he cried; "I have left my pistols behind! I can trust no others."

"Take this," said the marquis, drawing from beneath his cloak a shining, great weapon, ornamented with carven silver. "There are none truer. But guard it closely, for it bears my arms and crest, and already I am suspected. Me, I must put many leagues between myself and Paris this night. Tomorrow must find me in my château. After you, dear countess."

The marquis puffed out the candle. The lady, well cloaked, and the two gentlemen softly descended the stairway and flowed into the crowd that roamed along the narrow pavements of the Rue Conti.

David sped. At the south gate of the king's residence a halberd was laid to his breast, but he turned its point with the words: "The falcon has left his nest."

"Pass, brother," said the guard, "and go quickly."

On the south steps of the palace they moved to seize him, but again the *mot de passe* charmed the watchers. One among them stepped forward and began: "Let him strike——" But a flurry among the guards told of a surprise. A man of keen look and soldierly stride suddenly pressed through them and seized the letter which David held in his hand. "Come with me," he said, and led him inside the great hall. Then he tore open the letter and read it. He beckoned to a man uniformed as an officer of musketeers, who was passing. "Captain Tetreau, you will have the guards at the south entrance and the south gate arrested and confined. Place men known to be loyal in their places." To David he said: "Come with me."

He conducted him through a corridor and an anteroom into a spacious chamber, where a melancholy man, sombrely dressed, sat brooding in a great leather-covered chair. To that man he said:

"Sire, I have told you that the palace is as full of traitors and spies as a sewer is of rats. You have thought, sire, that it was my fancy. This man penetrated to your very door by their connivance. He bore a letter which I have intercepted. I have brought him here that your majesty may no longer think my zeal excessive."

"I will question him," said the king, stirring in his chair. He looked at David with heavy eyes dulled by an opaque film. The poet bent his knee.

"From where do you come?" asked the king.

"From the village of Vernoy, in the province of Eure-et-Loir, sire,"

"What do you follow in Paris?"

"I—I would be a poet, sire."

"What did you in Vernoy?"

"I minded my father's flock of sheep."

The king stirred again, and the film lifted from his eyes.

"Ah! in the fields?"

"Yes, sire."

"You lived in the fields; you went out in the cool of the morning and lay among the hedges in the grass. The flock distributed itself upon the hillside; you drank of the living stream; you ate your sweet brown bread in the shade; and you listened, doubtless, to blackbirds piping in the grove. Is not that so, shepherd?"

"It is, sire," answered David, with a sigh; "and to the bees at the flowers, and, maybe, to the grape gatherers singing on the hill."

"Yes, yes," said the king, impatiently; "maybe to them; but surely to the blackbirds. They whistled often, in the grove, did they not?"

"Nowhere, sire, so sweetly as in Eure-et-Loir. I have

endeavored to express their song in some verses that I have written."

"Can you repeat those verses?" asked the king, eagerly. "A long time ago I listened to the blackbirds. It would be something better than a kingdom if one could rightly construe their song. And at night you drove the sheep to the fold and then sat, in peace and tranquillity, to your pleasant bread. Can you repeat those verses, shepherd?"

"They run this way, sire," said David, with respectful ardor:

> *"Lazy shepherd, see your lambkins*
> *Skip, ecstatic, on the mead;*
> *See the firs dance in the breezes,*
> *Hear Pan blowing at his reed.*

> *"Hear us calling from the tree-tops,*
> *See us swoop upon your flock;*
> *Yield us wool to make our nests warm*
> *In the branches of the——"*

"If it please your majesty," interrupted a harsh voice, "I will ask a question or two of this rhymester. There is little time to spare. I crave pardon, sire, if my anxiety for your safety offends."

"The loyalty," said the king, "of the Duke d'Aumale is too well proven to give offence." He sank into his chair, and the film came again over his eyes.

"First," said the duke, "I will read you the letter he brought:

"Tonight is the anniversary of the dauphin's death. If he goes, as is his custom, to midnight mass to pray for the soul of his son, the falcon will strike, at the corner of the Rue Esplanade. If this be his intention, set a red light in the upper room at the southwest corner of the palace, that the falcon may take heed.

"Peasant," said the duke, sternly, "you have heard these words. Who gave you this message to bring?"

"My lord duke," said David, sincerely, "I will tell you. A lady gave it me. She said her mother was ill, and that this writing would fetch her uncle to her bedside. I do not know the meaning of the letter, but I will swear that she is beautiful and good."

"Describe the woman," commanded the duke, "and how you came to be her dupe."

"Describe her!" said David with a tender smile. "You would command words to perform miracles. Well, she is made of sunshine and deep shade. She is slender, like the alders, and moves with their grace. Her eyes change while you gaze into them; now round, and then half shut as the sun peeps between two clouds. When she comes, heaven is all about her; when she leaves, there is chaos and a scent of hawthorn blossoms. She came to me in the Rue Conti, number twenty-nine."

"It is the house," said the duke, turning to the king, "that we have been watching. Thanks to the poet's tongue, we have a picture of the infamous Countess Quebedaux."

"Sire and my lord duke," said David, earnestly, "I hope my poor words have done no injustice. I have looked into that lady's eyes. I will stake my life that she is an angel, letter or no letter."

The duke looked at him steadily. "I will put you to the proof," he said, slowly. "Dressed as the king, you shall, yourself, attend mass in his carriage at midnight. Do you accept the test?"

David smiled. "I have looked into her eyes," he said. "I had my proof there. Take yours how you will."

Half an hour before twelve the Duke d'Aumale, with his own hands, set a red lamp in a southwest window of the palace. At ten minutes to the hour, David, leaning on his arm, dressed as the king, from top to toe, with his head bowed in his cloak, walked slowly from the royal apartments to the waiting carriage. The duke assisted him inside and closed the door. The carriage whirled away along its route to the cathedral.

On the *qui vive* in a house at the corner of the Rue Esplanade was Captain Tetreau with twenty men, ready to pounce upon the conspirators when they should appear.

But it seemed that, for some reason, the plotters had slightly altered their plans. When the royal carriage had reached the Rue Christopher, one square nearer than the Rue Esplanade, forth from it burst Captain Desrolles, with his band of would-be regicides, and assailed the equipage. The guards upon the carriage, though surprised at the premature attack, descended and fought valiantly. The noise of conflict attracted the force of Captain Tetreau, and they came pelting down the street to the rescue. But, in the meantime, the desperate Desrolles had torn open the door of the king's carriage, thrust his weapon against the body of the dark figure inside, and fired.

Now, with loyal reinforcements at hand, the street rang with cries and the rasp of steel, but the frightened horses had dashed away. Upon the cushions lay the dead body of the poor mock king and poet, slain by a ball from the pistol of Monseigneur, the Marquis de Beaupertuys.

THE MAIN ROAD

Three leagues, then, the road ran, and turned into a puzzle. It joined with another and a larger road at right angles. David stood, uncertain, for a while, and then sat himself to rest upon its side.

Whither those roads led he knew not. Either way there seemed to lie a great world full of chance and peril. And then, sitting there, his eye fell upon a bright star, one that he and Yvonne had named for theirs. That set him thinking of Yvonne, and he wondered if he had not been too hasty. Why should he leave her and his home because a few hot words had come between them? Was love so brittle a thing that jealousy, the very proof of it, could break it? Mornings always brought a cure for the little heartaches of evening. There was yet time for him to return home without anyone in the sweetly sleeping village of Vernoy being the wiser. His heart was Yvonne's; there where he lived always he could write his poems and find his happiness.

David rose, and shook off his unrest and the wild mood that had tempted him. He set his face steadfastly back, along the road he had come. By the time he had retraveled the road to Vernoy, his desire to rove was gone. He passed the sheepfold, and the sheep scurried, with a drumming flutter, at his late footsteps, warming his heart by the homely sound. He crept without noise into his little room and lay there, thankful that his feet had escaped the distress of new roads that night.

How well he knew woman's heart! The next evening Yvonne was at the well in the road where the young congregated in order that the *curé* might have business. The corner of her eye was engaged in a search for David, albeit her set mouth seemed unrelenting. He saw the look; braved the mouth, drew from it a recantation and, later, a kiss as they walked homeward together.

Three months afterward they were married. David's father was shrewd and prosperous. He gave them a wedding that was heard of three leagues away. Both the young people were favorites in the village. There was a procession in the streets, a dance on the green; they had the marionettes and a tumbler out from Dreux to delight the guests.

Then a year, and David's father died. The sheep and the cottage descended to him. He already had the seemliest wife in the village. Yvonne's milk pails and her brass kettles were bright—*ouf!* they blinded you in the sun when you passsed that way. But you must keep your eyes upon her yard, for her flower beds were so neat and gay they restored to you your sight. And you might hear her sing, aye, as far as the double chestnut tree above Père Gruneau's blacksmith forge.

But a day came when David drew out paper from a long-shut drawer, and began to bite the end of a pencil. Spring had come again and touched his heart. Poet he must have been, for now Yvonne was well-nigh forgotten. This fine new loveliness of earth held him with its witchery and grace. The perfume from her woods and meadows stirred him strangely. Daily had he gone forth with his flock, and brought it safe at night. But now he stretched himself under the hedge and pieced words together on his bits of paper. The sheep strayed, and the wolves, perceiving that difficult poems make easy mutton, ventured from the woods and stole his lambs.

David's stock of poems grew larger and his flock smaller. Yvonne's nose and temper waxed sharp and her talk blunt. Her pans and kettles grew dull, but her eyes had caught their flash. She pointed out to the poet that his neglect was reducing the flock and bringing woe upon the household. David hired a boy to guard the sheep, locked himself in the little room in the top of the cottage, and wrote more poems. The boy, being a poet by nature, but not furnished with an outlet in the way of writing, spent his time in slumber. The wolves lost no time in discovering that poetry and sleep are practically the same; so the flock steadily grew smaller. Yvonne's ill temper increased at an equal rate. Sometimes she would stand in the yard and rail at David through his high window. Then you could hear her as far as the double chestnut tree above Père Gruneau's blacksmith forge.

M. Papineau, the kind, wise, meddling old notary, saw this, as he saw everything at which his nose pointed. He went to David, fortified himself with a great pinch of snuff, and said:

"Friend Mignot, I affixed the seal upon the marriage certificate of your father. It would distress me to be obliged to attest a paper signifying the bankruptcy of his son. But that is what you are coming to. I speak as an old friend. Now, listen to what I have to say. You have your heart set, I perceive, upon poetry. At Dreux, I have a friend, one Monsieur Bril—Georges Bril. He lives in a little cleared space in a houseful of books. He is a learned man; he visits Paris each year; he himself has written books. He will tell you when the catacombs were made, how they found out the names of the stars, and why the plover has a long bill. The meaning and the form of poetry is to him as intelligent as the baa of a sheep is to you. I will give you a letter to him, and you shall take him your poems and let him read them. Then you will know if you shall write more, or give your attention to your wife and business."

"Write the letter," said David. "I am sorry you did not speak of this sooner."

At sunrise the next morning he was on the road to Dreux with the precious roll of poems under his arm. At noon he wiped the dust from his feet at the door of Monsieur Bril. That learned man broke the seal of M. Papineau's letter, and sucked up its contents through his gleaming spectacles as the sun draws water. He took David inside to his study and sat him down upon a little island beat upon by a sea of books.

Monsieur Bril had a conscience. He flinched not even at a mass of manuscript the thickness of a finger length and rolled to an incorrigible curve. He broke the back of the roll against his knee and began to read. He slighted nothing; he bored into the lump as a worm into a nut, seeking for a kernel.

Meanwhile, David sat, marooned, trembling in the spray of so much literature. It roared in his ears. He held no chart or compass for voyaging in that sea. Half the world, he thought, must be writing books.

Monsieur Bril bored to the last page of the poems. Then he took off his spectacles and wiped them with his handkerchief.

"My old friend, Papineau, is well?" he asked.

"In the best of health," said David.

"How many sheep have you, Monsieur Mignot?"

"Three hundred and nine, when I counted them yesterday. The flock has had ill fortune. To that number it has decreased from eight hundred and fifty."

"You have a wife and a home, and lived in comfort. The sheep brought you plenty. You went into the fields with them and lived in the keen air and ate the sweet bread of contentment. You had but to be vigilant and recline there upon nature's breast, listening to the whistle of the blackbirds in the grove. Am I right thus far?"

"It was so," said David.

"I have read all your verses," continued Monsieur Bril, his eyes wandering about his sea of books as if he conned the horizon for a sail. "Look yonder, through that window, Monsieur Mignot; tell me what you see in that tree."

"I see a crow," said David, looking.

"There is a bird," said Monsieur Bril, "that shall assist me where I am disposed to shirk a duty. You know that bird, Monsieur Mignot; he is the philosopher of the air. He is happy through submission to his lot. None so merry or full-crawed as he with his whimsical eye and rollicking step. The fields yield him what he desires. He never grieves that his plumage is not gay, like the oriole's. And you have heard, Monsieur Mignot, the notes that nature has given him? Is the nightingale any happier, do you think?"

David rose to his feet. The crow cawed harshly from his tree.

"I thank you, Monsieur Bril," he said, slowly. "There was not, then, one nightingale note among all those croaks?"

"I could not have missed it," said Monsieur Bril, with a sigh. "I read every word. Live your poetry, man; do not try to write it anymore."

"I thank you," said David, again. "And now I will be going back to my sheep."

"If you would dine with me," said the man of books, "and overlook the smart of it, I will give you reasons at length."

"No," said the poet, "I must be back in the fields cawing at my sheep."

Back along the road to Vernoy he trudged with his poems under his arm. When he reached his village he turned into the shop of one Zeigler, who sold anything that came to his hand.

"Friend," said David, "wolves from the forest harass my sheep on the hills. I must purchase firearms to protect them. What have you?"

"A bad day, this, for me, friend Mignot," said Zeigler, spreading his hands, "for I perceive that I must sell you a weapon that will not fetch a tenth of its value. Only last week I bought from a peddler a wagon full of goods that he procured at a sale by a *commissionaire* of the crown. The sale was of the château and belongings of a great lord—I know not his title— who has been banished for conspiracy against the king. There are some choice firearms in the lot. This pistol—oh, a weapon fit for a prince!—it shall be only forty francs to you, friend Mignot—if I lost ten by the sale. But perhaps an arquebus——"

"This will do," said David, throwing the money on the counter. "Is it charged?"

"I will charge it," said Zeigler. "And, for ten francs more, add a store of powder and ball."

David laid his pistol under his coat and walked to his cottage. Yvonne was not there. Of late she had taken to gadding much among the neighbors. But a fire was glowing in the kitchen stove. David opened the door of it and thrust his poems in upon the coals. As they blazed up they made a singing, harsh sound in the flue.

"The song of the crow!" said the poet.

He went up to his attic room and closed the door. So quiet was the village that a score of people heard the roar of the great pistol. They flocked thither, and up the stairs where the smoke, issuing, drew their notice.

The men laid the body of the poet upon his bed, awkwardly arranging it to conceal the torn plumage of the poor black crow. The women chattered in a luxury of zealous pity. Some of them ran to tell Yvonne.

M. Papineau, whose nose had brought him there among the first, picked up the weapon and ran his eye over its silver mountings with a mingled air of connoisseurship and grief.

"The arms," he explained, aside, to the *curé*, "and crest of Monseigneur, the Marquis de Beaupertuys."

Reading for Understanding _____

Main Idea

1. No matter what he did, David Mignot would have (a) become famous for his poetry (b) married the beautiful niece of the Marquis (c) died by the pistol of the Marquis (d) been faithful and true to Yvonne.

Details

2. In the first episode, David catches the attention of the Marquis by (a) sending him some poetry (b) freeing a carriage from the mud (c) writing a love letter to the niece (d) serving the Marquis at a table in the inn.

3. In the first episode, David did all the following EXCEPT (a) throw wine into the Marquis' face (b) propose marriage to the niece (c) have an argument with Yvonne (d) apologize to the Marquis.

4. In the second episode, there was a plot to (a) kill the king (b) kill Captain Desrolles (c) capture the Duke d'Aumale (d) kidnap the beautiful Countess Quebedaux.

5. In the third episode David (a) took good care of his sheep (b) inherited his father's estate (c) married someone other than Yvonne (d) became a famous poet.

Inferences

6. David's challenge of the Marquis to a duel must be considered extremely (a) wise (b) humorous (c) selfish (d) foolish.

7. The challenge was given because David was so (a) romantic (b) greedy (c) thoughtful (d) skillful a duelist.

8. In the second episode, David's part in the plot was as (a) a brave soldier (b) a leader of the conspiracy (c) a foolish messenger (d) an enemy of the king.

9. It may be inferred from the first two episodes that David (a) was a coward (b) fell easily into love (c) was an outstanding poet (d) didn't trust strangers.

10. In the third episode David (a) was mistaken about his poetic abilities (b) knew that someday he'd meet the Marquis (c) let his love for Yvonne dominate his life (d) loved city life more than country life.

Order of Events

11. Arrange the items in the order in which they occurred. Use letters only. Confine yourself to the first episode only.
    A.   David is of assistance to the Marquis on the road.
    B.   David is killed by the pistol of the Marquis.
    C.   David has an argument with Yvonne.
    D.   David is offered the niece's hand in marriage.
    E.   David challenges the Marquis to a duel.

Outcome

12. If there were a third path in the road to take and if David had taken it,   (a) his terrible fate would have been avoided   (b) he'd have returned home to Yvonne and lived to a ripe old age   (c) he and the Marquis would at last have become good friends   (d) somehow or other, he'd have been killed by the pistol of the Marquis.

Cause and Effect

13. In the second episode, David was chosen as a messenger because he had impressed the Countess by his

(a)   trickiness   (b)   understanding of the world
(c)   simplicity   (d) patriotism.

Fact or Opinion

Tell whether the following is a fact or an opinion.
14.   In his dealings with the world, David was impetuous, foolish, but courageous.

Author's Role

15.   The tone of the story is   (a) angry and hopeless (b)   bored   and   indifferent   (c)   honest   and straightforward   (d)   sensational and quite exaggerated.

Words in Context

1.   "When my poems are on every man's tongue," he told himself, in a fine *exhilaration*, "she will, perhaps, think of the hard words she spoke this day."
     Exhilaration (155) means state of   (a)   annoyance
     (b) depression   (c) laughter   (d) high spirits.
2.   Perhaps that light meant that she *rued*, sleepless, her anger, and that morning might—But no! His decision was made.
     Rued (156) means   (a) strengthened   (b) repeated
     (c) remembered   (d) regretted.
3, 4.   Some half an hour later these traces were verified by the sight of a *ponderous* carriage *mired* in a little brook at the bottom of a steep hill.
     Ponderous (156) means   (a) delicate
     (b) broken-down   (c) bulky   (d) colorful.
     Mired (156) means   (a) stuck in mud   (b) sliding
     along   (c) crossing swiftly   (d) easily seen.
5.   But as yet he held no key to it, for no word was spoken while he sat with his *impenetrable* companions.

Impenetrable (157) means   (a) nervous
(b) unapproachable   (c) hostile   (d) newfound.

6. In an hour's time David perceived through the window
    that the vehicle *traversed* the street of some town.
    Traversed (157) means   (a) avoided   (b) crossed
    through   (c) stopped suddenly   (d) severely
    damaged.

7. Shivering with chill and *apprehension*, the landlord of the
    Silver Flagon stood, half-clad, candle in hand, upon the
    threshold.
    Apprehension (158) means   (a) dread   (b) sickness
    (c) happiness   (d) curiosity.

8. He was startled from the contemplation of her *forlorn*
    loveliness by the booming voice of the Marquis.
    Forlorn (158) means   (a) sorrowful   (b) striking
    (c) natural   (d) painted.

9. "Do not *vex* me with words or questions."
    Vex (159) means   (a) address   (b) distress
    (c) humor   (d) amuse.

10. Her *imminent* need of long-denied help and kindness
    thawed her to sudden tears.
    Imminent (160) means   (a) clearly expressed
    (b) concealed   (c) pressing   (d) obvious.

11. You will forgive me for bringing this *vexation* upon you,
    monsieur.
    Vexation (160) means   (a) annoyance   (b) false tale
    (c) threat to life   (d) marriage.

12. "The devil that descended to her is there in her eyes and
    skin and mouth that stoop even to *beguile* a peasant."
    Beguile (161) means   (a) interest   (b) injure
    (c) deceive   (d) bother.

13, 14. Where once *gentility* abode was now but a *rancid* and
    rude incontinence.
    Gentility (164) means   (a) the mayor   (b) a band of
    merchants   (c) humble friendliness   (d) good
    manners.
    Rancid (164) means   (a) high-spirited   (b) foul
    (c) pleasant   (d) little understood.

15. But here David found housing *commensurate* to his scant purse.
    Commensurate (164) means   (a) lacking
    (b) expensive   (c) inexpensive   (d) adequate.

16. "Our *stanchest* men must accompany the royal carriage."
    (Also *staunchest*)
    Stanchest (166) means most   (a) cheerful   (b) strong
    (c) wise   (d) friendly.

17. "In this house lives a youth from the provinces as *guileless* and tender as the lambs he tended there."
    Guileless (167) means   (a) handsome   (b) poor
    (c) affectionate   (d) innocent.

18. He heard a *timorous* knock at his door, and opened it, with a great throb.
    Timorous (167) means   (a) timid   (b) loud
    (c) double   (d) emphatic.

19. "How I flew through the streets among the *swaggering* men!"
    Swaggering (167) means   (a) bold and boastful
    (b) quiet and thoughtful   (c) ugly but kindly
    (d) tried and true.

20. "This man penetrated to your very door by their *connivance*."
    Connivance (169) means   (a) goodwill   (b) scheming
    (c) resistance   (d) carelessness.

21. "It would be something better than a kingdom if one could rightly *construe* their song."
    Construe (170) means   (a) repeat   (b) appreciate
    (c) hear   (d) understand.

22. He saw the look; braved the mouth, drew from it a *recantation* and later, a kiss as they walked homeward together.
    Recantation (173) means a statement showing a
    (a) change of mind   (b) bitter repetition   (c) fierce loyalty   (d) friendly disagreement.

23. "It would distress me to be obliged to *attest* a paper signifying the bankruptcy of his son."

Attest (174) means   (a) reject   (b) discover
(c) certify   (d) handle.

24. "You had but to be *vigilant* and recline there upon
nature's breast, listening to the whistle of the blackbirds
in the grove."
Vigilant (175) means   (a) weary   (b) sleepy
(c) watchful   (d) indifferent.

25, 26. "There is a bird that shall assist me where I am
disposed to *shirk* a duty."
Disposed (175) means   (a) inclined   (b) unwilling
(c) eager   (d) careless.
Shirk (175) means   (a) follow   (b) avoid
(c) welcome   (d) force.

27, 28. None so merry or full-crawed as he with his *whimsical*
eye and *rollicking* step.
Whimsical (175) means   (a) teary   (b) sad
(c) colorful   (d) impish.
Rollicking (175) means   (a) unsteady   (b) carefree
(c) heavy   (d) tidy.

29. The women chattered in a luxury of *zealous* pity.
Zealous (177) means   (a) false   (b) unstated
(c) intense   (d) carefree.

30. M. Papineau picked up the weapon and ran his eye over
the silver mountings with a mingled air of *connoisseurship*
and grief.
Connoisseurship (177) means having the qualities of
(a) a duelist   (b) an expert   (c) a mourner
(d) a jeweler.

Thinking Critically About the Story _____

1. Why is the fable of the appointment in Samarra appropriate as an introduction to this story?

2. How does the author stimulate the reader's imagination
through the introduction of three separate stories?

3. Although David appears in three different stories, his

character is consistent throughout. What are some of the qualities that appear in all three stories?

4. Why do you think that the pistol of the Marquis was found in a kind of pawnshop (Story 3)? What clues in the second story suggest the possible fate of the Marquis?

5. Some people say, "I don't worry. When my time is up, it's up, and there's nothing I can do about it." Do you agree with this statement? Explain your point of view.

6. Why did Monsieur Bril (page 175) use the crow as a model for David to copy?

7. After getting the bad news about his poetry, David refuses dinner and says, "I must be back in the fields cawing at my sheep." Why does he use the word *cawing?* How does this reveal his bitterness?

8. Here's the beginning of a story:

    When David reached the fork in the road, he stood uncertain, for a while, and then sat himself to rest upon its side. As he sat, he noticed a footpath running off into the woods. David stood up suddenly, squared his shoulders and set off on the path.

    What happened next? Finish the story, inventing still another possible conclusion.

Stories in Words _____

Companions (157)   Two Latin words, *com* ("with") and *panis* ("bread") suggest the colorful origin of this word. A *companion* is, by derivation, someone we "break bread with," someone we eat with, a close associate.

Echo (163)   In Greek mythology, *Echo* was a nymph who fell in love with Narcissus. Her love was hopeless, for Narcissus was in love with his own beauty. She pined away until nothing was left of her but her voice. When you hear your voice returning to you across a canyon, perhaps it is but the voice of Echo picking up the call.

Oriole (175) The Latin word *aureolus* means "golden." By derivation, an oriole is a golden bird. Many birds in the large oriole family are golden yellow in part. A related word, *aureole*, refers to the halo around the heads of figures in religious paintings. It also refers to the band of light around the sun, as seen through a mist.

The Magic of Imagination

ACTIVITIES

Thinking Critically About the Stories ____

1. "Roads of Destiny," as the title suggests, is principally about fate and the part it may or may not play in our lives. At least two other stories also deal with fate and its effect on the characters' lives. Select two stories and show how fate seems to play a part.

2. Three major characters in these stories are Bubber, Giovanni Corte, and David Mignot. Which one did you find most sympathetic? Why?

3. Of all the settings (3), which one seemed to you the scariest. Why?

4. Imagination has been defined as "the power of creating mental images of something that is not present or even not in existence." Some critics add "the ability to see inner relationships." What does imagination mean to you? By your definition, which of the stories stimulated your imagination most? Explain why you chose it.

5. Except for "Lonesome Boy, Silver Trumpet," the endings were not happy ones. Would these have been spoiled by happy endings? Do you prefer happy endings to sad ones? If the former, do you still find that certain stories cannot reasonably have happy endings? Explain.

6. Did any of these stories remind you of a movie or television play you have seen? It may be just a character like Bubber or David Mignot. Or it may be a setting like the sanatorium in "Seven Floors." Point out any resemblances.

7. Except for a brief moment in Paris in "Roads of Destiny," the settings for the stories are rural areas. Even the sanatorium in "Seven Floors" is apparently out in the country. Are stories of the imagination easier to set away from the cities? Explain your point of view.

Writing and Other Activities _____

1. Stimulate *your* imagination. In a composition of 200–250 words, explain why dogs chase cats, where old coins finally end up, how your marvelous invention "the perpetual-motion machine" (or some other) works, how jokes can travel across an entire continent in a couple of days, who makes up all those jokes that travel so fast, or some other unlikely, but imaginative, topic. A bit of humor would be welcome.

2. Write a letter to a friend recommending one of the stories in this section. Tell why you liked it and why you think he or she would enjoy it. Use correct letter form.

3. Select one of the stories in this unit and select movie or television actors who you think would play the parts well.

4. "The Monkey's Paw" has a great deal of effective dialog. Select four characters to play the roles of Mr. White, Mrs. White, Herbert White, and Sergeant-Major Morris. If you wish, other classmates may be delegated to read the explanatory action and description.

5. Watch a television program or movie advertised as having suspense. Try to analyze the director's method of building tension and prepare to report to the class.

Stories in Words: A Review _____

A. alarmed   E. companions   I. jovially
B. apathy   F. cricket   J. oriole
C. caprice   G. echo   K. scurried
D. chauffeur   H. enthralled   L. telephone

Answer the following questions by choosing a word from the list above. Use letters only.

Which of the words above . . .

1. . . . comes from the name of a nymph in Greek mythology?
2. . . . comes from the name of a god in Roman mythology?
3. . . . has a prefix that means "not, without"?
4. . . . is related to the familiar *taxicab?*
5. . . . literally means "make a slave of"?
6. . . . is related to the metal gold.
7. . . . means "those who break bread together"?
8. . . . is related to an old call to action?
9. . . . may have developed like the words *harum-scarum* and *hubbub?*
10. . . . originally had to do with stoking a furnace?

3

The Surprise Ending

"Surprise!"

Why are surprise parties consistently popular, especially on special days like birthdays and anniversaries? How do *you* feel about surprises? Do you secretly enjoy a surprise? Do you like something out of the ordinary? Though you enjoy your familiar routines, do you occasionally enjoy a twist of the unexpected? Do you greet a long-absent relative or friend who turns up unexpectedly with greater enthusiasm than the expected visitor?

The popular short-story writer O. Henry built his reputation on surprise endings. Yet, even though readers know a surprise is coming, they have to read on to find out what the surprise is. "How is O. Henry going to surprise me this time?"

Unit Two contains an O. Henry story with a surprise that goes far beyond the usual, for there are three unexpected twists to the story. In Unit 3, the surprise ending is brought to perfection by four skilled short-story writers, with different styles and different approaches.

You will be touched by the fate of Mathilde in "The Necklace." You will gasp when you come to the end of "A Horseman in the Sky." There are surprises still to come. You will find "A Habit for the Voyage" and "The Point of Honor" quite unlike in the manner of storytelling, but each concludes with an unexpected revelation. The former suggests tension from the opening sentence and sustains that tension to the surprising conclusion. The latter uses a different style altogether. The storytelling is leisurely. The character of the Señor is developed slowly and inevitably. The sense of menace arises only gradually and subtly, and the conclusion is suggested but not confirmed. Like "The Lady, or the Tiger?" the story remains open-ended.

In all four stories, plot (1) is of major importance, but "The Point of Honor" adds something extra: keen characterization (2).

The Necklace

Guy de Maupassant

♦ **She removed the wraps, which covered her shoulders, before the glass, so as once more to see herself in all her glory. But suddenly she uttered a cry. She had no longer the necklace around her neck!**

The poet John Greenleaf Whittier once wrote that the saddest of all words are "It might have been." An opposing view is expressed in the proverb, "Don't cry over spilled milk." The conclusion of "The Necklace" leads us to wonder how the principal character will fare in the future, which philosophy she will adopt.

In this classic short story, Mathilde Loisel, the major character, faces the kind of stress that few people experience. As we observe her challenge, we witness the kind of character development so difficult within the pages of a short story. We come to know her as well as we know the characters in many novels. We share with her the misfortune that transforms her life and we put ourselves in her place.

"What would I have done if I had been she?"

The plot of "The Necklace" is simple, but it is dynamite. Though plot is of major importance, characterization is superbly presented—and not only in the person of Mathilde. "The Necklace" also provides a glimpse into the life and heart of Mathilde's husband, M. Loisel. We contrast the lives of the Loisels with that of Madame Forestier, who serves as a contrast to Mathilde. This perfectly organized short story will stay with you for many years to come.

THE NECKLACE

She was one of those pretty and charming girls who are sometimes, as if by a mistake of destiny, born in a family of clerks. She had no dowry, no expectations, no means of being known, understood, loved, wedded, by any rich and distinguished man; and she let herself be married to a little clerk at the Ministry of Public Instruction.

She dressed plainly because she could not dress well, but she was as unhappy as though she had really fallen from her proper station; since with women there is neither caste nor rank; and beauty, grace, and charm act instead of family and birth. Natural fineness, instinct for what is elegant, suppleness of wit, are the sole hierarchy, and make from women of the people the equals of the very greatest ladies.

She suffered ceaselessly, feeling herself born for all the delicacies and all the luxuries. She suffered from the poverty of her dwelling, from the wretched look of the walls, from the worn-out chairs, from the ugliness of the curtains. All those things, of which another woman of her rank would never even have been conscious, tortured her and made her angry. The sight of the little Breton peasant who did her humble housework aroused in her regrets which were despairing, and distracted dreams. She thought of the silent antechambers hung with Oriental tapestry, lit by tall bronze candelabra, and of the two great footmen in knee-breeches who sleep in the big armchairs, made drowsy by the heavy warmth of the hot-air stove. She thought of the long *salons* fitted up with ancient silk, of the delicate furniture carrying priceless curiosities, and of the coquettish perfumed boudoirs made for talks at five o'clock with intimate friends, with men famous and sought after, whom all women envy and whose attention they all desire.

When she sat down to dinner, before the round table covered with a tablecloth three days old, opposite her husband, who uncovered the soup tureen and declared with an enchanted air, "Ah, the good *pot-au-feu!* I don't know anything better than that," she thought of dainty dinners, of shining silverware, of tapestry which peopled the walls with ancient personages and with strange birds flying in the midst of a fairy forest; and she thought of delicious dishes served on marvelous plates, and of the whispered gallantries which you listen to with a sphinxlike smile, while you are eating the pink flesh of a trout or the wings of a quail.

She had no dresses, no jewels, nothing. And she loved nothing but that; she felt made for that. She would so have liked to please, to be envied, to be charming, to be sought after.

She had a friend, a former schoolmate at the convent, who was rich, and whom she did not like to go and see anymore, because she suffered so much when she came back.

But, one evening, her husband returned home with a triumphant air, and holding a large envelope in his hand.

"There," said he, "here is something for you."

She tore the paper sharply, and drew out a printed card which bore these words:

"The Minister of Public Instruction and Mme. Georges Ramponneau request the honor of M. and Mme. Loisel's company at the palace of the Ministry on Monday evening, January 18th."

Instead of being delighted, as her husband hoped, she threw the invitation on the table with disdain, murmuring:

"What do you want me to do with that?"

"But, my dear, I thought you would be glad. You never go out, and this is such a fine opportunity. I had awful trouble to get it. Everyone wants to go; it is very select, and they are not giving many invitations to clerks. The whole official world will be there."

She looked at him with an irritated eye, and she said, impatiently:

"And what do you want me to put on my back?"

He had not thought of that; he stammered:

"Why, the dress you go to the theatre in. It looks very well."

He stopped, distracted, seeing that his wife was crying. Two great tears descended slowly from the corners of her eyes towards the corners of her mouth. He stuttered:

"What's the matter? What's the matter?"

But, by a violent effort, she had conquered her grief, and she replied, with a calm voice, while she wiped her wet cheeks:

"Nothing. Only I have no dress, and therefore I can't go to this ball. Give your card to some colleague whose wife is better equipped than I."

He was in despair. He resumed:

"Come, let us see, Mathilde. How much would it cost, a suitable dress, which you could use on other occasions, something very simple?"

She reflected several seconds, making her calculations and wondering also what sum she could ask without drawing on herself an immediate refusal and a frightened exclamation from the economical clerk.

Finally, she replied, hesitatingly:

"I don't know exactly, but I think I could manage it with four hundred francs."

He had grown a little pale, because he was laying aside just that amount to buy a gun and treat himself to a little shooting next summer on the plain of Nanterre, with several friends who went to shoot larks down there, of a Sunday.

But he said:

"All right. I will give you four hundred francs. And try to have a pretty dress."

The day of the ball drew near, and Mme. Loisel seemed sad, uneasy, anxious. Her dress was ready, however. Her husband said to her one evening:

"What is the matter? Come, you've been so queer these last three days."

And she answered:

"It annoys me not to have a single jewel, not a single stone, nothing to put on. I shall look like distress. I should almost rather not go at all."

He resumed:

"You might wear natural flowers. It's very stylish at this time of the year. For ten francs you can get two or three magnificent roses."

She was not convinced.

"No; there's nothing more humiliating than to look poor among other women who are rich."

But her husband cried:

"How stupid you are! Go look up your friend Mme. Forestier, and ask her to lend you some jewels. You're quite thick enough with her to do that."

She uttered a cry of joy:

"It's true. I never thought of it."

The next day she went to her friend and told of her distress.

Mme. Forestier went to a wardrobe with a glass door, took out a large jewel box, brought it back, opened it, and said to Mme. Loisel:

"Choose, my dear."

She saw first of all some bracelets, then a pearl necklace, then a Venetian cross, gold and precious stones of admirable workmanship. She tried on the ornaments before the glass, hesitated, could not make up her mind to part with them, to give them back. She kept asking:

"Haven't you any more?"

"Why, yes. Look. I don't know what you like."

All of a sudden she discovered, in a black satin box, a superb necklace of diamonds; and her heart began to beat with an immoderate desire. Her hands trembled as she took it. She fastened it around her throat, outside her high-necked dress, and remained lost in ecstasy at the sight of herself.

Then she asked, hesitating, filled with anguish:

"Can you lend me that, only that?"

"Why, yes, certainly."

She sprang upon the neck of her friend, kissed her passionately, then fled with her treasure.

The day of the ball arrived. Mme. Loisel made a great success. She was prettier than them all, elegant, gracious, smiling, and crazy with joy. All the men looked at her, asked her name, endeavored to be introduced. All the attachés of the

Cabinet wanted to waltz with her. She was remarked by the minister himself.

She danced with intoxication, with passion, made drunk by pleasure, forgetting all, in the triumph of her beauty, in the glory of her success, in a sort of cloud of happiness composed of all this homage, of all this admiration, of all these awakened desires, and of that sense of complete victory which is so sweet to woman's heart.

She went away about four o'clock in the morning. Her husband had been sleeping since midnight, in a little deserted anteroom, with three other gentlemen whose wives were having a good time.

He threw over her shoulders the wraps which he had brought, modest wraps of common life, whose poverty contrasted with the elegance of the ball dress. She felt this and wanted to escape so as not to be remarked by the other women, who were enveloping themselves in costly furs.

Loisel held her back.

"Wait a bit. You will catch cold outside. I will go and call a cab."

But she did not listen to him, and rapidly descended the stairs. When they were in the street they did not find a carriage; and they began to look for one, shouting after the cabmen whom they saw passing by at a distance.

They went down towards the Seine, in despair, shivering with cold. At last they found on the quay one of those ancient noctambulant coupés which, exactly as if they were ashamed to show their misery during the day, are never seen round Paris until after nightfall.

It took them to their door in the Rue des Martyrs, and once more, sadly, they climbed up homeward. All was ended, for her. And as to him, he reflected that he must be at the Ministry at ten o'clock.

She removed the wraps, which covered her shoulders, before the glass, so as once more to see herself in all her glory. But suddenly she uttered a cry. She had no longer the necklace around her neck!

Her husband, already half-undressed, demanded:

"What is the matter with you?"

She turned madly towards him:

"I have—I have—I've lost Mme. Forestier's necklace."

He stood up, distracted.

"What!—how?—Impossible!"

And they looked in the folds of her dress, in the folds of her cloak, in her pockets, everywhere. They did not find it.

He asked:

"You're sure you had it on when you left the ball?"

"Yes, I felt it in the vestibule of the palace."

"But if you had lost it in the street we should have heard it fall. It must be in the cab."

"Yes. Probably. Did you take his number?"

"No. And you, didn't you notice it?"

"No."

They looked, thunderstruck, at one another. At last Loisel put on his clothes.

"I shall go back on foot," said he, "over the whole route which we have taken, to see if I can't find it."

And he went out. She sat waiting on a chair in her ball

dress, without strength to go to bed, overwhelmed, without fire, without a thought.

Her husband came back about seven o'clock. He had found nothing.

He went to Police Headquarters, to the newspaper offices, to offer a reward; he went to the cab companies—everywhere, in fact, whither he was urged by the least suspicion of hope.

She waited all day, in the same condition of mad fear before this terrible calamity.

Loisel returned at night with a hollow, pale face; he had discovered nothing.

"You must write to your friend," said he, "that you have broken the clasp of her necklace and that you are having it mended. That will give us time to turn round."

She wrote at his dictation.

At the end of a week they had lost all hope.

And Loisel, who had aged five years, declared:

"We must consider how to replace that ornament."

The next day they took the box which had contained it, and they went to the jeweler whose name was found within. He consulted his books.

"It was not I, madame, who sold that necklace; I must simply have furnished the case."

Then they went from jeweler to jeweler, searching for a necklace like the other, consulting their memories, sick both of them with chagrin and with anguish.

They found, in a shop at the Palais Royal, a string of diamonds which seemed to them exactly like the one they looked for. It was worth forty thousand francs. They could have it for thirty-six.

So they begged the jeweler not to sell it for three days yet. And they made a bargain that he should buy it back for thirty-four thousand francs, in case they found the other one before the end of February.

Loisel possessed eighteen thousand francs which his father had left him. He would borrow the rest.

He did borrow, asking a thousand francs of one, five hundred of another, five louis here, three louis there. He gave notes, took up ruinous obligations, dealt with usurers, and all the race of lenders. He compromised all the rest of his life, risked his signature without even knowing if he could meet it; and, frightened by the pains yet to come, by the black misery which was about to fall upon him, by the prospect of all the physical privations and of all the moral tortures which he was to suffer, he went to get the new necklace, putting down upon the merchant's counter thirty-six thousand francs.

When Mme. Loisel took back the necklace, Mme. Forestier said to her, with a chilly manner:

"You should have returned it sooner, I might have needed it."

She did not open the case, as her friend had so much feared. If she detected the substitution, what would she have thought, what would she have said? Would she not have taken Mme. Loisel for a thief?

Mme. Loisel now knew the horrible existence of the needy. She took her part, moreover, all of a sudden, with heroism. That dreadful debt must be paid. She would pay it. They dismissed their servant; they changed their lodgings; they rented a garret under the roof.

She came to know what heavy housework meant and the odious cares of the kitchen. She washed the dishes, using her rosy nails on the greasy pots and pans. She washed the dirty linen, the shirts, and the dishcloths, which she dried upon a line; she carried the slops down to the street every morning, and carried up the water, stopping for breath at every landing. And, dressed like a woman of the people, she went to the fruiterer, the grocer, the butcher, her basket on her arm, bargaining, insulted, defending her miserable money sou by sou.

Each month they had to meet some notes, renew others, obtain more time.

Her husband worked in the evening making a fair copy of some tradesman's accounts, and late at night he often copied manuscript for five sous a page.

And this life lasted ten years.

At the end of ten years they had paid everything, everything, with the rates of usury, and the accumulations of the compound interest.

Mme. Loisel looked old now. She had become the woman

of impoverished households—strong and hard and rough. With frowsy hair, skirts askew, and red hands, she talked loud while washing the floor with great swishes of water. But sometimes, when her husband was at the office, she sat down near the window, and she thought of that gay evening of long ago, of that ball where she had been so beautiful and so fêted.

What would have happened if she had not lost that necklace? Who knows? Who knows? How life is strange and changeful! How little a thing is needed for us to be lost or to be saved!

But, one Sunday, having gone to take a walk in the Champs-Élysées to refresh herself from the labors of the week, she suddenly perceived a woman who was leading a child. It was Mme. Forestier, still young, still beautiful, still charming.

Mme. Loisel felt moved. Was she going to speak to her? Yes, certainly. And now that she had paid, she was going to tell her all about it. Why not?

She went up.

"Good day, Jeanne."

The other, astonished to be familiarly addressed by this plain good wife, did not recognize her at all, and stammered:

"But—madame!—I do not know— You must have mistaken."

"No. I am Mathilde Loisel."

Her friend uttered a cry.

"Oh, my poor Mathilde! How you are changed!"

"Yes, I have had days hard enough, since I have seen you, days wretched enough—and that because of you!"

"Of me! How so?"

"Do you remember that diamond necklace which you lent me to wear at the ministerial ball?"

"Yes. Well?"

"Well, I lost it."

"What do you mean? You brought it back."

"I brought you back another just like it. And for this we have been ten years paying. You can understand that it was not easy for us, us who had nothing. At last it is ended, and I am very glad."

Mme. Forestier had stopped.

"You say that you bought a necklace of diamonds to replace mine?"

"Yes. You never noticed it, then! They were very like."

And she smiled with a joy which was proud and naive at once.

Mme. Forestier, strongly moved, took her two hands.

"Oh, my poor Mathilde! Why, my necklace was paste. It was worth at most five hundred francs!"

Reading for Understanding _____

Main Idea

1. The main idea, or theme, of the story is best represented by which of the following quotations?
    (a) She had become the woman of impoverished households—strong and hard and rough.
    (b) She was one of those pretty and charming girls who are sometimes, as if by a mistake of destiny, born in a family of clerks.
    (c) The day of the ball arrived. Mme. Loisel made a great success.
    (d) How little a thing is needed for us to be lost or to be saved.

Details

2. Mathilde knew Mme. Forestier   (a) in the Ministry of Public Instruction   (b) in school   (c) as the owner of a jewelry shop   (d) as a cousin on her mother's side.

3. The necklace was made of   (a) pearls   (b) rubies   (c) diamonds   (d) sapphires.

4. After the ball, Mathilde was ashamed of her   (a) wraps   (b) shoes   (c) dress   (d) necklace.

5. The period of time it took to repay all loans was
   (a) six months   (b) a year   (c) five years   (d) ten
   years.

Inferences

6. At the beginning of the story, Mathilde's major activity
   seemed to be   (a) doing housework   (b) daydreaming
   (c) assisting her husband   (d) visiting her wealthy
   friend.

7. Mathilde's husband might best be described as
   (a) dashing and handsome   (b) simple and honorable
   (c) tricky and unreliable   (d) bitter and hateful.

8. To get her husband to spend his money on her dress,
   Mathilde   (a) made him feel guilty   (b) flattered him
   (c) refused to cook for him   (d) said she'd make the
   dress herself.

9. In trying to find a substitute to match the lost necklace,
   the Loisels   (a) gave up after one or two tries
   (b) consulted Mme. Forestier's husband   (c) visited
   many jewelry shops without success   (d) bought an
   inexpensive copy.

10. Throughout the story, Mathilde's husband showed
    (a) jealousy of his wife's beauty   (b) a disregard for
    Mathilde's feelings   (c) a spirit of self-sacrifice
    (d) a desire to cheat Mme. Forestier.

Order of Events

11. Arrange the items in the order in which they occurred.
    Use letters only.
    A. Mathilde tells Mme. Forestier about the replacement
       of the necklace.
    B. M. Loisel uses his precious money for a dress for
       Mathilde.
    C. Mathilde is the hit of the ball.
    D. Mme. Forestier tells the truth about the necklace.
    E. Mathilde borrows the necklace for the ball.

Outcomes

12. If Mathilde had told Mme. Forestier immediately about
    the lost necklace, probably   (a) she would have had to
    replace the necklace at 36,000 francs anyway
    (b) Mme. Forestier would have told her that the necklace
    was inexpensive   (c) Mme. Forestier would have had
    Mathilde brought to court   (d) M. Loisel might have
    been blamed for the loss.

Cause and Effect

13. If Mathilde had not lost the necklace, ten years later she
    (a) would not have looked old and coarse   (b) might
    have been as wealthy as Mme. Forestier   (c) would have
    been divorced from M. Loisel   (d) would have become a
    famous beauty in town.

Fact or Opinion

Tell whether the following is a fact or an opinion.
14. The Loisels could have afforded the loss of a necklace
    worth 500 francs without going into debt.

Author's Role

15. The attitude of the author toward Mathilde was one of
    (a) bitter disapproval   (b) scornful dismissal
    (c) unrestrained approval   (d) deep sympathy.

Words in Context _____

1. She had no *dowry*, no expectations, no means of being
   known, understood, loved, wedded, by any rich and distinguished man.
   Dowry (191) means   (a) money that a bride brings to a

marriage (b) a mortgage on the family homestead
(c) a particular talent that can be profitable
(d) a famous member in a family.

2. With women there is neither *caste* nor rank.
    Caste (191) means (a) natural ability (b) social
    class (c) extraordinary charm (d) elaborate
    costume.

3. Natural fineness, instinct for what is elegant, *suppleness* of
    wit ... make from women of the people the equals of the
    very greatest ladies.
    Suppleness (191) means (a) lack (b) dullness
    (c) certain amount (d) flexibility.

4. The sight of the little Breton peasant aroused in her
    regrets which were despairing, and *distracted* dreams.
    Distracted (191) means (a) repeated (b) common-
    place (c) unsettled (d) pleasant.

5. She thought of the *coquettish* perfumed boudoirs made for
    talks at five o'clock with intimate friends.
    Coquettish (191) means (a) flirting (b) honest
    (c) painted (d) tiring.

6. Instead of being delighted, as her husband hoped, she
    threw the invitation on the table with *disdain*.
    Disdain (192) means (a) speed (b) hope
    (c) scorn (d) a shout.

7. "Give your card to some *colleague* whose wife is better
    equipped than I."
    Colleague (193) means (a) clerk (b) dress designer
    (c) fellow worker (d) interested person.

8. She danced with intoxication in a sort of cloud of happi-
    ness composed of all this *homage*.
    Homage (195) means (a) honor (b) sweet music
    (c) envy (d) jealousy.

9. Then they went from jeweler to jeweler, searching for a
    necklace like the other, consulting their memories, sick
    both of them with *chagrin* and anguish.
    Chagrin (197) means (a) faith (b) disappointment
    (c) mental cruelty (d) fatigue.

10. Frightened by the pains yet to come, by the prospect of all
     the physical *privations* and of all the moral tortures which
     he was to suffer, he went to get the new necklace.
     Privations (198) means   (a) tortures   (b) disappoint-
     ments   (c) reckless spending   (d) hardships.

11. She came to know what heavy housework meant and the
     odious cares of the kitchen.
     Odious (198) means   (a) worrisome   (b) hateful
     (c) tasteless   (d) frequent.

12. She had become the woman of *impoverished* households—
     strong and hard and rough.
     Impoverished (199) means   (a) peasant   (b) satisfied
     (c) honest   (d) poor.

13, 14. With *frowsy* hair, skirts *askew,* and red hands, she
     talked loud while washing the floor with great swishes of
     water.
     Frowsy (199) means   (a) tinted   (b) well-kept
     (c) long and waving   (d) untidy.
     Askew (199) means   (a) crooked   (b) reaching to the
     floor   (c) neatly folded   (d) ballooning outward.

15. And she smiled with a joy which was proud and *naive* at
     once.
     Naive (200) means   (a) restrained   (b) childlike
     (c) scornful   (d) obvious.

Thinking Critically About the Story _____

1. Mathilde is hurt by the difference in social standing be-
    tween herself and Mme. Forestier. Yet how does she feel
    toward the little Breton peasant who did her housework?
    What does that tell about Mathilde herself?

2. What is Mathilde's attitude toward her husband? Which
    one, in your opinion, is the nobler person? Explain.

3. Mathilde is much given to daydreams. Are daydreams
    harmless? Harmful? Can they play a constructive part in
    life? Explain.

4. "How little a thing is needed for us to be lost or to be saved!"

    Do you believe this statement to be true? Can you supply examples from television or from reading to prove your point?

5. Should the Loisels have gone directly to Mme. Forestier upon discovering the loss? Should they have explained what had happened? After all, didn't Mme. Forestier have a great many jewels?

6. What do you think happened next? Did Mme. Forestier sell the necklace and give the Loisels the amount in excess of 500 francs? Or had she already disposed of the necklace, not knowing its value? In a narrative of 200–250 words, continue the story and bring it to another conclusion.

Stories in Words

Calculations (193)   In Latin, a *calculus* is a pebble. In counting, the Romans used a crude kind of abacus, or counting board. Pebbles were used as counters. Thus to calculate is "to add and subtract by using pebbles." A modern calculator has nothing to do with pebbles, but the history of the word recalls the simple origins of *calculate*.

Ecstasy (194)   *Ecstasy* is derived from two Greek roots meaning "to put out of place." At the ball, Mathilde experienced the powerful emotion of joy and was "taken outside herself." Sometimes the word is used negatively. Upon discovering the loss of the necklace, Mathilde experienced an ecstasy of agony—again "taken outside herself."

Intoxication (195)   You have probably met the word *toxic* in *toxic substances:* poisonous, deadly substances. The Latin word for *poison* is *toxicum*. The current word *toxin* means the same thing. *Intoxicate* thus means "to poison." By derivation, intoxication is a poisonous state. Mathilde's condition was not quite so serious, but even so, *her* intoxication had an unhappy result.

A Horseman in the Sky

Ambrose Bierce

◆ **Lifting his eyes to the dizzy altitude of the summit, the officer saw an astonishing sight—a man on horseback riding down into the valley through the air.**

Straight upright sat the rider, in military fashion, with a firm seat in the saddle, a strong clutch upon the rein to hold his charger from too impetuous a plunge. From his bare head his long hair streamed upward, waving like a plume.

Ambrose Bierce is famous for half a dozen unusual short stories, of which "A Horseman in the Sky" is one of the best. Yet his stories are no more unusual than Bierce's own life. As a young man he served in the Civil War and later became a brilliant journalist in San Francisco. For a while, he went to England and made a name for himself as a magazine editor, writer, and publisher. Then he went back to San Francisco and a new career in journalism. There he also wrote poems, short stories, and an epic romance. After that he became a Washington correspondent for Hearst newspapers and tried many new challenges. He collected a series of witty definitions for *The Devil's Dictionary* and wrote *Fantastic Fables* about contemporary economics and politics.

All this success was not enough for Ambrose Bierce. He was restless. He was tired of fame and civilization. In 1913, he went off to war-torn Mexico . . . and was never seen again. Like so many of his stories, Bierce's life had a surprise ending worthy of his own pen.

"A Horseman in the Sky" has but the sketchiest of plots and little characterization. It is the slow development and rich description that make the story unforgettable, with a surprise ending worthy of the best.

A Horseman in the Sky

One sunny afternoon in the autumn of the year 1861 a soldier lay in a clump of laurel by the side of a road in western Virginia. He lay at full length upon his stomach, his feet resting upon the toes, his head upon the left forearm. His extended right hand loosely grasped his rifle. But for the somewhat methodical disposition of his limbs and a slight rhythmic movement of the cartridge box at the back of his belt, he might have been thought to be dead. He was asleep at his post of duty. But if detected he would be dead shortly afterward, death being the just and legal penalty of his crime.

The clump of laurel in which the criminal lay was in the angle of a road which, after ascending southward a steep acclivity to that point, turned sharply to the west, running along the summit for perhaps one hundred yards. There it turned southward again and went zigzagging downward through the forest. At the salient of that second angle was a large flat rock, jutting out northward, overlooking the deep valley from which the road ascended. The rock capped a high cliff; a stone dropped from its outer edge would have fallen sheer downward one thousand feet to the tops of the pines. The angle where the soldier lay was on another spur of the same cliff. Had he been awake he would have commanded a view, not only of the short arm of the road and the jutting rock, but of the entire profile of the cliff below it. It might well have made him giddy to look.

The country was wooded everywhere except at the bottom of the valley to the northward, where there was a small natural meadow, through which flowed a stream scarcely visible from the valley's rim. This open ground looked hardly larger than an ordinary dooryard, but was really several acres in extent. Its green was more vivid than that of the enclosing forest. Away beyond it rose a line of giant cliffs similar to those upon which we are supposed to stand in our survey of the savage scene, and through which the road had somehow made its climb to the summit. The configuration of the valley, indeed, was such that from this point of observation it seemed entirely shut in, and one could but have wondered how the road which found a way out of it had found a way into it, and whence came and whither went the waters of the stream that parted the meadow more than a thousand feet below.

No country is so wild and difficult but men will make it a theater of war; concealed in the forest at the bottom of that military rattrap, in which half a hundred men in possession of the exits might have starved an army to submission, lay five regiments of Federal infantry. They had marched all the previous day and night, and were resting. At nightfall they would take to the road again, climb to the place where their unfaithful sentinel now slept, and descending the other slope of the ridge fall upon a camp of the enemy at about midnight. Their hope was to surprise it, for the road led to the rear of it. In case of failure, their position would be perilous in the extreme; and fail they surely would should accident or vigilance apprise the enemy of the movement.

II

The sleeping sentinel in the clump of laurel was a young Virginian named Carter Druse. He was the son of wealthy parents, an only child, and had known such ease and cultivation and high living as wealth and taste were able to command in the mountain country of western Virginia. His home was but a few miles from where he now lay. One morning he had risen from the breakfast table and said, quietly but gravely, "Father, a Union regiment has arrived at Grafton. I am going to join it."

The father lifted his leonine head, looked at the son a moment in silence, and replied, "Well, go, sir, and whatever may occur, do what you conceive to be your duty. Virginia, to which you are a traitor, must get on without you. Should we both live to the end of the war, we will speak further of the matter. Your mother, as the physician has informed you, is in a most critical condition; at the best she cannot be with us longer than a few weeks, but that time is precious. It would be better not to disturb her."

So Carter Druse, bowing reverently to his father, who returned the salute with a stately courtesy that masked a breaking heart, left the home of his childhood to go soldiering. By conscience and courage, by deeds of devotion and daring, he soon commended himself to his fellows and his officers; and it was to these qualities and to some knowledge of the country that he owed his selection for his present perilous duty at the extreme outpost. Nevertheless, fatigue had been stronger than resolution, and he had fallen asleep. What good or bad angel came in a dream to rouse him from his state of crime, who shall say? Without a movement, without a sound, in the profound silence and the languor of the late afternoon, some invisible messenger of fate touched with unsealing finger the eyes of his consciousness—whispered into the ear of his spirit the mysterious awakening word which no human lips ever have spoken, no human memory ever has recalled. He quietly raised his forehead from his arm and looked between the masking stems of the laurels, instinctively closing his right hand about the stock of his rifle.

His first feeling was a keen artistic delight. On a colossal pedestal, the cliff—motionless at the extreme edge of the capping rock and sharply outlined against the sky—was an equestrian statue of impressive dignity. The figure of the man sat on the figure of the horse, straight and soldierly, but with the repose of a Grecian god carved in the marble which limits the suggestion of activity. The gray costume harmonized with its aerial background; the metal of accouterment and caparison was softened and subdued by the shadow; the animal's skin had no points of highlight. A carbine strikingly foreshortened lay across the pommel of the saddle, kept in place by the right hand grasping it at the "grip"; the left hand, holding the bridle rein, was invisible. In silhouette against the sky the profile of the horse was cut with the sharpness of a cameo; it looked across the heights of air to the confronting cliffs beyond. The face of the rider, turned slightly away, showed only an outline of temple and beard; he was looking downward to the bottom of the valley. Magnified by its lift against the sky and by the soldier's testifying sense of the formidableness of a near enemy, the group appeared of heroic, almost colossal, size.

For an instant Druse had a strange, half-defined feeling that he had slept to the end of the war and was looking upon a noble work of art reared upon that eminence to commemorate the deeds of a heroic past of which he had been an inglorious part. The feeling was dispelled by a slight movement of the group: the horse, without moving its feet, had drawn its body slightly back from the verge; the man remained immobile as before. Broad awake and keenly alive to the significance of the situation, Druse now brought the butt of his rifle against his cheek by cautiously pushing the barrel forward through the bushes, cocked the piece, and glancing through the sights covered a vital spot of the horseman's breast. A touch upon the trigger and all would have been well with Carter Druse. At that instant the horseman turned his head and looked in the direction of his concealed foeman—seemed to look into his very face, into his eyes, into his brave, compassionate heart.

Is it then so terrible to kill an enemy in war—an enemy who has surprised a secret vital to the safety of one's self and comrades—an enemy more formidable for his knowledge than all his army for its numbers? Carter Druse grew pale; he shook in every limb, turned faint, and saw the statuesque group before him as black figures, rising, falling, moving unsteadily in arcs of circles in a fiery sky. His hand fell away from his weapon, his head slowly dropped until his face rested on the leaves in which he lay. This courageous gentleman and hardy soldier was near swooning from intensity of emotion.

It was not for long; in another moment his face was raised from earth, his hands resumed their places on the rifle, his forefinger sought the trigger; mind, heart, and eyes were clear, conscience and reason sound. He could not hope to capture that enemy; to alarm him would but send him dashing to his camp with his fatal news. The duty of the soldier was plain: the man must be shot dead from ambush—without warning, without a moment's spiritual preparation, with never so much as an unspoken prayer, he must be sent to his account. But no—there is a hope; he may have discovered nothing—perhaps

he is but admiring the sublimity of the landscape. If permitted, he may turn and ride carelessly away in the direction whence he came. Surely it will be possible to judge at the instant of his withdrawing whether he knows. It may well be that his fixity of attention—Druse turned his head and looked through the deeps of air downward, as from the surface to the bottom of a translucent sea. He saw creeping across the green meadow a sinuous line of figures of men and horses—some foolish commander was permitting the soldiers of his escort to water their beasts in the open, in plain view from a dozen summits!

Druse withdrew his eyes from the valley and fixed them again upon the group of man and horse in the sky, and again it was through the sights of his rifle. But this time his aim was at the horse. In his memory, as if they were a divine mandate, rang the words of his father at their parting: "Whatever may occur, do what you conceive to be your duty." He was calm now. His teeth were firmly but not rigidly closed; his nerves were as tranquil as a sleeping babe's—not a tremor affected any muscle of his body; his breathing, until suspended in the act of taking aim, was regular and slow. Duty had conquered; the spirit had said to the body: "Peace, be still." He fired.

III

An officer of the Federal force, who in a spirit of adventure or in quest of knowledge had left the hidden bivouac in the valley, and with aimless feet had made his way to the lower edge of a small open space near the foot of the cliff, was considering what he had to gain by pushing his exploration further. At a distance of a quarter-mile before him, but apparently at a stone's throw, rose from its fringe of pines the gigantic face of rock, towering to so great a height above him that it made him giddy to look up to where its edge cut a sharp, rugged line against the sky. It presented a clean, vertical profile against a background of blue sky to a point half the way down, and of distant hills, hardly less blue, thence to the tops of the trees at its base. Lifting his eyes to the dizzy altitude of its summit the officer saw an astonishing sight—a man on horseback riding down into the valley through the air!

Straight upright sat the rider, in military fashion, with a firm seat in the saddle, a strong clutch upon the rein to hold his charger from too impetuous a plunge. From his bare head his long hair streamed upward, waving like a plume. His hands were concealed in the cloud of the horse's lifted mane. The animal's body was as level as if every hoof-stroke encountered the resistant earth. Its motions were those of a wild gallop, but even as the officer looked they ceased, with all the legs thrown sharply forward as in the act of alighting from a leap. But this was a flight!

Filled with amazement and terror by this apparition of a horseman in the sky—half believing himself the chosen scribe of some new Apocalypse, the officer was overcome by the intensity of his emotions; his legs failed him and he fell. Almost at the same instant he heard a crashing sound in the trees—a sound that died without an echo—and all was still.

The officer rose to his feet, trembling. The familiar sensation of an abraded shin recalled his dazed faculties. Pulling himself together he ran rapidly obliquely away from the cliff to a point distant from its foot; thereabout he expected to find his man; and thereabout he naturally failed. In the fleeting instant of his vision his imagination had been so wrought upon by the apparent grace and ease and intention of the marvelous performance that it did not occur to him that the line of march of aerial cavalry is directly downward, and that he could find the objects of his search at the very foot of the cliff. A half hour later he returned to camp.

This officer was a wise man; he knew better than to tell an incredible truth. He said nothing of what he had seen. But when the commander asked him if in his scout he had learned anything of advantage to the expedition he answered:

"Yes, sir. There is no road leading down into this valley from the southward."

The commander, knowing better, smiled.

IV

After firing his shot, Private Carter Druse reloaded his rifle and resumed his watch. Ten minutes had hardly passed when a Federal sergeant crept cautiously to him on hands and knees. Druse neither turned his head nor looked at him, but lay without motion or sign of recognition.

"Did you fire?" the sergeant whispered.

"Yes."

"At what?"

"A horse. It was standing on yonder rock—pretty far out. You see it is no longer there. It went over the cliff."

The man's face was white, but he showed no other sign of emotion. Having answered, he turned away his eyes and said no more. The sergeant did not understand.

"See here, Druse," he said, after a moment's silence, "it's no use making a mystery. I order you to report. Was there anybody on the horse?"

"Yes."

"Well?"

"My father."

The sergeant rose to his feet and walked away. "Good God!" he said.

Reading for Understanding _____

Main Idea

1. Which of the following best summarizes the main idea of the story?
    (a) Military strategy is a very difficult study to understand.
    (b) There were many cruel episodes in the Civil war.
    (c) In the conflict between duty and family affection, duty won.
    (d) In war, it's a good idea to win the high ground.

Details

2. The purpose of the Federal campaign was to (a) get new supplies   (b) win control of a railroad (c) surprise the enemy   (d) try out new recruits.

3. Carter Druse was a   (a) Confederate officer   (b) civilian   (c) traitor to the Union   (d) Virginian.

4. Druse's mother was   (a) critically ill   (b) proud of Carter's decision   (c) divorced from his father (d) a Union sympathizer.

5. The horseman in the sky was observed by   (a) a Confederate sharpshooter   (b) a Federal officer   (c) a civilian on the mountain   (d) the commander.

Inferences

6. The Union forces could be said to be   (a) in a risky position   (b) perfectly in control of the mountains (c) always on the alert   (d) less courageous than the Confederate forces.

7. The father's advice to Carter Druse was   (a) angry and excited   (b) honorable but sorrowful   (c) insulting and thoughtless   (d) pleased but uncertain.

8. The reason for Druse's awakening at just the right moment was   (a) a noise in the camp below   (b) the blast of a horn on the ridge   (c) an insect bite on his leg   (d) not really explained.

9. Carter Druse grew pale when he   (a) saw the face of the horseman   (b) realized he had been sleeping on duty   (c) left his post   (d) fired the shot at the horseman.

10. "The march of aerial cavalry is directly downward" (page 213) is another way of saying that   (a) different cavalry regiments have different formations   (b) a foolish commander watered the horses in plain sight   (c) there was no road leading down into the valley   (d) the horseman fell down directly to his death.

Order of Events

11. Arrange the items in the order in which they occurred. Use letters only.
    A. The horseman plunges to his death.
    B. Carter Druse tells his father about joining the Union forces.
    C. Carter Druse falls asleep at his post.
    D. A foolish Union commander exposes his men and beasts in the open.
    E. Carter decides to fire.

Outcomes

12. At the end of the story after the sergeant walked away, he probably   (a) told Carter he had made a great mistake   (b) asked to be transferred to another unit   (c) immediately went to the bottom of the cliff   (d) told his commanding officer about the shot.

Cause and Effect

13. If the horseman had not seen the exposed Union soldiers, (a) Carter might not have shot him   (b) he would have

gone over to the Union side (c) Carter would have deserted the Union forces for the Confederacy (d) the nervous horse might have jumped anyway.

Fact or Opinion

Tell whether the following is a fact or an opinion.
14. Carter Druse did the right thing in killing his father.

Author's Role

15. The style of the author might be characterized as (a) nervous and jumpy (b) leisurely but effective (c) light and hilarious (d) critical and unfavorable.

Words in Context _____

1, 2. But for the somewhat *methodical disposition* of his limbs and a slight rhythmic movement of the cartridge box at the back of his belt, he might have been thought to be dead.
Methodical (207) means (a) strange (b) orderly (c) unnatural (d) jumbled.
Disposition (207) means (a) personality quirk (b) sickness (c) arrangement (d) appearance.
  3. The *configuration* of the valley, indeed, was such that from this point of observation it seemed entirely shut in.
Configuration (208) means (a) shape (b) height (c) roads (d) low spot.
4, 5, 6. In case of failure, their position would be *perilous* in the extreme; and fail they surely would should accident or *vigilance apprise* the enemy of the movement.
Perilous (208) means (a) secure (b) foolish (c) careless (d) risky.
Vigilance (208) means (a) watchfulness (b) treason (c) disaster (d) bad weather.
Apprise (208) means (a) impress (b) conceal (c) inform (d) welcome.

7, 8. The father lifted his *leonine* head, looked at the son a
moment in silence, and replied, "Well, go, sir, and whatever may occur, do what you *conceive* to be your duty."
Leonine (208) means   (a) white   (b) like a lion
(c) finely shaped   (d) weary.
Conceive (208) means   (a) read   (b) hope   (c) hint
(d) understand.

9. Nevertheless, fatigue had been stronger than *resolution*.
Resolution (209) means   (a) wakefulness
(b) determination   (c) fear   (d) anxiety.

10. He quietly raised his forehead from his arm and looked
between the masking stems of the laurels, *instinctively*
closing his right hand about the stock of his rifle.
Instinctively (209) means   (a) hurriedly and grimly
(b) without thinking   (c) loosely but effectively
(d) with great speed.

11. The figure of the man sat on the figure of the horse,
straight and soldierly, with the *repose* of a Grecian god.
Repose   (209) means   (a) easy calm   (b) slight
haste   (c) clever handling   (d) obvious vigor.

12. In silhouette against the sky the profile of the horse was
cut with the sharpness of a *cameo*.
Cameo (209) means   (a) knife   (b) photograph
(c) carved gem   (d) paintbrush.

13, 14. Druse had a strange, half-defined feeling that he had
slept to the end of the war and was looking upon a noble
work of art reared upon that *eminence* to commemorate
the deeds of a heroic past of which he had been an
inglorious part.
Eminence (210 means   (a) height   (b) meadow
(c) base   (d) ground.
Inglorious (210) means   (a) famous   (b) proud
(c) hopeless   (d) unimportant.

15. The horse, without moving its feet, had drawn its body
slightly backward from the verge; the man remained
immobile as before.
Immobile (210) means   (a) restless   (b) cold
(c) curious   (d) motionless.

16. At that instant the horseman turned his head and looked
    in the direction of his concealed foeman—seemed to look
    into his very face, into his eyes, into his brave,
    compassionate heart.
    Compassionate (210) means   (a) excitable
    (b) sympathetic   (c) victorious   (d) hostile.

17. This courageous gentleman and hardy soldier was near
    swooning from intensity of emotion.
    Swooning (210) means   (a) tripping   (b) laughing
    (c) weeping   (d) fainting.

18. Perhaps he is but admiring the *sublimity* of the landscape.
    Sublimity (211) means   (a) appearance   (b) hills and
    valleys   (c) magnificence   (d) twists and turns.

19. Druse turned his head and looked through the deeps of air
    downward, as from the surface to the bottom of a
    translucent sea.
    Translucent (211) means   (a) cold and muddy
    (b) allowing light to pass through   (c) filled with
    seaweed   (d) inhabited by many sea creatures.

20. He saw creeping across the green meadow a *sinuous* line
    of figures of men and horses.
    Sinuous (211) means   (a) winding   (b) irregular
    (c) lengthy   (d) disorganized.

21. Not a *tremor* affected any muscle of his body.
    Tremor (212) means   (a) pain   (b) regret
    (c) trembling   (d) comfort.

22. Straight upright sat the rider, with a strong clutch upon
    the rein to hold his charger from too *impetuous* a plunge.
    Impetuous (212) means   (a) sudden   (b) rash
    (c) rapid   (d) uncertain.

23. Filled with amazement and terror by this *apparition* of a
    horseman in the sky, the officer was overcome by the
    intensity of his emotions.
    Apparition (212) means   (a) brief episode   (b) emo-
    tional experience   (c) keen observation   (d) strange
    figure.

24. The familiar sensation of an *abraded* shin recalled his
    dazed faculties.

Abraded (213) means   (a) scraped   (b) sunburned
(c) itchy   (d) smooth.

25. Pulling himself together he ran rapidly *obliquely* away
from the cliff to a point distant from its foot.
Obliquely (213) means   (a) fearfully   (b) at an angle
(c) without looking back   (d) silently.

Thinking Critically About the Story _____

1. What evidence does the story supply to suggest that Carter
Druse made his decision after much soul searching? What
two things finally influenced him to shoot?
2. Why did Druse aim at the horse instead of the man?
3. Why does the author start the story with a sleeping sentry?
How does this provide a good introduction to Carter?

Stories in Words _____

Colossal (209)   Once upon a time, in the harbor of Rhodes, a
gigantic bronze statue more than 100 feet high dominated
the landscape. It was called the *Colossus of Rhodes*. The
statue was one of the Seven Wonders. *Colossal* thus describes anything especially large.

Ambush (210)   An ambush is a surprise attack. What better
place for such an attack than a heavily wooded area that
conceals the attackers? The word is derived from the Latin
in and *boscus* ("woods"). A prime example of ambush is a
surprise attack "in the woods."

Pommel (209)   The knob on a saddle and the knob at the end of
some swords are both identified by the word *pommel*. It
comes from the Latin *pomum* ("apple"). What connection
is there between the objects and an apple? Think of their
shapes. They are rounded and firm—like an apple.

A Habit for the Voyage

Robert Edmond Alter

♦ Krueger and the victim were quite alone in the whispering, sea-running night. And the unsuspecting victim thought that he was all alone. It wouldn't take much; just a sudden short rush and a bit of a push, catching Bicker on his side, and propelling him sideways right out into that empty waiting space.

Grinning tightly, Krueger broke into a cat-footed, avid rush.

The tramp steamer leaves the dock with its cargo of bananas and a handful of passengers. The stage is set for a peaceful cruise and a relaxing vacation for the passengers. But not for all. One of the passengers has a deadly assignment; to eliminate one of the other passengers. As a professional assassin, he has made a study of his job. He understands the unconscious habits that reveal our identities even if we prefer them to be unknown. He moves on to the deadly conclusion, ready for anything that might happen.

Here is a story that repays study. All four ingredients—*plot, character, setting,* and *theme*—are neatly woven together. The *plot* moves onward with speed and tension. It cleverly baffles the reader, forcing patience till the very last sentence. The *character* of Krueger is revealed in a dozen little events, as well as in the thoughts we tune in on. The *setting* is crucial, for it limits the action to a steamer, concentrating the tension in a small area. The *theme,* suggesting the importance of habit, is intimately connected with the other elements.

Were the three deadly close calls accidents? Was there a pattern in the events? The final sentence tells all. Don't peek.

A HABIT FOR THE VOYAGE

The moment Krueger stepped aboard the steamer he was aware of a vague sense of something gone wrong. He had never understood the atavism behind these instinctive warnings, but he had had them before and usually he had been right.

He paused at the head of the gangplank, standing stock-still on the little bit of railed deck overlooking the after well deck. Down in the well, the Brazilian stevedores were just finishing with the last of the cargo. The steward was standing just inside a door marked *De Segunda Clase*, with Krueger's shabby suitcase in his hand. He looked back at Krueger with an air of incurious impatience.

Krueger took a last look around, saw nothing out of the ordinary, and stepped across the deck to follow the steward.

It came again—a last split-second premonition of danger—so sharply that he actually flinched. Then, as a black, blurred mass hurtled by his vision, he threw himself to one side, and the object, whatever it was, smacked the deck with an appalling crash, right at his feet.

He shot but one glance at it—a metal deck bucket filled to the brim with nuts and bolts and other nameless, greasy odds and ends. He moved again, stepping quickly to the right, rooting his hand under and around to the back of his raincoat to get at the snub-nosed pistol in his right hip-pocket, staring upward at the shadowy promenade deck just above him and at the railed edge of the boat deck above that.

He couldn't see anyone. Nothing moved up there.

The steward was coming back with a look of shocked disbelief.

"*¡Nombre de Dios, señor! ¿Qué pasa?*"

Krueger realized that the stevedores were also watching

him from below. He quickly withdrew his empty hand from under his coat.

"Some idiot almost killed me with that bucket! That's what happened!"

The steward stared at the loaded bucket wonderingly. "Those deckhands are careless dogs."

Krueger was getting back his breath. The steward was right; it had been an accident, of course.

Krueger was a linguist. He felt perfectly at home with seven languages; it was important in his business. He said, *"Lléveme usted a mi camarote."* The steward nodded and led him down a sickly lit corridor to his second-class stateroom.

It was on the starboard and there wasn't much to it. A verdigris-crusted porthole, a sink on the right, a wardrobe on the left, and one uncomfortable-looking bunk. That was that.

Krueger gave the steward a moderate tip and sat down on the bunk with a sigh, as though prepared to relax and enjoy his voyage. He always maintained a calm, bland air in front of the serving class. Stewards, pursers, waiters, and desk clerks had an annoying way of being able to recall certain little mannerisms about you when questioned later.

The steward said, *"Gracias, señor,"* and closed the door after himself. Krueger stayed where he was for a moment, then he got up and went over to bolt the door. But there was no bolt. He could see the holes where the screws had once been driven into the woodwork of the door, but the bolt had been removed.

That was the trouble with second-class travel. Nothing was ever in its entirety; nothing ever functioned properly. The bunks were lumpy, the hot-water tap ran lukewarm, the portholes always stuck. Krueger had had to put up with this nonsense all his life. The Party's rigorous belief that a penny saved was a penny earned was frequently an annoying pain in the neck to Krueger. Still—they were his best clients.

He took a paper matchbook from his pocket and wedged it under the door. It just did the trick. He opened his case and got out a roll of adhesive tape, cut four eight-inch strips, then got down on his knees and placed his pistol up underneath the sink and taped it there. Second-class stewards also had a bad habit of going through your things when you were out of your compartment.

He never relied upon a firearm for his work. It was messy and much too obvious. He was a man who arranged innocent-looking accidents. The pistol was purely a weapon of self-defense, in case there was a hitch and he had to fight his way out, which had happened more than once in his checkered career.

He was fifty-three, balding, inclined to be stout, and had a face as bland as a third-rate stockbroker's, unless you looked close at his eyes, which he seldom allowed anyone to do. He had worked at his trade for thirty years. He was an assassin.

He sat back in his bunk and thought about the man he was going to kill aboard this ship.

Unconsciously his right hand went up to his ear and he began to tug at the lobe gently. Catching himself at it, he hurriedly snatched his hand away. That was a bad habit with him, one that he had to watch. They were dangerous in his line of work, bad habits, exceedingly dangerous. They pinpointed you, gave you away, gave an enemy agent a chance to spot you. It was like walking around in public wearing a sign reading: *I Am Krueger, the Assassin!*

He remembered only too vividly what had happened to his old friend Delchev. *He* had unconsciously developed a bad habit—the simple, involuntary gesture of tugging his tie knot and collar away from his Adam's apple with his forefinger. Through the years the word had gotten around; the habit had been noted and renoted. It went into all the dossiers on Delchev in all of the world's many secret service files. He was earmarked by his habit. No matter what alias or disguise or cover he adopted, sooner or later his habit gave him away. And they had nailed him in the end.

Krueger had known of another agent who used to break cigarettes in half, and still another who picked his ear, always the same ear. Both dead now—by arranged accidents.

And there was one colorful fellow who went by so many aliases that he was simply referred to by those in the business as Mister M. Krueger had always felt that he could have tracked M down within six months, had someone offered to make it worth his while. Because there was a notation in the dossiers on M of a bad habit that simply screamed for attention. M always tabbed himself by marking paper matchbooks with his thumbnail, orderly spaced little indentations all up and down the four edges.

Well, at least tugging your earlobe wasn't that bad. But it was bad enough and Krueger knew it. He must be more attentive to his idiosyncrasies in the future. He had to weed all mannerisms out of his character until he became as bland as a mud wall.

The distant clang of a ship's bell reached him. The deck began to vibrate. Then the engines went astern with a rattle that he felt up his spine. A pause and then the engines went ahead, throbbing peacefully.

All right. Time to go to work. Time to view the future victim.

The dining room adjoined the saloon and they were both very dingy affairs. Cramped, too. And you could see rust streaks down the white walls at the corners of the windows. It all added up to greasy, overseasoned, poorly prepared food. But Krueger remained calm and benign; never call attention to yourself by being a complainer.

He sandwiched himself between a fat lady and a Latin priest, picked up his napkin and started to tuck it in his collar, but caught himself in time and put it on his lap instead.

Watch it; watch that sort of thing. You were the napkin-in-the-collar type on the last assignment. Never repeat the same mannerisms! He smiled at the man across the table, saying, "Pass the menu if you will, please."

The man addressed was an ineffectual-looking little fellow of about forty, with thinning hair and spectacles. His name was Amos Bicker and he was slated for a fatal accident—arranged by Krueger.

Krueger studied him surreptitiously. He certainly didn't look like the sort who needed killing. He had that civil-service-employee aspect. However, some way or another, innocent or not, he must have placed himself in this position of jeopardy by getting in the Party's path. Krueger's instructions had called for Immediate Elimination. So be it. Now for the means . . .

He caught his hand halfway to his ear. *Dammit!* He carried the gesture through, switching its course to scratch the back of his neck. Then he studied the menu. Two of his favorites were there: oyster cocktail and New York cut. He ordered them, then turned to the priest, trying him first in Spanish, which worked. Actually he was thinking about the man across the table, Bicker, and the permanent removal of same.

Krueger always favored obvious accidents. So, when aboard ships, man overboard. This could be handled in a variety of ways. One, make friends with the victim, suggest a late stroll along the promenade deck; then a quick judo blow and . . . Two, again make friends and (if the victim were a drinking man) drink him under the table, and then . . . Or three (and this method had great appeal to Krueger, because it eliminated public observance of his contact with the victim) slip into the victim's room in the wee hours of the morning, and jab him with a small syringe which induced quick and total unconsciousness, and after that . . . well, what followed was simple enough. Man overboard.

The steward brought Krueger his oyster cocktail. Krueger reached for his small fork and gave a start. Something was rubbing his left leg under the table. He leaned back in his chair and raised the cloth. A mangy-looking old cat—ship's cat, probably—was busy stropping himself against Krueger's thick leg.

"Kitty, kitty," Krueger said. He loved animals. Had he led a more sedentary life, he would have had a home, and the home would have been filled with pets. And a wife too, of course.

A minor ship's officer appeared in the starboard doorway. "¿Dónde está Señor Werfel?" he asked at large.

"Here!" Krueger called. That was one thing he never slipped on; he could pick up and drop an alias like the snap of the fingers.

"The captain wishes to see you for a moment, señor."

A multitude of why's came clamoring alive in Krueger's brain. Then he caught the obvious answer and stood up, smiling. The accident with the bucket. It was annoying because the incident called undue attention to him—the steward, the stevedores, this officer, all the passengers, and now the captain.

He met the captain on the starboard wing of the flying bridge. The captain, originally some conglomeration of Mediterranean blood, was profuse in his apologies regarding the

accident. Krueger laughed it off. It was nothing, truly. Those things happened. He wished the captain would put it out of his mind, really. He shook the captain's hand, he accepted the captain's cigar. He even allowed the captain to allow him to inspect the bridge.

He returned to the dining room wearing his professional bland smile. But something had happened during his absence.

The passengers were against the walls. The cook and his assistants and the steward formed a more central ring. But the star of the scene was on the floor in the exact center of the room. It was the ship's cat and it was stretched out to an incredible length and going through the most grotesque mouth-foaming convulsions.

"*Ohh*, Mr. *Wer*fel!" the fat lady who had been seated next to Krueger cried. "I did a *ter*rible thing! No! Come to think of it, it was *for*tunate that I did! Certainly fortunate for *you!*"

"What?" Krueger said sharply, his eyes fixed on the convulsed cat. "What did you do?"

"That *poor* little dear jumped up on your seat after you left. He wanted your oysters! Of course I held him off, but you were so long in returning, and there are so many flies in here, you know.

"You gave him my oysters," Krueger said.

"Yes! I finally did! And before any of us knew it, the poor little thing went into those *awful . . .*"

"I'd better put the poor thing out of its misery," the priest said, coming forward. No one offered to help him.

Krueger stalled for an interval, until the passengers had thinned out, then he led the steward aside. "What was wrong with those oysters?" he demanded.

The steward seemed utterly flabbergasted. "*Señor*, I don't know! Ptomaine, you think? They were canned, of course."

"Let's see the can," Krueger said.

There was a faint scent of taint to the can—if held close to a sensitive nose. Krueger put it down and looked at the steward.

"Anyone else order oysters?

"No, *señor*. Only yourself."

Krueger forced up a smile. "Well, accidents will happen." But he certainly wished there were some way he could have had that can, more especially the dead cat, analyzed. He returned to his stateroom more angry than shaken.

Well, that had been close. Too close. Look at it either way you wanted to, he had been a very lucky man. Of course, it *could* have been ptomaine . . . those things happened, . . . but when you coupled it with the business about the bucket . . .

He went over to the sink and reached under for his gun.

It wasn't there. The tape was there, neatly, but not the gun.

Now wait, he warned himself, pulling at his earlobe. A sailor could have kicked over the bucket by accident. Bolts are frequently missing from doors in rumdum ships like this. Ptomaine does occur in carelessly canned meats. And stewards do rifle compartments.

But the combination still spelled suspicion. Yet, supposing his suspicions were right, what could he do about it? He couldn't disprove that the bucket and food poisoning were accidents; and if questioned about the missing pistol, the steward would appear to be the epitome of innocence.

I must tread carefully, he thought. Very, very carefully, until this business is over. It's just possible that the Party slipped up somewhere on this assignment. Or was it possible that the Party . . .

No! That was absurd. He had always given them faithful service; they *knew* that. And they knew, too, that he was one of the best in the business. No. No. Tugging furiously at his ear. Absurd.

He replaced the matchfolder under the door and, not satisfied with that, put his suitcase before it, flat, and, using the adhesive tape again, taped it to the deck. A man could get in, yes, but he would make a lot of noise doing it. He turned out the light and undressed and got into his bunk.

At first he thought it must be the wool blanket scratching him. Then he remembered that he had a sheet between his body and the blanket. Then he was really sure that it wasn't the blanket, because it moved when he didn't!

He felt the soft rasp of straggly fuzz across his bare belly, crawling sluggishly under the weight of the blanket, as a thing gorged with food. He started to raise the upper edge of the blanket and the thing, whatever it was, scrabbled anxiously toward his navel. He froze, sucking his breath, scared to move a muscle.

It stopped, too, as if waiting for the man to make the first decisive move. He could feel it on his naked stomach, squatting there, poised expectantly. It was alive, whatever it was, . . . it started moving again, he could feel the tiny feet (many of them) scuttling up toward his rib cage, the dry, hairy, fat little legs tickling his goose-fleshed skin, which rippled with loathsome revulsion.

He'd had it. With movements perfectly coordinated out of pure terror, he threw the blanket and sheet aside with his left and took a sweeping thrust across his stomach with his right forearm—as he rolled from the bunk to the deck.

He was up instantly and frantically fumbling for the light switch.

The thing scurried across the white desert of the bottom sheet—a thick-legged tarantula species, hideous, its furry body as fat as a bird's. Krueger snatched up a shoe and beat the thing over and over, and because of the give of the mattress the spider died the long, slow, frenziedly wiggly way.

Krueger threw the shoe aside and went to the sink to wash the clammy sweat from his face.

There was no call-button in the stateroom. He unbarricaded his door and shouted, "*¡Camarero!*"

A few minutes later the steward looked in with a sleepy smile. "*¿Si, señor? ¿Qué desea usted?*"

Krueger pointed at the crushed spider on his bed. The steward came over and looked at it. He made a face and grunted. He didn't seem overly surprised.

"*Si*, it happens. It is the cargo, *señor*. The bananas. They come aboard in the fruit. Some of these *diablos* find their way amidships."

It was the kind of answer Krueger had expected, a reasonable explanation that left no room for argument. But it was getting to be too much. The tarantula was the last straw. He took his hand away from his earlobe and started getting into his clothes.

"*Quisiera hablar con el capitán,*" he said flatly.

The steward shrugged fatalistically. If the unreasonable gringo wanted to bother the captain at this time of night, it was none of his concern.

Krueger shoved by the steward rudely, saying, "I won't need you to find him. You're about as much help as a third leg." He was starting to forget all of his rules.

The captain was no help at all. He repeated all of the old sad-apple excuses: clumsy seamen, careless canning, the bothersome little hazards of shipping on a cargo steamer hauling bananas . . .

"Now look here, Captain," Krueger said, angrily pulling at his ear. "I'm a reasonable man and I'll go along with everyday accidents, as long as they stay within the limits of probability. But all of these accidents have happened to *me*. Within one day."

"What is it that you're trying to say, Mr. Werfel? Surely you're not implying that someone aboard this ship is trying to kill you, are you? You don't have enemies, do you?"

Krueger balked at that. It was a subject that he wanted to stay away from. To get into it would be wading into a thick sea of endless, embarrassing explanations. He hedged.

"I said no such thing, Captain. All I'm saying is that these things keep happening to me aboard your ship, and I expect you to protect me from them."

"Certainly, Mr. Werfel. Let me see . . . yes! I can give you your choice of any of my officers' cabins. My own included. I can even assign a competent man to stay by your—"

"No, no, no!" Krueger said hastily. "That isn't at all necessary, Captain. I don't intend to act like a prisoner aboard this ship. Just assign me to a new cabin, one with a lock and bolt on the door."

Leaving the navigation deck, Krueger decided that he needed a drink. He would go down and see if the saloon was still open. His nerves were getting out of hand and no wonder! The whole game was going very badly, turning sour on him. He was breaking all his time-tested rules, calling more attention to himself than a brass band.

He paused on the companionway overlooking the dark, gusty boat deck. Someone was down there on the deck, someone familiar, leaning at the rail just to the stern of Number One starboard lifeboat.

Krueger took a quick swipe at his face, wiping away the tiny, moist needle-fingers of the sea mist, and came down another step . . . but quietly, ever so quietly. The man on the boat deck was Amos Bicker. He was mooning out at the black rambling sea, his forearms cocked up on the damp rail, his thin back to Krueger.

Krueger came down another quiet step, his narrowed eyes quickly checking out the points of professional interest.

Bicker had taken a position just inside the aft boat davit, to stand in the sheltering lee of the lifeboat's stern. He was leaning about a yard from the extreme corner of the rail; beyond that was nothing. There weren't even guard-chains, only the vacant space through which the davits swung the lifeboat. Below was the open sea.

Made to order. Krueger could finish the business here and now. Then he could concentrate all his wits on his own survival, guard himself against those recurring accidents . . . if that's what they were.

He came down the last step and put both feet on the boat deck.

Krueger and the victim were quite alone in the whispering, sea-running night. And the unsuspecting victim thought that he was all alone. It wouldn't take much; just a sudden short rush and a bit of a push, catching Bicker on his side, and propelling him sideways right out into that empty waiting space.

Grinning tightly, Krueger broke into a cat-footed, avid rush.

All the lifeboats had returned and the captain had received their reports. Shaking his head, he reentered his office and went behind his desk and resumed his seat.

"Well," he said, "this is certainly a sorry business. Unfortunate that you had to be subjected to it, Mr. Bicker."

Amos Bicker was sitting hunched and drawn in his chair facing the desk. The first mate had given him a shot of whisky but it didn't seem to be doing him much good. He was obviously in a bad state of nerves. His hands trembled, his voice too.

"You didn't recover the—uh—"

"Not a sign," the captain said. "Must have gone down like a stone. But please, Mr. Bicker, please do not let it prey upon you. You couldn't have done more than you did. You cried *man overboard* the moment it happened, and you even had the presence of mind to throw over a life ring. You behaved admirably."

Mr. Bicker shivered and wrapped both hands about the empty shot glass. It was just possible, the captain thought, that he was going into shock. "Have a smoke, Mr. Bicker," he offered solicitously, passing over a cigarette box and matches.

Mr. Bicker had trouble lighting up, his hands shook so.

"He must have been mad—deranged," he said finally, hoarsely. "I didn't know the man, had never seen him, except in the dining room this evening. I was just standing there at the rail minding my own business, watching the sea without a thought in my head, and—and then I heard a—a movement, a sort of quiet rushing motion, and I looked around and there he was. Coming right at me! And the look on his face!"

"Yes, yes, Mr. Bicker," the captain said sympathetically, "we quite understand. There's no doubt in anyone's mind that there was something—well, odd, in Mr. Werfel's behavior. I have reason to believe that the poor devil actually thought that someone aboard this ship was trying to kill him. Mental delusion. Lucky for you that you reacted by stepping backwards instead of sideways or he might have taken you over with him."

Mr. Bicker nodded, staring at the carpets. One of his thumbnails absentmindedly was making orderly-spaced little indentations down one edge of the captain's paper matchbook.

Reading for Understanding _____

Main Idea

1. Our habits   (a) are easily broken if proper thought is given to them   (b) become an unconscious part of our appearance and personality   (c) are nearly all negative in their effects upon us   (d) are among the proudest aspects of our personality.

Details

2. Werfel is   (a) the captain of the steamer   (b) the steward   (c) another name for Bicker   (d) another name for Krueger.

3. On the steamer, Krueger traveled   (a) first class   (b) second class   (c) third class   (d) as a member of the crew.

4. The "ineffectual-looking little fellow of about forty, with thinning hair and spectacles" identifies   (a) Bicker   (b) Krueger   (c) the priest   (d) Delchev.

5. The identity of the surviving killer is revealed by   (a) a tugging at the ear   (b) a tugging at a tie knot and

collar   (c) indenting a matchbook   (d) breaking cigarettes in half.

Inferences

6. The metal deck bucket was intended   (a) as a deadly
   weapon   (b) to give Krueger a warning   (c) to play a
   trick on Krueger   (d) to reveal that the steward was the
   assassin.

7. On board ship, Krueger's favorite method of assassination
   was   (a) poisoned oysters   (b) deadly tarantula
   (c) man overboard   (d) none of these.

8. After what he considered the third attempt on his life,
   Krueger   (a) made immediate arrangements to leave
   the ship   (b) gave up his idea of assassinating his victim
   (c) suspected the captain and the steward of working
   together   (d) lost some of his professional calm.

9. In reality, it might be said that Krueger   (a) looked like
   a deadly killer   (b) was himself the intended victim
   (c) planned the poisoning to look like an accident
   (d) had no habits that could identify him.

10. The captain really believed that Krueger was
    (a) slightly disturbed   (b) the ideal passenger   (c) a
    person unfairly treated by the crew   (d) an assassin.

Order of Events

11. Arrange the items in the order in which they occurred.
    Use letters only.
    A. Krueger finds a tarantula in the bed.
    B. Bicker and Krueger sit together at table.
    C. Bicker appears terrified at a terrible accident.
    D. A deck bucket falls from the deck above.
    E. The cat is poisoned.

Outcomes

12. After the story ended,   (a) Krueger turned up in another
    country under another name   (b) Bicker continued his

career as an assassin   (c) the captain was unmasked as an assassin   (d) the steward tugged at his earlobes.

Cause and Effect

13.   When Bicker stood alone at the rail, he was   (a) thinking of his home and family   (b) obviously seasick   (c) signaling to another ship at sea   (d) expecting Krueger's attack.

Fact or Opinion

Tell whether the following is a fact or an opinion.
14.   Bicker was an assassin.

Author's Role

15.   The author's major purpose in writing this story was to   (a) make a study of people's habits   (b) discourage people from boarding tramp steamers   (c) tell a gripping tale   (d) show that good always conquers evil.

Words in Context _____

1, 2.   It came again—a last split-second *premonition* of danger—so sharply that he actually *flinched.*
Premonition (221) means   (a) memory   (b) forewarning   (c) description   (d) disregard.
Flinched (221) means   (a) looked up   (b) gasped sharply   (c) drew back   (d) slipped down.
  3.   The object smacked the deck with an *appalling* crash, right at his feet.
Appalling (221) means   (a) horrifying   (b) noisy   (c) unexpected   (d) unexplained.

4. He always maintained a calm, *bland* air in front of the serving class.
   Bland (222) means   (a) alert and bright
   (b) aggressive and unyielding   (c) curious and questioning   (d) mild and colorless.

5. The Party's *rigorous* belief that a penny saved was a penny earned was frequently an annoying pain in the neck to Krueger.
   Rigorous (222) means   (a) constant   (b) cheap
   (c) strict   (d) often stated.

6. He must be more attentive to his *idiosyncrasies* in the future.
   Idiosyncrasies (224) means   (a) personal mannerisms
   (b) manner of dress   (c) way of speaking
   (d) revealed emotions.

7. But Krueger remained calm and *benign;* never call attention to yourself by being a complainer.
   Benign (224) means   (a) good-natured   (b) efficient
   (c) attentive   (d) eager.

8. The man addressed was an *ineffectual*-looking little fellow of about forty, with thinning hair and spectacles.
   Ineffectual (224) means   (a) bright   (b) unusual
   (c) handsome   (d) weak.

9. Krueger studied him *surreptitiously.*
   Surreptitiously (224) means   (a) intensely   (b) hurriedly   (c) effectively   (d) secretly.

10. However, some way or another, innocent or not, he must have placed himself in this position of *jeopardy* by getting in the Party's path.
    Jeopardy (224) means   (a) responsibility   (b) danger
    (c) honor   (d) sociability.

11. Had he led a more *sedentary* life, he would have had a home, and the home would have been filled with pets.
    Sedentary (225) means   (a) active   (b) settled
    (c) interesting   (d) dull.

12, 13.   The captain, originally some *conglomeration* of Medi-

terranean blood, was *profuse* in his apologies regarding
the accident.
Conglomeration (225) means   (a) reminder
(b) officer   (c) mixture   (d) classifier.
Profuse (225) means   (a) reluctant   (b) late
(c) generous   (d) choosy.

14. It was the ship's cat and it was stretched out to an
incredible length and going through the most *grotesque*
mouth-foaming convulsions.
Grotesque (226) means   (a) loud   (b) unnatural
(c) picturesque   (d) annoying.

15. Crawling sluggishly under the weight of the blanket was a
thing *gorged* with food.
Gorged (228) means   (a) discolored   (b) streaked
(c) ill   (d) crammed.

16. It stopped, too, as if waiting for the man to make the first
decisive move.
Decisive (228) means   (a) definite   (b) rapid
(c) careless   (d) defensive.

17, 18. He could feel the tiny feet (many of them) scuttling up
toward his rib cage, the dry, hairy, fat little legs tickling
his goose-fleshed skin, which rippled with *loathsome
revulsion*.
Loathsome (228) means   (a) tender   (b) disgusting
(c) secret   (d) lively.
Revulsion (228) means   (a) distaste   (b) novelty
(c) deceit   (d) groaning.

19. Because of the give of the mattress the spider died the
long, slow, *frenziedly* wiggly way.
Frenziedly (228) means   (a) swiftly   (b) lowly
(c) monotonously   (d) frantically.

20. The steward shrugged *fatalistically*.
Fatalistically (229) means   (a) without agreeing
(b) with a negative attitude   (c) with acceptance
(d) without hesitation.

21. Bicker had taken a position just inside the aft boat davit,
to stand in the sheltering *lee* of the lifeboat's stern.

Lee (230) means   (a) toward the front   (b) away from the wind   (c) toward the rear   (d) on the sunny side.

22. Then he could concentrate all his wits on his own survival, guard himself against those *recurring* accidents . . . if that's what they were.
   Recurring (230) means   (a) happening again
   (b) nearly fatal   (c) ever-present   (d) upsetting.

23. Grinning tightly, Krueger broke into a cat-footed, *avid* rush.
   Avid (231) means   (a) rapid   (b) silent   (c) careless
   (d) urgent.

24. "Have a smoke, Mr. Bicker," he offered *solicitously*.
   Solicitously (231) means   (a) mechanically
   (b) grudgingly   (c) gruffly   (d) concernedly.

25. "He must have been mad—*deranged*," he said finally, hoarsely.
   Deranged (231) means   (a) insane   (b) cruel
   (c) thoughtless   (d) unfriendly.

Thinking Critically About the Story _____

1. Titles sometimes tell a great deal about a story. Why is "A Habit for the Voyage" a particularly appropriate title for this story? How did the mannerisms of both Bicker and Krueger play a role in the development of the plot?

2. Krueger proudly thinks of himself as "the assassin." But there are two. Who is the second? How does the second prove himself the superior assassin?

3. The reader must infer certain things that are not directly stated. What is the Party? Who works for the Party? Who is

being taken advantage of? How? Might Bicker be a member of the Party?

4. In a good detective story, the clues are fairly presented. What clues are provided in this story? Concerning the "accidents," whom did you suspect? The captain? The steward? The lady at the table? Bicker? Explain.

5. Why is the setting so important to the plot of the story? How are the characters affected by the setting? Why would the story have been different if the setting had been a village, a city, or some other place?

6. Krueger says of himself, "He had to weed all mannerisms out of his character until he became as bland as a mud wall." What happens to this resolution? Why are Krueger's mannerisms finally unimportant to the outcome of the story?

7. Have you ever tried to break a habit? What methods did you try? Did you succeed? Why or why not? In a composition of 200–250 words analyze the importance of good habits and the difficulty of breaking bad ones. Use your own experiences to support your views.

Stories in Words _____

Habit (221)   The history of the word *habit* provides a fascinating insight into human behavior. *Habit* comes from the Latin *habere* meaning "to have, to hold." A habit is something that *takes hold of us*, that hangs on sometimes long after we'd like to be rid of it.

Atavism (221)   This is an uncommon word with an interesting history. *Avus* is the Latin word for *grandfather*. *At* plus *avus* means "beyond the grandfather," or "ancestor." *Atavism* thus means "the appearance in an individual of some characteristic from a distant ancestor." When Krueger was aware of something wrong as soon as he boarded the steamer, some warning from a distant ancestor put him on guard—some *atavism*.

Stevedore (221) This word tells a simple, colorful story. It comes from the Spanish *estivar*, "to ram tight." Thus, a stevedore is a longshoreman who takes cargo from the docks and "rams it tight" into the ship!

The Point of Honor

W. Somerset Maugham

> ◆ **Don Pedro laughed.**
> **"Of course I shall not withdraw. Your father is a**
> **thief and a rascal."**
> **Pepe did the only thing he could do. He sprang**
> **from his chair and with his open hand hit Don Pedro**
> **in the face. The outcome was inevitable.**

There is an old saying that important persons must not only be above evil but also above any *suspicion* of wrongdoing, even if the suspicion is unfounded. The saying is based on an old anecdote about Julius Caesar and his second wife, Pompeia. She was rumored to have had an affair with Publius Claudius, a notorious character. The rumor was untrue, but Caesar divorced his wife because "Caesar's wife should be above suspicion." The expression *Caesar's wife* is attached to a blameless person who suffers unfairly because of her high position.

You will find that the expression has something to do with this story. At what point does a sense of honor become foolish, exaggerated, even deadly? This story suggests some answers. The author examines the relationship between a man and his wife and explores the dangers of excessive pride.

Here is a story in which setting, character, plot, and theme are about equally important. The setting determines the strange code of honor that motivates the Señor and shapes his character. The plot is an outgrowth of that setting. The theme (3) suggests that pride may be an evil, life-destroying force. The device of having an outsider tell the story builds suspense and lets us share with the narrator a growing sense of unease and finally horror.

The ending qualifies the story for inclusion in Unit Three.

240

THE POINT OF HONOR

Some years ago, being engaged on writing a book about Spain in the Golden Age, I had occasion to read again the plays of Calderón. Among others I read one called *El Médico de Su Honra*, which means the Physician of His Honor. It is a cruel play and you can hardly read it without a shudder. But rereading it, I was reminded of an encounter I had had many years before which has always remained in my memory as one of the strangest I have ever had. I was quite young then and I had gone to Seville on a short visit to see the celebration of the Feast of Corpus Christi. It was the height of summer and the heat was terrific. Great sailcloths were drawn across the narrow streets, giving a grateful shade, but in the large squares the sun beat down mercilessly. In the morning I watched the procession. It was splendid and impressive. The crowd knelt down as the Host was solemnly carried past and the Civil Guards in full uniform stood at salute to do homage to the heavenly King. And in the afternoon I joined the dense throng which was making its way to the bullring. The cigarette girls and the sewing girls wore carnations in their dark hair and their young men were dressed in all their best. It was just after the Spanish-American War and the short, embroidered jacket, the skintight trousers and the broad-brimmed, low-crowned hat were still worn. Sometimes the crowd was scattered by a picador on the wretched hack that would never survive the afternoon, and the rider, with conscious pride in his picturesque costume, exchanged pleasantries with the facetious. A long line of carriages, dilapidated and shabby, overfilled with *aficionados*, that is to say fans, drove noisily along.

I went early, for it amused me to see the people gradually filling the vast arena. The cheaper seats in the sun were already packed and it was a curious effect that the countless fans made, like the fluttering of a host of butterflies, as men and women restlessly fanned themselves. In the shade, where I was sitting, the places were taken more slowly, but even there, an hour before the fight began, one had to look rather carefully for a seat. Presently a man stopped in front of me and with a pleasant smile asked if I could make room for him. When he had settled down, I took a sidelong glance at him and noticed that he was well dressed, in English clothes, and looked like a gentleman. He had beautiful hands, small but resolute, with thin, long fingers. Wanting a cigarette, I took out my case and thought it would be polite to offer him one. He gave me a glance and accepted. He had evidently seen that I was a foreigner, for he thanked me in French.

"You are English?" he went on.

"Yes."

"How is it you haven't run away from the heat?"

I explained that I had come on purpose to see the Feast of Corpus Christi.

"After all, it's something you must come to Seville for."

Then I made some casual remark about the vast concourse of people.

"No one would imagine that Spain was bleeding from the loss of all that remained of her Empire and that her ancient glory is now nothing but a name."

"There's a great deal left."

"The sunshine, the blue sky, and the future."

He spoke dispassionately, as though the misfortunes of his fallen country were no concern of his. Not knowing what to reply, I remained silent. We waited. The boxes began to fill up. Ladies in their mantillas of black or white lace entered them and spread their Manila shawls over the front of them so as to form a gay and many-colored drapery. Now and then, when one of them was of particular beauty, a round of applause would greet her appearance and she would smile and bow without embarrassment. At last the president of the bullfight made his entry, the band struck up, and the fighters, all glittering in their satin, in gold and silver, marched swaggering down across the ring. A minute later a great black bull charged in. Carried away by the horrible excitement of the contest I noticed, notwithstanding, that my neighbor remained cool. When a man fell and only escaped by a miracle the horns of the furious beast, and with a gasp thousands sprang to their feet, he remained motionless. The bull was killed and the mules dragged out the huge carcass. I sank back exhausted.

"Do you like bullfighting?" he asked me. "Most English do, though I have noticed that in their own country they say hard enough things about it."

"Can one like something that fills one with horror and loathing? Each time I come to a fight I swear I will never go to another. And yet I do."

"It's a curious passion that leads us to delight in the peril of others. Perhaps it's natural to the human race. The Romans had their gladiators and the moderns their melodramas. It may be that it is an instinct in man to find pleasure in bloodshed and torture."

I did not answer directly.

"Don't you think that the bullfight is the reason why human life is of so little account in Spain?"

"And do you think human life is of any great value?" he asked.

I gave him a quick look, for there was an ironical tone in his voice that no one could have missed, and I saw that his eyes were full of mockery. I flushed a little, for he made me on a sudden feel very young. I was surprised at the change of his expression. He had seemed rather an amiable man, with his large, soft, friendly eyes, but now his face bore a look of sardonic hauteur which was a trifle disquieting. I shrank back into my shell. We said little to one another during the rest of the afternoon, but when the last bull was killed and we all rose to our feet, he shook hands with me and expressed the hope that we might meet again. It was a mere politeness and neither of us, I imagine, thought that there was even a remote possibility of it.

But quite by chance, two or three days later, we did. I was in a quarter of Seville that I did not know very well. I had been that afternoon to the palace of the Duke of Alba which I knew had a fine garden and in one of the rooms a magnificent ceiling reputed to have been made by Moorish captives before the fall of Granada. It was not easy to gain admittance, but I wanted

very much to see it and I thought that now, in the height of
summer when there were no tourists, with two or three pesetas
I might be allowed in. I was disappointed. The man in charge
told me that the house was under repair and no stranger could
visit it without a written permission from the Duke's agent. So,
having nothing else to do, I went to the royal garden of the
Alcázar, the old palace of Don Pedro the Cruel, whose memory
lives still among the people of Seville. It was very pleasant
among the orange trees and cypresses. I had a book with me, a
volume of Calderón, and I sat there for a while and read. Then
I went for a stroll. In the older parts of Seville the streets are
narrow and tortuous. It is delicious to wander along them
under the awnings that stretch above, but not easy to find one's
way. I lost mine. When I had just made up my mind that I had
no notion in which direction to turn I saw a man walking
toward me and recognized my acquaintance of the bullring. I
stopped him and asked whether he could direct me. He
remembered me.

"You'll never find your way," he smiled, turning round.
"I'll walk a little with you until you can't mistake it."

I protested, but he would not listen. He assured me it was
no trouble.

"You haven't gone away then?" he said.

"I'm leaving tomorrow. I've just been to the Duke of Alba's
house. I wanted to see that Moorish ceiling of his, but they
wouldn't let me in."

"Are you interested in Arabic art?"

"Well, yes. I've heard that that ceiling is one of the finest
things in Seville."

"I think I could show you one as good."

"Where?"

He looked at me for a moment reflectively as though
wondering what sort of a person I was. If he was, he evidently
came to a satisfactory decision.

"If you have ten minutes to spare I will take you to it."

I thanked him warmly and we turned back and retraced
our steps. We chatted of indifferent things till we came to a
large house, washed in pale green, with the Arabic look of a
prison, the windows on the street heavily barred, which so
many houses in Seville have. My guide clapped his hands at the

gateway and a servant looked out from a window into the patio, and pulled a cord.

"Whose house is this?"

"Mine."

I was surprised, for I knew how jealously Spaniards guarded their privacy and how little inclined they were to admit strangers into their houses. The heavy iron gate swung open and we walked into the courtyard; we crossed it and went through a narrow passage. Then I found myself suddenly in an enchanted garden. It was walled on three sides, with walls as high as houses; and their old red brick, softened by time, was covered with roses. They clad every inch in wanton, scented luxuriance. In the garden, growing wildly, as if the gardeners had striven in vain to curb the exuberance of nature, were palm trees rising high into the air in their passionate desire for the sun, dark orange trees and trees in flower whose names I did not know, and among them roses and more roses. The fourth wall was a Moorish loggia, with horseshoe arches heavily decorated with tracery, and when we entered this I saw the magnificent ceiling. It was like a little bit of the Alcázar, but it had not suffered the restorations that have taken all the charm from that palace, and the colors were exquisitely tender. It was a gem.

"Believe me, you need not regret that you have not been able to see the Duke's house. Further, you can say that you have seen something that no other foreigner has seen within living memory.

"It's very kind of you to have shown it to me. I'm infinitely grateful."

He looked about him with a pride with which I could sympathize.

"It was built by one of my own ancestors in the time of Don Pedro the Cruel. It is very likely that the King himself more than once caroused under this ceiling with my ancestor."

I held out the book I was carrying.

"I've just been reading a play in which Don Pedro is one of the important characters."

"What is the book?"

I handed it to him and he glanced at the title. I looked about me.

"Of course, what adds to the beauty is that wonderful garden," I said. "The whole impression is incredibly romantic."

The Spaniard was evidently pleased with my enthusiasm. He smiled. I had already noticed how grave his smile was. It hardly dispelled the habitual melancholy of his expression.

"Would you like to sit down for a few minutes and smoke a cigarette?"

"I should love to."

We walked out into the garden and we came upon a lady sitting on a bench of Moorish tiles like those in the gardens of the Alcázar. She was working at some embroidery. She looked up quickly, evidently taken aback to see a stranger, and gave my companion an enquiring stare.

"Allow me to present you to my wife," he said.

The lady gravely bowed. She was very beautiful, with magnificent eyes, a straight nose with delicate nostrils and a pale smooth skin. In her black hair, abundant as with most

Spanish women, there was a broad white streak. Her face was quite unlined and she could not have been more than thirty.

"You have a very lovely garden, Señora," I said because I had to say something.

She gave it an indifferent glance.

"Yes, it is pretty."

I felt suddenly embarrassed. I did not expect her to show me any cordiality and I could not blame her if she thought my intrusion merely a nuisance. There was something about her that I could not quite make out. It was not an active hostility. Absurd as it seemed, since she was a young woman and beautiful, I felt that there was something dead in her.

"Are you going to sit here?" she asked her husband.

"With your permission. Only for a few minutes."

"I won't disturb you."

She gathered her silks and the canvas on which she had been working and rose to her feet. When she stood up I saw that she was rather taller than Spanish women generally are. She gave me an unsmiling bow. She carried herself with a sort of royal composure and her gait was stately. I was flippant in those days and I remember saying to myself that she was not the sort of girl you could very well think of being silly with. We sat down on the multicolored bench and I gave my host a cigarette. I held a match to it. He had still my volume of Calderón in his hands and now he idly turned the pages.

"Which of the plays have you been reading?"

"*El Médico de Su Honra.*"

He gave me a look and I thought I discerned in his large eyes a sardonic glint.

"And what do you think of it?"

"I think it's revolting. The fact is, of course, that the idea is so foreign to our modern notions."

"What idea?"

"The point of honor and all that sort of thing."

I should explain that the point of honor is the mainspring of much of the Spanish drama. It is the nobleman's code that impels a man to kill his wife, in cold blood, not only if she has been unfaithful to him, but even if, however little she was to blame, her conduct has given rise to scandal. In this particular play there is an example of this more deliberate than any I have ever read: the physician of his honor takes vengeance on his wife, though aware that she is innocent, simply as a matter of decorum.

"It's in the Spanish blood," said my friend. "The foreigner must just take it or leave it."

"Oh, come, a lot of water has flowed down the Guadalquivir since Calderón's day. You're not going to pretend that any man would behave like that now."

"On the contrary I pretend that even now a husband who finds himself in such a humiliating and ridiculous position can only regain his self-respect by the offender's death."

I did not answer. It seemed to me that he was pulling a romantic gesture and within me I murmured, Bosh. He gave me an ironic smile.

"Have you ever heard of Don Pedro Aguria?"

"Never."

"The name is not unknown in Spanish history. An ancestor was Admiral of Spain under Philip II and another was bosom friend to Philip IV. By royal command he sat for his portrait to Velásquez."

My host hesitated a moment. He gave me a long, reflective stare before he went on.

"Under the Philips the Agurias were rich, but by the time my friend Don Pedro succeeded his father their circumstances were much reduced. But still he was not poor, he had estates between Cordova and Aguilar, and in Seville his house retained at least traces of its ancient splendor. The little world of Seville was astonished when he announced his engagement to Soledad, the daughter of the ruined Count of Acaba, for though her family was distinguished her father was an old scamp. He was crippled with debts and the shifts he resorted to in order to keep his head above water were none too nice. But Soledad was beautiful and Don Pedro madly in love with her. They were married. He adored her with the vehement passion of which perhaps only a Spaniard is capable. But he discovered to his dismay that she did not love him. She was kind and gentle. She was a good wife and a good housekeeper. She was grateful to him. But that was all. He thought that when she had a child she would change, but the child came, and it made no difference.

The barrier between them that he had felt from the beginning was still there. He suffered. At last he told himself that she had a character too noble, a spirit too delicate, to descend to earthly passion, and he resigned himself. She was too high above him for mortal love."

I moved a little uneasily in my seat. I thought the Spaniard was unduly rhetorical. He went on.

"You know that here in Seville the Opera House is open only for six weeks after Easter, and since the Sevillans don't care very much for European music we go more to meet our friends than to listen to the singers. The Agurias had a box, like everybody else, and they went on the opening night of the season. *Tannhäuser* was being given. Don Pedro and his wife, like typical Spaniards, with nothing to do all day but always late, did not arrive till nearly the end of the first act. In the interval the Count of Acaba, Soledad's father, came into the box accompanied by a young officer of artillery whom Don Pedro had never seen before. But Soledad seemed to know him well.

" 'Here is Pepe Alvarez,' said the Count. 'He's just come back from Cuba and I insisted on bringing him to see you.'

"Soledad smiled and held out her hand, then introduced the newcomer to her husband.

" 'Pepe is the son of the attorney at Carmona. We used to play together when we were children.'

"Carmona is a small town near Seville and it was here that the Count had retired when his creditors in the city grew too troublesome. The house he owned there was almost all that was left him of the fortune he had squandered. He lived in Seville now through Don Pedro's generosity. But Don Pedro did not like him and he bowed stiffly to the young officer. He guessed that his father the attorney and the Count had been concerned together in transactions that were none too reputable. In a minute he left the box to talk with his cousin, the Duchess of Santaguador, whose box was opposite his own. A few days later he met Pepe Alvarez at his club in the Sierpes and had a chat with him. To his surprise he found him a very pleasant young fellow. He was full of his exploits in Cuba and he related them with humor.

"The six weeks about Easter and the great Fair are the

gayest in Seville and the world meets to exchange gossip and laughter at one festivity after another. Pepe Alvarez with his good nature and high spirits was in great request and the Agurias met him constantly. Don Pedro saw that he amused Soledad. She was more vivacious when he was there and her laughter, which he had so seldom heard, was a delight to him. Like other members of the aristocracy he took a booth for the Fair where they danced, supped, and drank champagne till dawn. Pepe Alvarez was always the life and soul of the parties.

"One night Don Pedro was dancing with the Duchess of Santaguador and they passed Soledad with Pepe Alvarez.

" 'Soledad is looking very beautiful this evening,' she remarked.

" 'And happy,' he replied.

" 'Is it true that once she was engaged to be married to Pepe Alvarez?'

" 'Of course not.'

"But the question startled him. He had known that Soledad and Pepe had known one another when they were children, but it had never crossed his mind that there could have been anything between them. The Count of Acaba, though a rogue, was a gentleman by birth and it was inconceivable that he could have thought of marrying his daughter to the son of a provincial attorney. When they got home Don Pedro told his wife what the duchess had said and what he had replied.

" 'But I was engaged to Pepe,' she said.

" 'Why did you never tell me?'

" 'It was finished and done with. He was in Cuba. I never expected to see him again.'

" 'There must be people who know you were engaged to him.'

" 'I daresay. Does it matter?'

" 'Very much. You shouldn't have renewed your acquaintance with him when he returned.'

" 'Does that mean that you have no confidence in me?'

" 'Of course not. I have every confidence in you. All the same I wish you to discontinue it now.'

" 'And if I refuse?'

" 'I shall kill him.'

"They looked long into one another's eyes. Then she gave

him a little bow and went to her room. Don Pedro sighed. He wondered whether she still loved Pepe Alvarez and whether it was on account of this that she had never loved him. But he would not allow himself to give way to the unworthy emotion of jealousy. He looked into his heart and was sure that it harbored no feeling of hatred for the young artilleryman. On the contrary, he liked him. This was not an affair of love or hate, but of honor. On a sudden he remembered that a few days before when he went to his club he noticed that the conversation suddenly failed and, looking back, he seemed to remember that several of the group who were sitting there and chatting eyed him curiously. Was it possible that he had been the subject of their conversation? He shivered a little at the thought.

"The Fair was drawing to its end and when it was over the Agurias had arranged to go to Cordova where Don Pedro had an estate which it was necessary for him to visit from time to time. He had looked forward to the peace of a country life after the turmoil of Seville. The day after this conversation Soledad, saying she was not well, stayed in the house, and she did the same the day following. Don Pedro visited her in her room morning and evening and they talked of indifferent things. But on the third day his cousin Conchita de Santaguador was giving a ball. It was the last of the season and everyone in her exclusive set would be there. Soledad, saying she was still indisposed, announced that she would stay at home.

" 'Are you refusing to go because of our conversation of the other night?' Don Pedro asked.

" 'I have been thinking over what you said. I think your demand unreasonable, but I shall accede to it. The only way I can cease my friendship with Pepe is by not going to places where I am likely to meet him.' A tremor of pain passed over her lovely face. 'Perhaps it is best.'

" 'Do you love him still?'

" 'Yes.'

"Don Pedro felt himself go cold with anguish.

" 'Then why did you marry me?'

" 'Pepe was away, in Cuba, no one knew when he would come back. Perhaps never. My father said that I must marry you.'

" 'To save him from ruin?'

" 'From worse than ruin.'

" 'I am very sorry for you.'

" 'You have been very kind to me. I have done everything in my power to prove to you that I am grateful.'

" 'And does Pepe love you?'

"She shook her head and smiled sadly.

" 'Men are different. He's young. He's too gay to love anyone very long. No, to him I'm just the friend with whom he used to play when he was a child and flirt when he was a boy. He can make jokes about the love he once had for me.'

"He took her hand and pressed it, then kissed it and left her. He went to the ball by himself. His friends were sorry to hear of Soledad's indisposition, but after expressing a proper sympathy devoted themselves to the evening's amusement. Don Pedro drifted into the card room. There was room at a table and he sat down to play *chemin de fer*. He played with extraordinary luck and made a good deal of money. One of the players laughingly asked where Soledad was that evening. Don Pedro saw another give him a startled glance, but he laughed and answered that she was safely in bed and asleep. Then an unlucky incident occurred. Some young man came into the room and addressing an artillery officer who was playing asked where Pepe Alvarez was.

" 'Isn't he here?' said the officer.

" 'No.'

"An odd silence fell upon the party. Don Pedro exercised all his self-control to prevent his face from showing what he suddenly felt. The thought flashed through his mind that Pepe was with Soledad and that those men at the table suspected it too. Oh, the shame! The indignity! He forced himself to go on playing for another hour and still he won. He could not go wrong. The game broke up and he returned to the ballroom. He went up to his cousin.

" 'I've hardly had a word with you,' he said. 'Come into another room and let us sit down for a little.'

" 'If you like.'

"The room, Conchita's boudoir, was empty.

" 'Where is Pepe Alvarez tonight?' he asked casually.

" 'I can't think.'

" 'You were expecting him?'

" 'Of course.'

"She was smiling as he was, but he noticed that she looked at him sharply. He dropped his mask of casualness and, though they were alone, lowered his voice.

" 'Conchita, I beseech you to tell me the truth. Are they saying that he is Soledad's lover?'

" 'Pedrito, what an incredible question to put to me.'

"But he had seen the terror in her eyes and the sudden instinctive movement of her hand to her face.

" 'You've answered it.'

"He got up and left her. He went home and looking up from the patio saw a light in his wife's room. He went upstairs and knocked at the door. There was no answer, but he went in. To his surprise, for it was late, she was sitting up working at the embroidery upon which much of her time was spent.

" 'Why are you working at this hour?'

" 'I couldn't sleep, I couldn't read. I thought it would distract my mind if I worked.'

"He did not sit down.

" 'Soledad, I have something to tell you that must cause you pain. I must ask you to be brave. Pepe Alvarez was not at Conchita's tonight.'

" 'What is that to me?'

" 'It is unfortunate that you were not there either. Everyone at the ball thought that you were together.'

" 'That's preposterous.'

" 'I know, but that doesn't help matters. You could have opened the gate for him yourself and let him out, or you could have slipped out yourself without anyone seeing you go or come.'

" 'But do you believe it?'

" 'No. I agreed with you that the thing was preposterous. Where was Pepe Alvarez?'

" 'How do I know? How should I know?'

" 'It is very strange that he should not have come to the most brilliant party, the last party, of the season.'

"She was silent for a minute.

" 'The night after you spoke to me about him I wrote and told him that in view of the circumstances I thought it would be better if in the future we saw no more of one another than could be helped. It may be that he did not go to the ball for the same reason that I did not.'

"They were silent for a while. He looked down at the ground, but he felt that her eyes were fixed on him. I should have told you before that Don Pedro possessed one accomplishment which raised him above his fellows, but at the same time was a drawback. He was the best shot in Andalusia. Everyone knew this and it would have been a brave man who ventured to offend him. A few days earlier there had been pigeon-shooting at Tablada, the wide common outside Seville along the Guadalquivir, and Don Pedro had beaten everybody. Pepe Alvarez on the other hand had shown himself so indifferent a marksman that everyone had laughed at him. The young artilleryman had borne the chaff with good humor. Cannon were his weapon, he said.

" 'What are you going to do?' Soledad asked.

" 'You know that there is only one thing I can do.'

"She understood. But she tried to treat what he said as a pleasantry.

" 'You're childish. We're not living anymore in the sixteenth century.'

" 'I know. That is why I am talking to you now. If I have to challenge Pepe I shall kill him. I don't want to do that. If he will resign his commission and leave Spain I will do nothing.'

" 'How can he? Where is he to go?'

" 'He can go to South America. He may make his fortune.'

" 'Do you expect me to tell him that?'

" 'If you love him.'

" 'I love him too much to ask him to run away like a coward. How could he face life without honor?'

"Don Pedro laughed.

" 'What has Pepe Alvarez, the son of the attorney at Carmona, to do with honor?'

"She did not answer, but in her eyes he saw the fierce hatred she bore him. That look stabbed his heart, for he loved her, he loved her as passionately as ever.

"Next day he went to his club and joined a group who were

sitting at the window looking out at the crowd passing up and down the Sierpes. Pepe Alvarez was in it. They were talking of last night's party.

" 'Where were you, Pepe?' someone asked.

" 'My mother was ill. I had to go down to Carmona,' he answered. 'I was dreadfully disappointed, but perhaps it was all for the best.' He turned laughingly to Don Pedro. 'I hear you were in luck and won everybody's money.'

" 'When are you going to give us our revenge, Pedrito?' asked another.

" 'I'm afraid you'll have to wait for that,' he answered. 'I have to go to Cordova. I find that my attorney has been robbing me. I know that all attorneys are thieves, but I stupidly thought this one was honest.'

"He seemed to speak quite lightly and it was as lightly that Pepe Alvarez put in his word.

" 'I think you exaggerate, Pedrito. Don't forget that my father is an attorney and he at least is honest.'

" 'I don't believe it for a minute,' laughed Don Pedro. 'I have no doubt your father is as big a thief as any.'

"The insult was so unexpected and so unprovoked that for a moment Pepe Alvarez was staggered. The others were startled into sudden seriousness.

" 'What do you mean, Pedrito?'

" 'Exactly what I say.'

" 'It's a lie and you know it's a lie. You must withdraw that at once.'

"Don Pedro laughed.

" 'Of course I shall not withdraw. Your father is a thief and a rascal.'

"Pepe did the only thing he could do. He sprang from his chair and with his open hand hit Don Pedro in the face. The outcome was inevitable. Next day the two men met on the frontier of Portugal. Pepe Alvarez, the attorney's son, died like a gentleman with a bullet in his heart."

The Spaniard ended his story on such a casual note that for the first moment I hardly took it in. But when I did I was profoundly shocked.

"Barbarous," I said. "It was just cold-blooded murder."

My host got up from his chair.

"You're talking nonsense, my young friend. Don Pedro did the only thing he could do in the circumstances."

I left Seville next day and from then till now have never been able to discover the name of the man who told me this strange story. I have often wondered whether the lady I saw, the lady with the pale face and the lock of white hair, was the unhappy Soledad.

Reading for Understanding _____

Main Idea

1. Which of the following statements best expresses the main idea of the story?
   (a) Dueling is a dangerous and illegal activity.
   (b) A cruel sense of honor may have disastrous results.
   (c) Bullfighting, though a Spanish sport, has fans outside Spain.
   (d) A man must struggle constantly for the honor of his family.

Details

2. Between the nobleman and the narrator, the discussion of honor arose because of   (a) an insult by the narrator   (b) a bullfight   (c) a mistake   (d) a play.

3. The narrator was in Spain for the purpose of   (a) trying out Spanish food   (b) meeting Don Pedro   (c) visiting Spanish shrines   (d) writing a book.

4. Pepe Alvarez had once   (a) served in Cuba   (b) been a toreador   (c) been an attorney   (d) been acclaimed as the best shot in Spain.

5. Conchita is   (a) another name for Pedro's wife   (b) the beloved of Pepe Alvarez   (c) the narrator's friend   (d) Pedro's cousin.

Inferences

6. A good adjective to describe Soledad is   (a) tricky
   (b) plain   (c) evil   (d) honest.

7. A good adjective to describe the narrator's new acquaintance, the Señor, is   (a) uncontrolled   (b) silly
   (c) cool   (d) sympathetic.

8. As a host, the new acquaintance proved to be
   (a) courteous   (b) uncertain   (c) antagonistic
   (d) weak.

9. Of the supposed romance between Pepe and Soledad, it
   might reasonably be said that   (a) Pepe was still madly
   in love with Soledad   (b) Soledad really disliked Pepe
   (c) the rumor was untrue   (d) Soledad's husband was a
   forgiving man.

10. When the narrator congratulates the Señora about her
    garden, her reply is   (a) enthusiastic   (b) without
    warmth   (c) hostile   (d) too soft to be heard.

Order of Events

11. Arrange the items in the order in which they occurred.
    Use letters only.
    A. Pedro insults Pepe.
    B. Soledad introduces Pedro to Pepe.
    C. Pedro marries Soledad.
    D. Soledad and Pepe are engaged.
    E. Pepe is killed in a duel.

Outcomes

12. After the duel,   (a) Soledad grieved and was saddened
    by the death   (b) Pedro apologized to the attorney
    (c) Soledad and Pedro were united happily   (d) Pedro
    divorced Soledad.

Cause and Effect

13. It might be said that Pepe lost his life because of
    (a) his cowardice   (b) gossip   (c) Pedro's personal ha-
    tred of him   (d) Calderón's play.

Fact or Opinion

Tell whether the following is a fact or an opinion.

14. Pepe's father was indeed a dishonest attorney.

Author's Role

15. The attitude of the writer toward Don Pedro is one of
    (a) disapproval (b) understanding (c) support
    (d) indifference.

Words in Context _____

1. The rider, with conscious pride in his picturesque costume, exchanged pleasantries with the *facetious*.
   Facetious (241) means (a) silly (b) somber
   (c) well dressed (d) excited.

2. He had beautiful hands, small but *resolute*, with thin, long fingers.
   Resolute (242) means (a) wrinkled (b) firm
   (c) muscular (d) bony.

3. He spoke *dispassionately*, as though the misfortunes of his fallen country were no concern of his.
   Dispassionately (242) means (a) correctly (b) slowly
   (c) sadly (d) calmly.

4. The fighters, all glittering in their satin, in gold and silver, marched *swaggering* down across the ring.
   Swaggering (242) means (a) strutting (b) limping
   (c) plodding (d) hiking.

5. "Can one like something that fills one with horror and *loathing*?"
   Loathing (243) means (a) fear (b) panic (c) disgust
   (d) strong interest.

6. He had seemed rather an *amiable* man, with his large, soft, friendly eyes.
   Amiable (243) means (a) violent (b) burned-out
   (c) childish (d) friendly.

7. Now his face bore a look of *sardonic* hauteur (haughtiness) which was a trifle disquieting.
Sardonic (243) means   (a) elated   (b) scornful (c) puzzling   (d) amused.

8. In the older parts of Seville the streets are narrow and *tortuous*.
Tortuous (244) means   (a) twisting   (b) muddy (c) clearly marked   (d) bumpy.

9, 10. The roses clad every inch in *wanton*, scented *luxuriance*.
Wanton (245) means   (a) lacking   (b) permanent (c) wild   (d) wandering.
Luxuriance (245) means   (a) comfort   (b) narrowness (c) color   (d) abundance.

11. The gardeners had striven in vain to curb the *exuberance* of nature.
Exuberance (245) means   (a) rich growth (b) occasional dry spells   (c) slow progress (d) shrubs.

12. It is very likely that the King himself more than once *caroused* under this ceiling with my ancestor.
Caroused (245) means   (a) sang   (b) slept (c) frolicked   (d) argued.

13. It hardly *dispelled* the habitual melancholy of his expression.
Dispelled (246) means   (a) increased   (b) drove away (c) made more interesting   (d) captured.

14. I did not expect her to show me any *cordiality* and I could not blame her if she thought my intrusion was merely a nuisance.
Cordiality (247) means   (a) anger   (b) friendliness (c) interest   (d) response.

15. She carried herself with a sort of royal *composure* and her gait was stately.
Composure (247) means   (a) conceit   (b) command (c) poise   (d) upset.

16. I was *flippant* in those days and I remember saying to myself that she was not the sort of girl you could very well

think of being silly with.
Flippant (247) means   (a) handsome   (b) wise
(c) quiet   (d) impertinent.

17. The physician of his honor takes vengeance on his wife,
     though aware that she is innocent, simply as a matter of
     decorum.
     Decorum (248) means   (a) suitable behavior
     (b) inner cruelty   (c) legal requirement   (d) slight
     misunderstanding.

18. He gave me a long, *reflective* stare before he went on.
     Reflective (248) means   (a) baffling   (b) unchanging
     (c) humorous   (d) thoughtful.

19. He adored her with the *vehement* passion of which perhaps
     only a Spaniard is capable.
     Vehement (248) means   (a) intense   (b) changeable
     (c) considerate   (d) cool.

20. The house he owned there was almost all that was left
     him of the fortune he had *squandered*.
     Squandered (249) means   (a) gathered together
     (b) spent foolishly   (c) inherited from his father
     (d) mislaid.

21. Soledad, saying she was still *indisposed,* announced that
     she would stay at home.
     Indisposed (251) means   (a) violently angry
      (b) confused   (c) slightly ill   (d) aloof and
     indifferent.

22. Oh, the shame! The *indignity!* He forced himself to go on
     playing for another hour and still he won.
     Indignity (252) means   (a) advertising   (b) legend
     (c) loss of value   (d) disgrace.

23. He had seen the terror in her eyes and the sudden
     instinctive movement of her hand to her face.
     Instinctive (253) means done without   (a) delay
     (b) thought   (c) shame   (d) sympathy.

24. "That's *preposterous*."
     Preposterous (253) means   (a) surprising   (b) serious
     (c) ridiculous   (d) reasonable.

25. The insult was so unexpected and so *unprovoked* that for a moment Pepe Alvarez was staggered.
    Unprovoked (255) means (a) timely (b) without reason (c) finally understandable (d) feeble.

Thinking Critically About the Story _____

1. This is a story that has two narrators, with a story within a story. Is this a successful device for storytelling? Explain your point of view.

2. The central character, the owner of the beautiful house and garden, is a contradiction. He is both kind and cruel, sympathetic and heartless, sophisticated but with a cruel fault in his nature. Does he strike you as a realistic creation? Are people in real life contradictions? Can you mention some examples in public life of people who demonstrate those contradictions?

3. As in "The Lady, or the Tiger?" the author leaves the ending open. Was the Señor's wife actually Soledad? Why was there "something dead in her"? What do you think? What evidence can you suggest to prove your point?

4. Pepe Alvarez has been called the most tragic character in the story. Others vote for Soledad. Which would you choose?

5. The title of the story includes the word *honor*. What is honor? Is it a good thing? Can it be a bad thing? Refer to the story in discussing this question.

6. In discussions about the bullring, Spaniards often make the point that American football and hockey are distastefully more violent than bullfighting. How would you respond to such a statement?

7. "The Point of Honor" is a perfectly balanced story in which plot, character, setting, and theme carry almost equal weight.
   In a composition of 200–250 words discuss the truth or falsity of the statement. Refer to the story to prove your point.

Stories in Words _____

Dilapidated (241) *Lapis* is Latin for *stone*. Originally, *dilapidated* meant "to have stones missing." Thus, a stone building might be dilapidated. Over the years, however, the specific meaning has disappeared. Now the word just means "falling apart." Wooden houses may be dilapidated! The carriages on the streets of Seville were dilapidated. The word is now used as a general synonym for *decaying, shabby,* even *threadbare.*

Enthusiasm (246) This word suggests keen interest, eagerness, the joy of participation. The history of the word provides a clue to its present meaning. It has as its root *theos,* the Greek word for a *god.* Thus, a person who is enthusiastic is "seized by a god." The intense interest signals that a "god has taken possession" of the happy victim.

Sardonic (243) *Sardonic* means *sneering, ironic, sarcastic, generally unpleasant.* It comes from the name *Sardinia.* In Roman times, a plant grew on that island. It was so bitter if eaten, it forced the mouth muscles to contract into a painful grin. Though the idea of physical pain has left the word *sardonic,* the idea of bitterness and unpleasantness remains.

The Surprise Ending

ACTIVITIES

Thinking Critically About the Stories ____

1. Which of the four stories has the most headlong pace? How is this pace sustained?
2. Which of the stories has the most interesting, most complicated character? Give reasons for choosing this person.
3. In which two stories does fate play an especially important role? Tell why and how.
4. Which one of the four titles do you consider most appropriate and most stimulating? Explain.
5. How does social class play a major role in both "The Necklace" and "The Point of Honor"?
6. "A Habit for the Voyage" and "The Point of Honor" resemble detective stories in some respects. In each there is a puzzle element. Does the writer of each story provide some clues to prepare the reader for the ending? Explain.
7. Of the characters presented in the four stories, which do you find most admirable? Why?
8. Do you enjoy stories with surprise endings? Why or why not?

Writing and Other Activities ____

1. What is honor? What does *honor* mean? What role does honor play in "The Necklace" and "The Point of Honor"?

In a composition of 150–200 words explain how Mathilde and Don Pedro both lived by what they considered a code of honor. Explain your attitude toward each character.

2. In all four stories, the unexpected plays a major role. Choose an episode from your own life in which the unexpected played a role. In a composition of 150–200 words, retell the episode.

3. The movies and television plays often rely on surprise endings. Think of a movie or TV program that used the surprise-ending device and prepare to report to the class.

4. In *The Devil's Dictionary*, Ambrose Bierce provides interesting meanings for common words. Here's a sample:

Architect.   One who drafts a plan of your house, and plans a draft of your money.

Apologize.   To lay the foundation of a future offense.

Absurdity.   A statement of belief manifestly inconsistent with one's own opinion.

Auctioneer.   The man who proclaims with a hammer that he has picked a pocket with his tongue.

Consult.   To seek another's approval of a course already decided on.

Discussion.   A method of confirming others in their errors.

Egotist.   A person of low taste, more interested in himself than in me.

Positive.   Mistaken at the top of one's voice.

Choose three of the definitions above and explain the meaning of each. How does each differ from a dictionary definition?

5. What is the characteristic mood of the definitions above? What do you tell about Bierce himself? Do you like them? Can you make up a humorous definition of your own?

Stories in Words: A Review _____

A. atavism   E. dilapidated   I. intoxication
B. ambush   F. ecstasy   J. pommel
C. calculations   G. enthusiasm   K. sardonic
D. colossal   H. habit   L. stevedore

Answer the following questions by choosing a word from the list above. Use letters only.

Which of the words above . . .

1. . . . suggests an inspiration from a god?

2. . . . comes from a plant on a Mediterranean island?

3. . . . is derived from the name of one of the Seven Wonders of the Ancient World?

4. . . . comes from a Latin word meaning "pebbles to count with"?

5. . . . is related, in the original meaning, to the expression "left no stone unturned"?

6. . . . suggests that a certain state of the body is poisoned?

7. . . . identifies something that can happen anywhere, even though the original meaning limited the action to the woods?

8. . . . derives from the word for an ancestor?

9. . . . comes from Spanish words meaning "ram tight"?

10. . . . suggests an apple?

4

All
in Fun

A glance at a wordbook will reveal many synonyms for *laugh: cackle, chortle, chuckle, giggle, guffaw, roar, shriek, snicker,* and *snort.* To these may be added words like *grin* and *smile,* which express a more restrained sense of amusement, without sound. Apparently, humor is a serious business since there are so many words associated with it!

One of a person's most prized possessions is a sense of humor, an ability to laugh at the oddities in the world and the weaknesses in oneself. Why some people seem to have a more keenly developed sense of humor than others is a source of puzzlement and a subject for debate.

In the Thinking Critically section of "The Noblest Instrument," you will be invited to present your idea of what makes something funny. You will try, along with your classmates, to decide what humor is, a question that has challenged scholars for hundreds of years.

The four stories that follow will help you make a decision. "The Noblest Instrument" will introduce you to one of the funniest characters in literature: Father Day. Part of the fun is that Father has no idea just how funny he is. "The Secret Life of Walter Mitty" presents another, quite different character. Father's major characteristics are assertiveness and self-assurance. Walter Mitty presents an altogether different face to the world.

In "Tobermory," the humor grows out of an outrageously impossible situation. Tobermory is not only a talking cat but a most insightful, sneering, and sarcastic one. In "Is He Living or Is He Dead?" Mark Twain, the master of exaggeration (sometimes called *hyperbole*), asks the readers to believe an unlikely, though somewhat plausible, tale of the art world. Here the humor is more subtle than in many other works by Twain.

All four stories present a study of humor—all different. Get ready to grin, smile, chuckle, giggle, or guffaw, however the mood takes you!

The Noblest Instrument

Clarence Day

♦ **My teacher, Herr M., looked as though he had suddenly taken in a large glass of vinegar. He sucked in his breath. His lips were drawn back from his teeth, and his eyes tightly shut. Of course, he hadn't expected my notes to be sweet at the start; but still, there was something unearthly about that first cry.**

Among the great humorous characters in literature, certain ones stand out: Sir John Falstaff, created by Shakespeare; Mr. Micawber, by Charles Dickens; Huckleberry Finn, by Mark Twain. In this illustrious company belongs Father Day, the central character in *Life with Father,* by Clarence Day, Jr.

This episode from *Life with Father* suggests the atmosphere of the book. Father is a completely self-centered tyrant who thinks the world should think as he does, act in the way he suggests, and conform to all his beliefs and prejudices. If Father decides Clarence, Jr., should learn to play the violin, Clarence must learn to play "the noblest instrument." Such matters as Clarence's feelings and abilities do not enter into the discussion.

Yet there is a good side to Clarence, Sr. His bark is usually worse than his bite. Though he is antifeminist and seems to dominate his wife, Mother Day has strategies of her own and usually wins the day.

In this episode, young Clarence somehow manages to survive his violin lessons, but for those who must listen to him, survival is not enough. As you read, notice the subtle touches of humor. Contrasting poor Herr M., the violin teacher, with his untalented pupil provides many chuckles. There are others. Meet Father Day at his best.

THE NOBLEST INSTRUMENT

Father had been away, reorganizing some old upstate railroad. He returned in an executive mood and proceeded to shake up our home. In spite of my failure as a singer, he was still bound to have us taught music. We boys were summoned before him and informed that we must at once learn to play on something. We might not appreciate it now, he said, but we should later on. "You, Clarence, will learn the violin. George, you the piano. Julian—well, Julian is too young yet. But you older boys must have lessons."

I was appalled at this order. At the age of ten it seemed a disaster to lose any more of my freedom. The days were already too short for our games after school; and now here was a chunk to come out of playtime three days every week. A chunk every day, we found afterward, because we had to practice.

George sat at the piano in the parlor, and faithfully learned to pound out his exercises. He had all the luck. He was not an inspired player, but at least he had some ear for music. He also had the advantage of playing on a good robust instrument, which he didn't have to be careful not to drop, and was in no danger of breaking. Furthermore, he did not have to tune it. A piano had some good points.

But I had to go through a blacker and more gruesome experience. It was bad enough to have to come in from the street and the sunlight and go down into our dark little basement where I took my lessons. But that was only the opening chill of the struggle that followed.

The whole thing was uncanny. The violin itself was a queer, fragile, cigar-boxy thing, that had to be handled most gingerly. Nothing sturdy about it. Why, a fellow was liable to crack it putting it into its case. And then my teacher, he was queer too. He had a queer pickled smell.

I dare say he wasn't queer at all really, but he seemed so to me, because he was different from the people I generally met. He was probably worth a dozen of some of them, but I didn't know it. He was one of the violins in the Philharmonic, and an excellent player; a grave, middle-aged little man—who was obliged to give lessons.

He wore a black, wrinkled frock coat, and a discolored gold watch chain. He had small, black-rimmed glasses; not tortoise-shell, but thin rims of metal. His violin was dark, rich, and polished, and would do anything for him.

Mine was balky and awkward, brand new, and of a light, common color.

The violin is intended for persons with a passion for music. I wasn't that kind of person. I liked to hear a band play a tune that we could march up and down to, but try as I would, I could seldom whistle such a tune afterward. My teacher didn't know this. He greeted me as a possible genius.

He taught me how to hold that contraption, tucked under my chin. I learned how to move my fingers here and there on its handle or stem. I learned how to draw the bow across the strings, and thus produce sounds. . . .

Does a mother recall the first cry of her baby, I wonder? I still remember the strange cry at birth of that new violin.

My teacher, Herr M.,* looked as though he had suddenly taken a large glass of vinegar. He sucked in his breath. His lips were drawn back from his teeth, and his eyes tightly shut. Of course, he hadn't expected my notes to be sweet at the start; but still, there was something unearthly about that first cry. He snatched the violin from me, examined it, readjusted its pegs, and comforted it gently, by drawing his own bow across it. It was only a new and not especially fine violin, but the sounds it made for him were more natural—they were classifiable sounds. They were not richly musical, but at least they had been heard before on this earth.

He handed the instrument back to me with careful direc-

---

* *Herr*   German title of respect, equivalent of *Mr.*

tions. I tucked it up under my chin again and grasped the end tight. I held my bow exactly as ordered. I looked up at him, waiting.

"Now," he said, nervously.

I slowly raised the bow, drew it downward. . . .

This time there were *two* dreadful cries in our little front basement. One came from my new violin and one from the heart of Herr M.

Herr M. presently came to, and smiled bravely at me, and said if I wanted to rest a moment he would permit it. He seemed to think I might wish to lie down awhile and recover. I didn't feel any need of lying down. All I wanted was to get through the lesson. But Herr M. was shaken. He was by no means ready to let me proceed. He looked around desperately, saw the music book, and said he would now show me that. We sat down side by side on the window seat, with the book in his

lap, while he pointed out the notes to me with his finger, and told me their names.

After a bit, when he felt better, he took up his own violin, and instructed me to watch him and note how he handled the strings. And then at last, he nerved himself to let me take my violin up again. "Softly, my child, softly," he begged me, and stood facing the wall. . . .

We got through the afternoon somehow, but it was a ghastly experience. Part of the time he was maddened by the mistakes I kept making, and part of the time he was plain wretched. He covered his eyes. He seemed ill. He looked often at his watch, even shook it as though it had stopped; but he stayed the full hour.

That was Wednesday. What struggles he had with himself before Friday, when my second lesson was due, I can only dimly imagine, and of course I never even gave them a thought at the time. He came back to recommence teaching me, but he had changed—he had hardened. Instead of being cross, he was stern; and instead of sad, bitter. He wasn't unkind to me, but we were no longer companions. He talked to himself, under his breath; and sometimes he took bits of paper, and did little sums on them, gloomily, and then tore them up.

During my third lesson I saw the tears come to his eyes. He went up to Father and said he was sorry but he honestly felt sure I'd never be able to play.

Father didn't like this at all. He said he felt sure I would. He dismissed Herr M. briefly—the poor man came stumbling back down in two minutes. In that short space of time he had gallantly gone upstairs in a glow, resolved upon sacrificing his earnings for the sake of telling the truth. He returned with his earnings still running, but with the look of a lost soul about him, as though he felt that his nerves and his sanity were doomed to destruction. He was low in his mind, and he talked to himself more than ever. Sometimes he spoke harshly of America, sometimes of fate.

But he no longer struggled. He accepted this thing as his destiny. He regarded me as an unfortunate something, outside the human species, whom he must simply try to labor with as well as he could. It was a grotesque, indeed a hellish experience, but he felt he must bear it.

He wasn't the only one—he was at least not alone in his sufferings. Mother, though expecting the worst, had tried to be hopeful about it, but at the end of a week or two I heard her and Margaret talking it over. I was slaughtering a scale in the front basement, when Mother came down and stood outside the door in the kitchen hall and whispered, "Oh, Margaret!"

I watched them. Margaret was baking a cake. She screwed up her face, raised her arms, and brought them down with hands clenched.

"I don't know what we shall do, Margaret."

"The poor little feller," Margaret whispered. "He can't make the thing go."

This made me indignant. They were making me look like a lubber. I wished to feel always that I could make anything go. . . .

I now began to feel a determination to master this thing. History shows us many examples of the misplaced determinations of men—they are one of the darkest aspects of human life, they spread so much needless pain: but I knew little history. And I viewed what little I did know romantically—I should have seen in such episodes their heroism, not their futility. Any role that seemed heroic attracted me, no matter how senseless.

Not that I saw any chance for heroism in our front basement, of course. You had to have a battlefield or something. I saw only that I was appearing ridiculous. But that stung my pride. I hadn't wanted to learn anything whatever about fiddles or music, but since I was in for it, I'd do it, and show them I could. A boy will often put in enormous amounts of his time trying to prove he isn't as ridiculous as he thinks people think him.

Meanwhile Herr M. and I had discovered that I was nearsighted. On account of the violin's being an instrument that sticks out in front of one, I couldn't stand close enough to the music book to see the notes clearly. He didn't at first realize that I often made mistakes from that cause. When he and I finally comprehended that I had this defect, he had a sudden new hope that this might have been the whole trouble, and that when it was corrected I might play like a human being at last.

Neither of us ventured to take up this matter with Father. We knew that it would have been hard to convince him that my

eyes were not perfect, I being a son of his and presumably
made in his image; and we knew that he immediately would
have felt we were trying to make trouble for him, and would
have shown an amount of resentment which it was best to
avoid. So Herr M. instead lent me his glasses. These did fairly
well. They turned the dim grayness of the notes into a queer
bright distortion, but the main thing was they did make them
brighter, so that I now saw more of them. How well I remember
those little glasses. Poor, dingy old things. Herr M. was nervous
about lending them to me; he feared that I'd drop them. It
would have been safer if they had been spectacles: but no, they
were pince-nez*; and I had to learn to balance them across my
nose as well as I could. I couldn't wear them up near my eyes
because my nose was too thin there; I had to put them about
halfway down where there was enough flesh to hold them. I
also had to tilt my head back, for the music stand was a little
too tall for me. Herr M. sometimes mounted me on a stool,
warning me not to step off. Then when I was all set, and when
he without his glasses was blind, I would smash my way into
the scales again.

All during the long winter months I worked away at this
job. I gave no thought, of course, to the family. But they did to
me. Our house was heated by a furnace, which had big warm
air pipes; these ran up through the walls with wide outlets into
each room, and sound traveled easily and ringingly through
their roomy, tin passages. My violin could be heard in every
part of the house. No one could settle down to anything while
I was practicing. If visitors came they soon left. Mother
couldn't even sing to the baby. She would wait, watching the
clock, until my long hour of scalework was over, and then come
downstairs and shriek at me that my time was up. She would
find me sawing away with my forehead wet, and my hair wet
and stringy, and even my clothes slowly getting damp from my
exertions. She would feel my collar, which was done for, and
say I must change it. "Oh, Mother! Please!"—for I was in a
hurry now to run out and play. But she wasn't being fussy
about my collar, I can see, looking back; she was using it

* *pince-nez*　　eyeglasses that clip to bridge of nose—without side-
pieces

merely as a barometer or gauge of my pores. She thought I had better dry myself before going out in the snow.

It was a hard winter for Mother. I believe she also had fears for the baby. She sometimes pleaded with Father; but no one could ever tell Father anything. He continued to stand like a rock against stopping my lessons.

Schopenhauer*, in his rules for debating, shows how to win a weak case by insidiously transferring an argument from its right field, and discussing it instead from some irrelevant but impregnable angle. Father knew nothing of Schopenhauer, and was never insidious, but nevertheless, he had certain natural gifts for debate. In the first place his voice was powerful and stormy, and he let it out at full strength, and kept on letting it out with a vigor that stunned his opponents. As a second gift, he was convinced at all times that his opponents were wrong. Hence, even if they did win a point or two, it did them no good, for he dragged the issue to some other ground then, where he and Truth could prevail. When Mother said it surely was plain enough that I had no ear, what was his reply? Why, he said that the violin was the noblest instrument invented by man. Having silenced her with this solid premise he declared that it followed that any boy was lucky to be given the privilege of learning to play it. No boy should expect to learn it immediately. It required persistence. Everything, he had found, required persistence. The motto was, Never give up.

All his life, he declared, he had persevered in spite of discouragement, and he meant to keep on persevering, and he meant me to, too. He said that none of us realized what he had had to go through. If he had been the kind that gave up at the very first obstacle, where would he have been now—where would any of the family have been? The answer was, apparently, that we'd either have been in a very bad way, poking round for crusts in the gutter, or else nonexistent. We might have never even been born if Father had not persevered.

Placed beside this record of Father's vast trials overcome, the little difficulty of my learning to play the violin seemed a trifle. I faithfully spurred myself on again, to work at the

* *Schopenhauer*   nineteenth-century German philosopher and writer

puzzle. Even my teacher seemed impressed with these views on persistence. Though older than Father, he had certainly not made as much money, and he bowed to the experience of a practical man who was a success. If he, Herr M., had been a success he would not have had to teach boys; and sitting in this black pit in which his need of money had placed him, he saw more than ever that he must learn the ways of this world. He listened with all his heart, as to a god, when Father shook his forefinger, and told him how to climb to the heights where financial rewards were achieved. The idea he got was that perseverance was sure to lead to great wealth.

Consequently our front basement continued to be the home of lost causes.

Of course, I kept begging Herr M. to let me learn just one tune. Even though I seldom could whistle them, still I liked tunes, and I knew that, in my hours of practicing, a tune would be a comfort. That is, for myself. Here again I never gave a thought to the effect upon others.

Herr M., after many misgivings, to which I respectfully listened—though they were not spoken to me, they were muttered to himself, pessimistically—hunted through a worn old book of selections, and after much doubtful fumbling chose as simple a thing as he could find for me—for me and the neighbors.

It was spring now, and windows were open. That tune became famous.

What would the musician who had tenderly composed this air, years before, have felt if he had foreseen what an end it would have, on Madison Avenue; and how, before death, it would be execrated by that once peaceful neighborhood. I engraved it on their hearts; not in its true form but in my own eerie versions. It was the only tune I knew. Consequently I played and replayed it.

Even horrors when repeated grow old and lose part of their sting. But those I produced were, unluckily, never the same. To be sure, this tune kept its general structure the same, even in my sweating hands. There was always the place where I climbed unsteadily up to its peak, and that difficult spot where it wavered, or staggered, and stuck; and then a sudden jerk of resumption—I came out strong on that. Every afternoon when

I got to that difficult spot, the neighbors dropped whatever they were doing to wait for that jerk, shrinking from the moment, and yet feverishly impatient for it to come.

But what made the tune and their anguish so different each day? I'll explain. The strings of a violin are wound at the end around pegs, and each peg must be screwed in and tightened till the string sounds just right. Herr M. left my violin properly tuned when he went. But suppose a string broke, or that somehow I jarred a peg loose. Its string then became slack and soundless. I had to retighten it. Not having an ear, I was highly uncertain about this.

Our neighbors never knew at what degree of tautness I'd put such a string. I didn't myself. I just screwed her up tight enough to make a strong reliable sound. Neither they nor I could tell which string would thus appear in a new role each day, nor foresee the profound transformations this would produce in that tune.

All that spring this unhappy and ill-destined melody floated out through my window, and writhed in the air for one hour daily, in sunshine or storm. All that spring our neighbors and I daily toiled to its peak, and staggered over its hump, so to speak, and fell wailing through space.

Things now began to be said to Mother which drove her to act. She explained to Father that the end had come at last. Absolutely. "This awful nightmare cannot go on," she said.

Father pooh-poohed her.

She cried. She told him what it was doing to her. He said that she was excited, and that her descriptions of the sounds I made were exaggerated and hysterical—must be. She was always too vehement, he shouted. She must learn to be calm.

"But you're downtown, *you* don't have to hear it!"

Father remained wholly skeptical.

She endeavored to shame him. She told him what awful things the neighbors were saying about him, because of the noise I was making, for which he was responsible.

He couldn't be made to look at it that way. If there really were any unpleasantness then I was responsible. He had provided me with a good teacher and a good violin—so he reasoned. In short, he had done his best, and no father could have done more. If I made hideous sounds after all that, the

fault must be mine. He said that Mother should be stricter with
me, if necessary, and make me try harder.

This was the last straw. I couldn't try harder. When
Mother told me his verdict I said nothing, but my body
rebelled. Self-discipline had its limits—and I wanted to be out:
it was spring. I skimped my hours of practice when I heard the
fellows playing outside. I came home late for lessons—even
forgot them. Little by little they stopped.

Father was outraged. His final argument, I remember, was
that my violin had cost twenty-five dollars; if I didn't learn it
the money would be wasted, and he couldn't afford it. But it
was put to him that my younger brother, Julian, could learn it
instead, later on. Then summer came, anyhow, and we went for
three months to the seashore; and in the confusion of this
Father was defeated and I was set free.

In the autumn little Julian was led away one afternoon,
and imprisoned in the front basement in my place. I don't
remember how long they kept him down there, but it was
several years. He had an ear, however, and I believe he learned
to play fairly well. This would have made a happy ending for
Herr M. after all; but it was some other teacher, a younger
man, who was engaged to teach Julian. Father said Herr M.
was a failure.

Reading for Understanding _____

Main Idea

1. Young Clarence's attempts to play the violin were
    (a) a comic disaster   (b) Clarence's own idea
    (c) sometimes successful, sometimes not   (d) generally
    approved by Mother.

Details

2. A major reason for Clarence's reluctance to play the violin
    was   (a) a   preference   for   learning   the   trumpet

(b) a loss of valuable play time   (c) jealousy of his youngest brother   (d) a desire to anger Father.

3. The instrument assigned to brother George was the (a) clarinet   (b) violin   (c) flute   (d) piano.

4. Clarence admits that Herr M. was really   (a) a cruel person   (b) an admirer of Clarence's playing (c) an excellent player himself   (d) one person who was not afraid of Father.

5. Clarence was finally saved during the   (a) Easter holidays   (b) summer   (c) autumn   (d) winter.

Inferences

6. As a music student, George could be said to be (a) similar to Father   (b) the best student Herr M. ever had   (c) a better student than Clarence   (d) as good as Julian.

7. On page 272, Herr M. has "the look of a lost soul about him" because   (a) Father refused to pay him (b) Father asked him to teach George as well as Clarence (c) Mother had asked that he be dismissed   (d) he had been beaten down by Father.

8. At one point Clarence, heroically but unwisely, resolves to (a) yell back at Father   (b) master the violin (c) ask the assistance of his brother George   (d) cause Mother to plead for further lessons.

9. "It was a hard winter for Mother" because   (a) she couldn't stand the sound of Clarence's violin (b) she couldn't get her finances straight   (c) Margaret quit   (d) Father had to travel abroad.

10. The worst torture for listeners was   (a) Clarence's playing the same tune over and over   (b) Herr M.'s screams (c) noisy defects in the heating system   (d) learning that Clarence had broken his violin.

Order of Events

11. Arrange the items in the order in which they occurred. Use letters only.

A. Clarence learns to play one tune.
B. Little Julian is given music lessons.
C. Father hires Herr M.
D. Clarence determines to prove his musical ability.
E. The family goes to the seashore for the summer.

Outcomes

12. After the episode with the violin, Father probably
(a) sold the violin for a profit (b) donated money to a musical charity (c) did not change his personality
(d) learned his lesson and did not try to boss others around.

Cause and Effect

13. If Clarence had had some musical talent, (a) he would have joined Herr M.'s orchestra, the Philharmonic
(b) Father would have stopped his playing after the summer anyway (c) Mother would still have disliked his playing (d) Herr M. would have been a happier man.

Fact or Opinion

Tell whether the following is a fact or an opinion.
14. Father assigned music lessons after returning from a trip upstate.

Author's Role

15. The author assumes that the reader (a) has at one time or other played a musical instrument (b) has some idea how horrible a violin sounds when it is played poorly
(c) agrees with Father that Clarence should have been given lessons (d) thinks that Clarence's problem isn't funny.

Words in Context

1. The whole thing was *uncanny.*
   Uncanny (269) means   (a) exciting   (b) weird
   (c) simple   (d) breathtaking.

2. He wore a black, wrinkled *frock* coat, and a discolored
   gold watch chain.
   Frock (270) means   (a) black   (b) formal, ¾ length
   (c) worn   (d) expensive.

3. He had small, black-rimmed glasses; not *tortoise shell,* but
   thin rims of metal.
   Tortoise shell (270) means with rims of   (a) brown and
   yellow plastic   (b) thick and rigid metal   (c) gold
   imitation   (d) silver imitation.

4. In that short space of time he had gallantly gone upstairs
   in a glow, resolved upon sacrificing his earnings for the
   sake of telling the truth.
   In a glow (272) means   (a) embarrassed   (b) eager
   (c) annoyed   (d) hurriedly.

5. It was a *grotesque,* indeed a hellish experience, but he felt
   he must bear it.
   Grotesque (272) means   (a) weird   (b) dangerous
   (c) exciting   (d) fatal.

6. This made me *indignant.*
   Indignant (273) means   (a) angry   (b) embarrassed
   (c) determined   (d) discouraged.

7. And I viewed what little I did know *romantically*—
   Romantically (273) means   (a) fondly   (b) impracti-
   cally   (c) confidently   (d) dreamily.

8. I should have seen in such episodes their heroism, not
   their *futility.*
   Futility (273) means   (a) significance   (b) uselessness
   (c) beauty   (d) sternness.

9. We knew that it would have been hard to convince him
   that my eyes were not perfect, I being his son and
   presumably made in his image . . .

Presumably (274) means   (a) obviously   (b) fortunately
(c) probably   (d) unfortunately.

10. They turned the dim grayness of the notes into a queer
bright *distortion* . . .
Distortion (274) means   (a) symbol   (b) set of tree
trunks   (c) being twisted out of shape   (d) mass of
mixed colors.

11. . . . discussing it instead from some *irrelevant but
impregnable* angle.
Irrelevant but impregnable (275) means   (a) provable
but farfetched   (b) interesting but untrue
(c) dramatic but unprovable   (d) unrelated but
unconquerable.

12. All his life, he declared, he had *persevered* in spite of
discouragement, and he meant to keep on persevering,
and he meant me to, too.
Persevered (275) means   (a) continued trying
(b) gave up easily   (c) failed   (d) reached victory.

13. The answer was, apparently, that we'd either have been in
a very bad way, poking round for crusts in the gutter, or
else *nonexistent*.
Nonexistent (275) means   (a) imaginary   (b) famous
(c) powerfully rich   (d) politically powerful.

14. All that spring this unhappy and *ill-destined* melody
floated out through my window . . .
Ill-destined (277) means   (a) little known   (b) loud
(c) ill-spoken of   (d) unlucky.

15. Father remained wholly *skeptical*.
Skeptical (277) means   (a) enthusiastic
(b) determined   (c) trusting   (d) inclined to doubt.

Thinking Critically About the Story _____

1. If a powerfully built, muscular athlete comes along leading
a tiny dog on a chain, people will snicker. Why? The

experts have long debated the nature of humor. What makes something funny? Is it the element of surprise? Is it the placement side by side of two or more quite different ideas, pictures, or experiences? (Note that the athlete with the tiny dog satisfies both possibilities.) Is it an exaggeration of reality? Is it the contagion of someone else's laughter? Is it the ability to laugh at oneself? Why is Father funny? What makes "The Noblest Instrument" humorous?

2.   How is Father's personality suggested by his saying, "You, Clarence, will learn the violin. George, you the piano"?

3.   Sometimes a single word will give a clue to a personality or a situation. Herr M. is described as "a grave, middle-aged little man—who was obliged to give lessons." What does the word *obliged* tell us about Herr M.'s fortunes?

Stories in Words _____

Philharmonic (270)   Two Greek roots suggest the meaning of this word. *Phil,* meaning "love," appears in words like *Philip,* a "lover of horses"; *philosophy,* a "love of wisdom,"; and *Philadelphia,* the city of "brotherly love." *Harmos,* originally meaning a "fitting," has come to mean a "fitting together of sounds for a pleasing result." *Philharmonic* suggests a "love of music."

Vinegar (270)   Two Latin roots create this word. The root *vin,* meaning "wine," appears in *vine* and *vintage.* The root *egar* comes from the Latin *acer,* meaning *sharp, sour. Acer* appears in *acute, acrid, acumen,* and *acrimony,* all having something to do with sharpness, sourness. Thus *vinegar,* by derivation, is "sharp, sour wine."

Pince-nez (274)   The first syllable, *pince,* comes from a French word, *pincer,* "to pinch." The second comes from the French *nez,* "the nose." *Pince-nez* thus means "pinch the nose." And that is exactly what these glasses do: pinch the nose. There are no side pieces to go over the ears.

The Secret Life of Walter Mitty

James Thurber

◆ **War thundered and whined around the dugout and battered at the door. There was a rending of wood, and splinters flew through the room. "A bit of a near thing," said Captain Mitty carelessly. "The box barrage is closing in," said the sergeant. "We only live once, Sergeant," said Mitty, with his faint, fleeting smile. "Or do we?"**

Captain Walter Mitty, with his usual fearlessness, faces death once again, as he has faced it in a hundred adventures, all equally hair-raising. In this story, you will follow Captain Mitty into the very jaws of death, only to be. . . .

A *Romeo,* from Shakespeare's *Romeo and Juliet,* is a young lover. A *Cassandra,* from Homer's *Iliad,* is a prophetess whose accurate prophecies of misfortune are destined never to be believed. A *Pollyanna,* from a novel of Eleanor H. Porter's, is an excessively optimistic person. On the other hand, a *Uriah Heep,* from Charles Dickens' *David Copperfield,* is an evil hypocrite. Many characters from literature have become so famous for certain characteristics that they find their way into dictionaries. Their names almost become common nouns.

"Oh, Paul's a Walter Mitty!"

In both *Webster's New Collegiate Dictionary* and in the *Random House Dictionary of the English Language,* Second Edition, Unabridged, the name of *Walter Mitty* appears as a word to be familiar with. If the word is applied to a person, what does it mean? By the time you finish the story, you'll know exactly what a Walter Mitty is . . . and you may secretly sympathize with the source of this name.

James Thurber is one of the noted humorists of modern times. His drawings, sketches, and stories display a wonderful sense of fun. You will find "The Secret Life of Walter Mitty" a story to chuckle over . . . and remember.

THE SECRET LIFE OF WALTER MITTY

"**W**e're going through!" The Commander's voice was like thin ice breaking. He wore his full-dress uniform, with the heavily braided white cap pulled down rakishly over one cold gray eye. "We can't make it, sir. It's spoiling for a hurricane, if you ask me." "I'm not asking you, Lieutenant Berg," said the Commander. "Throw on the power lights! Rev her up to 8,500! We're going through!" The pounding of the cylinders increased: ta-pocketa-pocketa-pocketa-*pocketa-pocketa*. The Commander stared at the ice forming on the pilot window. He walked over and twisted a row of complicated dials. "Switch on No. 8 auxiliary!" he shouted. "Switch on No. 8 auxiliary!" repeated Lieutenant Berg. "Full strength in No. 3 turret!" shouted the Commander. "Full strength in No. 3 turret!" The crew, bending to their various tasks in the huge, hurtling eight-engined Navy hydroplane, looked at each other and grinned. "The Old Man'll get us through," they said to one another. "The Old Man ain't afraid of Hell!" . . .

"Not so fast! You're driving too fast!" said Mrs. Mitty. "What are you driving so fast for?"

"Hmm?" said Walter Mitty. He looked at his wife, in the seat beside him, with shocked astonishment. She seemed grossly unfamiliar, like a strange woman who had yelled at him in a crowd. "You were up to fifty-five," she said. "You know I don't like to go more than forty. You were up to fifty-five." Walter Mitty drove on toward Waterbury in silence, the roaring of the SN202 through the worst storm in twenty years of Navy flying fading in the remote, intimate airways of

his mind. "You're tensed up again," said Mrs. Mitty. "It's one
of your days. I wish you'd let Dr. Renshaw look you over."

Walter Mitty stopped the car in front of the building where
his wife went to have her hair done. "Remember to get those
overshoes while I'm having my hair done," she said. "I don't
need overshoes," said Mitty. She put her mirror back into her
bag. "We've been all through that," she said, getting out of the
car. "You're not a young man any longer." He raced the engine
a little. "Why don't you wear your gloves? Have you lost your
gloves?" Walter Mitty reached in a pocket and brought out the
gloves. He put them on, but after she had turned and gone into
the building and he had driven on to a red light, he took them
off again. "Pick it up, brother!" snapped a cop as the light
changed, and Mitty hastily pulled on his gloves and lurched
ahead. He drove around the streets aimlessly for a time, and

then he drove past the hospital on his way to the parking lot. ... "It's the millionaire banker, Wellington McMillan," said the pretty nurse. "Yes!" said Walter Mitty, removing his gloves slowly. "Who has the case?" "Dr. Renshaw and Dr. Benbow, but there are two specialists here, Dr. Remington from New York and Mr. Pritchard-Mitford from London. He flew over." A door opened down a long, cool corridor and Dr. Renshaw came out. He looked distraught and haggard. "Hello, Mitty," he said. "We're having the devil's own time with McMillan, the millionaire banker and close personal friend of Roosevelt. Obstreosis of the ductal tract. Tertiary. Wish you'd take a look at him." "Glad to," said Mitty.

In the operating room there were whispered introductions: "Dr. Remington, Dr. Mitty. Mr. Pritchard-Mitford, Dr. Mitty." "I've read your book on streptothricosis," said Pritchard-Mitford, shaking hands. "A brilliant performance, sir." "Thank you," said Walter Mitty. "Didn't know you were in the States, Mitty," grumbled Remington. "Coals to Newcastle, bringing Mitford and me up here for a tertiary." "You are very kind," said Mitty. A huge, complicated machine, connected to the operating table, with many tubes and wires, began at this moment to go pocketa-pocketa-pocketa. "The new anesthetizer is giving way!" shouted an interne. "There is no one in the East who knows how to fix it!" "Quiet, man!" said Mitty, in a low, cool voice. He sprang to the machine, which was now going pocketa-pocketa-queep-pocketa-queep. He began fingering delicately a row of glistening dials. "Give me a fountain pen!" he snapped. Someone handed him a fountain pen. He pulled a faulty piston out of the machine and inserted the pen in its place. "That will hold for ten minutes," he said. "Get on with the operation." A nurse hurried over and whispered to Renshaw, and Mitty saw the man turn pale. "Coreopsis has set in," said Renshaw nervously. "If you would take over, Mitty?" Mitty looked at him and at the craven figure of Benbow, who drank, and at the grave, uncertain faces of the two great specialists. "If you wish," he said. They slipped a white gown on him; he adjusted a mask and drew on thin gloves; nurses handed him shining ...

"Back it up, Mac! Look out for that Buick!" Walter Mitty jammed on the brakes. "Wrong lane, Mac," said the parking-lot attendant, looking at Mitty closely. "Gee. Yeh," muttered Mitty. He began cautiously to back out of the lane marked "Exit Only." "Leave her sit there," said the attendant. "I'll put her away." Mitty got out of the car. "Hey, better leave the key." "Oh," said Mitty; handing the man the ignition key. The attendant vaulted into the car, backed it up with insolent skill, and put it where it belonged.

They're so damn cocky, thought Walter Mitty, walking along Main Street; they think they know everything. Once he had tried to take his chains off, outside New Milford, and he had got them wound around the axles. A man had had to come out in a wrecking car and unwind them, a young, grinning garageman. Since then Mrs. Mitty always made him drive to a garage to have the chains taken off. The next time, he thought, I'll wear my right arm in a sling; they won't grin at me then. I'll have my right arm in a sling and they'll see I couldn't possibly take the chains off myself. He kicked at the slush on the sidewalk. "Overshoes," he said to himself, and he began looking for a shoe store.

When he came out into the street again, with the overshoes in a box under his arm, Walter Mitty began to wonder what the other thing was his wife had told him to get. She had told him twice, before they set out from their house for Waterbury. In a way he hated these weekly trips to town—he was always getting something wrong. Kleenex, he thought, Squibb's, razor blades? No. Toothpaste, toothbrush, bicarbonate, Carborundum, initiative, and referendum? He gave it up. But she would remember it. "Where's the what's-its-name?" she would ask. "Don't tell me you forgot the what's-its-name." A newsboy went by shouting something about the Waterbury trial.

. . . "Perhaps this will refresh your memory." The District Attorney suddenly thrust a heavy automatic at the quiet figure on the witness stand. "Have you ever seen this before?" Walter Mitty took the gun and examined it expertly. "This is my Webley-Vickers 50.80," he said calmly. An excited buzz ran around the courtroom. The judge rapped for order. "You are a crack shot with any sort of firearms, I believe?" said the District Attorney, insinuatingly. "Objection!" shouted Mitty's attorney. "We have shown that the defendant could not have fired the shot. We have shown that he wore his right arm in a sling on the night of the fourteenth of July." Walter Mitty raised his hand briefly and the bickering attorneys were stilled. "With any known make of gun," he said evenly, "I could have killed Gregory Fitzhurst at three hundred feet *with my left hand*." Pandemonium broke loose in the courtroom. A woman's scream rose above the bedlam and suddenly a lovely, dark-haired girl was in Walter Mitty's arms. The District Attorney struck at her savagely. Without rising from his chair, Mitty let the man have it on the point of the chin. "You miserable cur!" . . .

"Puppy biscuit," said Walter Mitty. He stopped walking and the buildings of Waterbury rose up out of the misty courtroom and surrounded him again. A woman who was passing laughed. "He said 'Puppy biscuit,'" she said to her companion. "That man said 'Puppy biscuit' to himself." Walter Mitty hurried on. He went into an A & P, not the first one he came to but a smaller one farther up the street. "I want some biscuit for small, young dogs," he said to the clerk. "Any special brand, sir?" The greatest pistol shot in the world thought a moment. "It says 'Puppies Bark for It' on the box," said Walter Mitty.

His wife would be through at the hairdresser's in fifteen minutes, Mitty saw in looking at his watch, unless they had trouble drying it; sometimes they had trouble drying it. She didn't like to get to the hotel first; she would want him to be there waiting for her as usual. He found a big leather chair in the lobby, facing a window, and he put the overshoes and the puppy biscuit on the floor beside it. He picked up an old copy of *Liberty* and sank down into the chair. "Can Germany Conquer the World Through the Air?" Walter Mitty looked at the pictures of bombing planes and of ruined streets.

. . . "The cannonading has got the wind up in young Raleigh, sir," said the sergeant. Captain Mitty looked up at him through tousled hair. "Get him to bed," he said wearily. "With the others. I'll fly alone." "But you can't, sir," said the sergeant anxiously. "It takes two men to handle that bomber and the Archies are pounding hell out of the air. Von Richtman's circus is between here and Saulier." "Somebody's got to get that ammunition dump," said Mitty. "I'm going over. Spot of brandy?" He poured a drink for the sergeant and one for himself. War thundered and whined around the dugout and battered at the door. There was a rending of wood, and splinters flew through the room. "A bit of a near thing," said Captain Mitty carelessly. "The box barrage is closing in," said the sergeant. "We only live once, Sergeant," said Mitty, with his faint, fleeting smile. "Or do we?" He poured another brandy and tossed it off. "I never see a man could hold his brandy like you, sir," said the sergeant. "Begging your pardon, sir." Captain Mitty stood up and strapped on his huge Webley-Vickers automatic. "It's forty kilometers through hell, sir," said the sergeant. Mitty finished one last brandy. "After all," he said softly, "what isn't?" The pounding of the cannon increased; there was the rat-tat-tatting of machine guns, and from somewhere came the menacing pocketa-pocketa-pocketa of the new flamethrowers. Walter Mitty walked to the door of the dugout humming "Auprès de Ma Blonde." He turned and waved to the sergeant. "Cheerio!" he said . . .

Something struck his shoulder. "I've been looking all over this hotel for you," said Mrs. Mitty. "Why do you have to hide in this old chair? How did you expect me to find you?" "Things close in," said Walter Mitty vaguely. "What?" Mrs. Mitty said. "Did you get the what's-its-name? The puppy biscuit? What's in that box?" "Overshoes," said Mitty. "Couldn't you have put them on in the store?" "I was thinking," said Walter Mitty. "Does it ever occur to you that I am sometimes thinking?" She looked at him. "I'm going to take your temperature when I get you home," she said.

They went out through the revolving doors that made a faintly derisive whistling sound when you pushed them. It was two blocks to the parking lot. At the drugstore on the corner she said, "Wait here for me. I forgot something. I won't be a minute." She was more than a minute. Walter Mitty lighted a cigarette. It began to rain, rain with sleet in it. He stood up against the wall of the drugstore, smoking. . . . He put his shoulders back and his heels together. "To hell with the handkerchief," said Walter Mitty scornfully. He took one last drag on his cigarette and snapped it away. Then, with that faint, fleeting smile playing about his lips, he faced the firing squad; erect and motionless, proud and disdainful, Walter Mitty the Undefeated, inscrutable to the last.

Reading for Understanding _____

Main Idea

1. Walter Mitty   (a) lived a life full of rich and dangerous adventure   (b) was a famous surgeon   (c) was a daydreamer   (d) was a war hero.

Details

2. "The Old Man" in paragraph 1 is   (a) Lieutenant Berg   (b) Dr.   Remington   (c) the   District   Attorney   (d) Walter Mitty.

3. In the hospital episode, Walter Mitty repairs the anesthetizer with a   (a) pair of gloves   (b) fountain pen   (c) piston   (d) handkerchief.

4. At one point, Walter Mitty   (a) entered the parking lot in the wrong lane   (b) got to the hotel after his wife   (c) bawled out a traffic cop   (d) bought bread instead of puppy biscuit.

5. Walter's wife urged him to wear   (a) overshoes   (b) a hat   (c) a raincoat   (d) an initialed handkerchief.

Inferences

6. Walter Mitty is driving fast because in his imagination he's   (a) performing an operation   (b) flying a plane   (c) in a courtroom   (d) on the firing line.

7. When Mitty says, "I don't need overshoes," he's thinking that   (a) his wife really does understand him   (b) it's not going to rain   (c) Commander Mitty would not wear overshoes   (d) he'll be driving anyway.

8. The cop says, "Pick it up, brother," because Mitty   (a) has dropped his gloves   (b) has lost an overshoe   (c) is going too slow   (d) hasn't noticed the light change.

9. In all the episodes, Mitty is   (a) timid and thoughtful

(b) brave and dramatic   (c) cruel and thoughtless
(d) courageous but second-rate.

10. Walter Mitty's daydreams are usually triggered by
(a) a car radio   (b) his wife's creative imagination
(c) sounds and events around him   (d) the parking attendant's sympathetic smile.

Order of Events

11. Arrange the items in the order in which they appear in the
story. Use letters only.
A. Walter Mitty strikes the District Attorney.
B. Walter Mitty faces the firing squad bravely.
C. Mrs. Mitty complains that Walter is driving too fast.
D. Surgeon Mitty prepares for a critical operation.
E. Walter Mitty remembers the puppy biscuits.

Outcomes

12. Not long after his "death" by the firing squad, Walter
Mitty   (a) is engaged in another imaginary experience
(b) throws his gloves into a wastebasket   (c) has a terrible argument with his wife   (d) becomes a skilled
pilot.

Cause and Effect

13. Walter Mitty didn't pay attention entering the parking lot
because   (a) his brakes were bad   (b) he resented the
young garageman   (c) he was about to "perform an
operation"   (d) the car's pistons were misfiring.

Fact or Opinion

Tell whether the following is a fact or an opinion.
14. Walter Mitty was a good, if absentminded, husband.

Author's Role

15. The style of the author might be characterized as
(a) solemn and heavy   (b) light and amusing
(c) dull and repetitive   (d) artificial and offensive.

Words in Context

1. "Switch on No. 8 *auxiliary!*" he shouted.
   Auxiliary (285) means   (a) supporting   (b) outdated
   (c) absolute   (d) repeating.

2. She seemed *grossly* unfamiliar, like a strange woman who
   had yelled at him in a crowd.
   Grossly (285) means   (a) strangely   (b) totally
   (c) realistically   (d) gently.

3. Mitty hastily pulled on his gloves and *lurched* ahead.
   Lurched (286) means   (a) went faster than the speed
   limit   (b) sprang ahead   (c) moved slowly but
   steadily   (d) turned sharply to the right.

4, 5. He looked *distraught* and *haggard*.
   Distraught (287) means   (a) quietly efficient
   (b) remarkably calm   (c) deeply troubled
   (d) fiercely independent.
   Haggard (287) means having a   (a) possible solution
   (b) lot of energy   (c) careful organization
   (d) wasted look.

6. "The new anesthetizer is giving way!" shouted an *interne*.
   Interne (287) means   (a) student doctor   (b) skilled
   specialist   (c) experienced surgeon   (d) hospital
   administrator.

7. Mitty looked at him and at the *craven* figure of Benbow,
   who drank.
   Craven (287) means   (a) bent   (b) proud   (c) bold
   (d) cowardly.

8, 9. The attendant *vaulted* into the car, backed it up with
   insolent skill, and put it where it belonged.
   Vaulted (288) means   (a) crashed   (b) drove
   (c) leaped   (d) fell.
   Insolent (288) means   (a) weary   (b) uncertain
   (c) disrespectful   (d) cruel.

10. *Pandemonium* broke loose in the courtroom.
    Pandemonium (289) means   (a) dangerous fire

(b) contagious disease   (c) mild disagreement
(d) utter confusion.

11.   A woman's scream rose above the *bedlam*.
      Bedlam (289) means   (a) duel   (b) loudspeaker
      (c) uproar   (d) building.

12.   There was a *rending* of wood, and splinters flew through
      the room.
      Rending (290) means   (a) splitting   (b) explosion
      (c) hissing   (d) sawing.

13.   They went out through the revolving doors that made a
      faintly *derisive* whistling sound when you pushed them.
      Derisive (290) means   (a) pleasant   (b) mocking
      (c) noisy   (d) unrecognizable.

14, 15.   Then, with that faint, fleeting smile playing about his
      lips, he faced the firing squad; erect and motionless,
      proud and *disdainful*, Walter Mitty the Undefeated,
      inscrutable to the last.
      Disdainful (290) means   (a) calm   (b) agreeable
      (c) weary   (d) scornful.
      Inscrutable (290) means   (a) mysterious
      (b) talkative   (c) unbearable   (d) humorous.

Thinking Critically About the Story _____

1.   Now that you have read the story, how do you think the
     dictionary defines *Walter Mitty?* What are Walter's major
     characteristics?

2.   Compatibility is a sufficient similarity of personality traits
     to allow two people to live harmoniously together. Were
     Walter Mitty and his wife compatible? Is it possible for two
     incompatible people to have a successful marriage? Ex-
     plain. What does the statement, "He was always getting
     something wrong," tell about the relationship.

3.   There is usually a link between the outside world and
     Walter Mitty's daydreams. For example, the sound of his

automobile's engines ("pocketa-pocketa-pocketa-pocketa") helped develop his daydream about the Navy hydroplane. Point out similar links with the daydreams that follow.

4. It has been said that every person is the hero of his or her life story. How does this statement relate to the story?

5. Add a brief chapter to "The Secret Life of Walter Mitty." In a composition of 200–250 words, imagine still another daydream of Walter Mitty's, perhaps as he opens his front door and hears a clock chiming.

Stories in Words

Ignition (288)   This word reminds us that our automobiles run on explosions. The root is the Latin word *ignis* meaning "fire." Ignition is at the heart of the auto engine's power. The explosive gas mixture in each cylinder is *ignited* in turn, forcing the cylinders up and down. This motion of the cylinders is the driving force of the car. The root *ignis* also appears in *ignite*, "to set on fire," and *igneous*, "a kind of rock formed by volcanic action."

Pandemonium (289)   *Demon* is the recognizable root in *pandemonium*. *Pan*, meaning "all," is found in *pan-American* and *panorama* ("unlimited view in all directions"). In *Paradise Lost*, the English poet John Milton coined *pandemonium* to represent the capital of Hell, where all the demons assembled. It was a place of utter noise and confusion, and that is the association with the word today.

Bedlam (289)   The history of this word tells us something about the historical attitude toward the mentally disturbed. Many of these unfortunate people were housed in the Hospital of St. Mary of Bethlehem in London. The name *Bethlehem* was corrupted to *Bedlam*. The word came to mean a place of extreme noise and confusion. Though Bedlam was a place of unhappy disorder, it is notable for being England's first hospital for the mentally disturbed.

Tobermory

Saki (H. H. Munro)

◆ "And do you really ask us to believe," Sir Wilfrid
was saying, "that you have discovered a means for
instructing animals in the art of human speech and
that dear old Tobermory has proved your first successful pupil?"

Fiction is based on a "willing suspension of disbelief." In order for us to
become emotionally involved in a story, we must be willing to accept the
reality that the author presents.

Yes, this story opens with Cornelius Appin calmly claiming that he has
met a cat with so high a level of intelligence and ability that it has learned to
converse in English! If at this point, you say, "Rubbish! That's impossible!"—
that would end the author's chances of enticing you into becoming emotionally involved in what he claims has happened.

But, on the other hand, let's suppose that you say—as most readers
do—"I'll accept the author's facts." Now where will it lead you?

If the author is hard and tough, the story line could involve robbery,
murder, intrigue in high places. If the writer is a humanitarian, you would
learn what Tobermory could teach about the oneness of life. If the author is
a skillful humorist, he could have his story cat—but why go on. Let's let Saki
himself tell you what he did with the talking supercat.

TOBERMORY

It was a chill, rainwashed afternoon of a late August day, that indefinite season when partridges are still in security or cold storage, and there is nothing to hunt—unless one is bounded on the north by the Bristol Channel*, in which case one may lawfully gallop after fat red stags. Lady Blemley's house party was not bounded on the north by the Bristol Channel, hence there was a full gathering of her guests round the tea table on this particular afternoon. And, in spite of the blankness of the season and the triteness of the occasion, there was no trace in the company of that fatigued restlessness which means a dread of the pianola and a subdued hankering for the game of bridge. The undisguised open-mouthed attention of the entire party was fixed on the homely, negative personality of Mr. Cornelius Appin. Of all her guests, he was the one who had come to Lady Blemley with the vaguest reputation. Someone had said he was "clever," and he had got his invitation in the moderate expectation, on the part of his hostess, that some portion at least of his cleverness would be contributed to the general entertainment. Until teatime that day she had been unable to discover in what direction, if any, his cleverness lay. He was neither a wit nor a croquet champion, a hypnotic force nor a begetter of amateur theatricals. Neither did his exterior suggest the sort of man in whom women are willing to pardon a generous measure of mental deficiency. He had subsided into mere Mr. Appin, and the Cornelius seemed a piece of transparent baptismal bluff. And now he was claiming to have launched on the world a discovery beside which the invention of gunpowder, of the printing press,

* *Bristol Channel*   waterway on the west coast of England

297

and of steam locomotion were inconsiderable trifles. Science had made bewildering strides in many directions during recent decades, but this thing seemed to belong to the domain of miracle rather than to scientific achievement.

"And do you really ask us to believe," Sir Wilfrid was saying, "that you have discovered a means for instructing animals in the art of human speech, and that dear old Tobermory has proved your first successful pupil?"

"It is a problem at which I have worked for the last seventeen years," said Mr. Appin, "but only during the last eight or nine months have I been rewarded with glimmerings of success. Of course I have experimented with thousands of animals, but latterly only with cats, those wonderful creatures which have assimilated themselves so marvelously with our civilization while retaining all their highly developed feral instincts. Here and there among cats one comes across an outstanding superior intellect, just as one does among the ruck of human beings, and when I made the acquaintance of Tobermory a week ago, I saw at once that I was in contact with a 'Beyond—cat' of extraordinary intelligence. I had gone far along the road to success in recent experiments; with Tobermory, as you call him, I have reached the goal."

Mr. Appin concluded his remarkable statement in a voice which strove to divest of the triumphant inflection. No one said "Rats," though Clovis's lips moved in a monosyllabic contortion which probably invoked those rodents of disbelief.

"And do you mean to say," asked Miss Resker, after a slight pause, "that you have taught Tobermory to say and understand easy sentences of one syllable?"

"My dear Miss Resker," said the wonder-worker patiently, "one teaches little children and savages and backward adults in that piecemeal fashion; when one has once solved the problem of making a beginning with an animal of highly developed intelligence one has no need for those halting methods. Tobermory can speak our language with perfect correctness."

This time Clovis very distinctly said, "Beyond—rats!" Sir Wilfrid was more polite, but equally skeptical.

"Hadn't we better have the cat in and judge for ourselves?" suggested Lady Blemley.

Sir Wilfrid went in search of the animal, and the company settled themselves down to the languid expectation of witnessing some more or less adroit drawing room ventriloquism.

In a minute Sir Wilfrid was back in the room, his face white beneath its tan and his eyes dilated with excitement.

"By Gad, it's true!"

His agitation was unmistakably genuine, and his hearers started forward in a thrill of awakened interest.

Collapsing into an armchair he continued breathlessly: "I found him dozing in the smoking room, and called out to him to come for his tea. He blinked at me in his usual way, and I said, 'Come on, Toby; don't keep us waiting'; and, by Gad! he drawled out in a most horribly natural voice that he'd come when he dashed well pleased! I nearly jumped out of my skin!"

Appin had preached to absolutely incredulous hearers; Sir Wilfrid's statement carried instant conviction. A Babel-like chorus of startled exclamation arose, amid which the scientist sat mutely enjoying the firstfruit of his stupendous discovery.

In the midst of the clamor Tobermory entered the room and made his way with velvet tread and studied unconcern across to the group seated round the tea table.

A sudden hush of awkwardness and constraint fell on the company. Somehow there seemed an element of embarrassment in addressing on equal terms a domestic cat of acknowledged mental ability.

"Will you have some milk, Tobermory?" asked Lady Blemley in a rather strained voice.

"I don't mind if I do," was the response, couched in a tone of even indifference. A shiver of suppressed excitement went through the listeners, and Lady Blemley might be excused for pouring out the saucerful of milk rather unsteadily.

"I'm afraid I've spilt a good deal of it," she said apologetically.

"After all, it's not my Axminster*," was Tobermory's rejoinder.

Another silence fell on the group, and then Miss Resker, in her best district-visitor manner, asked if the human language had been difficult to learn. Tobermory looked squarely at her

---

* *Axminster*   a type of rug

for a moment and then fixed his gaze serenely on the middle distance. It was obvious that boring questions lay outside his scheme of life.

"What do you think of human intelligence?" asked Mavis Pellington lamely.

"Of whose intelligence in particular?" asked Tobermory coldly.

"Oh, well, mine for instance," said Mavis, with a feeble laugh.

"You put me in an embarrassing position," said Tobermory, whose tone and attitude certainly did not suggest a shred of embarrassment. "When your inclusion in this house party was suggested Sir Wilfrid protested that you were the most brainless woman of his acquaintance, and that there was a wide distinction between hospitality and the care of the feebleminded. Lady Blemley replied that your lack of brain-power was the precise quality which had earned you your invitation, as you were the only person she could think of who might be idiotic enough to buy their old car. You know, the one they call 'The Envy of Sisyphus*,' because it goes quite nicely uphill if you push it."

Lady Blemley's protestations would have had greater effect if she had not casually suggested to Mavis only that morning that the car in question would be just the thing for her down at her Devonshire home. Major Barfield plunged in heavily to effect a diversion.

"How about your carryings-on with the tortoiseshell puss up at the stables, eh?"

The moment he said it everyone realized the blunder.

"One does not usually discuss these matters in public," said Tobermory frigidly. "From a slight observation of your ways since you've been in this house, I should imagine you'd find it inconvenient if I were to shift the conversation on to your own little affairs."

The panic which ensued was not confined to the Major.

"Would you like to go and see if cook has got your dinner ready?" suggested Lady Blemley hurriedly, affecting to ignore the fact that it wanted at least two hours to Tobermory's dinnertime.

"Thanks," said Tobermory, "not quite so soon after my tea. I don't want to die of indigestion."

"Cats have nine lives, you know," said Sir Wilfrid heartily.

"Possibly," answered Tobermory; "but only one liver."

"Adelaide!" said Mrs. Cornett, "do you mean to encourage that cat to go out and gossip about us in the servants' hall?"

The panic had indeed become general. A narrow ornamental balustrade ran in front of most of the bedroom windows at the Towers, and it was recalled with dismay that this had formed a favorite promenade for Tobermory at all hours, whence he could watch the pigeons—and heaven knew what

* *Sisyphus*   the mythical giant condemned forever to roll a boulder uphill only to have it constantly slip away and fall

else besides. If he intended to become reminiscent in his present outspoken strain, the effect would be something more than disconcerting. Mrs. Cornett, who spent much time at her toilet table, and whose complexion was reputed to be of a nomadic though punctual disposition, looked as ill at ease as the Major. Miss Scrawen, who wrote fiercely sensuous poetry and led a blameless life, merely displayed irritation; if you are methodical and virtuous in private you don't necessarily want everyone to know it. Bertie van Tahn, who was so depraved at seventeen that he had long ago given up trying to be any worse, turned a dull shade of gardenia-white, but he did not commit the error of dashing out of the room like Odo Finsberry, a young gentleman who was understood to be reading for the Church and who was possibly disturbed at the thought of scandals he might hear concerning other people. Clovis had the presence of mind to maintain a composed exterior; privately he was calculating how long it would take to procure a box of fancy mice through the agency of the *Exchange and Mart* as a species of hush money.

Even in the delicate situation like the present, Agnes Resker could not endure to remain too long in the background.

"Why did I ever come down here?" she asked dramatically.

Tobermory immediately accepted the opening.

"Judging by what you said to Mrs. Cornett on the croquet lawn yesterday, you were out for food. You described the Blemleys as the dullest people to stay with that you knew, but said they were clever enough to employ a first-rate cook; otherwise they'd find it difficult to get anyone to come down a second time."

"There's not a word of truth in it! I appeal to Mrs. Cornett—" exclaimed the discomfited Agnes.

"Mrs. Cornett repeated your remark afterwards to Bertie van Tahn," continued Tobermory, "and said, 'That woman is a regular Hunger Marcher; she'd go anywhere for four square meals a day,' and Bertie van Tahn said—"

At this point the chronicle mercifully ceased. Tobermory had caught a glimpse of the big yellow Tom from the Rectory working his way through the shrubbery toward the stable wing. In a flash he had vanished through the open French window.

With the disappearance of his too-brilliant pupil Cornelius Appin found himself beset by a hurricane of bitter upbraiding, anxious inquiry, and frightened entreaty. The responsibility for the situation lay with him, and he must prevent matters from becoming worse. Could Tobermory impart his dangerous gift to other cats? was the first question he had to answer. It was possible, he replied, that he might have initiated his intimate friend the stable puss into his new accomplishment, but it was unlikely that his teaching could have taken a wider range as yet.

"Then," said Mrs. Cornett, "Tobermory may be a valuable cat and a great pet; but I'm sure you'll agree, Adelaide, that both he and the stable cat must be done away with without delay."

"You don't suppose I've enjoyed the last quarter of an hour, do you?" said Lady Blemley bitterly. "My husband and I are very fond of Tobermory—at least, we were before this horrible accomplishment was infused into him; but now, of course, the only thing is to have him destroyed as soon as possible."

"We can put some strychnine in the scraps he always gets at dinnertime," said Sir Wilfrid, "and I will go and drown the stable cat myself. The coachman will be very sore at losing his pet, but I'll say a very catching form of mange has broken out in both cats and we're afraid of its spreading to the kennels."

"But my great discovery!" expostulated Mr. Appin; "after all my years of research and experiment—"

"You can go and experiment on the shorthorns at the farm, who are under proper control," said Mrs. Cornett, "or the elephants at the Zoological Gardens. They're said to be highly intelligent, and they have this recommendation, that they don't come creeping about our bedrooms and under chairs, and so forth."

An archangel ecstatically proclaiming the Millennium, and then finding that it clashed unpardonably with Henley and would have to be indefinitely postponed, could hardly have felt more crestfallen than Cornelius Appin at the reception of his wonderful achievement. Public opinion, however, was against him—in fact, had the general voice been consulted on the subject it is probable that a strong minority vote would have been in favor of including him in the strychnine diet.

Defective train arrangements and a nervous desire to see matters brought to a finish prevented an immediate dispersal of the party, but dinner that evening was not a social success. Sir Wilfrid had had rather a trying time with the stable cat and subsequently with the coachman. Agnes Resker ostentatiously limited her repast to a morsel of dry toast, which she bit as though it were a personal enemy; while Mavis Pellington maintained a vindictive silence throughout the meal. Lady Blemley kept up a flow of what she hoped was conversation, but her attention was fixed on the doorway. A plateful of carefully dosed fish scraps was in readiness on the sideboard, but sweets and savory and dessert went their way, and no Tobermory appeared either in the dining room or kitchen.

The sepulchral dinner was cheerful compared with the subsequent vigil in the smoking room. Eating and drinking had at least supplied a distraction and cloak to the prevailing embarrassment. Bridge was out of the question in the general tension of nerves and tempers, and after Odo Finsberry had given a lugubrious rendering of "Mélisande in the Wood" to a frigid audience, music was tacitly avoided. At eleven the servants went to bed, announcing that the small window in the pantry had been left open as usual for Tobermory's private use. The guests read steadily through the current batch of magazines, and fell back gradually on the "Badminton Library" and bound volumes of *Punch*[*], Lady Blemley made periodic visits to the pantry, returning each time with an expression of listless depression which forestalled questioning.

At two o'clock Clovis broke the dominating silence.

"He won't turn up tonight. He's probably in the local newspaper office at the present moment, dictating the first installment of his reminiscences. Lady What's-her-name's book won't be in it. It will be the event of the day."

Having made this contribution to the general cheerfulness, Clovis went to bed. At long intervals the various members of the house party followed his example.

The servants taking round the early tea made a uniform announcement in reply to a uniform question. Tobermory had not returned.

Breakfast was, if anything, a more unpleasant function than dinner had been, but before its conclusion the situation

[*] *Punch*   British humor magazine

was relieved. Tobermory's corpse was brought in from the shrubbery, where a gardener had just discovered it. From the bites on his throat and the yellow fur which coated his claws it was evident that he had fallen in unequal combat with the big Tom from the Rectory.

By midday most of the guests had quitted the Towers, and after lunch Lady Blemley had sufficiently recovered her spirits to write an extremely nasty letter to the Rectory about the loss of her valuable pet.

Tobermory had been Appin's one successful pupil, and he was destined to have no successor. A few weeks later an elephant in the Dresden Zoological Garden, which had shown no previous signs of irritability, broke loose and killed an Englishman who had apparently been teasing it. The victim's name was variously reported in the papers as Oppin and Eppelin, but his front name was faithfully rendered Cornelius.

"If he was trying German irregular verbs on the poor beast," said Clovis, "he deserved all he got."

Reading for Understanding _____

Main Idea

1. Which of the following best states the main idea of the story?
   (a) Neither people nor animals are ready for conversational communication with each other.
   (b) To remain alive and safe, cats should not be taught to speak.
   (c) People are more fearful of having their weaknesses exposed than they are of seeing progress made.
   (d) Cats are fundamentally bright, sensitive to the needs of people.

Details

2. The story takes place in (a) New York City (b) London (c) a French villa (d) a British country estate.

3. Late August is   (a) the hunting season   (b) the opera
   season   (c) the horseracing season   (d) in between
   seasons.

4. Lady Blemley has invited Cornelius Appin to the house
   party because   (a) he is a member of the group
   (b) he has asked her to invite him   (c) she hopes the
   group will find him entertaining   (d) he promises to
   make the party a success.

5. Tobermory is   (a) one of the many Appin has taught to
   speak   (b) the only pupil Appin has ever had
   (c) the only pupil Appin has ever succeeded with
   (d) an unwilling pupil.

Inferences

6. All the people, except Appin, singled out by Tobermory or
   the   author   (a) are   hardworking   and   earnest
   (b) are striving to help others   (c) have something to
   hide from others   (d) are without a conscience.

7. Cornelius   Appin   (a) envies   the   other   guests
   (b) is not easily discouraged   (c) has a well-developed
   sense of humor   (d) experiments only in controlled environments.

8. When Tobermory fails to return, the guests   (a) fear for
   his   safety   (b) are   relieved   (c) decide   to   leave
   (d) fear further exposure.

9. Lady   Blemley's   husband   is   (a) Major   Barfield
   (b) Odo   Finsberry   (c) Sir   Wilfrid   (d) Bertie   van
   Tahn.

10. The guests do not fear that   (a) Tobermory would teach
    cats to talk   (b) the other guests would learn their
    secrets   (c) the secrets would be made known to the
    servants   (d) Appin would tell the secrets to others.

Order of Events

11. Arrange the items in the order in which they occurred.
    Use letters only.
    A. Tobermory's knowledge threatens the intimate lives of
       the members of the group.

    B. Cornelius Appin meets an unwilling pupil for the last time.

    C. Odo Finsberry sings to an unappreciative audience.

    D. Appin meets Tobermory for the first time.

    E. Lady Blemley sends a note of protest to the Rectory.

Outcomes

12. A major outcome of the experience is that   (a) training animals beyond their nature can bring unforeseen trouble (b) Cornelius Appin tries to blackmail Lady Blemley (c) Lady Blemley misses Tobermory   (d) Lady Blemley publishes her autobiography.

Cause and Effect

13. The undoing of Tobermory is caused by his (a) intelligence   (b) curiosity   (c) self-confidence (d) love of gossip.

Fact or Opinion

Tell whether the following is a fact or an opinion.

14. Tobermory is at least the equal of the partygoers in intelligence and quickness of wit.

Author's Role

15. Which of the following least expresses the author's purpose.

    (a) To satirize the social behavior of a class of society

    (b) To poke fun at cattiness of human beings and animals

    (c) To carry a humorous idea to a logical conclusion

    (d) To encourage experimentation in communicating with animals

Words in Context

Group One: Quips and Twists

Readers turn to Saki not only for his unusual plots and skillful character portrayal but also for his ability to manipulate words. How many of the following five samples did you get?

1.   . . . that indefinite season when partridges are still in
      security or cold storage. (page 297)
      It is the time when   (a) people become vegetarians
      (b) shooting game-birds is illegal   (c) the hunting
      crowd goes north   (d) the weather turns cold.

2.   . . . there was no trace of that fatigued restlessness which
      means a dread of the pianola and a subdued hankering for
      a bridge game. (page 297)
      The group is   (a) looking forward to listening to a
      recital or playing bridge   (b) bored   (c) very noisy
      (d) interested in what is going on.

3.   Neither did his exterior suggest the sort of man in whom
      women are willing to pardon a generous measure of
      mental deficiency. (page 297)
      Cornelius Appin   (a) is handsome   (b) has an
      outgoing personality   (c) is an awkward, shy person
      (d) is not physically appealing to women.

4.   . . . and the [name] Cornelius seemed a piece of transpar-
      ent baptismal bluff. (page 297)
      The name Cornelius   (a) is stuffy   (b) implies a more
      exciting personality than Appin's   (c) is too
      old-fashioned   (d) was given to Appin to make him
      successful.

5.   . . . those wonderful creatures which have assimilated
      themselves so marvelously with our civilization while
      retaining all their highly developed feral instincts. (page
      298)
      The author praises cats because   (a) they are pleasant
      companions   (b) they can be both pets and wild
      animals   (c) they can be trained easily   (d) they can
      take care of themselves.

Group Two: Words

6.   . . . but only during the last eight or nine months have I
      been rewarded with *glimmerings* of success.
      Glimmerings (298) means   (a) glimpses   (b) rewards
      (c) knowledge   (d) chances.

7.   Here and there among cats one comes across an outstand-

ing superior intellect, just as one does among the *ruck* of human beings . . .
Ruck (298) means   (a) students   (b) leaders
(c) great mass   (d) lowest.

8. No one said "Rats," though Clovis's lips moved in a *monosyllabic contortion* which probably invoked those rodents of disbelief.
Monosyllabic contortion (298) means   (a) one-syllable twist   (b) noisy grunt   (c) silent grin   (d) hurried nod.

9. Appin had preached to absolutely *incredulous* hearers . . .
Incredulous (299) means   (a) fascinated   (b) loyal
(c) bored   (d) unbelieving.

10. "I don't mind if I do," was the response, couched in a tone of even *indifference*.
Indifference (299) means   (a) not caring   (b) anger
(c) sarcasm   (d) politeness.

11. Tobermory looked squarely at her for a moment and then fixed his gaze *serenely* on the middle distance.
Serenely (300) means   (a) proudly   (b) slyly
(c) calmly   (d) quickly.

12. Major Barfield plunged in heavily to effect a *diversion*.
Diversion (301) means   (a) comedy   (b) difficulty
(c) distraction   (d) way out.

13. "One does not usually discuss these matters in public," said Tobermory *frigidly*.
Frigidly (301) means   (a) proudly   (b) politely
(c) icily   (d) softly.

14. The panic which *ensued* was not confined to the Major.
Ensued (301) means   (a) ended   (b) multiplied
(c) exploded   (d) followed.

15. Clovis had the presence of mind to maintain a *composed exterior* . . .
Composed exterior (302) means   (a) calm appearance
(b) fixed smile   (c) sad look   (d) look of disbelief.

16. At this point the *chronicle* mercifully ceased.
Chronicle (302) means   (a) record   (b) torture
(c) search   (d) scandals.

17. "But my great discovery!" *expostulated* Mr. Appin; "after all my years of research and experiment—"
    Expostulated (303) means   (a) shouted   (b) groaned   (c) joked   (d) demanded.

18. The *sepulchral* dinner was cheerful compared with the subsequent vigil in the smoking room.
    Sepulchral (304) means   (a) noisy   (b) hearty   (c) meager   (d) tomblike.

19. The servants taking round the early tea made a *uniform* announcement in reply to a *uniform* question.
    Uniform (304) means   (a) unchanging   (b) searching   (c) troublesome   (d) unanswerable.

20. Tobermory had been Appin's one successful pupil, and he was *destined* to have no successor.
    Destined (305) means   (a) ordered   (b) fated   (c) required   (d) discovered.

Thinking Critically About the Story _____

1. Did the author make maximum mileage from the gimmick of a talking animal? How does "Tobermory" compare with TV stories that you have seen, stories that contain live animals with dubbed in voices. Would "Tobermory" make a successful TV drama?

2. By referring to the situation dramas (soap operas) that come regularly onto your TV screen at home, test the truth of the following statement.

    The characters in "Tobermory" seem to come right out of the situation comedies and soap operas that we find on TV.

3. Are the characters in Tobermory true to life? Would you be willing to have the group as your friends? Is there missing in their lives anything that you feel is important?

4. What seems to be Cornelius Appin's attitude toward research? How significant was the discovery that he made? To what use did he put his discovery? How does he compare

with the research scientists in your family? With those you have read about? How would you have controlled the experimentation to prevent the problems he ran into? What would you have done to make the results more meaningful?

Stories in Words _____

Hypnotic (297)   The Greek god of sleep was Hypnos. Hypnosis is a sleeplike condition in which the subject responds to the suggestions of a hypnotist. An earlier word for hypnosis was *mesmerism*. F. A. Mesmer was a Viennese physician who treated certain kinds of ailments by the process now known as *hypnosis*.

Ventriloquism (299)   A skilled ventriloquist seems to "throw his or her voice," making it seem as though someone else or something (usually a dummy) is saying the words. Since a dummy doesn't speak and since a good ventriloquist doesn't move the lips when performing, the voice must come from somewhere. But where? The word *ventriloquism* suggests that the voice comes from the entertainer's stomach! *Venter*, the root for *stomach*, appears in certain scientific words like *ventral* and *ventricle*. *Loqu*, the root for speaking, appears in words like *loquacious* and *elocution*.

Pantry (304)   One of the most interesting processes in language is called "folk etymology." Over a period of time, some words have changed spellings to provide an apparent connection with another, more common, word. A *pickax* for example, by word derivation is not connected with *ax*. A *penthouse* is not connected with *house*. A *primrose* is not a *rose*. A *muskrat* is not a *rat*. *Curtail* doesn't mean "cut the tail off." *Cutlet* did not come from *cut*. *Pantry* is another such word. It is derived from the Latin word *panis*, "bread." By word history, the pantry is the place where "the bread is kept." Most people, however, think of it as the place where "the pans are kept."

Is He Living or Is He Dead?

Mark Twain

♦ "Yes, one of us must die to save the others—and himself. We will cast lots. The one chosen shall be illustrious, all of us shall be rich . . ."

We all spend so much time enjoying humor that releases tension and makes us laugh that we forget that humor can be serious—and bitter. Instead of causing us to roll in the aisles, it can make us grit our teeth in a frozen smile, protesting with "That wasn't funny!"

"Is He Living or Is He Dead" was written by one of America's best-known humorists, Mark Twain, but it is on the dark side. Twain made his reputation as the writer that made the world laugh. As he grew older and personal misfortunes buffeted him, he turned more and more toward themes that made fun of rather than laughed with.

In this story, Twain used one of his favorite formats, that of the tall story. A tall story involves an absurdity, something that couldn't be true, and builds it up with such realistic details that the reader feels it really could happen: a frog that won jumping contests until it was given a ballast of iron pellets, a lumberjack who was so tall and powerful that his sneeze would denude trees of their leaves for a mile around.

The central character of this story is Jean-François Millet, the beloved French painter who lived from 1814 to 1875. Mark Twain carefully tells us in the first sentence that the time the story opens is March 1892. Looking at dates we realize that at the time this most famous painter was no longer among the living—or was he?

So—there it is! The story involves a real celebrity, someone that history verifies as not the creation of an author. Read on and give Mark Twain a chance to let you decide whether the bitter taste of dark humor is to your liking.

IS HE LIVING OR IS HE DEAD?

I was spending the month of March, 1892, at Mentone, on the Riviera. At this retired spot one has all the advantages, privately, which are to be had at Monte Carlo and Nice, a few miles farther along, publicly. That is to say, one has the flooding sunshine, the balmy air, and the brilliant blue sea, without the marring additions of human powwow and fuss and feathers and display. Mentone is quiet, simple, restful, unpretentious; the rich and the gaudy do not come there. As a rule, I mean, the rich do not come there. Now and then a rich man comes, and I presently got acquainted with one of these. Partially to disguise him I will call him Smith. One day, in the Hôtel des Anglais, at the second breakfast, he exclaimed:

"Quick! Cast your eye on the man going out at the door. Take in every detail of him."

"Why?"

"Do you know who he is?"

"Yes. He spent several days here before you came. He is an old, retired, and very rich silk manufacturer from Lyons, they say, and I guess he is alone in the world, for he always looks sad and dreamy, and doesn't talk with anybody. His name is Théophile Magnan."

I supposed that Smith would now proceed to justify the large interest which he had shown in Monsieur Magnan; but instead he dropped into a brown study, and was apparently lost to me and to the rest of the world during some minutes. Now and then he passed his fingers through his flossy white hair, to assist his thinking, and meantime he allowed his breakfast to go on cooling. At last he said:

313

"No, it's gone; I can't call it back."

"Can't call what back?"

"It's one of Hans Andersen's beautiful little stories. But it's gone from me. Part of it is like this: A child has a caged bird, which it loves, but thoughtlessly neglects. The bird pours out its song unheard and unheeded; but in time, hunger and thirst assail the creature, and its song grows plaintive and feeble and finally ceases—the bird dies. The child comes, and is smitten to the heart with remorse; then, with bitter tears and lamentations, it calls its mates, and they bury the bird with elaborate pomp and the tenderest grief, without knowing, poor things, that it isn't children only who starve poets to death and then spend enough on their funerals and monuments to have kept them alive and made them easy and comfortable. Now—"

But here we were interrupted. About ten that evening I ran across Smith, and he asked me up to his parlor to help him smoke and drink hot toddy. It was a cozy place, with its comfortable chairs, its cheerful lamps, and its friendly open fire of seasoned olive wood. To make everything perfect, there was the muffled booming of the surf outside. After the second hot toddy and much lazy and contented chat, Smith said:

"Now we are properly primed—I to tell a curious history, and you to listen to it. It has been a secret for many years—a secret between me and three others; but I am going to break that seal now. Are you comfortable?"

"Perfectly. Go on."

Here follows what he told me:

A long time ago I was a young artist—a very young artist, in fact—and I wandered about the country parts of France, sketching here and sketching there, and was presently joined by a couple of young Frenchmen who were at the same kind of thing that I was doing. We were as happy as we were poor, or as poor as we were happy—phrase it to suit yourself. Claude Frère and Carl Boulanger—these are the names of those boys; likable companions, and the sunniest spirits that ever laughed at poverty and had a noble good time in all weathers.

At last we ran hard aground in a Breton village, and an artist as poor as ourselves took us in and literally saved us from starving—François Millet—

What! the *great* François Millet?"

Great? He wasn't any greater than we were, then. He hadn't any fame, even in his own village; and he was so poor that he hadn't anything to feed us on but turnips, and even the turnips failed us sometimes. We four became fast friends, doting friends, inseparables. We painted away together with all our might, piling up stock, piling up stock, but very seldom getting rid of any of it. We had wonderful times together, but, O my soul! how we were pinched now and then!

For a little over two years this went on. At last, one day, Claude said:

"Boys, we've come to the end. Do you understand that?—absolutely to the end. Everybody has struck—there's a league formed against us. I've been all around the village and it's just as I tell you. They refuse to credit us for another centime* until all the odds and ends are paid up."

This struck us cold. Every face was blank with dismay. We realized that our circumstances were desperate, now. There was a long silence. Finally, Millet said with a sigh:

"Nothing occurs to me—nothing. Suggest something, lads."

There was no response, unless a mournful silence may be called a response. Carl got up, and walked nervously up and down awhile, then said:

"It's a shame! Look at these canvases: stacks and stacks of as good pictures as anybody in Europe paints—I don't care who he is. Yes, and plenty of lounging strangers have said the same—or nearly that, anyway."

"But didn't buy," Millet said.

"No matter, they said it; and it's true, too. Look at your Angelus,† there! Will anybody tell me—"

"Pah, Carl—my 'Angelus'! I was offered five francs for it."

"When?"

"Who offered it?"

"Where is he?"

"Why didn't you take it?"

"Come—don't all speak at once. I thought he would give

* *centime*　　French penny
† *Angelus*　　Millet's masterpiece

more—I was sure of it—he looked it—so I asked him eight."

"Well—and then?"

"He said he would call again."

"Thunder and lightning! Why, François—"

"Oh, I know—I know! It was a mistake, and I was a fool. Boys, I meant for the best; you'll grant me that, and I—"

"Why, certainly, we know that, bless your dear heart; but don't you be a fool again."

"I? I wish somebody would come along and offer us a cabbage for it—you'd see!"

"A cabbage! Oh, don't name it—it makes my mouth water. Talk of things less trying."

"Boys," said Carl, "*do* these pictures lack merit? Answer me that."

"No!"

"Aren't they of very great and high merit? Answer me that."

"Yes."

"Of such great and high merit that, if an illustrious name were attached to them, they would sell at splendid prices. Isn't it so?"

"Certainly it is. Nobody doubts that."

"But—I'm not joking—*isn't* it so?"

"Why, of course it's so—and *we* are not joking. But what of it? What of it? How does that concern us?"

"In this way, comrades—we'll *attach* an illustrious name to them!"

The lively conversation stopped. The faces were turned inquiringly upon Carl. What sort of riddle might this be? Where was an illustrious name to be borrowed? And who was to borrow it?

Carl sat down, and said:

"Now, I have a perfectly serious thing to propose. I think it is the only way to keep us out of the almshouse, and I believe it to be a perfectly sure way. I base this opinion upon certain multitudinous and long-established facts in human history. I believe my project will make us all rich."

"Rich! You've lost your mind."

"No, I haven't."

"Yes, you have—you've lost your mind. What do you *call* rich?"

"A hundred thousand francs apiece."

"He *has* lost his mind. I knew it."

"Yes, he has. Carl, privation has been too much for you, and—"

"Carl, you want to take a pill and get right to bed."

"Bandage him first—bandage his head, and then—"

"No, bandage his heels; his brains have been settling for weeks—I've noticed it."

"Shut up!" said Millet, with ostensible severity, "and let the boy say his say. Now, then—come out with your project, Carl. What is it?"

"Well, then, by way of preamble I will ask you to note this fact in human history: that the merit of many a great artist has never been acknowledged until after he was starved and dead. This has happened so often that I make bold to found a law upon it. This law: that the merit of *every* great unknown and neglected artist must and will be recognized, and his pictures climb to high prices after his death. My project is this: we must cast lots—one of us must die."

The remark fell so calmly and so unexpectedly that we almost forgot to jump. Then there was a wild chorus of advice again—medical advice—for the help of Carl's brain; but he waited patiently for the hilarity to calm down, then went on again with his project:"

"Yes, one of us must die, to save the others—and himself. We will cast lots. The one chosen shall be illustrious, all of us shall be rich. Hold still, now—hold still; don't interrupt—I tell you I know what I am talking about. Here is the idea. During the next three months the one who is to die shall paint with all his might, enlarge his stock all he can—not pictures, *no!* skeleton sketches, studies, parts of studies, fragments of studies, a dozen dabs of the brush on each—meaningless, of course, but *his* with his cipher on them; turn out fifty a day, each to contain some peculiarity or mannerism, easily detectable as his—*they're* the things that sell you know, and are collected at fabulous prices for the world's museums, after the great man is gone; we'll have a ton of them ready—a ton! And all that time the rest of us will be busy supporting the moribund, and working Paris and the dealers—preparations for the coming event, you know; and when everything is hot and just right, we'll spring the death on them and have the notorious funeral. You get the idea?"

"N-o; at least, not qu—"

"Not quite? Don't you see? The man doesn't really die; he changes his name and vanishes; we bury a dummy, and cry over it, with all the world to help. And I—"

But he wasn't allowed to finish. Everybody broke out into a rousing hurrah of applause; and all jumped up and capered about the room in transports of gratitude and joy. For hours we talked over the great plan, without ever feeling hungry; and at last, when all the details had been arranged satisfactorily, we cast lots and Millet was elected—elected to die, as we called it. Then we scraped together those things which one never parts with until he is betting them against future wealth—keepsake trinkets and such like—and these we pawned for enough to furnish us a frugal farewell supper and breakfast, and leave us a few francs over for travel, and a stake of turnips and such for Millet to live on for a few days.

Next morning, early, the three of us cleared out, straightway after breakfast—on foot, of course. Each of us carried a dozen of Millet's small pictures, purposing to market them. Carl struck for Paris, where he would start the work of building up Millet's fame against the coming great day. Claude and I were to separate, and scatter abroad over France.

Now, it will surprise you to know what an easy and comfortable thing we had. I walked two days before I began business. Then I began to sketch a villa in the outskirts of a big town—because I saw the proprietor standing on an upper veranda. He came down to look on—I thought he would. I worked swiftly, intending to keep him interested. Occasionally he fired off a little ejaculation of approbation, and by and by he spoke up with enthusiasm, and said I was a master!

I put down my brush, reached into my satchel, fetched out a Millet, and pointed to the cipher in the corner. I said, proudly:

"I suppose you recognize *that?* Well, he taught me! I should *think* I ought to know my trade!"

The man looked guiltily embarrassed, and was silent. I said, sorrowfully:

"You don't mean to intimate that you don't know the cipher of François Millet!"

Of course he didn't know that cipher; but he was the gratefulest man you ever saw, just the same, for being let out of an uncomfortable place on such easy terms. He said:

"No! Why, it *is* Millet's, sure enough! I don't know what I could have been thinking of. Of course I recognize it now."

Next, he wanted to buy it; but I said that although I wasn't rich I wasn't *that* poor. However, at last, I let him have it for eight hundred francs.

"Eight hundred!"

Yes. Millet would have sold it for a pork-chop. Yes, I got eight hundred francs for that little thing. I wish I could get it back for eighty thousand. But that time's gone by. I made a very nice picture of that man's house, and I wanted to offer it to him for ten francs, but that wouldn't answer, seeing I was the pupil of such a master, so I sold it to him for a hundred. I sent the eight hundred francs straight back to Millet from that town and struck out again next day.

But I didn't walk—no. I rode. I have ridden ever since. I sold one picture every day, and never tried to sell two. I always said to my customer:

"I am a fool to sell a picture of François Millet's at all, for that man is not going to live three months, and when he dies his pictures can't be had for love or money."

I took care to spread that little fact as far as I could, and prepare the world for the event.

I take credit to myself for our plan of selling the pictures— it was mine. I suggested it that last evening when we were laying out our campaign, and all three of us agreed to give it a good fair trial before giving it up for some other. It succeeded with all of us. I walked only two days, Claude walked two— both of us afraid to make Millet celebrated too close to home—but Carl walked only half a day, the bright conscience- less rascal, and after that he traveled like a duke.

Every now and then we got in with a country editor and started an item around through the press; not an item announc- ing that a new painter had been discovered, but an item which

let on that everybody knew François Millet; not an item
praising him in any way, but merely a word concerning the
present condition of the "master"—sometimes hopeful, sometimes despondent, but always tinged with fears for the worst.
We always marked these paragraphs, and sent the papers to all
the people who had bought pictures of us.

Carl was soon in Paris, and he worked things with a high
hand. He made friends with the foreign reporters, and got
Millet's condition reported to England and all over the continent, and America, and everywhere.

At the end of six weeks from the start, we three met in Paris
and called a halt, and stopped sending back to Millet for
additional pictures. The boom was so high, and everything so
ripe, that we saw that it would be a mistake not to strike now,
right away, without waiting any longer. So we wrote Millet to
go to bed and begin to waste away pretty fast, for we should
like him to die in ten days if he could get ready.

Then we figured up and found that among us we had sold
eighty-five small pictures and studies, and had sixty-nine

thousand francs to show for it. Carl had made the last sale and the most brilliant one of all. He sold the "Angelus" for twenty-two hundred francs. How we did glorify him!—not foreseeing that a day was coming by and by when France would struggle to own it and a stranger would capture it for five hundred and fifty thousand, cash.

We had a wind-up champagne supper that night, and next day Claude and I packed up and went off to nurse Millet through his last days and keep busybodies out of the house and send daily bulletins to Carl in Paris for publication in the papers of several continents for the information of a waiting world. The sad end came at last, and Carl was there in time to help in the final mournful rites.

You remember that great funeral, and what a stir it made all over the globe, and how the illustrious of two worlds came to attend it and testify their sorrow. We four—still inseparable—carried the coffin, and would allow none to help. And we were right about that, because it hadn't anything in it but a wax figure, and any other coffin-bearers would have found fault with the weight. Yes, we same old four, who had lovingly shared privation together in the old hard times now gone forever, carried the cof—

"Which four?"

"*We* four—for Millet helped to carry his own coffin. In disguise, you know. Disguised as a relative—distant relative."

"Astonishing!"

"But true, just the same. Well, you remember how the pictures went up. Money? We didn't know what to do with it. There's a man in Paris today who owns seventy Millet pictures. He paid us two million francs for them. And as for the bushels of sketches and studies which Millet shoveled out during the six weeks that we were on the road, well, it would astonish you to know the figure we sell them at nowadays—that is, when we consent to let one go!"

"It is a wonderful history, perfectly wonderful!"

"Yes—it amounts to that."

"Whatever became of Millet?"

"Can you keep a secret?"

"I can."

"Do you remember the man I called your attention to in the dining room today? *That was François Millet.*"

"Great—"

"Scott! Yes. For once they didn't starve a genius to death and then put into other pockets the rewards he should have had himself. *This* songbird was not allowed to pipe out its heart unheard and then be paid with the cold pomp of a big funeral. We looked out for that."

Reading for Understanding _____

Main Idea

1. Which of the following quotations best expresses the main idea of the story?
    (a) "Now we are properly primed—I to tell you a curious history and you to listen to it."
    (b) "For once they didn't starve a genius to death and then put into other pockets the rewards he should have himself."
    (c) "The man doesn't really die; he changes his name and vanishes; we bury a dummy and cry over it, with all the world to help."
    (d) "He wasn't any greater than we were then. He hadn't any fame even in his own village; and he was so poor that he hadn't anything to feed us but turnips."

Details

2. This short story is called a framed story or a story within a story because   (a) the story is told by an English painter about a French painter   (b) the story is told in Mentone about a painter who lived in Brittany   (c) the story is told by two different *I*'s   (d) the public was tricked.

3. Three of the friends meet while   (a) they are in Paris   (b) they are attending a school for painters   (c) they are looking for work   (d) they are painting in the country.

4. They join Millet because   (a) he is famous   (b) they can learn from him   (c) he is well-to-do   (d) he can offer them food.

5. Millet is chosen to die because   (a) he is the best painter in the group   (b) he is the oldest   (c) he volunteers   (d) he loses.

Inferences

6. Smith is   (a) an American writer   (b) a French businessman   (c) a wealthy Englishman   (d) a French nobleman.

7. Magnan has come to Mentone rather than to Monte Carlo because   (a) he dislikes popular, crowded resorts   (b) it has pleasanter weather   (c) there are more things to do   (d) there is less chance of meeting old acquaintances.

8. After the hoax succeeds, all four painters   (a) continue to paint   (b) continue to live together   (c) give up their comradeship   (d) become famous painters.

9. Smith tells the story about the child and the caged bird because   (a) he has just read it   (b) he doesn't want to reveal Théophile Magnan's true identity   (c) he is asked to recall it   (d) he wants to finish his meal.

10. In recalling Andersen's tale, Smith compares Millet to   (a) the child   (b) Hans Andersen himself   (c) the bird   (d) the child's friends.

Order of Events

11. Arrange the items in the order in which they occurred. Use letters only.
    A. Millet does his last painting.
    B. The three younger painters turn salesmen.
    C. Twain meets Millet.
    D. The world mourns the passing of Millet.
    E. Millet paints his famous "Angelus."

Outcomes

12. Which of the following is not a result of the hoax?
    (a) Millet becomes very wealthy.
    (b) Millet is unable to use his talents.
    (c) Millet feels forced to live alone, without companionship.
    (d) Millet lives to enjoy his international fame.

Cause and Effect

13. In planning the hoax, the four painters do not take into consideration   (a) the moral wrong they are committing   (b) their chances of making money
    (c) the fame Millet will gain   (d) the sale of the "dead" artist's estate.

Fact or Opinion

Tell whether the following is a fact or an opinion.
14. Reading this story makes the public more sympathetic toward young painters.

Author's Role

15. Twain tells the story as it is told to him by one of the participants in order to   (a) speed up the pace of the story   (b) convince the reader of its truthfulness
    (c) add another character to the story   (d) add a moral to the story.

Words in Context _____

1. That is to say, one has the flooding sunshine, the *balmy* air, and the brilliant blue sea . . .
   Balmy (313) means   (a) cool   (b) clear   (c) gentle
   (d) pollution-free.

2. ... The bird pours out its song unheard and unheeded, but in time, hunger and thirst *assail* the creature ...
   Assail (314) means   (a) find   (b) destroy   (c) attack   (d) weaken.

3. The child comes and is smitten to the heart with *remorse*.
   Remorse (314) means   (a) deep regret   (b) fear   (c) horror   (d) disappointment.

4. ... then with bitter tears and *lamentations*, it calls its mates, and they bury the bird ...
   Lamentations (314) means   (a) fearful cries   (b) loud shouts   (c) loud grief   (d) long sermons.

5. Now we are properly *primed*—I to tell a curious history, and you to listen to it.
   Primed (314) means   (a) set for use   (b) seated   (c) rested   (d) dressed.

6. We were as happy as we were poor, or as poor as we were happy—*phrase* it to suit yourself.
   Phrase (314) used as a verb means   (a) thought   (b) analyze   (c) commit   (d) express.

7. ... and an artist as poor as ourselves took us in and *literally* saved us from starvation.
   Literally (314) means   (a) generously   (b) actually   (c) in time   (d) humanely.

8. We four became fast friends, *doting* friends, inseparables.
   Doting (315) means   (a) lavishly fond   (b) sensitive   (c) giving   (d) most thoughtful.

9. It is the only way to keep out of the *almshouse*.
   Almshouse (316) means   (a) factories   (b) poorhouse   (c) prisons   (d) breadlines.

10. I base this opinion upon certain *multitudinous* and long-established facts in human history.
    Multitudinous (316) means   (a) trustworthy   (b) universal   (c) very numerous   (d) beneficial.

11. "Shut up!" said Millet with *ostensible severity*, "and let the boy say his say."
    Ostensible severity (317) means   (a) visible harshness   (b) understandable firmness   (c) quiet humor   (d) intense feeling.

12. . . . and when everything is hot and just right, we'll spring
     the death on them and have the *notorious* funeral.
     Notorious (318) means   (a) horrible   (b) widely
     publicized   (c) criminal   (d) subdued.

13. Then I began to sketch a *villa* in the outskirts of a big
     town.
     Villa (318) means   (a) farmhouse   (b) suburban
     cottage   (c) country mansion   (d) village.

14. . . . because I saw the proprietor standing on an upper
     veranda.
     Veranda (318) means   (a) level   (b) wide breezeway
     (c) street   (d) long porch.

15. . . . not an item praising him in any way, but merely a
     word concerning the present condition of the master—
     sometimes hopeful, sometimes despondent, but always
     tinged with fears for the worst.
     Tinged with (320) means   (a) filled with
     (b) overloaded with   (c) colored slightly with
     (d) spoiled by.

Thinking Critically About the Story _____

1. Are the young painters justified in their bitterness toward
    the buying public? Give the reasons for your answer. Has
    the situation improved since this story was written? Ex-
    plain. What do you think should be done to aid young
    artists?

2. In this story two wrongs are used to make a right: the
    young painters are allowed to starve and the painters plan
    their hoax. Were the painters justified in going through
    with the hoax? Explain. What risks did they take? If you
    had been one of the four friends, what would you have
    done?

3. Was the reward that Millet received worth it? Explain.

4. The humor in this story is based on a hoax, on trickery. It

is angry and bitter. This is the humor of ridicule, and sarcasm. Have you met other examples of this black humor in real life? in other readings? How effective is it as a means of educating or changing people?

5. What devices did Twain use to give reality to this tall story? How effective was each of the devices?

Stories in Words

Powwow (313)   The American Indians have given a number of common words to English: *caucus, hickory, moccasin, moose, muskrat, opossum, pecan, raccoon, skunk, squaw.* One of the most interesting Indian words is *powwow*. Originally, it meant a "priest" or "medicine man." Then it came to mean a kind of "ceremony led by medicine men." Then it came to mean a "conference, a meeting for discussion." It is now used informally for "conversations."

Preamble (317)   The Preamble to the Constitution is an "introduction," and that is the meaning of *preamble*. The origin of the word suggests a concealed metaphor. The prefix *pre,* "before" is combined with the root *ambulare,* "to walk, go." A *preamble* "walks before" something else. The *ambulare* root also appears in *amble, ambulance,* and *ambulatory.* The impressive word *somnambulist* merely means "sleepwalker."

Trinket (318)   How could the word *trinket,* meaning a "small ornament or piece of jewelry," come from a Latin root meaning "to cut"? Tracing the history of the word shows how language changes. In Middle English a *trenket* was a "shoemaker's knife." But a knife may be used to carve ornaments and decorations, so the meaning was extended to the results of the carving. The word has further extended its meaning to include "trifle, something of little worth."

All in Fun

ACTIVITIES

Thinking Critically About the Stories ___

1. Compare and contrast the characters of Father Day and Walter Mitty. Mention such things as self-confidence, public manner, sense of reality, and attitude of others.

2. Consider each of the stories in turn. What makes each funny? How does each appeal to a sense of humor in a different way?

3. A distinction is often made between wit and humor. Wit is verbal. It relies upon a knowledge of language and is intellectual in appeal. Humor is a more general term. It doesn't depend upon words or keen intelligence. A baby will laugh at its parents' crazy antics, as they play peekaboo or some other game. The baby finds real humor in the sudden apparent childishness of otherwise serious adults. The baby recognizes this discrepancy and begins to develop a sense of humor. An appreciation of wit comes later. Which movie or television comics depend upon humor for their success and which upon wit? Which do you prefer? Why?

4. Talking animals are a tradition in folklore and fairy tales. *Aesop's Fables*, for example, use talking animals to point to a moral, like "Necessity is the mother of invention." Cartoon characters like the cat Garfield replace human beings as sources of fun. Walt Disney made Mickey Mouse and his friends a part of every child's experience. Why do you suppose storytellers use talking animals to tell a tale or express a point of view?

5. The modern television sitcom attempts to amuse. Why does the sitcom as a type survive, even though individual sitcoms come and go? Which is your favorite? Why?

Writing and Other Activities _____

1. As a contribution to the school or class Bulletin Board, write the items you would want to see included in the Ten Commandments for each of the following:
   (a) Parents of young teenagers
   (b) Getting and keeping friends
   (c) Daydreaming
   (d) Teenagers with younger siblings
   (e) Getting even.
2. Write the setting and the dialog between Father Day and his son Clarence on one of the following:
   (a) Clarence comes home after being gone over by the class bully
   (b) Clarence asks his father when he can begin to take Driver's Education
   (c) Clarence tells his father that he feels he isn't college material
   (d) Clarence feels unhappy because his parents "don't understand him."
3. Lead a class discussion on one of the following topics:
   (a) Advantages and disadvantages of having a pet animal: choosing a pet; training and raising a pet; sharing responsibilities; handling an aging pet.
   (b) Trouble in budgeting time: time-wasters for teenagers; handling TV and telephone; homework time; time to relax; reading time.
4. In a collection of Tall Tales find one that you can retell to the class. Be prepared to explain why you choose the tale. Write the plot outline of a Tall Tale on a topic of your own choosing or on one of the following:
   (a) Why erasures always leave telltale marks
   (b) Why dogs and cats don't usually get along

(c) Why peanut butter tastes like peanut butter
(d) Why shoelaces break
(e) Why adults change their minds so often.

5. Write the inner dialog of a family pet cat or dog (or of a bright pet goldfish swimming in its bowl in the living room) watching one of the following:
   (a) an animated cartoon on the TV screen
   (b) the family deciding on the TV fare for the evening
   (c) the children of the family quarreling about division of chores
   (d) the adult members of the family relaxing while viewing a favorite soap opera
   (e) a teenager-to-teenager telephone marathon.

Stories in Words: A Review

A. bedlam
B. hypnotic
C. ignition
D. pandemonium
E. pantry
F. philharmonic
G. pince-nez
H. powwow
I. preamble
J. trinket
K. ventriloquism
L. vinegar

Answer the following questions by choosing a word from the list above. Use letters only.

Which of the words above . . .

1. . . . takes its name from a London hospital?
2. . . . literally means "all the devils"?
3. . . . suggests "talking through the stomach"?
4. . . . was borrowed from the American Indians?
5. . . . literally means "walking before"?
6. . . . has something to do with *nose?*

7 . . . is derived from the word for bread, not a utensil?

8. . . . literally means "sharp wine"?

9. . . . comes from a word for *fire?*

10. . . . is named for the Greek god of sleep?

5

Short Shorts

During the first half of the nineteenth century, the short short story became a feature of many daily newspapers. It was also used as a filler in the monthly magazines. The short short of that period relied almost solely on the surprise ending for its punch and purpose.

In the hands of the writers of today, it has become an equal partner of the full-length short story. Whatever a short story can do, the short short does—more compactly and in fewer words. Unit Five contains four contemporary short shorts that sample this range and breadth.

The first story, "Johanna," has the traditional surprise ending—but with a difference. "Bees and People," a folk tale of social protest, is a glimpse into a time slot and way of life so different from ours. "Zoo" in fewer than four pages plunges us into the world of science fiction. "Good-by, Herman" focuses our attention on people struggling with middle-class values in contemporary America.

Whatever the longer story does, the short short of today can do. You have to decide: Is the short short just as effective?

Johanna

Jane Yolen

♦ **Still this was the first night she had ever been out
in the forest, though she had lived by it all her life. It
was tradition—no, more than that—that members of
the Chevril family did not venture into the midnight
forest.**

The story opens with a deceptive directness of narration. The reader is
plunged immediately into a moment of decision. Johanna's mother is ill, and
Johanna must go through the midnight forest to fetch the doctor. In times
past, other members of her family—including her father—had gone at night
into the darkened land of trees and shrubs, but they had never returned.
Nevertheless, Johanna does not hesitate. She loves her mother dearly.

And then . . . suddenly . . . Be on the alert! The twist comes quickly.
Don't fight the author's pace or try too hard to guess in advance the gimmick
that makes this story a modern classic. To enjoy a short short fully, you must
be willing to read for understanding and let the ending catch you by surprise.

JOHANNA

The forest was dark and the snow-covered path was merely an impression left on Johanna's moccasined feet.

If she had not come this way countless daylit times, Johanna would never have known where to go. But Hartwood* was familiar to her, even in the unfamiliar night. She had often picnicked in the cool, shady copses and grubbed around the tall oak trees. In a hard winter like this one, a family could subsist for days on acorn stew.

Still, this was the first night she had ever been out in the forest, though she had lived by it all her life. It was tradition— no, more than that—that members of the Chevril family did not venture into the midnight forest. "Never, never go to the woods at night," her mother said, and it was not a warning so much as a command. "Your father went though he was told not to. He never returned."

And Johanna had obeyed. Her father's disappearance was still in her memory, though she remembered nothing else of him. He was not the first of the Chevrils to go that way. There had been a great-uncle and two girl cousins who had likewise "never returned." At least, that was what Johanna had been told. Whether they had disappeared into the maw of the city that lurked over several mountains to the west, or into the hungry jaws of a wolf or bear, was never made clear. But Johanna, being an obedient girl, always came into the house with the setting sun.

For sixteen years she had listened to that warning. But tonight, with her mother pale and sightless, breathing brokenly in the bed they shared, Johanna had no choice. The doctor, who

* *Hartwood*   name of forest (Deer Forest)

lived on the other side of the wood, must be fetched. He lived in the cluster of houses that rimmed the far side of Hartwood, a cluster that was known as "the village," though it was really much too small for such a name. The five houses of the Chevril family that clung together, now empty except for Johanna and her mother, were not called a village, though they squatted on as much land.

Usually the doctor himself came through the forest to visit the Chevrils. Once a year he made the trip. Even when the grandparents and uncles and cousins had been alive, the village doctor came only once a year. He was gruff with them and called them "strong as beasts" and went away, never even offering a tonic. They needed none. They were healthy.

But the long, cruel winter had sapped Johanna's mother's strength. She lay for days silent, eyes cloudy and unfocused, barely taking in the acorn gruel that Johanna spooned for her. And at last Johanna had said: "I will fetch the doctor."

Her mother had grunted "no" each day, until this evening. When Johanna mentioned the doctor again, there had been no answering voice. Without her mother's no, Johanna made up her own mind. She *would* go.

If she did not get through the woods and back with the doctor before dawn, she felt it would be too late. Deep inside she knew she should have left before, even when her mother did not want her to go. And so she ran as quickly as she dared, following the small, twisting path through Hartwood by feel.

At first Johanna's guilt and the unfamiliar night were a burden, making her feel heavier than usual. But as she continued running, the crisp night air seemed to clear her head. She felt unnaturally alert, as if she had suddenly begun to discover new senses.

The wind molded her short dark hair to her head. For the first time she felt graceful and light, almost beautiful. Her feet beat a steady tattoo on the snow as she ran, and she felt neither cold nor winded. Her steps lengthened as she went.

Suddenly a broken branch across the path tangled in her legs. She went down heavily on all fours, her breath caught in her throat. As she got to her feet, she searched the darkness ahead. Were there other branches waiting?

Even as she stared, the forest seemed to grow brighter. The

light from the full moon must be finding its way into the heart of the woods. It was a comforting thought.

She ran faster now, confident of her steps. The trees seemed to rush by. There would be plenty of time.

She came at last to the place where the woods stopped, and cautiously she ranged along the last trees, careful not to be silhouetted against the sky. Then she halted.

She could hear nothing moving, could see nothing that threatened. When she was sure, she edged out onto the short meadow that ran in a downward curve to the back of the village.

Once more she stopped. This time she turned her head to the left and right. She could smell the musk of the farm animals on the wind, blowing faintly up to her. The moon beat down upon her head and, for a moment, seemed to ride on her broad, dark shoulder.

Slowly she paced down the hill toward the line of houses that stood like teeth in a jagged row. Light streamed out of the rear windows, making threatening little earthbound moons on the graying snow.

She hesitated.

A dog barked. Then a second began, only to end his call in a whine.

A voice cried out from the house farthest on the right, a woman's voice, soft and soothing. "Be quiet, Boy."

The dog was silenced.

She dared a few more slow steps toward the village, but her fear seemed to precede her. As if catching its scent, the first dog barked lustily again.

"Boy! Down!" It was a man this time, shattering the night with authority.

She recognized it at once. It was the doctor's voice. She edged toward its sound. Shivering with relief and dread, she came to the backyard of the house on the right and waited. In her nervousness, she moved one foot restlessly, pawing the snow down to the dead grass. She wondered if her father, her great-uncle, her cousins had felt this fear under the burning eye of the moon.

The doctor, short and too stout for his age, came out of the back door, buttoning his breeches with one hand. In the other he carried a gun. He peered out into the darkness.

"Who's there?"

She stepped forward into the yard, into the puddle of light. She tried to speak her name, but she suddenly could not recall it. She tried to tell why she had come, but nothing passed her closed throat. She shook her head to clear the fear away.

The dog barked again, excited, furious.

"By gosh," the doctor said, "it's a deer."

She spun around and looked behind her, following his line of sight. There was nothing there.

"That's enough meat to last the rest of this cruel winter," he said. He raised the gun, and fired.

Reading for Understanding _____

Main Idea

1. Which of the following quotations best expresses the main idea of the story?
   (a) "Your father went though he was told not to. He never returned."

(b) And at last Johanna had said: "I will fetch the doctor."

(c) "That's enough meat to last the rest of this cruel winter."

(d) "By gosh," the doctor said, "it's a deer."

Details

2. The story opens in   (a) late autumn   (b) early winter   (c) midwinter   (d) early spring.

3. Johanna is about   (a) five years old   (b) ten years old   (c) twelve years old   (d) sixteen years old.

4. Johanna thinks of the doctor immediately because (a) the neighbors have been suggesting calling for him (b) her mother has been thinking of going to him (c) he examines them annually   (d) he has been so friendly and helpful in the past.

5. Hartwood is the name of   (a) the doctor's village (b) Johanna's family   (c) the doctor   (d) the forest.

6. The dangers of the night in Johanna's trip to the doctor do not include   (a) wolves   (b) hunters   (c) snow on the ground   (d) fallen branches. ᾽

Inferences

7. The statement that Johanna and her mother are able to live on acorn stew does not reveal their true identity because   (a) deer can subsist on a diet of acorns (b) farmers sell acorns in the produce markets (c) acorns are found in abundance in oak forests (d) people are known to eat acorns in bad times.

8. Johanna is careful to stay among the trees as long as possible   (a) to avoid detection   (b) to avoid stumbling   (c) to avoid the snowdrifts   (d) to avoid missing the doctor's house.

9. The doctor is awakened by   (a) Johanna's cry for help (b) the coldness of the night   (c) Johanna's footsteps (d) the barking of the dogs.

10. When the doctor exclaims that he sees a deer,

(a) Johanna spins around to flee   (b) Johanna does not realize that he is referring to her   (c) Johanna's fears disappear   (d) the dogs run toward Johanna.

Order of Events

11. Arrange the items in the order in which they occurred. Use letters only.
    A. Fear overcomes Johanna.
    B. Johanna's father disappears in the midnight forest.
    C. The doctor begins his annual visits.
    D. A shot is fired.
    E. Johanna's mother becomes ill.

Outcomes

12. By suddenly changing the point of view from Johanna to the doctor, the author   (a) creates a surprise ending   (b) attempts to save Johanna's life   (c) shows human cruelty   (d) shows animal stupidity.

Cause and Effect

13. Johanna did not know about human beings'   (a) innate cruelty to wild animals   (b) dual standards toward wild animals   (c) love for their dogs   (d) ability to help.

Fact or Opinion

Tell whether each of the following is a fact or an opinion.
14. The cruelty of winter and the food needs of stronger creatures wiped out the last of the Chevril family.
15. Individual identity is usually not involved in the processing of the food chain.

Words in Context _____

1. She had often picnicked in the cool, shady *copses* . . .
   Copses (335) means   (a) towering forest giants

(b) babbling brooks   (c) tall grasses   (d) groups of bushes and small trees.

2. She . . . *grubbed* around the tall oak trees.
   Grubbed (335) means   (a) dug in the ground
   (b) slept   (c) hid   (d) covered herself with leaves.

3. In a hard winter like this one, a family could *subsist* for days on acorn stew.
   Subsist (335) means   (a) fatten   (b) continue existing on   (c) content itself   (d) extend itself.

4. Whether they had disappeared into the *maw* of the city . . . or the hungry jaws of a wolf or bear, was never made clear.
   Maw (335) means   (a) confusion   (b) turmoil
   (c) mouth   (d) crowds.

5. Whether they had disappeared into the maw of the city that *lurked* over several mountains to the west . . . was never made clear.
   Lurked (335) means   (a) lay in wait   (b) sprawled
   (c) beckoned   (d) stood in full view.

6. The five houses of the Chevril family . . . were not called a village, though they *squatted on* as much land.
   Squatted on (336) means   (a) farmed   (b) settled on without owning   (c) claimed   (d) continued.

7. He was *gruff with* them and called them "strong as beasts" and went away, never even offering a tonic.
   Gruff with (336) means   (a) sensitive and considerate
   (b) gentle and loving   (c) blunt and harsh   (d) cruel and harmful.

8. But the long, cruel winter had *sapped* Johanna's mother's strength.
   Sapped (336) means   (a) taken away   (b) weakened
   (c) developed   (d) restored.

9. . . . she ranged along the last trees, careful not to be *silhouetted* against the sky.
   Silhouetted (337) means   (a) outlined   (b) painted
   (c) visible   (d) identified.

10. She could smell the *musk* of the farm animals on the wind, blowing faintly up to her.
     Musk (337) means   (a) heat   (b) breath   (c) food
     (d) odor.

Thinking Critically About the Story _____

1. What are some of the details the author included in order to hide the true identity of Johanna? How effective is the use of these devices? Was the author unfair to the reader? Give the reasons for your choice.

2. Why don't Johanna's natural instincts protect her from the doctor's gun? Is the doctor justified in shooting her? Give the reasons for your choice.

3. How can we justify raising animals in protected environments like fish hatcheries or game farms and then releasing them into the wild to become fair game for a fisherman or hunter?

4. The story contains many examples of irony, incidents in which the opposite of what is intended results from a given action: Johanna's desire to save her mother's life leads to her own death. What other examples can you cite from the story? From your readings? From real life? Is there any way we can protect ourselves from the ironies in real life? Explain your choice. Why is irony a favorite device of storytellers? Can an author overuse irony? Explain.

Stories in Words _____

Picnicked (335)   Two French words, *piquer*, "to pick," and *nique*, "a trifle," combine to make the word *picnic*. As you sit nibbling the sandwiches and potato chips on your next picnic, remember that word history suggests you are "picking trifles or snacks"!

Unfocused (336)   The heart of this word is *focus*, which comes directly and unchanged from the Latin *focus*, "hearth." *Focus* means "the point where heat or light rays come together." It also means "the center of activity or attention." The Roman focus, or hearth, was the place where all the family members came together. From a very specific meaning, the word *focus* has expanded its meanings to include many different activities. This *generalization* is a common tendency of language. The opposite, *specialization*, is a narrowing of meaning. Once *meat* meant "food, any solid food."

Silhouette (337)   Many common names are derived from proper names. *Herculean*, from Hercules, the Roman god of strength, means "having great size, strength, and courage." *Atlas*, from the mythical Greek giant who held up the pillars of the world, is now remembered by a book of maps. *Sandwich* is named for the fourth Earl of Sandwich, who supposedly invented that quick snack. Similarly, the word *silhouette* was named after Etienne de Silhouette, a French author and politician of the 18th century. Words from names abound in English.

Bees and People

Mikhail Zoshchenko

♦ "Bees absolutely will not stand for being pushed around by indifferent bureaucrats. You probably treated them the way you treat people—and you see what you get."

The short short story can be more than just a means of entertainment and revelation of human nature. In the hands of a skilled writer, it can become a strong voice of protest. During the dark days of the 1940's in Russia under Stalin, the opposition was mercilessly suppressed. Huge prison camps were filled with those who dared to find fault and look for solutions.

But the voice of protest was not to be silenced. The short short that follows shows one of the areas available to writers who were willing to risk exile and possibly death for poking fun at Russian officialdom.

"Bees and People" is not a mild story filled with folk humor. The key to the story is the realization that the author is talking about people and not bees. If bees are mistreated, what do they do? If people are mistreated, what can they do? Is this story based on incidents that really happened? Could it happen today? In Russia? In our own country?

BEES AND PEOPLE

A Red Army soldier came to a certain collective farm for a visit. And as a present for his relatives he brought a jar of flower honey.

And everyone liked that honey so much that the farm decided to set up a beekeeping operation of its own.

But no one around there kept bees, so the members of the collective had to do everything from the ground up—build the hives and then get the bees out of the forest and into their new apartments.

When they saw what a long time all this would take, they lost their enthusiasm. "There's no end to it," they said. "We'll be running here and there and first thing you know it'll be winter and we won't see that honey till next year. And now's when we need it."

But one of the collective farmers was a certain Ivan Panfilich, a fine man, no longer in his first youth, aged seventy-two. As a young man he had kept bees.

So he says, "If we're going to have our tea with honey this year, then somebody has got to go somewhere where there's bees being kept and buy what we're thinking about."

The farmers say, "This farm is loaded. Money is no object. Let's buy bees in full production, already perched in the hives. Because if we went and got bees out of the woods they might turn out to be no good. They might start turning out some kind of horrible honey like linden or something. But we want flower honey."

And so they gave Ivan Panfilich some money and sent him off to the city of Tambov.

He arrives in Tambov and the people there tell him, "You did the right thing coming to us. We've just had three villages relocated to the Far East and there's one extra beekeeping setup left behind. We can let you have it for next to nothing. But the thing is—how are you going to transport these bees? That's what we don't know. This is what you might call loose goods. In fact it has wings on. The least little thing and it'll fly every which way. We're afraid you'll get to the addressee with nothing but hives and eggs."

Panfilich says, "One way or another I'll get them there. I know bees. Been associated with bees my whole life."

And so he took sixteen hives to the station on two carts. At the station he managed to get hold of a flatcar and he put his hives on that flatcar and covered them up with a tarpaulin. And it wasn't long before the freight train took off and our flatcar rolling along with it.

Panfilich struck a pose on the flatcar and addressed the bees: "It's okay, boys," said he, "we'll make it! Just hang on in there in the dark a little while and when we get there I'll put you out in the flowers. And I think you'll find what you want there. But whatever you do, don't get upset about me carrying you in the dark. I covered you all with that tarpaulin on purpose so nobody would be crazy enough to fly out while the train's running. Something might happen and you wouldn't be able to hop back on board."

And so the train traveled on for a day. And another day.

By the third day Panfilich was getting a little worried. The train was going slowly. Stopping at every station. Standing there for hours. And he couldn't tell when they were going to get to where he was going.

At Polya Station Panfilich got down off his flatcar and looked up at the stationmaster. "Tell me, sir," he asked, "are we going to be stopping long at your station?"

"I really couldn't tell you," the stationmaster answered. "You could be here till evening."

"If we'll be here till evening," Panfilich said, "then I'm taking off the tarpaulin to let my bees out into your fields. Otherwise they'll be worn out from this trip. This makes three days they've been sitting under the tarpaulin. They're perishing. They haven't had anything to eat or drink and they can't feed the little ones."

"Do whatever you like! What do I care about your flying

passengers! I've got my hands full without them. And I should get excited about your little ones—that's the limit! Of all the stupid . . . !''

Panfilich went back to his flatcar and took off the tarpaulin.

And the weather was magnificent. Blue sky. Good old July sun. Fields all around. Flowers. A grove of chestnuts in bloom.

So Panfilich took the tarpaulin off the flatcar and all at once a whole army of bees took off into the blue.

The bees circled, looked around, and headed straight for the fields and forests.

A crowd of passengers surrounded the flatcar, and Panfilich used it as a platform to lecture them on the usefulness of bees. But while the lecture was going on, the stationmaster came out of the station and began signaling the engineer to start the train.

Panfilich gasped "Ach!" when he saw these signals, got

terribly upset, and said to the stationmaster, "But my dear sir, don't send the train on, all my bees are out!"

The stationmaster said, "Well, you just whistle them back into their seats! I can't hold the train longer than three minutes."

Panfilich said, *"Please!* Just hold the train till sundown. At sundown the bees will be back in their seats. Or at least unhook my flatcar. I can't go without the bees. I only have a thousand left here; there are fifteen thousand in the fields. Try to understand the fix I'm in! Don't harden your heart to this tragedy!"

The stationmaster said, "I'm not running a health farm for bees! I'm running a railroad! The bees flew away! Beautiful! And on the next train they'll tell me the flies have flown away! Or the fleas have jumped out of the sleeping car! What am I supposed to do—hold up the train for that? Don't make me laugh!" And with that he signaled the engineer again.

And the train started off.

Panfilich, white as a sheet, stood on his flatcar, his arms spread wide, his gaze sweeping from side to side, his body trembling with indignation.

But the train goes on.

Well, a certain number of bees did manage to jump on while the train was moving. But most of them stayed behind in the fields and groves of trees. Soon the train was out of sight.

The stationmaster returned to the station and settled down to work. He was writing something in the log and drinking tea with lemon. Suddenly he heard a kind of racket on the station platform.

He opened the window to see what had happened and he saw that the passengers waiting there were in a frenzy, hopping and lurching around. The stationmaster asked, "What happened?"

"Bees have stung three passengers here," they answered, "and now they're attacking the rest. The sky is black with them!"

Then the stationmaster saw that a whole dark cloud of bees were circling around his station. They were looking for their flatcar, naturally. But there wasn't any flatcar. It had left.

So they were attacking people and whatever else got in the way.

No sooner had the stationmaster left the window to go out on the platform than in through the window flew a swarm of bees, mad as hell. He grabbed a towel and began waving it about to drive the bees out of the room.

But evidently that was his great mistake.

Two bees got him on the neck, a third on the ear, and a fourth stung him on the forehead.

The stationmaster wrapped himself up in a towel and lay down on the sofa and commenced to give out these pitiful groans. Soon his assistant ran in and said, "The bees have stung other people besides you. The telegraph operator got stung on the cheek and now won't work."

The stationmaster, lying on his couch, said, "Oy! What are we going to do?"

At this point another employee ran up and said, "The ticket seller—I mean to say, your wife, Klavdia Ivanovna—just got stung on the nose. Now her appearance has been ruined for good."

The stationmaster let out even louder groans and said, "We've got to get that flatcar with that crazy beekeeper back here at once." He jumped off his sofa and grabbed the telephone. From the next station down the line he heard: "Okay. We'll uncouple that flatcar right away. Only we don't have an engine to pull it to you."

The stationmaster screamed, "We'll send you the engine! Uncouple that flat at once! The bees have already stung my wife! My station Polya is deserted! All the passengers are hiding in the shed! There's nothing but bees flying around in the air! And I absolutely refuse to go outside—let there *be* train wrecks!"

And it wasn't long before the flatcar was delivered. Everyone gave a sigh of relief when they saw the flatcar, with Panfilich standing on it.

Panfilich ordered the flatcar to be placed precisely where it had been before, and the bees, when they saw their car, instantly flew up to it. But there were so many bees, and they were in such a hurry to take their seats, that there was a crush.

And they raised such a buzzing and humming that a dog started howling and the pigeons scattered into the sky.

Panfilich, standing on the platform, spoke to them: "Easy, boys, don't rush. Plenty of time! Everybody sit where their boarding pass says!" In ten minutes all was quiet. When he'd made sure everything was in order, Panfilich stepped down off his platform. And the people standing around the station began to clap. And Panfilich, like an actor, bowed to thank them and said: "Turn your collars down! Show your faces! And stop trembling—the stinging is over!"

When he'd said this, Panfilich went to the stationmaster. The stationmaster, wrapped in his towel, was still lying on his sofa gasping and groaning. When Panfilich entered he groaned even louder.

"My dear sir," said Panfilich, "I'm very sorry that my bees stung you. But it was your own fault. You can't be so indifferent to things, whether they're big or little. Bees can't stand that. Bees sting people for that without giving it a second thought."

The stationmaster groaned even louder, and Panfilich went on: "Bees absolutely will not stand for being pushed around by indifferent bureaucrats. You probably treated them the way you treat people—and you see what you get."

Panfilich glanced out the window and added, "The sun's gone down. My fellow travelers have taken their seats. I have the honor to bid you good day! We're off!"

The stationmaster feebly nodded his head as though saying, "Be off quickly!" And in a low whisper he added, "Sure you've got all the bees? See you don't leave any!"

Panfilich said, "If two or three bees get left they can be of help to you. Their buzzing will remind you of what has happened." With this, he left the room.

The next day toward evening our splendid Panfilich reached his destination with his live merchandise. They greeted him with a band.

Reading for Understanding _____

Main Idea

1. Which of the following statements best expresses the
   main idea of this story?
   (a) Raising bees can become very complex.
   (b) Bees will react strongly if they are not treated with
   consideration.
   (c) The welfare of the people should be the basis of all
   rules and regulations.
   (d) Innocent people must suffer when some official makes
   a wrong decision.

Details

2. The Red Army soldier in this story   (a) brings a beehive
   as   a   present   (b) raises   bees   for   their   honey
   (c) organizes the collective   (d) gives away a container
   of honey.
3. The members of the collective do not want   (a) to raise
   bees for their honey   (b) to sell their excess honey
   (c) to wait too long for a supply of honey   (d) to buy
   commercial honey.
4. Ivan Panfilich is   (a) the leader of the collective
   (b) the Red Army soldier   (c) the owner of the bees
   (d) an elderly member of the collective.
5. Panfilich's   greatest   problem   is   (a) transportation
   (b) money   (c) finding a bee colony   (d) getting the
   approval of his fellow collectivists.

Inferences

6. Panfilich speaks to the bees   (a) fearfully   (b) plead-
   ingly   (c) joyfully   (d) as to a group of cooperators.
7. The   bees   he   buys   (a) produce   linden   honey

(b) number about sixteen thousand　(c) are from the Far East　(d) disobey Panfilich's orders.

8. Panfilich's troubles begin when　(a) he cannot find transportation　(b) the tarpaulin falls off　(c) the train makes too many long stops　(d) the bees become drowsy.

9. The trainmaster's troubles begin when　(a) Panfilich decides to take revenge　(b) the passengers object to Panfilich and his charges　(c) he ignores Panfilich's request　(d) he orders the train to return.

10. The bees become angry when　(a) the passengers bother them　(b) they are not allowed to feed　(c) their hives disappear　(d) the stationmaster lectures them.

Order of Events

11. Arrange the items in the order in which they occurred. Use letters only.
    A. The stationmaster signals the train to leave.
    B. The bees go without food for more than 48 hours.
    C. Panfilich receives a hero's welcome.
    D. Panfilich sees a bargain and grabs it.
    E. The cooperators have their own honey to sweeten their .tea.

Outcomes

12. As a result of this story,　(a) the bees produce more honey　(b) Panfilich decides never to travel again by train　(c) the cooperators ration the honey　(d) the readers are aware that officials can be criticized.

Cause and Effect

13. At the railroad station, Panfilich accomplishes his purpose by　(a) denouncing the stationmaster　(b) appealing to the passengers for justice　(c) angering the bees　(d) following a foolish order.

Fact or Opinion

Tell whether the following is a fact or an opinion.
14. Panfilich handled with the same courtesy and calmness both the bees and the people he had dealings with.

Author's Role

15. The author's purpose in this story is to   (a) ridicule the speech patterns of the cooperators   (b) expose officials who feel more important than the average citizens (c) reveal the significance of bees in the lives of the average citizen   (d) show the oneness of all creatures on earth.

Words in Context _____

1. A Red Army soldier came to a certain *collective* farm for a visit.
   Collective (345) as used in this sentence means
   (a) Russian   (b) wealthy   (c) cooperatively run under government supervision   (d) privately owned and operated for profit.

2. The farmers say, *"This farm is loaded . . ."*
   This farm is loaded (345), a translation of Russian slang into American slang, means   (a) the farm is well run (b) it is a wealthy community   (c) the crop is in (d) there are too many members in this cooperative.

3. "We've just had three villages *relocated* in the Far East."
   Relocated (346) means   (a) destroyed   (b) exiled to Siberia   (c) go into bankruptcy   (d) invited to migrate.

4. "This is what you might call *loose goods.*"

Loose goods (346) means   (a) without ownership
(b) of unknown quality   (c) in poor condition
(d) unpackaged material.

5. "We're afraid you'll get to the *addressee* with nothing but hives and eggs."
    The word *addressee* (346) refers to   (a) the sellers
    (b) the buyers   (c) the government officials
    (d) the bees.

6. At the station he managed to get hold of a *flatcar* . . .
    A *flatcar* (346) is   (a) a large truck without a top
    (b) a topless, sideless freight car   (c) a wagon for transporting vegetables   (d) a horseless carriage.

7. . . . he put his hives on that flatcar and covered them with a *tarpaulin.*
    A *tarpaulin* (346) is a   (a) canvas cover   (b) thin layer of soil   (c) heavy netting   (d) wooden roof.

8. Panfilich *struck a pose* on the flatcar and addressed the bees . . .
    When he *struck a pose* (346), Panfilich   (a) sat down
    (b) clapped his hands   (c) took the posture of a public speaker   (d) laughed several times.

9. . . . and all at once the whole army of bees *took off into the blue.*
    Took off into the blue (347) means   (a) gathered together   (b) tried to escape   (c) flew skyward
    (d) came out of the hives.

10. Panfilich, white as a sheet, stood on his flatcar . . . his body trembling with *indignation.*
    Indignation (348) means   (a) scornful anger
    (b) fatigue   (c) horror   (d) fear.

11. . . . he saw that the passengers waiting there were in a *frenzy* . . .
    Frenzy (348) means   (a) large group   (b) state of great excitement   (c) great hurry   (d) need for relaxation.

12. . . . he saw that the passengers . . . were hopping and *lurching* around.

Lurching (348) means (a) laughing (b) staggering
(c) rushing (d) flailing.

13. The stationmaster wrapped himself up in a towel . . . and
commenced to give out these pitiful groans.
Commenced (349) means (a) refused (b) began
(c) stopped (d) decided.

14. "You can't be so *indifferent to* things, whether they're big
or little."
Indifferent to (350) means (a) concerned about
(b) moved by (c) not caring about (d) forgetful of.

15. Bees absolutely will not stand for being pushed around by
indifferent *bureaucrats*.
Bureaucrats (350) means (a) beekeepers
(b) supervisors (c) cooperators (d) government
officials.

Thinking Critically About the Story _____

1. What does this story reveal about life in Russia during the
1940s? How does living in Russia then compare with living
in the United States today? What avenues of protest that
are available to us were lacking in Russia then?

2. In handling the stationmaster, Panfilich showed his control
of passive resistance. How far would he have gotten with
open refusal? Which is the more effective approach, passive
resistance or open refusal? Which of the two approaches is
used most frequently by teenagers? In your home, which
brings better results?

3. To what extent is the author's condemnation of 1940
Russia applicable to the United States today? If you were
to write a satire, what would you attack in living with your
family? In adjusting to friends? In school life? In the
political world?

4. It is ironic that the decision maker, the stationmaster, suffered little from the backfire that followed his commands. The passengers and the workers around the station were the ones who had to suffer loss of time and physical discomfort. Is such the case in real life—the instigators go scot-free or almost scot-free while the innocent bystanders receive the punishment? Give examples to justify your stand.

5. Based on your own experiences and what you have read, to what extent is the following quotation valid?

"Satire is not a perfect weapon. All too often the satire is so subtle that the audience misses the intended point. The satire can be so bitter that only negative faultfinding results. The audience never reaches for positive solutions to the evils exposed. However, on the other hand, satire can dig deep and create the type of anger that leads to the corrections."

Stories in Words

Tarpaulin (346) As we have seen (page 311), guessing word origins can be tricky. *Pantry* has nothing to do with *pan* and *primrose* has nothing to do with *rose*. Sometimes, though, the obvious guess is correct. *Tarpaulin* does come from *tar*, but what of the second part? *Paulin* comes from the Latin *pallium*, a "cover." A *tarpaulin* is a *tarry covering*. *Pall* is the same word found in a smoky *pall*, a dark or gloomy, smoky *covering*.

Chestnut (347) The *nut* in *chestnut* is pure folk etymology. The word *chestnut* comes directly from the Spanish *castanea*, which in turn comes from a similar Greek word. A related word is *castanet*. Castanets, which look like chestnuts, are small, hollowed pieces of wood or some other material. They are clicked together with the fingers in time with the music, especially in Spanish dances.

Precise (349)   *Precise* means "accurate, definite, exact." The two parts of *precise* are the Latin prefix *pre*, "before," and *cidere*, "to cut." How did the meaning of *precise* change from "cut before" to "exact"? *To cut off* is "to shorten." A shorter version of a message must be more exact than a longer one. Thus the meaning of *precise* has come to mean "exact." Without the final *e*, *precise* becomes *précis*, "a shorter version of a message, a summary."

Zoo

Edward Hoch

♦ **"Peoples of Earth, this year you see a real treat for your single dollar . . . brought to you across a million miles of space at great expense.**

People have an abiding curiosity about the forms of life on our planet. The zoo and the aquarium have been main attractions for centuries.

With the development of exploration in space, interest has widened to include the possibilities of life outside our own sphere. The likelihood of life elsewhere in the universe is a favorite field of exploration of science fiction.

In this short short, Edward Hoch has projected his imagination into the world of tomorrow and created a folktale that seems so realistic that many feel it really happened! It has the direct approach and tone of a news item.

One word of warning: Read it slowly; it will be over before you realize it! Did it really happen? Could it happen? Will it happen? Will creatures of outer space be so varied and gentle? This story, as a good story should, raises more questions than it answers.

Zoo

The children were always good during the month of August, especially when it began to get near the twenty-third. It was on this day that the great silver spaceship carrying Professor Hugo's Interplanetary Zoo settled down for its annual six-hour visit to the Chicago area.

Before daybreak the crowds would form, long lines of children and adults both, each one clutching his or her dollar, and waiting with wonderment to see what race of strange creatures the Professor had brought this year.

In the past they had sometimes been treated to three-legged creatures from Venus, or tall, thin men from Mars, or even snakelike horrors from somewhere more distant. This year, as the great round ship settled slowly to earth in the huge tricity parking area just outside of Chicago, they watched with awe as the sides slowly slid up to reveal the familiar barred cages. In them were some wild breed of nightmare—small, horselike animals that moved with quick, jerking motions and constantly chattered in a high-pitched tongue. The citizens of Earth clustered around as Professor Hugo's crew quickly collected the waiting dollars, and soon the good Professor himself made an appearance, wearing his many-colored rainbow cape and top hat. "Peoples of Earth," he called into his microphone.

The crowd's noise died down and he continued. "Peoples of Earth, this year you see a real treat for your single dollar—the little-known horse-spider people of Kaan—brought to you across a million miles of space at great expense. Gather around, see them, study them, listen to them, tell your friends about them. But hurry! My ship can remain here only six hours!"

And the crowds slowly filed by, at once horrified and fascinated by these strange creatures that looked like horses but ran up the walls of their cages like spiders. "This is certainly worth a dollar," one man remarked, hurrying away. "I'm going home to get the wife."

All day long it went like that, until ten thousand people had filed by the barred cages set into the side of the spaceship. Then, as the six-hour limit ran out, Professor Hugo once more took microphone in hand. "We must go now, but we will return next year on this date. And if you enjoyed our zoo this year, phone your friends in other cities about it. We will land in New York tomorrow, and next week on to London, Paris, Rome, Hong Kong, and Tokyo. Then on to other worlds!"

He waved farewell to them, and as the ship rose from the ground the Earth peoples agreed that this had been the very best Zoo yet. . . .

Some two months and three planets later, the silver ship of Professor Hugo settled at last onto the familiar jagged rocks of Kaan, and the queer horse-spider creatures filed quickly out

of their cages. Professor Hugo was there to say a few parting words, and then they scurried away in a hundred different directions, seeking their homes among the rocks.

In one, the she-creature was happy to see the return of her mate and offspring. She babbled a greeting in the strange tongue and hurried to embrace them. "It was a long time you were gone. Was it good?"

And the he-creature nodded. "The little one enjoyed it especially. We visited eight worlds and saw many things."

The little one ran up the wall of the cave. "On the place called Earth it was the best. The creatures there wear garments over their skins, and they walk on two legs."

"But isn't it dangerous?" asked the she-creature.

"No," her mate answered. "There are bars to protect us from them. We remain right in the ship. Next time you must come with us. It is well worth the nineteen commocs* it costs."

And the little one nodded. "It was the very best Zoo ever. . . ."

Reading for Understanding _____

Main Idea

1. Which of the following statements sums up the main idea of the story?
   (a) There are many unusual ways to make money.
   (b) Someday there will be an interchange of life-forms throughout the universe.
   (c) There are living creatures in other parts of the universe.
   (d) Curiosity about other forms of life does not belong exclusively to human beings.

* *commocs*   made-up word for units of money

Details

2. August 23 is the day   (a) the spaceship was launched
   (b) the story closes   (c) the spaceship lands near Chicago
   (d) the specimens were gathered.

3. The visiting creatures on exhibit resemble   (a) human
   beings   (b) fish   (c) horses   (d) snakes.

4. We are not told   (a) how the visitors communicate with
   each other   (b) how Professor Hugo communicates with
   the visitors   (c) what type of creature Professor Hugo is
   (d) why the creatures are being exhibited.

5. Professor Hugo exhibits his zoo   (a) only on Earth
   (b) only on Earth and Kaan   (c) on many planets
   (d) only in Chicago.

Inferences

6. According to the story, the cages are barred to
   (a) make the exhibited creatures more clearly visible
   (b) separate the exhibition from the audience
   (c) protect the audience from attack   (d) protect the
   exhibited creatures from attack.

7. Kaan is an imaginary planet   (a) in a nearby
   star-cluster   (b) in the solar system   (c) outside the
   solar system   (d) in a distant nebula.

8. Dr. Hugo wears the costume of a   (a) circus announcer
   (b) laboratory worker   (c) jungle explorer   (d) TV
   news reporter.

9. It is called the "best zoo yet" because   (a) the exhibit is
   the largest ever   (b) more people attend it   (c) it is
   more varied   (d) of the unusual appearance of the creatures exhibited.

10. The exhibition changes   (a) every ten years
    (b) every year   (c) every five years   (d) every few
    months.

Order of Events

11. Arrange the items in the order in which they occurred.
Use letters only.
A. The spaceship lands in Tokyo with a group of horse-like creatures.
B. The inhabitants of Kaan pay for a trip to Earth.
C. Dr. Hugo establishes his zoo.
D. Interplanetary travel becomes a reality.
E. A happy mother greets her family after their long journey.

Outcomes

12. As a result of the exhibit   (a) new industries are started
(b) horizons are enlarged   (c) life is prolonged
(d) scientific discoveries are made.

Cause and Effect

13. One of the major outcomes of Dr. Hugo's project could be that a familiar slogan would be changed to
(a) Peace in the Solar System and Goodwill to All.
(b) Time and Tide Wait for No Creature.
(c) One Good Voyage Deserves Another.
(d) A Trip in Time Saves Nine.

Fact or Opinion

Tell whether each of the following is a fact or an opinion.
14. Dr. Hugo's exhibit pleased all of the spectators.
15. The admission fee charged was reasonable.

Words in Context _____

1. It was on this day that the great silver spaceship carrying Professor Hugo's *Interplanetary* Zoo settled down.

Interplanetary (359) means that it was used in travel
(a) to the moon   (b) throughout the world   (c) in the
solar system   (d) throughout the universe.

2.   ... and waiting *with wonderment* to see what race of
strange creatures the Professor brought this year.
With wonderment (359) means that the spectators were
(a) on a holiday   (b) ordered to do so   (c) filled with
curiosity   (d) very enthusiastic.

3.   This year, as the great round ship settled slowly to earth
in the huge *tricity* parking area. . . .
The landing field was most likely labeled *tricity* (359)
because   (a) it was so large   (b) it was near Chicago
(c) it was on continental America   (d) it serviced more
than one area.

4.   The citizens of Earth *clustered* around as Professor Hugo's
crew quickly collected the waiting dollars.
Clustered (359) means   (a) hurried   (b) looked
(c) sat   (d) gathered.

5.   ... the sides slowly slid up to reveal the familiar *barred*
cages.
Barred (359) means   (a) painted in varied colors
(b) large and comfortable   (c) having rods across the
opening   (d) lined with strange scenery.

6.   Some two months and three planets later, the silver ship
of Professor Hugo settled at last onto the familiar *jagged*
rocks of Kaan.
Jagged (360) means   (a) slippery   (b) covered with
greenery   (c) tall   (d) uneven.

7.   ... and then they *scurried* away in a hundred different
directions.
Scurried (361) means   (a) rushed   (b) limped
(c) crawled   (d) strolled.

8.   It is well worth the nineteen *commocs* it costs.
Commocs (361) means   (a) units of money   (b) rocks
(c) chips   (d) cents.

9.   In one, the she-creature was happy to see the return of her
mate and *offspring*.

Offspring (361) means (a) companion (b) provider
(c) teacher (d) child.

10. She *babbled* a greeting *in the strange tongue* and hurried to
embrace them.
Babbled . . . in the strange tongue (361) means
(a) spoke in a language unfamiliar to us (b) spoke in
a high-pitched voice (c) spoke in sign language
(d) shouted with great emotion.

Thinking Critically About the Story _____

1. How does Dr. Hugo's zoo differ from the ones you have
visited or know about? Which is more considerate of the
living creatures involved? Is it fair to imprison for life
those chosen to be exhibited? How have exhibition areas
been changed in recent years?

2. What are some of the dangers in bringing to Earth forms of
life found elsewhere in the Universe? How have space
scientists attempted to overcome some of the known possibilities of danger? Should such explorations be stopped
to prevent contamination of our planet?

3. What assumptions did the author make about the physical
and emotional makeup of creatures outside our planet?
How does this picture differ from that of writers who
imagine extraterrestrials that are cannibalistic or filled
with a desire to dominate and destroy our civilization?
With whom do you tend to agree?

4. What makes people like Dr. Hugo willing to risk their lives
in order to make us more aware of our living space? Would
you be willing to find your lifework as a naturalist or
worker in a museum or zoo? Give reasons to support your
choice.

5. Our daily lives are constantly being bombarded by TV programs, movies, videocassettes, and books dealing with aspects of life and living outside of our Earth. Which is your favorite story? What makes such stories so fascinating? To what extent do you believe them to be true to reality?

6. Would you be interested in space travel?
> As a pioneer?
> As an explorer?
> As a settler?
> As a tourist?

Given its present stage of development, would you choose a career in space exploration?

Stories in Words _____

August (359)   The ancient Egyptians had a twelve-month calendar with thirty days each. Some extra days had to be provided. The primitive Roman calendar had only ten months with extra months added to complete the year. Then January and February were added to make twelve. Things were confused until Julius Caesar called for calendar reform. In honor of his achievements, the month named "Sextilis" was changed to *July*, from the name *Julius*. Caesar Augustus changed the name of "Quintilis" to *August*, in *his* own honor.

Month (359)   Calendars based on the moon are called "lunar calendars." "Solar calendars," based on the sun, are not quite so complicated. Our present calendar is a solar calendar. Yet the motions of the moon have not been forgotten. Our word *month* has within it the word *moon* itself.

Planets (360)   The word *planet* comes from a Greek word meaning "to wander." Under the brilliantly starry skies of ancient times, stargazers noticed that some points of light in the sky moved in relationship to the other points, the "fixed stars." A nearer planet, like Venus, seems to change its position almost overnight. Even distant planets are seen to move against the background of stars. The planets thus have earned the name "wanderers," and the word history reminds us of their special quality.

Good-By, Herman

John O'Hara

◆ **"There's a man in there. He came to see you. He's been here for an hour and he's driving me crazy."**

In the days before electric shavers, injector blades, and the latest bearded generations, the barbershop was an important, if not the most important, center of urban communities. It was more than the haircutting emporium for the entire male population.

The barbershop was where you went to find out who was who and what was happening. All of the important men came there for their daily shaves and to gather the news and opinions of the day.

Lining the walls of the establishment were elaborately decorated one- or two-eared glazed mugs with the name of the owner imprinted in large letters. To the young, owning such a cup symbolized maturity. To the mature, the cup proclaimed the arrival of social standing. That it served merely as the base for the lather used in the shave was only incidental.

The mug remained in the barber's collection until the owner moved or passed away. It was then returned to become part of the family heirlooms.

This short short proves that, in the hands of a master, the readers' interest need not depend on a surprise ending or unusual characters.

GOOD-BY, HERMAN

Miller was putting his key in the lock. He had two afternoon papers folded under one arm, and a package—two dress shirts which he had picked up at the laundry because he was going out that night. Just when the ridges of the key were fitting properly, the door was swung open and it was his wife. She was frowning. "Hello," he said.

She held up her finger. "Come in the bedroom," she said. She was distressed about something. Throwing his hat on a chair in the foyer, he followed her to the bedroom. She turned and faced him as he put down his bundle and began taking off his coat.

"What's up?" he said.

"There's a man in there. He came to see you. He's been here for an hour and he's driving me crazy."

"Who is he? What's it all about?"

"He's from Lancaster, and he said he was a friend of your father's."

"Well, has he been causing any trouble?"

"His name is Wasserfogel, or something like that."

"Oh, I know. Herman Wasservogel. He was my father's barber. I knew he was coming. I just forgot to tell you."

"Oh, you did. Well, thanks for a lovely hour. Hereafter, when you're expecting somebody, I wish you'd let me know beforehand. I tried to reach you at the office. Where were you? I tried everywhere I could think of. You don't know what it is to suddenly have a perfectly strange man—"

"I'm sorry, darling. I just forgot. I'll go in."

He went to the living room, and there sat a little old man. In his lap was a small package, round which he had wrapped his hands. He was looking down at the package, and there was

369

a faint smile on his face, which Miller knew to be the man's customary expression. His feet, in high, black shoes, were flat on the floor and parallel with each other, and Miller guessed that this was the way the little old man had been sitting ever since he first arrived.

"Herman, how are you? I'm sorry I'm late."

"Oh, that's all right. How are you, Paul?"

"Fine. You're looking fine, Herman. I got your letter and I forgot to tell Elsie. I guess you know each other by now," he said as Elsie came into the room and sat down. "My wife, Elsie, this is Herman Wasservogel, an old friend of mine."

"Pleased to meet you," said Herman.

Elsie lit a cigarette.

"How about a drink, Herman? A little schnapps? Glass of beer?"

"No, thank you, Paul. I just came; I wanted to bring this here. I just thought maybe you would want it."

"I was sorry I didn't see you when I was home for the funeral, but you know how it is. It's such a big family, I never got around to the shop."

"Henry was in. I shaved him three times."

"Yes, Henry was there longer than I was. I was only there overnight. I had to come right back to New York after the funeral. Sure you won't have a beer?"

"No, I just wanted to bring this in to give to you." Herman stood up and handed the little package to Paul.

"Gee, thanks a lot, Herman."

"What's that? Mr. Wasserfogel wouldn't show it to me. It's all very mysterious." Elsie spoke without looking at Herman, not even when she mentioned his name.

"Oh, he probably thought I'd told you."

Herman stood while Paul undid the package, revealing a shaving mug. "This was my father's. Herman shaved him every day of his life, I guess."

"Well, not every day. The Daddy didn't start shaving till he was I guess eighteen years old, and he used to go away a lot. But I guess I shaved him more than all the other barbers put together."

"Darn right you did. Dad always swore by you, Herman."

"Yes, I guess that's right," said Herman.

"See, Elsie?" said Paul, holding up the mug. He read the gold lettering: "J.D. Miller, M.D.' "

"Mm. Why do you get it? You're not the oldest boy. Henry's older than you," said Elsie.

Herman looked at her and then at Paul. He frowned a little. "Paul, will you give me a favor? I don't want Henry to know it that I give you this mug. After the Daddy died, I said, 'Which one will I give the mug to?' Henry was entitled to it, being the oldest and all. In a way he should have got it. But not saying anything against Henry—well, I don't know."

"Mr. Wasserfogel liked you better than he did Henry, isn't that it, Mr. Wasserfogel?" said Elsie.

"Oh, well," said Herman.

"Don't you worry, Herman, I'll keep quiet about it. I never see Henry anyway," said Paul.

"The brush I didn't bring. Doc needed a new one this long time, and I used to say to him. 'Doc, are you so poor yet you won't even buy a new shaving brush?' 'I am,' he'd say to me. 'Well,' I said, 'I'll give you one out of my own pocket for a gift.' 'You do,' he'd say, 'and I'll stop coming here. I'll go to the hotel.' Only joking, we were, Mrs. Miller. The Doc was always saying he'd stop coming and go to the hotel, but I knew better. He was always making out like my razors needed sharpening, or I ought to get new lights for my shop, or I was shaving him too close. Complain, complain, complain. Then around the first of last year I noticed how he'd come in, and all he'd say was, 'Hello Herman. Once over, not too close,' and that's all he'd say. I knew he was a sick man. He knew it, too."

"Yes, you're right," said Paul. "When'd you get in, Herman?"

"Just today. I came by bus."

"When are you going back? I'd like to see some more of you before you go away. Elsie and I, we're going out tonight, but tomorrow night—"

"Not tomorrow night. Tomorrow night is Hazel's," said Elsie.

"Oh, I don't have to go to that," said Paul. "Where are you stopping, Herman?"

"Well, to tell you the truth, I ain't stopping. I'm going back to Lancaster this evening."

"Why, no! You can't. You just got here. You ought to stick around, see the sights. Come down to my office and I'll show you Wall Street."

"I guess I know enough about Wall Street; all I want to know. If it wasn't for Wall Street, I wouldn't be barbering at my age. No. Thanks very much, Paul, but I got to get back. Got to open the shop in the morning. I only have this relief man for one day. Young Joe Meyers. He's a barber now."

"Well, why not? Keep him on for another day or two. I'll pay him. You've got to stick around. How long is it since you've been to New York?"

"Nineteen years last March I was here, when young Hermie went to France with the Army."

"Herman had a son. He was killed in the war."

"He'd be forty years old, a grown man," said Herman. "No. Thank you, Paul, but I think I better be going. I wanted to take a walk down to where the bus leaves from. I didn't get my walk in today yet, and that will give me the chance to see New York City."

"Oh, come on, Herman."

"Don't be so insistent, Paul. You can see Mr. Wasserfogel wants to go back to Lancaster. I'll leave you alone for a few minutes. I've got to start dressing. But not too long, Paul. We've got to go all the way down to Ninth Street. Good-by, Mr. Wasserfogel. I hope we'll see you again sometime. And thank you for bringing Paul the cup. It was very sweet of you."

"Oh, that's all right, Mrs. Miller."

"Well, I really must go," said Elsie.

"I'll be in in a minute," said Paul. "Herman, you sure you won't change your mind?"

"No, Paul. Thank you, but I have the shop to think of. And you better go in and wash up, or you'll catch the dickens."

Paul tried a laugh. "Oh, Elsie isn't always like that. She's just fidgety today. You know how women get."

"Oh, sure, Paul. She's a nice girl. Very pretty-looking. Well."

"If you change your mind—"

"Nope."

"We're in the phone book."

"Nope."

"Well, just remember, if you *do* change your mind; and I really don't know how to thank you, Herman. You know I mean it, how much I appreciate this."

"Well, your Dad was always good to me. So were you, Paul. Only don't tell Henry."

"That's a promise, Herman. Good-by, Herman. Good luck, and I hope I'll see you soon. I may get down to Lancaster this fall, and I'll surely look you up this time."

"Mm. Well, *auf Wiedersehen*, Paul."

Auf Wiedersehen, Herman."

Paul watched Herman going the short distance to the elevator. He pushed the button, waited a few seconds until the elevator got there, and then he got in without looking back. "Good-by, Herman," Paul called, but he was sure Herman did not hear him.

Reading for Understanding _____

Main Idea

1. Which of the following best expresses the main idea of the story?
   (a) The customs of one generation are not easily understood by the next.
   (b) Each generation attempts to leave monuments as guidelines to the succeeding generations.
   (c) Customs and values change from generation to generation.
   (d) Small town customs lose their significance in the melting pot of the big cities.

Details

2. "The Daddy" was　(a) Elsie's father　(b) the barber　(c) a town doctor　(d) the town mayor.

3. Herman's son　(a) is the assistant barber　(b) is the new town doctor　(c) died fighting for his country　(d) is Paul's best friend.

4. Paul most likely　(a) followed in his father's footsteps　(b) manages a large factory　(c) works in a large department store　(d) works for an investment company.

5. Which of the following is not true of Paul?
   (a) He accepts goodnaturedly his wife's anger and impatience.
   (b) He is most grateful to receive the mug.
   (c) He is impatient with Herman.
   (d) He hoped his wife would show Herman proper courtesy.

Inferences

6. Herman gives the cup to Paul because　(a) Paul has asked him to　(b) the father had told him to　(c) the lawyer has advised him to.　(d) he likes Paul better than Henry.

7. Herman arrives at Paul Miller's home (a) on appointment (b) without an appointment (c) frequently (d) at Elsie's request.

8. Elsie is annoyed because (a) Herman is rude (b) Paul scolds her (c) Paul tries to brush Herman off (d) Paul forgot to alert her.

9. Which of the following is most likely true?
   (a) Elsie grew up in Lancaster.
   (b) Elsie is a practicing physician.
   (c) Elsie and Paul had their home in Lancaster for years.
   (d) Paul met and married Elsie in the big city.

10. The old Doctor (a) quit going to the barbershop (b) kept going to the barbershop when he was sick (c) forbade the boys from going to the barbershop (d) mentioned the mug in his will.

Order of Events

11. Arrange the items in the order in which they occurred. Use letters only.
    A. Paul becomes acquainted with Herman.
    B. Herman meets Paul's wife.
    C. Paul's father buys the mug.
    D. Paul moves to the big city.
    E. Paul's father dies.

Outcome

12. Which of the following statements is most likely true?
    (a) The mug is put on display for Elsie's guests to admire.
    (b) Herman regrets having made the trip.
    (c) Herman feels that he has shown the proper respect to his former customer.
    (d) Paul boasts to his brother that he now has their father's shaving cup.

Cause and Effect

13. The most likely reason for Paul's not telling Elsie of the appointment with Herman is (a) he knew how busy

they were   (b) she would have refused to let him keep it
(c) he wanted to be inconsiderate   (d) he hoped Herman would not come.

Fact or Opinion

Tell whether each of the following is a fact or opinion.
14. Elsie is not aware of the part Herman played in Paul's
growing-up years.
15. Paul calls out, "Good-by, Herman" to signify that a phase
of his life has ended.

Words in Context _____

1. Throwing his hat on a chair in the *foyer*, he followed her to
the bedroom.
Foyer (369) means   (a) hall closet   (b) bedroom
closet   (c) dressing room   (d) entrance hallway.

2. Just when the *ridges* of the key were fitting properly, the
door was swung open and it was his wife.
Ridges (369) means   (a) high spots   (b) indentations
(c) top and bottom   (d) holes.

3. He was looking down at the package, and there was a
faint smile on his face, which Miller knew to be the man's
customary expression.
Customary (370) means   (a) hurt   (b) friendly
(c) sad   (d) usual.

4. "How about a drink, Herman? A little *schnapps?* Glass of
beer?"
Schnapps (370) means   (a) a light tea
(b) carbonated water   (c) soda pop   (d) strong
alcoholic drink.

5. "Dad *always swore by you*, Herman."
Always swore by you (371) means   (a) enjoyed your
company   (b) had great confidence in you   (c) told
stories about you   (d) invested in your tips.

6. "Henry *was entitled to* it, being the oldest and all. In a way he should have got it. But not saying anything against Henry—well, I don't know."
   Was entitled to (371) means   (a) had a right to
   (b) worked for   (c) paid for   (d) wanted.

7. Got to open the shop in the morning. I only have this *relief man* for one day.
   Relief man (372) means   (a) client   (b) customer
   (c) replacement   (d) agent.

8. "And you better go in and wash up, or you'll *catch the dickens.*"
   Catch the dickens (373) means   (a) make a mistake
   (b) be complimented   (c) be scolded   (d) get into a fight.

9. "She's just *fidgety* today. You know how women get."
   Fidgety (373) means   (a) fussy   (b) angry   (c) unhappy   (d) talkative.

10. "Mm. Well, *auf Wiedersehen*, Paul."
    Auf Wiedersehen (373) means   (a) Stay well
    (b) Don't fight with her about this   (c) Enjoy whatever you do   (d) Until we meet again.

Thinking Critically About the Story _____

1. From this story, what do we learn about the contrast between life in the small town that Paul grew up in and life in the big city?

2. By citing examples from the story show the extent to which the following statement is true:
   The dialog shows that the characters understand the inner drama in each other, the feelings and reactions that they do not allow to come to the surface.

3. Why does Paul feel obligated to show Herman the town? Why does Herman refuse? How does Elsie signal her reactions to Paul? To Herman? Do any go beyond the limits

of proper conduct in letting wishes be known? Why don't they openly state how they feel? Is it fair to the others to disguise feelings in this way? Explain.

4. To what extent is the following statement true of the characters in this story?
    > In "Good-by, Herman" John O'Hara depicts no heroes or villains. Instead, he uses merciless humor to expose the pettiness of everyday people.

5. Are the characters in this story true to life? Do they remind you of any adults in your neighborhood? Among your relatives? Among your favorite TV characters? Would you be willing to have any one of them as your best friend?

Stories in Words

Parallel (370) The two parts of this word give a perfect description of its meaning. The Greek prefix *para* means "side by side." The root *allel* comes from the Greek *allelos,* "one another." Parallel lines run beside one another, "side by side," but supposedly never cross. *Para* also appears in words like *paragraph, parachute,* and *parasite.*

Barber (372) The history of this word is simple, direct, and clear. The Latin word *barba* means "beard." A barber trims beards. During the Middle Ages, the barber was also a surgeon, but this meaning of the word *barber* is obsolete (out-of-date, no longer in use). A related word *barb* tells an interesting story. *Barb* means "a beardlike growth near the mouth of certain animals"; "the sharp point of a fishhook, harpoon, or arrow"; "a cutting remark"; or "a hooked hair." Though the meanings have traveled far from the original *beard*, it is still possible to trace the changes. The beard's bristles can be sharp, pointed, cutting. A person's remarks may also be sharp, pointed, cutting.

Minute (373)   Have you ever been called by a family member and replied, "In a minute"? What you intended was to assure the caller that you'd be there in a very short time. This phrase gives a clue to the origin of *minute*. The word is derived from the Latin "to lessen, to make smaller." A minute is a "small" part of an hour. There is an adjective *minute*, pronounced "my-NYOOT," which means "very small, of little importance."

Short Shorts

ACTIVITIES

Thinking Critically About the Stories ___

1. Compare Ivan Panfilich and Herman Wasservogel. Why are they survivors? How do they compare with the men you know in your grandfather's generation? ·

2. Both Ivan Panfilich and Professor Hugo look toward the future. Herman, on the other hand, is concerned mainly with the past. Can you explain why they are so oriented? Which is the better way to look at events—for youth? For parents? For older people?

3. How does Johanna's attitude toward family obligations compare—with Paul Miller's? With your own? To what extent should we feel obligated toward other members of our family—our parents? Our siblings? Our grandparents? Our cousins? Our friends?

4. The stories in this Unit have a wide range of ideas. Which one has the most significance for you? Which one stretched your imagination most? Which one do you think you will remember longest? Which one do you think is most effective? Justify each of your choices.

5. Which scene revealed most about human nature? Explain.

Writing and Other Activities _____

1. Occasionally in real life a surprise ending occurs—as in "Johanna." Write the plot of a story involving such an

incident that you heard about or that happened to you or someone you know.

2. Write the setting and dialog for one of the following, involving an explorer from Kaan who had visited Earth, unobserved, and is now telling his wife what he had seen and experienced.

   (a) He had slipped into the school cafeteria during lunchtime.

   (b) He had visited the local football stadium just when the local hero broke a tie with a touchdown run of 45 yards.

   (c) He had visited a teenage no-alcohol discotheque.

   (d) He had landed at the main intersection in your hometown at 5:15 P.M., the peak of rush hour.

   (e) He had gone to a mall filled with last-minute Christmas shoppers.

3. Be prepared to retell briefly the science-fiction story you like best. Justify your choice.

4. Be prepared to lead a class panel in a discussion of one of the following:

   (a) Officiousness. How to handle officious people—like the stationmaster. What are symptoms of officiousness? What causes people to become officious? How can they be managed without damage to either side?

   (b) Patience and Impatience. How did Ivan Panfilich show his patience? How did Elsie Miller show her impatience? What are the advantages of patience? When does it become a handicap? What are the disadvantages of impatience? When does impatience become an advantage? How can we control impatience? Patience? How can we help others to become less impatient? Less patient?

5. Write the setting and dialog for the first three minutes of a short-short story on one of the following:

   (a) Grandfather has just knocked on the door of the neighbor who threatened to have his dogs attack the children if they continue to play punchball near his house or car.

   (b) You are about to knock on the front door of the

neighborhood miser to ask for a contribution for the local Scout Chapter.

(c) The last person in the world you would want to be seen with has just asked you in front of your friends to go on a date or double date.

(d) Your best friend has asked to borrow the jacket or trinket that you plan to wear to the same affair that he (she) wants it for.

(e) Your father insists that you call his client's son or daughter and invite him or her to the party that your friends are planning to have.

Stories in Words: A Review

A. August	E. month	I. precisely
B. barber	F. parallel	J. silhouette
C. chestnut	G. picnicked	K. tarpaulin
D. minute	H. planets	L. unfocused

Answer the following questions by choosing a word from the list above. Use letters only.

Which of the words above . . .

1. . . . is named for a French author?
2. . . . has something to do with "a sharp point"?
3. . . . is named for a Roman emperor?
4. . . . contains a root that means "cut"?
5. . . . is related to Spanish *castanets?*

6. . . . has earned the name *wanderers?*
7. . . . means "picked a trifle"?
8. . . . has something to do with a hearth or fireplace?
9. . . . really means "something small"?
10. . . . describes lines that never cross?

6

Fellow Creatures

Stories in which major characters are animals are part of the heritage of all cultures. In the fables and legends of many lands, the animals of storyland are endowed with human emotions and human thinking patterns. In most instances the animals think and speak like the people listening to or reading the tale. Modern TV cartoons have carried on this tradition from Mickey Mouse, Pluto, Roadrunner, and Woody Woodpecker down through Snoopy, Garfield, the creations of Dr. Seuss, the companions of Dennis the Menace, and the weird ones of Sendak.

Today's writers of short stories have not abandoned animals as central or supporting characters. The appeal to readers of all ages is too great to be ignored. The contemporary author's approach, however, is much more varied. Our fellow creatures are presented as having minds and emotions of their own species, as well as ours. They are closer in behavior to that of real-life tamed and untamed earthlings.

Unit Six samples the variety. "My Friend Flicka" unfolds the taming of the untamable yearling. In "The Apprentice" we share the swing of moods of a young collie and his teenage owner. In "Leiningen Versus the Ants" human ingenuity is pitted against the merciless discipline of killer ants. What would happen if the birds of the world lost their fear of human beings? That is the frightening question answered in "The Birds." You too will find a most interesting world of fellow creatures in these stories.

My Friend Flicka

Mary O'Hara

♦   "It isn't the school marks alone, but I just don't
want things to go on any longer with Ken never
coming out at the right end of anything."

This story begins at a critical time in the lives of a boy and a horse on a
ranch in Wyoming. Both are on self-destructing courses. Kennie's self-
confidence and will to keep trying are being shattered by his endless stream
of failures. Even his father is becoming resigned to accepting Kennie on a
slower track.

The thoroughbred, Flicka, has been branded as untamable. She
unhesitatingly risks death rather than being deprived of her freedom to roam
the hills.

No turnabout is in sight for either one! What follows is one of the
best-loved animal stories of our time!

MY FRIEND FLICKA

Report cards for the second semester were sent out soon after school closed in mid-June.

Kennie's was a shock to the whole family.

"If I could have a colt all for my own," said Kennie, "I might do better."

Rob McLaughlin glared at his son. "Just as a matter of curiosity," he said, "how do you go about it to get a *zero* in an examination? Forty in arithmetic; seventeen in history! But a *zero*? Just as one man to another, what goes on in your head?"

"Yes, tell us how you do it, Ken," chirped Howard.

"Eat your breakfast, Howard," snapped his mother.

Kennie's blond head bent over his plate until his face was almost hidden. His cheeks burned.

McLaughlin finished his coffee and pushed his chair back. "You'll do an hour a day on your lessons all through the summer."

Nell McLaughlin saw Kennie wince as if something had actually hurt him.

Lessons and study in the summertime, when the long winter was just over and there weren't hours enough in the day for all the things he wanted to do!

Kennie took things hard. His eyes turned to the wide-open window with a look almost of despair.

The hill opposite the house, covered with arrow-straight jack pines, was sharply etched in the thin air of the eight-thousand-foot altitude. Where it fell away, vivid green grass ran up to meet it; and over range and upland poured the strong Wyoming sunlight that stung everything into burning color. A

387

big jackrabbit sat under one of the pines, waving his long ears
back and forth.

Ken had to look at his plate and blink back tears before he
could turn to his father and say carelessly, "Can I help you in
the corral with the horses this morning, Dad?"

"You'll do your study every morning before you do anything else." And McLaughlin's scarred boots and heavy spurs
clattered across the kitchen floor. "I'm disgusted with you.
Come, Howard."

Howard strode after his father, nobly refraining from
looking at Kennie.

"Help me with the dishes, Kennie," said Nell McLaughlin
as she rose, tied on a big apron, and began to clear the table.

Kennie looked at her in despair. She poured steaming
water into the dishpan and sent him for the soap powder.

"If I could have a colt," he muttered again.

"Now get busy with that dishtowel, Ken. It's eight o'clock.
You can study till nine and then go up to the corral. They'll still
be there."

At supper that night Kennie said, "But Dad, Howard had a
colt all of his own when he was only eight. And he trained it and
schooled it all himself; and now he's eleven, and Highboy is
three, and he's riding him. I'm nine now and even if you did give
me a colt now I couldn't catch up to Howard because I couldn't
ride it till it was a three-year-old and then I'd be twelve."

Nell laughed. "Nothing wrong with that arithmetic."

But Rob said, "Howard never gets less than seventy-five
average at school, and hasn't disgraced himself and his family
by getting more demerits than any other boy in his class."

Kennie didn't answer. He couldn't figure it out. He tried
hard; he spent hours poring over his books. That was supposed
to get you good marks, but it never did. Everyone said he was
bright. Why was it that when he studied he didn't learn? He
had a vague feeling that perhaps he looked out the window too
much, or looked through the walls to see clouds and sky and
hills and wonder what was happening out there. Sometimes it
wasn't even a wonder, but just a pleasant drifting feeling of
nothing at all, as if nothing mattered, as if there was always
plenty of time, as if the lessons would get done of themselves.
And then the bell would ring, and study period was over.

If he had a colt . . .

When the boys had gone to bed that night, Nell McLaughlin sat down with her overflowing mending basket and glanced at her husband.

He was at his desk as usual, working on account books and inventories.

Nell threaded a darning needle and thought, "It's either that whacking big bill from the vet for the mare that died or the last half of the tax bill."

It didn't seem just the auspicious moment to plead Kennie's cause. But then, these days, there was always a line between Rob's eyes and a harsh note in his voice.

"Rob," she began.

He flung down his pencil and turned around.

"How could they make such a law!" he exclaimed.

"What law?"

"The state law that puts high taxes on pedigreed stock. I'll have to do as the rest of 'em do—drop the papers."

"Drop the papers! But you'll never get decent prices if you don't have registered horses."

"I don't get decent prices now."

"But you will someday if you don't drop the papers."

"Maybe." He bent again over the desk.

Rob, thought Nell, was a lot like Kennie himself. He set his heart. Oh, how stubbornly he set his heart on just some one thing he wanted above everything else. He had set his heart on horses and ranching way back when he had been a crack rider at West Point; and he had resigned and thrown away his army career just for the horses. Well, he'd got what he wanted. . . .

She drew a deep breath, snipped her thread, laid down the sock, and again looked across at her husband as she unrolled another length of darning cotton.

To get what you want is one thing, she was thinking. The three-thousand-acre ranch and the hundred head of horses. But to make it pay—for a dozen or more years they had been trying to make it pay. People said ranching hadn't paid since the beef barons ran their herds on public land; people said the only prosperous ranchers in Wyoming were the dude ranchers; people said . . .

But suddenly she gave her head a little rebellious, gallant

shake. Rob would always be fighting and struggling against something, like Kennie; perhaps like herself, too. Even those first years when there was no water piped into the house, when every day brought a new difficulty or danger, how she had loved it! How she still loved it!

She ran the darning ball into the toe of a sock, Kennie's sock. The length of it gave her a shock. Yes, the boys were growing up fast, and now Kennie—Kennie and the colt . . .

After a while she said, "Give Kennie a colt, Rob."

"He doesn't deserve it." The answer was short. Rob pushed away his papers and took out his pipe.

"Howard's too far ahead of him, older and bigger and quicker, and his wits about him, and—"

"Ken doesn't half try, doesn't stick at anything."

She put down her sewing. "He's crazy for a colt of his own. He hasn't had another idea in his head since you gave Highboy to Howard."

"I don't believe in bribing children to do their duty."

"Not a bribe." She hesitated.

"No? What would you call it?"

She tried to think it out. "I just have the feeling Ken isn't going to pull anything off, and"—her eyes sought Rob's—"it's time he did. It isn't the school marks alone, but I just don't want things to go on any longer with Ken never coming out at the right end of anything."

"I'm beginning to think he's just dumb."

"He's not dumb. Maybe a little thing like this—if he had a colt of his own, trained him, rode him—"

Rob interrupted. "But it isn't a little thing, nor an easy thing, to break and school a colt the way Howard has schooled Highboy. I'm not going to have a good horse spoiled by Ken's careless ways. He goes woolgathering. He never knows what he's doing."

"But he'd *love* a colt of his own, Rob. If he could do it, it might make a big difference in him."

"*If* he could do it! But that's a big if."

At breakfast next morning Kennie's father said to him, "When you've done your study come out to the barn. I'm going in the car up to section twenty-one this morning to look over the brood mares. You can go with me."

"Can I go, too, Dad?" cried Howard.

McLaughlin frowned at Howard. "You turned Highboy out last evening with dirty legs."

Howard wriggled. "I groomed him—"

"Yes, down to his knees."

"He kicks."

"And whose fault is that? You don't get on his back again until I see his legs clean."

The two boys eyed each other, Kennie secretly triumphant and Howard chagrined. McLaughlin turned at the door, "And, Ken, a week from today I'll give you a colt. Between now and then you can decide what one you want."

Kennie shot out of his chair and stared at his father. "A—a spring colt, Dad, or a yearling?"

McLaughlin was somewhat taken aback, but his wife concealed a smile. If Kennie got a yearling colt he would be even up with Howard.

"A yearling colt, your father means, Ken," she said smoothly. "Now hurry with your lessons. Howard will wipe."

Kennie found himself the most important personage on the ranch. Prestige lifted his head, gave him an inch more of height and a bold stare, and made him feel different all the way through. Even Gus and Tim Murphy, the ranch hands, were more interested in Kennie's choice of a colt than anything else.

Howard was fidgety with suspense. "Who'll you pick, Ken? Say—pick Doughboy, why don't you? Then when he grows up he'll be sort of twins with mine, in his name anyway. Doughboy, Highboy, see?"

The boys were sitting on the worn wooden step of the door which led from the tack room into the corral, busy with rags and polish, shining their bridles.

Ken looked at his brother with scorn. Doughboy would never have half of Highboy's speed.

"Lassie, then," suggested Howard. "She's black as ink, like mine. And she'll be fast—"

"Dad says Lassie'll never go over fifteen hands."

Nell McLaughlin saw the change in Kennie, and her hopes

rose. He went to his books in the morning with determination and really studied. A new alertness took the place of the daydreaming. Examples in arithmetic were neatly written out, and as she passed his door before breakfast she often heard the monotonous drone of his voice as he read his American history aloud.

Each night, when he kissed her, he flung his arms around her and held her fiercely for a moment, then, with a winsome and blissful smile into her eyes, turned away to bed.

He spent days inspecting the different bands of horses and colts. He sat for hours on the corral fence, very important, chewing straws. He rode off on one of the ponies for half the day, wandering through the mile-square pastures that ran down toward the Colorado border.

And when the week was up he announced his decision. "I'll take that yearling filly of Rocket's. The sorrel with the cream tail and mane."

His father looked at him in surprise. "The one that got tangled in the barbed wire? That's never been named?"

In a second all Kennie's new pride was gone. He hung his head defensively. "Yes."

"You've made a bad choice, son. You couldn't have picked a worse."

"She's fast, Dad. And Rocket's fast—"

"It's the worst line of horses I've got. There's never one amongst them with real sense. The mares are hellions and the stallions outlaws; they're untamable."

"I'll tame her."

Rob guffawed. "Not I, nor anyone, has ever been able to really tame any one of them."

Kennie's chest heaved.

"Better change your mind, Ken. You want a horse that'll be a real friend to you, don't you?"

"Yes." Kennie's voice was unsteady.

"Well, you'll never make a friend of that filly. She's all cut and scarred up already with tearing through barbed wire after that mother of hers. No fence'll hold 'em—"

"I know," said Kennie, still more faintly.

"Change your mind?" asked Howard briskly.

"No."

Rob was grim and put out. He couldn't go back on his word. The boy had to have a reasonable amount of help in breaking and taming the filly, and he could envision precious hours, whole days, wasted in the struggle.

Nell McLaughlin despaired. Once again Ken seemed to have taken the wrong turn and was back where he had begun; stoical, silent, defensive.

But there was a difference that only Ken could know. The way he felt about his colt. The way his heart sang. The pride and joy that filled him so full that sometimes he hung his head so they wouldn't see it shining out of his eyes.

He had known from the very first that he would choose that particular yearling because he was in love with her.

The year before, he had been out working with Gus, the big Swedish ranch hand, on the irrigation ditch, when they had noticed Rocket standing in a gully on the hillside, quiet for once, and eyeing them cautiously.

"I bet she got a colt," said Gus, and they walked carefully up the draw. Rocket gave a wild snort, thrust her feet out, shook her head wickedly, then fled away. And as they reached the spot they saw standing there the wavering, pinkish colt, barely able to keep its feet. It gave a little squeak and started after its mother on crooked, wobbling legs.

"Gee, look at the little *flicka!*" said Gus.

"What does *flicka* mean, Gus?"

"Swedish for little girl, Ken."

Ken announced at supper, "You said she'd never been named. I've named her. Her name is Flicka."

The first thing to do was to get her in. She was running with a band of yearlings on the saddleback, cut with ravines and gullies, on section twenty.

They all went out after her, Ken, as owner, on old Rob Roy, the wisest horse on the ranch.

Ken was entranced to watch Flicka when the wild band of youngsters discovered that they were being pursued and took off across the mountain. Footing made no difference to her. She floated across the ravines, always two lengths ahead of the others. Her pink mane and tail whipped in the wind. Her long delicate legs had only to aim, it seemed, at a particular spot, for her to reach it and sail on. She seemed to Ken a fairy horse.

He sat motionless, just watching and holding Rob Roy in, when his father thundered past on Sultan and shouted, "Well, what's the matter? Why didn't you turn 'em?"

Kennie woke up and galloped after.

Rob Roy brought in the whole band. The corral gates were closed, and an hour was spent shunting the ponies in and out and through the chutes, until Flicka was left alone in the small round corral in which the baby colts were branded. Gus drove the others away, out the gate, and up the saddleback.

But Flicka did not intend to be left. She hurled herself against the poles which walled the corral. She tried to jump them. They were seven feet high. She caught her front feet over the top rung, clung, scrambled, while Kennie held his breath for fear the slender legs would be caught between the bars and snapped. Her hold broke; she fell over backward, rolled, screamed, tore around the corral. Kennie had a sick feeling in the pit of his stomach, and his father looked disgusted.

One of the bars broke. She hurled herself again. Another went. She saw the opening and, as neatly as a dog crawls

through a fence, inserted her head and forefeet, scrambled through, and fled away, bleeding in a dozen places.

As Gus was coming back, just about to close the gate to the upper range, the sorrel whipped through it, sailed across the road and ditch with her inimitable floating leap, and went up the side of the saddleback like a jackrabbit.

From way up the mountain Gus heard excited whinnies, as she joined the band he had just driven up, and the last he saw of them they were strung out along the crest running like deer.

"Gee whiz!" said Gus, and stood motionless and staring until the ponies had disappeared over the ridge. Then he closed the gate, remounted Rob Roy, and rode back to the corral.

Rob McLaughlin gave Kennie one more chance to change his mind. "Last chance, son. Better pick a horse that you have some hope of riding one day. I'd have got rid of this whole line of stock if they weren't so fast that I've had the fool idea that someday there might turn out one gentle one in the lot—and I'd have a racehorse. But there's never been one so far, and it's not going to be Flicka."

"It's not going to be Flicka," chanted Howard.

"Perhaps she *might* be gentled," said Kennie; and Nell, watching, saw that although his lips quivered, there was fanatical determination in his eye.

"Ken," said Rob, "it's up to you. If you say you want her we'll get her. But she won't be the first of that line to die rather than give in. They're beautiful and they're fast, but let me tell you this, young man, they're *loco!*"

Kennie flinched under his father's direct glance.

"If I go after her again I'll not give up whatever comes; understand what I mean by that?"

"Yes."

"What do you say?"

"I want her."

They brought her in again. They had better luck this time. She jumped over the Dutch half door of the stable and crashed inside. The men slammed the upper half of the door shut, and she was caught.

The rest of the band was driven away, and Kennie stood outside of the stable, listening to the wild hoofs beating, the screams, the crashes. His Flicka inside there! He was drenched with perspiration.

"We'll leave her to think it over," said Rob when dinnertime came. "Afterward we'll go up and feed and water her."

But when they went up afterward there was no Flicka in the barn. One of the windows, higher than the mangers, was broken.

The window opened onto a pasture an eighth of a mile square, fenced in barbed wire six feet high. Near the stable stood a wagonload of hay. When they went around the back of the stable to see where Flicka had hidden herself they found her between the stable and the hay wagon, eating.

At their approach she leaped away, then headed east across the pasture.

"If she's like her mother," said Rob, "she'll go right through the wire."

"I bet she'll go over," said Gus. "She jumps like a deer."

"No horse can jump that," said McLaughlin.

Kennie said nothing because he could not speak. It was, perhaps, the most terrible moment of his life. He watched Flicka racing toward the eastern wire.

A few yards from it she swerved, turned, and raced diagonally south.

"It turned her! It turned her!" cried Kennie, almost sobbing. It was the first sign of hope for Flicka. "Oh, Dad! She has got sense. She has! She has!"

Flicka turned again as she met the southern boundary of the pasture, again at the northern; she avoided the barn. Without abating anything of her whirlwind speed, following a precise, accurate calculation and turning each time on a dime, she investigated every possibility. Then, seeing that there was no hope, she raced south toward the range where she had spent her life, gathered herself, and shot into the air.

Each of the three men watching had the impulse to cover his eyes, and Kennie gave a sort of a howl of despair.

Twenty yards of fence came down with her as she hurled herself through. Caught on the upper strands, she turned a complete somersault, landing on her back, her four legs dragging the wires down on top of her, and tangling herself in them beyond hope of escape.

"Curse the wire!" shouted McLaughlin. "If I could afford decent fences . . ."

Kennie followed the men miserably as they walked to the filly. They stood in a circle watching, while she kicked and fought and thrashed until the wire was tightly wound and knotted about her, cutting, piercing, and tearing great three-cornered pieces of flesh and hide. At last she was unconscious, streams of blood running on her golden coat, and pools of crimson widening and spreading on the grass beneath her.

With the wire cutter which Gus always carried in the hip pocket of his overalls he cut all the wire away, and they drew her into the pasture, repaired the fence, placed hay, a box of oats, and a tub of water near her, and called it a day.

"I don't think she'll pull out of it," said McLaughlin.

Next morning Kennie was up at five, doing his lessons. At six he went out to Flicka.

She had not moved. Food and water were untouched. She was no longer bleeding, but the wounds were swollen and caked over.

Kennie got a bucket of fresh water and poured it over her mouth. Then he leaped away, for Flicka came to life, scrambled up, got her balance, and stood swaying.

Kennie went a few feet away and sat down to watch her. When he went in to breakfast she had drunk deeply of the water and was mouthing the oats.

There began then a sort of recovery. She ate, drank, limped about the pasture, stood for hours with hanging head and weakly splayed-out legs, under the clump of cottonwood trees. The swollen wounds scabbed and began to heal.

Kennie lived in the pasture too. He followed her around; he talked to her. He, too, lay snoozing or sat under the cottonwoods; and often, coaxing her with hand outstretched, he walked very quietly toward her. But she would not let him come near her.

Often she stood with her head at the south fence, looking off to the mountain. It made the tears come to Kennie's eyes to see the way she longed to get away.

Still Rob said she wouldn't pull out of it. There was no use putting a halter on her. She had no strength.

One morning, as Ken came out of the house, Gus met him and said, "The filly's down."

Kennie ran to the pasture, Howard close behind him. The right hind leg which had been badly swollen at the knee joint had opened in a festering wound, and Flicka lay flat and motionless, with staring eyes.

"Don't you wish now you'd chosen Doughboy?" asked Howard.

"Go away!" shouted Ken.

Howard stood watching while Kennie sat down on the ground and took Flicka's head on his lap. Though she was conscious and moved a little she did not struggle nor seem frightened. Tears rolled down Kennie's cheeks as he talked to her and petted her. After a few moments Howard walked away.

"Mother, what do you do for an infection when it's a horse?" asked Kennie.

"Just what you'd do if it was a person. Wet dressings. I'll help you, Ken. We mustn't let those wounds close or scab over until they're clean. I'll make a poultice for that hind leg and help you put it on. Now that she'll let us get close to her, we can help her a lot."

"The thing to do is see that she eats," said Rob. "Keep up her strength."

But he himself would not go near her. "She won't pull out of it," he said. "I don't want to see her or think about her."

Kennie and his mother nursed the filly. The big poultice was bandaged on the hind leg. It drew out much poisoned matter, and Flicka felt better and was able to stand again.

She watched for Kennie now and followed him like a dog, hopping on three legs, holding up the right hind leg with its huge knob of a bandage in comical fashion.

"Dad, Flicka's my friend now; she likes me," said Ken.

His father looked at him. "I'm glad of that, son. It's a fine thing to have a horse for a friend."

Kennie found a nicer place for her. In the lower pasture the brook ran over cool stones. There was a grassy bank, the size of a corral, almost on a level with the water. Here she could lie softly, eat grass, drink fresh running water. From the grass, a twenty-foot hill sloped up, crested with overhanging trees. She was enclosed, as it were, in a green, open-air nursery.

Kennie carried her oats morning and evening. She would watch for him to come, eyes and ears pointed to the hill. And one evening Ken, still some distance off, came to a stop and a wide grin spread over his face. He had heard her nicker. She had caught sight of him coming and was calling to him!

He placed the box of oats under her nose, and she ate while he stood beside her, his hand smoothing the satin-soft skin under her mane. It had a nap as deep as plush. He played with her long, cream-colored tresses, arranged her forelock neatly between her eyes. She was a bit dish-faced, like an Arab, with eyes set far apart. He lightly groomed and brushed her while she stood turning her head to him whichever way he went.

He spoiled her. Soon she would not step to the stream to drink but he must hold a bucket for her. And she would drink, then lift her dripping muzzle, rest it on the shoulder of his blue chambray shirt, her golden eyes dreaming off into the distance, then daintily dip her mouth and drink again.

When she turned her head to the south and pricked up her ears and stood tense and listening, Ken knew she heard the other colts galloping on the upland.

"You'll go back there someday, Flicka," he whispered. "You'll be three, and I'll be eleven. You'll be so strong you won't know I'm on your back, and we'll fly like the wind. We'll stand on the very top where we can look over the whole world and smell the snow from the Neversummer Range. Maybe we'll see antelope. . . ."

This was the happiest month of Kennie's life.

With the morning Flicka always had new strength and would hop three-legged' up the hill to stand broadside to the early sun, as horses love to do.

The moment Ken woke he'd go to the window and see her there, and when he was dressed and at his table studying he sat so that he could raise his head and see Flicka.

After breakfast she would be waiting at the gate for him and the box of oats, and for Nell McLaughlin with fresh bandages and buckets of disinfectant. All three would go together to the brook, Flicka hopping along ahead of them as if she were leading the way.

But Rob McLaughlin would not look at her.

One day all the wounds were swollen again. Presently they

opened, one by one, and Kennie and his mother made more poultices.

Still the little filly climbed the hill in the early morning and ran about on three legs. Then she began to go down in flesh and almost overnight wasted away to nothing. Every rib showed; the glossy hide was dull and brittle and was pulled over the skeleton as if she were a dead horse.

Gus said, "It's the fever. It burns up her flesh. If you could stop the fever she might get well."

McLaughlin was standing in his window one morning and saw the little skeleton hopping about three-legged in the sunshine, and he said, "That's the end. I won't have a thing like that on my place."

Kennie had to understand that Flicka had not been getting well all this time; she had been slowly dying.

"She still eats her oats," he said mechanically.

They were all sorry for Ken. Nell McLaughlin stopped disinfecting and dressing the wounds. "It's no use, Ken," she said gently, "you know Flicka's going to die, don't you?"

"Yes, Mother."

Ken stopped eating. Howard said, "Ken doesn't eat anything anymore. Don't he have to eat his dinner, Mother?"

But Nell answered, "Leave him alone."

Because the shooting of wounded animals is all in the day's work on the western plains, and sickening to everyone, Rob's voice, when he gave the order to have Flicka shot, was as flat as if he had been telling Gus to kill a chicken for dinner.

"Here's the Marlin, Gus. Pick out a time when Ken's not around and put the filly out of her misery."

Gus took the rifle. *"Yes, boss. . . ."*

Ever since Ken had known that Flicka was to be shot he had kept his eye on the rack which held the firearms. His father allowed no firearms in the bunkhouse. The gun rack was in the dining room of the ranch house, and going through it to the kitchen three times a day for meals, Ken's eye scanned the weapons to make sure that they were all there.

That night they were not all there. The Marlin rifle was missing.

When Kennie saw that he stopped walking. He felt dizzy. He kept staring at the gun rack, telling himself that it surely was there—he counted again and again—he couldn't see clearly. . . .

Then he felt an arm across his shoulders and heard his father's voice.

"I know, son. Some things are awful hard to take. We just have to take 'em. I have to, too."

Kennie got hold of his father's hand and held on. It helped steady him.

Finally he looked up. Rob looked down and smiled at him and gave him a little shake and squeeze. Ken managed a smile too.

"All right now?"

"All right, Dad."

They walked in to supper together.

Ken even ate a little. But Nell looked thoughtfully at the ashen color of his face and at the little pulse that was beating in the side of his neck.

After supper he carried Flicka her oats but he had to coax her, and she would only eat a little. She stood with her head hanging but when he stroked it and talked to her she pressed her face into his chest and was content. He could feel the burning heat of her body. It didn't seem possible that anything so thin could be alive.

Presently Kennie saw Gus come into the pasture carrying the Marlin. When he saw Ken he changed his direction and sauntered along as if he was out to shoot some cottontails.

Ken ran to him. "When are you going to do it, Gus?"

"I was goin' down soon now, before it got dark. . . ."

"Gus, don't do it tonight. Wait till morning. Just one more night, Gus."

"Well, in the morning then, but it got to be done, Ken. Your father gives the order."

"I know. I won't say anything more."

An hour after the family had gone to bed Ken got up and put on his clothes. It was a warm moonlit night. He ran down to the brook, calling softly. "Flicka! Flicka!"

But Flicka did not answer with a little nicker; and she was not in the nursery nor hopping about the pasture. Ken hunted for an hour.

At last he found her down the creek, lying in the water. Her head had been on the bank, but as she lay there the current of the stream had sucked and pulled at her, and she had had no strength to resist; and little by little her head had slipped down until when Ken got there only the muzzle was resting on the bank, and the body and legs were swinging in the stream.

Kennie slid into the water, sitting on the bank, and he hauled at her head. But she was heavy, and the current dragged like a weight; and he began to sob because he had no strength to draw her out.

Then he found a leverage for his heels against some rocks in the bed of the stream and he braced himself against these and pulled with all his might; and her head came up onto his knees, and he held it cradled in his arms.

He was glad that she had died of her own accord, in the cool water, under the moon, instead of being shot by Gus. Then, putting his face close to hers, and looking searchingly into her eyes, he saw that she was alive and looking back at him.

And then he burst out crying and hugged her and said, "Oh, my little Flicka, my little Flicka."

The long night passed.

The moon slid slowly across the heavens.

The water rippled over Kennie's legs and over Flicka's body. And gradually the heat and fever went out of her. And the cool running water washed and washed her wounds.

When Gus went down in the morning with the rifle they hadn't moved. There they were, Kennie sitting in water over his thighs and hips, with Flicka's head in his arms.

Gus seized Flicka by the head and hauled her out on the grassy bank and then, seeing that Kennie couldn't move, cold and stiff and half-paralyzed as he was, lifted him in his arms and carried him to the house.

"Gus," said Ken through chattering teeth, "don't shoot her, Gus."

"It ain't for me to say, Ken. You know that."

"But the fever's left her, Gus."

"I'll wait a little, Ken. . . ."

Rob McLaughlin drove to Laramie to get the doctor, for Ken was in violent chills that would not stop. His mother had him in bed wrapped in hot blankets when they got back.

He looked at his father imploringly as the doctor shook down the thermometer.

"She might get well now, Dad. The fever's left her. It went out of her when the moon went down."

"All right, son. Don't worry. Gus'll feed her, morning and night, as long as she's—"

"As long as I can't do it," finished Kennie happily.

The doctor put the thermometer in his mouth and told him to keep it shut.

All day Gus went about his work, thinking of Flicka. He had not been back to look at her. He had been given no more orders. If she was alive the order to shoot her was still in effect. But Kennie was ill, McLaughlin making his second trip to town taking the doctor home, and would not be back till long after dark.

After their supper in the bunkhouse Gus and Tim walked down to the brook. They did not speak as they approached the filly, lying stretched out flat on the grassy bank, but their eyes were straining at her to see if she was dead or alive.

She raised her head as they reached her.

"By the powers!" exclaimed Tim. "There she is!"

She dropped her head, raised it again, and moved her legs and became tense as if struggling to rise. But to do so she must use her right hind leg to brace herself against the earth. That was the damaged leg, and at the first bit of pressure with it she gave up and fell back.

"We'll swing her onto the other side," said Tim. "Then she can help herself."

"Good. . . ."

Standing behind her, they leaned over, grabbed hold of her left legs, front and back, and gently hauled her over. Flicka was as lax and willing as a puppy. But the moment she found herself lying on her right side, she began to scramble, braced herself with her good left leg, and tried to rise.

"Gee whiz!" said Gus. "She got plenty strength yet."

"Hi!" cheered Tim. "She's up!"

But Flicka wavered, slid down again, and lay flat. This time she gave notice that she would not try again by heaving a deep sigh and closing her eyes.

Gus took his pipe out of his mouth and thought it over. Orders or no orders, he would try to save the filly. Ken had gone too far to be let down.

"I'm goin' to rig a blanket sling for her, Tim, and get her on her feet, and keep her up."

There was bright moonlight to work by. They brought down the posthole digger and set two aspen poles deep into the ground either side of the filly, then, with ropes attached to the blanket, hoisted her by a pulley.

Not at all disconcerted, she rested comfortably in the blanket under her belly, touched her feet on the ground, and reached for the bucket of water Gus held for her.

Kennie was sick a long time. He nearly died. But Flicka picked up. Every day Gus passed the word to Nell, who carried it to Ken. "She's cleaning up her oats." "She's out of the sling." "She bears a little weight on the bad leg."

Tim declared it was a real miracle. They argued about it, eating their supper.

"Na," said Gus. "It was the cold water, washin' the fever outa her. And more than that—it was Ken—you think it don't count? All night that boy sits there and says, 'Hold on, Flicka, I'm here with you. I'm standin' by, two of us, together'. . . ."

Tim stared at Gus without answering, while he thought it over. In the silence a coyote yapped far off on the plains, and the wind made a rushing sound high up in the jack pines on the hill.

Gus filled his pipe.

"Sure," said Tim finally. "Sure. That's it."

Then came the day when Rob McLaughlin stood smiling at the foot of Kennie's bed and said, "Listen! Hear your friend?"

Ken listened and heard Flicka's high, eager whinny.

"She don't spend much time by the brook anymore. She's up at the gate of the corral half the time, nickering for you."

"For me!"

Rob wrapped a blanket around the boy and carried him out to the corral gate.

Kennie gazed at Flicka. There was a look of marveling in his eyes. He felt as if he had been living in a world where everything was dreadful and hurting but awfully real; and *this* couldn't be real; this was all soft and happy, nothing to struggle over or worry about or fight for anymore. Even his father was proud of him! He could feel it in the way Rob's big arms held him. It was all like a dream and far away. He couldn't, yet, get close to anything.

But Flicka—Flicka—alive, well, pressing up to him, recognizing him, nickering . . .

Kennie put out a hand—weak and white—and laid it on her face. His thin little fingers straightened her forelock the way he used to do, while Rob looked at the two with a strange expression about his mouth and a glow in his eyes that was not often there.

"She's still poor, Dad, but she's on four legs now."

"She's picking up."

Ken turned his face up, suddenly remembering. "Dad! She did get gentled, didn't she?"

"Gentle—as a kitten. . . ."

They put a cot down by the brook for Ken, and boy and filly got well together.

Reading for Understanding _____

Main Idea

1. The main idea of the story is summed up in which of the following statements?
   (a) Determination alone is sufficient for success.
   (b) Love is a strong medicine.
   (c) Daydreams cannot help us to shape our lives.
   (d) Parents must set reasonable limits for their children.

Details

2. At the beginning of the story, Kennie is   (a) nine years old   (b) twelve years old   (c) fourteen years old   (d) sixteen years old.

3. Rob can't understand   (a) how Kennie could spend so
    much time daydreaming   (b) why Kennie forgets to do
    his chores   (c) why Howard does so much better than
    Kennie   (d) how Kennie could get marks that are so
    low.

4. Which one of the following statements is true?
    (a) From the start, Rob approved of Kennie's choice of
    Flicka.   (b) Rob planned to have Flicka shot because
    she was so rebellious.   (c) Rob named the yearling
    Flicka at Gus's suggestion.   (d) Rob trusted Nell's judg-
    ment rather than his own in letting Kenny have his own
    horse.

5. The poultice   (a) almost kills Flicka   (b) is prepared
    by Gus at Rob's suggestion   (c) helps temporarily
    (d) cures Flicka.

Inferences

6. Rob feels that Flicka is a poor choice because
    (a) Flicka is too fast   (b) her mother was untrainable
    (c) Flicka has never been saddled   (d) Kennie has not
    proved he can tame a horse.

7. Gus shows that he wants to help Kennie by   (a) putting
    the shells into the rifle   (b) agreeing to shoot Flicka
    (c) building the sling   (d) calling the colt Flicka.

8. At the beginning of the story, Kennie's brother Howard
    (a) treats Kennie as an equal   (b) doesn't want Kennie
    to succeed with Flicka   (c) mistrusts Kennie
    (d) feels superior to Kennie.

9. Kennie's model for his deep ability to love comes from
    (a) his mother   (b) his father   (c) Gus   (d) Flicka.

10. Rob gave up his army career because   (a) he had done
    poorly at West Point   (b) he wanted to build and not
    destroy   (c) he was injured in maneuvers   (d) he was
    not promoted.

Order of Events

11. Arrange the items in the order in which they occurred.
    Use letters only.

A. Kennie names the yearling Flicka.
B. Flicka fails to jump over a barbed wire barrier.
C. Flicka jumps out of a high stable window.
D. His illness almost kills Kennie.
E. Gus is told to shoot Flicka.

Outcomes

12. Flicka is tamed by   (a) Kennie's almost sacrificing his own life   (b) Kennie's showing her who the master was   (c) her fear of the barbed wire   (d) her contacts with Kennie and other human beings.

Cause and Effect

13. Which of the following is not a result of Kennie's staying in the stream?   (a) Kennie prevents Gus from shooting Flicka   (b) Kennie saves Flicka from drowning   (c) Kennie almost becomes a victim   (d) Kennie loses his father's cooperation in handling Flicka.

Fact or Opinion

Tell whether each of the following is a fact or an opinion.
14. Rob does not question his right to punish or reward his sons.

15. Flicka's mother, Rocket, could have been tamed if Rob had treated her with the same love Kennie had for Flicka.

Words in Context _____

1. Nell McLaughlin saw Kennie *wince* as if something had actually hurt him.
   Wince (387) means   (a) frown   (b) draw back suddenly   (c) grow angry for a moment   (d) tremble.

2. Howard strode after his father, *nobly refraining from* looking at Kennie.
   Nobly refraining from (388) means (a) feeling very sorry while (b) refusing to lower himself by (c) talking quietly while (d) pleased with himself while.

3. I'll have to do as the rest of 'em do—drop the papers. In the above statement (389) Rob revealed his fear that he would have to (a) sell the horses (b) sell the ranch (c) take a mortgage (d) not register his thoroughbreds.

4. McLaughlin was somewhat *taken aback*, but his wife concealed a smile.
   Taken aback (391) means (a) surprised (b) angered (c) pleased (d) unwilling.

5. The boys were sitting on the worn wooden step of the door which led from the *tack room* into the corral.
   Tack room (391) is the place where (a) bridles and saddles are stored (b) rain gear is kept (c) food is prepared (d) the help live.

6. I'll take that yearling filly of Rocket's. The *sorrel* with the cream tail and mane.
   Sorrel (392) means (a) thoroughbred (b) reddish brown (c) tall gray (d) leader.

7. The mares are *hellions* and the stallions outlaws; they're untamable.
   Hellions (392) means that the horses were (a) playful (b) stubborn (c) troublemakers (d) delicate.

8. Rob *guffawed*. "Not I, nor anyone, has ever been able to really tame any one of them."
   Guffawed (392) means (a) laughed loudly (b) sneered (c) shouted (d) frowned.

9. Rob was *grim and put out*. He couldn't go back on his word.
   Grim and put out (393) means (a) hurt and bewildered (b) scowling and annoyed (c) confused and upset (d) serious and emphatic.

10. And as they reached the spot they saw standing there the *wavering* pinkish colt, barely able to keep its feet.
    Wavering (393) means   (a) small   (b) frightened
    (c) wild   (d) unsteady.

11. Ken was *entranced* to watch Flicka when the wild band of youngsters discovered that they were being pursued . . .
    Entranced (393) means   (a) eager   (b) upset
    (c) ordered   (d) delighted.

12. The corral gates were closed, and an hour was spent *shunting* the ponies in and out and through the chutes until Flicka was left alone in the small round corral . . .
    Shunting (394) means   (a) switching   (b) riding
    (c) following   (d) observing.

13. As Gus was coming back, just about to close the gate to the upper range, the sorrel whipped through it, sailed across the road and ditch with her *inimitable* floating leap . . .
    Inimitable (395) means   (a) graceful   (b) splendid
    (c) unmatched   (d) speedy.

14. Without *abating* anything of her whirlwind speed . . . she investigated every possibility.
    Abating (396) means   (a) lessening   (b) considering
    (c) revealing   (d) developing.

15. She . . . stood for hours with hanging head and weakly *splayed-out* legs, under the clump of cottonwood trees.
    Splayed-out (397) means   (a) controlled
    (b) trembling   (c) displayed   (d) spread out.

Thinking Critically About the Story _____

1. Why were both Kennie and Flicka apparently doomed to failure? What was the turning point for Kennie? For Flicka? In what way was it similar for both? Are people born doomed to failure? Justify your answer.

2. In the beginning was Rob too much of a disciplinarian? Did his character change as the story developed? Which incidents support your point of view? Do adults change or does our understanding of them change as events bring them closer to us? Cite examples to support your point of view.

3. Why did Kennie select Flicka? Why do people select the pets that they do? How successful were you with the ones you chose?

4. Is tender loving care a cure-all in real life as it was in this story?

5. Did Kennie's older brother help or hinder him? What evidence of sibling rivalry did you find in the story? Does it happen that way in real life? What should be the relationship between siblings? To what extent does such jealousy exist in your family? How could it be controlled?

Stories in Words _____

Corral (388)   What possible connection is there between *corral* and *currency?* Both are derived ultimately from the Latin word *currere,* "to run." Currency is money in circulation, "running" through people's hands. A corral is a place where horses "run." *Corral* comes from the Latin through the Spanish *corro,* "a ring, circle," but it has the same root as *currency, curriculum, courier, concourse,* and *recur.*

Auspicious (389)   Here's a word for the birds. *Auspicious* comes from two Latin roots meaning "bird" and "look, observe." We have enthusiastic birdwatchers now, but to the Romans, watching birds was a more serious business. Ancient soothsayers studied the flight, feeding, and singing of birds to predict the future. Optimism always suggested good things for the future. *Auspicious* means "of good omen, favorable for the future." In the short story "The Birds," (page 462), the arrival of the birds is anything but auspicious.

Stoical (393)   The Greek philosopher Zeno taught that the wise man should follow virtue, accept what comes, and remain indifferent to emotion. We use the word *stoical* to mean "silent, showing no emotion." The Greek word *stoa* meant "porch," usually a "covered walk." Zeno and his pupils gathered in one of the principal porches of Athens. Hence, his followers were called "Stoics."

The Apprentice

Dorothy Canfield Fisher

◆ **The day had been one of the unbearable ones,
when every sound had set her teeth on edge like
chalk creaking on a blackboard, when every word her
father and mother said to her or did not say to her
seemed an intentional injustice.**

Dorothy Canfield Fisher, a leading American novelist of the preceding
generation, invites you to spend an hour or so with teenager Peg and her
collie, Rollie. What unfolds is not a high adventure story. It has no surprise
ending. It has no moral attached to it. "The Apprentice" belongs to that rarest
group of stories in which the author stops the clock for a brief moment and
gazes at the awesome mystery and beauty of life itself.

The test of such stories is in the reader's reactions. The question before
you is: Has the author treated her characters fairly and given us a picture that
is true to life as you see it? Read and find out for yourself!

THE APPRENTICE

The day had been one of the unbearable ones, when every sound had set her teeth on edge like chalk creaking on a blackboard, when every word her father or mother said to her or did not say to her seemed an intentional injustice. And of course it would happen, as the fitting end to such a day, that just as the sun went down back of the mountain and the long twilight began, she noticed that Rollie was not around.

Tense with exasperation at what her mother would say, she began to call him in a carefully casual tone—she would simply explode if mother got going: "Here Rollie! He-ere boy! Want to go for a walk, Rollie?" Whistling to him cheerfully, her heart full of wrath at the way the world treated her, she made the rounds of his haunts: the corner of the woodshed, where he liked to curl up on the wool of father's discarded old sweater; the hay barn, the cow barn, the sunny spot on the side porch. No Rollie.

Perhaps he had sneaked upstairs to lie on her bed, where he was not supposed to go—not that *she* would have minded! That rule was a part of mother's fussiness, part, too, of mother's bossiness. It was *her* bed, wasn't it? But was she allowed the say-so about it? Not on your life. They *said* she could have things the way she wanted in her own room, now she was in her teens, but—her heart burned at unfairness as she took the stairs stormily, two steps at a time, her pigtails flopping up and down on her back. If Rollie was there, she was just going to let him stay there, and mother could say what she wanted to.

But he was not there. The bedspread and pillow were crumpled, but that was where she had flung herself down to cry that afternoon. Every nerve in her had been twanging

413

discordantly, but she couldn't cry. She could only lie there, her hands doubled up hard, furious that she had nothing to cry about. Not really. She was too big to cry just over father's having said to her severely, "I told you if I let you take the chess set, you were to put it away when you got through with it. One of the pawns was on the floor of our bedroom this morning. I stepped on it. If I'd had my shoes on I'd have broken it."

Well, he *had* told her that. And he hadn't said she mustn't ever take the set again. No, the instant she thought about that, she knew she couldn't cry about it. She could be, and was, in a rage about the way father kept on talking, long after she'd got his point: "It's not that I care so much about the chess set. It's because if you don't learn how to take care of things, you yourself will suffer for it. You'll forget or neglect something that will be really important for *you*. We *have* to try to teach you to be responsible for what you've said you'll take care of. If we—" on and on.

She stood there, dry-eyed, by the bed that Rollie had not crumpled and thought, *I hope mother sees the spread and says something about Rollie—I just hope she does. . . .*

She heard her mother coming down the hall, and hastily shut her door. She had a right to shut the door to her own room, hadn't she? She had *some* rights, she supposed, even if she was only thirteen and the youngest child. If her mother opened it to say, "What are you doing in here that you don't want me to see? she'd say—she'd just say—

But her mother did not open the door. Her feet went steadily on along the hall, and then, carefully, slowly, down the stairs. She probably had an armful of winter things she was bringing down from the attic. She was probably thinking that a tall, thirteen-year-old daughter was big enough to help with a chore like that. But she wouldn't *say* anything. She would just get out that insulting look of a grownup silently putting up with a crazy unreasonable kid. She had worn that expression all day; it was too much to be endured.

Up in her bedroom behind her closed door the thirteen-year-old stamped her foot in a gust of uncontrollable rage, none the less savage and heartshaking because it was mysterious to her.

But she had not located Rollie. She would be cut into little pieces before she would let her father and mother know she had lost sight of him, forgotten about him. They would not scold her, she knew. They would do worse; they would look at her. And in their silence she would hear, droning on reproachfully, what they had said when she had been begging to keep for her own the sweet, woolly collie puppy in her arms.

How warm he had felt! Astonishing how warm and alive a puppy was compared with a doll! She had never liked her dolls much after she had held Rollie, feeling him warm against her chest, warm and wriggling, bursting with life, reaching up to lick her face. He had loved her from that first instant. As he felt her arms around him his liquid, beautiful eyes had melted in trusting sweetness. And they did now, whenever he looked at her. Her dog was the only creature in the world who *really* loved her, she thought passionately.

And back then, at the very minute when, as a darling baby dog, he was beginning to love her, her father and mother were saying, so cold, so reasonable—gosh, how she *hated* reasonableness!—"Now, Peg, remember that, living where we do, with sheep on the farms around us, it is a serious responsibility to have a collie dog. If you keep him, you've got to be the one to take care of him. You'll have to be the one to train him to stay at home. We're too busy with you children to start bringing up a puppy too."

Rollie, nestling in her arms, let one hind leg drop awkwardly. It must be uncomfortable. She looked down at him tenderly, tucked his leg up under him and gave him a hug. He laughed up in her face—he really did laugh, his mouth stretched wide in a cheerful grin. Now he was snug in a warm little ball.

Her parents were saying, "If you want him, you can have him. But you must be responsible for him. If he gets to running sheep, he'll just have to be shot, you know that."

They had not said, aloud, "Like the Wilsons' collie." They never mentioned that awfulness—her racing unsuspectingly down across the fields just at the horrible moment when Mr. Wilson shot their collie, caught in the very act of killing sheep. They probably thought that if they never spoke about it, she would forget it—*forget* the crack of that rifle, and the collapse of the great beautiful dog! Forget the red blood spurting from the hole in his head. She hadn't forgotten. She never would. She knew as well as they did how important it was to train a collie puppy about sheep. They didn't have to rub it in like that. They always rubbed everything in. She had told them, fervently, indignantly, that of *course* she would take care of him, be responsible for him, teach him to stay at home. Of course. Of course. *She* understood!

And now, when he was six months old, tall, rangy, power-ful, standing up far above her knee, nearly to her waist, she didn't know where he was. But of course he must be somewhere around. He always was. She composed her face to look natural and went downstairs to search the house. He was probably asleep somewhere. She looked every room over carefully. Her mother was nowhere visible. It was safe to call him again, to give the special piercing whistle which always brought him racing to her, the white-feathered plume of his tail waving in elation that she wanted him.

But he did not answer. She stood still on the front porch to think.

Could he have gone up to their special place in the edge of the field where the three young pines, their branches growing close to the ground, made a triangular, walled-in space, com-pletely hidden from the world? Sometimes he went up there with her, and when she lay down on the dried grass to dream he, too, lay down quietly, his head on his paws, his beautiful eyes fixed adoringly on her. He entered into her every mood. If she wanted to be quiet, all right, he did too. It didn't seem as though he would have gone alone there. Still—She loped up the steep slope of the field rather fast, beginning to be anxious.

No, he was not there. She stood irresolutely in the roofless, green-walled triangular hideout, wondering what to do next.

Then, before she knew what thought had come into her mind, its emotional impact knocked her down. At least her knees crumpled under her. The Wilsons had, last Wednesday, brought their sheep down from the far upper pasture, to the home farm! They were—she herself had seen them on her way to school, and like an idiot had not thought of Rollie—on the river meadow.

She was off like a racer at the crack of the starting pistol, her long, strong legs stretched in great leaps, her pigtails flying. She took the short cut, regardless of the brambles. Their thorn-spiked, wiry stems tore at her flesh, but she did not care. She welcomed the pain. It was something she was doing for Rollie, for her Rollie.

She was in the pine woods now, rushing down the steep, stony path, tripping over roots, half falling, catching herself just in time, not slackening her speed. She burst out on the open knoll above the river meadow, calling wildly, "Rollie, here, Rollie, here, boy! Here! Here!" She tried to whistle, but she was crying too hard to pucker her lips.

There was nobody to see or hear her. Twilight was falling over the bare, grassy knoll. The sunless evening wind slid down the mountain like an invisible river, engulfing her in cold. Her teeth began to chatter. "Here, Rollie, here, boy, here!" She strained her eyes to look down into the meadow to see if the sheep were there. She could not be sure. She stopped calling him as she would a dog, and called out his name despairingly, as if he were her child, "Rollie! Oh, *Rollie*, where are you?"

The tears ran down her cheeks in streams. She sobbed loudly, terribly; she did not try to control herself, since there was no one to hear. "Hou! Hou! Hou!" she sobbed, her face contorted grotesquely. "Oh, Rollie! Rollie! Rollie!" She had wanted something to cry about. Oh, how terribly now she had something to cry about.

She saw him as clearly as if he were there beside her, his muzzle and gaping mouth all smeared with the betraying blood (like the Wilsons' collie). "But he didn't *know* it was wrong!" she screamed like a wild creature. "Nobody *told* him it was wrong. It was my fault. I should have taken better care of him. I will now. I will!"

But no matter how she screamed, she could not make herself heard. In the cold gathering darkness, she saw him stand, poor, guiltless victim of his ignorance, who should have been protected from his own nature, his beautiful soft eyes looking at her with love, his splendid plumed tail waving gently. "It was my fault. I promised I would bring him up. I should have *made* him stay at home. I was responsible for him. It was my fault."

But she could not make his executioners hear her. The shot

rang out. Rollie sank down, his beautiful liquid eyes glazed, the blood spurting from the hole in his head—like the Wilsons' collie. She gave a wild shriek, long, soul-satisfying, frantic. It was the scream at sudden, unendurable tragedy of a mature, full-blooded woman. It drained dry the girl of thirteen. She came to herself. She was standing on the knoll, trembling and quaking with cold, the darkness closing in on her.

Her breath had given out. For once in her life she had wept all the tears there were in her body. Her hands were so stiff with cold she could scarcely close them. How her nose was running. Simply streaming down her upper lip. And she had no handkerchief. She lifted her skirt, fumbled for her slip, stooped, blew her nose on it, wiped her eyes, drew a long quavering breath—and heard something! Far off in the distance, a faint sound, like a dog's muffled bark.

She whirled on her heels and bent her head to listen. The sound did not come from the meadow below the knoll. It came from back of her, from the Wilsons' maple grove higher up. She held her breath. Yes, it came from there. She began to run again, but now she was not sobbing. She was silent, absorbed in her effort to cover ground. If she could only live to get there, to see if it really were Rollie. She ran steadily till she came to the fence, and went over this in a great plunge. Her skirt caught on a nail. She impatiently pulled at it, not hearing or not heeding the long sibilant tear as it came loose. She was in the dusky maple woods, stumbling over the rocks as she ran. As she tore on up the slope she knew it was Rollie's bark.

She stopped short and leaned weakly against a tree, sick with the breathlessness of her straining lungs, sick in the reaction of relief, sick with anger at Rollie, who had been here having a wonderful time while she had been dying, just dying in terror about him.

For she could not only hear that it was Rollie's bark; she could hear, in the dog language she knew as well as he, what he was saying in those excited yips; that he had run a woodchuck into a hole in the tumbled stone wall, that he almost had him, that the intoxicating wild-animal smell was as close to him— almost—as if he had his jaws on his quarry. Yip! Woof! Yip! Yip!

The wild, joyful quality of the dog talk enraged the girl.

She was trembling in exhaustion, in indignation. So that was where he had been, when she was killing herself trying to take care of him. Plenty near enough to hear her calling and whistling to him, if he had paid attention. Just so set on having his foolish good time, he never thought to listen for her call.

She stooped to pick up a stout stick. She would teach him! It was time he had something to make him remember to listen. She started forward.

But she stopped, stood thinking. One of the things to remember about collies—everybody knew that—was their sensitiveness. A collie who had been beaten was never "right" again. His spirit was broken. "Anything but a broken-spirited collie," the farmers often said. They were no good after that.

She threw down her stick. Anyhow, she thought, he was too young to know, really, that he had done wrong. He was still only a puppy. Like all puppies, he got perfectly crazy over wild-animal smells. Probably he really and truly hadn't heard her calling and whistling.

All the same, all the same—she stared intently into the twilight—he couldn't be let to grow up just as he wanted to. She would have to make him understand that he mustn't go off this way by himself. He must be trained to know how to do what a good dog does—not because *she* wanted him to, but for his own sake.

She walked on now, steady, purposeful, gathering her inner strength together. Olympian in her understanding of the full meaning of the event.

When he heard his own special young god approaching, he turned delightedly and ran to meet her, panting, his tongue hanging out. His eyes shone. He jumped up on her in an ecstasy of welcome and licked her face.

But she pushed him away. Her face and voice were grave. "No, Rollie, *no!*" she said severely. "You're *bad.* You know you're not to go off in the woods without me! You are— a—*bad*—dog."

He was horrified. Stricken into misery. He stood facing her, frozen, the gladness going out of his eyes, the erect waving plume of his tail slowly lowered to slinking, guilty dejection.

"I know you were all wrapped up in that woodchuck. But that's no excuse. You *could* have heard me, calling you, whistling for you, if you'd paid attention," she went on. "You've got to learn, and I've got to teach you."

With a shudder of misery he lay down, his tail stretched out limp on the ground, his head flat on his paws, his ears drooping—ears ringing with doomsday awfulness of the voice he so loved and revered. He must have been utterly wicked. He trembled, and turned his head away from her august look of blame, groveling in remorse for whatever mysterious sin he had committed.

She sat down by him, as miserable as he. "I don't *want* to scold you. But I have to! I have to bring you up right, or you'll get shot, Rollie. You *mustn't* go away from the house without me, do you hear, *never!*"

Catching, with his sharp ears yearning for her approval, a faint overtone of relenting affection in her voice, he lifted his eyes to her, humbly, soft in imploring fondness.

"Oh, Rollie!" she said, stooping low over him. "I *do* love you. I do. But I *have* to bring you up. I'm responsible for you, don't you see?"

He did not see. Hearing sternness, or something else he did not recognize, in the beloved voice, he shut his eyes tight in sorrow, and made a little whimpering lament in his throat.

She had never heard him cry before. It was too much. She sat down by him and drew his head to her, rocking him in her arms, soothing him with inarticulate small murmurs.

He leaped in her arms and wriggled happily as he had when he was a baby; he reached up to lick her face as he had then. But he was no baby now. He was half as big as she, a great, warm, pulsing, living armful of love. She clasped him closely. Her heart was brimming full, but calmed, quiet. The blood flowed in equable gentleness all over her body. She was deliciously warm. Her nose was still running a little. She sniffed and wiped it on her sleeve.

It was almost dark now. "We'll be late to supper, Rollie," she said responsibly. Pushing him gently off, she stood up. "Home, Rollie, home!"

Here was a command he could understand. At once he trotted along the path toward home. His plumed tail, held high, waved cheerfully. His short dog memory had dropped into oblivion the suffering just back of him.

Her human memory was longer. His prancing gait was as carefree as a young child's. Plodding heavily like a serious adult, she trod behind him. Her very shoulders seemed bowed by what she had lived through. She felt, she thought like an old, old woman of thirty. But it was all right now. She knew she had made an impression on him.

When they came out into the open pasture, Rollie ran back to get her to play with him. He leaped around her in circles, barking in cheerful yawps, jumping up on her, inviting her to run a race with him, to throw him a stick, to come alive.

His high spirits were ridiculous. But infectious. She gave one little leap to match his. Rollie pretended that this was a threat to him, planted his forepaws low and barked loudly at her, laughing between yips. He was so funny, she thought, when he grinned that way. She laughed back, and gave another mock-threatening leap at him. Radiant that his sky was once more clear, he sprang high on his spring-steel muscles in an explosion of happiness, and bounded in circles around her.

Following him, not noting in the dusk where she was going, she felt the grassy slope drop steeply. Oh, yes, she knew where she was. They had come to the rolling-down hill just back of the house. All the kids rolled down there, even the little ones, because it was soft grass without a stone. She had rolled down that slope a million times—years and years ago, when she was a kid herself. It was fun. She remembered well the whirling dizziness of the descent, all the world turning over and over crazily. And the delicious giddy staggering when you first stood up, the earth still spinning under your feet.

"All right, Rollie, let's go," she cried, and flung herself down in the rolling position, her arms straight up over her head.

Rollie had never seen this skylarking before. It threw him into almost hysterical amusement. He capered around the rapidly rolling figure, half scared, mystified, enchanted.

His wild frolicsome barking might have come from her own throat, so accurately did it sound the way she felt—crazy, foolish, like a little kid, no more than five years old, the age she had been when she had last rolled down that hill.

At the bottom she sprang up, on muscles as steel-strong as Rollie's. She staggered a little, and laughed aloud.

The living room windows were just before them. How yellow lighted windows looked when you were in the darkness going home. How nice and yellow. Maybe mother had waffles for supper. She was a swell cook, mother was, and she certainly gave her family all the breaks, when it came to meals.

"Home, Rollie, home!" She burst open the door to the living room. "Hi, Mom, what you got for supper?"

From the kitchen her mother announced coolly, "I hate to break the news to you, but it's waffles."

"Oh, *Mom!*" she shouted in ecstasy.

Her mother could not see her. She did not need to. "For goodness sakes, go and wash," she called.

In the long mirror across the room she saw herself, her hair

hanging wild, her long bare legs scratched, her broadly smiling face dirt-streaked, her torn skirt dangling, her dog laughing up at her. Gosh, was it a relief to feel your own age, just exactly thirteen years old!

Reading for Understanding

Main Idea

1. Which of the following quotations states the main idea of the story?
   (a) His short dog memory had dropped into oblivion the suffering just back of him.
   (b) She had wanted something to cry about. Oh, how terribly now she had something to cry about.
   (c) Gosh, was it a relief to feel your own age, just exactly thirteen years old.
   (d) Her dog was the only creature in the world who *really* loved her, she thought passionately.

Details

2. The story takes place   (a) on a farm   (b) in a big city   (c) in a small town   (d) at a summer home.

3. Peg is   (a) a twin (b) the youngest child (c) the oldest child (d) an only child.

4. Which of the following is not a factor that helps create Peg's mood at the opening of the story?
   (a) She does not know where Rollie is.
   (b) Her father almost smashes a chess piece.
   (c) She has left her bedspread and pillow mussed up.
   (d) She has done poorly in school that day.

5. At the beginning of the story Rollie is not   (a) an untrained puppy   (b) as much a learner as Peg   (c) a new arrival at the farm   (d) almost unmanageable.

6. The title, "The Apprentice," refers to   (a) the parents   (b) Peg   (c) the collie that is shot   (d) the farmer who shoots the collie.

7. According to the author, a collie at six months is equiva-
    lent to   (a) a mature person   (b) a ten-year-old girl
    (c) a young adult person   (d) a teenager.

8. Peg's parents   (a) are worried about Peg's moods
    (b) use corporal punishment in handling Peg
    (c) are too busy to supervise Peg   (d) use love and
    understanding to guide Peg.

9. Peg was given a pet collie   (a) to train the dog to handle
    sheep   (b) to teach Peg to be responsible   (c) because
    the neighbor's children all have pets   (d) because her
    parents had one when they were growing up.

10. Peg rolls down the hill   (a) to irritate her mother
    (b) to   please   Rollie   (c) to   change   her   mood
    (d) because she is loved.

Order of Events

11. Arrange the items in the order in which they occurred.
    Use letters only.
    A. Peg finds something to cry about.
    B. Peg flings herself on her bed to cry.
    C. Peg clearly remembers seeing a sheep killer being shot.
    D. Peg considers using corporal punishment in training
       Rollie.
    E. Rollie's love for her changes her mood.

Outcomes

12. Peg   (a) teaches Rollie a lasting lesson   (b) becomes
    aware   of   how   understanding   her   parents   are
    (c) saves Rollie's life   (d) finds support in Rollie.

Cause and Effect

13. Peg's swing in moods from one extreme to another
    (a) irritates   her   parents   (b) is   enjoyed   by   Rollie
    (c) worries Peg   (d) is unusual for a thirteen-year-old.

Fact or Opinion

Tell whether each of the following is a fact or an opinion.

14. Peg fears that Rollie cannot be trained to handle sheep properly.
15. Both Rollie and Peg are apprentices.

Words in Context _____

1. Tense with *exasperation* at what her mother would say, she began to call to him in a carefully casual tone . . .
   Exasperation (413) means   (a) irritation   (b) concern
   (c) fear   (d) expectation.

2. Whistling to him cheerfully, her heart full of *wrath* at the way the world treated her, she made her rounds of his haunts.
   Wrath (413) means   (a) self-pity   (b) envy
   (c) sorrow   (d) anger.

3. Every nerve in her had been *twanging discordantly,* but she couldn't cry.
   Twanging discordantly (413) means   (a) pounding irregularly   (b) beating impatiently   (c) pulsating heavily   (d) throbbing slowly.

4. She had told them *fervently, indignantly,* that of course she would take care of him, be responsible for him . . .
   Fervently, indignantly (416) means,   (a) quietly and sincerely   (b) earnestly and angrily   (c) loud and clear   (d) quickly and with certainty.

5. It was safe to call him again, to give the special piercing whistle which always brought him racing to her, the white-feathered plume of his tail waving *in elation* that she wanted him.
   In elation (416) means   (a) joyously   (b) proudly
   (c) excitedly   (d) rapidly.

6. She burst out on the open *knoll* above the river meadow, calling wildly . . .

Knoll (417) means   (a) meadow   (b) hill   (c) field
(d) dell.

7. "Hou! Hou! Hou!" she sobbed, her face *contorted grotesquely.*
Contorted grotesquely (417) means   (a) filled with fear
b) twisted unnaturally   (c) frozen with grief
(d) tense and subdued.

8. It was the scream at sudden, *unendurable tragedy* of a mature, full-blooded woman.
Unendurable tragedy (418) means   (a) sudden disaster
(b) total defeat   (c) unbearable misfortune
(d) great losses.

9. She ... wiped her eyes, drew a long *quavering* breath—and heard something!
Quavering (418) means   (a) painful   (b) gasping
(c) loud   (d) with a trembling sound.

10. She impatiently pulled at it, not hearing or not heeding the long *sibilant* tear as it came loose.
Sibilant (418) means   (a) hissing   (b) jagged
(c) noisy   (d) destructive.

11. She walked on now, steady, purposeful, gathering her inner strength together. *Olympian* in her understanding of the full meaning of the event.
Olympian (419) means   (a) grown-up   (b) godlike
(c) jubilant   (d) melancholy.

12. With a shudder of misery he lay down ... ears ringing with *doomsday awfulness* of the voice he so loved ...
Doomsday awfulness (420) means   (a) dreadfulness of Judgment Day   (b) horrifying fear   (c) inescapable horror   (d) harsh spitefulness.

13. He trembled ... *groveling in remorse* for whatever mysterious sin he had committed.
Groveling in remorse (420) means   (a) cringing with regret   (b) twisting in the grass   (c) filled with a willingness to please   (d) filled with unhappiness.

14. Catching ... a faint overtone of *relenting* affection in her voice, he lifted his eyes to her, humbly ...

Relenting (420) means (a) deep (b) increased
(c) less harsh (d) universal.

15. . . . he lifted his eyes to her, humbly, soft in *imploring*
fondness.
Imploring (420) means (a) everlasting (b) begging
(c) bargaining (d) great.

16. . . . he shut his eyes tight in sorrow, and made a little
whimpering lament in his throat.
Whimpering lament (420) means (a) low growl
(b) series of barks (c) high-pitched yips (d) sobbing
whine.

17. His short dog memory had dropped into *oblivion* the
suffering just back of him.
Oblivion (420) means (a) the past (b) complete
forgetfulness (c) the future (d) the lap of the gods.

18. *Plodding* heavily like a serious adult, she trod behind him.
Plodding (421) means (a) running (b) racing
(c) trudging (d) shouting.

19. He *capered* around the rapidly rolling figure, half scared,
mystified, enchanted.
Capered (421) means (a) stumbled (b) barked and
ran (c) yipped and nipped (d) leaped and frolicked.

20. His wild *frolicsome* barking might have come from her
own throat, so accurately did it sound the way she felt . . .
Frolicsome (421) means (a) hysterical (b) playful
(c) hoarse (d) untamed.

Thinking Critically About the Story _____

1. Parents usually know all about what to expect of their
children and what the children should expect of them. *But,
it's the mix that counts!* The magical combination of to
what extent the parents should (a) instruct
(b) punish (c) be strict (d) overlook is not always

available to mothers and fathers who have so many additional responsibilities.

How close to ideal parents are Peg's? What are their pluses and minuses? Have you met "ideal parents" in other stories? In real life? How would you go about parenting? Could you be an "ideal parent"?

2. Do your parents allow you to have a pet animal? Advantages? Disadvantages? Are your rewards similar to those Peg received?

3. Is Peg a typical 13-year-old girl? This story deals with a Peg who grew up fifty years ago. Have 13-year-old girls changed?

4. Evaluate the training process Peg used on Rollie. In your opinion, what are the major *do's* and *don't's* in training pets?

5. How does Peg compare with the teenagers in current TV and movie fare?

6. Which incidents in the story did you most closely identify with? Which, if any, did you find painful?

7. Is Peg a fair representation of both boy and girl 13-year-olds? If not, how do boys differ from girls?

Stories in Words _____

Discordantly (414) "Let's have a heart-to-heart talk." "My heart isn't in it." "Have a heart!" How often do we use the word *heart* to express an emotion, like a "heartfelt desire"? The word *discordantly* is right in step. The Latin prefix *dis* means "apart." The root *cord* means "heart." When the heart is "torn apart," there is discord, conflict, disagreement. The prefix *con* means "together." Therefore, *concord* means "agreement, harmony, peace." This is an antonym (word with opposite meaning) of *discord*.

Fervently (416) *Fervently* means "warmly, passionately, enthusiastically, earnestly, excitedly, intensely, vehemently, zealously." Note the wealth of synonyms in English. Because English has so many roots and has borrowed from many languages, the number of synonyms (words with the same or nearly the same meaning) is extensive. When Rollie's owner says (416) "fervently, indignantly, that of *course* she would take care of him," we can picture her statement as fiery and emotional—in no way lukewarm. Appropriately, *fervently* comes from the Latin *fervere*, "to glow, boil, rage." Though the meaning was originally physical, dealing with fire, the English word extends the meaning to include emotions like fire. This comparison without *like* or *as* is called "metaphor."

Remorse (420)   Here is another example of metaphor. *Remorse* has the Latin prefix *re*, "again," and the root *mors*, "to bite." *Remorse* literally means "bite again." But the English word *remorse* has nothing to do with biting, or does it? *Remorse* suggests that state of mind involving a deep sense of guilt, repentance. If you have ever felt guilt over something that you knew you had done wrong, you had a constantly returning painful feeling. The thought kept "biting again": *remorse*.

Leiningen Versus the Ants

Carl Stephenson

◆   **A dispassionate observer would have estimated the odds against him at a thousand to one. But then such an onlooker would have reckoned only by what he saw—the advance of myriad battalions of ants against the futile efforts of a few defenders—and not by the unseen activity that can go on in a man's brain.**

Here is a modern story with a plot that is forever old and forever new. It is a tale that will always have a widespread appeal. It tells of one man's struggle against natural forces that are huge and hostile.

In very few stories are the lines so clearly drawn: a plantation owner fights to protect his land and his loyal workers from the destructive power of an incredibly large army of killer ants out to devour every living organism in its path.

The suspense begins to build from the very first sentence when the reader is made aware of the danger ahead. It increases as Leiningen reveals the devices he has planned to outwit the flesh-eating enemy. It reaches its height in his final effort to end forever the forward march of incredible devastation.

Leiningen Versus the Ants

"**U**nless they alter their course and there's no reason why they should, they'll reach your plantation in two days at the latest."

Leiningen sucked placidly at a cigar about the size of a corncob and for a few seconds gazed without answering at the agitated District Commissioner. Then he took the cigar from his lips, and leaned slightly forward. With his bristling grey hair, bulky nose, and lucid eyes, he had the look of an aging and shabby eagle.

"Decent of you," he murmured, "paddling all this way just to give me the tip. But you're pulling my leg of course when you say I must do a bunk. Why, even a herd of saurians* couldn't drive me from this plantation of mine."

The Brazilian official threw up lean and lanky arms and clawed the air with wildly distended fingers. "Leiningen!" he shouted. "You're insane! They're not creatures you can fight— they're an elemental—an 'act of God!' Ten miles long, two miles wide—ants, nothing but ants! And every single one of them a fiend from hell; before you can spit three times they'll eat a full-grown buffalo to the bones. I tell you if you don't clear out at once there'll be nothing left of you but a skeleton picked as clean as your own plantation."

Leiningen grinned. "Act of God, my eye! Anyway, I'm not an old woman; I'm not going to run for it just because an elemental's on the way. And don't think I'm the kind of fathead who tries to fend off lightning with his fists, either. I use my intelligence, old man. With me, the brain isn't a second blind gut; I know what it's there for. When I began this model

* *saurians*   lizards

431

farm and plantation three years ago, I took into account all that could conceivably happen to it. And now I'm ready for anything and everything—including your ants."

The Brazilian rose heavily to his feet. "I've done my best," he gasped. "Your obstinacy endangers not only yourself, but the lives of your four hundred workers. You don't know these ants!"

Leiningen accompanied him down to the river, where the Government launch was moored. The vessel cast off. As it moved downstream, the exclamation mark neared the rail and began waving its arms frantically. Long after the launch had disappeared round the bend, Leiningen thought he could still hear that dimming, imploring voice, "You don't know them, I tell you! *You don't know them!*"

But the reported enemy was by no means unfamiliar to the planter. Before he started work on his settlement, he had lived long enough in the country to see for himself the fearful devastations sometimes wrought by these ravenous insects in their campaigns for food. But since then he had planned measures of defense accordingly, and these, he was convinced, were in every way adequate to withstand the approaching peril.

Moreover, during his three years as a planter, Leiningen had met and defeated drought, flood, plague and all other "acts of God" which had come against him—unlike his fellow-settlers in the district, who had made little or no resistance. This unbroken success he attributed solely to the observance of his lifelong motto: *The human brain needs only to become fully aware of its powers to conquer even the elements.* Dullards reeled senselessly and aimlessly into the abyss; cranks, however brilliant, lost their heads when circumstances suddenly altered or accelerated and ran into stone walls, sluggards drifted with the current until they were caught in whirlpools and dragged under. But such disasters, Leiningen contended, merely strengthened his argument that intelligence, directed aright, invariably makes man the master of his fate.

Yes, Leiningen had always known how to grapple with life. Even here, in this Brazilian wilderness, his brain had triumphed over every difficulty and danger it had so far encountered. First he had vanquished primal forces by cunning and organization, then he had enlisted the resources of modern science to increase miraculously the yield of his plantation. And now he was sure he would prove more than a match for the "irresistible" ants.

That same evening, however, Leiningen assembled his workers. He had no intention of waiting till the news reached their ears from other sources. Most of them had been born in the district; the cry "The ants are coming!" was to them an imperative signal for instant, panic-stricken flight, a spring for life itself. But so great was the Indians' trust in Leiningen, in Leiningen's word, and in Leiningen's wisdom, that they received his curt tidings, and his orders for the imminent struggle, with the calmness with which they were given. They waited, unafraid, alert, as if for the beginning of a new game or hunt which he had just described to them. The ants were indeed mighty, but not so mighty as the boss. Let them come!

They came at noon the second day. Their approach was announced by the wild unrest of the horses, scarcely controllable now either in stall or under rider, scenting from afar a vapor instinct with horror.

It was announced by a stampede of animals, timid and savage, hurtling past each other; jaguars and pumas flashing by nimble stags of the pampas, bulky tapirs, no longer hunters, themselves hunted, outpacing fleet kinkajous, maddened herds of cattle, heads lowered, nostrils snorting, rushing through tribes of loping monkeys, chattering in a dementia of terror; then followed the creeping and springing denizens of bush and steppe, big and little rodents, snakes, and lizards.

Pell-mell the rabble swarmed down the hill to the plantation, scattered right and left before the barrier of the water-filled ditch, then sped onwards to the river, where, again hindered, they fled along its bank out of sight.

This water-filled ditch was one of the defense measures which Leiningen had long since prepared against the advent of the ants. It encompassed three sides of the plantation like a huge horseshoe. Twelve feet across, but not very deep, when dry it could hardly be described as an obstacle to either man or beast. But the ends of the "horseshoe" ran into the river which formed the northern boundary, and fourth side, of the plantation. And at the end nearer the house and outbuildings in the middle of the plantation, Leiningen had constructed a dam by means of which water from the river could be diverted into the ditch.

So now, by opening the dam, he was able to fling an imposing girdle of water, a huge quadrilateral with the river as its base, completely around the plantation, like the moat encircling a medieval city. Unless the ants were clever enough to build rafts, they had no hope of reaching the plantation, Leiningen concluded.

The twelve-foot water ditch seemed to afford in itself all the security needed. But while awaiting the arrival of the ants, Leiningen made a further improvement. The western section of the ditch ran along the edge of a tamarind wood, and the branches of some great trees reached over the water. Leiningen now had them lopped so that ants could not descend from them within the "moat."

The women and children, then the herds of cattle, were escorted by peons on rafts over the river, to remain on the other side in absolute safety until the plunderers had departed. Leiningen gave this instruction, not because he believed the noncombatants were in any danger, but in order to avoid hampering the efficiency of the defenders. "Critical situations first become crises," he explained to his men, "when oxen or parents get excited."

Finally, he made a careful inspection of the "inner moat"—a smaller ditch lined with concrete, which extended around the hill on which stood the ranch house, barns, stables and other buildings. Into this concrete ditch emptied the inflow pipes from three great petrol tanks. If by some miracle the ants managed to cross the water and reach the plantation, this "rampart of petrol" would be an absolutely impassable protection for the besieged and their dwellings and stock. Such, at least, was Leiningen's opinion.

He stationed his men at irregular distances along the water ditch, the first line of defense. Then he lay down in his hammock and puffed drowsily away at his pipe until a peon came with the report that the ants had been observed far away in the South.

Leiningen mounted his horse, which at the feel of its master seemed to forget its uneasiness, and rode leisurely in

the direction of the threatening offensive. The southern stretch
of ditch—the upper side of the quadrilateral—was nearly three
miles long; from its center one could survey the entire countryside. This was destined to be the scene of the outbreak of
war between Leiningen's brain and twenty square miles of
life-destroying ants.

It was a sight one could never forget. Over the range of
hills, as far as eye could see, crept a darkening hem, ever longer
and broader, until the shadow spread across the slope from
east to west, then downwards, downwards, uncannily swift,
and all the green herbage of that wide vista was being mown as
by a giant sickle, leaving only the vast moving shadow,
extending, deepening, and moving rapidly nearer.

When Leiningen's men, behind their barrier of water,
perceived the approach of the long-expected foe, they gave vent
to their suspense in screams and imprecations. But as the
distance began to lessen between the "sons of hell" and the
water ditch, they relapsed into silence. Before the advance of
that awe-inspiring throng, their belief in the powers of the boss
began to steadily dwindle.

Even Leiningen himself, who had ridden up just in time to
restore their loss of heart by a display of unshakable calm, even
he could not free himself from a qualm of malaise. Yonder were

thousands of millions of voracious jaws bearing down upon
him and only a suddenly insignificant, narrow ditch lay between him and his men and being gnawed to the bones "before
you can spit three times."

Hadn't his brain for once taken on more than it could
manage? If the blighters decided to rush the ditch, fill it to the
brim with their corpses, there'd still be more than enough to
destroy every trace of that cranium of his. The planter's chin
jutted; they hadn't got him yet, and he'd see to it they never
would. While he could think at all, he'd flout both death and
the devil.

The hostile army was approaching in perfect formation; no
human battalions, however well-drilled, could ever hope to
rival the precision of that advance. Along a front that moved
forward as uniformly as a straight line, the ants drew nearer
and nearer to the water-ditch. Then, when they learned
through their scouts the nature of the obstacle, the two outlying
wings of the army detached themselves from the main body
and marched down the western and eastern sides of the ditch.

This surrounding maneuver took rather more than an hour
to accomplish; no doubt the ants expected that at some point
they would find a crossing.

During this outflanking movement by the wings, the army
on the center and southern front remained still. The besieged
were therefore able to contemplate at their leisure the thumb-
long, reddish-black, long-legged insects; some of the Indians
believed they could see, too, intent on them, the brilliant, cold
eyes, and the razor-edged mandibles, of this host of infinity.

It is not easy for the average person to imagine that an
animal, not to mention an insect, can *think*. But now both
Leiningen and the Indians began to stir with the unpleasant
foreboding that inside every single one of that deluge of insects
dwelt a thought. And that thought was: Ditch or no ditch, we'll
get to your flesh!

Not until four o'clock did the wings reach the "horseshoe"
ends of the ditch, only to find these ran into the great river.
Through some kind of secret telegraphy, the report must then
have flashed very swiftly indeed along the entire enemy line.
And Leiningen, riding—no longer casually—along his side of
the ditch, noticed by energetic and widespread movements of

troops that for some unknown reason the news of the check had its greatest effect on the southern front, where the main army was massed. Perhaps the failure to find a way over the ditch was persuading the ants to withdraw from the plantation in search of spoils more easily attainable.

An immense flood of ants, about a hundred yards in width, was pouring in a glimmering-black cataract down the far slope of the ditch. Many thousands were already drowning in the sluggish creeping flow, but they were followed by troop after troop, who clambered over their sinking comrades, and then themselves served as dying bridges to the reserves hurrying on in their rear.

Shoals of ants were being carried away by the current into the middle of the ditch, where gradually they broke asunder and then, exhausted by their struggles, vanished below the surface. Nevertheless, the wavering, floundering hundred-yard front was remorselessly if slowly advancing towards the besieged on the other bank. Leiningen had been wrong when he supposed the enemy would first have to fill the ditch with their bodies before they could cross; instead, they merely needed to act as stepping-stones, as they swam and sank, to the hordes ever pressing onwards from behind.

Near Leiningen a few mounted herdsmen awaited his orders. He sent out to the weir—the river must be dammed more strongly to increase the speed and power of the water coursing through the ditch.

A second peon was dispatched to the outhouses to bring spades and petrol sprinklers. A third rode away to summon to the zone of the offensive all the men, except the observation posts, on the nearby sections of the ditch, which were not yet actively threatened.

The ants were getting across far more quickly than Leiningen would have deemed possible. Impelled by the mighty cascade behind them, they struggled nearer and nearer to the inner bank. The momentum of the attack was so great that neither the tardy flow of the stream nor its downward pull could exert its proper force; and into the gap left by every submerging insect, hastened forward a dozen more.

When reinforcements reached Leiningen, the invaders were halfway over. The planter had to admit to himself that it

was only by a stroke of luck for him that the ants were
attempting the crossing on a relatively short front: had they
assaulted simultaneously along the entire length of the ditch,
the outlook for the defenders would have been black indeed.

Even as it was, it could hardly be described as rosy, though
the planter seemed quite unaware that death in a gruesome
form was drawing closer and closer. As the war between his
brain and the "act of God" reached its climax, the very shadow
of annihilation began to pale to Leiningen, who now felt like a
champion in a new Olympic game, a gigantic and thrilling
contest, from which he was determined to emerge victor. Such,
indeed, was his aura of confidence that the Indians forgot their
fear of the peril only a yard or two away; under the planter's
supervision, they began fervidly digging up to the edge of the
bank and throwing clods of earth and spadefuls of sand into the
midst of the hostile fleet.

The petrol sprinklers, hitherto used to destroy pests and
blights on the plantation, were also brought into action.
Streams of evil-reeking oil now soared and fell over an enemy
already in disorder through the bombardment of earth and
sand.

The ants responded to these vigorous and successful measures of defense by further developments of their offensive.
Entire clumps of huddling insects began to roll down the
opposite bank into the water. At the same time, Leiningen
noticed that the ants were now attacking along an ever-
widening front. As the numbers both of his men and his petrol
sprinklers were severely limited, this rapid extension of the
line of battle was becoming an overwhelming danger.

To add to his difficulties, the very clods of earth they flung
into that black floating carpet often whirled fragments towards
the defenders' side, and here and there dark ribbons were
already mounting the inner bank. True, wherever a man saw
these they could still be driven back into the water by spadefuls of earth or jets of petrol. But the file of defenders was too
sparse and scattered to hold off at all points these landing
parties, and though the peons toiled like madmen, their plight
became momently more perilous.

One man struck with his spade at an enemy clump, did not
draw it back quickly enough from the water; in a trice the

wooden shaft swarmed with upward scurrying insects. With a curse, he dropped the spade into the ditch; too late, they were already on his body. They lost no time; wherever they encountered bare flesh they bit deeply; a few, bigger than the rest, carried in their hindquarters a sting which injected a burning and paralyzing venom. Screaming, frantic with pain, the peon danced and twirled like a dervish.

Realizing that another such casualty, yes, perhaps this alone, might plunge his men into confusion and destroy their morale, Leiningen roared in a bellow louder than the yells of the victim: "Into the petrol, idiot! Douse your paws in the petrol!" The dervish ceased his pirouette as if transfixed, then tore off his shirt and plunged his arm and the ants hanging to it up to the shoulder in one of the large open tins of petrol. But even then the fierce mandibles did not slacken; another peon had to help him squash and detach each separate insect.

Distracted by the episode, some defenders had turned away from the ditch. And now cries of fury, a thudding of spades, and a wild trampling to and fro, showed that the ants had made full use of the interval, though luckily only a few had managed to get across. The men set to work again desperately with the barrage of earth and sand. Meanwhile an old Indian, who acted as medicine man to the plantation workers, gave the bitten peon a drink he had prepared some hours before, which, he claimed, possessed the virtue of dissolving and weakening ants' venom.

Leiningen surveyed his position. A dispassionate observer would have estimated the odds against him at a thousand to one. But then such an onlooker would have reckoned only by what he saw—the advance of myriad battalions of ants against the futile efforts of a few defenders—and not by the unseen activity that can go on in a man's brain.

For Leiningen had not erred when he decided he would fight elemental with elemental. The water in the ditch was beginning to rise; the stronger damming of the river was making itself apparent.

Visibly the swiftness and power of the masses of water increased, swirling into quicker and quicker movement its living black surface, dispersing its pattern, carrying away more and more of it on the hastening current.

Victory had been snatched from the very jaws of defeat. With a hysterical shout of joy, the peons feverishly intensified their bombardment of earth clods and sand.

And now the wide cataract down the opposite bank was thinning and ceasing, as if the ants were becoming aware that they could not attain their aim. They were scurrying back up the slope to safety.

All the troops so far hurled into the ditch had been sacrificed in vain. Drowned and floundering insects eddied in thousands along the flow, while Indians running on the bank destroyed every swimmer that reached the side.

Not until the ditch curved towards the east did the scattered ranks assemble again in a coherent mass. And now, exhausted and half-numbed, they were in no condition to ascend the bank. Fusillades of clods drove them round the bend toward the mouth of the ditch and then into the river, wherein they vanished without leaving a trace.

The news ran swiftly along the entire chain of outposts, and soon a long scattered line of laughing men could be seen hastening along the ditch toward the scene of victory.

For once they seemed to have lost all their native reserve, for it was in wild abandon now they celebrated the triumph— as if there were no longer thousands of millions of merciless, cold and hungry eyes watching them from the opposite bank, watching and waiting.

The sun sank behind the rim of the tamarind wood and twilight deepened into night. It was not only hoped but expected that the ants would remain quiet until dawn. But to defeat any forlorn attempt at a crossing, the flow of water through the ditch was powerfully increased by opening the dam still further.

In spite of this impregnable barrier, Leiningen was not yet altogether convinced that the ants would not venture another surprise attack. He ordered his men to camp along the bank overnight. He also detailed parties of them to patrol the ditch in two of his motorcars and ceaselessly to illuminate the surface of the water with headlights and electric torches.

After having taken all the precautions he deemed necessary, the farmer ate his supper with considerable appetite and went to bed. His slumbers were in no wise disturbed by the memory of the waiting, live, twenty square miles.

Dawn found a thoroughly refreshed and active Leiningen riding along the edge of the ditch. The planter saw before him a motionless and unaltered throng of besiegers. He studied the wide belt of water between them and the plantation, and for a moment almost regretted that the fight had ended so soon and so simply. In the comforting, matter-of-fact light of morning, it seemed to him now that the ants hadn't the ghost of a chance to cross the ditch. Even if they plunged headlong into it on all three fronts at once, the force of the now powerful current would inevitably sweep them away. He had got quite a thrill out of the fight—a pity it was already over.

He rode along the eastern and southern sections of the ditch and found everything in order. He reached the western section, opposite the tamarind wood, and here, contrary to the other battle fronts, he found the enemy very busy indeed. The trunks and branches of the trees and the creepers of the lianas, on the far bank of the ditch, fairly swarmed with industrious insects. But instead of eating the leaves there and then, they were merely gnawing through the stalks, so that a thick green shower fell steadily to the ground.

No doubt they were victualing columns sent out to obtain provender for the rest of the army. The discovery did not surprise Leiningen. He did not need to be told that ants are intelligent, that certain species even use others as milch cows, watchdogs and slaves. He was well aware of their power of adaptation, their sense of discipline, their marvelous talent for organization.

His belief that a foray to supply the army was in progress was strengthened when he saw the leaves that fell to the ground being dragged to the troops waiting outside the wood. Then all at once he realized the aim that rain of green was intended to serve.

Each single leaf, pulled or pushed by dozens of toiling insects, was borne straight to the edge of the ditch. Even as Macbeth watched the approach of Birnam Wood in the hands of his enemies, Leiningen saw the tamarind wood move nearer and nearer in the mandibles of the ants. Unlike the fey Scot, however, he did not lose his nerve; no witches had prophesied his doom, and if they had he would have slept just as soundly. All the time, he was forced to admit to himself that the situation was now far more ominous than that of the day before.

He had thought it impossible for the ants to build rafts for themselves—well, here they were, coming in thousands, more than enough to bridge the ditch. Leaves after leaves rustled down the slope into the water, where the current drew them away from the bank and carried them into midstream. And every single leaf carried several ants. This time the farmer did not trust to the alacrity of his messengers. He galloped away, leaning from his saddle and yelling orders as he rushed past outpost after outpost: "Bring petrol pumps to the southwest front! Issue spades to every man along the line facing the wood!" And arrived at the eastern and southern sections, he dispatched every man except the observation posts to the menaced west.

Then, as he rode past the stretch where the ants had failed to cross the day before, he witnessed a brief but impressive scene. Down the slope of the distant hill there came toward him a singular being, writhing rather than running, an animal-like blackened statue with a shapeless head and four quivering feet that knuckled under almost ceaselessly. When the creature reached the far bank of the ditch and collapsed opposite Leiningen, he recognized it as a pampas stag, covered over and over with ants.

It had strayed near the zone of the army. As usual, they had attacked its eyes first. Blinded, it had reeled in the madness of hideous torment straight into the ranks of its persecutors, and now the beast swayed to and fro in its death agony.

With a shot from his rifle Leiningen put it out of its misery. Then he pulled out his watch. He hadn't a second to lose, but for life itself he could not have denied his curiosity the satisfaction of knowing how long the ants would take—for personal reasons, so to speak. After six minutes the white polished bones alone remained. That's how he himself would look before you can—Leiningen spat once, and put spurs to his horse.

The sporting zest with which the excitement of the novel contest had inspired him the day before had now vanished; in its place was a cold and violent purpose. He would send these vermin back to the hell where they belonged, somehow, anyhow. Yes, but how was indeed the question; as things stood at present it looked as if the devils would raze him and his men from the earth instead. He had underestimated the might of the enemy; he really would have to bestir himself if he hoped to outwit them.

The biggest danger now, he decided, was the point where the western section of the ditch curved southward. And having arrived there, he found his worst expectations justified. The very power of the current had huddled the leaves and their crews of ants so close together at the bend that the bridge was almost ready.

True, streams of petrol and clumps of earth still prevented a landing, but the number of floating leaves was increasing ever more swiftly. It could not be long now before a stretch of water a mile in length was decked by a green pontoon over which the ants could rush in millions.

Leiningen galloped to the weir. The damming of the river was controlled by a wheel on its bank. The planter ordered the man at the wheel first to lower the water in the ditch almost to vanishing point, next to wait a moment, then suddenly to let the river in again. This maneuver of lowering and raising the surface, of decreasing then increasing the flow of water through the ditch was to be repeated over and over again until further notice.

This tactic was at first successful. The water in the ditch sank, and with it the film of leaves. The green fleet nearly reached the bed and the troops on the far bank swarmed down the slope to it. Then a violent flow of water at the original depth raced through the ditch, overwhelming leaves and ants, and sweeping them along.

This intermittent rapid flushing prevented just in time the almost completed fording of the ditch. But it also flung here and there squads of the enemy vanguard simultaneously up the inner bank. These seemed to know their duty only too well, and lost no time accomplishing it. The air rang with the curses of bitten Indians. They had removed their shirts and pants to detect the quicker the upwards-hastening insects; when they saw one, they crushed it; and fortunately the onslaught as yet was only by skirmishers.

Again and again, the water sank and rose, carrying leaves

and drowned ants away with it. It lowered once more nearly to
its bed; but this time the exhausted defenders waited in vain
for the flush of destruction. Leiningen sensed disaster; something must have gone wrong with the machinery of the dam.
Then a sweating peon tore up to him—

"They're over!"

While the besieged were concentrating upon the defense of
the stretch opposite the wood, the seemingly unaffected line
beyond the wood had become the theatre of decisive action.
Here the defenders' front was sparse and scattered; everyone
who could be spared had hurried away to the south.

Just as the man at the weir had lowered the water almost
to the bed of the ditch, the ants on a wide front began another
attempt at a direct crossing like that of the preceding day. Into
the emptied bed poured an irresistible throng. Rushing across
the ditch, they attained the inner bank before the fatigued
Indians fully grasped the situation. Their frantic screams
dumbfounded the man at the weir. Before he could direct the
river anew into the safeguarding bed he saw himself surrounded by raging ants. He ran like the others, ran for his life.

When Leiningen heard this, he knew the plantation was
doomed. He wasted no time bemoaning the inevitable. For as
long as there was the slightest chance of success, he had stood
his ground, and now any further resistance was both useless
and dangerous. He fired three revolver shots into the air—the
prearranged signal for his men to retreat instantly within the
"inner moat." Then he rode towards the ranch house.

This was two miles from the point of invasion. There was
therefore time enough to prepare the second line of defense
against the advent of the ants. Of the three great petrol cisterns
near the house, one had already been half emptied by the
constant withdrawals needed for the pumps during the fight at
the water ditch. The remaining petrol in it was now drawn off
through underground pipes into the concrete trench which
encircled the ranch house and its outbuildings.

And there, drifting in twos and threes, Leiningen's men
reached him. Most of them were obviously trying to preserve
an air of calm and indifference, belied, however, by their
restless glances and knitted brows. One could see their belief in

a favorable outcome of the struggle was already considerably shaken.

The planter called his peons around him.

"Well, lads," he began, "we've lost the first round. But we'll smash the beggars yet, don't you worry. Anyone who thinks otherwise can draw his pay here and now and push off. There are rafts enough and to spare on the river and plenty of time still to reach 'em."

Not a man stirred.

Leiningen acknowledged his silent vote of confidence with a laugh that was half a grunt. "That's the stuff, lads. Too bad if you'd missed the rest of the show, eh? Well, the fun won't start till morning. Once these blighters turn tail, there'll be plenty of work for everyone and higher wages all round. And now run along and get something to eat; you've earned it all right."

In the excitement of the fight the greater part of the day had passed without the men once pausing to snatch a bite. Now that the ants were for the time being out of sight, and the "wall of petrol" gave a stronger feeling of security, hungry stomachs began to assert their claims.

The bridges over the concrete ditch were removed. Here and there solitary ants had reached the ditch; they gazed at the petrol meditatively, then scurried back again. Apparently they had little interest at the moment for what lay beyond the evil-reeking barrier; the abundant spoils of the plantation were the main attraction. Soon the trees, shrubs and beds for miles around were hulled with ants zealously gobbling the yield of long weary months of strenuous toil.

As twilight began to fall, a cordon of ants marched around the petrol trench, but as yet made no move toward its brink. Leiningen posted sentries with headlights and electric torches, then withdrew to his office, and began to reckon up his losses. He estimated these as large, but, in comparison with his bank balance, by no means unbearable. He worked out in some detail a scheme of intensive cultivation which would enable him, before very long, to more than compensate himself for the damage now being wrought to his crops. It was with a contented mind that he finally betook himself to bed where he slept deeply until dawn, undisturbed by any thought that next day little more might be left of him than a glistening skeleton.

He rose with the sun and went out on the flat roof of his house. And a scene like one from Dante lay around him; for miles in every direction there was nothing but a black, glittering multitude, a multitude of rested, sated, but nonetheless voracious ants: yes, look as far as one might, one could see nothing but that rustling black throng, except in the north, where the great river drew a boundary they could not hope to pass. But even the high stone breakwater, along the bank of the river, which Leiningen had built as a defense against inundations, was, like the paths, the shorn trees and shrubs, the ground itself, black with ants.

So their greed was not glutted in razing that vast plantation? Not by a long chalk; they were all the more eager now on a rich and certain booty—four hundred men, numerous horses, and bursting granaries.

At first it seemed that the petrol trench would serve its purpose. The besiegers sensed the peril of swimming it, and made no move to plunge blindly over its brink. Instead they devised a better maneuver; they began to collect shreds of bark, twigs and dried leaves and dropped these into the petrol. Everything green, which could have been similarly used, had long since been eaten. After a time, though, a long procession could be seen bringing from the west the tamarind leaves used as rafts the day before.

Since the petrol, unlike the water in the outer ditch, was perfectly still, the refuse stayed where it was thrown. It was several hours before the ants succeeded in covering an appreciable part of the surface. At length, however, they were ready to proceed to a direct attack.

Their storm troops swarmed down the concrete side, scrambled over the supporting surface of twigs and leaves, and impelled these over the few remaining streaks of open petrol until they reached the other side. Then they began to climb up this to make straight for the helpless garrison.

During the entire offensive, the planter sat peacefully, watching them with interest, but not stirring a muscle. Moreover, he had ordered his men not to disturb in any way whatever the advancing horde. So they squatted listlessly along the bank of the ditch and waited for a sign from the boss.

The petrol was now covered with ants. A few had climbed the inner concrete wall and were scurrying towards the defenders.

"Everyone back from the ditch!" roared Leiningen. The men rushed away, without the slightest idea of his plan. He stooped forward and cautiously dropped into the ditch a stone which split the floating carpet and its living freight, to reveal a gleaming patch of petrol. A match spurted, sank down to the oily surface—Leiningen sprang back; in a flash a towering rampart of fire encompassed the garrison.

This spectacular and instant repulse threw the Indians into ecstasy. They applauded, yelled and stamped, like children at a pantomime. Had it not been for the awe in which they held the boss, they would infallibly have carried him shoulder high.

It was some time before the petrol burned down to the bed of the ditch, and the wall of smoke and flame began to lower. The ants had retreated in a wide circle from the devastation, and innumerable charred fragments along the outer bank showed that the flames had spread from the holocaust in the ditch well into the ranks beyond, where they had wrought havoc far and wide.

Yet the perseverance of the ants was by no means broken; indeed, each setback seemed only to whet it. The concrete cooled, the flicker of the dying flames wavered and vanished, petrol from the second tank poured into the trench—and the ants marched forward anew to the attack.

The foregoing scene repeated itself in every detail, except that on this occasion less time was needed to bridge the ditch, for the petrol was now already filmed by a layer of ash. Once again they withdrew; once again petrol flowed into the ditch. Would the creatures never learn that their self-sacrifice was utterly senseless? It really was senseless, wasn't it? Yes, of course if was senseless—provided the defenders had an *unlimited* supply of petrol.

When Leiningen reached this stage of reasoning, he felt for the first time since the arrival of the ants that his confidence was deserting him. His skin began to creep; he loosened his collar. Once the devils were over the trench there wasn't a chance in hell for him and his men. God, what a prospect, to be eaten alive like that!

For the third time the flames immolated the attacking troops, and burned down to extinction. Yet the ants were coming on again as if nothing had happened. And meanwhile Leiningen had made a discovery that chilled him to the bone—petrol was no longer flowing into the ditch. Something must be blocking the outflow pipe of the third and last cistern—a snake or a dead rat? Whatever it was, the ants could be held off no longer, unless petrol could by some method be led from the cistern into the ditch.

Then Leiningen remembered that in an outhouse nearby were two old disused fire engines. Spry as never before in their lives, the peons dragged them out of the shed, connected their pumps to the cistern, uncoiled and laid the hose. They were just in time to aim a stream of petrol at a column of ants that had already crossed and drive them back down the incline into the ditch. Once more an oily girdle surrounded the garrison, once more it was possible to hold the position—for the moment.

It was obvious, however, that this last resource meant only the postponement of defeat and death. A few of the peons fell on their knees and began to pray; others, shrieking insanely, fired their revolvers at the black, advancing masses, as if they felt their despair was pitiful enough to sway fate itself to mercy.

At length, two of the men's nerves broke: Leiningen saw a naked Indian leap over the north side of the petrol trench, quickly followed by a second. They sprinted with incredible speed towards the river. But their fleetness did not save them; long before they could attain the rafts, the enemy covered their bodies from head to foot.

In the agony of their torment, both sprang blindly into the wide river, where enemies no less sinister awaited them. Wild screams of mortal anguish informed the breathless onlookers that crocodiles and sword-toothed piranhas* were no less ravenous than ants, and even nimbler in reaching their prey.

In spite of this bloody warning, more and more men showed they were making up their minds to run the blockade. Anything, even a fight midstream against alligators, seemed

* *piranhas*   ferocious flesh-eating fish of South America

better than powerlessly waiting for death to come and slowly consume their living bodies.

Leiningen flogged his brain till it reeled. Was there nothing on earth could sweep this devils' spawn back into the hell from which it came?

Then out of the inferno of his bewilderment rose a terrifying inspiration. Yes, one hope remained, and one alone. It might be possible to dam the great river completely, so that its waters would fill not only the water ditch but overflow into the entire gigantic "saucer" of land in which lay the plantation.

The far bank of the river was too high for the waters to escape that way. The stone breakwater ran between the river and the plantation; its only gaps occurred where the "horseshoe" ends of the water-ditch passed into the river. So its waters would not only be forced to inundate into the plantation, they would also be held there by the breakwater until they rose to its own high level. In half an hour, perhaps even earlier, the plantation and its hostile army of occupation would be flooded.

The ranch house and outbuildings stood upon rising ground. Their foundations were higher than the breakwater, so the flood would not reach them. And any remaining ants trying to ascend the slope could be repulsed by petrol.

It was possible yes, if one could only get to the dam! A distance of nearly two miles lay between the ranch house and the weir—two miles of ants. Those two peons had managed only a fifth of that distance at the cost of their lives. Was there an Indian daring enough after that to run the gauntlet five times as far? Hardly likely; and if there were, his prospect of getting back was almost nil.

No, there was only one thing for it, he'd have to make the attempt himself; he might just as well be running as sitting still, anyway, when the ants finally got him. Besides, there *was* a bit of a chance. Perhaps the ants weren't so almighty, after all; perhaps he had allowed the mass suggestion of that evil black throng to hypnotize him, just as a snake fascinates and overpowers.

The ants were building their bridges. Leiningen got up on a chair. "Hey, lads, listen to me!" he cried. Slowly and listlessly, from all sides of the trench, the men began to shuffle towards him, the apathy of death already stamped on their faces.

"Listen, lads!" he shouted. "You're frightened of those beggars, but you're a damn sight more frightened of me, and I'm proud of you. There's still a chance to save our lives—by flooding the plantation from the river. Now one of you might manage to get as far as the weir—but he'd never come back. Well, I'm not going to let you try it; if I did I'd be worse than one of those ants. No, I called the tune, and now I'm going to pay the piper.

"The moment I'm over the ditch, set fire to the petrol. That'll allow time for the flood to do the trick. Then all you have to do is to wait here all snug and quiet till I'm back. Yes, I'm coming back, trust me"—he grinned—"when I've finished my slimming-cure."

He pulled on high leather boots, drew heavy gauntlets over his hands, and stuffed the spaces between breeches and boots, gauntlets and arms, shirt and neck, with rags soaked in petrol. With close-fitting mosquito goggles he shielded his eyes, knowing too well the ants' dodge of first robbing their victim of sight. Finally, he plugged his nostrils and ears with cotton-wool, and let the peons drench his clothes with petrol.

He was about to set off, when the old Indian medicine man came up to him; he had a wondrous salve, he said, prepared from a species of chafer whose odor was intolerable to ants. Yes, this odor protected these chafers from the attacks of even the most murderous ants. The Indian smeared the boss' boots, his gauntlets, and his face over and over with the extract.

Leiningen then remembered the paralyzing effect of ants' venom, and the Indian gave him a gourd full of the medicine he had administered to the bitten peon at the water-ditch. The planter drank it down without noticing its bitter taste; his mind was already at the weir.

He started off towards the northwest corner of the trench. With a bound he was over—and among the ants.

The beleaguered garrison had no opportunity to watch Leiningen's race against death. The ants were climbing the inner bank again—the lurid ring of petrol blazed aloft. For the fourth time that day the reflection from the fire shone on the sweating faces of the imprisoned men, and on the reddish-black cuirasses of their oppressors. The red and blue, dark-edged flames leaped vividly now, celebrating what? The funeral pyre of the four hundred, or of the hosts of destruction?

Leiningen ran. He ran in long, equal strides, with only one thought, one sensation, in his being—he *must* get through. He dodged all trees and shrubs; except for the split seconds his soles touched the ground the ants should have no opportunity to alight on him. That they would get to him soon, despite the salve on his boots, the petrol in his clothes, he realized only too well, but he knew even more surely that he must, and that he would, get to the weir.

Apparently the salve was some use after all; not until he had reached halfway did he feel ants under his clothes, and a few on his face. Mechanically, in his stride, he struck at them, scarcely conscious of their bites. He saw he was drawing appreciably nearer the weir—the distance grew less and less—sank to five hundred—three—two—one hundred yards.

Then he was at the weir and gripping the ant-hulled wheel. Hardly had he seized it when a horde of infuriated ants flowed over his hands, arms and shoulders. He started the wheel—before it turned once on its axis the swarm covered his face. Leiningen strained like a madman, his lips pressed tight; if he opened them to draw breath. . . .

He turned and turned; slowly the dam lowered until it reached the bed of the river. Already the water was overflowing the ditch. Another minute, and the river was pouring through the nearby gap in the breakwater. The flooding of the plantation had begun.

Leiningen let go the wheel. Now, for the first time, he realized he was coated from head to foot with a layer of ants. In spite of the petrol, his clothes were full of them; several had got to his body or were clinging to his face. Now that he had completed his task, he felt the smart raging over his flesh from the bites of sawing and piercing insects.

Frantic with pain, he almost plunged into the river. To be ripped and slashed to shreds by piranhas? Already he was running the return journey, knocking ants from his gloves and jacket, brushing them from his bloodied face, squashing them to death under his clothes.

One of the creatures bit him just below the rim of his goggles; he managed to tear it away, but the agony of the bite and its etching acid drilled into the eye nerves; he saw now through circles of fire into a milky mist, then he ran for a time almost blinded, knowing that if he once tripped and fell. . . . The old Indian's brew didn't seem much good; it weakened the poison a bit, but didn't get rid of it. His heart pounded as if it would burst; blood roared in his ears; a giant's fist battered his lungs.

Then he could see again, but the burning girdle of petrol appeared infinitely far away; he could not last half that distance. Swift-changing pictures flashed through his head, episodes in his life, while in another part of his brain a cool and impartial onlooker informed this ant-blurred, gasping, exhausted bundle named Leiningen that such a rushing panorama of scenes from one's past is seen only in the moment before death.

A stone in the path . . . too weak to avoid it . . . the planter stumbled and collapsed. He tried to rise . . . he must be pinned under a rock . . . it was impossible . . . the slightest movement was impossible. . . .

Then all at once he saw, starkly clear and huge, and, right before his eyes, furred with ants, towering and swaying in its death agony, the pampas stag. In six minutes—gnawed to the bones. God, he *couldn't* die like that! And something outside him seemed to drag him to his feet. He tottered. He began to stagger forward again.

Through the blazing ring hurtled an apparition which, as soon as it reached the ground on the inner side, fell full length and did not move. Leiningen, at the moment he made that leap through the flames, lost consciousness for the first time in his life. As he lay there, with glazing eyes and lacerated face, he appeared a man returned from the grave. The peons rushed to him, stripped off his clothes, tore away the ants from a body that seemed almost one open wound; in some places the bones were showing. They carried him into the ranch house.

As the curtain of flames lowered, one could see in place of the illimitable host of ants an extensive vista of water. The thwarted river had swept over the plantation, carrying with it the entire army. The water had collected and mounted in the great "saucer," while the ants had in vain attempted to reach the hill on which stood the ranch house. The girdle of flames held them back.

And so imprisoned between water and fire, they had been delivered into the annihilation that was their god. And near the farther mouth of the water-ditch, where the stone mole had its second gap, the ocean swept the lost battalions into the river, to vanish forever.

The ring of fire dwindled as the water mounted to the petrol trench, and quenched the dimming flames. The inundation rose higher and higher; because its outflow was impeded by the timber and underbrush it had carried along with it, its surface required some time to reach the top of the high stone breakwater and discharge over it the rest of the shattered army.

It swelled over ant-stippled shrubs and bushes, until it washed against the foot of the knoll whereon the besieged had taken refuge. For a while an alluvial of ants tried again and again to attain this dry land, only to be repulsed by streams of petrol back into the merciless flood.

Leiningen lay on his bed, his body swathed from head to foot in bandages. With fomentations and salves, they had managed to stop the bleeding, and had dressed his many wounds. Now they thronged around him, one question in every face. Would he recover? "He won't die," said the old man who had bandaged him, "if he doesn't want to."

The planter opened his eyes. "Everything in order?" he asked.

"They're gone," said his nurse. "To hell." He held out to his master a gourd full of a powerful sleeping draught. Leiningen gulped it down.

"I told you I'd come back," he murmured, "even if I am a bit streamlined." He grinned and shut his eyes. He slept.

Reading for Understanding _____

Main Idea

1. Which of the following bits of dialog best expresses the main idea of the story?
    (a) "I tell you if you don't clear out at once there'll be nothing left of you but a skeleton picked as clean as your own plantation."
    (b) "The human brain needs only to become fully aware of its powers to conquer even the elements."
    (c) "Ten miles long, two miles wide—ants, nothing but ants! And every single one of them a fiend from hell."
    (d) "Your obstinacy endangers not only yourself, but the lives of your four hundred workers."

Details

2. The story takes place in   (a) Africa   (b) Asia   (c) Mexico   (d) Brazil.

3. Which one of the following statements is true?
    (a) The District Commissioner ordered Leiningen to leave the plantation to the ants.
    (b) The ants had chosen to attack the plantation because of the wealth of food in its storehouses.
    (c) The women and children were barricaded in the ranch house.
    (d) Leiningen fired his gun to drive off ants and as a signal to his men.

4. Leiningen shot the deer   (a) to gain time   (b) to end its suffering   (c) to feed the ants   (d) to show the men what the real danger was.

5. The ants made rafts of leaves to cross the   (a) ditch   (b) river   (c) swamp   (d) cascades.

Inferences

6. Rather than flee, the workers stayed   (a) to protect their homes   (b) to protect their families   (c) because Lein-

ingen forced them to   (d) because they trusted his judgment.

7. The water-filled ditch failed as a defense measure because (a) it was too narrow   (b) Leiningen was careless (c) human error occurred   (d) there was no way to renew the water level.

8. Leiningen did not make use of bulldozers, dynamite, flame-throwers, poisoned spray, or heat-rays because (a) he was not sure of himself   (b) he did not want to harm the workers   (c) he had faith in elemental weaponry   (d) he lacked the imagination necessary to consider them.

9. Leiningen ran to the dam himself because   (a) he had lost faith in his workers   (b) he couldn't ask another to face almost certain death   (c) the men refused to volunteer   (d) he was confident that he would return unharmed.

10. The final choice offered the ants was:
    (a) Retreat or die.
    (b) Drown or be burned alive.
    (c) Swerve away from the plantation or face the dangers of the river.
    (d) Let the plantation survive or be destroyed by the petrol.

Order of Events

11. Arrange the items in the order in which they occurred. Use letters only.
    A. A ring of fire protects the men.
    B. The ants use rafts to cross the water.
    C. A peon opens and closes the dam.
    D. Leiningen forces the river water to overflow the dam.
    E. Leiningen retreats to the ranch house.

Outcomes

12. The final and successful tactic   (a) destroyed the army of ants   (b) set up a water barrier between the ants and

what remained of the plantation   (c) forced the ants to retreat   (d) cost Leiningen his life.

Cause and Effect

13. The workers could not escape by swimming across the river because   (a) Leiningen threatened to kill anyone who tried   (b) that would make them appear cowardly   (c) they would be eaten alive   (d) the river was too wide.

Fact or Opinion

Tell whether each of the following is a fact or an opinion.

14. The ants were willing to sacrifice many thousands in their ranks in order to obtain the food on the plantation.

15. Leiningen would be able to reclaim his land by redirecting the flow of the river.

Words in Context _____

1. "And don't think I'm the kind of fathead who tries to *fend off* lightning with his fists, either."
   Fend off (431) means   (a) avoid   (b) attack   (c) destroy   (d) repel.

2. "Your *obstinacy* endangers not only yourself, but the lives of your four hundred workers."
   Obstinacy (432) means   (a) carelessness   (b) stubbornness   (c) foolishness   (d) overconfidence.

3. As it moved downstream, the *exclamation mark* neared the rail and began waving its arms frantically.
   What looked like an *exclamation mark* (432) in the distance was   (a) Leiningen himself   (b) the ants   (c) the District Commissioner   (d) the pilot of the boat.

4. Before he started work on his settlement, he had lived long enough in the country to see for himself the fearful

devastations sometimes wrought by these *ravenous* insects in their campaigns for food.
Ravenous (432) means   (a) cruel   (b) very hungry
(c) thoughtless   (d) very reckless.

5. This unbroken success he *attributed solely to* the observance of his lifelong motto . . .
Attributed solely to (432) means   (a) gave credit completely to   (b) blamed totally on   (c) solved through   (d) lost as the result of.

6. *Dullards reeled senselessly and aimlessly into the abyss* . . .
The above statement (432) means   (a) only the rich succeeded   (b) action should precede thought
(c) stupid people were unaware of why they lost
(d) to the strong belong the winnings.

7. Yes, Leiningen had always known how to *grapple with* life.
Grapple with (432) means   (a) wrestle with
(b) compromise with   (c) understand   (d) overcome obstacles in.

8. It was announced by a stampede of animals, timid and savage, *hurtling past* each other . . .
Hurtling past (433) means   (a) crushing   (b) rushing wildly ahead of   (c) fighting savagely against
(d) bruising.

9. The water-filled ditch was one of the defense measures which Leiningen had long since prepared against the *advent* of the ants.
Advent (433) means   (a) conquest   (b) rumors
(c) savagery   (d) coming.

10. It *encompassed* three sides of the plantation like a huge horseshoe.
Encompassed (433) means   (a) excluded   (b) encircled   (c) defended   (d) exposed.

11. . . . Leiningen had constructed a dam by means of which water could be *diverted into* the ditch.
Diverted into (434) means   (a) turned into
(b) pumped from   (c) stored in   (d) converted into.

12. This was *destined* to be the scene of the outbreak of war between Leiningen's brain and twenty square miles of life-destroying ants.
Destined (435) means   (a) pictured   (b) bound
(c) boasted   (d) considered.

13. The *besieged* were therefore able to contemplate at their leisure the thumb-long, reddish-black, long-legged insects . . .
The *besieged* (436) were those who were   (a) going to fight   (b) surrounded and attacked   (c) planning to destroy the men   (d) not afraid of the ants.

14. Many thousands were already drowning in the *sluggish* creeping flow . . .
Sluggish (437) means   (a) brownish   (b) clear
(c) icy   (d) slow-moving.

15. Nevertheless, the *wavering*, floundering hundred-yard front was remorselessly if slowly advancing . . .
Wavering (437) means moving   (a) cautiously
(b) inch-by-inch   (c) unsteadily   (d) daringly.

16. . . . the Indians . . . began . . . throwing *clods* of earth and spadefuls of sand into the midst of the hostile fleet.
Clods (438) means   (a) cartloads   (b) lumps
(c) pounds   (d) masses.

17. . . . *their plight became momently more perilous.*
The above statement (438) means   (a) The danger decreased gradually   (b) The danger increased second by second   (c) Things could not get worse   (d) The men knew that they had no hope.

18. The men set to work again desperately with the *barrage* of earth and sand.
Barrage (439) means   (a) loads   (b) bombardment
(c) bullets   (d) barriers.

19. For Leiningen had not *erred* when he decided that he would fight elemental with elemental.
Erred (439) means   (a) gone wrong   (b) lost
(c) gained   (d) been stupid.

20. The sporting *zest* with which the excitement of the novel contest had inspired him the day before had now vanished; in its place was a cold and violent purpose.
    Zest (442) means (a) enjoyment (b) sorrow (c) fear (d) hope.

21. . . . he really would have to *bestir himself* if he hoped to outwit them.
    Bestir himself (443) means (a) outdo (b) get going (c) not fall asleep (d) arm himself.

22. . . . and fortunately the onslaught as yet was only by *skirmishers.*
    Skirmishers (443) means (a) weaklings (b) scouts (c) main force (d) few in number.

23. Now that the ants were for the time being out of sight . . . hungry stomachs began to *assert* their claims.
    Assert (445) means (a) state strongly (b) deny (c) recall (d) forget.

24. . . . *in a flash a towering rampart of fire encompassed the garrison.*
    The above statement (447) means (a) the ants were killed (b) the defenders were severely burned (c) a wall of fire surrounded the besieged (d) the house went up in flames.

25. Hardly likely; and if there were, his prospect of getting back was almost *nil.*
    Nil (449) means (a) a certainty (b) impossible (c) nothing (d) an even bet.

Thinking Critically About the Story _____

1. Was Leiningen foolhardy or courageous in his decision to defend the plantation? What would you have done in his place?

2. What details did the author add to increase the sense of horror? The suspense?

3. Although the other characters are not developed, we are given a fuller picture of Leiningen. What were some of his admirable qualities? Some of his faults? How does he resemble some of the adults in your life? Would you seek him out as a friend or adviser? Explain your choice.

4. To what extent do you think Leiningen reached a fundamental truth in his faith in the ability of people to think their way through all difficulties?

5. How does Leiningen compare to those people who trust their instincts or emotions more than they do their intelligence? Which group has the better chance of achieving success? Of achieving happiness?

Stories in Words

Ravenous (432) The raven is a large bird of the crow family, with bright black feathers and a powerful, sharp beak. The word *ravenous* means "greedily, wildly hungry." It might seem that *ravenous* comes from the name of the bird, but it doesn't. *Ravenous* comes from an altogether different root, meaning "to snatch, seize." The name of the bird, on the other hand, comes from an imitation of the bird's cry. (See *murmured* below.) A fascinating aspect of word study is discovering that sometimes seemingly obviously connected words are not connected at all, while dissimilar words have similar histories.

Pantomime (447) We have already met the Greek prefix *pan* meaning "all" (page 295). *Panto* is another form of the same root. What of *mime*? Mime is an actor who uses gestures and actions rather than words. *Pantomime* is the performance given by such an actor. The word *pantomime* has acquired a larger meaning. If a friend signals a message to another across a room, he or she is using pantomime. The root *mimus* means "imitator, actor." It appears in *mimic* and *mimicry*.

Murmured (453)   If you say the word *murmur* softly to yourself, you will understand how the word arose. The sound of the word is perfectly suited to its meaning. This formation of a word by imitating the natural sound is called *onomatopoeia,* as in words like *crash, buzz, hiss.* A famous line of poetry by Alfred Lord Tennyson uses onomatopoeia to suggest the sounds: "The moan of doves in immemorial elms, And murmuring of innumerable bees." See also *Cricket,* page 129.

The Birds

Daphne du Maurier

♦ **"It is thought that the Arctic airstream at present covering the British Isles is causing birds to migrate south in immense numbers, and the intense hunger may drive these birds to attack human beings."**

We are accustomed to life going on as usual with the human race dominating the creatures of Earth. What would result if the birds of the world united to wrest control from us by destroying every living person?

The story opens on the first day of the great offensive. The birds swarm in on the attack, not by hundreds or thousands, but in flocks of hundreds of thousands of each variety.

What then happens is told through the eyes of a war veteran, a simple, part-time farm laborer. The events of the first 48 hours of the assault are related so factually that the horror and suspense come as an aftershock.

We can guarantee that when you finish this example of science fiction, you will be glad that it is all based on the vivid imagination of a writer rather than on any semblance to reality!

THE BIRDS

On December the third the wind changed overnight and it was winter. Until then the autumn had been mellow, soft. The earth was rich where the plow had turned it.

Nat Hocken, because of a wartime disability, had a pension and did not work full time at the farm. He worked three days a week, and they gave him the lighter jobs. Although he was married, with children, his was a solitary disposition; he liked best to work alone.

It pleased him when he was given a bank to build up, or a gate to mend, at the far end of the peninsula, where the sea surrounded the farmland on either side. Then, at midday, he would pause and eat the meat pie his wife had baked for him and, sitting on the cliff's edge, watch the birds.

In autumn great flocks of them came to the peninsula, restless, uneasy, spending themselves in motion; now wheeling, circling in the sky; now settling to feed on the rich, new-turned soil; but even when they fed, it was as though they did so without hunger, without desire.

Restlessness drove them to the skies again. Crying, whistling, calling, they skimmed the placid sea and left the shore.

Make haste, make speed, hurry and begone; yet where, and to what purpose? The restless urge of autumn, unsatisfying, sad, had put a spell upon them, and they must spill themselves of motion before winter came.

Perhaps, thought Nat, a message comes to the birds in autumn, like a warning. Winter is coming. Many of them will perish. And like people who, apprehensive of death before their time, drive themselves to work or folly, the birds do likewise; tomorrow we shall die.

The birds had been more restless than ever this fall of the

year. Their agitation more remarked because the days were still.

As Mr. Trigg's tractor traced its path up and down the western hills, and Nat, hedging, saw it dip and turn, the whole machine and the man upon it were momentarily lost in the great cloud of wheeling, crying birds.

Nat remarked upon them to Mr. Trigg when the work was finished for the day.

"Yes," said the farmer, "there are more birds about than usual. I have a notion the weather will change. It will be a hard winter. That's why the birds are restless."

The farmer was right. That night the weather turned.

The bedroom in the cottage faced east. Nat woke just after two and heard the east wind, cold and dry. It sounded hollow in the chimney, and a loose slate rattled on the roof. Nat listened, and he could hear the sea roaring in the bay. He drew the blanket round him, leaned closer to the back of his wife, deep in sleep. Then he heard the tapping on the windowpane. It continued until, irritated by the sound, Nat got out of bed and went to the window. He opened it; and as he did so something brushed his hand, jabbing at his knuckles, grazing the skin. Then he saw the flutter of wings and the thing was gone again, over the roof, behind the cottage.

It was a bird. What kind of bird he could not tell. The wind must have driven it to shelter on the sill.

He shut the window and went back to bed, but feeling his knuckles wet, put his mouth to the scratch. The bird had drawn blood.

Frightened, he supposed, bewildered, seeking shelter, the bird had stabbed at him in the darkness. Once more he settled himself to sleep.

Presently the tapping came again—this time more forceful, more insistent. And now his wife woke at the sound, and turning in the bed, said to him, "See to the window, Nat; it's rattling."

"I've already been to it," he told her. "There's some bird there, trying to get in."

"Send it away," she said. "I can't sleep with that noise."

He went to the window for the second time, and now when he opened it, there was not one bird on the sill but half a dozen; they flew straight into his face.

He shouted, striking out at them with his arms, scattering them; like the first one, they flew over the roof and disappeared.

He let the window fall and latched it.

Suddenly a frightened cry came from the room across the passage where the children slept.

"It's Jill," said his wife, roused at the sound.

There came a second cry, this time from both children. Stumbling into their room, Nat felt the beating of wings about him in the darkness. The window was wide open. Through it came the birds, hitting first the ceiling and the walls, then swerving in midflight and turning to the children in their beds.

"It's all right. I'm here," shouted Nat, and the children flung themselves, screaming, upon him, while in the darkness the birds rose, and dived, and came for him again.

"What is it, Nat? What's happened?" his wife called. Swiftly he pushed the children through the door to the passage and shut it upon them, so that he was alone in their bedroom with the birds.

He seized a blanket from the nearest bed, and using it as a weapon, flung it to right and left about him.

He felt the thud of bodies, heard the fluttering of wings; but the birds were not yet defeated, for again and again they returned to the assault, jabbing his hands, his head, their little stabbing beaks sharp as pointed forks.

The blanket became a weapon of defense. He wound it about his head, and then in greater darkness, beat at the birds with his bare hands. He dared not stumble to the door and open it lest the birds follow him.

How long he fought with them in the darkness he could not tell; but at last the beating of the wings about him lessened, withdrew; and through the dense blanket he was aware of light.

He waited, listened; there was no sound except the fretful crying of one of the children from the bedroom beyond.

He took the blanket from his head and stared about him. The cold gray morning light exposed the room.

Dawn and the open window had called the living birds; the dead lay on the floor.

Sickened, Nat went to the window and stared out across his patch of garden to the fields.

It was bitter cold, and the ground had all the hard, black look of the frost that the east wind brings. The sea, fiercer now with turning tide, whitecapped and steep, broke harshly in the bay. Of the birds there was no sign.

Nat shut the window and the door of the small bedroom and went back across the passage to his own room.

His wife sat up in bed, one child asleep beside her; the smaller one in her arms, his face bandaged.

"He's sleeping now," she whispered. "Something must have cut him; there was blood at the corners of his eyes. Jill said it was the birds. She said she woke up and the birds were in the room."

His wife looked up at Nat, searching his face for confirmation. She looked terrified, bewildered. He did not want her to know that he also was shaken, dazed almost, by the events of the past few hours.

"There are birds in there," he said. "Dead birds, nearly fifty of them." He sat down on the bed beside his wife.

"It's the hard weather," he said. "It must be that; it's the hard weather. They aren't the birds, maybe, from around here. They've been driven down from upcountry."

"But Nat," whispered his wife, "it's only this night that the weather turned. They can't be hungry yet. There's food for them out there in the fields."

"It's the weather," repeated Nat. "I tell you, it's the weather."

His face, too, was drawn and tired, like hers. They stared at one another for a while without speaking.

Nat went to the window and looked out. The sky was hard and leaden, and the blown hills that had gleamed in the sun the day before looked dark and bare. Black winter had descended in a single night.

The children were awake now. Jill was chattering, and young Johnny was crying once again. Nat heard his wife's voice, soothing, comforting them as he went downstairs.

Presently they came down. He had breakfast ready for them.

"Did you drive away the birds?" asked Jill.

"Yes, they've all gone now," Nat said. "It was the east wind brought them in."

"I hope they won't come again," said Jill.

"I'll walk with you to the bus," Nat said to her.

Jill seemed to have forgotten her experience of the night before. She danced ahead of him, chasing the leaves, her face rosy under her pixy hood.

All the while Nat searched the hedgerows for the birds, glanced over them to the fields beyond, looked to the small wood above the farm where the rooks and jackdaws gathered; he saw none. Soon the bus came ambling up the hill.

Nat saw Jill onto the bus, then turned and walked back toward the farm. It was not his day for work, but he wanted to satisfy himself that all was well. He went to the back door of the farmhouse; he heard Mrs. Trigg singing, the wireless making a background for her song.

"Are you there, missus?" Nat called.

She came to the door, beaming, broad, a good-tempered woman.

"Hullo, Mr. Hocken," she said. "Can you tell me where this cold is coming from? Is it Russia? I've never seen such a change. And it's going on, the wireless says. Something to do with the Arctic Circle."

"We didn't turn on the wireless this morning," said Nat. "Fact is, we had trouble in the night."

"Kiddies poorly?"

"No." He hardly knew how to explain. Now, in daylight, the battle of the birds would sound absurd.

He tried to tell Mrs. Trigg what had happened, but he could see from her eyes that she thought his story was the result of a nightmare following a heavy meal.

"Sure they were real birds?" she said, smiling.

"Mrs. Trigg," he said, "there are fifty dead birds—robins, wrens, and such—lying now on the floor of the children's bedroom. They went for me; they tried to go for young Johnny's eyes."

Mrs. Trigg stared at him doubtfully. "Well, now," she answered. "I suppose the weather brought them; once in the bedroom they wouldn't know where they were. Foreign birds maybe, from that Arctic Circle."

"No," said Nat. "They were the birds you see about here every day."

"Funny thing," said Mrs. Trigg. "No explaining it, really. You ought to write up and ask the *Guardian*. They'd have some answer for it. Well, I must be getting on."

Nat walked back along the lane to his cottage. He found his wife in the kitchen with young Johnny.

"See anyone?" she asked.

"Mrs. Trigg," he answered. "I don't think she believed me. Anyway, nothing wrong up there."

"You might take the birds away," she said. "I daren't go into the room to make the beds until you do. I'm scared."

"Nothing to scare you now," said Nat. "They're dead, aren't they?"

He went up with a sack and dropped the stiff bodies into it, one by one. Yes, there were fifty of them all told. Just the ordinary, common birds of the hedgerow; nothing as large even as a thrush. It must have been fright that made them act the way they did.

He took the sack out into the garden and was faced with a fresh problem. The ground was frozen solid, yet no snow had fallen; nothing had happened in the past hours but the coming of the east wind. It was unnatural, queer. He could see the white-capped seas breaking in the bay. He decided to take the birds to the shore and bury them.

When he reached the beach below the headland, he could scarcely stand, the force of the east wind was so strong. It was low tide; he crunched his way over the shingle* to the softer sand, then, his back to the wind, opened up his sack.

He ground a pit in the sand with his heel, meaning to drop the birds into it; but as he did so, the force of the wind lifted them as though in flight again, and they were blown away from him along the beach, tossed like feathers, spread and scattered.

The tide will take them when it turns, he said to himself.

He looked out to sea and watched the crested breakers, combing green. They rose stiffly, curled, and broke again; and because it was ebb tide, the roar was distant, more remote, lacking the sound and thunder of the flood.

Then he saw them. The gulls. Out there, riding the seas.

* *shingle*   stony beach

What he had thought at first were the whitecaps of the waves were gulls. Hundreds, thousands, tens of thousands.

They rose and fell in the troughs of the seas, heads to the wind, like a mighty fleet at anchor, waiting on the tide.

Nat turned; leaving the beach, he climbed the steep path home.

Someone should know of this. Someone should be told. Something was happening, because of the east wind and the weather, that he did not understand.

As he drew near the cottage, his wife came to meet him at the door. She called to him, excited. "Nat," she said, "it's on the wireless. They've just read out a special news bulletin. It's not only here, it's everywhere. In London, all over the country. Something has happened to the birds. Come listen; they're repeating it."

Together they went into the kitchen to listen to the announcement.

"Statement from the Home Office, at eleven A.M. this morning. Reports from all over the country are coming in hourly about the vast quantity of birds flocking above towns, villages, and outlying districts, causing obstruction and damage and even attacking individuals. It is thought that the Arctic airstream at present covering the British Isles is causing birds to migrate south in immense numbers, and that intense hunger may drive these birds to attack human beings. Householders are warned to see to their windows, doors, and chimneys, and to take reasonable precautions for the safety of their children. A further statement will be issued later."

A kind of excitement seized Nat. He looked at his wife in triumph. "There you are," he said. "I've been telling myself all morning there's something wrong. And just now, down on the beach, I looked out to sea and there were gulls, thousands of them, riding on the sea, waiting."

"What are they waiting for, Nat?" she asked.

He stared at her. "I don't know," he said slowly.

He went over to the drawer where he kept his hammer and other tools.

"What are you going to do, Nat?"

"See to the windows and the chimneys, like they tell you to."

"You think they would break in with the windows shut? Those wrens and robins and such? Why, how could they?"

He did not answer. He was not thinking of the robins and the wrens. He was thinking of the gulls.

He went upstairs and worked there the rest of the morning, boarding the windows of the bedrooms, filling up the chimney bases.

"Dinner's ready." His wife called him from the kitchen.

"All right. Coming down."

When dinner was over and his wife was washing up, Nat switched on the one o'clock news. The same announcement was repeated, but the news bulletin enlarged upon it. "The flocks of birds have caused dislocation in all areas," said the announcer, "and in London the mass was so dense at ten o'clock this morning that it seemed like a vast black cloud. The birds settled on rooftops, on window ledges, and on chimneys. The species included blackbird, thrush, the common house sparrow, and as might be expected in the metropolis, a vast quantity of pigeons, starlings, and that frequenter of the London river, the black-headed gull. The sight was so unusual that traffic came to a standstill in many thoroughfares, work was abandoned in shops and offices, and the streets and pavements were crowded with people standing about to watch the birds."

The announcer's voice was smooth and suave; Nat had the impression that he treated the whole business as he would an elaborate joke. There would be others like him, hundreds of them, who did not know what it was to struggle in darkness with a flock of birds.

Nat switched off the wireless. He got up and started work on the kitchen windows. His wife watched him, young Johnny at her heels.

"What they ought to do," she said, "is to call the Army out and shoot the birds."

"Let them try," said Nat. "How'd they set about it?"

"I don't know. But something should be done. They ought to do something."

Nat thought to himself that "they" were no doubt considering the problem at that very moment, but whatever "they" decided to do in London and the big cities would not help them here, nearly three hundred miles away.

"How are we off for food?" he asked.

"It's shopping day tomorrow, you know that. I don't keep uncooked food about. Butcher doesn't call till the day after. But I can bring back something when I go in tomorrow."

Nat did not want to scare her. He looked in the larder for himself and in the cupboard where she kept her tins.

They could hold out for a couple of days.

He went on hammering the boards across the kitchen windows. Candles. They were low on candles. That must be another thing she meant to buy tomorrow. Well, they must go early to bed tonight. That was, if—

He got up and went out the back door and stood in the garden, looking down toward the sea.

There had been no sun all day, and now, at barely three o'clock, a kind of darkness had already come; the sky was sullen, heavy, colorless like salt. He could hear the vicious sea drumming on the rocks.

He walked down the path halfway to the beach. And then he stopped. He could see the tide had turned. The gulls had risen. They were circling, hundreds of them, thousands of them, lifting their wings against the wind.

It was the gulls that made the darkening of the sky.

And they were silent. They just went on soaring and circling, rising, falling, trying their strength against the wind. Nat turned. He ran up the path back to the cottage.

"I'm going for Jill," he said to his wife.

"What's the matter?" she asked. "You've gone quite white."

"Keep Johnny inside," he said. "Keep the door shut. Light up now and draw the curtains."

"It's only gone three," she said.

"Never mind. Do what I tell you."

He looked inside the toolshed and took the hoe.

He started walking up the lane to the bus stop. Now and again he glanced back over his shoulder; and he could see the gulls had risen higher now, their circles were broader, they were spreading out in huge formation across the sky.

He hurried on. Although he knew the bus would not come before four o'clock, he had to hurry.

He waited at the top of the hill. There was half an hour still to go.

The east wind came whipping across the fields from the higher ground. In the distance he could see the clay hills, white and clean against the heavy pallor of the sky.

Something black rose from behind them, like a smudge at first, then widening, becoming deeper. The smudge became a cloud; and the cloud divided again into five other clouds, spreading north, east, south, and west; and then they were not clouds at all, but birds.

He watched them travel across the sky, within two or three hundred feet of him. He knew, from their speed, that they were bound inland; they had no business with the people here on the peninsula. They were rooks, crows, jackdaws, magpies, jays, all birds that usually preyed upon the smaller species, but bound this afternoon on some other mission.

He went to the telephone call box, stepped inside, lifted the receiver. The exchange would pass the message on. "I'm speaking from the highway," he said, "by the bus stop. I want to report large formations of birds traveling upcountry. The gulls are also forming in the bay."

"All right," answered the voice, laconic, weary.

"You'll be sure and pass this message on to the proper quarter?"

"Yes. Yes." Impatient now, fed up. The buzzing note resumed.

She's another, thought Nat. She doesn't care.

The bus came lumbering up the hill. Jill climbed out.

"What's the hoe for, Dad?"

"I just brought it along," he said. "Come on now, let's get home. It's cold; no hanging about. See how fast you can run."

He could see the gulls now, still silent, circling the fields, coming in toward the land.

"Look, Dad; look over there. Look at all the gulls."

"Yes. Hurry now."

"Where are they flying to? Where are they going?"

"Upcountry, I dare say. Where it's warmer."

He seized her hand and dragged her after him along the lane.

"Don't go so fast. I can't keep up."

The gulls were copying the rooks and the crows. They were spreading out, in formation, across the sky. They headed, in bands of thousands, to the four compass points.

"Dad, what is it? What are the gulls doing?"

They were not intent upon their flight, as the crows, as the jackdaws, had been. They still circled overhead. Nor did they fly so high. It was as though they waited upon some signal; as though some decision had yet to be given.

"I wish the gulls would go away," Jill was crying. "I don't like them. They're coming closer to the lane."

He started running, swinging Jill after him. As they went past the farm turning he saw the farmer backing his car into the garage. Nat called to him.

"Can you give us a lift?" he said.

Mr. Trigg turned in the driver's seat and stared at them. Then a smile came to his cheerful, rubicund face. "It looks as though we're in for some fun," he said. "Have you seen the gulls? Jim and I are going to take a crack at them. Everyone's gone bird crazy, talking of nothing else. I hear you were troubled in the night. Want a gun?"

Nat shook his head.

The small car was packed, but there was room for Jill on the back seat.

"I don't want a gun," said Nat, "but I'd be obliged if you'd run Jill home. She's scared of the birds."

"Okay," said the farmer. "I'll take her home. Why don't you stop behind and join the shooting match? We'll make the feathers fly."

Jill climbed in, and turning the car, the driver sped up the lane. Nat followed after. Trigg must be crazy. What use was a gun against a sky of birds?

They were coming in now toward the farm, circling lower in the sky. The farm, then, was their target. Nat increased his pace toward his own cottage. He saw the farmer's car turn and come back along the lane. It drew up beside him with a jerk.

"The kid has run inside," said the farmer. "Your wife was

watching for her. Well, what do you make of it? They're saying in town the Russians have done it. The Russians have poisoned the birds."

"How could they do that?" asked Nat.

"Don't ask me. You know how stories get around."

"Have you boarded your windows?" asked Nat.

"No. Lot of nonsense. I've had more to do today than to go round boarding up my windows."

"I'd board them now if I were you."

"Garn. You're windy. Like to come to our place to sleep?"

"No, thanks all the same."

"All right. See you in the morning. Give you a gull breakfast."

The farmer grinned and turned his car to the farm entrance. Nat hurried on. Past the little wood, past the old barn, and then across the stile to the remaining field. As he jumped the stile, he heard the whir of wings. A black-backed gull dived down at him from the sky. It missed, swerved in flight, and rose to dive again. In a moment it was joined by others—six, seven, a dozen.

Nat dropped his hoe. The hoe was useless. Covering his head with his arms, he ran toward the cottage.

They kept coming at him from the air—noiseless, silent, save for the beating wings. The terrible, fluttering wings. He could feel the blood on his hands, his wrists, upon his neck. If only he could keep them from his eyes. Nothing else mattered.

With each dive, with each attack, they became bolder. And they had no thought for themselves. When they dived low and missed, they crashed, bruised and broken, on the ground.

As Nat ran he stumbled, kicking their spend bodies in front of him.

He found the door and hammered upon it with his bleeding hands. "Let me in," he shouted. "It's Nat. Let me in."

Then he saw the gannet, poised for the dive, above him in the sky.

The gulls circled, retired, soared, one with another, against the wind.

Only the gannet remained. One single gannet, above him in the sky. Its wings folded suddenly to its body. It dropped like a stone.

Nat screamed; and the door opened.

He stumbled across the threshold, and his wife threw her weight against the door.

They heard the thud of the gannet as it fell.

His wife dressed his wounds. They were not deep. The backs of his hands had suffered most, and his wrists. Had he not worn a cap, the birds would have reached his head. As for the gannet—the gannet could have split his skull.

The children were crying, of course. They had seen the blood on their father's hands.

"It's all right now," he told them. "I'm not hurt."

His wife was ashen. "I saw them overhead," she whispered. "They began collecting just as Jill ran in with Mr. Trigg. I shut the door fast, and it jammed. That's why I couldn't open it at once when you came."

"Thank God the birds waited for me," he said. "Jill would have fallen at once. They're flying inland, thousands of them. Rooks, crows, all the bigger birds. I saw them from the bus stop. They're making for the towns."

"But what can they do, Nat?"

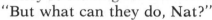

"They'll attack. Go for everyone out in the streets. Then they'll try the windows, the chimneys."

"Why don't the authorities do something? Why don't they get the Army, get machine guns?"

"There's been no time. Nobody's prepared. We'll hear what they have to say on the six o'clock news."

"I can hear the birds," Jill said. "Listen, Dad."

Nat listened. Muffled sounds came from the windows, from the door. Wings brushing the surface, sliding, scraping, seeking a way of entry. The sound of many bodies pressed together, shuffling on the sills. Now and again came a thud, a crash, as some bird dived and fell.

Some of them will kill themselves that way, he thought, but not enough. Never enough.

"All right," he said aloud. "I've got boards over the windows, Jill. The birds can't get in."

He went and examined all the windows. He found wedges—pieces of old tin, strips of wood and metal—and fastened them at the sides of the windows to reinforce the boards.

His hammering helped to deafen the sound of the birds, the shuffling, the tapping, and—more ominous—the splinter of breaking glass.

"Turn on the wireless," he said.

He went upstairs to the bedrooms and reinforced the windows there. Now he could hear the birds on the roof—the scraping of claws, a sliding, jostling sound.

He decided the whole family must sleep in the kitchen and keep up the fire. He was afraid of the bedroom chimneys. The boards he had placed at their bases might give way. In the kitchen they would be safe because of the fire.

He would have to make a joke of it. Pretend to the children they were playing camp. If the worst happened and the birds forced an entry by way of the bedroom chimneys, it would be hours, days perhaps, before they could break down the doors. The birds would be imprisoned in the bedrooms. They could do no harm there. Crowded together, they would stifle and die. He began to bring the mattresses downstairs.

At sight of them, his wife's eyes widened in apprehension.

"All right," he said cheerfully. "We'll all sleep together in the kitchen tonight. More cozy, here by the fire. Then we won't be worried by those silly old birds tapping at the windows."

He made the children help him rearrange the furniture, and he took the precaution of moving the dresser against the windows.

We're safe enough now, he thought. We're snug and tight. We can hold out. It's just the food that worries me. Food and coal for the fire. We've enough for two or three days, not more. By that time—

No use thinking ahead as far as that. And they'd be given directions on the wireless.

And now, in the midst of many problems, he realized that only dance music was coming over the air. He knew the reason. The usual programs had been abandoned; this only happened at exceptional times.

At six o'clock the records ceased. The time signal was given. There was a pause, and then the announcer spoke. His voice was solemn, grave. Quite different from midday.

"This is London," he said. "A national emergency was proclaimed at four o'clock this afternoon. Measures are being taken to safeguard the lives and property of the population, but it must be understood that these are not easy to effect immediately, owing to the unforeseen and unparalleled nature of the present crisis. Every householder must take precautions about his own building. Where several people live together, as in flats and hotels, they must unite to do the utmost that they can to prevent entry. It is absolutely imperative that every individual stay indoors tonight.

"The birds, in vast numbers, are attacking anyone on sight, and have already begun an assault upon buildings; but these, with due care, should be impenetrable.

"The population is asked to remain calm.

"Owing to the exceptional nature of the emergency, there will be no further transmission from any broadcasting station until seven A.M. tomorrow."

They played "God Save the Queen." Nothing more happened.

Nat switched off the set. He looked at his wife. She stared back at him.

"We'll have supper early," suggested Nat. "Something for a treat—toasted cheese, eh? Something we all like."

He winked and nodded at his wife. He wanted the look of dread, of apprehension, to leave her face.

He helped with the supper, whistling, singing, making as much clatter as he could. It seemed to him that the shuffling and the tapping were not so intense as they had been at first, and presently he went up to the bedrooms and listened. He no longer heard the jostling for place upon the roof.

They've got reasoning powers, he thought. They know it's hard to break in here. They'll try elsewhere.

Supper passed without incident. Then, when they were clearing away, they heard a new sound, a familiar droning.

His wife looked up at him, her face alight.

"It's planes," she said. "They're sending out planes after the birds. That will get them. Isn't that gunfire? Can't you hear guns?"

It might be gunfire, out at sea. Nat could not tell. Big naval guns might have some effect upon the gulls out at sea, but the gulls were inland now. The guns couldn't shell the shore because of the population.

"It's good, isn't it," said his wife, "to hear the planes?"

Catching her enthusiasm, Jill jumped up and down with Johnny. "The planes will get the birds."

Just then they heard a crash about two miles distant. Followed by a second, then a third. The droning became more distant, passed away out to sea.

"What was that?" asked his wife.

"I don't know," answered Nat. He did not want to tell her that the sound they had heard was the crashing of aircraft.

It was, he had no doubt, a gamble on the part of the authorities to send out reconnaissance forces, but they might have known the gamble was suicidal. What could aircraft do against birds that flung themselves to death against propeller and fuselage but hurtle to the ground themselves?

"Where have the planes gone, Dad?" asked Jill.

"Back to base," he said. "Come on now, time to tuck down for bed."

There was no further drone of aircraft, and the naval guns had ceased. Waste of life and effort, Nat said to himself. We can't destroy enough of them that way. Cost too heavy. There's always gas. Maybe they'll try spraying with gas, mustard gas.

We'll be warned first, of course, if they do. There's one thing, the best brains of the country will be on it tonight.

Upstairs in the bedrooms all was quiet. No more scraping and stabbing at the windows. A lull in battle. The wind hadn't dropped, though. Nat could still hear it roaring in the chimneys. And the sea breaking down on the shore.

Then he remembered the tide. The tide would be on the turn. Maybe the lull in battle was because of the tide. There was some law the birds obeyed, and it had to do with the east wind and the tide.

He glanced at his watch. Nearly eight o'clock. It must have gone high water an hour ago. That explained the lull. The birds attacked with the flood tide.

He reckoned the time limit in his head. They had six hours to go without attack. When the tide turned again, around 1:20 in the morning, the birds would come back.

He called softly to his wife and whispered to her that he would go out and see how they were faring at the farm, see if the telephone was still working there so that they might get news from the exchange.

"You're not to go," she said at once, "and leave me alone with the children. I can't stand it."

"All right," he said, "all right. I'll wait till morning. And we can get the wireless bulletin then, too, at seven. But when the tide ebbs again, I'll try for the farm; they may let us have bread and potatoes."

His mind was busy again, planning against emergency. They would not have milked, of course, this evening. The cows would be standing by the gate, waiting; the household would be inside, battened behind boards as they were here at the cottage.

That is, if they had had time to take precautions.

Softly, stealthily, he opened the back door and looked outside.

It was pitch-dark. The wind was blowing harder than ever, coming in steady gusts, icy, from the sea.

He kicked at the step. It was heaped with birds. These were the suicides, the divers, the ones with broken necks. Wherever he looked, he saw dead birds. The living had flown seaward with the turn of the tide. The gulls would be riding the seas now, as they had done in the forenoon.

In the far distance on the hill, something was burning. One of the aircraft that had crashed; the fire, fanned by the wind, had set light to a stack.

He looked at the bodies of the birds. He had a notion that if he stacked them, one upon the other, on the window sills, they would be added protection against the next attack.

Not much, perhaps, but something. The bodies would have to be clawed at, pecked and dragged aside before the living birds gained purchase on the sills and attacked the panes.

He set to work in the darkness. It was queer. He hated touching the dead birds, but he went on with his work. He noticed grimly that every windowpane was shattered. Only the boards had kept the birds from breaking in.

He stuffed the cracked panes with the bleeding bodies of the birds and felt his stomach turn. When he had finished, he went back into the cottage and barricaded the kitchen door, making it doubly secure.

His wife had made him cocoa; he drank it thirstily. He was very tired. "All right," he said, smiling, "don't worry. We'll get through."

He lay down on his mattress and closed his eyes.

He dreamed uneasily because, through his dreams, ran the dread of something forgotten. Some piece of work that he should have done. It was connected, in some way, with the burning aircraft.

It was his wife, shaking his shoulder, who awoke him finally.

"They've begun," she sobbed. "They've started this last hour. I can't listen to it any longer alone. There's something smells bad too, something burning."

Then he remembered. He had forgotten to make up the fire.

The fire was smoldering, nearly out. He got up swiftly and lighted the lamp.

The hammering had started at the windows and the door, but it was not that he minded now. It was the smell of singed feathers.

The smell filled the kitchen. He knew what it was at once. The birds were coming down the chimney, squeezing their way down to the kitchen range.

He got sticks and paper and put them on the embers, then reached for the can of kerosene.

"Stand back," he shouted to his wife. He threw some of the kerosene onto the fire.

The flame roared up the pipe, and down into the fire fell the scorched, blackened bodies of the birds.

The children waked, crying. "What is it?" asked Jill. "What's happened?"

Nat had no time to answer her. He was raking the bodies from the chimney, clawing them out onto the floor.

The flames would drive away the living birds from the chimney top. The lower joint was the difficulty though. It was choked with the smoldering, helpless bodies of the birds caught by fire.

He scarcely heeded the attack on the windows and the door. Let them beat their wings, break their backs, lose their lives, in the desperate attempt to force an entry into his home. They would not break in.

"Stop crying," he called to the children. "There's nothing to be afraid of. Stop crying."

He went on raking out the burning, smoldering bodies as they fell into the fire.

This'll fetch them, he said to himself. The draft and the flames together. We're all right as long as the chimney doesn't catch.

Amid the tearing at the window boards came the sudden homely striking of the kitchen clock. Three o'clock.

A little more than four hours to go. He could not be sure of the exact time of high water. He reckoned the tide would not turn much before half past seven.

He waited by the range. The flames were dying. But no more blackened bodies fell from the chimney. He thrust his poker up as far as it could go and found nothing.

The danger of the chimney's being choked up was over. It could not happen again, not if the fire was kept burning day and night.

I'll have to get more fuel from the farm tomorrow, he thought. I can do all that with the ebb tide. It can be worked; we can fetch what we need when the tide's turned. We've just got to adapt ourselves, that's all.

They drank tea and cocoa, ate slices of bread. Only half a loaf left, Nat noticed. Never mind, though; they'd get by.

If they could hang on like this until seven, when the first news bulletin came through, they would not have done too badly.

"Give us a smoke," he said to his wife. "It will clear away the smell of the scorched feathers."

"There's only two left in the packet," she said. "I was going to buy you some."

"I'll have one," he said.

He sat with one arm around his wife and one around Jill, with Johnny on his lap, the blankets heaped about them on the mattress.

"You can't help admiring the beggars," he said. "They've got persistency. You'd think they'd tire of the game, but not a bit of it."

Admiration was hard to sustain. The tapping went on and on; and a new, rasping note struck Nat's ear, as though a sharper beak than any hitherto had come to take over from its fellows.

He tried to remember the names of birds; he tried to think which species would go for this particular job.

It was not the tap of the woodpecker. That would be light and frequent. This was more serious; if it continued long, the wood would splinter as the glass had done.

Then he remembered the hawks. Could the hawks have taken over from the gulls? Were there buzzards now upon the sills, using talons as well as beaks? Hawks, buzzards, kestrels, falcons; he had forgotten the birds of prey. He had forgotten the gripping power of the birds of prey. Three hours to go; and while they waited, the sound of the splintering wood, the talons tearing at the wood.

Nat looked about him, seeing what furniture he could destroy to fortify the door.

The windows were safe because of the dresser. He was not certain of the door. He went upstairs; but when he reached the landing, he paused and listened.

There was a soft patter on the floor of the children's bedroom. The birds had broken through.

The other bedroom was still clear. He brought out the

furniture to pile at the head of the stairs should the door of the children's bedroom go.

"Come down, Nat. What are you doing?" called his wife.

"I won't be long," he shouted. "I'm just making everything shipshape up here."

He did not want her to come. He did not want her to hear the pattering in the children's bedroom, the brushing of those wings against the door.

After he suggested breakfast, he found himself watching the clock, gazing at the hands that went so slowly around the dial. If his theory was not correct, if the attack did not cease with the turn of the tide, he knew they were beaten. They could not continue through the long day without air, without rest, without fuel.

A crackling in his ears drove away the sudden, desperate desire for sleep.

"What is it? What now?" he said sharply.

"The wireless," said his wife. "I've been watching the clock. It's nearly seven."

The comfortable crackling of the wireless brought new life.

They waited. The kitchen clock struck seven.

The crackling continued. Nothing else. No chimes. No music.

They waited until a quarter past. No news bulletin came through.

"We heard wrong," he said. "They won't be broadcasting until eight o'clock."

They left the wireless switched on. Nat thought of the battery, wondered how much power was left in the battery. If it failed, they would not hear the instructions.

"It's getting light," whispered his wife. "I can't see it but I can feel it. And listen! The birds aren't hammering so loud now."

She was right. The rasping, tearing sound grew fainter every moment. So did the shuffling, the jostling for place upon the step, upon the sills. The tide was on the turn.

By eight there was no sound at all. Only the wind. And the crackling of the wireless. The children, lulled at last by the stillness, fell asleep.

At half past eight, Nat switched the wireless off.

"We'll miss the news," said his wife.

"There isn't going to be any news," said Nat. "We've got to depend upon ourselves."

He went to the door and slowly pulled away the barricades. He drew the bolts and kicking the broken bodies from the step outside the door, breathed the cold air.

He had six working hours before him, and he knew he must reserve his strength to the utmost, not waste it in any way.

Food and light and fuel; these were the most necessary things. If he could get them, they could endure another night.

He stepped into the garden; and as he did so, he saw the living birds. The gulls had gone to ride the sea, as they had done before. They sought seafood and the buoyancy of the tide before they returned to the attack.

Not so the land birds. They waited, and watched.

Nat saw them on the hedgerows, on the soil, crowded in the trees, outside in the field—line upon line of birds, still, doing nothing. He went to the end of his small garden.

The birds did not move. They merely watched him.

I've got to get food, Nat said to himself. I've got to go to the farm to get food.

He went back to the cottage. He saw to the windows and the door.

"I'm going to the farm," he said.

His wife clung to him. She had seen the living birds from the open door.

"Take us with you," she begged. "We can't stay here alone. I'd rather die than stay here alone."

"Come on, then," he said. "Bring baskets and Johnny's pram. We can load up the pram."

They dressed against the biting wind. His wife put Johnny in the pram, and Nat took Jill's hand.

"The birds," Jill whimpered. "They're all out there in the fields."

"They won't hurt us," he said. "Not in the light."

They started walking across the field toward the stile, and the birds did not move. They waited, their heads turned to the wind.

When they reached the turning to the farm, Nat stopped and told his wife to wait in the shelter of the hedge with the two children. "But I want to see Mrs. Trigg," she protested. "There are lots of things we can borrow if they went to market yesterday, and—"

"Wait here," Nat interrupted. "I'll be back in a moment."

The cows were lowing, moving restlessly in the yard, and he could see a gap in the fence where the sheep had knocked their way through to roam unchecked in the front garden before the farmhouse.

No smoke came from the chimneys. Nat was filled with misgiving. He did not want his wife or children to go down to the farm.

He went down alone, pushing his way through the herd of lowing cows, who turned this way and that, distressed, their udders full.

He saw the car standing by the gate. Not put away in the garage.

All the windows of the farmhouse were smashed. There were many dead gulls lying in the yard and around the house.

The living birds perched on the group of trees behind the farm and on the roof of the house. They were quite still. They watched him. Jim's body lay in the yard. What was left of it. His gun was beside him.

The door of the house was shut and bolted, but it was easy to push up a smashed window and climb through.

Trigg's body was close to the telephone. He must have been trying to get through to the exchange when the birds got him. The receiver was off the hook, the instrument was torn from the wall.

No sign of Mrs. Trigg. She would be upstairs. Was it any use going up? Sickened, Nat knew what he would find there.

Thank God, he said to himself, there were no children.

He forced himself to climb the stairs, but halfway up he turned and descended again. He could see Mrs. Trigg's legs protruding from the open bedroom door. Beside her were the bodies of black-backed gulls and an umbrella, broken. It's no use doing anything, Nat thought. I've only got five hours; less than that. The Triggs would understand. I must load up with what I can find.

He tramped back to his wife and children.

"I'm going to fill up the car with stuff," he said. "We'll take it home and return for a fresh load."

"What about the Triggs?" asked his wife.

"They must have gone to friends," he said.

"Shall I come and help you then?"

"No, there's a mess down there. Cows and sheep all over the place. Wait; I'll get the car. You can sit in the car."

Her eyes watched his all the time he was talking. He believed she understood. Otherwise she certainly would have insisted on helping him find the bread and groceries.

They made three journeys altogether, to and from the farm, before he was satisfied they had everything they needed. It was surprising, once he started thinking, how many things were necessary. Almost the most important of all was planking for the windows. He had to go around searching for timber. He wanted to renew the boards on all the windows at the cottage.

On the final journey he drove the car to the bus stop and got out and went to the telephone box.

He waited a few minutes, jangling the hook. No good, though. The line was dead. He climbed onto a bank and looked over the countryside, but there was no sign of life at all, nothing in the fields but the waiting, watching birds.

Some of them slept; he could see their beaks tucked into their feathers.

You'd think they'd be feeding, he said to himself, not just standing that way.

Then he remembered. They were gorged with food. They had eaten their fill during the night. That was why they did not move this morning.

He lifted his face to the sky. It was colorless, gray. The bare trees looked bent and blackened by the east wind.

The cold did not affect the living birds, waiting out there in the fields.

This is the time they ought to get them, Nat said to himself. They're a sitting target now. They must be doing this all over the country. Why don't our aircraft take off now and spray them with mustard gas? What are all our chaps doing? They must know; they must see for themselves.

He went back to the car and got into the driver's seat.

"Go quickly past that second gate," whispered his wife. "The postman's lying there. I don't want Jill to see."

It was a quarter to one by the time they reached the cottage. Only an hour to go.

"Better have dinner," said Nat. "Hot up something for yourself and the children, some of that soup. I've no time to eat now. I've got to unload all this stuff from the car."

He got everything inside the cottage. It could be sorted later. Give them all something to do during the long hours ahead.

First he must see to the windows and the door.

He went around the cottage methodically, testing every window and the door. He climbed onto the roof also, and fixed boards across every chimney except the kitchen's.

The cold was so intense he could hardly bear it, but the job had to be done. Now and again he looked up, searching the sky for aircraft. None came. As he worked, he cursed the inefficiency of the authorities.

He paused, his work on the bedroom chimney finished, and looked out to sea. Something was moving out there. Something gray and white among the breakers.

"Good old Navy," he said. "They never let us down. They're coming down channel; they're turning into the bay."

He waited, straining his eyes toward the sea. He was wrong, though. The Navy was not there. It was the gulls rising from the sea. And the massed flocks in the fields, with ruffled feathers, rose in formation from the ground and, wing to wing, soared upward to the sky.

The tide had turned again.

Nat climbed down the ladder and went inside the cottage. The family were at dinner. It was a little after two.

He bolted the door, put up the barricade, and lighted the lamp.

"It's nighttime," said young Johnny.

His wife had switched on the wireless once again. The crackling sound came, but nothing else.

"I've been all round the dial," she said, "foreign stations and all. I can't get anything but the crackling."

"Maybe they have the same trouble," he said. "Maybe it's the same right through Europe."

They ate in silence.

The tapping began at the windows, at the door, the rustling, the jostling, the pushing for position on the sills. The first thud of the suicide gulls upon the step.

When he had finished dinner, Nat planned, he would put the supplies away, stack them neatly, get everything shipshape. The boards were strong against the windows and across the chimneys. The cottage was filled with stores, with fuel, with all they needed for the next few days.

His wife could help him, the children too. They'd tire themselves out between now and a quarter to nine, when the tide would ebb; then he'd tuck them down on their mattresses, see that they slept good and sound until three in the morning.

He had a new scheme for the windows, which was to fix barbed wire in front of the boards. He had brought a great roll of it from the farm. The nuisance was, he'd have to work at this in the dark, when the lull came between nine and three. Pity he had not thought of it before. Still, as long as the wife and kids slept—that was the main thing.

The smaller birds were at the windows now. He recognized the light tap-tapping of their beaks and the soft brush of their wings.

The hawks ignored the windows. They concentrated their attack upon the door.

Nat listened to the tearing sound of splintering wood, and wondered how many million years of memory were stored in those little brains, behind the stabbing beaks, the piercing eyes, now giving them this instinct to destroy mankind with all the deft precision of machines.

"I'll smoke that last cigarette," he said to his wife. "Stupid of me. It was the one thing I forgot to bring back from the farm."

He reached for it, switched on the crackling wireless.

He threw the empty packet onto the fire and watched it burn.

Reading for Understanding

Main Idea

1. Which of the following quotations best expresses the main idea of the story?
    (a) "It will be a hard winter. That's why the birds are restless."
    (b) "... million years of memory ... now giving them this instinct to destroy mankind with all the deft precision of machines."
    (c) "Maybe it's the same right through Europe."
    (d) There was some law the birds obeyed, and it had to do with the east wind and the tide.

Details

2. Nat Hocken lived   (a) in a suburb of London   (b) on a finger of land jutting into the sea   (c) high in the forested mountains   (d) on an island off the coast of England.

3. Which of the following is *not* true of Nat Hocken?
    (a) He had his own farm.
    (b) His wartime injury limited him to part-time employment.
    (c) He was used to making his own decisions.
    (d) He was used to working alone.

4. The usual wind came from the   (a) north   (b) south   (c) east   (d) west.

5. Nat almost lost his life when   (a) he went to the farm   (b) the door jammed   (c) the window broke   (d) he drove the car.

Inferences

6. Nat was approximately   (a) 18 years old   (b) 20 years old   (c) 30 years old   (d) 50 years old.

7. Nat was   (a) reckless   (b) cautious   (c) hesitant   (d) impulsive.

8. The wireless Nat relied on was equivalent to the American
   (a) television   (b) radio   (c) tape recorder
   (d) duplicator.

9. Even though messages ceased coming through, Nat kept
   the wireless in operation   (a) in order not to lose all
   hope   (b) to see if he could help others   (c) to report
   on how his area was surviving   (d) to find out how
   severe the disaster really was.

10. Which of the following is not true of the birds?
    (a) Their attack was effective because there were so many
    of them.   (b) Their concern was the destruction of man-
    kind and not their own survival.   (c) They did not use
    mankind as a source of food.   (d) Bombs and airplanes
    were ineffective against them.

Order of Events

11. Arrange the events in the order in which they occurred.
    Use letters only.
    A. Nat stocked up with provisions from the farmhouse.
    B. Nat went to the farmhouse for supplies.
    C. Mr. Trigg felt that his gun would give him sufficient
       protection.
    D. The birds came into the children's room through the
       open window.
    E. Nat put barbed wire around the boarded windows.

Outcomes

12. Nat proved that   (a) he and his family could survive the
    attacks indefinitely   (b) the birds would destroy all of
    mankind   (c) to survive we must be adaptable
    (d) national leadership is necessary for survival.

Cause and Effect

13. The tragic mistake Mr. Trigg made was   (a) not stocking
    up with food   (b) following the advice given over the
    wireless   (c) relying on traditional means of protection
    (d) refusing to assist Nat.

Fact or Opinion

Tell whether each of the following is a fact or an opinion.

14. Nat was better trained to follow orders than was Mr. Trigg.

15. If the weather had not changed, the birds would not have attacked.

Words in Context

1. Their *agitation* more remarked because the days were still.
   Agitation (464) means   (a) frenzy   (b) emotional upset   (c) quiet acceptance   (d) quarrelsomeness.

2. As Mr. Trigg's tractor traced its path up and down the western hills, and Nat, *hedging*, saw it dip and turn . . .
   Hedging (464) means   (a) plowing   (b) weeding
   (c) repairing the equipment   (d) repairing the fencing.

3. . . . the whole machine and the man upon it were *momentarily* lost in the great cloud of wheeling, crying birds.
   Momentarily (464) means   (a) for a second
   (b) quickly   (c) after a while   (d) thoroughly.

4. He waited, listened; there was no sound except the *fretful* crying of one of the children from the bedroom beyond.
   Fretful (465) means   (a) cranky   (b) panicky
   (c) loud   (d) sad.

5. His wife looked up at Nat, searching his face for *confirmation*.
   Confirmation (466) means   (a) denial   (b) confidence
   (c) comfort   (d) agreement.

6. Soon the bus came *ambling* up the hill.
   Ambling (467) means   (a) chugging   (b) racing
   (c) slowly   (d) noisily.

7. Statement from the *Home Office*, at eleven A.M. this morning.

The *Home Office* (469) is the British equivalent of our
(a) public broadcasting system   (b) Department of
Justice   (c) mayor   (d) agencies dealing with
internal affairs.

8. The announcer's voice was smooth and *suave*.
    Suave (470) means   (a) threatening   (b) agreeable
    (c) pitying   (c) direct.

9. They were not *intent upon* their flight, as the crows, as the
    jackdaws, had been.
    Intent upon (473) means   (a) settling on   (b) forgetful
    of   (c) concentrating on   (d) discontinuing.

10. His wife was *ashen*.
    Ashen (475) means   (a) speechless   (b) hysterical
    (c) concerned   (d) pale.

11. A national emergency was *proclaimed* at four o'clock this
    afternoon.
    Proclaimed (477) means   (a) enacted   (b) declared
    (c) vetoed   (d) planned.

12. The birds, in vast numbers, are attacking anyone on sight,
    and have already begun an assault upon buildings; but
    these, with due care, should be *impenetrable*.
    Impenetrable (477) means cannot be   (a) lost
    (b) sold   (c) protected   (d) entered.

13. It was, he had no doubt, a gamble on the part of the
    authorities to send out *reconnaissance* forces, but they
    might have known the gamble was suicidal.
    Reconnaissance (478) means   (a) bombing
    (b) powerful   (c) exploratory   (d) considerable.

14. What could aircraft do against the birds that flung them-
    selves to death against propeller and fuselage but *hurtle* to
    the ground themselves?
    Hurtle (478) means   (a) plunge   (b) drift   (c) follow
    (d) descend.

15. A *lull* in battle.
    Lull (479) means   (a) defeat   (b) purpose   (c) pause
    (d) decision.

16. He called softly to his wife and whispered to her that he
    would go out and see how they were *faring* at the farm . . .

Faring (479) means	(a) recovering	(b) protected
(c) provisioned	(d) getting along.

17.	He got sticks and paper and put them on the *embers*, then
reached for the can of kerosene.
Embers (481) means	(a) birds	(b) fire bed
(c) stove	(d) pile of wood.

18.	Three hours to go; and while they waited, the sound of the
splintering wood, the *talons* tearing at the wood.
Talons (482) means	(a) birds	(b) hawks	(c) beaks
(d) claws.

19.	They sought seafood and the *buoyancy* of the tide before
they returned to the attack.
Buoyancy (484) means	(a) protection	(b) warmth
(c) direction	(d) floating power.

20.	They were *gorged with* food.
Gorged with (486) means	(a) looking for	(b) hungry
for	(c) stuffed with	(d) completely without.

Thinking Critically About the Story _____

1.	As the author wrote it, the story has no ending. How effective
is such a conclusion? How would you have ended it?

2.	Nat Hocken and Farmer Trigg are in sharp contrast. Which
one was better prepared to survive in the world of today?
In the battle with the birds?

3.	What qualities did Nat possess to make him a survivor? To
what extent do most people have such qualities?

4.	How did the author make use of realistic details to make
this story have the ring of truth?

5.	How did the author intensify our sense of horror as we read
the story? Why did she relate incidents that included Nat's
wife and children? Was she taking unfair advantage of the
reader?

6.	What are the possibilities of a story like this ever really happening? Why do so many people become so fascinated by stories of this genre that they become fans for life? Are you ready to become one? Justify your answer.

Stories in Words

Peninsula (463)   A *peninsula* is a land area that juts out into the water and is connected to the mainland by a narrow strip of land. Here is a word whose history gives a clue that will help you to remember it always. The first portion is the Latin *paene*, "almost." The second, *insula*, means "island." A peninsula is "almost an island," a perfect interpretation of the word's meaning.

Bewildered (464)   This is a fascinating word to track down. The first syllable, *be*, means "thoroughly." *Bewhiskered* means "thoroughly whiskered." *Befuddled* means "thoroughly confused." *Bejeweled* means "thoroughly covered with jewels." The two parts of *wildered* mean "wild deer." From *wildered* came *wilderness*, the "place of wild deer." *Bewildered* is "being lost in the deep forest, the place of the wild deer; confused."

Laconic (472)   The Laconians of ancient Greece inhabited a portion of Greece that had Sparta as the capital. Because the military arts were cultivated from early childhood, the Laconians were awesome in battle. They also had a reputation for wasting no words. Once a messenger from Athens told them, "If we come to your city, we will burn it to the ground." The Laconians answered with one word: *If*. Laconic speech is brief and to the point.

Fellow Creatures

ACTIVITIES

Thinking Critically About the Stories ___

1. How does Ken's mother, Nell, compare with Peg's mother? How close do they come to your idea of an ideal parent? Are they too good to be true? How do they compare with the mother in a movie you saw recently?

2. Compare Nat Hocken's approach to his problem with Farmer Trigg's. With Peg's. With Ken's. With Leiningen's. With your own. Which do you think is most effective?

3. Compare Ken and Peg. What do they have in common? Are they "typical teenagers"? How do they compare with your friends? Would you be willing to have either or both as friends?

4. Compare the "fellow creatures" in the four stories: Flicka, Rollie, the ants, the birds. How true to life are they? Justify your answer.

5. Compare how the author of each of the stories built up suspense and fear. Be prepared to read to the class excerpts from the stories to prove your statements.

Writing and Other Activities ___

1. From the daily newspaper clip an item that reports:
   (a) How someone saved another's life through quick thinking. Retell the story from the point of view of the near-victim.

(b) The details of a natural disaster. Retell the story from the point of view of someone who was caught in it—and escaped.

(c) The story of an automobile accident in which several people were injured. Retell the story from the point of view of the driver of the car that was hit.

2. Write an informal editorial to appear in the school newspaper on one of the following:

(a) A tribute to the patience of our family pet.

(b) Recollection of the most pleasant experience I had with our family pet.

(c) Recall a day you could have spent with the dog you never had.

(d) Why my neighbor's dog and I can never be friends.

3. Plan to lead a class discussion on one of the following:

(a) Having a pet dog or cat in a large public housing unit or in the crowded inner city.

(b) Reasons for choosing and not choosing to own a pet.

(c) Sharing responsibility for the family pet.

(d) Getting along with pet animals of your friends and relatives.

4. Plan a panel discussion to be held by the class on one of the following:

(a) To what extent are we responsible for the lives and welfare of our fellow creatures?

(b) Why should we save any species from extinction?

(c) Should scientists be allowed to experiment on living creatures?

(d) Should we keep other creatures imprisoned in cages in zoos as permanent exhibits?

5. Describe the scene and write the inner dialog for a slice-of-life story dealing with one of the following:

(a) Younger teenager talking to parent (parents) about "going easy" with older sibling who is having a crisis.

(b) Dismissed member asking the coach for "a second chance."

(c) Older sibling explaining to young teenager why parents "act that way."

(d) Parent discussing with a child the fear brought on by a horror movie.

(e) Parent handling strong feelings of guilt that have depressed teenager who has "broken off" with his best friend.

Stories in Words: A Review

A. auspicious	E. fervently	I. peninsula
B. bewildered	F. laconic	J. ravenous
C. corral	G. murmured	K. remorse
D. discordantly	H. pantomime	L. stoical

Answer the following questions by choosing a word from the list above. Use letters only.

Which of the words above . . .

1. . . . means "almost an island"?

2. . . . suggests using birds for fortune-telling?

3. . . . holds the vivid image "biting again"?

4. . . . is associated with the place where a Greek philosopher taught?

5. . . . comes from the name of an ancient Greek warlike people?

6. . . . has the word for *heart* at its root?

7. . . . suggests a word origin that seems obvious but is incorrect?

8. . . . has a sound that suggests the meaning?

9. . . . has the word for *deer* in it?

10. . . . contains the root word for *imitator*?

7

World of People

"Fiction is a fulcrum that can lift us out of our daily lives and for a brief time involve us in events with people we could never meet otherwise."

When we read a traditional story of adventure we consciously or unconsciously identify with the hero. Once we are in the story we become the knight in white armor, the cowboy wearing the white hat, the courageous princess in a white dress. We easily turn against the dark-clothed bully, the witch in black, or the black-mustached swindler who is either sloppily dressed or too elegantly dressed.

Great is our satisfaction when, as expected, the evil ones go down in defeat, and the forces for good ride into the sunset with happiness assured.

The traditional story is assured lasting popularity; it dominates TV, movies, and current best-selling books. However, the modern short story has added to the variety of plots, characters, and settings. The characters we are asked to identify with are not all good or all bad. They approach the complexity of real-life people who are always a mixture of both admirable and unadmirable traits.

The four stories in Unit Seven will give you a chance to meet this newer genre. Don't try to decide which type of story you like better. Learn to like both, the story that brings adventure into your life and the story that brings you into the reality that real or almost-real people have to face.

One Thousand Dollars

O. Henry

♦ "A thousand dollars," he said, "means much or little. One man may buy a happy home with it and laugh at Rockefeller . . . *You* could count upon a half hour's diversion with it at faro . . . "

All too often a story that deserves wide acceptance is overlooked because time in its endless march toward change has dated a minor aspect of the plot. To find excitement and tension in this story of young love, you have to be willing to accept the fact that when it was written, a thousand dollars then was the equivalent of twenty thousand today, and that the interest from $50,000 could support a life of ease and luxury.

But . . . this is a story written by O. Henry, the master of the surprise ending, the explorer into the unexpected byways of human nature. Let the author weave the web to catch your imagination and interest!

ONE THOUSAND DOLLARS

"One thousand dollars," repeated Lawyer Tolman, solemnly and severely, "and here is the money."

Young Gillian gave a decidedly amused laugh as he fingered the thin package of new fifty-dollar notes.

"It's such a confoundedly awkward amount," he explained, genially, to the lawyer. "If it had been ten thousand a fellow might wind up with a lot of fireworks and do himself credit. Even fifty dollars would have been less trouble."

"You heard the reading of your uncle's will," continued Lawyer Tolman, professionally dry in his tones. "I do not know if you paid much attention to its details. I must remind you of one. You are required to render to us an account of the manner of expenditure of this $1,000 as soon as you have disposed of it. The will stipulates that. I trust that you will so far comply with the late Mr. Gillian's wishes."

"You may depend upon it," said the young man, politely, "in spite of the extra expense it will entail. I may have to engage a secretary. I was never good at accounts."

Gillian went to his club. There he hunted out one whom he called Old Bryson.

Old Bryson was calm and forty and sequestered. He was in a corner reading a book, and when he saw Gillian approaching he sighed, laid down his book and took off his glasses.

"Old Bryson, wake up," said Gillian. "I've a funny story to tell you."

"I wish you would tell it to someone in the billiard room," said Old Bryson. "You know how I hate your stories."

"This is a better one than usual," said Gillian, rolling a cigarette; "and I'm glad to tell it to you. It's too sad and funny to go with the rattling of billiard balls. I've just come from my

501

late uncle's firm of legal corsairs. He leaves me an even thousand dollars. Now, what can a man possibly do with a thousand dollars?"

"I thought," said Old Bryson, showing as much interest as a bee shows in a vinegar cruet, "that the late Septimus Gillian was worth something like half a million."

"He was," assented Gillian, joyously, "and that's where the joke comes in. He's left his whole cargo of doubloons to a microbe. That is, part of it goes to the man who invents a new bacillus and the rest to establish a hospital for doing away with it again. There are one or two trifling bequests on the side. The butler and the housekeeper get a seal ring and $10 each. His nephew gets $1,000."

"You've always had plenty of money to spend," observed Old Bryson.

"Tons," said Gillian. "Uncle was the fairy godmother as far as an allowance was concerned."

"Any other heirs?" asked Old Bryson.

"None." Gillian frowned at his cigarette and kicked the upholstered leather of a divan uneasily. "There is a Miss Hayden, a ward of my uncle's, who lived in his house. She's a quiet thing—musical—the daughter of somebody who was unlucky enough to be his friend. I forgot to say that she was in on the seal ring and $10 joke, too. I wish I had been. Then I could have had two bottles of brut, tipped the waiter with the ring, and had the whole business off my hands. Don't be superior and insulting, Old Bryson—tell me what a fellow can do with a thousand dollars."

Old Bryson rubbed his glasses and smiled. And when Old Bryson smiled, Gillian knew that he intended to be more offensive than ever.

"A thousand dollars," he said, "means much or little. One man may buy a happy home with it and laugh at Rockefeller. Another could send his wife South with it and save her life. A thousand dollars would buy pure milk for one hundred babies during June, July, and August and save fifty of their lives. You could count upon a half hour's diversion with it at faro* in one of the fortified art galleries. It would furnish an education to an

* *faro*   gamblers' favorite game

ambitious boy. I am told that a genuine Corot* was secured for that amount in an auction room yesterday. You could move to a New Hampshire town and live respectably two years on it. You could rent Madison Square Garden for one evening with it, and lecture your audience, if you should have one, on the precariousness of the profession of heir presumptive."

"People might like you, Old Bryson," said Gillian, almost unruffled, "if you wouldn't moralize. I asked you to tell me what I could do with a thousand dollars."

"You?" said Bryson, with a gentle laugh. "Why, Bobby Gillian, there's only one logical thing you could do. You can go buy Miss Lotta Lauriere a diamond pendant with the money, and then take yourself off to Idaho and inflict your presence upon a ranch. I advise a sheep ranch, as I have a particular dislike for sheep."

"Thanks," said Gillian, rising. "I thought I could depend upon you, Old Bryson. You hit on the very scheme. I wanted to chuck the money in a lump, for I've got to turn in an account for it, and I hate itemizing."

Gillian phoned for a cab and said to the driver:

"The stage entrance of the Columbine Theatre."

Miss Lotta Lauriere was assisting nature with a powder puff, almost ready for her call at a crowded matinée, when her dresser mentioned the name of Mr. Gillian.

"Let it in," said Miss Lauriere. "Now, what is it, Bobby? I'm going on in two minutes."

"Rabbit-foot your right ear a little," suggested Gillian, critically. "That's better. It won't take two minutes for me. What do you say to a little thing in the pendant line? I can stand three ciphers with a figure one in front of 'em."

"Oh, just as you say," caroled Miss Lauriere.

"My right glove, Adams. Say, Bobby, did you see that necklace Della Stacey had on the other night? Twenty-two hundred dollars it cost at Tiffany's. But, of course—pull my sash a little to the left, Adams."

"Miss Lauriere for the opening chorus!" cried the call boy without.

Gillian strolled out to where his cab was waiting.

* *Corot*   nineteenth-century French painter

"What would you do with a thousand dollars if you had it?" he asked the driver.

"Open a s'loon," said the cabby promptly and huskily. "I know a place I could take money in with both hands. It's a four-story brick on a corner. I've got it figured out. Second story—chow mein and chop suey; third floor—manicures and foreign missions; fourth floor—poolroom. If you was thinking of putting up the cap—"

"Oh, no," said Gillian, "I merely asked from curiosity. I take you by the hour. Drive till I tell you to stop."

Eight blocks down Broadway Gillian poked up the trap with his cane and got out. A blind man sat upon a stool on the sidewalk selling pencils. Gillian went out and stood before him.

"Excuse me," he said, "but would you mind telling me what you would do if you had a thousand dollars?"

"You got out of that cab that just drove up, didn't you?" asked the blind man.

"I did," said Gillian.

"I guess you are all right," said the pencil dealer, "to ride in a cab by daylight. Take a look at that, if you like."

He drew a small book from his coat pocket and held it out. Gillian opened it and saw that it was a bank deposit book. It showed a balance of $1,785 to the blind man's credit.

Gillian returned the book and got into the cab.

"I forgot something," he said. "You may drive to the law offices of Tolman & Sharp, at——Broadway."

Lawyer Tolman looked at him hostilely and inquiringly through his gold-rimmed glasses.

"I beg your pardon," said Gillian, cheerfully, "but may I ask you a question? It is not an impertinent one, I hope. Was Miss Hayden left anything by my uncle's will besides the ring and the $10?"

"Nothing," said Mr. Tolman.

"I thank you very much, sir," said Gillian, and out he went to his cab. He gave the driver the address of his late uncle's home.

Miss Hayden was writing letters in the library. She was small and slender and clothed in black. But you would have noticed her eyes. Gillian drifted in with his air of regarding the world as inconsequent.

"I've just come from old Tolman's," he explained. "They've been going over the papers down there. They found a"—Gillian searched his memory for a legal term—"they found an amendment or a postscript or something to the will. It seemed that the old boy loosened up a little on second thoughts and willed you a thousand dollars. I was driving up this way and Tolman asked me to bring you the money. Here it is. You'd better count it to see if it's right." Gillian laid the money beside her hand on the desk.

Miss Hayden turned white. "Oh!" she said, and again "Oh!"

Gillian half turned and looked out of the window.

"I suppose, of course," he said, in a low voice, "that you know I love you."

"I am sorry," said Miss Hayden, taking up her money.

"There is no use?" asked Gillian, almost lightheartedly.

"I am sorry," she said again.

"May I write a note?" asked Gillian, with a smile. He seated himself at the big library table. She supplied him with paper and pen, and then went back to her secrétaire.

Gillian made out his account of his expenditure of the thousand dollars in these words:

"Paid by the black sheep, Robert Gillian, $1,000 on account of the eternal happiness, owed by Heaven to the best and dearest woman on earth."

Gillian slipped his writing into an envelope, bowed and went his way.

His cab stopped again at the offices of Tolman & Sharp.

"I have expended the thousand dollars," he said, cheerily, to Tolman of the gold glasses, "and I have come to render account of it, as I agreed. There is quite a feeling of summer in the air—do you not think so, Mr. Tolman?" He tossed a white envelope on the lawyer's table. "You will find there a memorandum, sir, of the *modus operandi* of the vanishing of the dollars."

Without touching the envelope, Mr. Tolman went to a door and called his partner, Sharp. Together they explored the caverns of an immense safe. Forth they dragged as trophy of their search a big envelope sealed with wax. This they forcibly invaded, and wagged their venerable heads together over its contents. Then Tolman became spokesman.

"Mr. Gillian," he said, formally, "there was a codicil to your uncle's will. It was entrusted to us privately, with instructions that it be not opened until you had furnished us with a full account of your handling of the $1,000 bequest in the will. As you have fulfilled the conditions, my partner and I have read the codicil. I do not wish to encumber your understanding with its legal phraseology, but I will acquaint you with the spirit of its contents.

"In the event that your disposition of the $1,000 demonstrates that you possess any of the qualifications that deserve reward, much benefit will accrue to you. Mr. Sharp and I are named as the judges, and I assure you that we will do our duty strictly according to justice—with liberality. We are not at all unfavorably disposed toward you, Mr. Gillian. But let us return to the letter of the codicil. If your disposal of the money in question has been prudent, wise, or unselfish, it is in our power to hand you over bonds to the value of $50,000, which have been placed in our hands for that purpose. But if—as our client, the late Mr. Gillian, explicitly provides—you have used this money as you have used money in the past—I quote the late Mr. Gillian—in reprehensible dissipation among disreputable associates—the $50,000 is to be paid to Miriam Hayden, ward of the late Mr. Gillian, without delay. Now, Mr. Gillian, Mr. Sharp and I will examine your account in regard to the $1,000. You submit it in writing, I believe. I hope you will repose confidence in our decision."

Mr. Tolman reached for the envelope. Gillian was a little the quicker in taking it up. He tore the account and its cover leisurely into strips and dropped them into his pocket.

"It's all right," he said, smilingly. "There isn't a bit of need to bother you with this. I don't suppose you'd understand these itemized bets, anyway. I lost the thousand dollars on the races. Good day to you, gentlemen."

Tolman & Sharp shook their heads mournfully at each other when Gillian left, for they heard him whistling happily in the hallways as he waited for the elevator.

Understanding the Story _____

Main Idea

1. Which of the following best expresses the main idea of the story?
   (a) Love is a fragile thing.
   (b) Love can feed on self-sacrifice.
   (c) Love can overcome all obstacles.
   (d) Lasting love must be mutual.

Details

2. Gillian's previous source of income was   (a) his winnings at the gambling tables   (b) his salary for work accomplished   (c) his uncle   (d) Miriam Hayden.

3. Gillian did not give the $1,000 to Lotta Lauriere because
   (a) she laughed at him
   (b) it would not get her what she wanted

(c) she was in love with another
(d) she refused it.

4. The cab driver offered to   (a) place Gillian's bets
(b) have Gillian as his partner   (c) share the money
with Gillian   (d) sell him the cab.

5. We are told   (a) why Septimus Gillian had left Miss
Hayden so little   (b) why the bulk of the estate was left
to medical research   (c) that Miriam Hayden accepted
Gillian's offer   (d) that Gillian promised to give an
accounting to the lawyers.

Inferences

6. The uncle who died   (a) disliked his nephew intensely
(b) questioned the lawyers' honesty   (c) hoped Gillian
would reform   (d) felt obligated to continue providing
in his will for his ward, Miriam Hayden.

7. Outwardly Gillian was a   (a) shrewd businessman
(b) serious   student   (c) pleasure-seeker   (d) young
man in love.

8. Miriam Hayden was   (a) in love with Gillian
(b) left out of the uncle's will   (c) a professor of music
(d) not concerned about Gillian's future.

9. Gillian whistled happily in the hall as he left the lawyers'
office because   (a) he had outwitted his uncle
(b) he had secured Miss Hayden's future   (c) Miss Hayden proved her love for him   (d) he had spent his entire
inheritance.

10. Which of the following statements is true?   (a) Gillian
was accustomed to telling the truth at all costs.
(b) Gillian expected respect and admiration from others.
(c) The lawyers were not told what Gillian had really
done with the money.   (d) Gillian was fearful of what
the future had in store for him.

Order of Events

11. Arrange the items in the order in which they occurred.
Use letters only.

A. Gillian is about to receive $50,000.
B. Gillian tells Old Bryson about his legacy.
C. The blind man reveals his wealth to Gillian.
D. The lawyers become judges.

Outcomes

12. Gillian's final sacrifice shows   (a) his devotion to his uncle   (b) his need for admiration   (c) his ambition (d) his true feelings.

Cause and Effect

13. If Gillian had let the truth be known   (a) he could still have assisted Miss Hayden   (b) the lawyers would have rejected him   (c) the medical research would have stopped   (d) Miss Hayden would have accepted his proposal.

Fact or Opinion

Tell whether each of the following is a fact or an opinion.
14. Gillian's uncle must have regretted his lavish treatment of his nephew.
15. Gillian made possible Miss Hayden's ability to continue her interest in music.

Words in Context _____

1. "It's such a confoundedly awkward amount," he explained, *genially*, to the lawyer.
   Genially (501) means   (a) angrily   (b) emphatically (c) quietly   (d) pleasantly.
2. One thousand dollars in 1900, the time of this story,

would be worth how much in terms of today's purchasing power?
(a) $1,000   (b) $10,000   (c) $20,000   (d) $100,000

3. You are required to *render* to us an account of the manner of expenditure of this $1,000 as soon as you have disposed of it.
    Render (501) means   (a) hand over   (b) explain
    (c) certify   (d) pay.

4. I trust that you will so far *comply with* the late Mr. Gillian's wishes.
    Comply with (501) means   (a) reject   (b) question
    (c) agree with   (d) disregard.

5. He's left his whole cargo of doubloons to a microbe.
    In the above sentence (502) Gillian states that his uncle
    (a) made his money in Spain   (b) had been a pirate
    (c) left all his money to medical research   (d) divided his estate among his relatives and friends.

6. Uncle was the fairy godmother as far as an allowance was concerned.
    In the above statement (502) Gillian admits that
    (a) his uncle refused to support him   (b) his uncle spoiled him   (c) his uncle limited his spending
    (d) he had an income independent of his uncle.

7. I forgot to say that she was in on the seal ring and $10 joke, too.
    According to Gillian (502) the amount given to Miss Hayden in the will was   (a) considerable   (b) barely enough for her future needs   (c) as large as that which he had received   (d) shamefully little.

8. Then I could have had two bottles of *brut*, tipped the waiter with the ring, and had the whole business off my hands.
    Brut (502) means   (a) brewed tea   (b) champagne
    (c) imported beer   (d) club soda.

9. You could count upon a half hour's diversion (amusement) with it *at faro in one of the fortified art galleries*.
    Bryson suggests (502) that Gillian could spend the money in thirty minutes   (a) entertaining his friends

(b) playing the stock markets   (c) investing in a business   (d) gambling in a casino.

10. You could rent Madison Square Garden for one evening with it, and lecture your audience . . . on the precariousness of the profession of heir presumptive.
    Bryson suggests (503) in addition that Gillian could hire a hall to tell people   (a) how he had failed in business   (b) the secrets of his success at gambling   (c) why his uncle had not left him a fortune   (d) how easily the only relative can be left out of a rich man's will.

11. "People might like you, Old Bryson," said Gillian, almost *unruffled.*
    Unruffled (503) means   (a) irritated   (b) calm   (c) amused   (d) pleased.

12. It is not an *impertinent* one, I hope.
    Impertinent (504) means   (a) disrespectful   (b) childish   (c) humorous   (d) searching.

13. Gillian drifted in with his air of regarding the world as inconsequent (senseless).
    Gillian (504) looked   (a) bashful   (b) bored   (c) worried   (d) pleased.

14. She supplied him with paper and pen and then went back to her *secrétaire.*
    Secrétaire (505) means   (a) desk   (b) corner   (c) sofa   (d) assistant.

15. " . . . and I assure you that we will do our duty strictly according to justice—with *liberality."*
    Liberality (506) means   (a) understanding   (b) skill   (c) fair-mindedness   (d) money.

Thinking Critically About the Story _____

1. The skill of O. Henry comes through in the plausibility of his surprise endings. Although we rarely can predict what the ending will be, when it does come, we realize that it has

been possible and almost inevitable all along. How did O. Henry prepare us for the ending of this story?

2. "Most of the main characters in the short stories of O. Henry are not likable people, but they do have one redeeming trait and usually the story revolves around that characteristic."

    To what extent is the above quotation true of Gillian, the main character in this story? What makes him not likable? What is his redeeming trait? Would you choose him as a friend?

3. If you had been in Gillian's place would you have acted the way he did? Do people in other stories make sacrifices similar to one made by Gillian? Can you cite examples? Do people in real life react similarly?

4. Would you characterize Gillian as a weakling or as a strong character? Explain.

5. The basic plot of "One Thousand Dollars" is far removed from reality. There is no doubt that few readers would be able to cite from real life any such uncles and such bequests. Yet, when we read the story, we can hear the dialog as it is spoken and actually see the characters living and breathing. What devices did O. Henry use to persuade the reader to accept as truth in the plot?

Stories in Words _____

Awkward (501) Words from Anglo-Saxon provide the commonest, most frequently used words in English, especially in everyday conversation. These words are familiar, and their histories are obvious. The origin of a word like *houseboat*, for example, is clear, but some words from Anglo-Saxon are a bit trickier. *Awkward* comes from two Anglo-Saxon roots meaning "toward" and "in the wrong direction." An *awkward* person moves "in the wrong direction." An *awkward* comment moves "in the wrong direction." The word is commonplace, but the history adds color.

Divan (502) The commonest meaning of *divan* is "couch, sofa," but this is a far cry from its original meaning. It comes from Persian through Turkish. In its original form, it meant "a bundle of written sheets." From this came the meaning "accounts." From this came the meaning "customhouse," then "council room," and then "the appropriate furniture in such a room."

Musical (502) The Nine Muses of ancient Greek myth presided over all phases of the arts. The dance, drama, comedy, poetry, history, and music were among the arts covered. *Mousike tekhne* was "the art of the Muses." Gradually, the first word became *music*, one of the special arts covered. Other words from *Muse* include the verb *to muse, museum,* and *amusement.*

All Gold Canyon

♦ **Suddenly there came to him a premonition of danger. It seemed a shadow had fallen upon him. But there was no shadow. His heart had given a great jump up into his throat and was choking him. Then his blood slowly chilled and he felt the sweat of his shirt cold against his flesh.**

The lure of get-rich-quick has long reached deep within the inner selves of humankind. Its appeal today is through lotteries, gambling tables, stock deals, business ventures. But the most enduring of all fortune-seeking adventures has been the age-old search for a pocket of gold hidden by nature in the vast reaches of the mountains and rivers of the world.

In "All Gold Canyon" Jack London takes us into the High Sierras of our West at the beginning of the twentieth century. He introduces us to Bill, an experienced placer miner, a searcher for deposits of gold that geology had settled among the peaks and valleys.

As the story unfolds, we find out how far Bill will go to locate and then keep a fortune in finders-keepers gold. This, however, is more than just a tale of adventure that gives the reader a lesson in panning for a placer mine, but—let's let Jack London tell you the rest!

ALL GOLD CANYON

It was the green heart of the canyon, where the walls swerved back from the rigid plan and relieved their harshness of line by making a little sheltered nook and filling it to the brim with sweetness and roundness and softness. Here all things rested. Even the narrow stream ceased its turbulent downrush long enough to form a quiet pool. Knee-deep in the water, with drooping head and half-shut eyes, drowsed a red-coated, many-antlered buck.

On one side, beginning at the very lip of the pool, was a tiny meadow, a cool, resilient surface of green that extended to the base of the frowning wall. Beyond the pool a gentle slope of earth ran up and up to meet the opposing wall. Fine grass covered the slope—grass that was spangled with flowers, with here and there patches of color, orange and purple and golden. Below, the canyon was shut in. There was no view. The walls leaned together abruptly and the canyon ended in a chaos of rocks, moss-covered and hidden by a green screen of vines and creepers and boughs of trees. Up the canyon rose far hills and peaks, the big foothills, pine-covered and remote. And far beyond, like clouds upon the border of the sky, towered minarets of white, where the Sierra's eternal snows flashed austerely the blazes of the sun.

There was no dust in the canyon. The leaves and flowers were clean and bright. The grass was young velvet. Over the pool three cottonwoods sent their snowy fluffs fluttering down the quiet air. On the slope the blossoms of the wine-wooded manzanita filled the air with springtime odors, while the leaves, wise with experience, were already beginning their vertical twist against the coming aridity of summer. In the open spaces on the slope, beyond the farthest shadow-reach of the manzanita, poised the mariposa lilies, like so many flights of jeweled moths suddenly arrested and on the verge of trembling into flight again. Here and there that wood's harlequin, the madroña, permitting itself to be caught in the act of changing its pea-green trunk to madder red, breathed its fragrance into the air from great clusters of waxen bells. Creamy white were these bells, shaped like lilies of the valley, with the sweetness of perfume that is of the springtime.

There was not a sigh of wind. The air was drowsy with its weight of perfume. It was a sweetness that would have been cloying had the air been heavy and humid. But the air was sharp and thin. It was as starlight transmuted into atmosphere, shot through and warmed by sunshine, and flower-drenched with sweetness.

An occasional butterfly drifted in and out through the patches of light and shade. And from all about rose the low and sleepy hum of mountain bees—feasting sybarites that jostled one another good-naturedly at the board, nor found time for rough discourtesy. So quietly did the little stream drip and ripple its way through the canyon that it spoke only in faint and occasional gurgles. The voice of the stream was as a drowsy whisper, ever interrupted by dozings and silences, ever lifted again in the awakenings.

The motion of all things was a drifting in the heart of the canyon. Sunshine and butterflies drifted in and out among the trees. The hum of the bees and the whisper of the stream were a drifting of sound. And the drifting sound and drifting color seemed to weave together in the making of a delicate and intangible fabric which was the spirit of the place. It was a spirit of peace that was not of death, but of smooth-pulsing life, of quietude that was not silence, of movement that was not action, of repose that was quick with existence without being violent with struggle and travail. The spirit of the place was the spirit of the peace of the living, somnolent with the easement and content of prosperity, and undisturbed by rumors of far wars.

The red-coated, many-antlered buck acknowledged the lordship of the spirit of the place and dozed knee-deep in the cool, shaded pool. There seemed no flies to vex him and he was languid with rest. Sometimes his ears moved when the stream awoke and whispered; but they moved lazily, with foreknowledge that it was merely the stream grown garrulous at discovery that it had slept.

But there came a time when the buck's ears lifted and tensed with swift eagerness for sound. His head was turned down the canyon. His sensitive, quivering nostrils scented the air. His eyes could not pierce the green screen through which the stream rippled away, but to his ears came the voice of a man. It was a steady, monotonous, singsong voice. Once the buck heard the harsh clash of metal upon rock. At the sound he snorted with a sudden start that jerked him through the air from water to meadow, and his feet sank into the young velvet, while he raised his ears again to listen, and faded away out of the canyon like a wraith, soft-footed and without sound.

The clash of steel-shod soles against the rocks began to be heard, and the man's voice grew louder. It was raised in a sort of chant and became distinct with nearness, so that the words could be heard:

> Tu'n around an' tu'n yo' face
> Untoe them sweet hills of grace.
> (D' pow'rs of sin yo' am scornin'!)
> Look about an' look aroun'.
> Fling yo' sin pack on d' groun'.
> (Yo' will meet wid d' Lord in d' mornin'!)

A sound of scrambling accompanied the song, and the spirit of the place fled away on the heels of the red-coated buck. The green screen was burst asunder, and a man peered out at the meadow and the pool and the sloping sidehill. He was a deliberate sort of man. He took in the scene with one embracing glance, then ran his eyes over the details to verify the general impression. Then, and not until then, did he open his mouth in vivid and solemn approval.

"Smoke of life an' snakes of purgatory! Will you just look at that! Wood an' water an' grass an' a sidehill! A pocket* hunter's delight an' a cayuse's paradise! Cool green for tired

---

* *pocket*   large natural deposit of gold

eyes! Pink pills for pale people ain't in it. A secret pasture for prospectors and a resting place for tired burros."

He was a sandy-complexioned man in whose face geniality and humor seemed the salient characteristics. It was a mobile face, quick-changing to inward mood and thought. Thinking was in him a visible process. Ideas chased across his face like windflaws across the surface of a lake. His hair, sparse and unkempt of growth, was as indeterminate and colorless as his complexion. It would seem that all the color of his frame had gone into his eyes, for they were startlingly blue. Also they were laughing and merry eyes, within them much of the naïveté and wonder of the child; and yet, in an unassertive way, they contained much of calm self-reliance and strength of purpose founded upon self-experience and experience of the world.

From out the screen of vines and creepers he flung ahead of him a miner's pick and shovel and gold pan. Then he crawled out himself into the open. He was clad in faded overalls and black cotton shirt, with hobnailed brogans on his feet, and on his head a hat whose shapelessness and stains advertised the rough usage of wind and rain and sun and camp smoke. He stood erect, seeing wide-eyed the secrecy of the scene and sensuously inhaling the warm, sweet breath of the canyon garden through nostrils that dilated and quivered with delight. His eyes narrowed to laughing slits of blue, his face wreathed itself in joy, and his mouth curled in a smile as he cried aloud:

"Jumping dandelions and happy hollyhocks, but that smells good to me! Talk about your attar o' roses an' cologne factories! They ain't in it!"

He had the habit of soliloquy. His quick-changing facial expressions might tell every thought and mood, but the tongue, perforce, ran hard after, repeating, like a second Boswell.

The man lay down on the lip of the pool and drank long and deep of its water. "Tastes good to me," he murmured, lifting his head and gazing across the pool at the sidehill, while he wiped his mouth with the back of his hand. The sidehill attracted his attention. Still lying on his stomach, he studied the hill formation long and carefully. It was a practiced eye that traveled up the slope to the crumbling canyon wall and

back and down again to the edge of the pool. He scrambled to his feet and favored the sidehill with a second survey.

"Looks good to me," he concluded, picking up his pick and shovel and gold pan.

He crossed the stream below the pool, stepping agilely from stone to stone. Where the sidehill touched the water he dug up a shovelful of dirt and put it into the gold pan. He squatted down, holding the pan in his two hands, and partly immersing it in the stream. Then he imparted to the pan a deft circular motion that sent the water sluicing in and out through the dirt and gravel. The larger and the lighter particles worked to the surface, and these, by a skillful dipping movement of the pan, he spilled out and over the edge. Occasionally, to expedite matters, he rested the pan and with his fingers raked out the large pebbles and pieces of rock.

The contents of the pan diminished rapidly until only fine dirt and the smallest bits of gravel remained. At this stage he began to work very deliberately and carefully. It was fine washing, and he washed fine and finer, with a keen scrutiny and delicate and fastidious touch. At last the pan seemed empty of everything but water; but with a quick semicircular flirt that sent the water flying over the shallow rim into the stream, he disclosed a layer of black sand on the bottom of the pan. So thin was this layer that it was like a streak of paint. He examined it closely. In the midst of it was a tiny golden speck. He dribbled a little water in over the depressed edge of the pan. With a quick flirt he sent the water sluicing across the bottom, turning the grains of black sand over and over. A second tiny golden speck rewarded his effort.

The washing had now become very fine—fine beyond all need of ordinary placer* mining. He worked the black sand, a small portion at a time, up the shallow rim of the pan. Each small portion he examined sharply, so that his eyes saw every grain of it before he allowed it to slide over the edge and away. Jealously, bit by bit, he let the black sand slip away. A golden speck, no larger than a pinpoint, appeared on the rim, and by his manipulation of the water it returned to the bottom of the pan. And in such fashion another speck was disclosed, and another. Great was his care of them. Like a shepherd he herded his flock of golden specks so that not one should be lost. At last, of the pan of dirt nothing remained but his golden herd. He counted it, and then, after all his labor, sent it flying out of the pan with one final swirl of water.

But his blue eyes were shining with desire as he rose to his feet. "Seven," he muttered aloud, asserting the sum of the specks for which he had toiled so hard and which he had so wantonly thrown away. "Seven," he repeated, with the emphasis of one trying to impress a number on his memory.

He stood still a long while, surveying the hillside. In his eyes was a curiosity, new-aroused and burning. There was an exultance about his bearing and a keenness like that of a hunting animal catching the fresh scent of game.

* *placer*   glacial deposit of gold

He moved down the stream a few steps and took a second panful of dirt.

Again came the careful washing, the jealous herding of the golden specks, and the wantonness with which he sent them flying into the stream when he had counted their number.

"Five," he muttered, and repeated, "five."

He could not forbear another survey of the hill before filling the pan farther down the stream. His golden herds diminished. "Four, three, two, two, one," were his memory tabulations as he moved down the stream. When but one speck of gold rewarded his washing he stopped and built a fire of dry twigs. Into this he thrust the gold pan and burned it till it was blue-black. He held up the pan and examined it critically. Then he nodded approbation. Against such a color background he could defy the tiniest yellow speck to elude him.

Still moving down the stream, he panned again. A single speck was his reward. A third pan contained no gold at all. Not satisfied with this, he panned three times again, taking his shovels of dirt within a foot of one another. Each pan proved empty of gold, and the fact, instead of discouraging him, seemed to give him satisfaction. His elation increased with each barren washing, until he arose, exclaiming jubilantly:

"If it ain't the real thing, may destiny knock off my head with sour apples!"

Returning to where he had started operations, he began to pan up the stream. At first his golden herds increased—increased prodigiously. "Fourteen, eighteen, twenty-one, twenty-six," ran his memory tabulations. Just above the pool he struck his richest pan—thirty-five colors.

"Almost enough to save," he remarked regretfully as he allowed the water to sweep them away.

The sun climbed to the top of the sky. The man worked on. Pan by pan he went up the stream, the tally of results steadily decreasing.

"It's just beautiful, the way it peters out," he exulted when a shovelful of dirt contained no more than a single speck of gold.

And when no specks at all were found in several pans, he straightened up and favored the hillside with a confident glance.

"Aha! Mr. Pocket!" he cried out as though to an auditor hidden somewhere above him beneath the surface of the slope. "Aha! Mr. Pocket! I'm a-comin', I'm a comin', an' I'm shorely gwine to get yer! You heah me, Mr. Pocket? I'm gwine to get yer as shore as punkins ain't cauliflowers!"

He turned and flung a measuring glance at the sun poised above him in the azure of the cloudless sky. Then he went down the canyon, following the line of shovel holes he had made in filling the pans. He crossed the stream below the pool and disappeared through the green screen. There was little opportunity for the spirit of the place to return with its quietude and repose, for the man's voice, raised in ragtime song, still dominated the canyon with possession.

After a time, with a greater clashing of steel-shod feet on rock, he returned. The green screen was tremendously agitated. It surged back and forth in the throes of a struggle. There was a loud grating and clanging of metal. The man's voice leaped to a higher pitch and was sharp with imperativeness. A large body plunged and panted. There was a snapping and ripping and rending, and amid a shower of falling leaves a horse burst through the screen. On its back was a pack, and from this trailed broken vines and torn creepers. The animal gazed with astonished eyes at the scene into which it had been precipitated, then dropped its head to the grass and began contentedly to graze. A second horse scrambled into view, slipping once on the mossy rocks and regaining equilibrium when its hoofs sank into the yielding surface of the meadow. It was riderless, though on its back was a high-horned Mexican saddle, scarred and discolored by long usage.

The man brought up the rear. He threw off pack and saddle, with an eye to camp location, and gave the animals their freedom to graze. He unpacked his food and got out frying pan and coffeepot. He gathered an armful of dry wood, and with a few stones made a place for his fire.

"My," he said, "but I've got an appetite! I could scoff iron filings an' horseshoe nails an' thank you kindly, ma'am, for a second helpin'."

He straightened up, and while he reached for matches in the pocket of his overalls his eyes traveled across the pool to the sidehill. His fingers had clutched the matchbox, but they relaxed their hold and the hand came out empty. The man wavered perceptibly. He looked at his preparations for cooking and he looked at the hill.

"Guess I'll take another whack at her," he concluded, starting to cross the stream.

"They ain't no sense in it, I know," he mumbled apologetically. "But keepin' grub back an hour ain't goin' to hurt none, I reckon."

A few feet back from his first line of test pans he started a second line. The sun dropped down the western sky, the shadows lengthened, but the man worked on. He began a third line of test pans. He was crosscutting the hillside, line by line, as he ascended. The center of each line produced the richest pans, while the ends came where no colors showed in the pan. And as he ascended the hillside the lines grew perceptibly shorter. The regularity with which their length diminished served to indicate that somewhere up the slope the last line would be so short as to have scarcely length at all, and that beyond could come only a point. The design was growing into an inverted V. The converging sides of this V marked the boundaries of the gold-bearing dirt.

The apex of the V was evidently the man's goal. Often he ran his eye along the converging sides and on up the hill, trying to divine the apex, the point where the gold-bearing dirt must cease. Here resided "Mr. Pocket"—for so the man familiarly addressed the imaginary point above him on the slope, crying out:

"Come down out o' that, Mr. Pocket! Be right smart an' agreeable, an' come down!"

"All right," he would add later, in a voice resigned to determination. "All right, Mr. Pocket. It's plain to me I got to come right up an' snatch you out bald-headed. An' I'll do it! I'll do it!" he would threaten still later.

Each pan he carried down to the water to wash, and as he went higher up the hill the pans grew richer, until he began to save the gold in an empty baking powder can which he carried carelessly in his lap pocket. So engrossed was he in his toil that he did not notice the long twilight of oncoming night. It was not until he tried vainly to see the gold colors in the bottom of the pan that he realized the passage of time. He straightened up abruptly. An expression of whimsical wonderment and awe overspread his face as he drawled:

"Gosh darn my buttons, if I didn't plumb forget dinner!"

He stumbled across the stream in the darkness and lighted his long-delayed fire. Flapjacks and bacon and warmed-over beans constituted his supper. Then he smoked a pipe by the smoldering coals, listening to the night noises and watching the moonlight stream through the canyon. After that he unrolled his bed, took off his heavy shoes, and pulled the blankets up to his chin. His face showed white in the moonlight, like the face of a corpse. But it was a corpse that knew its resurrection, for the man rose suddenly on one elbow and gazed across at his hillside.

"Good night, Mr. Pocket," he called sleepily. "Good night."

He slept through the early gray of morning until the direct rays of the sun smote his closed eyelids, when he awoke with a start and looked about him until he had established the continuity of his existence and identified his present self with the days previously lived.

To dress, he had merely to buckle on his shoes. He glanced at his fireplace and at his hillside, wavered, but fought down the temptation and started the fire.

"Keep yer shirt on, Bill; keep yer shirt on," he admonished himself. "What's the good of rushin'? No use in gettin' all het up an' sweaty. Mr. Pocket'll wait for you. He ain't a-runnin' away before you can get yer breakfast. Now what you want, Bill, is something fresh in yer bill o' fare. So it's up to you to go an' get it."

He cut a short pole at the water's edge and drew from one of his pockets a bit of line and a draggled fly that had once been a royal coachman.

"Mebbe they'll bite in the early morning," he muttered as he made his first cast into the pool. And a moment later he was gleefully crying: "What'd I tell you, eh? What'd I tell you?"

He had no reel or any inclination to waste time, and by main strength, and swiftly, he drew out of the water a flashing ten-inch trout. Three more, caught in rapid succession, furnished his breakfast. When he came to the stepping-stones on his way to his hillside, he was struck by a sudden thought, and paused.

"I'd just better take a hike downstream a ways," he said. "There's no tellin' what cuss may be snoopin' around."

But he crossed over on the stones, and with a "I really oughter take that hike" the need of the precaution passed out of his mind and he fell to work.

At nightfall he straightened up. The small of his back was stiff from stooping toil, and as he put his hand behind him to soothe the protesting muscles he said:

"Now what d'ye think of that? I clean forgot my dinner again! If I don't watch out I'll sure be degeneratin' into a two-meal-a-day crank."

"Pockets is the worst things I ever see for makin' a man absentminded," he communed that night as he crawled into his blankets. Nor did he forget to call up the hillside. "Good night, Mr. Pocket! Good night!"

Rising with the sun, and snatching a hasty breakfast, he was early at work. A fever seemed to be growing in him, nor did the increasing richness of the test pans allay this fever. There was a flush in his cheek other than that made by the heat of the sun, and he was oblivious to fatigue and the passage of time. When he filled a pan with dirt he ran down the hill to wash it; nor could he forbear running up the hill again, panting and stumbling profanely, to refill the pan.

He was now a hundred yards from the water, and the inverted V was assuming definite proportions. The width of the pay dirt steadily decreased, and the man extended in his mind's eye the sides of the V to their meeting place far up the hill. This was his goal, the apex of the V, and he panned many times to locate it.

"Just about two yards above that manzanita bush an' a yard to the right," he finally concluded.

Then the temptation seized him. "As plain as the nose on your face," he said as he abandoned his laborious crosscutting and climbed to the indicated apex. He filled a pan and carried it down the hill to wash. It contained no trace of gold. He dug deep, and he dug shallow, filling and washing a dozen pans, and was unrewarded even by the tiniest golden specks. He was enraged at having yielded to the temptation, and cursed himself blasphemously and pridelessly. Then he went down the hill and took up the crosscutting.

"Slow an' certain, Bill; slow an' certain," he crooned. "Shortcuts to fortune ain't in your line, an' it's about time you know it. Get wise, Bill, get wise. Slow an' certain's the only hand you can play; so go to it, an' keep to it, too."

As the crosscuts decreased, showing that the sides of the V were converging, the depth of the V increased. The gold trace was dipping into the hill. It was only at thirty inches beneath the surface that he could get colors in his pan. The dirt he found at twenty-five inches from the surface, and at thirty-five inches, yielded barren pans. At the base of the V, by the water's edge, he had found the gold colors at the grass roots. The higher he went up the hill; the deeper the gold dipped. To dig a hole three feet deep in order to get one test pan was a task of no mean magnitude; while between the man and the apex intervened an untold number of such holes to be dug. "An' there's no tellin' how much deeper it'll pitch," he sighed in a moment's pause, while his fingers soothed his aching back.

Feverish with desire, with aching back and stiffening muscles, with pick and shovel gouging and mauling the soft brown earth, the man toiled up the hill. Before him was the smooth slope, spangled with flowers and made sweet with their breath. Behind him was devastation. It looked like some terrible eruption breaking out on the smooth skin of the hill. His slow progress was like that of a slug, befouling beauty with a monstrous trail.

Though the dipping gold trace increased the man's work, he found consolation in the increasing richness of the pans. Twenty cents, thirty cents, fifty cents, sixty cents, were the values of the gold found in the pans, and at nightfall he washed his banner pan, which gave him a dollar's worth of gold dust from a shovelful of dirt.

"I'll just bet it's my luck to have some inquisitive cuss come buttin' in here on my pasture," he mumbled sleepily that night as he pulled the blankets up to his chin.

Suddenly he sat upright. "Bill!" he called sharply. "Now listen to me, Bill; d'ye hear! It's up to you, tomorrow mornin', to mosey round an' see what you can see. Understand? Tomorrow morning, an' don't forget it!"

He yawned and glanced across at his sidehill. "Good night, Mr. Pocket," he called.

In the morning he stole a march on the sun, for he had finished breakfast when its first rays caught him, and he was climbing the wall of the canyon where it crumbled away and gave footing. From the outlook at the top he found himself in the midst of loneliness. As far as he could see, chain after chain of mountains heaved themselves into his vision. To the east his eyes, leaping the miles between range and range and between many ranges, brought up at last against the white-peaked Sierras—the main crest, where the backbone of the Western world reared itself against the sky. To the north and south he could see more distinctly the cross systems that broke through the main trend of the sea of mountains. To the west the ranges fell away, one behind the other, diminishing and fading into the gentle foothills that, in turn, descended into the great valley which he could not see.

And in all that mighty sweep of earth he saw no sign of man nor of the handiwork of man—save only the torn bosom of the hillside at his feet. The man looked long and carefully. Once, far down his own canyon, he thought he saw in the air a faint hint of smoke. He looked again and decided that it was the purple haze of the hills made dark by a convolution of the canyon wall at its back.

"Hey, you, Mr. Pocket!" he called down into the canyon. "Stand out from under! I'm a-comin', Mr. Pocket! I'm a-comin'!"

The heavy brogans on the man's feet made him appear clumsy-footed, but he swung down from the giddy height as lightly and airily as a mountain goat. A rock, turning under his foot on the edge of the precipice, did not disconcert him. He seemed to know the precise time required for the turn to culminate in disaster, and in the meantime he utilized the false footing itself for the momentary earth contact necessary to carry him on into safety. Where the earth sloped so steeply that it was impossible to stand for a second upright, the man did not hesitate. His foot pressed the impossible surface for but a fraction of the fatal second and gave him the bound that carried him onward. Again, where even the fraction of a second's footing was out of the question, he would swing his body past by a moment's handgrip on a jutting knob of rock, a crevice, or a precariously rooted shrub. At last, with a wild leap and yell, he exchanged the face of the wall for an earth slide and finished the descent in the midst of several tons of sliding earth and gravel.

His first pan of the morning washed out over two dollars in coarse gold. It was from the center of the V. To either side the diminution in the values of the pans was swift. His lines of crosscutting holes were growing very short. The converging sides of the inverted V were only a few yards apart. Their meeting point was only a few yards above him. But the pay streak was dipping deeper and deeper into the earth. By early afternoon he was sinking the test holes five feet before the pans could show the gold trace.

For that matter the gold trace had become something more than a trace; it was a placer mine in itself, and the man resolved to come back after he had found the pocket and work over the ground. But the increasing richness of the pans began to worry him. By late afternoon the worth of the pans had grown to three and four dollars. The man scratched his head perplexedly and looked a few feet up the hill at the manzanita bush that marked approximately the apex of the V. He nodded his head and said oracularly:

"It's one o' two things, Bill; one o' two things. Either Mr. Pocket's spilled himself all out an' down the hill, or else Mr. Pocket's that rich you maybe won't be able to carry him all away with you. And that'd be tough, wouldn't it, now?" He chuckled at contemplation of so pleasant a dilemma.

Nightfall found him by the edge of the stream, his eyes wrestling with the gathering darkness over the washing of a five-dollar pan.

"Wisht I had an electric light to go on working," he said.

He found sleep difficult that night. Many times he composed himself and closed his eyes for slumber to overtake him; but his blood pounded with too strong desire, and as many times his eyes opened and he murmured wearily, "Wisht it was sunup."

Sleep came to him in the end, but his eyes were open with the first paling of the stars, and the gray of dawn caught him with breakfast finished and climbing the hillside in the direction of the secret abiding place of Mr. Pocket.

The first crosscut the man made, there was space for only three holes, so narrow had become the pay streak and so close was he to the fountainhead of the golden stream he had been following for four days.

"Be ca'm, Bill; be ca'm," he admonished himself as he broke ground for the final hole where the sides of the V had at last come together in a point.

"I've got the almighty cinch on you, Mr. Pocket, an' you can't lose me," he said many times as he sank the hole deeper and deeper.

Four feet, five feet, six feet, he dug his way down into the earth. The digging grew harder. His pick grated on broken rock. He examined the rock. "Rotten quartz," was his conclusion as, with the shovel, he cleared the bottom of the hole of loose dirt. He attacked the crumbling quartz with the pick, bursting the disintegrating rock asunder with every stroke.

He thrust his shovel into the loose mass. His eye caught a gleam of yellow. He dropped the shovel and squatted suddenly on his heels. As a farmer rubs the clinging earth from fresh-dug potatoes, so the man, a piece of rotten quartz held in both hands, rubbed the dirt away.

"Sufferin' Sardanopolis!" he cried. "Lumps an' chunks of it! Lumps an' chunks of it!"

It was only half rock he held in his hand. The other half was pure gold. He dropped it into his pan and examined another piece. Little yellow was to be seen, but with his strong fingers he crumbled the rotten quartz away till both hands were filled with glowing yellow. He rubbed the dirt away from fragment after fragment, tossing them into the gold pan. It was a treasure hole. So much had the quartz rotted away that there was less of it than there was of gold. Now and again he found a piece to which no rock clung—a piece that was all gold. A chunk, where the pick had laid open the heart of the gold, glittered like a handful of yellow jewels, and he tilted his head at it and slowly turned it around and over to observe the rich play of the light upon it.

"Talk about yer Too Much Gold diggin's!" the man snorted contemptuously. "Why, this diggin'd make it look like thirty cents. This diggin' is all gold. An' right here an' now I name this yere canyon 'All Gold Canyon,' b' gosh!"

Still squatting on his heels, he continued examining the fragments and tossing them into the pan. Suddenly there came to him a premonition of danger. It seemed a shadow had fallen upon him. But there was no shadow. His heart had given a great jump up into his throat and was choking him. Then his blood slowly chilled and he felt the sweat of his shirt cold against his flesh.

He did not spring up nor look around. He did not move. He was considering the nature of the premonition he had received, trying to locate the source of the mysterious force that had warned him, striving to sense the imperative presence of the unseen thing that threatened him. There is an aura of things hostile, made manifest by messengers too refined for the senses to know; and this aura he felt, but knew not how he felt it. His was the feeling as when a cloud passes over the sun. It seemed that between him and life had passed something dark and smothering and menacing; a gloom, as it were, that swallowed up life and made for death—his death.

Every force of his being impelled him to spring up and confront the unseen danger, but his soul dominated the panic, and he remained squatting on his heels, in his hands a chunk of gold. He did not dare to look around, but he knew by now that there was something behind him and above him. He made believe to be interested in the gold in his hand. He examined it critically, turned it over and over, and rubbed the dirt from it. All all the time he knew that something behind him was looking at the gold over his shoulder.

Still feigning interest in the chunk of gold in his hand, he listened intently and he heard the breathing of the thing behind him. His eyes searched the ground in front of him for a weapon, but they saw only the uprooted gold, worthless to him now in his extremity. There was his pick, a handy weapon on occasion; but this was not such an occasion. The man realized his predicament. He was in a narrow hole that was seven feet deep. His head did not come to the surface of the ground. He was in a trap.

He remained squatting on his heels. He was quite cool and collected; but his mind, considering every factor, showed him only his helplessness. He continued rubbing the dirt from the quartz fragments and throwing the gold into the pan. There was nothing else for him to do. Yet he knew that he would have to rise up, sooner or later, and face the danger that breathed at his back. The minutes passed, and with the passage of each minute he knew that by so much he was nearer the time when he must stand up or else—and his wet shirt went cold against his flesh again at the thought—or else he might receive death as he stooped there over his treasure.

Still he squatted on his heels, rubbing dirt from gold and debating in just what manner he should rise up. He might rise up with a rush and claw his way out of the hole to meet whatever threatened on the even footing aboveground. Or he might rise up slowly and carelessly, and feign casually to discover the thing that breathed at his back. His instinct and every fighting fiber of his body favored the mad, clawing rush to the surface. His intellect, and the craft thereof, favored the slow and cautious meeting with the thing that menaced and which he could not see. And while he debated, a loud, crashing noise burst on his ear. At the same instant he received a stunning blow on the left side of the back, and from the point of impact felt a rush of flame through his flesh. He sprang up in the air, but halfway to his feet collapsed. His body crumpled in like a leaf withered in sudden heat, and he came down, his chest across his pan of gold, his face in the dirt and rock, his legs tangled and twisted because of the restricted space at the bottom of the hole. His legs twitched convulsively several times. His body was shaken as with a mighty ague. There was a slow expansion of the lungs, accompanied by a deep sigh. Then the air was slowly, very slowly, exhaled, and his body as slowly flattened itself down into inertness.

Above, revolver in hand, a man was peering down over the edge of the hole. He peered for a long time at the prone and motionless body beneath him. After a while the stranger sat down on the edge of the hole so that he could see into it, and rested the revolver on his knee. Reaching his hand into a pocket, he drew out a wisp of brown paper. Into this he dropped a few crumbs of tobacco. The combination became a cigarette, brown and squat, with the ends turned in. Not once did he take his eyes from the body at the bottom of the hole. He lighted the cigarette and drew its smoke into his lungs with a caressing intake of the breath. He smoked slowly. Once the cigarette went out and he relighted it. And all the while he studied the body beneath him.

In the end he tossed the cigarette stub away and rose to his feet. He moved to the edge of the hole. Spanning it, a hand resting on each edge, and with the revolver still in the right hand, he muscled his body down into the hole. While his feet were yet a yard from the bottom he released his hands and dropped down.

At the instant his feet struck bottom he saw the pocket miner's arm leap out, and his own legs knew a swift, jerking grip that overthrew him. In the nature of the jump his revolver hand was above his head. Swiftly as the grip had flashed about his legs, just as swiftly he brought the revolver down. He was still in the air, his fall in process of completion, when he pulled the trigger. The explosion was deafening in the confined space. The smoke filled the hole so that he could see nothing. He struck the bottom on his back, and like a cat's the pocket miner's body was on top of him. Even as the miner's body passed on top, the stranger crooked in his right arm to fire; and even in that instant the miner, with a quick thrust of elbow, struck his wrist. The muzzle was thrown up and the bullet thudded into the dirt of the side of the hole.

The next instant the stranger felt the miner's hand grip his wrist. The struggle was now for the revolver. Each man strove to turn it against the other's body. The smoke in the hole was clearing. The stranger, lying on his back, was beginning to see dimly. But suddenly he was blinded by a handful of dirt deliberately flung into his eyes by his antagonist. In that moment he felt a smashing darkness descend upon his brain, and in the midst of the darkness even the darkness ceased.

But the pocket miner fired again and again, until the revolver was empty. Then he tossed it from him and, breathing heavily, sat down on the dead man's legs.

The miner was sobbing and struggling for breath. "Measly skunk!" he panted; "a-campin' on my trail an' lettin' me do the work, an' then shootin' me in the back!"

He was half crying from anger and exhaustion. He peered at the face of the dead man. It was sprinkled with loose dirt and gravel, and it was difficult to distinguish the features.

"Never laid eyes on him before," the miner concluded his

scrutiny. "Just a common an' ordinary thief! An' he shot me in the back! He shot me in the back!"

He opened his shirt and felt himself, front and back, on his left side.

"Went clean through, and no harm done!" he cried jubilantly. "I'll bet he aimed all right, all right; but he drew the gun over when he pulled the trigger—the cuss! But I fixed 'm! Oh, I fixed 'm!"

His fingers were investigating the bullet hole in his side, and a shade of regret passed over his face. "It's goin' to be sorer'n anything," he said. "An' it's up to me to get mended an' get out o' here."

He crawled out of the hole and went down the hill to his camp. Half an hour later he returned, leading his pack horse. His open shirt disclosed the rude bandages with which he had dressed his wound. He was slow and awkward with his left-hand movements, but that did not prevent his using the arm.

The bight of the pack rope under the dead man's shoulders enabled him to heave the body out of the hole. Then he set to work gathering up his gold. He worked steadily for several hours, pausing often to rest his stiffening shoulder and to exclaim:

"He shot me in the back, the measly skunk! He shot me in the back!"

When his treasure was quite cleaned up and wrapped securely into a number of blanket-covered parcels, he made an estimate of its value.

"Four hundred pounds, or I'm a Hottentot," he concluded. "Say two hundred in quartz an' dirt—that leaves two hundred pounds of gold. Bill! Wake up! Two hundred pounds of gold! Over a million dollars! An' it's yourn—all yourn!"

He scratched his head delightedly and his fingers blundered into an unfamiliar groove. They quested along it for several inches. It was a crease through his scalp where the second bullet had plowed.

He walked angrily over to the dead man.

"You would, would you?" he bullied. "You would, eh? Well, I fixed you good an' plenty, an' I'll give you decent burial, too. That's more'n you'd have done for me."

He dragged the body to the edge of the hole and toppled it

in. It struck the bottom with a dull crash, on its side, the face twisted up to the light. The miner peered down at it.

"An' you shot me in the back!" he said accusingly.

With pick and shovel he filled the hole. Then he loaded the gold on his horse. It was too great a load for the animal, and when he had gained his camp he transferred part of it to his saddle horse. Even so, he was compelled to abandon a portion of his outfit—pick and shovel and gold pan, extra food and cooking utensils, and divers odds and ends.

The sun was at the zenith when the man forced the horses at the screen of vines and creepers. To climb the huge boulders the animals were compelled to uprear and struggle blindly through the tangled mass of vegetation. Once the saddle horse fell heavily and the man removed the pack to get the animal on its feet. After it started on its way again the man thrust his head out from among the leaves and peered up at the hillside.

"The measly skunk!" he said, and disappeared.

There was a ripping and tearing of vines and boughs. The trees surged back and forth marking the passage of the animals through the midst of them. There was a clashing of steel-shod hoofs on stone, and now and again an oath or a sharp cry of command. Then the voice of the man was raised in song:

> Tu'n around an' tu'n yo' face
> Untoe them sweet hills of grace.
>   (D' pow'rs of sin yo' am scornin'!)
> Look about an' look aroun'
> Fling yo' sin pack on d' groun'.
>   (Yo' will meet wid d' Lord in d' mornin'!)

The song grew faint and fainter, and through the silence crept back the spirit of the place. The stream once more drowsed and whispered; the hum of the mountain's bees rose sleepily. Down through the perfume-weighed air fluttered the snowy fluffs of the cottonwoods. The butterflies drifted in and out among the trees, and over all blazed the quiet sunshine. Only remained the hoofmarks in the meadow and the torn hillside to mark the boisterous trail of the life that had broken the peace of the place and passed on.

Reading for Understanding _____

Main Idea

1. Which of the following quotations best expresses the main idea of the story?
   (a) Up the canyon rose far hills and peaks, the big foothills, pine-covered and remote.
   (b) "Just a common an' ordinary thief! An' he shot me in the back! He shot me in the back!"
   (c) "Slow an' certain's the only hand you can play; so go to it, and keep to it, too."
   (d) "I'd just better take a hike downstream a ways," he said. "There's no tellin' what cuss may be snoopin' around."

Details

2. Mr. Pocket was (a) Bill himself (b) the man who attacked him (c) the canyon (d) the source of the gold.

3. The only weapon Bill had with him in the hole was (a) his knife (b) the pickax (c) a gun (d) the pan.

4. A trick that Bill did not use to foil the attacker was (a) not moving for minutes (b) throwing dirt (c) grabbing the gun in the attacker's hand (d) waiting until the man jumped into the hole.

5. Which of the following was not true of the gold deposit?
   (a) The rain was washing it gradually into the stream.
   (b) The animals in the canyon paid no attention to its presence.
   (c) Plant life had grown above it.
   (d) Before he left, Bill pledged that he would be back to recover the rest of the gold in the pocket.

Inferences

6. Bill was about (a) 15–17 years old (b) 22–25 years old (c) 35–40 years old (d) 65–67 years old.

7. Bill frequently thought out loud   (a) to quiet his horses
   (b) because he was fearful   (c) because he was alone
   (d) to frighten off the wild animals.

8. Which of the following was not used by the author to
   reveal Bill's growing excitement?   (a) Bill's forgetting
   to eat on time   (b) Bill's forgetting to take his gun with
   him   (c) Bill's rising before dawn   (d) Bill's running
   up and down the hill.

9. The attacker lit a cigarette to   (a) check the gold
   (b) have a better view of Bill   (c) signal to his
   companion   (d) make certain of Bill's condition.

10. Bill sang as he entered and left the valley   (a) to keep
    the bears away   (b) because he was at peace
    (c) to warn other prospectors of his presence
    (d) to guide his horses.

Order of Events

11. Arrange the items in the order in which they occurred.
    Use letters only.
    A. Bill abandoned his pick and shovel.
    B. Bill pretended to be dead.
    C. Bill completed the V.
    D. Bill threw away small pieces of gold.
    E. Bill emptied the gun.

Outcomes

12. If Bill had been more cautious, he could have
    (a) found the intruder before the intruder found him
    (b) found the gold pocket sooner   (c) saved the life of
    the intruder   (d) carried more gold back from the moun-
    tains.

Cause and Effect

13. Bill's knowledge and skill was not in evidence when he
    (a) released his horses to graze and possibly wander off
    (b) prepared his elaborate meals   (c) explored the area
    only once   (d) dug his exploratory holes.

Fact or Opinion

Tell whether each of the following is a fact or an opinion.

14. The attacker had followed Bill on foot.
15. Bill had plans on how he intended to spend his newfound wealth.

Words in Context _____

1. Even the narrow stream ceased its *turbulent* downrush long enough to form a quiet pool.
   Turbulent (515) means   (a) usual   (b) swift   (c) gigantic   (d) violent.

2. The walls leaned together abruptly and the canyon ended in a *chaos* of rocks, moss-covered and hidden by a green screen of vines and creepers and boughs of trees.
   Chaos (515) means   (a) great confusion   (b) blind alley   (c) orderly grouping   (d) massive set.

3. In the open spaces on the slope, beyond the farthest shadow-reach of the manzanita, poised the mariposa lilies, like so many flights of jeweled moths suddenly arrested and *on the verge of* trembling into flight again.
   On the verge of (516) means   (a) filled with   (b) about to   (c) known for   (d) set for.

4. And from all about rose the low and sleepy hum of mountain bees . . . that *jostled* one another good-naturedly . . . nor found time for rough discourtesy.
   Jostled (516) means   (a) crowded noisily   (b) nudged   (c) commanded   (d) followed.

5. Then, and not until then, did he open his mouth in *vivid* and solemn approval.
   Vivid (517) means   (a) wordy   (b) silent   (c) intense   (d) argumentative.

6. He was a sandy-complexioned man in whose face *geniality* and humor seemed the salient (outstanding) features.

Geniality (518) means   (a) pleasantness   (b) greed
(c) gentleness   (d) intelligence.

7. He dribbled a little water in over the *depressed* edge of
the pan.
Depressed (520) means   (a) unhappy   (b) glistening
(c) battered   (d) pushed down.

8. There was little opportunity for the spirit of the place to
return with its quietude and repose, for the man's voice,
raised in ragtime song, still *dominated* the canyon with
possession.
Dominated (522) means   (a) controlled   (b) spoiled
(c) explored   (d) encountered.

9. The man *wavered perceptibly*.
Wavered perceptibly (523) means   (a) acted quickly
(b) shouted clearly   (c) laughed quietly   (d) clearly
hesitated.

10. But it was a corpse that knew its *resurrection*, for the man
rose suddenly on one elbow and gazed across at his
hillside.
Resurrection (524) means   (a) revival   (b) resting
place   (c) past   (d) hopes.

11. When he filled a pan with dirt he ran down the hill to
wash it, nor could he forbear (keep from) running up the
hill again, panting and *stumbling profanely*, to refill the
pan.
Stumbling profanely (525) means that he   (a) laughed
and joked   (b) tripped and cursed   (c) toiled and
sweated   (d) fell often.

12. He was enraged at having yielded to the temptation and
cursed himself *blasphemously* and pridelessly.
Blasphemously (526) means   (a) using strong language
(b) in very loud tones   (c) humorously
(d)   gently.

13. To the north and south he could see more distinctly the
cross systems that broke through the main *trend* of the sea
of mountains.
Trend (527) means   (a) heights   (b) expanse
(c) direction   (d) color scheme.

14. He seemed to know the precise time required for the turn
to *culminate in* disaster . . .
Culminate in (527) means   (a) control   (b) avert
(c) end   (d) end in.

15. Again, where even the fraction of a second's footing was
out of the question, he would swing his body past by a
moment's handgrip on a jutting knob of rock, a *crevice*, or
a precariously (insecurely) rooted shrub.
Crevice (528) means   (a) narrow split   (b) branch
(c) platform   (d) vine.

16. The first crosscut the man made, there was space for only
three holes, so narrow had become the pay streak and so
close was he to the *fountainhead* of the golden stream he
had been following for four days.
Fountainhead (529) means   (a) source   (b) limits
(c) total   (d) value.

17. Suddenly there came to him a *premonition* of danger.
Premonition (530) means   (a) warning   (b) cause
(c) reality   (d) result.

18. Every force of his being impelled him to spring up and
confront the unseen danger . . .
Confront (530) means   (a) avoid   (b) face
(c) conquer   (d) run away from.

19. . . . but his soul *dominated* the panic, and he remained
squatting on his heels, in his hands a chunk of gold.
Dominated (530) means   (a) gave in to   (b) examined
(c) disregarded   (d) controlled.

20. Still feigning (pretending) interest in the chunk of gold in
his hand, he listened *intently* and he heard the breathing
of the thing behind him.
Intently (530) means   (a) with close attention
(b) with heart beating wildly   (c) quietly   (d) stubbornly.

21. But suddenly he was blinded by a handful of dirt deliberately flung into his eyes by his *antagonist*.
Antagonist (532) means   (a) weight   (b) opponent
(c) confederate   (d) carelessness.

22. "*Measly* skunk!" he panted, "a-campin' on my trail an'

lettin' me do the work, and then shootin' me in the back!"
Measly (532) means   (a) contemptibly small
(b) dirty, smelly   (c) miserable   (d) traitorous.

23. Say, two hundred in quartz an' dirt—that leaves *two
     hundred pounds of gold!*
     Two hundred pounds of gold (533) today would be worth
     close to   (a) $50,000   (b) $500,000   (c) $1,500,000
     (d) $10,000,000.

24. His open shirt *disclosed* the rude bandages with which he
     had dressed his wound.
     Disclosed (533) means   (a) covered   (b) exposed
     (c) tested   (d) discolored.

25. They *quested* along it for several inches.
     Quested (533) means   (a) traveled   (b) dug
     (c) searched   (d) poked.

Thinking Critically About the Story _____

1. How would the environmentalists react to Bill's treatment
    of the canyon? Does mankind have the right to upset
    nature and endanger the existence of the other forms of life
    that share this planet? Explain your answer.

2. What were the major characteristics that led to Bill's
    successful prospecting? How do these traits compare with
    those of a successful executive? Teacher? Scientific re-
    searcher? Student? Parent?

3. Was Bill justified in killing the intruder? When, if ever, is
    homicide justified? To whom did the gold really belong?
    Was Bill as much a thief as the attacker?

4. How did Jack London use contrast to show that this is a
    story of life at a most elemental level?

5. To what extent is this a story of greed? How does Jack
    London show his reaction to greed? To what extent is greed
    justifiable? What emotion would you suggest as a replace-
    ment for greed?

Stories in Words

Soliloquy (518)   *Monolog* and *soliloquy* are an interesting pair of words. *Monolog* comes from two Greek words meaning "speaking alone." *Soliloquy* comes from two Latin words meaning "speaking alone." Including the pair demonstrates why English is so rich in synonyms. It borrows from all languages. *Soliloquy* is the narrower word, usually restricted to the stage. A *soliloquy* usually presents an actor's private thoughts to the audience. Like *soliloquy*, *monolog* has a dramatic use, but it is also applied to social situations when a speaker monopolizes the conversation. In this sense, it has a negative *connotation*, or suggested meaning.

Antagonist (532)   The Greek root *agon*, "struggle," appears in the English words *agony* and *agonize*. It also appears in an interesting pair of words. In ancient Greek tragedy, the *protagonist* was the leading character. The person who struggled against (*anti*) him was the *antagonist*. The latter word has become much more general.

Zenith (534)   During the Middle Ages, the Arabs excelled in science and mathematics. As a result, English has picked up many Arabic words dealing with those two subjects: *algebra, alkali, caliber, chemistry, cipher, zero. Zenith* comes from two Arabic words meaning "way over the head." The meaning persists today. *Zenith* means "the point in the sky directly overhead." It has gradually extended its meaning to suggest any high point, as in "the zenith of Roman power." The opposite of *zenith* is *nadir*, "the point directly below the observer." This, too, has become more general to mean "the lowest point."

The Proverb

Marcel Aymé

> ◆ "At your age you ought to understand that if I am hard on you it is for your own good. Later on you'll see that I was right. There's nothing better for a boy than a father who knows how to be stern."

What was it like to grow up during the days when throughout the land a teenager was seen but not heard, when a teenager did not speak until spoken to, when the father's word was law to all in his household?

Dinnertime in the Jacotin home brings all the members together at the end of the day's turmoil. When the dessert is finished, no one rises to leave. It is the time when the father, M. Jacotin, sits in lordly judgment. His is the task to evaluate the deeds of the day. Ridicule and fear are his major weapons.

To the dismay of the others around the table, the son, Lucien, leaves himself wide open and without defenses. He had spent his school holiday, Thursday, with his friends rather than with his schoolwork. M. Jacotin readily accepts Lucien as his worthy prey.

However, do not rush to conclusions about weak sons and tyrannical fathers. Do not judge either the son or the father before you reach the end of the story. Lucien's final action brings the story into an unexpected but logical perspective.

THE PROVERB

By the light of the hanging bulbs in the kitchen M. Jacotin surveyed his assembled family, who sat with their heads bowed over their plates, betraying by sidelong glances their mistrust of the master's mood. A profound consciousness of his own devotion and self-abnegation, together with an acute sense of domestic justice, did indeed render M. Jacotin both unjust and tyrannical, and his choleric explosions, always unpredictable, created in his household an atmosphere of constraint which in its turn had an irritating effect upon him.

Having learned during the afternoon that his name had been put forward for the *palmes académiques*, he had resolved to await the ending of the meal before informing his nearest and dearest; and now, after drinking a glass of wine with his cheese, he was ready to make the pronouncement. But the general tone of the gathering seemed to him not altogether propitious to the reception of the great news. His gaze went slowly round the table, pausing first at his wife, whose sickly aspect and timid, melancholy expression did him so little credit with his colleagues. He turned next to Aunt Julie, who was seated by the fireside in manifestation of her advanced age and several incurable maladies, and who in the past seven years must certainly have cost him more than was to be looked for under her will. Then came his two daughters, aged seventeen and sixteen, shop assistants at five hundred francs a month but dressed like film stars, with wristwatches, gold brooches at the bosom of their blouses, a general look of being above their station so that one wondered where the money came from and was amazed. M. Jacotin had a sudden intolerable feeling that his substance was filched from him, that the sweat of his labors was sucked dry, and that he was long-suffering to the point of absurdity. The wine rose in a wave to his head, suffusing his broad face, which was noteworthy for its redness even in repose.

And while he was in the grip of this emotion his gaze fell upon his thirteen-year-old son, Lucien, who since the beginning of supper had been doing his best to escape notice. There was something suspect in the pallor of the boy's face. He did not look up, but feeling his father's eyes upon him he twisted a corner of his black, schoolboy's overall with both hands.

"Trying to tear it, are you?" said M. Jacotin in a voice filled with gloating. "You seem to be doing your best to destroy it."

Lucien let go his apron and put his hands on the table. He bent over his plate without daring to seek the comfort of his sisters' glance, lonely in the face of approaching calamity.

"Do you hear me speaking to you? Can't you answer? I'm beginning to think you aren't quite easy in your mind."

Lucien replied with a look of apprehension, not from any hope of disarming suspicion but because he knew his father would be disappointed not to see alarm in his eyes.

"No, your conscience is certainly not clear. Will you please tell me what you've been doing this afternoon?"

"I was with Pichon. He said he'd come and fetch me at two. Then we met Chapusot, who had to go to the doctor because his uncle's ill. The day before yesterday his uncle started having a pain on his liver and—"

But realizing that the anecdote was designed to divert his attention, M. Jacotin cut it short.

"Never mind about other people's livers. Nobody bothers about my liver. Tell me what you did this morning."

"I went with Fourmont to see the house in the Avenue Poincaré that was burnt down the other night."

"In fact, you've been out all day, from first thing in the morning until this evening. Well, if you can afford to spend the whole of your Thursday amusing yourself, I take it that means you've done all your homework."

M. Jacotin uttered these words in a voice of mildness that caused all his hearers to hold their breath.

"My homework?" murmured Lucien.

"Yes, your homework."

"I worked yesterday evening when I got back from school."

"I'm not asking whether you worked yesterday evening. I'm asking if you have done your homework for tomorrow."

The others felt the crisis approaching and longed to avert it, but experience had taught them that any intervention in these circumstances would only make things worse, transforming the choleric man's ill temper into fury. Lucien's sisters tactfully pretended to ignore the scene, while his mother, preferring not to be too close a witness, got up and went to a cupboard. M. Jacotin himself, not yet launched upon his wrath, was reluctant to postpone the news of the *palmes académiques*. But Aunt Julie, moved to sympathy, could not hold her tongue.

"The way you always go on at the poor boy! He told you he worked yesterday evening. He has to play sometimes."

M. Jacotin replied with dignity:

"I must ask you kindly not to interfere with my efforts to assist my son's education. Being his father, I act as such, and I shall continue to supervise his activities as I think fit. When you have children of your own you will be at liberty to indulge them in any way you choose."

Aunt Julie, being seventy-three, seemed to detect a hint of irony in this reference to her future offspring. Greatly offended, she rose and left the kitchen. Lucien, apprehensively watching her departure, saw her for an instant groping for the switch in the half-light of the spotlessly clean living room. When she had shut the door behind her M. Jacotin called the family to witness that he had said nothing to warrant her withdrawal, and he went on to protest at a scheming maneuver designed to show him in an unfavorable light. But neither his daughters, who had begun to clear the table, nor his wife could bring themselves to acquiesce, although by doing so they might have relieved the tension. Their silence did him further outrage and he returned furiously to Lucien:

"I'm still waiting for your answer. Have you finished your homework or not?"

Realizing that he had nothing to gain by prolonging the agony, Lucien threw in his hand.

"I haven't done my French."

A gleam of thankfulness appeared in M. Jacotin's eyes. It was agreeable to tackle this boy.

"And why not, may I ask?"

Lucien raised his shoulders in token of ignorance and even of astonishment, as though the question had taken him by surprise.

"I'm waiting," said M. Jacotin, gazing intently at him.

For a moment longer he sat meditating in silence upon the iniquity and abject state of this graceless son, who for no avowable reason and with no appearance of remorse had failed to do his French homework.

"It's as I thought," he said, his voice gradually rising with his eloquence. "Not only do you neglect your work, but you do so deliberately. This French homework was set last Friday, to be shown up tomorrow. That is to say, you had a week to do it in, but you haven't done it. And if I had said nothing you would have gone to school tomorrow with it still not done. Worst of all, you have spent the whole of today idling and loafing. And with whom? With Pichon, Fourmont, Chapusot— boys as lazy as yourself, all at the bottom of the class! Birds of a feather flock together. It would naturally never have occurred to you to visit Béruchard. You would think it a disgrace, I suppose, to go and play with a good boy. But in any case Béruchard wouldn't want you. I'm sure he doesn't waste his time playing. He's not an idler, like you. Béruchard is a worker, and the result is he's always near the top. Only last week he was nine places above you. You can imagine how pleasant that is for me, seeing that I have to spend all day at the office with his father. A man, I may add, who is less well thought of than I am. A hardworking fellow, no doubt, but lacking in ability. And as limited in his political outlook as he is in his work. He has never had any imagination and he knows it. When we're discussing general topics, the other men and I, he keeps pretty quiet. But that doesn't stop him scoring over me whenever he mentions his son. And it puts me in a very awkward position. I'm not lucky enough to have a son like Béruchard's, always first in French and math, a boy who walks off with all the prizes. Lucien, kindly stop fiddling with that napkin ring. I will not tolerate impertinence. Are you listening, or do you want a box on the ears to remind you that I'm your father? Idle, useless oaf that you are! Your French homework was set a week ago. You can't pretend that this would have happened if you had any feeling for me or any sense of the burden you are to me. When I think of all the work I have to do, and my worries and anxieties, both for the present and the future! There'll be no one to keep me when I have to retire. One has to rely upon oneself in this world, not on other people. I've never asked a halfpenny of anyone, or expected any help from my neighbor when I was in trouble. I got nothing from my family either. My father didn't let me stay at school. I started my apprenticeship when I was twelve. Out in all weathers pulling the barrow, chilblains in winter and the shirt clinging to my back in summer. But you just loaf your time away because by good luck you have an overindulgent father. But don't imagine it will last forever. The more I think of it—your French homework utterly neglected! Lazy young lout! It never pays to be kind; people mistake it for weakness. And just when I was planning to take you all to the theater on Wednesday, to see 'Les Burgraves.' Little did I think what I should find when I got home! It's always the same—when I'm not here the place is in a state of chaos, homework not done, nothing done properly. And of course you had to choose the very day when . . .''

Here M. Jacotin made a pause. A sense of delicacy, of coyness and modesty, caused him to lower his eyes.

". . . the day when I learnt that my name has been put forward for the *palmes académiques*. That is the day you have chosen!''

He paused again, awaiting the effect of these words. But, following so abruptly upon the lengthy exordium, they seemed not to have been understood. The others had heard the sound, as they had heard the rest of his discourse, without grasping the sense. Only Mme. Jacotin, who knew that for two years her husband had been hoping for some recognition of his services as Honorary Treasurer of the local Musical Society, had the impression that something of importance had fallen from his lips. The words "*palmes académiques*" reached her ears with a sound at once familiar and exotic, evoking in her mind an image of her husband, in his honorary musician's cap, seated astride the topmost branches of a coconut palm. Her fear of having been inattentive caused her at length to grasp the meaning of this poetic vision, and she opened her mouth, prepared to utter sounds of deferent rejoicing. But it was too late. M. Jacotin, taking an acid pleasure in his family's indifference, and fearing lest a word from his wife might soften the effect of their heavy silence, hastened to forestall her.

"To continue," he said with a mirthless laugh. "I was saying that you have had a week in which to do this French homework. A week! I should like to know when Béruchard did his. I'm quite sure it didn't take him a week, or even half a week. I've no doubt Béruchard got it done next day. And now will you tell me what the homework consists of?"

Lucien, who was not listening, let slip the interval for a reply. His father called him to attention in a voice that could be heard three doors away, startling Aunt Julie in her bedroom. In her night attire and with a woebegone countenance she came to inquire the cause of the disturbance.

"What's the matter? What are you doing to that child? I insist upon knowing!"

Misfortune willed it that at this moment M. Jacotin's mind was principally occupied with the thought of his *palmes académiques*, and for this reason his patience failed him. Even at the height of his rages he was accustomed to express himself with moderation. But that an old woman taken into his home for charitable motives should thus browbeat a man on the verge of being decorated, seemed to him a provocation warranting extreme language.

"As for you," he said, "I can tell you what you are in five letters."

Aunt Julie gaped, round-eyed and unbelieving, and when he stated specifically what the five letters spelt she swooned. There were cries of alarm and a prolonged, dramatic hubbub filled with the clatter of kettles, bottles, and cups and saucers. Lucien's mother and sisters busied themselves about the sufferer with words of sympathy and consolation, each one a dart in M. Jacotin's flesh. They avoided looking at him, and when by chance their heads turned his way their eyes were hard. Conscious of his guilt, and feeling sorry for the old girl, he genuinely regretted his coarseness. Indeed, he would have liked to apologize, but in face of this ostentatious condemnation his pride hardened. As Aunt Julie was being led back to her room he said in a loud, clear voice:

"For the third time, will you tell me what your French homework is?"

"It's an essay," said Lucien. "I have to illustrate the proverb, 'Nothing is gained by running: it is better to start in time.'"

"Well? That doesn't sound very difficult."

Lucien nodded as though in agreement but with a noncommittal expression.

"Anyway, get your books and start work. I want to see it finished."

Lucien fetched his satchel, which was lying in a corner of the kitchen, got out his rough notebook and wrote at the head of a virgin page. "Nothing is gained by running: it is better to start in time." Slowly though his hand moved, he could not make this take more than a minute or two. He then sucked the end of his pen while he brooded over the words with a hostile and sulky air.

"I can see you aren't really trying," said his father. "Well, please yourself. I'm in no hurry. I'm quite prepared to sit up all night."

He had settled himself comfortably and in an attitude of calm resolution that filled Lucien with despair. He tried to think about the proverb, "Nothing is gained by running: it is better to start in time." The thing seemed to him too obvious to call for demonstration, and he thought with scorn of La Fontaine's fable about the Hare and the Tortoise. Meanwhile his sisters, after getting Aunt Julie to bed, had begun to put the dishes and plates back in the dresser. Despite their attempts to do so silently they made rattling sounds that irritated M. Jacotin, who suspected them of trying to provide their brother with an excuse for doing nothing. And suddenly there was a hideous clatter. His wife had let fall an iron saucepan over the sink so that it rebounded on to the floor.

"Be careful, can't you?" snapped M. Jacotin. "It's really very trying. How do you expect the boy to work with this racket going on? Go away and don't disturb him. You've finished washing up. Go to bed."

The women left the kitchen at once. Lucien was left defenseless, at the mercy of his father and the night, and conjuring up a vision of death in the dawn, strangled by a proverb, he burst into tears.

"A lot of good that's going to do you," said his father. "Don't be a little child!"

Although he spoke roughly there was now a hint of compassion in his voice, for M. Jacotin, still upset by the crisis he had provoked, hoped to redeem himself by showing some clemency in his treatment of his son. Perceiving the change, Lucien's self-pity deepened and he wept the more. His father, genuinely touched, came round the table bringing a chair with him and seated himself at the boy's side.

"That'll do. Get out your handkerchief and stop crying. At your age you ought to understand that if I'm hard on you it's for your own good. Later on you'll see that I was right. There's nothing better for a boy than a father who knows how to be stern. Oddly enough, Béruchard was saying the same thing to me only the other day. He makes no bones about beating his lad. Sometimes he'll just give him a clout or a kick in the pants, but at other times it's the cane. And he gets good results, what's more. He knows the boy's on the right road and that he'll go far. But I could never bring myself to strike a child, except of course just now and then, on the spur of the moment. We all have our own methods, as I said to Béruchard. Personally I think it's better to use persuasion."

Disarmed by these soothing words, Lucien had stopped crying, a fact which caused his father to feel certain misgivings.

"Mind you, you mustn't mistake it for weakness on my part if I talk to you as though you were grown up!"

"Oh, no!" said Lucien in a voice of profound conviction.

Reassured, M. Jacotin mellowed again. As he considered the proverb on the one hand and his son's distress on the other, it seemed to him that he could afford to be generous, and he said amiably:

"I can see that if I don't lend you a hand we shall be here till breakfast. We'd better get started. We have to show that 'Nothing is gained by running: it is better to start in time.' Well, now let me see. Nothing is gained by running . . ."

Until this moment the subject of the essay had appeared to

M. Jacotin almost ludicrously simple; but now that he had taken over the job he began to see it in a different light. With a somewhat worried expression he reread the sentence several times and then murmured:

"It's a proverb."

"Yes," said Lucien, and sat confidently awaiting further enlightenment.

His innocent trustfulness touched M. Jacotin's heart, while at the same time the thought that his prestige as a father was at stake occasioned in him a certain dismay.

"Did your master say anything when he set the subject?" he asked.

"He said, 'Whatever else you do, don't quote the fable of the Hare and the Tortoise. You must find an example of your own.' That's what he said."

"Ha!" said M. Jacotin. "I must say, the Hare and the Tortoise is an excellent illustration. I hadn't thought of that."

"But it's forbidden."

"Yes, of course—forbidden. But good grief, if everything's forbidden——!"

His face a little suffused, M. Jacotin groped round for some other idea, or at the very least for a phrase which would serve as a point of departure. His imagination did not prove helpful. He began to consider the proverb with feelings of alarm and exasperation, and by degrees his face assumed the same expression of boredom that Lucien's had worn a short time before.

Finally a notion occurred to him arising out of a newspaper headline that had caught his eye only that morning—"The Armaments Race." It promised well. A certain country has for a long time been preparing for war, producing guns, tanks, bombs and aircraft, while its neighbor has been sluggish in its preparations, so that when war breaks out it is by no means ready and struggles in vain to catch up. Here was the material for an admirable essay.

But then M. Jacotin's countenance, which had momentarily lightened, again grew somber. He had recalled that his political creed did not permit him to choose an example so tendentious in its nature. He was too high-minded to do injury to his principles, but it was a great pity. Despite the firmness of

his convictions he could not help slightly regretting that he
was not the helot of one of the parties of reaction, which would
have allowed him to develop an idea with the approval of his
conscience. He consoled himself with the thought of the *palmes
académiques*, but gloomily, nonetheless.

Lucien sat placidly awaiting the outcome of his medita-
tions. Having, as he considered, been relieved of the task of
elucidating the proverb, he was no longer even thinking about
it. But his father's protracted silence made the time seem slow
in passing. His lids drooped and he yawned widely several
times. To M. Jacotin, tight-lipped with the effort of concentration, these yawns were a reproach, and his state of nervous
tension increased. Rack his brains as he would, he could think

of nothing else. The armaments race had become a hindrance. It seemed to have attached itself to the proverb, and his very attempts to dismiss it brought it the more vividly to his mind. From time to time he glanced covertly and anxiously at his son.

At length, when he had almost given up hope and was on the verge of admitting failure, he had another idea. It came to him as a sort of offshoot of the armaments race, dispelling that obsession from his mind. This time it was a sporting contest— two crews of oarsmen in training, the one going about it methodically, the other with a negligent air.

"Right," said M. Jacotin. "Take this down."

Lucien, who was dozing, started and reached hastily for his pen.

"What! Do you mean to say you were asleep?"

"Oh, no. I was thinking. I was thinking about the proverb. But I couldn't think of anything."

M. Jacotin chuckled indulgently. Then his gaze became fixed and he began slowly to dictate.

"On this glorious Sunday afternoon, comma, what are those long, comma, slender, comma, green objects that present themselves to our gaze? Seen at a distance one might suppose them to possess long arms, but those arms are none other than oars, and the green objects are in reality racing-boats rocking gently upon the waters of the Marne . . ."

Lucien at this point raised his head and looked at his father in some alarm, but M. Jacotin, absorbed in polishing a transitional phrase which would enable him to introduce the rival crews, paid no attention. With mouth half-open and eyes half-closed he was contemplating his oarsmen and grouping them within the structure of his argument. His hand groped for his son's pen.

"Give that to me. I'll write it myself. It's better than dictating."

He began to write feverishly and copiously. Thoughts and words came in an effortless flow, and in a sequence that was at once convenient and exhilarating, lending itself to lyrical treatment. He felt rich, master of a fruitful and abundant domain. For a few more moments, and still with apprehension, Lucien watched the inspired pen traveling rapidly across the page of his exercise book, and then he fell asleep with his head on the table. At eleven o'clock his father woke him and handed the book back.

"Now you must copy it out carefully. I'll go over it when you've finished. Take particular care with the punctuation."

"It's rather late," said Lucien. "Perhaps it would be better if I got up early in the morning."

"No, no. One must strike while the iron's hot. And there's another proverb for you!" M. Jacotin smiled delightedly and added: "What's more, it's another that I should have no difficulty in illustrating. I'd be quite ready to tackle it, if I could spare the time. A splendid subject. I could do you a dozen pages on it. Well, at least I hope you understand what it means."

"What?"

"I'm asking you if you know the meaning of the proverb, 'Strike while the iron's hot.' "

Lucien nearly gave way to despair. He pulled himself together and said very gently:

"Yes father, I understand it. But now I must copy this one."

"That's right, copy it out," said M. Jacotin in the tone of one who disdains the humbler activities.

A week later Lucien's form master returned the corrected essays.

"Taking them all round," he said, "they're a poor lot. Apart from Béruchard, who gets thirteen, and three or four others, none of you has understood the subject."

He went on to explain what should have been done, and then selected for comment three out of the pile of exercise books with their red-ink markings. The first was Béruchard's, which he praised. The third was Lucien's.

"When I read your essay, Jacotin, I was startled by a literary manner to which you have not accustomed me, and which I found so distasteful that I had no hesitation in giving you only three. If I have often in the past had occasion to complain of your flat-footedness, this time you have gone to the opposite extreme. You have managed to fill six pages with matter that is entirely beside the point. And what is most intolerable is the odiously florid style you have seen fit to adopt."

The master talked for some time about Lucien's essay, offering it to the class as a model of what not to do. He read out certain passages which he thought especially instructive. There were grins and giggles and even one or two bursts of prolonged laughter. Lucien turned very pale, deeply wounded in his sense of filial piety no less than in his self-esteem.

And at the same time he was furious with his father for having brought this mockery upon him. Indifferent scholar though he was, neither his negligence nor his ignorance had hitherto exposed him to ridicule. Whether the subject was French, Latin or algebra, he contrived in his very inadequacy to show a regard for the scholastic proprieties and even for scholastic elegance. When he had copied his father's text, his eyes half-closing with sleep, he had had little doubt as to how the essay would be received. In the morning, with his wits about him, he had been half-inclined not to show it up, being more than ever conscious of its many discordances and false notes in terms of what was acceptable in the classroom. But at the last moment an instinctive trust in his father's infallibility had decided the matter.

When he came home at midday he was still angrily brooding over that impulse of almost religious faith which had caused him to go against his better judgment. What business had his father to do his homework for him? It served him right that he had only got three out of twenty, and perhaps this would cure him of trying to write essays. And Béruchard had got thirteen. Father would find that hard to swallow. That would teach him!

As they sat down to lunch M. Jacotin appeared joyful and almost amiable, his looks and words invested with a slightly feverish liveliness. He coyly refrained from at once asking the question which was uppermost in his mind and his son's. The atmosphere round the table was not much different from that of other days. The father's high spirits, far from putting the rest at ease, were rather an added source of discomfort. Mme. Jacotin and her daughters struggled in vain to adapt their manner to his own, while Aunt Julie made a point of emphasizing, by her sulky demeanor and air of offended surprise, how strange this display of good humor appeared in the eyes of the family. M. Jacotin evidently felt it himself, because his mood rapidly darkened.

"Well," he said abruptly, "and what about the proverb?"

His voice betrayed an emotion more akin to nervousness than to mere impatience. And in that instant Lucien perceived that he had the power to do lasting injury to his father. He saw him suddenly with a detachment that delivered him into his hands. He realized that for many years the unhappy man had lived on the sense of his infallibility as head of the household, and that when he had set out to elucidate the proverb he had exposed his principle to a dangerous hazard. Not only was the domestic tyrant about to lose face in the eyes of his family, but the consideration in which he held himself would also be undermined. It would be a disaster. In the familiar setting of the kitchen, the group round the table, Aunt Julie ever-watchful for the chance to score a point, the crisis that a single word might provoke assumed a shattering reality. Confronted by the startling discovery of his father's weakness, Lucien's heart melted in generous commiseration.

"Have you gone to sleep? I'm asking you if your master has returned my essay," said M. Jacotin.

"Your essay? Yes, he gave it back."

"And how many marks did we get?"

"Thirteen."

"Well, that's not bad. How about Béruchard?"

"He got thirteen too."

"And what was the most anyone got?"

"Thirteen."

M. Jacotin was radiant. He turned to gaze fixedly at Aunt Julie, as though the thirteen marks had been awarded in her despite. Lucien had lowered his eyes and was communing with himself in secret gratification. M. Jacotin laid a hand on his shoulder and said kindly:

"You see, my dear boy, the most important thing, when one starts on a piece of work, is to think it over carefully. Thoroughly to understand one's task is more than half the battle. That is what I want to get firmly into your head. I shall succeed in the end. I shall spare no pains. From now on we will do all your essays together."

Reading for Understanding _____

Main Idea

1. Which of the following proverbs best expresses the main idea of the story?
   (a) A stitch in time saves nine.
   (b) Early to bed, early to rise, make Lucien an alert teenager.
   (c) Love giveth understanding.
   (d) Time and tide wait for no person.

Details

2. In the French household, wine and cheese are served
   (a) as an introduction   (b) between courses
   (c) at any time   (d) at the end of the meal.

3. The wine he drinks does not make M. Jacotin
   (a) sorry for himself   (b) feel put upon by his family
   (c) severely critical   (d) a willing listener.

4. Lucien is about   (a) 9 years old   (b) 13 years old
   (c) 17 years old   (d) 20 years old.

5. M. Jacotin does not fault Lucien for   (a) neglecting his schoolwork   (b) lying   (c) picking the "wrong" type of friends   (d) misusing his time.

6. Aunt Julie swoons because M. Jacotin   (a) is too sarcastic   (b) uses foul language   (c) is not sorry for his outburst   (d) causes Lucien to run out of the room.

Inferences

7. Lucien becomes the prime target for the evening because
   (a) he eats slowly   (b) he is too talkative   (c) he is pale and nervous   (d) he looks too relaxed.

8. The mother and sisters do not come to Lucien's defense because   (a) they enjoy seeing him the victim   (b) they see nothing wrong in M. Jacotin's behavior

(c) any interference would make the father more irritable
(d) Lucien had hurt their feelings.

9. The only one who has M. Jacotin's sympathy is
(a) his aunt   (b) his wife   (c) the neighbor
(d) himself.

10. The family misses M. Jacotin's announcement of the prize
because   (a) it is mumbled   (b) Lucien begins to cry
loudly   (c) it is tacked on to M. Jacotin's usual speech
(d) they do not know what the prize signifies.

Order of Events

11. Arrange the items in the order in which they occurred.
Use letters only.
A. Lucien lies for his father's sake.
B. M. Jacotin hurts Aunt Julie's feelings.
C. The teacher has a field day at Jacotin's expense.
D. M. Jacotin finds that Lucien is not listening to him.
E. Lucien breaks down and cries.

Outcomes

12. Which of the following is the logical outcome of the story?
(a) Lucien gets to know himself better.
(b) M. Jacotin learns to appreciate his son.
(c) M. Jacotin learns to control his use of anger as an
outlet for his own frustrations.
(d) Aunt Julie goes to a retirement home.

Cause and Effect

13. It is ironic that M. Jacotin feels closer to Lucien because
(a) Lucien wins the prize   (b) the teacher praises Lucien's honesty   (c) Lucien lies to him   (d) Lucien asks
M. Jacotin to assist him with his homework.

Fact or Opinion

Tell whether each of the following is a fact or an opinion.
14. The teacher criticizes Lucien's essay because he realizes
that the boy had not written it without adult help.

15. Lack of material success in life has made M. Jacotin a petty tyrant.

Words in Context _____

1. A profound consciousness of his own devotion ... did indeed *render* M. Jacotin both unjust and tyrannical.
   Render (543) means (a) cause to become (b) picture as (c) expose as (d) develop into.

2. ... and now, after drinking a glass of wine with his cheese, he was ready to make the *pronouncement*.
   Pronouncement (543) means (a) award (b) public statement (c) prediction (d) honor.

3. But realizing that the anecdote was designed to *divert* his attention, M. Jacotin cut it short.
   Divert (544) means (a) attract (b) cut short (c) develop (d) sidetrack.

4. The others felt the crisis approaching and longed to *avert* it ...
   Avert (545) means (a) intensify (b) control (c) solve (d) forestall.

5. "I will not *tolerate impertinence*."
   Tolerate impertinence (546) means (a) encourage delinquency (b) pardon laziness (c) permit rudeness (d) encourage deception.

6. "Idle, useless *oaf* that you are! Your French homework was set a week ago."
   Oaf (546) means (a) simpleton (b) deceiver (c) fraud (d) fox.

7. "Out in all weathers pulling the *barrow* ..."
   Barrow (547) means (a) handcart (b) nails (c) heavy loads (d) sled.

8. "... *chilblains* in winter and the shirt clinging to my back in summer."
   Chilblains (547) means (a) chills (b) fever (c) frostbite (d) itchy sores from the cold.

9. A sense *of delicacy, of coyness* and modesty, caused him to lower his eyes.
   Of delicacy, of coyness (547) means (a) of pride, of accomplishment (b) of weakness, of envy (c) of tact, of pretended shyness (d) of loyalty, of acceptance.

10. Although he spoke roughly there was now a hint of *compassion* in his voice . . .
    Compassion (550) means (a) self-pity (b) sternness (c) tenderness (d) gloating.

11. . . . for M. Jacotin, still upset by the crisis he had provoked, hoped to redeem himself by showing some *clemency* in his treatment of his son.
    Clemency (550) means (a) sternness (b) understanding (c) love (d) mercy.

12. "Yes," said Lucien, and sat confidently awaiting further *enlightenment*.
    Enlightenment (551) means (a) advice (b) instruction (c) remarks (d) questioning.

13. But then M. Jacotin's countenance, which had momentarily lightened, again grew *somber*.
    Somber (551) means (a) dark and gloomy (b) lively and concerned (c) defensive and sad (d) heavy-handed.

14. He was too *high-minded* to do injury to his principles, but it was a great pity.
    High-minded (551) means (a) realistic (b) moral (c) well educated (d) serious.

15. It came to him as a sort of offshoot of the armaments race, *dispelling that obsession from his mind*.
    Dispelling that obsession from his mind (553) means (a) making him think more originally (b) letting him think of something else (c) emptying his mind of false impressions (d) making him almost forget the assignment topic.

16. . . . but M. Jacotin, absorbed in polishing a *transitional* phrase which would enable him to introduce the rival crews, paid no attention.

Transitional (553) means   (a) dramatic   (b) suitable   (c) connecting   (d) simple.

17. "Give that to me. I'll write it myself. It's better than dictating." He began to write *feverishly and copiously.*
Feverishly and copiously (553) means   (a) slowly and cautiously   (b) coolly and deliberately   (c) hurriedly and plentifully   (d) at top speed and with very few erasures.

18. Thoughts and words came in an effortless flow, and in a sequence that was at once convenient and *exhilarating . . .*
Exhilarating (553) means   (a) stimulating   (b) annoying   (c) appropriate   (d) wordy.

19. Lucien turned very pale, deeply wounded in his sense of *filial piety* no less than in his self-esteem.
Filial piety (555) means   (a) child's respect for parent   (b) devotion to ideals   (c) child's religious obligations   (d) parents' obligations toward their children.

20. *Indifferent* scholar though he was, neither his negligence nor his ignorance had hitherto exposed him to ridicule.
Indifferent (555) means   (a) exceptional   (b) concerned   (c) hostile   (d) mediocre.

Thinking Critically About the Story _____

1. M. Jacotin is opposed to the use of corporal punishment in handling Julien. He calls his method persuasion. How effective is his method? Is there an alternative? Explain.

2. How far should parents go in assisting their children with their homework? When do they go too far? How can teachers help in this process?

3. How does M. Jacotin compare with a typical American parent? Is he exaggerated? Explain. Have you met other parents like him? How does he compare with the fathers of your acquaintances? What causes parents to react the way they do? How can they be made to see their own errors?

4. Why is Aunt Julie part of the household? Did she have an alternative? Should grandparents and elderly relatives live with members of the next generation? What are the advantages and disadvantages? What alternatives are available today?

5. M. Jacotin's favorite method of correction is holding himself up as a model. He retells stories from his own life so that the children can benefit from them. In your opinion do you think that this is an effective method? What are the advantages to be gained from using this approach? What are the disadvantages? Do your parents use this approach? How effective is it with you? When does it lose its effectiveness for you? What method, if any, do you find effective?

Stories in Words

Tyrannical (543)   In ancient Greece, a *tyrant*, "tyrannos," was "a ruler, a prince," but since rulers often abused their privileges, *tyrant* acquired a negative *connotation*, or flavor. It was a neutral word at one time, but the word went downhill, a process called *degeneration*. Now *tyrant* means "an absolute, cruel, oppressive ruler." The meaning is still neutral in the title of a famous Greek play, *Oedipus Tyrannos*. The title is usually translated in English as *Oedipus the King*. The opposite process of degeneration is called *elevation*. *Fond*, for example, once meant "foolish."

Choleric (545)   Many years ago it was believed that four fluids, or *humors*, controlled the body: phlegm, blood, black bile, and yellow bile. These humors determined the personalities of people. Persons dominated by *phlegm*—from the Greek *phlegma*—were *phlegmatic:* "sluggish, dull." Persons dominated by blood—from the Latin *sanguis*—were *sanguine:* "confident, optimistic." Persons dominated by black bile—from the Greek *melas* and *chole*—were *melancholy*: "gloomy, depressed." Persons dominated by yellow bile—from the Greek *chole*—were *choleric*: "irritable, hot-tempered." There are vestiges of these old beliefs in expressions like *good-humored*.

Napkin (546) What connection does *napkin* have with *map*? *Map* is derived from the Latin *mappa mundi*, "map of the world." *Mappa* was the Latin word for *cloth*. *Napkin* also comes from *mappa*, but something has happened to the word. The suffix *kin*, which has been added to the root, is a diminutive suffix. It makes smaller whatever it is attached to. By derivation, a *manikin* is a "little man." A *lambkin* is a "little lamb." Other diminutive suffixes include *ette—luncheonette, statuette, kitchenette—*and *let— booklet, wristlet, ringlet, piglet.* The diminutive suffix *y* or *ie* is often added to names to suggest affection: *Johnny, Susie, Tommy.*

The Old Woman

Joyce Marshall

♦ **He knew the country, but he had been away. And then he had returned alone to this place, where for so long every year the winter buried you, snow blinded you, the wind screamed up the hill at night, and the water thundered.**

Anteus, a giant in Greek mythology, was deemed unconquerable; he quickly and easily defeated all who dared to challenge him—until he met Hercules who had learned the source of the giant's strength. When the battle between Hercules and Anteus began, Hercules lifted Anteus and held him high off the ground. Without contact with the earth, Anteus quickly became powerless.

The defeat of Anteus by forces that robbed him of his source of strength has been retold in many different tales in many different countries. The Biblical tale of Sampson and Delilah has a similar theme.

The story you are about to read is a modern retelling, with a modern twist. It takes place in the snowbelt of Canada, in the first quarter of the twentieth century. The protective force for the main character, an engineer named Toddy, is not his physical strength but his mind.

The enemy, as with Anteus, attacks with relentless purpose. The end comes so swiftly that neither Toddy nor his wife can oppose it. But enough of this! Let the story tell you the tale! Who is the enemy? Read and find out.

THE OLD WOMAN

He has changed, Molly thought, the instant she glimpsed her husband in the station at Montreal. He has changed. . . . The thought thudded hollowly through her mind, over and over during the long train ride into northern Quebec.

It was more than the absence of uniform. His face seemed so still, and there was something about his mouth—a sort of slackness. And at times she would turn and find him looking at her, his eyes absorbed and watchful.

"I am glad to see you," he kept saying. "I thought you would never make it, Moll."

"I know," she said. "But I had to wait till Mother was really well. . . . It *has* been a long three years, hasn't it?"

Apart from repeating his gladness at her arrival, he seemed to have little to say. He was just strange with her, she tried to soothe herself. They had known each other less than a year when they married in England during the war, and he had left for Canada so soon without her. He must have found it hard to hold a picture of her, just as she had found it hard to hold a picture of him. As soon as they got home—whatever home might be in this strange romantic north to which the train was drawing them—he would be more nearly the Toddy she had known.

It was grey dawn faintly disturbed with pink when they left the train, the only passengers for this little town of Missawani, at the tip of Lake St. John. The name on the greyed shingle reassured Molly a little. How often she had spelled out the strange syllables on letters to Toddy—the double s, the unexpected single n. Somewhere beyond this huddle of low wooden shacks, she knew, was the big Mason paper mill, and Toddy's powerhouse—one of several that supplied it with electricity—was more than thirty miles away. There was a road, Toddy had told her, but it was closed in winter.

A sullen youth waited behind the station with the dogs. Such beautiful dogs, black brindled with cream, their mouths spread wide in what seemed to Molly happy smiles of welcome. She put a hand toward the nose of the lead dog, but he lunged and Toddy drew her back.

"They're brutes," he told her. "All of them wolfish brutes."

It was a long strange journey over the snow, first through pink-streaked grey, then into a sun that first dazzled and then inflamed the eyes.

Snow that was flung up coarse and stinging from the feet of the dogs, black brittle fir trees, birches gleaming like white silk. No sound but the panting breath of the dogs, the dry leatherlike squeak of the snow under the sleigh's runners, and Toddy's rare French-spoken commands to the dogs.

At last he poked her back wordlessly and pointed a mittened hand over her shoulder. For an instant the picture seemed to hang suspended before Molly's eyes: the bare hill with the square red house at its top, the dam level with the top of the hill, the waterfall steaming down to a white swirl of rapids, the powerhouse like a squat grey cylinder at its foot.

"My old woman," Toddy shouted, and she saw that he was pointing, not up the hill towards the house where they would live, but to the powerhouse below.

In England his habit of personalizing an electric generating plant had charmed her, fitting her picturesque notions of the Canadian north. But now she felt uneasiness prod her. It was such a sinister-looking building, and the sound of falling water was so loud and engulfing.

The kitchen of the red house had what Molly thought of as a "poor" smell about it. Still, no one expected a man to be a good housewife. As soon as she could shut the door and get rid of the sound of that water, she told herself, it would be better. She looked quickly behind her, but Toddy had shut the door already. There must be a window open somewhere. It couldn't be possible that the waterfall was going to live with them in the house like this. It couldn't be possible.

"Cheerful sort of sound," said Toddy.

Molly looked at him vaguely, half-hearing. A window somewhere—there must be a window she could close.

He showed her quickly over the house, which was fairly well furnished and comfortably heated by electricity. Then he turned to her almost apologetically.

"I hope you won't mind if I go down right away," he said. "I'd like to see what kind of shape the old woman's got herself into while I've been away."

He looked elated and eager, and she smiled at him.

"Go ahead," she said. "I'll be all right."

After he had gone she unpacked her bags and went down to the living room. It had a broad window, overlooking the powerhouse, the rapids, and a long snowfield disappearing into the black huddle of pine bush. Snow, she thought. I always thought snow was white, but it's blue. Blue and treacherous as steel. And fully for the first time she realized how cut off they were to be—cut off from town by thirty odd miles of snow and tangled bush and roadlessness.

She found a pail and mop and began to clean the kitchen. She would have it all fresh and nice by the time Toddy came back. She would have no time to look out into the almost instantly blinding glare of the snow. She might even be able to ignore the thundering of the water. She was going to have to spend a lot of time alone in this house. She would have to learn to keep busy.

Toddy did not come up till evening. The powerhouse was in very bad shape, he told her.

"Those French operators and assistants are a lazy bunch of bums. It's amazing how they can let things go to hell in just two days."

Molly had set dinner on a little table in the living room. Toddy had wolfed his meal, his face preoccupied.

He *was* different. She hadn't just been imagining it. She had thought he would seem closer to her here, but he was more withdrawn than ever. For an instant she had a curious sense that none of this was real to him—not the dinner, nothing but the turbines and generators in the plant below.

Well, so you married this man, she told herself briskly, because you were thirty-eight and he looked nice in his officer's uniform. You followed him here because you were entranced with the idea of a strange and different place. So it is strange and different. And you have to start imagining things, just because your husband is a busy man who seems scarcely to notice that you are here.

"I'm going to make this place ever so much cosier," she heard herself saying, in a voice so importunate she scarcely recognized it as her own.

"What—oh, yes—yes, fine. Make any changes you like."

He finished eating and stood up.

"Well, I must be going back now."

"Back?" He wasn't even apologizing this time, she realized dully. "Won't your old woman give you an evening off—even when your wife has just come from the old country?"

"I've still things to do," he said. "You needn't be lonely. There's a radio—though I'm afraid the static's pretty bad on account of the plant. And I'll be only fifty feet away."

It was a week before he considered the powerhouse in suitable shape to show her. He showed her around it proudly— the squat gleaming turbines lying like fat sleepers along the floor, one of the four dismantled so that he could explain the power generator within, the gauges on the wall.

"It's very interesting, dear," she said, trying to understand his love for these inanimates, his glowing delight in the meshing parts.

"Perhaps now she looks so slick," she added, "you won't have to give her so much of your time."

"You'd be surprised how quickly she can go wrong," said Toddy.

He continued to spend all his hours there, from eight in the morning until late at night, with only brief spaces for meals.

Molly worked vigorously about the house and soon it was cleaned and sparkling from top to bottom. After that it was harder to keep busy. She read all the books she had brought, even the ancient magazines she found about the house. She could not go out. It was impossible to do more than keep a path cleared down to the powerhouse. There were no skis or snow-shoes, and Toddy could not seem to find time to teach her to drive the dogs. There were no neighbors within miles, no telephone calls or visits from milkman or baker—only one of

Toddy's sweepers coming once a fortnight with supplies and mail from Missawani.

She looked forward almost wildly to these visits, for they meant a break as well as letters from home. The men all lived on the nearby concessions*—"ranges" they were called here in northern Quebec—six or seven or eight miles away, driving back and forth to the powerhouse by dog team. She tried to get them to tell her about their lives and their families, but they were taciturn, just barely polite, and she felt that they simply did not like this house of which she was a part.

She tried constantly to build up some sort of closeness between herself and Toddy. But he seemed only to become less talkative—he had always had a lot of cheerful small talk in England—and more absorbed in the powerhouse. He seemed to accept her presence as a fact which pleased him, but he had no companionship to spare for her.

"I wish," she said to him one day, "that you could go out with me soon and teach me to drive the dogs."

"But where would you go?" he asked.

"Oh," she said, "around. Over the snow."

"But I'm so busy," he said. "I'm sorry—but this is my work, and I'm so busy."

As he spoke, she saw in his eyes again that look that had terrified her so the first day. Now she thought she recognized what it was. It was a watchful look, a powerful look, as if he were still in the presence of his machinery.

"But couldn't you take an afternoon? Those machines look as if they practically ran themselves. Couldn't you even take a Sunday, Toddy?"

"What if something went wrong while I was away?"

"Oh, Toddy, it can't need you every minute. I'm your wife and I need you too. You seemed so anxious for the time when I'd be able to come here. I can imagine how a person might get to hate being here alone, with that water always roaring and—"

Toddy's face became suddenly angry and wild.

"What do you mean?" he demanded.

"Just that you had three years here alone," she began.

* *Concessions* small communities built on government land

"I have never been bushed," Toddy interrupted furiously. "How dare you suggest that such a thing could ever happen to me? My God, apart from the war, I've lived in this country for twenty years."

Bushed. The suggestion was his, and for a moment she allowed herself to think about it. She was familiar with the term. Toddy used it constantly about others who had come up north to live. He knew the country, but he had been away. And then he had returned alone to this place, where for so long every year the winter buried you, snow blinded you, the wind screamed up the hill at night, and the water thundered. . . .

"Toddy," she said, afraid of the thought, putting it out of her mind, "when spring comes, couldn't we get a cow or two. I *do* know about cattle—I wasn't in the Land Army all through the war for nothing. I think it would give me an interest."

Toddy stared at her.

"Aren't you my wife?" he asked.

"Why yes—yes, of course."

"Then how can you speak about needing an interest? Isn't there interest enough for you in simply being my wife?"

"But I'm—I'm left so much alone. You have your work, but I have so little to do."

Toddy turned on his heel, preparing to go again to the powerhouse. At the door he glanced back over his shoulder, not speaking, merely watching her.

He doesn't want me to have an interest, thought Molly, her mind bruised with horror and fear. He looks at me watchfully, as if I were one of his machines. Perhaps that's what he wants me to be—a generator, quiet and docile, waiting for him here, moving only when he tells me to move.

And I am the sort of woman who must have work to do. If I don't, my mind will grow dim and misty. Already I can feel the long sweep of the snow trying to draw my thoughts out till they become diffused and vague. I can feel the sound of the water trying to crush and madden me.

After that, it seemed as if Toddy were trying to spend more time with her. Several times he sat and talked with her after dinner, telling her about the powerhouse and the catastrophes he had averted that day. But always his eyes would be turning

to the window and the powerhouse showing grey and sullen against the snow.

"Oh, you can go down now, Toddy," Molly would say. "Obviously, that is where you wish to be."

And then one day she found the work she wanted.

She looked up from her dishes to see Louis-Paul, one of the powerhouse oilers, standing in the doorway, snow leaking from his great felt boots on to the floor.

"Madame—" he said.

"Oh Louis, hello," said Molly warmly, for she was friendlier with this slight, fair youth than with any of Toddy's other workmen. They had long solemn conversations—she practicing her French and he his English. "But don't tell the Curé," Louis would say. "He does not like it if we speak English."

"Did you come for my list?" Molly asked him. "Are you going to town?"

"No, Madame, I have—how you say it?—I am today in big trouble. My Lucienne—"

"Oh, the baby—has your baby been born, Louis-Paul?"

"Yes, madame—"

With a hopeless gesture he relinquished his English. From his rapid, desperate French, Molly learned that there was something that prevented Lucienne from nursing her child, and none of the cows on any of the ranges were giving milk that winter.

"If you could come, madame, you might know—you might do something—"

His team of yellow dogs was tied at the kitchen stoop. Together Louis-Paul and Molly dashed across the snow to the house at the first range. Just a little bit of a house that Louis-Paul's father had built for him six years ago when he divided his thin-soiled farm and his timber lots among his sons. Its roof was the warm grey of weathered wood, almost as deeply curved as the roof of a Chinese pagoda.

In the kitchen Lucienne's mother and sisters and aunts in all their black wept noisily, one of them holding the crying child. And in the bedroom the girl Lucienne was sobbing, because she realized that the presence of her relatives in their best black meant that her child could not be saved.

Molly looked at her for a moment—the swarthy broad cheeks, the narrow eyes, that showed a tinge of Indian blood.

"Would you be shy with me, Lucienne?" she asked. "Too shy to take off your nightgown while I am here?"

"I would never be shy with you, madame," said Lucienne.

Something hot came into Molly's throat as she eased the nightgown from the girl's shoulders and went into the kitchen for hot and cold water and a quantity of cloths.

Tenderly she bathed her chest with alternate hot and cold water, explaining that this should bring on the flow of milk. And before she left, Lucienne was holding the baby's dark head against her breast, weeping silently; the wailing in the kitchen had ceased, and Louis-Paul was fixing stiff portions of whisky blanc and homemade wine, passing the one wineglass around and around the assembly.

Not until she was back at the red house, actually stamping the snow from her boots on the kitchen stoop, did Molly realize that it was long past the early dinner that Toddy liked. She went in quickly.

Toddy was standing in the middle of the room, his hands dangling with a peculiar slackness at his sides. He looked at her, and there was a great empty bewilderment on his face.

"You have been out?" he asked.

"Yes," she said, elated still from her afternoon. "I went over to Louis-Paul's with him. His wife's had her baby and—"

"He asked you?" said Toddy.

"Yes," she said. "He was desperate, poor lad, so I just had to offer to do what I could."

He's afraid I'll go away, she thought. He must have come up here and found the stove cold and thought I had gone forever. The thought alternately reassured and chilled her. It was simple and ordinary for him to be anxious, but his expression was neither simple nor ordinary. Now that she had explained, he should not be staring at her still, his gaze thinned by surprise and fear.

"I'm sorry about dinner," she said, "but I'll hurry and fix something easy. You have a smoke and I'll tell you all about it."

She told him but he would not join in her enthusiasm.

"Another French-Canadian brat," he said. "Molly, you're a fool."

A few weeks later she realized she now had a place even in this barren land. Louis-Paul appeared again in the kitchen, less shy, for now she was his friend. His sister-in-law was having a baby and something was wrong. They would have taken her to Missawani, but there was every sign of a blizzard blowing up. Madame had been so good with Lucienne. Perhaps she could do something for Marie-Claire as well.

"I don't see how I could," said Molly. "I've helped bring little calves and pigs into the world, but never a baby—"

"She may die," said Louis. "They say the baby is placed wrong. They have given her blood of a newborn calf to drink, but still—"

"All right," said Molly, "I'll go."

She set a cold meal for Toddy and propped a note against his plate. The thought of him nudged her mind guiltily during the dash over the snow to the little house. But that was absurd. She would be away only a few hours. Toddy would have to learn to accept an occasional absence. He was a little—well, selfish about her. He would have to learn.

With some help from an ancient grandmother, Molly delivered a child on the kitchen table of the little house. An old Cornish farmhand had showed her once how to turn a calf that was breached. Much the same thing was involved now— deftness, daring, a strong hand timed to the bitter contractions of the girl on the table.

When she returned home late in the evening, she had not thought of Toddy for hours.

This time he was angry, mumblingly, shakingly angry.

"Molly," he shouted, "you must put an end to this nonsensical—"

"But it's not nonsensical," she said, serene still from the miracle of new life she had held across her hands. "I brought a nice little boy into the world. He might never have been born except for me."

"These women have been popping kids for years without you."

"I know," said Molly, "but sometimes they lose them. And they're so—superstitious. I can help them, Toddy. I can."

She paused, then spoke more gently.

"What is it, Toddy? Why don't you want me to go?"

The question caught him somehow, and his face, his whole expression became looser, as if suddenly he did not understand his own rage.

"You're my wife," he said, "I want you here."

"Well, cheer up," she said, speaking lightly because his look had chilled her so. "I am, usually."

After that, no woman in any of the ranges ever had a baby without her husband's dogs whisking over the fields to the red house.

Molly now was famed for miles. She was good luck at a birth, and when something unexpected happened she could act with speed and ingenuity. She liked the people and felt that they liked her. Even the Curé, who hated the powerhouse and all it represented, bowed and passed the time of day when he and Molly met in a farmhouse kitchen.

She sent away for government pamphlets and a handful of texts. Though it was true, as Toddy said, that these women had had babies without her, it pleased her that she was cutting down the percentage of early deaths.

Each of her errands meant a scene with Toddy. There was a struggle here, she felt, between her own need for life and work and what she tried to persuade herself was merely selfishness in him. In her new strength and happiness she felt that she ought to be able to draw Toddy into taking an interest in something beyond the powerhouse. But he would not be drawn.

Surely when the snows broke it would be possible. She would persuade him to take the old car in the barn and drive with her about the countryside. He was only a trifle bushed from the long winter. Though she had been shocked at first by the suggestion that he might be bushed, she found the hope edging into her mind more and more often now that it was nothing more.

And then one day it was Joe Blanchard's turn to come to get her. His wife was expecting her tenth child.

All day Molly was restless, going to the window to strain her eyes into the glare for a sight of Joe's sleigh and his tough yellow dogs winding out of the bush. Sunset came and she prepared dinner, and still he had not come.

Once she looked up from her plate and saw Toddy staring at her, his lips trembling in an odd small way.

"Is anything wrong?" she asked.

"No," he said, "nothing."

"Toddy," she said, gently, and under her gentleness afraid. "I'll probably be going out tonight. I promised Joe Blanchard I'd help Mariette."

Toddy looked at her, and his face blazed.

"No," he shouted, "by God—you will stay where you belong."

"Why?" she asked, as she had before. "Why don't you want me to go?"

He seemed to search through his mind for words.

"Because I won't have you going out at night with that ruffian—because, damn it, it's too dangerous."

"Then you come too," she said. "You come with us."

"Don't be a fool," he said. "How could I leave?"

"Well, stay home tonight," she said. "Stay here and—and rest. We'll decide what to do when Joe comes."

"Rest—what do you mean?"

"I think you're—tired," she said. "I think you should stay home just one evening."

Toddy scraped back his chair.

"Don't be a fool, Molly. Of course I can't stay. I can't."

He walked to the door, then turned back to her.

"I shall find you here," he said, "when I return."

The evening dragged between the two anxieties—between wondering when Joe would come and watching for Toddy's return.

Midnight came, and still neither Toddy nor Joe had come. Her anxiety grew. Toddy had never stayed this late before. It had been ten-thirty first, then eleven.

The sound of the back door opening sent her flying to the kitchen. Joe stood in the doorway, his broad face beaming.'

"You ready, madame?"

Molly began to put on her heavy clothes, her snowboots. Anxiety licked still in her mind. Past twelve o'clock and Toddy had not returned.

"Joe," she said, "you'll wait just a minute while I go down and tell my husband?"

Her feet slipped several times on the icy steps Toddy kept cut in the hillside. She felt a sudden terrible urgency. She must reassure herself of something. She didn't quite know what.

She pulled open the door of the powerhouse and was struck, as she had been before, by the way the thunder of the waterfall was suddenly replaced by a low, even whine.

For an instant she did not see Toddy. Louis-Paul was propped in a straight chair dozing, across the room. Then she saw Toddy, his back, leaning towards one of the turbines. As she looked, he moved, with a curious scuttling speed, to one of the indicators on the wall. She saw the side of his face then, its expression totally absorbed, gloating.

"Toddy!" she called.

He turned, and for a long moment she felt that he did not know who she was. He did not speak.

"I didn't want you to worry," she said. "I'm going with Joe. If I shouldn't be back for breakfast—"

She stopped, for he did not seem to be listening.

"I probably *will* be back for breakfast," she said.

He glared at her. He moved his lips as if to speak. Then his gaze broke and slid back to the bright indicator on the wall.

At that moment she understood. The struggle she had sensed without being able to give it a name had been between herself and the powerhouse. In an indistinct way Toddy had realized it when he said, "I want you here."

"Toddy!" she shouted.

He turned his back to her in a vague, automatic way, and she saw that his face was quite empty except for a strange glitter that spread from his eyes over his face. He did not answer her.

For a moment she forgot that she was not alone with him, until a sound reminded her of Louis-Paul, awake now and standing by the door. And from the expression of sick, shaking terror on his face she knew what the fear had been that she had never allowed herself to name.

"Oh Louis," she said.

"Come madame," he said. "We can do nothing here. In the morning I will take you to Missawani. I will bring the doctor back."

"But is he safe?" she asked. "Will he—damage the machines perhaps?"

"Oh no. He would never hurt these machines. For years I watch him fall in love with her. Now she has him for herself."

Reading for Understanding

Main Idea

1. Which of the following statements could not sum up the main idea of the story?
   (a) The harsh elements in a northern Canada winter can destroy one's sanity.
   (b) The fear of loneliness can destroy the human spirit.
   (c) Human beings cannot for long endure the harshness of northern Canadian winters.
   (d) Humanity's survival depends on cooperation.

Details

2. The war mentioned in this story was most likely
   (a) the French and Indian War   (b) the war in which

the United States won its independence   (c) World War
I   (d) World War II.

3. The   old   woman   in   the   story   is   (a) Canada
    (b) the Mason Paper Mill   (c) Molly   (d) the electric
    plant.

4. Molly has delayed coming to Missawani because
    (a) wartime restrictions prevented her   (b) her mother
    was   ill   (c) she   didn't   want   to   leave   England
    (d) she felt too old to make the trip.

5. Molly helps the other women because   (a) Toddy sug-
    gests that she do so   (b) she had taken courses in emer-
    gency care   (c) she is asked to   (d) she wants to get
    away from Toddy.

Inferences

6. Which of the following is a reason that Molly does not give
    for her marrying Toddy?
    (a) She was middle-aged.
    (b) He was attractive-looking.
    (c) They had fallen in love.
    (d) He was an officer.

7. At the beginning of the story Molly feels that Toddy has
    changed   because   (a) he   speaks   so   little   (b) he
    doesn't seem pleased to see her   (c) he is so concerned
    about the power plant   (d) he worries about how she
    will adjust.

8. Molly   leaves   England   to   join   Toddy   because
    (a) she enjoys wintry weather   (b) she feels it is her
    duty to do so   (c) her mother persuades her to
    (d) she wants a change.

9. The house and the plant were built near the waterfall
    because   (a) it was the source of power   (b) it was a
    safe place to build on   (c) the surroundings were
    beautiful   (d) it was near the paper mill.

10. Toddy accepts as a major responsibility   (a) seeking
    companionship with the crew   (b) helping Molly help
    others   (c) developing an outside hobby   (d) keeping
    the plant in operation.

Order of Events

11. Arrange the items in the order in which they occurred. Use letters only.
    A. Molly travels halfway across Canada.
    B. Molly learns to be alone for long stretches of time.
    C. Molly saves a baby's life.
    D. Molly realizes why Toddy refused to allow her to help strangers.
    E. Molly looks for an open window.

Outcomes

12. Molly does not realize until it is too late (a) why the workers look to her for help (b) why the power plant was built so far away from the mill (c) that it is Toddy and not she who needs to adjust (d) why Toddy calls the plant and not her his old woman.

Cause and Effect

13. Molly is unable to help Toddy avoid disaster because (a) she is unwilling to help him (b) she wants to go back to England (c) she is searching for her own solution (d) she enjoys seeing him angry.

Fact or Opinion

Tell whether the following is fact or an opinion.
14. The workers were taught not to speak English.

Author's Role

15. The major purpose of the author was to (a) show the evils of progress (b) compare the British and the Canadian ways of life (c) contrast people and their defenses (d) show how cruel people can be.

Words in Context _____

1. In England his habit ... had charmed her, fitting her *picturesque* notions of the Canadian north.

Picturesque (566) means   (a) charming   (b) drab
(c) remote   (d) appropriate.

2. But now she felt *uneasiness prod her.*
Uneasiness prod her (566) means   (a) fear grip her
(b) dislike overcome her   (c) disturbing feelings stir in
her   (d) relief fill her mind.

3. It was such a *sinister-looking* building . . .
Sinister-looking (566) means   (a) magnificent
(b) old-fashioned   (c) threatening   (d) tremendous.

4. He looked *elated* and eager, and she smiled at him.
Elated (567) means   (a) overjoyed   (b) proud
(c) anxious   (d) subdued.

5. Toddy had *wolfed* his meal . . .
Wolfed   (567)   means   (a) overlooked   (b) eaten
greedily   (c) picked at   (d) finished.

6. She had thought he would seem closer to her here, but he
was more *withdrawn* than ever.
Withdrawn (567) means   (a) talkative   (b) sullen
(c) pleased   (d) cooperative.

7. You followed him here because you were *entranced with*
the idea of a strange and different place.
Entranced with (568) means   (a) fascinated by
(b) tricked by   (c) fearful of   (d) suspicious of.

8. The men all lived on the nearby *concessions*—"ranges"
they were called here in northern Quebec . . .
Concessions (569) as used in this sentence refers to
(a) ranches   (b) small communities   (c) retail outlets
(d) manufacturing units.

9. "I have never been *bushed*," Toddy interrupted furiously.
Bushed (570) as used by Toddy means   (a) ambushed
(b) fired   (c) burned out   (d) impatient.

10. Already I can feel the long sweep of the snow trying to
draw my thoughts out till they become *diffused and vague.*
Diffused and vague (570) means   (a) unclear and
uncertain   (b) inaccurate and meaningless
(c) mixed-up and wrong   (d) long-winded and baseless.

11. Several times he sat and talked with her after dinner,

telling her about the powerhouse and the *catastrophes he had averted* that day.

Catastrophes he had averted (570) means the   (a) energy the plant produced   (b) disasters he had avoided   (c) time he had saved   (d) gossip he had overheard.

12. With a hopeless gesture he *relinquished* his English. *Relinquished* (571) means   (a) abandoned (b) practiced   (c) expressed   (d) improved.

13. A few weeks later she realized *she now had a place* even in this barren land.
She now had a place (573) means that   (a) she was popular   (b) she was earning her keep   (c) she had won her husband's respect   (d) she was needed.

14. "But it's not nonsensical," she said, *serene* still from the miracle of new life she had held across her hands.
Serene (574) means   (a) upset   (b) calm (c) separating   (d) pleased.

15. She was good luck at birth, and when something unexpected happened she could act with speed and *ingenuity*.
Ingenuity (574) means   (a) accuracy   (b) knowledge (c) cleverness   (d) skill.

Thinking Critically About the Story _____

1. In your opinion, what was the major cause of Toddy's breakdown? How did each of the following contribute?
    The endless cold and piling-up snow
    Toddy's being British-Canadian
    The power plant
    The waterfall
    Molly
    Loneliness

2. Why does Toddy finally turn to the powerhouse and not to Molly? Why does he call the plant—and not Molly—his old woman? How does the power plant protect him? What

price does he have to pay? How could he have prevented such a costly "rescue"?

3. How did you react to Molly's unromantic reasons for marrying Toddy, and following him to Canada? How did her thinking compare to the reactions of your favorite soap opera heroine? Would you be willing to accept a person like Molly as a close friend?

4. What role do the workers at the plant assign to Molly? Why does she accept it—without specific training and credentials?

5. How has Molly failed Toddy? Is it her fault? What does he not realize when he turns to her for help? Would a long engagement have changed his judgment? Explain.

6. What protects the crew at the plant from mental breakdown? What protects Molly? Why wasn't such protection available to Toddy?

Stories in Words _____

Docile (570)   The root of *docile* is the Latin *docere*, "to teach." The same root is found in *doctor, doctrine, document*, and *indoctrinate. Docile* originally meant "teachable, easy to teach." The meaning expanded to "easy to manage or discipline." Someone who is easy to teach and eager to learn is likely to be obedient.

Catastrophe (570)   The Greek prefix *cata* means "down." It appears in words like *catapult*, "hurl down," and *catalyst*, "breaking down or loosening." The Greek root *stroph* means "turn." It appears in *apostrophe*, originally "a turning away from the audience to address one person." *Catastrophe* is "a downturn, a disaster."

Automatic (577)   Many words in English are called *hybrids* because they borrow from two or more languages. *Automobile*, which by derivation means "self-moving," comes from the Greek *auto*, "self," and the Latin *movere*, "to move." *Automatic* is entirely Greek in origin and means "thinking for itself." This meaning gradually expanded to mean "acting for itself." Other *auto* words include *autograph, autocrat, autopsy,* and *autonomous.*

World of People

ACTIVITIES

Thinking Critically About the Stories ____

1. Which of the following characters had traits you would like to find in a friend?

    Lucien   M. Jacotin   Bill   Gillian
    Miriam Hayden   Septimus   Molly

2. Compare the strengths and weaknesses of character in:

    M. Jacotin   Bill   Gillian
    Molly   Toddy

    Which one would you consider most mature? Which one— or ones—do you admire? Explain.

3. What role did the setting (time and place) play in the making of the character of:

    Toddy   M. Jacotin   Bill

    Can changing environment change our character? Change what we want out of life?

4. Which story has the most significance for you? What are some of the *Do's* and *Don't's* emphasized in these four stories? What are the chances of achieving happiness for each of the following?

    M. Jacotin   Gillian   Lucien   Bill

5. Which story would make the most effective TV movie?

Writing and Other Activities _____

1. Write the setting and dialog when Bill meets a crony years later and tells him why and how he killed the intruder.

2. Write the setting and dialog twenty-five years later when Lucien tries to explain to his own son the best way of helping children with their homework.

3. Lead a class discussion based on one of the following quotations and series of questions:

   (a) "Bill and Molly are realists. They accept life as it is and try their best to cope. Gillian, on the other hand, is a romantic; he refuses to accept reality; he looks at life through rose-colored glasses and lives in a world of dreams."

   Which of the characters has the best approach to life? Which has the better chance of achieving happiness? Which approach is the one you take?

   (b) "Sometimes we can have too much of a good thing. Both Toddy and M. Jacotin have a highly developed sense of responsibility."

   What was the cause of their being overwhelmed by the results of their taking their responsibilities so seriously? How could they have prevented the unfortunate results from occurring? Could others have helped them? When should responsibilities be dropped?

4. Write the plot of a story in which a young teenager:

   (a) heads for a fall because of conceit, because of an over-developed sense of his or her own importance.

   (b) takes on the responsibility of correcting the ways of a friend who does not want to change.

   (c) is too easily discouraged and feels inferior.

   (d) learns how to accept the truism: "You win some, and you lose some."

   (e) tries to tell her parents how to react when her first date rings the doorbell.

5. Write the dialog of a story in which a high-school freshman and her (his) parent (parents) have a three-way discussion beginning with the freshman's request for:

(a) greater freedom in choosing clothing styles.
(b) greater freedom in deciding the decor of her (his) room.
(c) planning her (his) own allotment of time and curfew.
(d) increase of allowance and decrease in the number of unexpected chores suddenly coming her (his) way.
(e) less responsibility toward siblings and/or grandparents living nearby.

Stories in Words: A Review

A. antagonist
B. automatic
C. awkward
D. catastrophic

E. choleric
F. divan
G. docile
H. musical

I. napkin
J. soliloquy
K. tyrannical
L. zenith

Answer the following questions by choosing a word from the list above. Use letters only.

Which of the words above . . .

1. . . . is the Latin equivalent of the Greek *monolog*?
2. . . . was once the hero's enemy in a play?
3. . . . means "the part overhead?"
4. . . . is related to the word *map*?
5. . . . is associated with *sanguine, melancholy*, and *phlegmatic*?
6. . . . means "a turn for the worse, a turn downward"?
7. . . . originally meant "teachable?"
8. . . . comes from Persian through Turkish?
9. . . . is associated with the name for a Greek ruler?
10. . . . has the word for *self* within it?

GLOSSARY

The best way to build a vocabulary is to meet new words in helpful contexts. A word's context is the setting it appears in, all the other words that surround it. The following list contains a great many new words that are worth adding to your word store.

All the words in the list appear in the stories you have read. Here you will find helpful definitions. In addition, you will meet the words in new contexts, sentences designed to suggest the meaning of the listed words. These sentences, together with the contexts in which the words originally appeared, will help you add the words to your use vocabulary.

A

abate   to lessen; diminish
>We could not leave the house until the fury of the storm had *abated*.

abject   miserable; cringing
>He was a man made *abject* by his fears.

abraded   scraped; rubbed; worn away
>My knee was *abraded* from my fall on the hard surface of the tennis court.

abyss   bottomless pit; deep, empty space
>One false step on this mountain pass, and you will fall into the *abyss*.

accordingly   for that reason; suitably
>He is the principal of the school and should be treated *accordingly*.

acquiesce   to agree; consent
>I *acquiesced* to going in order not to upset her plans.

admonish   to scold; rebuke; warn
>The guard *admonished* the children who had not waited until the traffic signal had changed completely.

adroit skillful; clever
Only an *adroit* driver could wend his way through the crowded, narrow streets without an accident.

adversary opponent; enemy
In the finals of the tennis tournament, Boris Becker's *adversary* was his longtime opponent, Ivan Lendl.

affect to pretend
In order to avoid suspicion, he *affected* a foreign accent that could fool no one.

afford to give
The delay *afforded* us the time we needed to reconsider our decision to help them.

agility quickness; gracefulness
Though Owen seems to be half asleep part of the time, he can move with *agility* on the tennis court when the opponent makes a good shot.

ague fever with chills
Only when we wrapped the victim in heavy blankets were we able to control her shivering. How do you treat *ague*?

alacrity enthusiasm; agility; briskness
I expect you to respond with *alacrity* to my request for assistance.

allay to calm; ease; lessen
This is the medicine the doctor ordered to *allay* the pain.

alluvial water deposited
The *alluvial* soil deposited at the mouth of the river is the richest soil in the area.

amiable agreeable; sociable; genial
Helen's *amiable* manner masks an intensely competitive nature.

anguished suffering from grief, pain, or worry
When the coach saw the opponent's ball sail through the uprights for a field goal, he let out an *anguished* cry.

annihilation wiping out; complete destruction
No tyrant has ever been able to bring about the total *annihilation* of the forces of opposition.

antagonist opponent
His *antagonist* in the debate had better control of the facts.

antiquarian person interested in old things, like old books or
furniture
The flea market and the garage sale are often favorite
hunting grounds of the *antiquarian*.

apathy lack of interest or emotion
The drop in television ratings could be traced directly to
listeners' *apathy*.

apex highest point; summit
The winning of the Nobel Peace Prize was the *apex* of her
career.

appalling causing horror, shock, or dismay
Mt. Pelee, on the island of Martinique, erupted in 1902
with an *appalling* loss of life.

apparition ghost; spirit; unusual sight
When he rushed in to tell us of the accident, he looked like
an *apparition* out of a vampire horror story.

appease to quiet by giving in; to satisfy
Before World War II, the Allies tried to *appease* Hitler, but
his demands became impossible.

appreciable noticeable; obvious
There is an *appreciable* difference between the two trucks.

apprehension worry; dread
Though there was no one in sight, the traveler had an
uneasy *apprehension* that he was being followed.

apprise inform; notify
We have not yet been *apprised* of the surveyor's findings in
mapping our land.

approbation approval
This worthy project has received the *approbation* of our
highest officials.

archangel chief angel
In the pageant she was the *archangel* in charge of the
cherubim in the choir for the high holidays.

ardor emotional warmth; eagerness; enthusiasm
>Nothing can match the *ardor* of a stamp collector when he gazes upon a copy of the famous airmail stamp with inverted center.

arid very dry; parched; colorless; uninteresting
>The irrigation system changed an *arid* desert into highly productive farmland.

arrogance haughtiness; excessive pride
>Some diners are intimidated by the *arrogance* of head-waiters in expensive restaurants.

askew to one side; awry; crookedly
>Denny wears his hat *askew* because he thinks it makes him look devil-may-care.

assented agreed to
>When Bud proposed the site for the picnic, nearly everyone *assented*, and the date was set.

assert to state strongly; maintain; insist
>Helen was right when she *asserted* that the chair should have allowed her to read her report.

assimilate absorb; take in
>An attentive student *assimilates* knowledge quickly.

asunder apart; into pieces
>The issue of equal opportunity for all tore *asunder* the small community.

attar perfume made from petals of flowers
>I have always found *attar* of roses too strong an odor.

attest declare to be true or genuine; certify; make clear
>We can *attest* to the loyalty of our friends in the other party, even though we disagree with them.

attire to dress; garments; apparel
>It is customary in that country for mourners to be *attired* all in white.

attribute to blame on; charge to; credit
>The fatal accident was *attributed* to pilot error.

auditor one who listens; one who checks accounts
>I am not a student taking the course for credit. I have been given permission to attend as an *auditor*.

auf Wiedersehen good-by for now; until we meet again
This is not good-by; I say, *"Auf Wiedersehen"* because we
shall meet again—soon.

august awe-inspiring; magnificent; noble
Some day I hope to sit among the most *august* jurors in the
world, the Supreme Court of our country.

aura kind of atmosphere; air; quality
There was an *aura* of mystery about her that I could never
analyze but always felt.

auspicious favorable; successful; fortunate
The enthusiastic reception by the critics of his first play
was most *auspicious*.

austerity severe simplicity; extreme economy
Only by practicing *austerity* will we be able to meet our
financial obligations this month.

auxiliary supporting; helpful; acting in a subordinate capac-
ity
In addition to paid personnel, in our city there are *auxiliary*
volunteer units to help in civil emergencies.

avaricious greedy
King Midas was *avaricious* for more and more gold until
he lost his only daughter because of his greed.

avert to turn aside; prevent
The prompt arrival of the police *averted* a serious riot that
could have led to loss of life.

avid eager; enthusiastic
An *avid* stamp collector would give anything for a set of
Graf Zeppelins, airmail stamps issued during the De-
pression.

avowed acknowledged; confessed; admitted
How could the judge allow an *avowed* thief to be free while
awaiting sentencing!

awe respectful fear; astonishment; respect; to astonish
The sight of the Lincoln Memorial filled the visiting
students with *awe*.

azure   sky-blue; clear blue
   We made real progress as we sailed under *azure* skies with
   favorable breezes during four glorious, cloudless days.

B

babble   talk in a strange tongue; to talk a foreign language
   Modern equipment allows us to listen to the whales
   babbling in their peculiar way.

balky   stubborn; contrary
   These mules are too *balky* to be ridden by children.

barrow   handcart
   The *barrow* tipped several times before I learned how to
   balance it as I pushed it forward on its one wheel.

battened down   fastened secure with thin bars or strips
   As the storm approached, the crew *battened down* the
   hatches that led to the storage areas below deck.

bedlam   place or condition of noise and confusion
   When the kindergarteners were given time for free play,
   there was happy *bedlam* in the schoolyard.

begetter   producer; one who brings about; causes
   The *begetter* of evil must suffer the consequences.

beguile   mislead; trick; pass time pleasantly
   Beguiled by the song of the Sirens, Odysseus begged his
   men to set him free.

benign   good-natured; favorable; beneficial
   Santa Claus had a *benign* expression on his face as he
   awaited his first young visitor.

bequest   to leave by will; inheritance
   The grandparents left a *bequest* for each of the grandchil-
   dren.

beset   to attack on all sides; trouble persistently
   Beset by doubts, I no longer was willing to follow his
   advice.

bestir   to rouse to action
   If you don't *bestir* yourself, you will miss the bus.

betake oneself   to go
  Betake yourself to the office and register your complaint there.

bight   loop in a rope; bay
  The *bight* must be securely fastened before you attempt to pull on the rope.

bland   smooth; agreeable; mild
  By comparison with hot, spicy Szechuan food, Cantonese cooking is *bland*.

blight   plant disease; plague; to destroy
  The *blight* destroyed all the stately elm trees that had lined our main street.

bode   be an omen of; indicate; foretell
  The sloppy pass protection of the Falcons doesn't *bode* well for a successful season.

booty   plunder; loot; spoils
  The pirates buried their *booty* on the beach of the uninhabited island.

brazenly   boldly
  In *The Taming of the Shrew*, Kate *brazenly* insulted every suitor who came to woo her.

brindled   gray or tan with streaks or spots of dark color
  The *brindled* calf was easy to spot in the herd of black Jersey cows.

brochure   pamphlet
  The *brochure* set forth all the attractions of a cruise to the Caribbean.

brogan   coarse, heavy shoe
  Hiking and work shoes have replaced the term *brogans* so popular years back.

brown study   deep, serious thought; reverie
  When he is in a *brown study*, he really does not hear the telephone ring or the doorbell sound.

buoyancy   floating ability; lightness; enthusiasm
  Modern life preservers have a lasting *buoyancy*.

bureaucrats government officials; public servants
Were you ever able to get a definite answer to any question that you asked one of the local *bureaucrats*?

burly big; strong; muscular
Burly Tom Jenkins contrasted in size with his small, frail brother.

C

capered pranced and leaped; skipped
The young goats *capered* among the rocks near the peak.

caprice sudden impulsive action; whim
Through some *caprice* of Barbara's, we're all supposed to come to the party as characters in history.

careen cause to lean sideways; lurch from side to side
The dislodged boulder *careened* madly down the mountainside, threatening the hikers on the slope.

carouse have a noisy, merry time—perhaps too merry
In Hamlet, the king would often *carouse* through the night, keeping the merrymaking going till dawn.

casual accidental; halfhearted; vague; informal
I am not a devoted fan; I have only a *casual* interest in TV football.

cataract waterfall; rapids; downfall; torrent
Only experienced canoeists should attempt to ride the *cataracts* of the Colorado River.

catch the dickens be reprimanded; be scolded
If the manager ever learns about this, you will really *catch the dickens*.

chagrin embarrassment; annoyance; disappointment
The relief pitcher walked the winning run in, much to the *chagrin* of his manager.

chambray a fine variety of gingham
She bought a bolt of *chambray* from which she planned to make the shirts for the bowling team.

chaos great confusion; turmoil
Can you imagine the *chaos* that resulted when the angry bull crashed his way through the pottery display?

charnel place where corpses are deposited
The Holocaust provided a *charnel* house on a scale un-
dreamed of before the evils of the Nazi regime.

chilblains inflammation of hands or feet from exposure to
cold and moisture; itching sore from cold
While *chilblains* are not life threatening, I find them most
distressing.

choleric bad-tempered; cranky; angry
As the day went on, she became more and more *choleric*
until she was impossible to be with.

cipher zero; code; interwoven initials of a name
In the right hand corner of the painting, the artist had
placed his *cipher* to prove its authenticity.

cistern water tank
Although the heat wave had soured the water in the
cistern, we were so thirsty that it tasted like soda pop.

citation summons to appear before a law court; honorable
mention for bravery
I'd rather have a *citation* for some excellent achievement
than a *citation* for a traffic violation.

clamber to climb awkwardly
We *clambered* over the rocks for what seemed like hours
before we reached a ledge where we could rest.

clemency mercy; mildness
When an accused shows no remorse, the judge is very
unwilling to show *clemency* when sentencing.

cloyed tired from too much; glutted
Our tolerance for puns became *cloyed* as she continued her
tireless efforts despite our obvious reaction.

codicil addition to a will
Unfortunately the last sentence in the *codicil* canceled the
gifts mentioned in the original will.

coherent understandable; organized; clear
Only after she had calmed down was she able to give us a
coherent account of what had occurred.

colleague   fellow worker; associate
Ask every *colleague* in the office to sign the get-well card for
Jan.

collective   a cooperative organization; combined
I worked on the kibbutz for the summer in order to learn
how members of a *collective* share the work.

commensurate   adequate; equal in measure or size; propor-
tionate
A jury should try to make an award *commensurate* with the
damage done to the plaintiff.

commiserate   sympathize with; feel for; share another's sorrow
Friends slowly gathered in the living room to *commiserate*
with the sorrowing family.

commune   to share thoughts; communicate; a community
Her followers actually believe that she is able to *commune*
with the spirits of departed dear ones.

compassion   pity; sympathy; humanity
We chose her as our family physician because of the great
compassion she has for her patients.

competent   qualified; capable; fit
To rate the diving form in Olympic diving contests,
competent judges are desperately needed.

comply   to agree with; follow; obey
Unless you *comply* with the rules, you will be denied the
privilege of being a member.

composed   calm; quiet; coolheaded; controlled
The captain remained *composed* and fully in command of
himself and his crew during the entire storm.

composure   calmness of mind; poise; serenity
Even bitter disappointments cannot affect Betty's
composure, for she always maintains a calm and pleasant
manner.

conceivable   imaginable; possible; believable
I had always thought that there was no *conceivable* way for
him to escape; but he did!

condoled sympathized
> The nation *condoled* with the Kennedy family after the death of John F. Kennedy.

confirmation a making sure; proof; approval; acceptance
> Before we print this story, you will have to receive a *confirmation* of the facts from those involved.

conjure to practice magic; call forth; summon; bewitch
> Wizards and witches are supposed to be able to *conjure* up spirits who will follow their commands.

connivance secret cooperation, especially in wrongdoing
> With the *connivance* of disloyal servants, enemy spies made their way into the palace.

connoisseurship state of being an expert
> Being a successful collector of antiques requires a *connoisseurship* based on research and experience.

consign to hand over; deliver; entrust
> Some of the used clothes were *consigned* to the dust heap.

consolation comfort; cheer; support
> I find no *consolation* in the realization that none of the members of our class volunteered.

constitute to form; make up; establish
> What are the elements that *constitute* a balanced diet?

constrain to force; compel; curb; put down
> Please *constrain* your enthusiasm until all the names of the successful candidates have been announced.

construe analyze; explain; understand
> If you had properly *construed* what the teacher said, you would have prepared your term report properly.

contemplating studying intently; meditating
> As the visitors were quietly *contemplating* the Grand Canyon, one tourist stupidly said, "What a place for a roller coaster."

contend to fight; combat; debate; quarrel; claim
> It is difficult to *contend* with self-seeking leaders.

continuity connectedness; continuation
> We have a substitute always on hand so that, in an emergency, *continuity* of the work will not be broken.

contorted violently twisted; misshapen
Her face was so *contorted* by grief that I could not recognize her.

convergence coming together; meeting
At the place of *convergence* of the two rivers, the many whirlpools prevent the passage of canoes.

convolution turn or winding; coiling
I stared awestruck at the *convolutions* of the snake as it glided toward me.

convulsively shaking violently
The children laughed so *convulsively* at the magician's tricks that he had to slow his delivery.

copious in great plenty; abundant
Because I am fearful of missing something important, I always take *copious* notes of any important lecture.

copse a wood or thicket of small trees or bushes
Only small animals dared to find safety in the *copse*.

coquettish flirting
Marianne was too *coquettish* for Jason; he preferred a more down-to-earth, straightforward person.

cordiality warmth; friendly feeling
The newcomers to the party were greeted by the hostess with *cordiality* and made to feel at home.

cordon off to surround with a protective circle (of police)
The police *cordoned off* the area surrounding the demonstrators to protect them from hostile actions.

couched worded; drew up
She *couched* her demands in clear, simple, nonthreatening terms.

countenance face; look; feature; approval; to tolerate
I refuse to continue any longer to *countenance* such rude behavior.

covertly secretly; in a concealed manner
She *covertly* slipped the note into her purse while they were busy watching the video production.

coy pretending shyness; bashful
   She always becomes *coy* when asked to recite before an
   audience of relatives.

craven cowardly
   The soldiers around Falstaff in Shakespeare's *Henry IV*
   plays were a *craven* bunch, not the heroes they pretended
   to be.

crestfallen downhearted; downcast; depressed
   He looked so *crestfallen* when he thought I would refuse his
   request, I just had to say, "Yes!"

cruet small glass bottle for vinegar, oil, or some other liquid
   Place the *cruet* and sugar bowl on the table.

cuirass piece of armor protecting chest area
   We visited the museum and saw the *cuirass* that was part
   of the armor worn by former kings.

culminate to reach the high point, top, end, or result
   Their verbal disagreement almost *culminated* in physical
   violence.

cumbersome clumsy; burdensome
   Some of the earliest bicycles were too bulky, too
   cumbersome to handle easily.

curé parish priest
   Troubled by the turn of events, he sought advice and
   consolation from the concerned *curé*.

curt abrupt; short; snappy
   Her *curt* reply made me realize how deeply our objections
   had annoyed her.

customary usual; accustomed
   He greeted us with his *customary* good cheer.

D

decorum good taste in behavior, speech, dress
   Superficially, Ted is a model of *decorum*, but underneath
   that model behavior is a rebel waiting to break out.

deem to think; believe; consider
   Unfortunately, they *deemed* that his silence was an admission of guilt.

deferential   respectful; courteous; considerate
This skilled receptionist is known for her pleasant, *deferential* response to all visitors.

deft   skillful; expert; handy
With a few *deft* motions of the needle, the tailor repaired the torn buttonhole.

degenerate   to grow worse; decline; corrupt
Without a skilled leader, the panel discussion quickly *degenerated* into an angry shouting match.

deign   consent to do something beneath one's dignity
Will Cynthia *deign* to answer those unfair criticisms of her term of office?

deliberation   careful thought
The jury spent two days in *deliberation* of the man's guilt or innocence.

deluge   to overwhelm; a great flood
The rising rock star was *deluged* with requests for her autograph.

demeanor   conduct; behavior; bearing; manner
His is not the *demeanor* of someone willing to submit to unfair pressure.

dementia   insanity; irreversible mental deterioration
A person who suddenly resorts to odd, irresponsible behavior is soon suspected of suffering from *dementia*.

denizen   inhabitant; resident
The calls and cries of the *denizens* of the rain forest kept me up much of the night.

deplorable   regrettable; shocking; unfortunate
Conditions in the slums of 18th-century London were more *deplorable* than conditions in the slums of today.

depraved   evil; corrupt; wicked; degraded
Only a *depraved* person could treat children with such intense cruelty.

deprecating   belittling; playing down
Even as the manager was *deprecating* the skill of the opposing pitcher, player after player on his own team struck out.

depreciated   reduced in value or price; belittled
The use of cheap metal *depreciated* the value of many Roman coins.

deranged   insane; demented; disturbed
Because of the terrible accident, the driver of the bus was temporarily *deranged*.

derisive   showing ridicule; mocking; sarcastic; taunting
Bart's *derisive* laughter bothered the listeners more than his previous comments.

dervish   a Moslem monk
We were completely enchanted by the whirling dances and chants of the *dervishes*.

despondent   without hope; discouraged; depressed
It's so easy to get *despondent* when plans seem to be going wrong.

destined   fated; due to accomplish
The sorcerer predicted that the young prince was *destined* to become a world ruler in a time of peace.

devastation   great destruction; ruin
The forest fire caused the complete *devastation* of thousands of acres of forest land.

devious   not in a straight path; indirect; crooked; tricky
By various *devious* strategies, Paula finally got her parents to lend her the family car for the trip to Augusta.

diabolical   devilish; evil; fiendish
In *Othello*, the evil Iago made a *diabolical* attack on the innocence and trust of Othello.

diffuse   to spread out; scatter; longwinded; wordy
Her calm response and logical reasoning quickly *diffused* his anger.

dilated   opened wide; expanded
In dim light the iris of the eye is *dilated*, to catch as much light as possible.

dilemma   difficult choice; predicament
My *dilemma* is such that, regardless of the solution I choose, it is impossible for me to come out ahead.

diminution   lessening; shrinking; dwindling
The first storm of the season caused such a *diminution* of our stockpile of wood that we were alarmed.

dire   dreadful; terrible
Cassandra's *dire* predictions were never believed, even though the disasters she prophesied did eventually come to pass.

disarming   charming; winning; reducing weaponry
Her *disarming* smile and warm greeting made us much less alert than we should have been.

discomfiture   uneasiness; frustration; embarrassment
Because of his shyness, the winning contestant showed great *discomfiture* when called upon to speak.

discordant   not harmonious; conflicting
The *discordant* sound of the coughing audience destroyed for me the beauty inherent in the musical program.

discourse   talk; conversation; lecture
We listened to an enlightening *discourse* on police efforts to teach teenagers the evils of drugs.

disdain   contempt; scorn
The general treated the order to surrender with *disdain*, sending back a resounding NO.

disdainful   scornful; proud; insulting
Puffed with his own conceit, Fred was *disdainful* of the feelings and ideas of others.

dislocate   to upset; disarrange; put out of place
By changing my filing system, she has so *dislocated* many items that I will spend hours finding them.

dispassionate   impartial; cool; levelheaded
His *dispassionate* analysis of the problem cleared the air and forced us to center our efforts on a solution.

dispassionately   calmly; impartially
A juror should consider the case *dispassionately*, basing the decision strictly on the evidence.

dispel   to drive away; scatter; banish
An animated cartoon comedy is guaranteed to *dispel* the gloom.

dispelled   scattered; driven away
The crowds before Chile's presidential palace were *dispelled* by army troops.

dissipate   to destroy; scatter; squander
The sun soon *dissipated* the heavy mists of the morning.

distended   expanded; stretched; swollen
After the snake had swallowed the rat, its body looked abnormally *distended*.

distracted   having attention drawn away; preoccupied; puzzled; confused
Jeremy was so *distracted* by the television in the other room that he couldn't do his homework.

distraught   upset; anxious; troubled; mentally confused
Carla was extremely *distraught* over the loss of her wedding ring.

divers   several; various
I had to try *divers* models before I found one that was most suitable to my needs.

diversion   amusement; pastime; turning aside
The only *diversion* available to him during the long winter months was supplied by an electronic chess game.

divest   to take authority from; deprive; undress; strip
In the United States no law can be passed to *divest* an individual of the right to a fair trial.

divine   to foresee; figure out; heavenly; preacher; priest
Only in storybooks can a person have the gift of being able to *divine* the future.

docile   gentle; meek; mild
The *docile* brother is in sharp contrast with his aggressive and competitive twin.

doggedly   stubbornly; persistently
Though nearly all the contestants had already finished the marathon, Deirdre *doggedly* kept on to the finish line.

doleful   sad; mournful; melancholy
After losing his no-hitter, the pitcher looked *doleful* and weary.

dominate   to control; rise high above; tower over
He believes that a father's role is to *dominate*, to make all the family decisions.

doomsday   the end of the world; Judgment Day
She dreamed of the awe-filled scene that would greet the eye and ear on *doomsday*.

doubloon   old Spanish coin
Did the pirates of old ever bury any coins that were not *doubloons*?

doughty   valiant; brave
The *doughty* Super Bowl winners were met by their fans at the Washington airport.

dowry   property brought by a woman at marriage
In some societies the size of a woman's *dowry* determines whether or not the ceremony will take place.

draggle   to make wet and dirty by dragging in mud; lag
After the rough games, the children's faces and hands looked just as *draggled* as their clothing.

draught   drink
"Draft beer" in modern times has replaced *"draughts* of ale" in story land.

dubiously   doubtfully
The campaign manager spoke rather *dubiously* about the chances of her candidate in the coming elections.

dumbfounded   stunned; astonished; startled speechless
We were *dumbfounded* by her ability to predict the outcome of seven of the eight races.

E

ebony   black
The *ebony* of the frame contrasted sharply with the white marble of the counter.

eddy   to move in circles; small whirlpool
The bay in which the two rivers join is too dangerous for swimmers because of the *eddies*.

eerie   scary; weird; mysterious
An *eerie* wail from the canyon below the cabin frightened the visitors.

elation   great joy; high spirits
Pam Shriver and Zena Garrison showed great *elation* when they won the gold medal for tennis doubles in the Olympics.

elemental   primary; like natural force; fundamental
During the hurricane, the rains beat down on us with *elemental* violence.

elucidate   to explain; make clear; interpret; spell out
She has the reputation of being able to *elucidate* the most obscure points in the law.

emanated   came forth; issued
In the darkness of the night, a sliver of light *emanated* from a window in the cottage.

eminence   lofty position or rank; greatness; high spot
The governor rose to *eminence* from a lowly job as a stable hand.

encompassed   surrounded; enclosed; included; involved
The range of mountains completely *encompassed* the lake.

encumber   to burden; load down; hinder; slow down
Encumbered by the heavy pack, the hiker made his way with great difficulty up the steep mountain trail.

engrossed   fully attentive; absorbed; taken up
I was so *engrossed* in the TV drama that I was unaware that my parents had entered the room.

entail   to involve certain steps; require; include
My summer job *entails* setting up new newspaper delivery routes and hiring teenagers to handle them.

enthralled   enslaved; captivated as by a spell
Children often sit *enthralled* for hours in front of the television sets on Saturday mornings.

entranced   bewitched; charmed; delighted; hypnotized
The six-year-old was so *entranced* by the electric cart that he refused to leave the driver's seat.

envision see mentally
The dream that Martin Luther King *envisioned*, true equality, shall come to pass.

equable easygoing; calm; uniform; unvaried; unchanging
Southern California has a more *equable* climate than Maine or Wisconsin.

equilibrium balance
The beginning tightrope walker did not dare look down for fear that he would lose his *equilibrium* and fall.

err to make a mistake; slip up; do wrong
It is not the electronic calculator that *errs*; it is as accurate as the numbers fed into it.

etch to cut into the surface; draw on copper
The lesson that this tragedy taught me is *etched* into my innermost being.

evoke to call forth; summon; arouse; awaken
Her uncalled-for sarcasm *evoked* a response that she had not expected from so well-controlled a group of adults.

exasperate to annoy; irritate; vex; bother; offend
The speaker's curt reply *exasperated* Ron who had to control his urge to reply in kind.

execrable hateful; detestable; repulsive
In talking loud and constantly throughout the performance, the two moviegoers showed an *execrable* lack of good manners.

exhilaration liveliness; joy; high spirits
As the skaters glided across the ice, there was an expression of *exhilaration* on their faces.

exordium beginning; introduction
To have the attention of your audience when you reach your conclusion, keep your *exordium* brief and clear.

expedite to hasten; speed along; advance
To *expedite* the delivery of mail, you must be certain to include the correct zip code.

expend   to use up; spend; give; contribute
Don't *expend* so much energy on insignificant details.

explicit   clear and full; definite; frank; direct
Didn't you hear her *explicit* instructions that we were not
to leave the grounds without permission!

extortion   theft; getting money by threats or misuse of authority
The gangsters used *extortion* to force small storekeepers to
pay for "protection."

extremity   farthest end; outer edge; hand; foot
A gate will be built at the southern *extremity* of the pass.

exultant   very joyful; in high spirits; delighted
Exultant because of the unexpected victory, the spectators
gave the home team a standing ovation.

F

facetious   witty; joking (often inappropriately)
Winifred tried to cover her embarrassment by a *facetious*
remark that no one found funny.

facilitating   making easy or possible
By *facilitating* the purchase of all needed supplies, the
backer of the expedition sent it on its way sooner than
expected.

fastidious   fussy; particular; overrefined; choosy
He is too *fastidious* to enjoy going on an overnight along
the rough mountain trails.

fazed   disturbed; upset
Russ is so energetic he isn't *fazed* by the prospect of
cleaning windows in a thirty-window house.

feign   to pretend; make believe
When Monty heard his mother coming to the bedroom, he
put out the light and *feigned* sleep.

fend   to provide for; take care of; repel; avoid
Are you trained well enough to *fend* for yourself if you get
lost in a heavily wooded area?

feral   wild; savage
It is rare that a *feral* animal can be domesticated and made gentle enough to be trusted.

fervent   hot; burning; glowing; enthusiastic
Fervent admirers of Elvis Presley still visit his homestead, Graceland.

fervid   glowing; passionate; eager
Thomas Jefferson expressed the *fervid* hope that the Declaration of Independence would be acceptable to the delegates.

fetid   having a bad smell; decaying; putrid
Because the vegetables had rotted, the root cellar had an overpoweringly *fetid* smell.

fey   fated; visionary; crazy
I had always feared that this *fey* venture into unknown regions of the mind would end in disaster.

filial   relating to son or daughter; respectful
Through the years Sarah has shown a deep *filial* affection for both of her handicapped parents.

filly   young female horse; young mare
We placed the *filly* and her new colt in the corral nearest to the barn to keep a close watch on them.

flinched   drew back, as from a blow
When the dog showed his teeth, the passerby *flinched* and then walked on.

flippant   frivolous; disrespectful; impertinent
Though Martha often gives *flippant* replies to serious questions, she really is a shy, caring person.

florid   rosy; ruddy
Geraldine had a *florid* complexion, completely unlike the tanned complexion of her sister.

flossy   overfancy; glamorous
If you want to write for this slick news magazine, you will have to cultivate its *flossy*, elegant style.

floundering   struggling helplessly; blundering
You will soon find yourself *floundering* and hesitating if you let your mind wander while delivering a speech.

flout to show contempt; scorn; defy; laugh at
Sooner or later you will be called to account if you *flout* the conventions of a community.

fomentation hot compress to ease pain; act of stirring up
The ranger quickly made a *fomentation* from the hot ashes and his shirt to ease the pain in the victim's arm.

foray raid; invasion; expedition
The youthful gangs made *forays* into enemy territory to test the ability of their new members.

forbear to be patient; refrain; hold back
I had to *forbear* from taking over when I realized that they wanted to do the task by themselves.

forestall to prevent; avoid; guard against
The government official called a conference of the parties involved in order to *forestall* a strike.

forlorn lonely; unhappy; deserted; lone; forgotten
The stranger looked so *forlorn* sitting dejected on the park bench that we invited her to join our group.

formidableness impressive size or excellence
The *formidableness* of the Washington defensive line discouraged opposing runners from trying to find a hole off guard or tackle.

fortnight two-week period
The magazine makes its regular appearance every *fortnight*, twenty-six times a year.

foyer vestibule; anteroom; lobby; entrance hall
The delivery men waited in the *foyer* while Helen was deciding where to place the new desk.

frivolous trivial; silly; of little importance
In Shakespeare's plays, Prince Hal led a *frivolous* life until the time came for him to assume the responsibilities of kingship.

frolicsome playful; fun-loving
The *frolicsome* puppy is in ecstasy when the youngsters have him chase a rubber ball.

frowsy   dirty; untidy; slovenly
In *Pygmalion*, Henry Higgins took a *frowsy* flower girl and turned her into a lady.

frugal   thrifty; not wasteful; skimpy; not abundant
My *frugal* parents have a file of discount coupons that they take with them on food-shopping trips.

furtively   secretly
The conspirators met *furtively* to escape the notice of the authorities.

fuselage   body of airplane
The burst of hostile antiaircraft gunfire had hit the *fuselage* but fortunately had not struck the engines.

fusillade   continual firing; broadside; salvo; volley
The new movie never survived the *fusillade* of bad reviews that greeted its appearance.

futile   useless; ineffective
When the weather satellite failed, the ground personnel made a *futile* attempt to restart it, but it stayed dead.

G

garrulous   talkative; windy; wordy; gossipy
He is so *garrulous* that he can outtalk any tape recorder on the market.

gauntlet   heavy glove; challenge
The pot was so hot that he could feel its searing heat through the thickness of the leather *gauntlets*.

gingerly   with great caution
She *gingerly* put down the cage containing the two rattlesnakes.

gloat   to laugh at other's failure; rejoice; crow over
A good way to lose friends and not influence people is to *gloat* over petty successes.

grapple   large hook; to hold tightly; struggle; fight; face
I need a clearer head than I have now if I am ever to *grapple* successfully with this problem.

grimace   twisting of the face; express pain or unhappiness
> When Betsy tasted the dish made of hot peppers, she made a *grimace* and said, "No, thank you."

grotesque   strange; distorted; bizarre; fantastic
> The *grotesque* shapes of trees on the wind-battered slopes reminded the climbers of witches and wizards in a child's cartoon.

grovel   to humble oneself; crawl before a person
> I shall never be one to *grovel* before a supervisor.

grubbed   dug in the ground; toiled; drudged
> I have *grubbed* too long for bare necessities not to want luxuries for a change.

gruel   watery cereal; thin porridge
> The first food that he received after the operation was some hot *gruel* that tasted like a royal feast.

guffaw   hearty laugh; burst of laughter; to laugh heartily
> I was startled by the *guffaw* he let out when I had finished telling him the joke I had just heard.

guileless   innocent; candid; frank
> Though young Cheryl seems a *guileless* chess player, she is a shrewd, knowledgeable, clever opponent.

H

haft   handle of a weapon or tool
> To make certain that borrowers would not be keepers, I carved my initials into the *haft* of my new hammer.

haggard   having a wasted look; gaunt; drawn
> The cave explorers' *haggard* expressions revealed their fatigue and anxiety after the rescuers finally reached the trapped pair.

havoc   widespread damage; destruction; devastation
> Jealousy and suspicion played *havoc* with her attempts at lasting friendships.

heir apparent   next in line for the title
> The male English *heir apparent* is given the title of Prince of Wales.

hellion troublemaker; mischievous person
  If you don't curb that young *hellion*, he will destroy all the goodwill you have among your neighbors.

helot slave; serf
  The *helots* of ancient Sparta were the equivalents of slaves who were bought and sold in the Americas years later.

hierarchy group of persons arranged in order of rank
  In every business office one's place in the *hierarchy* is usually understood.

holocaust great destruction, especially by fire
  This generation will not forget the *holocaust* that destroyed so much of Yellowstone Park's woodlands.

homage respect; reverence; honor
  The speaker on Memorial Day paid *homage* to all those who had died in America's wars.

hordes big crowds; throngs
  Every evening during the summer months the *hordes* of mosquitoes drove us indoors at dusk.

host of infinity numberless enemy
  Edna insists that the *host of infinity* that impairs the divine in man are ignorance and selfishness.

I

idiosyncrasies personal mannerisms; individual reactions
  In marriage, learning to live with the *idiosyncrasies* of the partner is important for a successful union.

immerse to submerge; soak; involve deeply; absorb
  Immerse the cloth for twenty minutes into the warm solution before attempting to cut it.

imminent about to happen; threatening
  When the collapse of the Third Reich was *imminent*, Hitler chose to die in a bunker in Berlin.

immolate to sacrifice
  For too many of us, our creative ability is *immolated* on the altar of financial security.

impart to tell; pass on; make known; give
His presence at the meeting *imparted* dignity and national significance to our deliberations.

impartial fair; neutral; unprejudiced
The referee in a labor dispute must remain *impartial* until both sides have presented their arguments.

impede to get in the way of; slow down; block; stall
The overturned truck *impeded* highway traffic for hours until the towing service was able to remove it.

imperative expressing a command; necessary; essential
It is *imperative* that this message reach the general within fifteen minutes.

imperceptibly not noticeably
By very slight movements, the cat crawled *imperceptibly* closer to the bird.

imperious domineering; overbearing; dictatorial
The *imperious* manner of the movie star turned away many former admirers.

impetuous bold; rash; impulsive
The Light Brigade made an *impetuous* charge on the enemy lines but lost many men as a result.

implacably relentlessly; not able to be satisfied; harshly; persistently
President Roosevelt was *implacably* opposed to making any deal with the Nazis.

implore to beg; urge; plead with
I *implore* you not to take part in this rash effort that risks so much for so little.

imposing impressive; outstanding; striking
The *imposing* Twin Towers of the World Trade Center have permanently changed the Manhattan skyline.

imprecation curse
There was nothing new or novel in the angry *imprecations* of the quarreling truck drivers.

impregnable unconquerable; strong; mighty; unattackable
Before the perfection of modern missiles, towns built high in the mountains were considered *impregnable*.

inarticulate   unable to find words; mumbled; mute; inexpressive
   Stage fright kept him momentarily *inarticulate* as he stood on the platform, gazing at the thousands before him.

inconsequential   unimportant; trivial; slight
   The sum involved is so *inconsequential* that it would cost you considerably more to collect than to forget.

incorrigible   unable to be corrected, improved, or reformed
   Though Jed is an *incorrigible* tall-story teller, we find him both amusing and informative.

incorruptible   pure
   Through all the pressures of his job, the mayor remained *incorruptible* and free of undue influence.

indeterminate   not fixed; uncertain; not clear
   Because he received an *indeterminate* sentence, the length of his stay in prison depends on his conduct.

indifference   not caring; unconcern; lack of feeling
   I would have much preferred an outburst of anger to the complete *indifference* with which they treated us.

indignantly   angrily; with displeasure
   He replied *indignantly*, "I never said that!"

indignity   something that hurts one's self-respect; humiliation
   It was the *indignity* of losing so badly that bothered Myra, not just the losing.

indisposed   slightly ill
   Cheryl is *indisposed* and has decided not to enter the golf tournament.

indolently   lazily; idly
   Bart was *indolently* drifting on an inner tube, while his brothers swam and dived vigorously.

indulge   to humor; yield to whims of oneself or another
   Though Marcia is pretty strict in her dieting, she occasionally does *indulge* in her craving for chocolate.

ineffectual   ineffective; useless; not producing the desired result
   All efforts to get the horse to leap the last hurdle proved to be *ineffectual*.

inert   lifeless; motionless; inactive
The victim lay so *inert* on the pavement where the car had thrown him that we feared he had been killed.

infallible   unable to do wrong; faultless; unerring
Our next-door neighbor has long been my *infallible* source of information about local happenings.

infuse   to inspire; instill; pour into
How can we *infuse* confidence in a writer who is convinced that he cannot write!

inimitable   cannot be imitated; matchless; unique
Many have tried in vain to copy this painter's *inimitable* style.

iniquity   unfairness; wrongdoing; wickedness
Innocent children often have to suffer for the *iniquities* of their parents.

inscrutable   puzzling; mysterious; baffling; deep
Leona showed no emotion but kept an *inscrutable* expression at all times.

insidious   deceitful; treacherous; underhand
The habit-forming side effect of this *insidious* drug does not become apparent for many months.

intangible   vague; untouchable
An *intangible* feeling of trouble ahead made me uneasy all morning.

intricate   hard to follow; complicated; detailed
Agatha Christie's detective-story plots are *intricate*, but all the details are fully explained at the end.

ironic   meaning the opposite of what is said or shown
In *Oedipus Rex*, it is ironic that Oedipus is seeking to find the cause of the plague in Athens when he himself is the cause.

irresolute   indecisive; hesitating; changeable
A successful executive cannot be *irresolute*.

J

jostled   bumped; pushed; elbowed in a crowd
A huge, rude passenger *jostled* his way through the crowd to reach the open door of the train first.

L

lacerated   jaggedly torn; wounded; mangled
The berry pickers' arms were *lacerated* by the sharp thorns of the blackberry bushes.

laconic   brief in speech
He used a *laconic* "yep" to answer practically all requests for assistance.

lamentation   expression of mourning; grief; deep regret
On the death of his friend, Arthur Hallam, Alfred Tennyson wrote a poem, a *lamentation* in his memory.

languor   weakness; lack of interest; indifference; sluggishness
The heat of the midday sun induced in us a *languor* that we couldn't overcome.

larder   food storage place; pantry; storeroom
Confined by the storm for a week, we found our *larder* almost bare of necessities.

latterly   later; recently
Latterly, a rarely used adverb, refers to the second of two people or things.

loathsome   disgusting
To a student of spiders, even a tarantula may be beautiful rather than *loathsome*.

lop   to cut off
With one quick application of the chain saw, she *lopped* off the tree limb that was shading the house.

lout   an awkward, stupid person; a term of contempt
I will teach that lazy *lout* not to interfere with me!

lowing   mooing of a cow
The loud *lowing* of the cows in the barn meant that once again Paul was late at milking time.

lubber awkward person; unskilled seaman
Although I have always been a *lubber*, all thumbs and slow
to respond, I still love to sail my catamaran.

lucid clear; bright; understandable; clearheaded
The first obligation of the news reporter is to present a
lucid account of what has happened.

lugubrious melancholy; mournful; sorrowful; gloomy
I was greatly moved by the *lugubrious* account the young-
ster gave of the accidental death of his pet dog.

lulled quieted; soothed; calmed; eased
The sound of the waves breaking gently on the beach soon
lulled me to sleep.

lurch to lean to one side; tilt; stumble; stagger
I almost lost my balance every time the ship *lurched* in the
rough sea.

lurid glaring; glowing; fiery; vivid; sensational
I was in the mood to see a TV police story filled with *lurid*
details of violent crime in the big city.

M

malady illness; sickness; disorder; ailment
Harry has been stricken with one *malady* after another,
leaving him weak and depressed.

maligned spoken evil of; slandered
Though often *maligned* by the press, Andrew Jackson kept
to his course and changed the direction of the republic.

mandible jaw; mouth parts for holding or biting
When magnified under a microscope, the *mandibles* of
many insects become frightening weapons.

manifest coming into view; obvious; cargo list; to show
It was *manifest* to all that he was in no condition to
continue the contest.

maw animals' throat, mouth, jaws, or stomach
The farmer crammed grain down the *maw* of the geese
destined for the holiday table.

mazes   confusing, winding pathways
Mazes, those twisting corridors of mirrors or some other substance, are popular attractions at amusement parks.

meager   thin; lean; of poor quality or amount
The prisoners of war were given a *meager* amount of food each day, barely enough to keep them alive.

meticulous   scrupulous; excessively careful; fussy; petty
Jeremy is *meticulous* about the order in which his suits are arranged in his closet, from light to dark.

minaret   tall slender tower on a Moslem place of worship
The call to prayer is sounded from the *minaret* on top of the mosque.

minimal   smallest possible
Despite the efforts of the promoters, fan interest in the concert was *minimal*.

mired   stuck in the mud
After the heavy rains, a truck was *mired* in the dirt leading to our farmhouse.

misgivings   anxiety; fears; worry; feelings of doubt
I had some *misgivings* about setting out on the long trek through the woods without a guide.

modus operandi   method of operation; procedure
We will have to agree on a common *modus operandi* before we can work cooperatively on this project.

mole   animal; spot on skin; structure in water
Tons of debris and stones were dumped into the water to make the *mole* that will eventually form the pier.

momentum   the force of a moving object
Even if a train is moving very slowly, its *momentum* is considerable.

moor   to tie up
Moor the boat securely; a severe storm watch is on.

moribund   dying out; waning; fading out
Giving up one's seat in a crowded bus to an older person or a woman seems to be a *moribund* custom.

musky having a heavy odor like musk
The *musky* odor in the old barn showed that it had been in use for a long time.

myriad countless; measureless; untold; limitless
Myriad acts of courage in the daily lives of ordinary people go unnoted and unsung as their lives unfold.

N

naïveté innocence; simplicity; frankness; sincerity
Her *naïveté*—her willingness to tell her life story to everyone, her way of trusting everyone—bothers me.

negligible unimportant; trifling
Though nighttime temperatures remained below zero, inside the well-insulated cabin, the loss of heat was *negligible*.

niche an open space in a wall; a place suitable for something in it
Every *niche* in the clay wall was inhabited by a family of barn swallows.

O

obliquely indirectly; not straight
The teacher *obliquely* referred to the date for our term paper, but we all got the point!

oblivious unaware; unconscious of; heedless; forgetful
I was so absorbed in the work I was doing that I was completely *oblivious* to people around me.

obsession something that takes hold of the mind; fear
For Donna, collecting all the records of the Beatles was more than hobby; it was an *obsession*.

obverse the side of a coin bearing the main design
For many generations, United States one-cent coins have borne the head of Lincoln on the *obverse*.

odious hateful; evil; vile; repulsive
I find her conceit so *odious* that I refuse to be within earshot of her.

Olympian   Greek god; a superior being; lofty; majestic
She has an *Olympian* disregard for details that do not interest her.

ominous   threatening; sinister; unfavorable
As the sky filled with *ominous* dark clouds, we raced across the field, hoping to beat the rain.

onslaught   attack; charge; offensive; invasion
When the massive *onslaught* of the enemy began, we were fully prepared and easily repulsed them.

opaqueness   barrier to the passage of light
The *opaqueness* of the muddy stream didn't allow us to see the bottom.

oracular   wise; like a prophet; having hidden meaning
Since his *oracular* pronouncements never came to pass, this would-be prophet quickly lost his following.

ostentatious   fond of display; immodest; conspicuous; showy
We had learned not to be *ostentatious* when we put our contribution in the collection box.

outflank   go around
The German armies *outflanked* the Maginot Line instead of trying to overrun it in a costly frontal attack.

overindulgent   too lenient; too forgiving; too permissive
Are married couples to blame when their deprived childhood makes them *overindulgent* parents?

P

pagoda   towerlike temple
The children climbed the stairs to the top of the *pagoda* to get a view of the surrounding city.

pallor   paleness
Too many days spent cooped up inside his tiny office had given Brad's face an unhealthy *pallor*.

palpable   that which can be touched or felt; obvious
In the light of Mack's previous record of unreliability, we felt his latest story was a *palpable* lie.

pampas grass-covered plains of South America
The gaucho is the cowboy of the Argentine *pampas*.

pandemonium wild disorder; confusion; upset
When the candidate announced that his opponent had conceded the election, there was *pandemonium* in the winner's headquarters.

parapet wall; bank; railing
The *parapet* above the castle entrance was lined with archers, waiting for the onslaught.

pell-mell recklessly; hastily; heedlessly
At the sound of the alarm, the fire fighters rush *pell-mell* to their stations on the truck.

pendant something suspended; hanging ornament
She wears my graduation ring as a *pendant* on the gold chain around her neck.

peons farm laborers in South America
The *peons* on the ranch lived with their families in the rows of houses built along the roadway.

perceived observed; became aware of
Through the mist, the hiker dimly *perceived* the outline of an old barn.

perceptibly noticeably; obviously
We were perceptibly distressed by her behavior, and we made no attempt to hide our displeasure.

perforce of necessity
On the hike we *perforce* had to follow his lead at all times since he alone had the experience.

perplexing puzzling; confusing; mystifying
Only a Sherlock Holmes at his best could solve this *perplexing* problem within the set time limits.

persevere to persist; not give up; stick to it
We must learn to *persevere* in developing our inborn abilities if we are truly to succeed.

pertinent related; suitable
Unless your comments are *pertinent* to the matter under discussion, we ask you to hold them until later.

piety   religious devotion; reverence
The depth of her *piety* is evidenced in the intensity with which she stresses her religious obligations.

pirouette   to whirl on toes; rapid whirling about of the body
When she heard her name mentioned, she quickly *pirouetted* around to catch a glimpse of the speaker.

placid   peaceful; quiet; serene; undisturbed
The painting by John Constable showed a *placid* scene of Salisbury Cathedral, suggestive of a peaceful summer day.

plaintive   sorrowful; mournful; pitiful
I can still hear the *plaintive* tone in the voice of the sick child asking for the missing doll.

pomp   stately display; showiness; spectacle
The coronation of the British king is always performed with great *pomp*.

ponderous   heavy; bulky; massive
The *ponderous* furniture of an earlier day has given way to lighter pieces in keeping with modern life-styles and living quarters.

pontoon   floating support
The temporary bridge across the river floats on hundreds of *pontoons*.

pore over   to study carefully; examine; ponder
He *pored over* the report looking for any error that could delay its publication.

poultice   hot pack applied to sores
The *poultice* was so hot when it was applied, it almost burned the skin around the afflicted area.

precariously   uncertainly; riskily
The cup was perched *precariously* at the edge of the shelf; then down it fell.

precipice   steep cliff; crag; palisade
The road along the edge of the *precipice* with a 150-foot drop had no guardrail, and our car had dim headlights!

precipitated caused; provoked; stimulated
Rapidly rising prices *precipitated* a crisis in the American economy.

premise basis for reasoning; assumption
If you want a chance for happiness, one of your major *premises* must be that most people are on your side.

preoccupied lost in thought
From Lori's *preoccupied* expression, I could tell she was miles away, remembering her recent vacation.

presume to dare; take upon oneself
I don't *presume* to know what Angela is thinking, but my guess is that she's happy to be nominated for secretary.

presumptive based on likelihood, probability
As an only child David is the heir *presumptive* to his parents' holdings in the company.

presumptuous too bold or forward
It is *presumptuous* of a fan to interrupt a celebrity's meal for an autograph.

prevail succeed; be widespread; in style; win out
Gloom *prevailed* when we realized how small our chances of succeeding really were.

privation loss of some quality; lack of necessities
W. C. Fields, the great comedian, suffered *privation* as a child, but in later years he became a financial success.

procured obtained
For our hiking trip, Jed *procured* the best equipment available.

prod to poke; jab; stir; quicken; encourage
The prospector used a long stick to *prod* the reluctant mule along the steep path.

prodigious vast; huge; exceptional; tremendous
The government spent *prodigious* sums of money to develop devices to increase the speed of the missile.

profane worldly; not respectful; to foul; abuse
The use of *profane* language accomplished little other than bringing attention unnecessarily to the speaker.

profuse　generous; pouring forth freely
　　When the running messenger bumped into a pedestrian, he offered *profuse* apologies.

prone　inclined; likely; lying face down
　　Since he is *prone* to refuse a request at first, we prepared and waited for his second reaction.

propitious　favorable; fortunate; beneficial; happy
　　We are gathered on this *propitious* occasion to honor a founding father of this community.

prosaic　commonplace; ordinary
　　Even the most *prosaic* life has moments of high drama and excitement.

proffered　offered
　　When Nan *proffered* her friend Sue a share in the craft shop, Sue expressed her gratitude.

prostrated　lying flat
　　Mrs. Fuller couldn't attend the meeting, for she had been *prostrated* by the heat of the past few days.

protrude　to jut out; project; stick out
　　The nail head that *protruded* from the catch prevented the door from closing.

provender　dry feed for animals; food; victuals
　　The silos of the prosperous farmers were filled with winter *provender* for the cattle.

provoke　to incite; arouse; stimulate
　　The presence of the National Guard, planned to calm the crowd, *provoked* anger and almost caused a riot.

pulsating　beating rhythmically
　　The *pulsating* sound of the riveters shattered the quiet of the night.

pungent　sharp and piercing; biting
　　Hal's *pungent* wit, though clever, made no friends with those whose feelings he had hurt.

purgatory　place or state of temporary suffering
　　I suffered the tortures of *purgatory* while waiting for the results of the laboratory tests.

pyre pile of material to be burned
> The acrid odor of *pyres* of burning leaves is no longer permitted to pollute the air of our town.

Q

qualm uneasiness; nausea; doubt; pang of conscience
> I have no *qualms* when it comes to letting him know that he has not been playing fair with us.

quavering trembling; quiver; gasping; falter
> I believe that all of us suffer from *quavering* breath after a brisk run up four flights of stairs.

quested pursued; sought; searched; hunted
> The Spaniards *quested* for vast riches when they ransacked South America.

R

rabble insulting name for the general population; mob
> The candidate, labeled as a *rabble*-rouser, promised to find graft and corruption everywhere in the government.

rampart protective wall; fortification
> The nearby hills serve as a *rampart*, protecting the farmlands from spring floods.

rancid spoiled; having bad smell or taste
> The butter was *rancid*, unfit to use.

rapturous overcome with joy
> When Teddy saw his new bicycle, he shrieked with *rapturous* delight.

ravenous greedy; hungry; piggish; starving
> What makes us so *ravenous* the moment we reach the picnic area?

raze to tear down; level; wreck; destroy; ruin
> How quickly a wrecking crew *razes* blocks of houses that took years to build!

reconnaissance   inspect; survey; exploration; scouting
We plan a pre-Christmas *reconnaissance* trip through the mall, looking for new and different gift ideas.

rectory   minister's residence
We do not hesitate to go to the *rectory* when we need the counsel of the minister in emergency matters.

reflective   thoughtful
Sam turned from his long, *reflective* gaze upon the Grand Canyon and said, "This is the most overwhelming sight we've seen on the trip."

rejoinder   answer; reply; response
The ideal *rejoinder* to a pun is another pun or a smile of recognition—but never a groan.

relentless   persistent; never giving up
The *relentless* pursuit of the fox in fox hunts has been criticized by animal lovers everywhere.

relevant   relating to the matter; appropriate; suitable
Unless your proposal is *relevant* to the matter we're discussing, please leave it till a later time.

repose   rest; peacefulness; calm; to lie at rest
I deserve an hour of *repose* in front of the TV before I begin my evening task of watching the ball game.

reprehensible   disgraceful; inexcusable; shameful; vile
To me one of the most *reprehensible* crimes is selling state secrets to foreign governments.

reproach   to blame; criticize; condemn; condemnation
His older brother *reproached* him for his rude behavior and compelled him to apologize.

reputed   considered; supposed; deemed; believed
I have a tendency to steer clear of anyone who is *reputed* to associate with gangland figures.

resignation   a feeling of acceptance
When Ethan Frome survived the crash with Mattie Silver, he accepted his fate with patient *resignation*.

resilient   springing back; flexible; adaptable; hardy
I so admire her *resilient* spirit, her ability to take the consequences and come back fighting.

resolute firm of purpose; unwavering
Though all his classmates gave up the puzzle, Jim was *resolute*, trying for a solution over and over.

retorted replied, often sharply
When the television interviewer asked an embarrassing question, the candidate *retorted* with a sharp objection.

retribution repayment; deserved punishment
The law insists upon some *retribution* for criminal acts.

revere to love and respect; look up to; honor
The symbol of our country, our flag, is something to *revere* and display proudly.

reveries daydreams; thinking of pleasant things
Andrea's *reveries* often made her the steeplechase champion at the country fair.

revulsion sudden change of feeling; extreme disgust or shock
Finding a scorpion in the house caused a feeling of *revulsion* in the owner.

rhapsodies great delights; enthusiastic utterances; wild cries
The *rhapsodies* of the Chicago Bear fans could be heard a mile away after the championship game.

ricochet to rebound; skip off surfaces
The golf ball *ricocheted* off a tree and fell within ten feet of the pin.

rigorous strict; harsh; severe
Astronauts go into *rigorous* training to prepare for shuttle flights.

rites ceremony; formal procedure; service
The marriage *rites* vary widely from country to country.

rollicking romping; behaving in a carefree way
The children had a *rollicking* afternoon at Walt Disney World, enjoying all the rides and attractions.

rubicund reddish; ruddy; rosy
After long exposure to cold and sun, the Antarctic explorers' countenances were *rubicund*.

rue   regret; feel sorry
>   Hitler lived to *rue* the day he overran Poland and France.

run the gauntlet   experience an ordeal; accept the challenge
>   During my early years I *ran the gauntlet* of criticism and
>   faultfinding that greet a newcomer.

S

salient   prominent; obvious; striking; outstanding
>   A *salient* feature of this recorder is its ease of operation.

sapped   weakened; reduced; exhausted
>   Our enthusiasm and willingness to cooperate were *sapped*
>   by their endless quarreling among themselves.

sardonic   bitter; scornful; disdainful
>   Perry's bitter sense of humor was revealed in his *sardonic*
>   comments about the team's progress.

sated   filled; glutted; stuffed; gorged
>   This horror film to end all horror films *sated* for months
>   our urge to see Bela Lugosi in action.

scrupulously   carefully; conscientiously; exactly
>   As treasurer of the club, Edith was *scrupulously* careful to
>   account for every penny.

scrutiny   close examination; inspection; study
>   Close *scrutiny* of the ancient map revealed a few lines
>   showing the outline of the Cape of Good Hope.

scuttling   hurrying
>   We grew uneasy as we listened to the mice *scuttling* across
>   the attic floor in the otherwise silent house.

seasoned   changed by time; experienced; spiced; tempered
>   To avoid warping, we carefully choose *seasoned* boards for
>   the flooring.

sector   area; district
>   Each *sector* of the city has its own police and fire depart-
>   ments.

sedentary   inactive; sitting a great deal
>   Health authorities believe that an active life is better for
>   the heart than a *sedentary* one.

self-abnegation setting aside of self for the sake of others
> The endless hours she spent with the children is clear evidence of the *self-abnegation* that ruined her career.

sensuously pleasing the senses; deliciously; delightfully
> You feel alive and vibrant as you stand in the spring meadow, *sensuously* enjoying the sights, smells, and sounds.

sequestered set apart; isolated; banished; withdrawn
> The Grand Jury was *sequestered* for the duration of the entire term because of the people involved.

serene calm; tranquil; quiet; cool
> His *serene* smile made us realize how much in command he felt despite our objections.

shambles slaughterhouse; scene of great disorder
> Frisky Perry can soon make a *shambles* out of any playroom that is well stocked with toys.

shirk neglect doing something; evading duty
> A worker who *shirks* his or her duty endangers the lives and well-being of fellow workers.

shorn cut off close; deprived
> *Shorn* of all power, the exiled king lives simply and quietly on an isolated island far from cities.

shunting switching; diverting; shuttling; shifting
> The commuter *shunted* from suburb to inner city and back day after day for years.

sibilant hissing; sound of *s*
> When he whispers, the *sibilants* dominate, and I can scarcely make out what he is saying.

simultaneous occurring at the same time; coincident
> The general planned *simultaneous* bombardments by land, sea, and air.

singular unusual; peculiar; odd
> The lawyer had a *singular* way of using his hands, a habit that constantly called attention to himself.

sinuous winding; curving; twisting; crooked
> From the air, the route of the river is seen to be *sinuous*, curving back and forth.

skylarking   frolicking; merrymaking; romping
Saturday morning was our time for *skylarking*, for letting
go and just enjoying being young and alive.

sluicing   washing gold ore
Sluicing is based on the principle that the water will wash
away the lighter particles, leaving mainly gold.

slug   rounded metal piece; snaillike creature
A close relative of the snail, the *slug* is long and wormlike,
with a fairly thin shell.

sluggard   lazy person
You misjudge him completely if you think that you can
push that *sluggard* to work in high gear.

smitten   hard hit; having a crush on; infatuated
Smitten with pangs of conscience, Alice returned the borrowed book—months later.

smote   struck
With his mighty club, the giant *smote* the rock one blow
and turned it into gravel for his roadbed.

solemnized   celebrated with formal ceremony
The coronation of Queen Elizabeth II was *solemnized* in
Westminster Abbey.

solicitously   showing care or concern; eagerly
Terry's friend inquired *solicitously* about the ankle Terry
had sprained in the first game of the season.

soliloquy   talking to oneself; dramatic monolog
A *soliloquy* in which you calmly discuss the issues mentally
is not so upsetting as speaking out loud.

somnolent   drowsy; sleepy; sluggish; half-asleep
It was definitely the heavy eating and the high heat and
humidity in the room that made us so *somnolent*.

sorrel   plant; reddish brown horse with light tail and mane
The patient *sorrel* is the best horse for a rank beginner.

sparse   thinly scattered; spotty; meager; scant
The *sparse* meal of the athletes on the day of the contest
contrasted sharply with their daily fare.

splayed   spread out
  The experienced gymnast *splayed* her fingers out automatically before going into a handstand.

squandered   wasted; spent extravagantly
  Many a person has *squandered* a fortune at the gaming tables of Las Vegas or Monte Carlo.

squatted   sat down; obtained public land by settling on it
  It was so cold that I *squatted* before the campfire and refused to budge.

staccato   made up of short, abrupt, distinct sounds
  The woodpecker sent a burst of *staccato* sounds through the quiet forest.

stanchest   (also *staunchest*) most firm, loyal, or strong
  Even the *stanchest* supporters of the Olympic athlete fell away when it was discovered he had used drugs.

stealthily   slyly; secretly; cautiously
  The cat *stealthily* approached the bird, but a sudden motion frightened its prey away.

steppe   level, treeless plains of Europe and Asia
  How do the *steppes* in Russia differ from the American prairie and the Argentine pampas?

stile   turnstile; set of steps over fence or wall
  To go from one pasture to another, the farmer built a *stile* into the high stone fence.

stippled   painted with dots or strokes
  The sun coming up behind the leafy tree *stippled* the grassy fairway.

stipulate   to impose a condition; specify; state; provide
  We *stipulated* in the contract that final payment would be made when the work was completed to our satisfaction.

stoical   detached; accepting fate calmly; fatalistic
  His *stoical* attitude during times of great stress helped us all bear our sorrow.

subdued   mild; restrained; suppressed
  The candidate sensed the *subdued* hostility of her audience, but she proceeded with her speech anyway.

sublimity   nobility; majesty; stateliness
The *sublimity* of Beethoven's Ninth Symphony raises listeners to heights of joy.

subsist   to continue existing; barely exist; survive; nourish
Lost in the woods for days, the hikers *subsisted* on the scant emergency food in their knapsacks.

suffuse   to cover; overspread; fill; overfill
The rays of the setting sun *suffused* the western skies with varied shades of red and orange.

suppleness   adaptability; flexibility; ability to bend
The Olympic gymnastics events call for incredible *suppleness* on the part of the athletes.

suppressed   held back; subdued; crushed; controlled; hidden
The government tried in vain to *suppress* all news of the unrest among the workers.

surreptitious   done or acting in a secret way
The *surreptitious* message reached the authorities in time to prevent the act of terrorism.

swaggering   walking boldly and arrogantly; strutting
In *Romeo and Juliet*, the swaggering servants of the Capulets began a brawl with the servants of the Montagues.

swathed   wrapped; enveloped; bound
Swathed in old rags, the wily spy lived unnoticed among the noisy beggars of the marketplace.

swarthy   dark-skinned
After hours of unhealthy sunbathing, the lifeguard resembled a *swarthy* giant, sitting on his throne.

sybarites   ones fond of luxury; pleasure seekers
I don't mind enjoying myself, but I disagree with the *sybarites* who make pleasure the be-all and end-all.

T

tacit   silently implied; taken for granted; undeclared
The roommates and I have a *tacit* agreement that anything that we borrow from one another must be returned.

taciturn   silent; reserved; close-mouthed; quiet
  She is so *taciturn* that we never know whether she really enjoys being with us.

tack room   storage room for saddles and bridles
  You will find all the extra saddles in the *tack room*.

talisman   something supposed to bring good luck
  Like many other ballplayers, Andy has his own *talisman*, a ring inherited from his grandfather.

tattoo   mark on the skin; steady beat
  The rain beat a lively *tattoo* on the tin roof and kept us awake most of the night.

taut   drawn tight; tense; tidy; rigid; unbending
  The *taut* rope began to sing as the moored ship, tugged by the current, tried to move away from the dock.

tendentious   biased; prejudiced; having a special purpose
  I want the facts, not a mass of *tendentious* statements that present a one-sided approach to the issue.

throng   crowd; horde; to form a crowd; to gather
  The *throngs* of pre-Christmas shoppers milled around the counters displaying the latest holiday novelties.

thwarted   hindered; stopped; checked; foiled
  The alarm system *thwarted* the burglars when they attempted to break into the locked storerooms.

timorous   timid; fearful
  The prey animals must be *timorous* and watchful to survive the onslaught of the carnivores.

tortuous   winding; twisting; turning
  Instead of using the direct interstate, Marie took the *tortuous* Spartanburg Highway to get to Tryon.

transfix   to spear; run through; captivate; spellbind
  The audience sat *transfixed*, listening to the youthful pianist reveal his extraordinary talent.

transitional   passing from one stage to another; temporary
  The leader of the *transitional* government did his best to ease the passage from the old to the new.

transmute   to change forms; transform
The alchemists searched in vain for a formula to *transmute* base metals like iron or lead into gold.

traverse   to pass over; cross through
Before you reach the mountain hut for the night, you must *traverse* a snowfield with some dangerous gullies.

turbine   type of engine
The *turbine* converted the energy in the flowing water into power to operate the factory equipment.

U

unassertive   not confident; modest; shy
The counselor tried to persuade the *unassertive* applicant to accept job opportunities as a salesperson.

undermine   to weaken gradually; ruin; destroy
Your continual sarcasm has *undermined* the child's self-confidence and made her fearful and timid.

undulating   moving in waves
The sound of the fire engine's alarms kept *undulating* through the quiet streets.

unearthly   ghostly; supernatural; absurd; terrible
How could you have the gall to come visiting at this *unearthly* hour!

unendurable   intolerable; insufferable
The pain he was suffering seemed *unendurable*, and I was almost relieved when he lost consciousness.

unkempt   not tidy; uncombed; messy; rough; unpolished
I am positive that a bird could build a nest, unnoticed in his massive, *unkempt* beard.

unparalleled   unequaled; unique; matchless
How many events have been labeled as being *unparalleled* in the history of the world!

unpretentious simple; modest; free from showiness
This modest genius has lived in the same *unpretentious* three-room apartment most of his adult life.

untold unrevealed; countless; limitless
This scheme has robbed *untold* thousands of retirees of the money set aside for their old age.

untrammeled not confined, limited, or hindered
When traveling, pack modestly, *untrammeled* by huge packages and suitcases.

upbraid to scold; reprimand; find fault with
I am tired of having him *upbraid* me for something that my older brother has done.

V

vanguard front rank; leaders; trendsetters
She dresses as though she were the *vanguard* of fashion setters, the model for all teenagers to follow.

vanquish to overcome; defeat; gain mastery over
The first step in *vanquishing* shyness is to realize that everyone makes mistakes, why not you?

vehement violent; impetuous
At the town meeting, several citizens raised *vehement* objections to the proposed plan to widen Main Street.

venerable worthy of respect; honored; admired
I am firmly convinced of the truth in that *venerable* adage, "You are as old as you feel!"

verge to edge; border on; near; approach
He'll never succeed; his present course of action *verges* on stupidity.

vex to annoy; irritate; irk; bother
Nothing *vexes* him more than having one of his friends do better on a test than he did.

victualing feeding; nourishing
My uncle has been *victualing* his pantry free of charge for years from our shelves.

vigil   watch; watchfulness; period of wakefulness
  The guard dog keeps his lonely *vigil* inside the chain-link fence.

vindictive   wanting revenge; spiteful; unforgiving
  After being fired for irresponsibility, the *vindictive* salesman spread vicious rumors about the company.

visage   face
  When the shot went wide of the basket, the player's *visage* showed his feelings of disappointment.

vista   view; scene; outlook; mental picture
  There is a breathtaking *vista* of distant mountains from the front porch of their cottage.

voracious   greedy; limitless
  She is such a *voracious* TV viewer that at any one time she may watch three sets tuned to different programs.

W

wantonly   maliciously; needlessly; senselessly
  The gangleader was accused of *wantonly* destroying the heating system in the project building.

weir   dam in a stream
  We built a *weir* across the stream to create a swimming hole of our own.

wended   proceeded; went
  The river *wended* its way through thick forests and pleasant meadows.

whimsical   full of unusual or quaint ideas; fanciful
  Lewis Carroll, author of *Alice in Wonderland*, had a *whimsical* imagination, filled with odd and unusual characters.

wince   to flinch; draw back; make a face; cringe
  Doreen *winced* when the teacher held her paper up to show the class how not to head a theme.

windflaws gusts of wind
 I knew it had to happen: one of the unexpected *windflaws* seized my new hat and landed it in the mud.

winsome winning; charming; engaging
 Marie has a *winsome* smile that wins her many friends and admirers.

wistfully yearningly; longingly
 Cinderella looked *wistfully* at the elegant gowns of her stepsisters, little realizing she would soon have a beautiful gown of her own.

withdrawn shy; quiet; retiring; reserved; unfriendly
 As he grew older, he became more and more *withdrawn*, preferring the TV set to contact with real people.

woebegone distressed; troubled; miserable; dejected
 The *woebegone* look on his face told me without words that he and Lucy were in the midst of a quarrel.

woolgathering daydreaming
 It is much better to get real small satisfactions than to achieve greatness while *woolgathering*.

wonderment surprise
 To the *wonderment* of her classmates, when Phyllis sat down at the piano, she played popular songs beautifully.

wraith ghost; spirit; phantom; apparition
 According to legend, the *wraith* of the drowned sailor appears at midnight whenever danger threatens.

wrath anger; rage; fury; irritability; ire
 You will feel the full force of her *wrath* when she learns that you were the one who hid her notebook.

writhed distorted; twisted; wrenched
 To our horror, Alan fell to the floor, *writhing* in pain and calling for help.

wrought made; worked; formed; hammered; excited
 I still don't see why she let herself get all *wrought* up about an incident that did not concern her.

Z

zealous   eager; earnest; enthusiastic; intense

The candidate had to warn his most *zealous* followers to treat him as a human being, not as an infallible god.

zenith   climax; summit; highest point; point in the sky directly overhead

At the *zenith* of her career, Marie Curie was the acknowledged leader in her field.

ACKNOWLEDGMENTS

Grateful acknowledgment is made to the following sources for permission to reprint copyrighted stories.

"Runaway Rig," page 6. By Carl Henry Rathjen. From *The Saturday Evening Post*, October 5, 1957. Copyright © 1957 by Curtis Publishing Co. Reprinted by permission of Larry Sternig Literary Agency.

"The Most Dangerous Game," page 20. By Richard Connell. Copyright 1924 by Richard Connell. Copyright renewed 1952 by Louise Fox Connell. Reprinted by permission of Brandt & Brandt Literary Agents, Inc.

"Archetypes," page 66. By Robert Greenwood. Reprinted by permission of Talisman Literary Research, Inc.

"The Monkey's Paw," page 94. From THE LADY OF THE BARGE by W. W. Jacobs. Reprinted by permission of Dodd, Mead & Company, Inc. Canadian rights by The Society of Authors, Ltd.

"Lonesome Boy, Silver Trumpet," page 114. From LONESOME BOY by Arna Bontemps. Copyright 1955 by Arna Bontemps and Feliks Topolski. Copyright © renewed 1983 by Mrs. Arna (Alberta) Bontemps. Reprinted by permission of Houghton Mifflin Company.

"Seven Floors," page 130. From CATASTROPHE by Dino Buzzati. Translated by Judith Landry and Cynthia Jolly. Published in the United States by Riverrun Press, Inc., New York and reproduced by permission of John Calder (Publishers) Ltd.

"Roads of Destiny," page 154. By O. Henry. From THE COMPLETE WORKS OF O. HENRY. Published by Doubleday, a division of Bantam, Doubleday, Dell Publishing Group, Inc.

"A Habit for the Voyage," page 220. By Robert Edmond Alter. From *Alfred Hitchcock's Mystery Magazine*, February 1964. Copyright © 1964 by H. S. D. Publications. Reprinted by permission of Larry Sternig Literary Agency.

"The Point of Honor," page 240. Copyright 1947 by W. Somerset Maugham from THE COMPLETE SHORT STORIES OF W. SOMERSET MAUGHAM. Reprinted by permission of Doubleday, a division of Bantam, Doubleday, Dell Publishing Group, Inc. Canadian rights by William Heinemann Ltd.

"The Noblest Instrument," page 268. Copyright 1935 by Clarence Day and renewed 1963 by K. B. Day. Reprinted from THE BEST OF CLARENCE DAY, by permission of Alfred A. Knopf, Inc.

"The Secret Life of Walter Mitty," page 284. Copyright © 1942 by James Thurber. Copyright © 1970 by Helen Thurber and Rosemary A. Thurber. From MY WORLD—AND WELCOME TO IT, published by Harcourt Brace Jovanovich, Inc.

"Tobermory," page 296. From THE COMPLETE SHORT STORIES OF SAKI by H. H. Munro. Copyright 1930, renewed © 1958 by The Viking Press, Inc. All rights reserved. Reprinted by permission of Viking Penguin Inc.

"Johanna," page 334. From TALES OF WONDER by Jane Yolen. Copyright © 1983 by Jane Yolen. Reprinted by permission of Schocken Books, published by Pantheon Books, a Division of Random House, Inc.

"Bees and People," page 344. By Mikhail Zoshchenko. From THE PORTABLE TWENTIETH-CENTURY RUSSIAN READER. Edited by Clarence Brown. Copyright © 1985 by Viking Penguin Inc. All rights reserved. Reprinted by permission of Viking Penguin Inc.

"ZOO," page 358. By Edward D. Hoch. Copyright © 1958 by King Size Publications. Reprinted by permission of Larry Sternig Literary Agency.

"Good-by, Herman," page 368. Copyright 1939 and renewed 1967 by John O'Hara. Reprinted from COLLECTED STORIES OF JOHN O'HARA, edited by Frank MacShane. By permission of Random House, Inc.

"My Friend Flicka," page 386. By Mary O'Hara. Copyright © 1941 by Mary O'Hara. From *Story*, January/February 1941. Reprinted by permission of John Hawkins & Associates, Inc.

"The Apprentice," page 412. Copyright 1947 by Curtis Publishing Company, renewed 1975 by Downe Publishing Inc. From FOUR SQUARE by Dorothy Canfield Fisher, reprinted by permission of Harcourt Brace Jovanovich, Inc.

"Leiningen Versus the Ants," page 430. Reprinted with permission from *Esquire*. Copyright © 1938 by Esquire Associates.

"The Birds," page 462. By Daphne du Maurier. Copyright 1952 by Daphne du Maurier. From KISS ME AGAIN STRANGER. Reprinted by permission of Doubleday, a division of Bantam, Doubleday, Dell Publishing Group, Inc. Canadian rights by Curtis Brown on behalf of Dame Daphne du Maurier, Copyright © Daphne du Maurier 1959.

"One Thousand Dollars," page 500. By O. Henry. From THE COMPLETE WORKS OF O. HENRY. Published by Doubleday, a division of Bantam, Doubleday, Dell Publishing Group, Inc.

"The Proverb," page 542. From THE PROVERB AND OTHER SHORT STORIES by Marcel Aymé. Copyright Editions Gallimard © 1943.

"The Old Woman," page 564. By Joyce Marshall. Reprinted by permission of the author.